Mistress of Lust

Lily. She grew up in the teeming slums and bleak orphanages of 19th-century New York, lost her innocence to the practiced skill of an aristrocratic, amoral lover, and came to the San Francisco of 1856 with only her ravishing beauty and incredibly lovely body to offer in a wide-open world where gold was king.

Here is the passionate saga of an exquisite woman who became the most fabulous courtesan ever to sell her favors to the highest bidder—and who set out to make society forget her legacy of shame and accept her as its queen. It is the story of the rich and powerful men who became Lily's pawns, and of the only man who could ever reach her heart . . .

Lily Cigar

A fiery new peak of romance and passion—a drama of poverty and wealth, intrigue and violence, heartbreak and courage, tragedy and ultimate triumph—with the most magnificent heroine ever to take on the world. . . .

Big Bestsellers from SIGNET

LILY CIGAR

a novel by

TOM MURPHY

A SIGNET BOOK

NEW AMERICAN LIBRARY

TIMES MIRROR

Copyright © 1979 by Tom Murphy

SIGNET TRADEMARK REG. U.S. PAT. OFF. AND FOREIGN COUNTRIES
REGISTERED TRADEMARK—MARCA REGISTRADA
HECHO EN CHICAGO, U.S.A.

SIGNET, SIGNET CLASSICS, MENTOR, PLUME AND MERIDIAN BOOKS
are published by The New American Library, Inc.,
1301 Avenue of the Americas, New York, New York 10019

First Printing, August, 1979

1   2   3   4   5   6   7   8   9

PRINTED IN THE UNITED STATES OF AMERICA

This book would not have been possible without the extraordinary research of Mary Vanaman O'Gorman, who worked tirelessly, imaginatively, and with surgical precision to unearth exactly the right materials from the enormous bulk of histories, diaries, and journalism of the period.

❧ 1 ❧

Lily looked at her mother. Mary Malone lay very still, thin under the thin sheet and nearly that pale, worn thin and worn out by the working and the fevers. Her breath came shallow now, and with a rasp to it, and the rhythms of Ma's breathing were irregular.

The doctor himself had said there was nothing Lily could do but watch and try to get some broth into her mother. But Lily had one last hope, one desperate plan, and she would try it this very afternoon, even if she were damned for all eternity for leaving the bedside.

How fine he had been, the doctor, and how disdainful of their poor home! Tall he was, and all in black, with a fine clean shirt and hands he was always rubbing together as if to keep the dirt off, for the Malones' one-room flat was far from clean, try as Lily did since Ma fell ill. He'd looked quickly about him, the doctor, and wrinkled his nose, not even trying to hide his disgust, and then he'd sighed, as though somehow Mary Malone had brought this on herself, willfully. And Lily saw in the doctor's eyes a look she had seen too many times, a look that seemed to say: *"Well, sure and I'll be whistling for my fee from this sorry lot."* And the anger rose in Lily then, small as she was for her ten and a half years.

For they hadn't always been like this, so helpless, so trapped by the bad luck that seemed to follow them like some stray and hungry dog.

Now, looking at the still, sad figure of her mother, wondering when to make her move, Lily remembered her dad.

Big Fergus!

She always remembered Big Fergus Malone when she felt bad; when her belly hurt because there was nothing to feed it; when Fergy, her brother, misbehaved yet again; when Ma turned all quiet and like to cried.

What Lily remembered was the dash and color of him, the roar of his laugh and the way his green eyes flashed with fires from inside them, and he'd scoop her up in hands big as shovels, but gentle, too, for all their strength, and she'd go flying, flying, up to the very ceiling itself, he was that tall, but even beyond, near all the way to heaven itself. Nothing bad could happen when Big Fergus Malone was near.

A fine big flat they'd had then, the whole bottom floor of this very house, where now they huddled in one small chamber three flights up. And he'd found himself a fine job, too, tending bar at Broderick's Subterranean, which had led to nothing less than being invited to join the Red Rovers, the finest volunteer fire company in New York, a club, really, a good place to meet the kind of men who could help an ambitious fellow make his way. At least, that's what Ma said, and she said it sadly and with the kind of grim resignation Lily often heard in the women's voices, a tone of speaking that accepted the fact that their lot in life was not a happy one, that babies died and luck was fickle and the only thing quite sure to grow was debt.

Sometimes Lily herself couldn't tell the difference between what she remembered about Big Fergus and what she'd been told by Ma, by Fergy, or by friends.

Because Lily had been only five years old the night Big Fergus raced off in his bright Red Rover uniform to help fight a fire at a sperm-oil warehouse and never came back.

Ma was sleeping.

Still, it was with a covert, sneaking little hand that Lily reached into the pocket of her one summer dress and found the coin. Her fingers closed around the penny as if the very touch of it could help. *And help it might, help it must.*

Lily looked around the room where they'd lived these last five years. The ceiling was cracked and stained and there was no Big Fergus to fix it, nor talk to the landlord either, for all the good that might do.

Outside, three stories down, the thousand weekday sounds of Mulberry Street rose to greet her ears, muffled by the tight-shut window, closed against evil vapors at the insistence of the several women who came bustling in and out each day with scant gifts of food and large doses of advice.

Lily felt guilty about the penny: it was one of only six they had left. Still and all, as she had explained to her brother in a tight-lipped whispered argument that very morning, the saint might listen better if they made her a small gift. *"Not small to us, Lil,"* said Fergy, his green eyes gleaming dangerously close to anger. But Lily soothed him and reassured him, as she'd learned to do early on, even if he was more than two years older. For Fergy was like a wild thing and there was no sense trying to cage him in or give him reins: only love worked with Fergus Malone Junior, and often even that was not enough.

And where would he have got himself to now? Lily could imagine her brother, running with his rat pack of urchin friends, the despair of his mother when she had the strength to despair, a boy full of the devil, not bad or cruel, but wild, wild.

Her fingers clutched the worn penny as if it held the secret of her future.

Lily stood up from the low stool where she had been keeping her sick-watch. Ma looked exactly the way she had looked all morning, with no sign of getting better and no sign of getting worse. *If only she'll keep on sleeping,* Lily thought desperately, *if only she doesn't wake and want something and find me gone.* Yet the determination was strong in her. It could not be resisted: for if ever there were a prayer that deserved to be answered, it was this one. And was it so much to ask the saint? Was her father so lonely in heaven that he must have Ma's company while his very own flesh and blood needed Mary Malone so badly here in New York, on Mulberry Street, in the year of our Lord 1847?

Lily took a deep breath in the stifling room and walked softly to the door.

If Mulberry Street knew of Lily's troubles or her scheme to acquire some heavenly intervention, the street and its denizens kept their own counsel.

Lucky it was that the distance to St. Paddy's was no more than four and a half blocks. Lily knew that if she walked fast she could be there and back well within an hour, and didn't she know the way by heart, walking it as she did near every day of her life, to Mass and to classes?

Squinting a little against the bright August sunlight, Lily made her way briskly up Mulberry Street.

The air was clear for all the heat, and even the clamorous noise of the street was a welcome change after the morbid stillness of their flat.

Three days it had been since Lily set foot out of the apartment.

She picked her way over the hot Belgian-block paving stones, stepping around steaming piles of horse manure, around pyramids of tomatoes, cabbages, grapes, peaches, pears, past the pickle barrels, wrinkling her nose at the fishmonger's, whose brave gilt and painted sign had a lobster gaily embracing an amorous salmon, belying the fact that its owner, Signor Garabaldi, bought all his stock three days old from other vendors. Lily smiled over the stench, thinking of some things her mother had said about such practices. But the smile faded and the girl walked on.

Now Lily could see the blunt square spire of St. Patrick's Cathedral pointing its sturdy sandstone finger toward heaven. Their own church, the first church in New York built for the Irish, and proud they should be of it, Ma always said. *Ma! Why did all her thoughts begin and end with Ma? What would life be like if . . . ? Don't even think it, goose,* Lily told herself sternly, *you have more important things to think on, a prayer to say, a miracle to work!*

She turned right on Prince Street, sticking close to the churchyard wall.

"All full up it is, bless us for martyrs."

Who had said that, and why was she thinking it now? True, whoever said it, and sad, for the churchyard of St. Paddy's was not a small one, yet filled it surely had been these last several years, and wasn't her own dad buried in the other graveyard up on Twelfth Street? Close by the churchyard wall, half in the afternoon shadow, Lily stole a glance across the street at the building she dreaded most of any she knew.

The orphanage of St. Patrick's Cathedral was not an ugly building, four stories tall and fine-looking where it sat under the elm trees on its well-trimmed lawn.

But Lily knew from Fergy's tales and from the simpering gossip of Fat Bessie with some of the other neighbor ladies who kept coming and going until Lily could see no pattern to it: but whenever anyone spoke of the orphanage, it was in secret whispers that implied dark and scandalous doings, souls lost, cruelties and other nameless terrors. Lily never knew precisely what these things were, only that they were to be avoided. Yet there were worse fates than the orphanage— no one would deny that.

The Baptists might get you, or the streets.

Lily shuddered as she passed the big front entrance to the orphanage, and she quickly crossed herself to ward off bad luck.

Here was the corner. St. Jude was getting closer.

Lily turned left on Mott Street, quiet after the bustle of Mulberry. There were none here but the occupants of the churchyard and the birds in the trees. She passed the curling wrought-iron fence and walked in through the open gate. Up

[4]

the stone stairs and into the vast dim space of St. Patrick's Cathedral.

There were no clergy inside this afternoon.

Two old ladies in their eternal black dresses and blacker shawls knelt mumbling toothless prayers in the back row of pews. Suddenly, irreverently, Lily found herself wondering who the saint was that you might pray to, to have your teeth come back.

The iron rack of votive candles was down in front and to the left. The fat little candles guttered and smoked. Lily knelt on the cool stones and closed her eyes.

Will the prayer work better if I pay the penny first and light the candle? There was no one to ask this urgent question. Lily decided that if she were the saint, she'd want to see some hard evidence of good faith first. Before granting the wish. It was only fair.

Slowly then she stood up and reached out to steady herself against the iron candle rack. Its strength seemed to flow into her as she reached for the penny. Lily looked at the precious coin before dropping it into the iron slot. Worn it was, almost beyond identification, yet a penny for all that, and one of their last.

Would St. Jude know that it was more than a penny to them?

The coin rattled and clanged with a noise beyond its size or worth as Lily dropped it down the slot. Then she reached for one of the long, slender lighting tapers and lit it from a votive candle, hesitated for a moment until she found the ideal fresh candle to light, a fat new one right at the edge of the rack closest to the altar, where the saint and maybe even Himself might be sure to see it. Surprised at the steadiness of her hand, Lily held the long taper until the fat votive candle ignited. *Maybe I can get two for a penny!* But one was all she needed. Slowly, gently, Lily blew out the taper and knelt to pray. *"Oh, St. Jude, protectress of lost causes . . ."* Lily recited the whole prayer and then added a verse or two of her own. Then she crossed herself again and stood up and walked out of the dark church into the dazzling afternoon.

Lily was halfway home when the pains of hunger hit her with the force of a sudden knife wound in the belly.

She stopped, shivering, and looked about her. There was the greengrocer's. And on the counter in front of his shop was a neat pyramid of the best-looking pears Lily could ever remember seeing. She walked a few steps closer, transfixed. *If I hadn't spent the penny on a prayer . . .* But then Lily remembered why she had spent the penny. Still she stood, small and silent, staring. The pears seemed diffused now. Her eyes were misting. She turned, and just as she turned, Lily felt a hand on her shoulder.

It was the grocer's wife, a round, red woman who might be gruff or merry, you never knew. She smiled at Lily and handed her a pear.

"Here, child. Lily, isn't it?"

"Yes, ma'am."

Lily couldn't remember the lady's name.

"Take it, and good luck to you, Lily."

"Thank you, ma'am."

I will bring it to Ma. It's just what she needs, after all that broth.

Lily held the pear as if it were the most fragile crystal, hugged it close for fear of dropping the precious thing in her excitement, and walked faster now, down Mulberry Street and into her own dark doorway and up, up the stairs.

Ma looked exactly the same, only a little paler now. Or maybe it was just that everything outside was so very bright. So alive. Lily set the pear carefully on the dresser and moved closer to the bed. At least her mother hadn't woken up while Lily was out praying for miracles.

Lily looked around the little room. It was just as she'd left it. Fergy was still out, then. She wished him luck. Sometimes her brother would arrive out of breath and dirty, holding a few carrots, and even, once, a chicken. Lily never asked him where these treasures came from, for she was sure he'd not earned the things. Her eyes in their journey around the room alighted upon the pear. And wasn't it a little miracle, all on its own? Maybe the first answer from the saint!

There was a faint noise from the bed.

Lily moved closer. Ma's breathing had changed. It was coming faster now, with a kind of grating noise.

"Ma?"

Mary Malone's thin hand fluttered on the sheet. Lily reached out for it.

Ma's eyes slowly opened. With an effort that looked to Lily as though she might be going to move the whole city, Ma raised her head a little on the rumpled pillow and forced herself to smile, not knowing how like a skull her pretty face had become.

"I have a nice pear for you, Ma."

She was trying to say something, Lily could tell from the way her mother's lips were moving. Lily held the frail hand tighter, and blinked, because she could feel the tears building up, and Ma mustn't see her crying, it would only upset her.

Lily stood there, holding her mother's hand, blinking.

When Ma spoke, it was almost a shock to Lily, how clear her voice was, even with the fever, even with the trembling.

Mary Malone spoke low, but distinctly.

"Don't cry for me, Lily," she said. "Save your tears, child, for one day you may truly need them. Tears are not to be wasted on what we cannot help, Lily. If you must be brave, then be as brave as you can. After that . . . you can do no more, for 'tis in the hands of God and His angels and tears enough to fill Dublin Bay won't change things a bit, girl."

Lily felt her mother's hand trembling. And although she was very close, and touching, the girl suddenly felt as though she was all alone in the darkest night, a night filled with a thousand dangers, and no place to go, and no one to help her. *She is saying good-bye.*

Something like a smile flickered across Ma's lips.

"Do you understand me, child?"

Ma's voice was faint now, and it seemed to Lily that she could feel the strength draining out of her mother like water through a sieve.

"Sure I do."

"Will you make me a promise, Lily?"

"Anything. Anything."

Anything, so long as the saint makes you well, Ma. Anything so long as you don't leave me too, alone out here in the dark.

"Then take care of Fergy, Lily dear, and love him for me and try to get the wildness out of him . . ."

The voice trailed off, and if Lily hadn't clutched her mother's hand still tighter, it would have slipped away.

"Of course, Ma. Sure and I'll do that."

Mary Malone's head sank back the few inches to the pillow. A trembling shook her thin body from head to toe.

Then there was nothing, nothing at all, no sound, not even the harsh gasping of her breath, not a moan.

She was gone.

Lily held onto the dead hand because letting it go would be to admit the truth.

Ma had left her too, then.

There was a clatter on the stairs, the door banged open and shut. Without looking backward Lily knew her brother had come into the room. And without showing the anger she felt inside at the saint's betrayal, Lily Malone said quietly: "Run now, Fergy. Run and fetch a priest."

Then the blackness and danger that were the only future Lily could imagine, closed around her like a shroud.

❧ 2 ❧

Father William Reardon Gregory was not yet twenty-five, tall, and fond of games. But for all that he was nearly out of breath with the effort of keeping up with the darting, shifting mop of red hair that signaled Fergy's progress through the crowds of Mulberry Street.

Father Bill knew the Malones and their troubles, but he had not known the mother was this badly taken.

It was an old story and a common one, he reflected, striding after his nimble escort, and nonetheless sad for all that; just look into the churchyards or St. Paddy's orphanage, which he did nearly every day, to take the measure of what troubles could strike down a poor immigrant family.

Fergy waited at the street door of the old brick house, and held it, wordless, as the tall priest stepped in and up the stairs.

The stairwell was dark and smelled of spoiled food and dampness, and from halfway up the first flight of creaking stairs Father Bill could hear the unearthly banshee wail of the mourners. So she was dead, then. The boy hadn't told him. The boy might not have known.

The priest walked into the room and he wondered how many times he would have to look upon such scenes before he died. Three neighbor women stood at the foot of Mary Malone's bed, keening. The sound never failed to sicken the young priest, often as he heard it, the low, wavering, half-whine, half-wail of it, a noise that might come winding right down the dark haunted corridors of hell itself. He wondered what good it did, this keening, or who it helped.

Then Father Bill saw Lily.

She sat in a corner on a low stool, and in her thin arms she held a rag doll, cradling it protectively. The girl looked at the mourning women and at her mother's body without seeming to see them truly. The priest came up to her and touched her shoulder.

"God bless you, child, and I'm sorry for your troubles."

Lily looked up at him, startled. The women who had come rushing, keening into the room had hardly spoken to her at all.

"Thank you, Father."

He asked her many questions then, and Lily answered as best she could from the bottomless pit of her loneliness, from the icy prison of her fears.

"No, Father, we have no other family."

They will turn us out into the streets, and Ma's body with us, and we'll all rot, and there's be none to care nor remember us.

"Yes, Father, my dad is buried in the Twelfth Street ground."

And who would pay the gravediggers, not to say the coffinmakers? A pauper's funeral Ma would be having, and for sure, to the eternal shame of all of them!

Finally Father Bill made some sense of the tragedy, and arranged that the two children would spend the night with old Mrs. Flannagan, who lived across the hall. He said the prayer for the dead, and spoke softly to Lily and her brother.

"I'll see to it, children, that your mother gets a decent burial, and that there will be a place for you both in St. Paddy's."

For a moment neither Lily nor Fergy could think of a word to say. Finally, it was Lily who answered softly, "Thank you, Father, and God bless you."

She felt Fergy tensing beside her, and feared for some outburst, for when he was angry her brother cared naught for any authority, be it that of God or man.

But Fergy said nothing, and soon the priest was gone, and the mourning women too, soon to come back, Lily knew, to dress the corpse in the time-honored Irish fashion.

Now they were alone, for the first time, with their mother's body.

Lily sat down on her stool and sighed.

Fergy turned to her as though she'd struck out at him.

"Dammit to hell, Lil," he said, "we deserve better than this!"

Whatever Fergy gets, Lily thought almost idly, *he thinks he deserves a better break. Luck might have been invented for the personal use of Fergus Malone, Junior.*

But all Lily said was: "Hush, Fergus. She wouldn't like to hear you taking on so."

"And is she going to rise out of the grave and save us from the damned orphanage, I ask you?"

"I'm sorry about the penny."

Fergy softened then, and knelt beside his sister, and put an arm awkwardly around her thin shoulder.

"Ah, Lil, dear, it isn't the damned penny. It's what may become of us, can't you see?"

"We'll go to St. Paddy's."

As she said it, all of Lily's fears came galloping back at her: the stories about strange vices among the nuns and priests, the rumors of beatings and worse for the children, of poisoned food, and of boys and girls who entered the gates of St. Paddy's never to be seen again.

"Or to the workhouse," said Fergy bitterly, "or to the damned heathen Protestant orphanage where they put the devil right in you day and night. Ah, well, then, St. Paddy's may be better than the street at that."

Lily knew about the workhouse, and the Protestant orphanages, and she knew far more than she cared to about the street. It was the workhouses they all feared most, children and grown-ups too, where the dregs of the earth sat picking oakum til their fingers bled, where they got thin gruel if they were lucky, and death came for the luckiest. And the Protestant orphanages existed for no other reason than to seduce good little Catholics from the faith and turn them, forever damned, into the paths of sin and corruption.

Lily had feared St. Patrick's orphanage, but now that she considered the alternatives, now that she had seen Father Gregory and heard the kindness in his words, it seemed to her that St. Paddy's might not be so bad a thing after all.

The worst thing in the world had already happened to Lily. Both of her parents had left her, and for no fault of her doing. She looked at her brother, still dirty from running in the street, and decided she loved him more than anything in all the world.

"You must wash yourself," she said softly, "for the funeral."

Old Mrs. Flannagan welcomed them into her little room, where they would sleep on folded blankets on the floor. The neighbor lady got some food together and insisted that Lily and Fergus split the pear. It tasted bitter to Lily, for hadn't she first looked on the thing as a gift from St. Jude, and hadn't St. Jude betrayed them?

After the simple meal Mrs. Flannagan and some other neighbor women joined to help make Mary Malone's corpse ready for the grave. Lily and Fergy stayed in the Flannagan apartment and said very little, too well aware of what was

[11]

happening in their former home across the hall, and what the morning would bring.

At last Fergy dropped off to sleep.

But for Lily the night moved slowly, and it seemed to be approaching dawn at a mourner's pace, measured and sad, black outside and blacker within.

Lily lay still, and the thoughts that crept through her head were sad, sad thoughts. *Maybe it's true, what they say, that Ma has gone to a better place, all shining and fine and the angels singing for her, and Dad too, waiting with his big smile, arms reaching, those big green eyes flashing bright. I have his eyes,* she thought, *people are forever saying that. Jade green, they say, the spit and image of her dad. But the eyes were not enough, I want the laughter, too, and the joy of him, and where has all that gone now but to the cold grave?*

They have all left me, and what did I do to deserve that?

Lily could hear the voices from across the hall, keening, chatting, and the sounds of women moving about doing the secret things women do at such times, the priestesses of death. *They'll sell us up, for the burying money.* And little enough they'd find to sell, for hadn't it all gone to the pawnbroker's and the rag shops? Ma's thin gold wedding ring had kept them near two months, then their winter coats, then blankets. All the selling-up would do would be to clear out the little flat for its next victim.

Lily realized that never again would she sleep under this roof, and she realized, too, that this was not, in truth, a thing to make her sad. For what good had ever come to her here?

The last church bell Lily remembered hearing chimed five times. Then she dozed off at last and slept, if not deeply, at least for a little.

Fergus woke her gently at eight.

"Come, Lily," he said, touching her shoulder. " 'Tis time."

So it had happened. While she drifted into sleep, while her guard was lowered, the dreaded day had crept up on her just as she feared. Lily blinked her eyes open, not knowing what unspeakable catastrophes might await her glance. But the dingy little room was still there, and Fergus, splashing his face with water from a chipped white pitcher, and old Mrs. Flannagan, in the eternal black, moving silently in the shadows and almost indistinguishable from them.

Lily lay on the hard floor for a moment and tried the old trick of closing her eyes more tightly than ever in hopes that the day would roll back into night again. The trick, as usual, failed to work. Then she got up, shivering in her shift, and followed Fergus at the pitcher. From the shadows came the well-meaning croak of old Mrs. Flannagan.

"They're coming," she said, "at ten."

Lily knew about the undertakers. Dylan Brothers had set up their undertaking service only lately, the first in the city, too, and quickly had earned a reputation for decent burials at honest prices. How the Malones could afford Dylan Brothers or anything else was a mystery to Lily, who knew how very little was left in her mother's sugar bowl. Maybe the Red Rovers had passed the hat once again, out of respect for Big Fergus. The neighbors, as always happened when very poor people died, would help any way they could. But the sum of all their charity might not pay for a Dylan Brothers funeral, for most of the neighbors were just as badly off as the Malones had been, or worse, and had trouble enough of their own.

Lily got herself dressed, slowly, in her only black dress, a winter churchgoing dress, much patched now, and the stockings so mended there was more darning to them than stocking. Thin as she was, the dress was tight on her now. *And who will darn for me now,* she thought, *or let out my dresses, or cook, or sing the old songs?*

Fergy sat in Mrs. Flannagan's best chair nibbling on stale bread and jam, and looked at his sister. *Jesus, and wasn't she a tiny little thing, more like a bird than a girl, looks a damnsight younger than going on eleven.* There she was, all he had in this bloody world but for his luck and the sure knowledge he'd make something of himself, if they'd give him so much as half a chance. Not that he'd been given a thing but trouble to this date. He was always being blamed for things, even though they weren't his fault. He'd been caught and blamed so many times for mischief he hadn't really done—not on his own, anyway—that he'd long since decided, damn-all, he'd do his worst. And now this, this final stroke of bad luck, Ma going like she did, after Dad. Fergy felt the anger coming in him just at the thought of it. There was no justice, none, and that was that. You had to make your own luck in this world, take the breaks and run with them. If you got a break, that is. He saw Lily, and the rage in him turned all soft and protective. He'd take care of her, sure as God made trees grow. And when he was rich, Lily would have a palace to live in, not some old damned orphanage, and coaches with footmen, and jewels big as hen's eggs shining on her.

He smiled at Lily and, faintly, she returned his smile.

All at once Fergy felt better. Luck or no luck, the future was his, and starting right now, and coming fast.

All he needed was one break.

He remembered the day he'd taken Lily to see the statue. The kid had no idea in the world what he was up to, but Lily came with him anyway, laughing, hand in hand, glad of his company.

He led her through the crowds down to the corner of Bayard and Bowery, and suddenly there they were, looking across Bowery at the splendid gleaming white front of the North American Hotel, a full five stories tall and bursting with activity.

"Well, Lil, what do you think of it?"

" 'Tis beautiful, very grand."

"He had it carved from the very same tree."

"What tree?"

"The statue. It's carved from that tree."

"Are you fooling me?"

"Look up on the roof, there, girl, to the right!"

Lily's eyes traveled up, up the five stories of the great hotel to the rooftop, and there, sure enough, perched on the very peak of the roof, stood a wooden statue of a ragged young boy holding a flagpole in his left hand.

"What does it mean?"

"It was his lucky tree, Lily Malone. That's why I brought you here. To tell you the story of David Reynolds."

"Tell me, then."

"Well, years ago, Lil, he was a boy, see, not much older than me, and he ran away from home . . ."

"Why?"

"To seek his fortune, goose! Well, it was a long way from where he lived to here, and finally he came, near starving he was, like in the statue, all in rags too, and he leaned against a big tree that grew right on that spot, wondering what might become of him, when just at that moment along came a fine gentleman and asked the boy if he'd carry his trunk, and David Reynolds said sure, and the man gave him twenty-five cents. And what do you think he did then?"

"Took a room in the hotel?"

"Silly. The hotel wasn't there yet. It was still a tree. He went and bought some apples. And he stood under that tree and sold the apples. Then he bought more apples . . . and some pears, too. Soon David Reynolds had a fine little fruit stand. Then a house. Then several houses. And at last he tore down all his houses and built this hotel. Isn't it a fine place,

Lil? And to build this great thing, they had to chop down his lucky tree, so he had it made into the statue, that all the world might know his story. So there!"

" 'Tis a fine story, Fergy. Will you be having a fruit stand, too?"

"I might, I might."

He remembered the day fondly, but the affection of his memory quickly turned bitter. How Lily had been caught up in his own excitement then!

"I have," she had said gravely as they started to walk back home, "three pennies. And if you like, I will loan them to you, Fergy. It isn't a quarter, but 'twould be a start."

"Ah, thanks, you're a good little thing, Lil. Maybe I'll be taking you up on that one fine day soon."

But somehow the fine day never came.

It never had, for Fergus Malone Junior. He'd leave one grand scheme half a-borning because another, finer scheme always seemed to come along, smiling and filled with promises and magic.

Well, Fergy thought, finishing the stale bread and washing it down with the last of the water, *it's just a question of time. My chance will come, and sure as there's fires in hell, I will take it!*

There was a loud knock at the door.

Lily thought the stranger looked just like what he was: a messenger from the grave. Tall and stern he was, and all dressed in black. The man from Dylan Brothers, come to take them away, and her poor mother too. Lily stood and she heard the words Mrs. Flannagan spoke, kind words, explaining why the old lady wouldn't go to the grave with them, how she'd stay here and sort out clothes for them, so they'd be ready for St. Paddy's, and for the selling-up that would come later. *Later! Why wasn't it later right now?* Lily took her brother's hand and followed him out of the room and down the stairs.

Everything about the funeral rig looked worn and cheap to Lily. The clothes on the tall man from Dylan's were worn and didn't fit him right. *I'll bet he took 'em off a dead man.* The workhorse that pulled the cart they rode in was black and worn too, dusty with age. He moved with a slow and painful gait, as though he might be walking to his own grave. And the cart itself was a poor thing, a farmer's wagon splashed with black paint. Only the inescapable dignity of death itself made them look like anything but a pack of beggars.

There were two carts.

One was the hearse, although "hearse" was by far too fine a name to give it.

The plain unpainted white-wood box that held Ma's body was lowered onto the crude cart by two rough young men in shirtsleeves. It went on ahead. Lily and Fergy climbed up next to the driver of the second cart, and the sad old horse began his agonized approach to the funeral Mass at St. Patrick's.

It was market day on Mulberry Street, and the stray pigs were having a field day, rutting everywhere, stealing fresh vegetables and arousing the wrath of shopkeepers. Lily was tempted to smile, seeing it all from the vantage point of the cart.

Then she remembered where she was, and why, and that the last time she had ridden on a wagon was five years before, going to her father's funeral. *What pain I might have been spared, had it been my own!*

Mary Malone's funeral, Lily knew, would be only a poor imitation of her father's, for that had been a hero's burial, all brass and glitter, and a glass-windowed hearse with six black plumes and four sleek black stallions all decked out in purple.

Still and all, the form of it would be the same, the burial mass at St. Paddy's, the ride to Twelfth Street, the graveside prayers.

Lily closed her eyes to the bright summer morning and prayed. She prayed that it would be over quickly, and that she could manage to save her tears like Ma had asked.

The funeral carriage rounded the corner of Prince Street and Lily's glance was drawn to the front of the orphanage as if magnetized.

My future home. She noticed that Fergy was staring at the place too, his green eyes dark with anger. She reached out and touched his hand. He withdrew it fast, as though the touch of her burned him.

Lily looked away.

So there was where I walked, only yesterday, and here is where I turned, and in a minute I'll be walking down the self-same aisle where I went to pray for a miracle. And did the saint betray me, or just not hear, or is it all some kind of testing, to see how much I can bear? It was easy enough for Lily to think of such questions, and many more besides, but the answers seemed to hover somewhere out of her reach, dancing elusively in the shimmering August sunlight.

Mary Malone's pine casket lay on a black-covered bier before the altar.

There was only one small black wreath to cover the naked-looking wood, a sinister thing of black, leathery leaves with a wrinkled purple ribbon on it. Lily knew it was a reusable wreath, for she had seen it and wreaths like it many times before. Like the horse and the cart he pulled, the wreath itself seemed ready for the grave.

The coffin looked small and lonely in the soaring darkness of the church. Lily thought of her mother, alone and cold inside, but at least past suffering.

Maybe Ma was with the angels, with Big Fergus! If only she could be sure of that.

Father Gregory, impressive in his priestly robes, came out on the altar and began the funeral Mass.

There were five or six neighbors present, but not Fat Bessie Sullivan. That, thought Lily, was typical. Fat Bessie was probably eating pastries somewhere and gossiping about how the Malones had fallen on evil times.

Well, and wasn't it true?

The Mass crawled across Lily's mind with the numbing familiarity of long, long acquaintance. Then it was over and the young priest said a short eulogy. He had known Big Fergus, which did not surprise Lily in the least, since she had always assumed that everyone in the world, high and low alike, knew her father. Then Father Gregory led them in a short prayer and it was over.

Lily stood with Fergy at the door of the cathedral and spoke to the people who had taken the trouble to come.

They made death sound like a fine and glorious thing, as though life were a race and death was the prize. Lily heard well-meaning people telling her that Ma had gone to her reward, that she would know eternal happiness now, that she was in a better place.

Yet, as much as Lily wanted these things to be true, the memory of Ma's last days was too vivid in her to believe the kind sentiments entirely. *She suffered terribly,* Lily thought, bracing herself against the forbidden tears, *and if she's anywhere now where she can see what's probably going to become of Fergy and me, she'll be suffering even more!*

In the end it was Father Gregory who saved them.

He came out of the vestry in his black priest's suit and stepped up behind the Malone children and put one of his big red hands on each of their shoulders. Then he led them down the stairs to the waiting carriage.

"Come now, Lily, Fergus," he said, and with such vigor in his voice, you could hardly call it sad. "And may I be hitching a ride with ye to the graveyard?"

On the slow ride to Twelfth Street, Father Gregory spoke kindly to the children and tried to make them feel he understood their sorrow, and how bad their luck had been.

He spoke of St. Paddy's orphanage, too, and told Lily and her brother many things they hadn't known, or had only guessed about the place. Father Bill was well aware of the rumors that circulated about St. Paddy's, for his parish was a garden of superstition and the young priest saw it as his duty to weed and prune that garden on a regular basis.

Lily found herself delighted with much of what he told them.

"There'll be classes, then, I can learn to read?"

"If you apply yourself, Lily, that is very likely, and to write a good hand, too, and to sew if you like, and do other handy things, for many of our best girls go into service, and with some of the finest families in the city, at that."

"And we won't be beaten?"

"Not if you behave yourselves. The nuns of St. Paddy's are kindly, Lily; they like the little ones, or surely they wouldn't be devoting their lives to 'em, now, would they?"

Lily had no answer for this: she remembered the lurid tales of torture and unspeakable perversions. Then she looked at the smiling young priest beside her and decided that the rumors had been just that, and this man would not be a part of anything unspeakable. It was just then that she noticed the slow horse slowing further.

The carriage stopped. Lily and Fergy knew the graveyard well. They came every Sunday when the weather permitted, before their mother fell ill, to visit their father's grave and make sure it was being kept properly. They were proud of the fine white headstone, all they had left of Big Fergus other than the memory of him.

Mother's grave had been dug, a narrow trench that looked too small even for the small pine box. Lily looked at the hole and then looked away. Dylan's men were there, and they had a rough trestle waiting for the coffin. The hearse was not really a hearse in the proper sense. There were no cut-glass windowpanes, no bright silver, no black plumes or glossy black paintwork. Lily's mother arrived at her burial place on a cart, like a load of hay, and even though the cart had been smeared with dull black paint, it didn't seem right, somehow. Lily remembered her father's funeral, the glitter and spectacle of it, and shivered at the comparison. Still, it was the best that ten dollars could buy from Dylan's, and who were they to quibble? Who, indeed?

Father Gregory read the service. The day was bright and hot within the walls of the new burial ground. Lily looked around her as the familiar prayers filled her ears: this place had been in use only ten years, and already it was nearly filled. The trees hadn't had a chance to reach their full growth as yet, and before they did, this graveyard would be shut, finished, full-up as the old St. Patrick's graveyard had been filled up before it. And the new place that people were talking about even now, out on Long Island somewhere, a boat ride away, it might as well be in another country. How people died! The new St. Patrick's graveyard was like a little town inhabited only by dead people. Lily hoped her mother would find friends there, that she would not be lonely. There would be, of course, Big Fergus. Lily tried to imagine her parents lying side by side in the black earth of Twelfth Street as they had lain side by side in bed, and she prayed there would be comfort in it for both of them, that they'd really and truly know, each of them, that the other was there, at hand, inches away. Lily hoped they'd be able to sing again, to laugh as they once laughed, and even argue now and then, then kiss and forgive, and dream again and make plans. She wanted to ask Father Gregory if dead people could sing, could they hear, was it allowed, in heaven, to make plans? But it would be unseemly, she decided, at least here and now. Maybe she could ask such questions later.

Father Gregory finished the service. Dylan's men had thick ropes under the coffin now, and they gently lowered it into the earth. The priest came close to the children then and once more put his arms around the two of them as the first spadefuls of earth rattled down on the lid of the pine box. Lily could feel herself shuddering with that fearful hollow noise, and all at once she hoped that dead people really couldn't hear, even if it meant not hearing singing or jokes. This noise was too terrible to hear, dirt rattling down on your own coffin. They did not wait for the grave to be filled.

Father Gregory walked with them back to the carriage and then rode back down Mulberry Street to the old apartment. He would wait, and the carriage would wait, while they got their clothes to take to the orphanage.

Somehow, Lily thought, as she and Fergus climbed those worn stairs for the last time, it might not be so bad after all, being in the orphanage. There would be school, there would be other girls to play with, Fergus would be nearby, in the boy's section. Best of all, there would be regular meals: Fergus wouldn't have to be out on the streets scrounging for them all day. They got to the old apartment door. It was open.

The one big room was changed already. Lily looked at the place that had been her home these last five years, in happy times and sad times, and thought: *We never lived here. Where we lived was somewhere else.*

Mrs. Logan was there, and old Mrs. Flannagan resting on a stool, coughing softly. And Fat Bessie Sullivan. The furniture, what was left of it, had been moved against the far wall, and the room seemed bigger than Lily could remember. There was a small heap of linen on top of the old kitchen table, the table where her mother had lain last night. On a chair were two worn pillowcases stuffed full of Lily's things and Fergus' everyday clothing. Hortense—Lily's only toy, the rag doll—waited sadly, her head flopping down as if in mourning, perched on top of the pillowcase that held everything Lily Malone owned in the world.

It was hard to know what to say. Fergus spoke first, to no one in particular: "We're going to St. Paddy's!" He blurted it out like a challenge.

The ladies gathered around them then, clucking and murmuring platitudes of thanks, more expressions of sympathy, notes of encouragement, all to the rasping counterpoint of Mrs. Flannagan's incessant coughing. Lily decided that the next time she went into St. Patrick's she would say a prayer for old lady Flannagan. The children squirmed under the sudden flood of attention. Lily walked to the window and looked out, to see Father Gregory pacing anxiously back and forth in front of the carriage, the picture of a man with better things to do. She turned to Fergus. Fat Bessie was bending over him to whisper something in his ear. Fergus cringed.

It was then that Lily noticed her mother's favorite scarf carefully knotted around Fat Bessie's neck. It was a very old scarf, part of Mary Malone's dowry chest, made from the softest ivory-colored linen and edged with pure white lace made by Lily's grandmother's own hands. It was the one valuable thing that Mary refused to sell, come what may. Even after her own gold wedding band had gone, just a month before she died, Lily's mother would never part with that scarf. She would ask Lily to take it out sometimes, just so she could hold it, and think of the olden times, and remember Big Fergus, and smile. Lily stood for a moment, staring. Then she walked up to Fat Bessie and touched her on the arm. Bessie Sullivan's arms were the shape and color of large hams. She straightened up, smoothed her billowing skirts, and smiled at Lily. It was a large, false smile, the smile of a marzipan pig.

"Yes, my darlin'?"

"You are wearing my mother's best scarf."

Bessie's smile grew even wider, even more false. Her hands fluttered to her neck like overweight drunken butterflies.

"Dear Mary, God rest her soul, she wanted me to have it."

"She was dead before you ever came here."

Bessie's pink face flushed red. The little beady eyes seemed to grow smaller and darker and more vindictive. Lily watched Fat Bessie with a mixture of loathing and detachment: she would have her mother's scarf back if she died on the spot, getting it off this swine in mourning.

"Child, are you accusing me of stealing?"

"May I have my mother's scarf, please?"

"Well! I never in all my . . . after all I've . . ."

The other two women stood transfixed, and Fergus, too.

Only the booming authority of Father Gregory's voice cut through the bewildering scene: "Tell the pure truth now, Bessie Sullivan: did Lily's mother bequeath you that scarf?"

"She most certainly did!"

Bessie gathered herself up, nearly five feet of lard trembling with self-righteous indignation.

"And you are prepared to roast in the eternal fires of hell if that isn't God's own truth? Eternity is a long, long time, Bessie. And hell is a very hot place."

"I . . . I just know she wanted me to have it!"

"Because she said so?"

"Well, Father, not in so many words . . . but . . ."

"So you kindly filled in the gaps for the poor dying creature, is that it? And helped yourself to this scarf, which I see around your neck like the noose on the neck of a murderer. Is that what happened?"

Bessie stuttered and fumbled for words which never came. Her flushed face turned pale. Small beads of sweat appeared upon her upper lip and her forehead, and ran down her face. Her lips opened and shut spasmodically, like the lips of a beached fish, but no words came out. Instinctively Lily moved closer to Father Gregory and took his hand.

Still in silence, Fat Bessie reached to her throat, quickly

untied the scarf, hurled it to the floor, turned on her heels, and flounced indignantly out of the room.

The sound of her footsteps in heavy retreat down the stairs was drowned by Father Gregory's laughter.

"Lily, Lily," he roared, lifting her to the very ceiling, "if General Scott had you at Veracruz, it would have been over in an hour!"

Dizzy from the height and the unexpected triumph, Lily found herself laughing, and heard Fergus laugh in response. Even Mrs. Logan was seen to smile, and old lady Flannagan nodded her approval through the incessant coughing.

At last the priest set her down, and picked up the scarf where it lay crumpled on the floor. He smoothed it out and handed it to Lily with a bow. " 'Tis a lovely scarf, Lily, and you must keep it always as a memory of your dear mother. I think," he added with a wink, "that it is not too badly contaminated by its recent adventures. Sure, and Sister Mary Agnes at St. Paddy's knows everything about fine linens. She can show you how best to clean it, and mend it too, if ever need be."

Lily thanked him and folded the scarf and put it in the pillowcase with her other things. Then she went to Mrs. Flannagan. "Thank you," said Lily softly, "for you surely helped us when we needed it most."

She thanked Mrs. Logan, too, as did Fergus. Then they picked up their belongings and walked out of the room and down to the carriage.

No one spoke until the carriage was off and moving. Both Lily and her brother had thoughts enough of their own to keep them from idle chatter. For, though St. Patrick's Orphanage was six short blocks from where they had lived all their lives, it was as much of a new adventure as going to a foreign country, both scary and exciting, filled with promise and fraught with unknown dangers.

Lily's reverie was interrupted by an uncontrollable chuckle from Father Gregory. "Indeed, 'twill be a long time before I forget the sight of Bessie Sullivan, children, caught as she was in the act. And while we think on that, my darlings, do not feel ashamed to be laughing on the day of your poor mother's burial. It is a dark hour indeed that has no light at all in it, and 'tis sure I am if Mary Malone had been in that room—and who is to say she was not?—she would have been proud and happy to see her little girl so lively after what's right. Always stand up for yourselves, children, for often there may be no one else to do it for you."

The horse clip-clopped its mournful way up Mulberry Street. Finally they reached Prince Street and turned the familiar right-hand corner. The St. Patrick's orphanage lined the block on their right, three stories of immaculate red brick and a gabled story above that, neat behind its lawn, dappled by the shade of two ancient elm trees, softened by a new fringe of flowering shrubs along the line where the bricks met the lawn. There could be no doubt that this was an institution, but somehow it seemed welcoming in the late-afternoon light. The familiar cathedral was just across the street, with its old walled graveyard and its square bell tower and iron lacework. Father Gregory, they learned, taught in the school, and might in fact be teaching them.

"Surely, it isn't home, children," he said as they were about to climb down, "but there are good things here, things to learn, things to do. Three square meals every day, that can't be too bad, now, can it? And the good Sisters of Charity are kindly ladies. I think you will like it here, and if you don't, Lily and Fergus, tell me why, and if I can, I will try to help you."

He patted them on the shoulder for encouragement, then led them up the short walk to the front door. Even though she felt better now, it seemed to Lily the longest and the saddest walk she had ever taken. She reached for Fergy's hand and held it tight. *Their future was here, and they'd face it together!*

❧ 3 ❧

Lily looked up at the polished dark-wood doors.

They seemed big enough to be the very gates of heaven—
or hell. She remembered all the old gossip, of children who
went in through these same doors and never were seen again.
Lily turned.

The priest smiled, but Lily was not entirely reassured.

Fergy knocked. They waited in silence. He was just about
to repeat his knocking when the door swung silently open. A
small, old, smiling nun stood there, old as the hills she was,
and hardly bigger than Lily herself.

"Come in, come in, my dears, you must be the Malones, is
that right?"

Fergy mumbled something and they followed the old nun
into the orphanage.

The front door opened onto a long central hallway floored
in dark wood that had been polished almost to the brightness
of a mirror. Lily couldn't remember ever seeing a floor so
bright. At the end of the hallway an enormous crucifix stood
against the white wall with a bigger-than-life-size Jesus twisting in unspeakable agony against a heavy oak cross, flesh
pale as Ma's had been in the last days, blood pouring from
the several wounds with ghastly authenticity. *Christ*, thought
Lily with a shudder, *died for my sins. Sure and I must have
some pretty bad ones, to have caused all that.* Fergus, standing beside her in the doorway, was unnaturally silent, as he
had been all morning. Lily sensed that her brother must be
feeling the same doubts and hopes and fears that she felt.
And that he must be as little equipped to handle those doubts
and fears. Well. And what was there to do but make the best
of it, and be thankful to Almighty God that it wasn't worse?
For surely they could be out on the streets this very night,
with no roof at all over their heads, and not a thing in their
bellies, and no one to know the difference whether they lived
or died. More than ten thousand homeless children, Lily had
heard, were reported to be wandering the streets of this city,

sleeping in alleys and cellars, stealing, running wild, prey to criminals of all kinds, and the pimps, and even Protestants. There was no doubt about it: things could have been much, much worse. The old nun nodded to Father Gregory then and left them.

Smiling, Lily turned to Father Gregory. "And will you be leaving us now, Father?"

"Not till I see that you're properly introduced, my girl. 'Tis Sister Cathleen herself I'll be taking you to, the matron of the whole establishment. Just follow me."

That they did. The hallway seemed to go on forever, and the crucifix at the end of it got bigger and bigger as they followed the tall young priest down the gleaming expanse of oak. At the end of the hallway a nun glided past them, smiling, her pale benevolent face framed in starched white, trailing a wimple and gown of some sheer black material, looking not at all mournful despite the severe black-against-white of her attire. Somehow the grace of the woman and her expression cheered Lily. In a world filled with Fat Bessies and coughing old Mrs. Flannagans, serenity of any kind counted for a lot. Lily decided that she, too, would be serene. She would find contentment in the fields of the Lord. Lily smiled benevolently as Father Gregory turned a corner and led them down another, even longer hallway.

Then Fergus pinched her.

"Ow! That hurt, Fergus. Why did you do that?"

"You dropped something."

Lily looked behind her. Hortense lay crumpled on the polished floor, martyr to her owner's newfound spirituality. Blushing, Lily ran back and retrieved her doll. Then she gave Fergus a swift clout in the belly. He was about to escalate the battle when Father Gregory grabbed his arm.

"Now, then, that will be enough of that, Fergus Malone. And on your mother's burial day, too. Get on with you, lad—here's Sister Cathleen's office now."

He knocked and was bid to enter.

Sister Cathleen's office was a small room paneled in oak up to the height of a chair back, and painted a cheerful pale yellow above that. One big window looked out on the back garden, which was a fair picture of fresh green lawns and new-leaved trees, with here and there great clumps of red and white and pink roses in full and fragrant bloom. The window was half-opened in the warmth of the afternoon, and Lily could smell the sweetness of the huge blossoms over the inside smells of furniture oil and dry paper and chalk. The

[25]

walls of the room were bare except for one small black-and-white engraving of St. Christopher wading a swift-flowing river with the Christ Child on his back. St. Christopher gazed hopefully at something just beyond the frame of the picture. The Christ Child waved cheerfully, confident in his mount. Lily felt better and better about St. Patrick's orphanage, but she still wondered why Fergus had pinched her in the hall.

Sister Cathleen was a tiny woman, one of the smallest grown-ups Lily had ever seen, but somehow she gave the impression of being very strong. She was slender and well-proportioned, as much as Lily could see of her under the wimple and robes, and she had the face of an inquisitive bird. Sister Cathleen's most prominent feature was her eyes. They were large and so dark brown they might have been black. The size and the darkness of her eyes, and the quick way they moved in her tiny face, all accentuated the impression that here was a very intelligent, not unkindly bird, but a bird nevertheless.

She sat at a specially built tall stool which compensated admirably for her shortness, while having the unfortunate side effect of looking exactly like a bird's perch.

Sister Cathleen looked up as Father Gregory opened the door, and smiled, a quick, intense, birdlike smile.

"Well, Father G.," she said brightly, speaking rather fast, "so you have brought me some new fledglings!"

He smiled. "That I have, Sister, and a fine pair they are, too: may I be presenting Miss Lillian Malone, and Mr. Fergus Malone, recently of Mulberry Street, in our very parish, and a true hero their father was, Big Fergus, who died fighting the Great Fire of Forty-two."

Sister Cathleen nodded agreeably through this rather long speech. Then she put her small, slender hands together on top of the papers she had been reading, making a small cathedral of her fingers.

"Well, children, we have a few more than two hundred young people here at St. Paddy's, and 'tis fair to say that more of them are happy than are not. We do have rules, not, mind you, because we love rules, but rather because 'tis the only way we'll ever get the lot of you fed and washed and educated."

She paused then, and stepped down from her stool, and walked around the desk. Lily watched, fascinated. Sister Cathleen was no taller standing than she was sitting on the curious stool! And yet, this tiny creature with the kind face had got to be matron of the best and biggest Catholic orphanage in New York. Sister Cathleen paused in front of Lily, reached down and touched her under the chin, and raised Lily's face to look into her own face, which in truth was not all that far above it. And she spoke:

"Lillian . . . Lily, is it, that they call you?"

"Yes, Sister. Lily."

"And your doll? What is her name?"

"Hortense."

"Ah. French, she is, then?"

"She's French," Lily said quietly, and then suddenly added: ". . . and she is a princess."

"A very beautiful princess, at that. Well, Lily, and Fergus, we must be getting you settled in time for the evening meal. Now, St. Patrick's is really two orphanages, one for girls and one for boys. You'll not be far away, for the boys are just over there, in that wing, and the girls here in this one. But the times when you can be together must be limited. As little limited as we can manage."

Lily looked at Fergus. *The dreaded moment had come. She was going to be sold into slavery! She'd never see Fergus again.* Lily clutched Hortense closer to her thin chest, and took one step closer to her brother.

Sister Cathleen went on: "On Saturday afternoons, after lunch, you can play together. You can visit after Mass on Sunday. And, of course, you may write letters as often as you like. We encourage that."

Sister Cathleen smiled brightly, but to Lily it still sounded like exile of the darkest, most remote order. She took another step closer to Fergus, and silently reached out for his hand. She caught his hand and squeezed it. Sister Cathleen continued, but now her voice seemed far away to Lily, and she only half-heard what the matron was saying.

"We have three dormitories for girls, and they're divided by ages, thirty girls to the dormitory. It is the same for the boys, except that we have four boys' dormitories. And a great new luxury has come to us since the Croton Reservoir opened five years ago: indoor plumbing! You'll have classes every day but Sunday, and fine classes they are, too: Father Gregory here teaches some of them, and other fine priests and nuns. Last year five of our boys went on to university: what do you think of that, Fergus?"

Fergus looked at the floor, still in the death grip of Lily's small hand.

"It's a fine thing, Sister."

"This world is filled with hope, children, even though it

may not seem so today. You can make your own way, by your own efforts, and prayers, and the grace of God Almighty. Even as Father Gregory has done, who once was an orphan boy just like Fergus here. Always remember that, Lily and Fergus: the future is what you make of it. Now. Let me take Lily to her new home, and, Father G., perhaps you'll see Fergus to the boys' wing?"

Lily stood transfixed. One more parting. She knew, somewhere deep inside her, that this was not a parting like death. But it was a parting from the last fragment of family love that the little girl knew, and it stung worse than knives, loomed darker than death, had the chill and finality of permanent exile. Together, with Fergus, things would somehow be all right. Alone, Lily had no idea how she could survive even for an hour, let alone the rest of her life. And she had similar doubts about Fergus, older as he was, and bigger and physically stronger. She read his fears in his silence, and she felt her own fear welling up in her, starting at the shivering tips of her toes and mounting like a fever, like a brushfire, first burning and then threatening to turn to tears. *"Save your tears, child, for one day you may truly need them."* Lily looked at the bright room and the garden beyond, and at the two fine smiling faces of Sister Cathleen and Father Gregory, smiling now over their obvious anxiety about the scene they feared was coming on them: Lily gulped and decided that this was no time for tears. All the sadness, all the fear, was from within. These people meant her no harm, nor Fergus either. The orphanage of St. Patrick's was the best they could do, and grateful they must be for the fact that it was opening up to them.

Still clutching her brother's hand, Lily stood up on tiptoe and kissed his cheek.

"God be with you, Fergus."

He looked at her then, and his ruddy face had turned pale. His eyes started to fill with tears, but no tear fell. He tried to smile at her, but the smile melted into quivering sadness.

"It won't be long, Lil, I promise it won't."

"We can write."

She said this without believing it: Fergus' struggles with the written word had been the despair of his teachers on those few days he deigned not to play hooky. And Lily herself was barely beginning to learn. Well, all the more reason to get on with it, then! They might try to keep her from Fergus, and Fergus from her, but Lily knew she'd find a way around their wicked rule. If writing must be part of it, well, then, she would learn to write. Fired with determination, Lily looked at Sister Cathleen. She was ready.

"Don't despair, children," said Sister Cathleen softly. "It may seem like you're apart, but in truth, you'll not be farther away than the length of this building."

Then she took Lily's hand and led her out of the small office and down the hall. Fergus and Father Gregory started off in the other direction, in silence.

On the way down the halls and up the stairs and around the bend, Sister Cathleen kept up a busy stream of talk. Lily learned that she would be in the middle level of the three girls' dormitories, containing thirty girls from ages seven to eleven. There was a nursery for infants of both sexes, and then the youngest dorm, ages three through seven. The older girls, who had decided to stay on in the orphanage and help with the young ones, or to stay on and consider their vocation as nuns, had a third dormitory of their own. It was these girls who helped supervise the younger ones, who acted as monitors in class and in study hall, who helped keep order in the sleeping quarters, and who also supervised the children's work programs.

"What sort of work will I be doing?"

Like all poor children in New York, Lily had grown up on frightening stories of the public workhouses, where charity wards of the city were worked sometimes literally to death in conditions of unspeakable filth, on almost nothing to eat.

"That," said Sister Cathleen, "depends on what you'd most like to learn. We help in the kitchen, where you could learn to cook. We have a great deal of sewing to do, and a wonderfully clever nun is in charge of all that, Sister Mary Agnes. We make our own uniforms, Lily, and mend all our own linen, and sometimes we even make altar cloths for St. Patrick's, costumes for the pageants, that sort of thing. And even fine linen to sell, when there's a spare moment, although I fear we have few enough of those these days. In any event, the work isn't that hard, nor the work time so long. Three hours per day per child is the rule, and often 'tis less. What we try to do here, Lily, is teach our children useful things, things that will let them go on to better jobs, should they decide to leave us."

"What sort of jobs might that be?"

"For girls, perhaps being a serving maid in some fine household. That's not at all a bad life, let me tell you. Or, if you were of an academic inclination, you might go for a governess, or nursemaid. Many of our brighter girls do that.

Then, there are always positions opening up in the shops, although that seems less appealing to me than being truly well-looked-after in a rich home. As for the lads, some of them, with luck, go on to college. Few, in truth, are so inclined, but it does happen, and we are proud when it does. More of our lads go into trade, as apprentices of one sort or another. And, of course, some of them get the calling and become priests. Even as Father Gregory himself did. And by the same token, some of our best girls become nuns, and stay with us always."

Lily had been so absorbed in what the matron was saying, she hadn't noticed where they were walking. They had climbed two flights of stairs, turned several corners, walked down one very long hallway and another, shorter one. Everything gleamed. The windowpanes themselves sparkled. The green grass outside seemed to be sparkling too, in the bright clear sunlight of the summer afternoon. The idea of staying here forever seemed not at all unattractive to Lily. One day, perhaps, she might be the matron, escorting some poor little orphan down this same hallway, giving her hope for a future that, just minutes ago, had seemed hopelessly dark and fraught with hidden perils.

They paused at a big oak door.

"Well, now," said Sister Cathleen brightly, "here we are."

She opened the door. Lily's eyes widened as she saw the size of the room that was to be her new home. It was one of the biggest rooms she had ever been in, outside of church, or the big hallway downstairs. The room was long and airy and sparkling clean, like everything else in St. Patrick's orphanage. It was up under the dormered roof, and the walls were truly vertical only up to a height of about five feet. Like Sister Cathleen's office, the walls were paneled to chair-back height. Above that, they were painted gleaming white. On both sides of a wide aisle, pairs of white-painted iron cots marched the length of the room, fifteen to the side. Next to each cot was a small wooden table, and on each table, a small pitcher and basin to wash in. There were hooks on the wall, four to each cot. Under the beds Lily could see woven wicker hampers that, she imagined, must contain the girls' extra clothing. It all looked neat and cheerful.

The big room had only two occupants: at the far end of the central aisle a broad-shouldered, sullen-looking girl with a very low forehead was lazily pushing a broom. Halfway down the row of beds, on the left, and facing away from them, a thin girl sat busily sewing something blue. Both girls wore what Lily soon learned was the summer weekday uniform of indigo-blue cotton twill jumper, with skirts to the floor, over a thin cotton shirt in a paler shade of blue.

"Bertha, Frances, come here."

The girls walked quickly to Sister Cathleen.

"Good afternoon, Sister Cathleen," they said in unison, at the same time bobbing in half-curtsy.

"Good afternoon, girls. I'd like you to meet our newest guest, Lillian Malone, called Lily."

"How do you do, Lily?"

"Fine, thank you," said Lily in a small voice, wishing it were true. Bertha was the sullen broom-pusher. The sewing girl was Frances. Lily wondered how the matron ever learned to remember all their names. Sister Cathleen walked away from them, seemed to be looking for something, then found it.

"Here we are! Lily, your bed will be this one. Right next to Frances. Frances, please help Lily get settled in, show her the water closet, where to get her uniform, how to store her things away, and introduce her to the others when they get back. Can you do all that, dear?"

Frances smiled. Lily decided she had a nice face, thin though it was. Frances looked as though she worried a lot. That is all right, thought Lily, so do I.

"Sure, and gladly, Sister Cathleen."

"Then I'll be off, Lily, my dear, but we'll have a chance to get better acquainted later on, won't we?"

It was the kind of question that didn't seem to need an answer. Lily simply nodded and stood by her new bed. The matron smiled benevolently and left them.

No sooner had the door closed behind her than the girl called Bertha was up and mincing down the hallway, squealing in a comic falsetto: "We'll have a chance, la-di-da, to get better acquainted later on, la-di-da, won't we?" Then she dissolved in giggles and sat on one of the beds. "You'd think"—Bertha snickered—"that this rat hole was bloody Delmonico's, and this little guttersnipe the Princess of Wales, la-di-da." And she laughed again, a deep, unhumorous laugh.

The girl named Frances came to Lily, put one arm around her protectively, and said quietly: "Hush, now, Dolan! If you were capable of feelings, you'd know how it feels on your first day. Pick on someone your own size, if you can locate 'em with a microscope. I'm sorry, Lily, but Bertha Dolan has spent so much time groveling with the pigs, she comes by that kind of behavior naturally. We aren't all like that, thanks be to God."

Bertha Dolan got up again, her face purple. She stood in the aisle with her hands on her hips and hissed like a mongoose: "Thanks be to God, is it, Miss la-di-da Frances O'Farrelley? Grovel with piggies, do I? Let me tell you, fair lady, we are all lower than pigshit in this place. We're Irish, aren't we, we're orphans, aren't we? Lower than low, that's what we are. Lower than low."

"And so determined to stay that way, Bertha, darlin'? And you not even an orphan, but masquerading as one?" Frances turned away from the purple-faced Bertha and said very distinctly, "Think of it, Lily, her parents are alive and well and want nothing more to do with the sad creature. I can't imagine why, lovable thing that she is, can you?"

Lily said nothing, but bowed her head, trying to imagine parents so heartless they'd turn a child out on the streets.

"Ah," said Bertha, "to hell with ye all."

She stomped down the aisle and took up her broom and punished invisible specks of dust as if she were flailing all her enemies.

"Now, then," said Frances with a smile, "this is your bed, Lily, and your stuff that you've brought goes under it, in the wicker chest. Your uniforms and nightgown get hung from these hooks, you fetch your own washwater from the faucet down in the W.C., which I'll be showing you in a minute, and that's about that except for learning your way around, which won't take all that long. Now. Let me run and see if we can still get you a uniform before 'tis time for supper."

Frances O'Farrelley walked briskly down the aisle and out of the door. Lily sat on her bed for the first time. It was a better bed than any she could remember from Mulberry Street. Then she got up and walked to the window nearest her bed. Sunk into its dormer, it made a small box just big enough for one little girl. She stood on tiptoe to see out: there across Prince Street was St. Patrick's in all its glory! Lily could see over the churchyard wall into the filled-up graveyard, with its white scallop-topped stones, its crosses and marble benches and willow trees rippling in the breeze like strands of seaweed under the ocean. Then she walked across the dormitory and looked out the other window. Here were the gardens, the playing field of the boys' orphanage, and all the back gardens of the row houses between Mott Street and Mulberry. Lily could see flowers and tomato plants twining, and chickens and pigs and an occasional goat. She opened the window. Here were the familiar noises of her old neighborhood, but more distant now, comforting and remote at the same time. She remembered her lonely walk up Mulberry Street to light the candle in St. Patrick's, and wondered when, if ever, she would be allowed to take such a walk again.

The big room was silent but for the noise of Bertha Dolan's broom sliding over the clean floor. That noise stopped, and Lily turned from the window. Bertha stood at the foot of Lily's bed, staring at Hortense with a kind of dull fascination, as though the little rag doll might bite.

"A pretty doll, that is."

Bertha's voice was heavy for a young girl, and there was a coarseness about it that Lily thought sounded more like the voice of a man, and a big man at that.

"Thank you."

"Might I be holdin' her?"

Lily didn't want the bigger girl to hold Hortense. Lily didn't like Bertha Dolan at all. But it was her first day, and the older girl frightened Lily. She picked up Hortense and handed her to Bertha. "My mother made her."

Instantly on holding the doll, Bertha's dull face changed. A lurid grin spread across her potato-shaped countenance. She laughed a shrill maniac's laugh, and held Hortense high over her head, as though holding the doll up for sale. "Ooooh! Did she, now? Hee-hee-hee! And would that be what the poor lady died of, making such ugly things for the likes of you? Hee-hee!"

Bertha danced and pranced the length of the big dormitory, tossing Hortense high in the air, catching her roughly.

Lily ran after her. "Stop that now. Give her back!"

"You'll be having better things to think on than silly dolls, my fine lady, for 'tis kissing the matron's ass, you'll be, and doing God knows what for the pleasurement of the priests!" Bertha eluded Lily easily. The bigger girl led Lily around the beds, back and forth, down the central aisle, until at last she made her way back to where the torment had begun, at the head of Lily's own bed, near the window.

"Please," said Lily, frantic now, on the brink of tears, "give her back to me."

"Here's what I think of your damned ugly old dolly, little miss, la-di-da, and good-bye to her!" Lily watched, horrified, as Bertha Dolan threw Hortense out of the open window. The doll spun in the air and fell in a heap on the lawn three stories below.

"No!" But Lily's cry was too late.

[33]

"It's grateful ye should be, little slut, that I'm not flinging you after her."

Both girls stood there for a moment in silence, Bertha looming over Lily, Lily not knowing whether to fight or cry or run away. Neither of them heard the door opening. The new voice came as a surprise.

"And what devilment have you been up to this time, Bertha Dolan?"

A young nun stood at the end of the room with a clean blanket folded over her arm. She was a pretty girl with pink-and-white skin and lively blue eyes. Lily thought that if she could have seen the nun's hair, it must be blond. Yet pleasant as she was to look on, there was authority in her voice, and a touch of anger. Obviously this was not the first time the strange nun had found herself at odds with Dolan.

"Nothing at all, Sister Claudia. I was just trying to help this poor little girl, Sister, she was so upset she went and threw her nice dolly out the window, sure as you're born."

Lily could only gape in speechless wonder at the speed and smoothness of Bertha's lie. The nun came up to Lily and touched her on the shoulder.

"We haven't met, my dear. I'm Sister Claudia, and I am in charge of the middle dormitory. What is your name?"

"Lily, Sister. Lillian Malone."

"I see. Tell me, Lily, and you needn't be afraid, not of Dolan here, nor of anyone in this place. Is it true, what Bertha told me?"

Lily looked at Bertha Dolan, scowling in silence by the bed, and saw her brute strength and the promise of vengeance in her eyes. Lily looked at Bertha, and at Sister Claudia. Lily had met bullies before. Fat Bessie was a bully. Lily made her decision. When she spoke, she spoke quietly.

"Bertha asked to hold my doll. She threw it out the window."

There was a pause then, and Bertha's face, which was already flushed from her dance around the big room, turned from red to purple.

"I didn't ever do no such a thing, Sister. It's lying she is, the little divil."

"Bertha, Bertha, what are we ever going to do with you?"

There was genuine wonderment in Sister Claudia's soft voice.

"Your reputation for truthfulness, Bertha, is not such that I have any special reason to take your word over Lily's, even though Lily is new here. The first part of your punishment will be to go fetch back Lily's doll, and quickly, please. Run along with you. We shall decide what else needs to be done about this when you get back."

Glowering in all directions, Bertha skulked out of the room. Sister Claudia turned to Lily and smiled. When Sister Claudia smiled, it seemed to Lily that her whole face lit up, as though someone had a hundred bright lanterns concentrating their beams there. Sister Claudia's voice had a special lightness to it when she spoke. Lily could sense that severity did not come naturally to this young nun.

"I apologize for Bertha, Lily," she began. "Most of our girls are good, friendly children, and the boys too, for that matter. Bertha is a problem, there's no denying it, and I hope you will bear with us. We try to help her, and sometimes it seems a thankless job of work. Yet try we must. Now. Tell me about yourself."

"I have a brother. Fergus. He's here now, too."

"I hope you will introduce me, Lily, and it's a fine thing to have a brother. I often wish I did. Alas, I've only got sisters. Sometimes it seems to me we're always wishing for what we have not, and maybe not appreciating what we have in this world."

"I like Fergus."

"I'm sure you do, Lily, and we must arrange that you see him as much as possible. I'll be taking that up with Father James, who is the headmaster of the boys' orphanage, and a kindly man at that."

"Thank you, Sister."

"I know, on your first day especially, dear, some things will be hard for you here. But truly, 'tis not a bad place. I only wish we had space enough for all the poor young things whose families have been taken away from them: often the poor creatures end up living in the streets, like the pigs, with nary a roof over their heads. 'Tis enough to break your heart."

Lily looked at Sister Claudia and thought it might not be such a bad thing to be a St. Patrick's orphan. It might not be such a bad thing to become a nun, like Sister Claudia. Lily was thinking these pleasant thoughts when Bertha Dolan came back into the room.

"Give Lily her doll, Bertha. And apologize."

"I'm sorry." Bertha did not meet Lily's eyes, nor the eyes of Sister Claudia. Instead, she looked at the floor, at the toes of her scuffed shoes, at the iron leg of the bed.

"Thank you."

"I have no further punishment for you, Bertha: your unhappiness is punishment enough. You may go back to your chores."

Bertha bobbed in an awkward imitation of a curtsy, turned, and walked quickly to the other end of the room, where she had left the broom. Lily had the uneasy feeling she hadn't heard the end of the incident. Hortense looked none the worse for her aerial adventures. Lily placed the doll gently on the bed.

"It might be wise," said Sister Claudia gently, "to keep the doll in your wicker trunk, Lily. Out of harm's way, if you take my meaning."

Frances O'Farrelley came bursting into the room. "Good afternoon, Sister," she began breathlessly. "Look, Lily, I think it'll just fit."

Frances held up one of the dark blue summer jumpers and its contrasting light blue blouse. Embarrassed at first, getting undressed in front of strangers, Lily nevertheless struggled out of her old go-to-church dress and into the jumper and blouse. The skirt was an inch too long, but the blouse fit perfectly. Frances ran for her sewing kit and pinned up the hem of the jumper right then and there.

"We'll sew it up properly tonight," Frances said, surveying her handiwork proudly, "and it's a fine sight you are, Lily, don't you think so, Sister?"

"I do," said Sister Claudia. "The color suits you, Lily, you should always wear blue, with that hair, blues or maybe greens, like your eyes."

Lily blushed. No one at home had time for compliments.

"It's a fine dress." The dress, Lily could tell, was not new. Yet it was freshly laundered and crisply ironed and it felt good after the too-tight woolen dress she had worn to the funeral. Lily turned in place, a small dancer's spin, and raised her arms up to get used to the feel of the uniform. She felt free, all of a sudden, as though some great weight had been lifted from her. She'd be one of them now. She'd belong in this strange, formal, frightening, fascinating new world. Lily finished her shy pirouette, and smiled at her audience of two. She liked Frances, and she liked Sister Claudia. "Thank you, Frances," Lily said, "for taking the trouble with me."

"Sure, and 'tis nothing. My job it is, Lily, to be the head seamstress in this dorm. Sister Mary Agnes is teaching me, and I'm teaching all as wants to learn. Tonight I'll teach you how to take up a hem, if you like."

"I would like that."

Lily decided then and there to become a seamstress first, and then, when she could sew something as fine as her mother's wedding scarf, then she would become a nun like Sister Claudia, then the matron of St. Patrick's.

"Now," said Frances, all business again, "I am to be giving you the grand tour, says Matron. Come with me, Lily, and I'll show you some fine sights, beginning with our well-known indoor water faucets."

She took Lily by the hand and led her past the glowering Bertha Dolan to the door. Sister Claudia watched them go, and a thoughtful expression came over the young nun's face as she took in Lily's shyness, her eagerness to please, a kind of quiet gallantry. *And to think*, thought Sister Claudia, *on this very day she buried her mother*.

4

The sun that poured so generously through the drawing-room windows of his parents' mansion on Washington Square did little to cheer Master Brooks Chaffee.

The boy sat on the ivory-and-blue Persian carpet, his long legs folded under him—like a red Indian, Mama said, but where was the harm in it? His armies spread out in front of him, the French to the left, the British to the right, brightly painted lead figures by the dozens, detailed to the tiniest sword and bandolier, horses rearing, flags permanently fluttering in an imaginary wind.

But it wasn't much fun unless Neddy would play with him, and Neddy had decided just a few weeks ago that he was too grown up for such games.

Brooks reviewed his troops, decided that the British lancers would be better deployed in a flanking maneuver, and proceeded to rearrange them. When his older brother's voice reached him, it came as a surprise.

"Thirteen years old and still playing with toys, is he? And he looked like such a clever lad. What a shame."

Brooks turned, flushing. Maybe he was too old to be commanding lead armies. Still, the bright little figures fascinated him. Even now, in the face of Ned's mockery, he could almost hear the bugle calls.

"Someday, when I'm grown, I'll be a famous general, Ned Chaffee, and you will be in distress somewhere and need rescuing, and I—"

"Will somehow contrive to snatch defeat from the jaws of victory, as they say. I've no doubt of it, old bean."

Brooks stood up and faced his brother, not quite sure how far removed his laughter was from tears. Neddy always had a quick, smooth answer. Brooks worshiped his brother, it was as simple as that. The two-year difference in their ages was only a pale measure of the superiority with which Brooks endowed his brother in all things. No one could run, leap, climb a tree, tie a knot, make a joke, or charm a girl with the disarming ease of Ned Chaffee. Sometimes, as in the present, this could be infuriating. Most of the time it was pure delight. And Brooks had long since learned that the only way to deal with his brother was to try, however much in vain, to match wit with wit, laughter with laughter.

"And to think," said Brooks, trying for mockery, "that I was going to let you be Wellington."

Neddy came over to him and put a hand on Brooks's shoulder.

"It's all right, don't you know, old turnip? I didn't mean to spoil your game. It's just that your dashing brother has an appointment. Someone has to defend the Chaffee honor, wouldn't you say?"

It was a girl, of course. It was always a girl these days, for Neddy, and always a different one. Girls were silly. Brooks hoped this didn't mean his brother was getting silly, too. He sighed.

"If you," said Brooks, in perfect imitation of their father at his gruffest and most intimidating, "are all we poor Chaffees have to defend our sacred honor, then I fear it is lost!"

And they both dissolved in hoots of laughter.

Neddy went off to his appointment, and Brooks stood in the window for a moment watching the older boy striding briskly across the dappled sun and shade of the park. Then he turned and looked at his soldiers for a while, and carefully packed them away in the wooden case that had been especially made for them. Each foot soldier, cavalryman, and officer had his own small felt-lined niche. When the big case was full, Brooks Chaffee shut it and clasped the latch and carried it upstairs to the old nursery. Then he put the case on the highest shelf beside a threadbare stuffed tiger and an incomplete deck of playing cards.

Lily could hardly believe that a year had passed, but pass it had, and no denying it. *Not that I'd want to.* In many ways, this had been a happy year. She had made fast friends with Frances O'Farrelley, and other friends, too: Sarah Fitzgerald for one, and Molly Sheehan for another. Bertha Dolan was still a menace, but she was a menace to the whole of St. Paddy's, a universal menace like influenza or the pox. Even the bishop himself was said to be aware of Dreadful Dolan, a name that Lily had invented for her old tormentor.

It was a relief not to worry about food, or if Ma would last the night. So many bad things had happened to Lily before St. Paddy's that the orphanage itself was an ease for her troubles. Most of the nuns were kindly, and although the orphans did more chores than schoolwork, Lily was learning to read a bit, and she could form the entire alphabet and even write her name and a few other words. And, under the friendly tutelage of Frances, Lily was learning to sew and care for linens.

St. Paddy's was a relief, but one thing it did not relieve her from was her continual worrying about Fergy.

It was all very well to have promised Ma on her deathbed to look out for her brother, to get the wildness out of him, but it was quite another matter to actually do anything effective in the way of achieving those goals.

Sometimes Lily felt there was no more hope of taming her brother than riding the wind. Strange fires burned in Fergy, and his sister had no idea what fed them, nor how to cool them down.

Yet there he was, past fourteen and nearly grown, and fast making a name for himself at St. Paddy's, a name worse than Dreadful Dolan's.

When Fergy found a friend in the boys' section of the orphanage, you could be sure the friend would be a wild one. Twice Fergy had run away and twice they'd brought him back. A third time they might not think him worth the bother, and that was more than speculation, for Lily had heard it from a despairing Father Gregory's own lips. And every time her brother ran away, Lily felt her small world tremble, for ever since Ma died her greatest fear was to be completely abandoned, and running away meant a lad might just as well be dead, considering the life of the streets in New York and the dangers that lurked anywhere a boy like Fergy might go.

But Fergy would hear no warnings. He was bound and determined to break away and win the fortune that was waiting for him sure as sunrise, and no words from Lily would sway him.

In the darkest corner of her heart Lily knew it was only a question of time, but this knowledge was too great a burden to bear thinking on, and she avoided it with the pathetic skill of practice.

Lily had come to dread their Sunday meetings in the big visitors' parlor on the ground-floor front of the orphanage. Today was such a Sunday, and Lily came as always to their appointed meeting. You never knew, this time God might give her the grace to say the right thing, to make the right gesture, to bring about the miracle that would be the saving of Fergus Malone Junior, and Lily too, for all that.

Before he even spoke a word, Lily could tell her brother had gotten himself into trouble again. His head hung a certain way, and a sly defiant glare crept into his eyes, which roamed the big heavily furnished room incessantly as if in search of lurking enemies.

"How are you, Fergy?" she asked, kissing him. He squirmed away from her touch.

"Right as rain, Lil, how's yourself?"

His voice carried its burden of false cheer unsteadily.

She looked at her brother. "What's wrong, Fergy?" Lily sometimes found herself slipping into the language of her babyhood: "Fergy" was her first name for her brother, and it usually had the magic power to make him smile. The magic worked. He flashed her a quick and dazzling grin and leaned closer to whisper, the two red-gold heads melding into one spot of color in the dark reception room where they had their Sunday meetings.

"Can you keep a secret, Lil?"

"You know I can."

"There's gold in California, Lil!"

"Yes?"

"Well, Barry and me, we figure to go out there and get us some. Lots. We'll make our fortunes, Lil, I can support you in style."

"Fergus Malone, you are fourteen years old and penniless. How in the name of the good Lord are you planning to get to California?"

His look changed then. The color rose in his face the way Lily had seen it rise many times, times when fate frustrated his plans, when reality came knocking upon the door of his castle of dreams. Fergus looked away from his sister. He had no answer. The gold was there. He would get it. The connecting links in this very long chain had not been filled in. It was a magical idea, instant riches, and it would therefore happen magically. That was all the logic Fergus needed for any scheme, the mere ghost of it floating in the air just beyond his reach.

"California, Fergy, is three thousand miles away. There are deserts and grizzly bears and wild Indians."

"Barry and me can lick 'em."

"Barry and you can't even get through one day in St. Paddy's orphanage without finding yourselves in some kind of trouble, Fergy. 'Tis a fine mess you'd be in, alone on the great desert when the Indians come to get you."

"Laugh, will you? Just see if I give you my gold."

Lily did laugh, then. Her native sense of humor had been some time coming back to her, but come it did, and stronger than ever, after those first bad months of grieving for her lost parents.

"Sure, Fergy, and don't think your scalp wouldn't make a fine prize for some wild heathen Indian chief, red as it is. Your scalp would have the place of honor on his flagpole, or wherever it is they hang such things, and it might just be the first place of honor my old Fergy ever won, isn't it the truth, now?"

"I'll be rich and famous and ride by in my silver coach and splash mud on you, and not even look your way."

"Fergy, Fergy, get on with you, now. 'Tis a fine dream, but it is a dream after all, then, isn't it?"

He turned away from her then and walked to the window and looked out. "It is a dream. And maybe you're right. But someday I'll get out of this prison, Lil, and go out into the great world and do fine things, things you'll be proud of."

"I truly hope you will, Fergy."

"Then why do you laugh at me?"

"Sometimes I wonder that myself. Sometimes maybe I'm laughing because if I weren't, 'tis crying I'd be, have you ever thought of that, Fergy?"

Lily knew he hadn't, for Fergus seemed hardly to think at all, except for the inventing of new and wilder schemes. He turned away from the window and walked up to his sister and awkwardly put his thin arms around her.

"There, now. I'm not the easiest brother in the world to put up with, am I, Lil?"

She looked up at him and smiled. This was better. At least this was human. "You're about the only one I have, Fergy, 'tis why I value you so. You're a bit of a scarce commodity, don't you know?"

"I love you, Lil, can you believe that?"

"Sure I can."

The bell rang then, and it was time for Fergus to go back to the boys' orphanage. They had an hour to themselves every Sunday afternoon, and sometimes half an hour on Saturdays. Otherwise, the two parts of the orphanage were kept strictly apart, for some of the girls and a few of the boys were of an age and disposition to cause some concern among the nuns should they be allowed to mingle.

So Lily got to see her brother for an hour or a bit more each week. Sometimes these sessions were fine and friendly, sometimes sullen and strained. It all depended on Fergus, whose moods changed like the weather. And while her worries about Fergy and what Fergy seemed about to do continued, life at the orphanage of St. Patrick's Cathedral went on with a consistency that Lily found reassuring.

She did not question her lot, for she knew that poor as she was, and orphaned, she was yet better off than many girls her age. *It's alive I am, after all, and I've got my health, and I'm learning things that will be useful one day in a shop or in service somewhere.*

For the most part, Lily enjoyed her life at St. Paddy's.

Frances, going on thirteen, was her closest friend.

Together they studied sewing with Sister Mary Agnes, English with Sister Claudia, religion with Matron herself, and mathematics with Sister Hilda, who was a bully. Together they fended off Dreadful Dolan, exchanged secrets, and speculated almost nightly upon the mystery of Sister Claudia.

For there was, beyond any doubt, a mystery.

Sister Claudia, on wings of rumor and fragments of fact, had become the focus of a glamorous and provocative legend at St. Paddy's. One of four daughters from a very rich family, she was said to have retreated to the convent to nurse a broken heart. No one knew, or would tell, exactly how or when this valuable organ had been so damaged, but this ignorance only fed the fires of speculation. There was, to begin with, the undeniable fact of Sister Claudia's beauty. Surely that alone was sufficient to break hearts left and right, and inevitably to run the risk of having one's own heart broken in return.

The girls would have it no other way, and since Frances and Lily were perhaps Sister Claudia's greatest admirers, they were also the most vulnerable to the legend, which they embroidered to the best of their small experience and soaring imaginations.

"She loved," said Frances darkly, "a man who loved another."

"Another what?"

"Another woman, silly. That's what happens. And then you get a broken heart. Sometimes you even die of it. You pine away."

"Maybe," said Lily in a voice of the utmost gravity, "he was married."

"Maybe he was . . . is . . . a p-r-i-e-s-t!"

[43]

"Never!"

"How do you know?"

"It would be a mortal sin."

"Lily Malone, it's *all* a mortal sin."

It was usually Lily who started laughing first, as their inventions got wilder and wilder. She did this now, and stuck her finger with the needle she was wielding.

"Ow! Anyway, it's a real tragedy. And she so young."

"Maybe he had a broken heart, too. Do men get them?"

"I think so. Only not so often. They're very often heartless, I believe."

Frances had the advantage over Lily in these discussions. She had thought about it more.

"Maybe," said Lily, her eyes gleaming with vicarious pleasure, "he became a priest, and she became a nun to follow him, don't you know?"

"Then maybe they'll run away together."

"And be defrocked!"

"Exactly."

"Wouldn't that be thrilling? They'd have to flee the country."

"In disgrace!"

"Heavily disguised!"

"At midnight!"

"Just imagine."

The deep and sullen tones of Bertha Dolan then came rumbling out of the night. "If you two don't shut up right now, I'll call Sister Claudia and tell her exactly what you said."

This was greeted with derisive giggles, more whispers, secrets, and promises that eventually trailed off into drowsiness. Dreadful Dolan would get hers one of these days—that, at least, was for sure.

The very next day Lily discovered a way of getting back at Dreadful Dolan.

She was walking in the back garden with Frances, coming from their afternoon sewing lesson with Sister Mary Agnes. Lily had her own sewing bag now, just like Frances'. It was made from a scrap of the same blue cotton twill as their uniforms, sewn with a drawstring, filled with odds and ends of fabric, needlepointing canvas, needles, pins, and thread.

"There," said Lily, pointing, "is a lovely little friend for Dreadful."

Sunbathing at the foot of a rosebush was a small brown-and-yellow-striped garter snake. He was lazy with the late-afternoon heat, and easy to catch. Lily quickly did this, held him up for Frances to admire, then popped him into her sewing bag.

The deed was done in darkness.

There was no giggling that night in the middle dormitory. Sister Claudia came by to turn the lantern off at nine P.M., just as she always did, and to wish her charges a good night.

"Good night, Sister Claudia," a chorus of sleepy-sounding voices responded, and the young nun vanished down the hall. All was silence for the next few minutes, until Bertha Dolan came back from the lavatory and stumbled into her bed. Still there was silence. For a moment Lily and Frances thought the snake had made his getaway. Then Dolan's scream came, long and high-pitched and deliciously satisfying.

"Eeeeeeeeeee! Eeee! Eeeeee!"

If Bertha Dolan, menace of the middle dormitory, were being slowly torn apart by the wild Indians, she could hardly have made more of a fuss.

"It's in me bed! It's in me bed!" Her voice was so shrill with terror that the words were almost indistinguishable, one from the other.

"Yes, Bertha Dolan," replied Lily in a deep basso profundo, "and it's a cobra, and you have about five minutes to live."

"Eeeeeeeeeeee!"

"Make your peace with God, Bertha, your time is nigh."

The room filled with giggles then, and three nuns appeared in the doorway, led by Sister Claudia with a lantern, prepared to fight off the devil himself.

"Girls, girls, what is this?"

"Eeeeeeeeeee!" was the only reply. "Eeeeee's in me bed, Sister. A cobra!"

The flickering lantern revealed Bertha Dolan standing on her pillow, the skirts of her nightdress drawn up to her fat thighs, screaming mindlessly.

"All right, Bertha, you're not dying, are you, anyone with strength enough to make this much noise can hardly be wounded." Sister Claudia was not amused.

"But he's in me bed."

"Let me have a look, Bertha, and do come down from there."

Sister Claudia drew back the sheet and the blanket and discovered the very frightened garter snake coiled at the foot of the bed. Sister Claudia brought the lantern closer. The snake's black eyes sparkled like jet. His tiny forked tongue flicked in and out nervously.

"Goodness, Bertha, 'tis only one of the little fellows from the garden." Sister Claudia picked up the snake gently. "And quite a fright he's had, poor creature. A cobra indeed! You're too big for such ideas, Bertha Dolan. Why, sure and he's more frightened than you are, by the look of him. I'll see that he gets safely back to his garden. But now, girls, I must know who has done this mischief. I'm sure 'twas someone's idea of a good joke, but the fact is, someone might have been hurt by it. Poor Bertha might have had a fit, for heaven's sake. Now. Who did it?"

For a moment there was silence, and a muffled giggle or two. No one answered.

"If the culprit," said Sister Claudia sternly, "doesn't come forth and confess her crime, why, then, I'll simply have to punish the lot of you, much as I'd hate to do that."

Slowly, fearfully, Lily stood up beside her bed. She had taken great pains never to get into trouble at St. Patrick's. God only knew, Fergus got into trouble enough for the both of them.

"I did it, Sister Claudia," she said in a small voice, "and I am sorry." This was a lie before God and all his angels, for Lily wasn't sorry at all. Dreadful Dolan deserved it, and worse.

"I'm truly surprised at you, Lily. You may come see me in Sister Cathleen's office tomorrow morning after breakfast. We will see what the matron makes of all this. Now, for the last time, good night, children."

"Good night, Sister Claudia."

The three nuns disappeared, and there was a moment of silence. Then the laughter broke out, gales of laughter, ripples and currents of stored-up mirth.

"To hell with ye all," said Bertha, sullen as ever.

"That," said an unidentifiable voice from the darkness, "was a wonderful performance, Dolan. Have you considered a career in the opera?"

More giggles followed, then silence. Lily did not look forward to her interview with the matron in the morning. Sleep was a long time coming.

Sister Cathleen's door had never looked more forbidding than it did to Lily on the morning after the Dreadful Dolan snake incident, which was fast becoming one of the basic legends of St. Patrick's orphanage. Freshly scrubbed, combed, and fearful, Lily knocked on the big oak door.

"Come in."

Sister Cathleen sat on her perch, tiny as ever, and wearing an unfamiliar frown. Sister Claudia was not in the room.

"Sit down, Lily."

As always, the matron had piles of papers on her desk, neatly stacked, and a ledger, and fresh quills to write with. She looked at the papers, then at Lily. The frown did not go away.

"You have been with us more than a year, Lily, and until last night, all reports have been most favorable. Sister Claudia, in particular, has good things to say about your progress here. Now. Is there anything you'd like to say about the events of last night?"

Lily sat on the edge of a chair that was much too big for her. At first she looked at the floor, then remembered Fergus, who did just that when in trouble, and looked at Sister Cathleen.

"If I had known," Lily began, "how very frightened she'd be, Sister, I never would have done it."

"I can believe that, Lily. A joke was all you meant, something to tease Bertha. But I think you girls don't understand Bertha. There is a sad, sad child, Lily. Bertha is the way she is because she thinks no one cares for her. And, in truth, no one does. We try, of course. We have tried, and we continue to try. Her rude ways, Lily, are the only means Bertha has of defending herself against the world. The story of her family is a sad one, and not like yours, or like the story of most orphans, where accident or illness has broken up a home. I won't burden you with that tale, but 'tis enough to make you weep, thinking on it. So let me say this, Lily, my dear: try to help poor Bertha, for there is a deeply unhappy child, and showing every sign of getting worse, I'm afraid. And where you, or Frances, or most of our other children can take a joke, it's worse, don't you see, for Bertha. Do you understand that, Lily?"

"I think so."

"Then let your punishment be this: to try to be a friend to Bertha Dolan. I know that is not the easiest thing I can ask of you, Lily, but the poor child has no friends at all, and she is her own enemy on top of it all. Do you think you can help her?"

"I'll try, Sister."

"Well, then. That's all any of us can do, isn't it? Try, Lily, and report to me in a week and we'll see what comes of it."

"Thank you, Sister."

"Pray for Bertha, Lily, and for all the poor ones in this world whom no one loves."

"I shall."

"Get on with you, then, Lily, and try to be better."

Pray for Bertha! Lily had never thought of being loved, or not loved. Now she did, and the effort confused and saddened her. *Ah, and a fine lot of good it does you if they love you and die, or run away as Fergy will. What kind of love is that, if all it leaves is a memory? But at the worst of it, Ma loved me, I do remember that, the sadness was in the leaving, and to think of poor Dolan with her family alive, and still leaving her. No wonder she is what she is.*

Lily thought much about Bertha Dolan, and went to find the bigger girl in the afternoon, in the dormitory, where she might be alone, sweeping.

But Bertha was not sweeping this afternoon. She sat huddled on the edge of her cot, trembling with sorrow, making low sobbing noises that seemed more animal than human, a beast in pain.

Lily went up to her and touched her on the shoulder. It was a gentle touch, but Bertha jumped as though Lily had nudged her with a red-hot poker. She wheeled around on the bed and looked at Lily with wild eyes. When Bertha spoke it was more like spitting than speaking.

"And to hell with ye, too, Lily!"

It was not going to be easy to be Bertha's friend. Lily looked at the girl, and remembered all Sister Cathleen had said. The look of Bertha confirmed the matron's words, if they needed confirming.

"What's wrong, Bertha?"

"And what the hell do ye care?"

"Why, I'd like to help, if I can."

"Help, would ye? Put more snakes in me bed, that's the way you help, slut."

"I said I was sorry for that, Bertha, and truly, I am. I never thought you'd be so upset."

"Slimy, nasty creatures they are, serpents."

"They do some good, like all of God's creatures. The gardeners like them."

"Well, 'tis sure and I don't. So just keep your damned slimy serpents to yourself, then."

"What's troubling you, Bertha? Why were you crying just now? Surely it wasn't just the snake?"

Bertha was sitting up now. Her hair was wet, and it fell across her forehead in greasy strings. In truth, Bertha Dolan was not an attractive-looking girl, even at her best. And right now she was far from her best. Lily sighed. Bertha looked at her, and slowly the resentment in her eyes changed to a kind of dull acceptance of an unjust fate. When she spoke, it was no more than a whisper.

"Ah, Lily," she said, "in all this damned world there's no one cares if I live or die."

"I care. So do the sisters. Sister Cathleen cares, and Sister Claudia too. Lots of people would care, Bertha, if you only let them."

"Not truly care."

"They would, too!"

"Not for Dreadful Dolan, they wouldn't."

"I cared last night, because I thought you were going to have a seizure. You scared the very devil out of me. I thought I was going to be a murderess, Bertha, and me not even twelve years old."

Bertha laughed then. It was a short, harsh laugh, and it went as quick as it came. But it was a real laugh, there was humor in it, not the mockery or scorn that usually animated Bertha's laughter.

Having found a note that produced some response, Lily pursued it: "Can you see me, then, all in chains, being led to the gallows?"

"Ha!"

"And would you pray for me, Bertha? As I went to my doom?"

"I might."

"I'd pray for you."

"Would you? Truly?"

"Truly."

"Then maybe I'd pray for you. But not if you put snakes in me bed."

"I won't do that anymore, you can be sure of it."

"Promise?"

"I promise."

Bertha sniffed. She brushed the vagrant hair out of her eye and sat up quite properly and looked at Lily Malone. "I never had a friend," said Bertha shyly, looking away with the cringing attitude of a small animal who thinks it may be beaten, "not ever a one."

"If you let me, I'll try to be your friend."

"Would you? Truly?"

"Really and truly. Just like Frances."

Lily looked at Bertha solemnly as she said those words,

thinking that God was going to strike her dead for a liar, and he might as well get it over with here and now. *So this was martyrdom! This was how it felt when they tied you to the stake and piled up the faggots, just like Joan of Arc in the history book Sister Claudia read to them.* It seemed to Lily that she could smell the smoke and feel the flames singeing her toes.

"You'd try, then?"

"Yes. Yes, I will."

"Shall I tell ye a secret?"

Lily wasn't sure she wanted to know Bertha's secrets. From what the matron had said, they might be truly terrible ones. "Sure."

"Do ye remember the first day you came here, and I threw your dolly out the window?"

"Yes?"

"I never had a dolly. Not one. Not ever."

"Would you like one now?"

"Oh, yes!"

"Well, we'll make you one. It isn't hard. I'll get Frances to show me, and even Sister Mary Agnes."

Bertha looked at Lily doubtfully, thinking it might be a joke.

"Ye'd truly do that?"

"If I say a thing, Bertha, I will do it, may the good Lord let me."

Lily looked at the object of her penance. *Being a martyr isn't going to be easy. When God was giving out graces, he surely forgot poor Dolan. It fair to hurts your eyes just looking at her, and wouldn't I hate to have been hanging since the last time she took a bath.* Still, Lily took a deep breath and plunged in: she walked around Bertha trying to think of ways to improve the girl's looks. A bath was definitely in order, and when Lily suggested it, she was surprised at how readily Dolan agreed. Then the church bells chimed four and Lily realized she was behind in her work.

"Well, now," said Lily briskly, "I've got to get back to my sewing. But I'll speak to Frances this very day, Bertha, and we'll be making you the finest doll in all of St. Paddy's."

There was a pause while this sank in. Then a slow, gentle smile came flowing across Bertha Dolan's face and for the first time Lily could remember, the girl looked almost pleasant.

"I thank ye."

That was all Bertha could say, but for Lily it was more than enough. A human response from Dreadful Dolan! There were truly more wonders in the world than anyone could imagine. Lily smiled as she walked half the length of the big dormitory to her own cot. Maybe the little snake had magic in him, maybe he was a manifestation! Maybe it was preordained that Lily go out into the world and save people, helping the helpless, the hope and inspiration of people even worse than Bertha Dolan. To cure the sick, the lame, and the halt! If the smallest kindness could start such a change in Bertha, who was to say what more effort could achieve in worse cases? She would become a nun, and more than a nun, and more even than Matron. Maybe a saint! It was possible. All kinds of girls of humble origin became saints. Sister Claudia was filled with their stories, and she often told them to the girls. There was St. Valerie, patron saint of Limoges. She had been a poor girl. And St. Theresa of Avila. Not to mention the Blessed Mother herself.

Lily took up her sewing in a transcendent haze of spiritual renewal. She saw herself wearing not the tough cotton twill of the orphanage uniform, but gauzy, floating veils that made long graceful trails in the breeze as she, St. Lillian of Mulberry Street, was wafted ever higher and higher upon a raft of the softest pink clouds, and the rays of the golden sun made a special glow around her head as she smiled down on all the poor unfortunate unloved and unwanted wretches whose lives she had changed with her kindness, and the angels themselves wept at the glory of it all.

It was only when Lily jabbed herself in the thumb with her needle that her mystic vision cleared up a bit. But still and all, she was a girl with a mission, and she would not rest until the complete and total salvation of Dreadful Dolan had been effected.

At first, Frances O'Farrelley was less than enthusiastic. "Get on with you, Lil, she's hopeless. I say more snakes in 'er bed, or maybe a mouse or two."

Lily looked at her best friend and smiled a gentle, saintly smile. She would put in a good word for Frances when she, St. Lillian, was on more intimate terms with God and all the other saints.

"There is," she said softly, "some good in everyone, Frances, and God has put us here to find it."

"What you say may be true, Lily," said Frances with a laugh, "but with someone like Dreadful, we could wear out many a shovel in the diggin', and don't tell me that ain't the truth."

"The harder the task, the greater the reward," said St. Lillian, making light of it, "and what's more, the matron will

[51]

have my head if I don't do some good with poor Bertha. So come on, Fran, help me with the damned dolly."

St. Lillian had not completely abandoned her sense of humor. They made the doll, and Bertha was a changed girl once she saw that Lily's promise had been a sincere one. Frances and Lily and Sister Claudia made a project of Bertha Dolan's renaissance, and soon the other girls were helping too. Bertha got more attention in the next few weeks than she had ever received in her short life. And once she realized she was not being made the object of mockery, as had so often been the case, she truly became a better girl. Bertha would never be beautiful to look at, but she kept herself neater now, and bathed more often, and washed her hair, which proved to be quite beautiful, a glossy dark chestnut. Sister Claudia brought Bertha a blue ribbon for her hair, and the girl was as touched as if it had been a rare jewel. Bertha would never be a scholar or a wit, but she gradually began to direct the energy that had once been wasted in rage to more productive efforts. She asked to help in the kitchen and proved to have a talent for cooking. Soon the whole orphanage was sampling Bertha's pound cake and Bertha's rice puddings. Sister Cathleen was delighted with all this and told Lily so. And even when the first urgency of Bertha's salvation had passed, Lily recalled her promise to Matron, and was kind to the lonely girl. Bertha would never be as close to Lily as was Frances, yet they remained friends of a kind for as long as Bertha remained at St. Paddy's.

The routine at the orphanage seemed to flow on with the steady, unruffled force of some wide and mighty river. Lily never thought about such questions as happiness, but worked steadily and learned what she could and took her fun as it came—seldom and innocently.

The core and focus of Lily's life was Fergy, and her fears for his future and her own, should he leave her. And in this she felt a terrible helplessness, for how could you keep a lad like Fergy in chains when even his mind couldn't stay in the room with you for five consecutive minutes, but rather was always flying about the great world outside like some mad thing filled with half-formed dreams and promises? *It wasn't fair of Ma to make me promise! 'Tis Fergy who should be looking after me, not the other way around.*

Her concern for Fergy filled much of Lily's small world, but there were now other concerns to speculate on.

There was, for instance, the deepening mystery of Sister Claudia.

5

Of all the nuns in St. Patrick's, Sister Claudia was Lily's favorite. Matron was fine, but Matron operated on a higher plane and had little part in the day-to-day routine. Sister Mary Agnes, who taught them sewing, was a good person but rather dry; Sister Hilda was a bully and had warts; Sister Sophia had such a high opinion of herself that whenever possible she spoke only to God and his bishop.

But Sister Claudia was perfection. Young she was, just in her early twenties, young enough to still have a girl's spirit in her, and pretty too, fair as morning, and with blue eyes that knew how to smile.

"And," Fran had summed her up, "she is decidedly a lady."

When I grow up, if I could be even a little bit like her, what a grand thing that would be, and wouldn't I be happy?

Nun though she was, it took no wild imagination to see Sister Claudia as the object of a man's desire. And Sister Claudia, Lily was sure, had a lover.

Lily knew this because she had seen the young man with her own eyes, met him, even.

It was the Sunday after Fergy and Sam Dougherty had been caught raiding the kitchen larder and sentenced to two hours' extra work time every day for a month. Lily had hated the thought of confronting her brother with yet another of his silly escapades, yet who else was there to do it? The memory of that promise she had made to her mother was never far from Lily's consciousness, and futile as it might seem, she would not stop trying to change Fergy's wild ways. He was silent as he walked into the room. Lily greeted him with a kiss, and he turned away from her, waiting, she knew, for the inevitable questions.

"And was it fun, Fergy? Was it worth a month's extra chores, and disgracing yourself again?"

"Ah, Lil, for the Lord's love, don't you be tormenting me too. We just did it for larks."

"Stealing is a lark, then?"

"I was hungry."

"And you asked, and they'd give you nothing? That's hard to believe, Fergy."

"Why are you always picking on me, anyway? You're just like the rest of them, after me like rats after cheese."

"And you such a picture of innocence, the victim of the world's injustice? You should see yourself, Fergus Malone, and think before you get into more such foolishness."

"You don't understand me, Lil, no one does, but you'll see, I can swear to that, and soon. They'll all see!" Raging still, he ran from the room.

Lily was shaken to her toes, for in her indignation she had done the thing she most feared, driven him from her. She reached for the nearest piece of furniture, a big stiff armchair, and pulled herself into its shadowy recesses. *I should have said it different, or not at all, for sure it is I've only provoked him more, and what good will that do, to him or me?* She felt the hot tears welling up in her and fought them back in silence.

She didn't hear them until they were in the room.

Sister Claudia spoke first. Lily would have known that sweet voice anywhere, yet now she trembled to hear it. Suppose Sister Claudia thought she was spying?

"Ah, Gerry, glad as I am to see you, can't anything I say make a difference?"

So there was a man! Lily detected an underlying tension in the well-known voice, usually so light and warm and filled with joy. There was a sadness in it now: Sister Claudia's voice was shaded darker, tinged with regret.

And a strange man answered: "No, Claudia. Not then, not now, not ever."

Lily stirred in her chair.

She knew they thought they were alone, and the idea of being uncovered as an eavesdropper terrified her. *She must do something!*

Gathering every last atom of courage into one small tight lump, Lily coughed loudly and got to her feet. There followed an instant of silence that seemed to Lily to last for hours.

Then the nun spoke: "Why, Lily! This is a surprise. Have you been visiting with your brother?"

"Yes, Sister," said Lily quietly, wishing that the carpet would open and swallow her up right then and there, "and he had to leave early."

"Gerald," said Sister Claudia too brightly, "meet one of my best pupils. Mr. Gerald St. Clair, Miss Lillian Malone."

Trembling, Lily curtsied as Sister Claudia had taught her, hoping and praying she was doing it properly. Her eyes were on the deep red of the flower-patterned carpet. Slowly, then, she raised them.

The young man was tall and dark-complexioned and beautifully dressed. He had a thin face, almost an eagle's face, with big dark eyes and a prominent nose. Lily did not find him beautiful to look at, but surely those great eyes were big enough to hold a tragedy. He smiled.

"I am pleased to meet you, Lillian."

"Good afternoon, sir, good afternoon, Sister Claudia. I must be going now."

"Good afternoon, then, Lily."

Sister Claudia smiled, but it was a pale imitation of her usual good cheer. *And how hard it must be to smile when you have a broken heart.* For here, Lily was sure, must be the ardent lover she had left behind when she Took the Vow, still in hot pursuit in defiance of all the laws of God and man! Lily somehow got herself out of the reception room without fainting, then raced back to the dormitory. She ran to the window facing out onto Prince Street. There was a sleek new cabriolet, glittering with bright paint and polished brass, two matched bays jingling their harness brasses in the crisp March afternoon breeze. *Suppose Sister Claudia let herself be persuaded!* Lily saw the empty carriage, imagined the lovers running out of St. Paddy's and leaping into it and galloping off into a life of passion and wickedness.

Of course, people who did things like that came to a bad end, there was no denying it, and a bad end was quite the opposite of what Lily wished for Sister Claudia. Yet, what an adventure! Suddenly Lily's narrow world was crowded with possibilities, all of them romantic.

But in a few minutes she saw the tall figure of Gerald St. Clair walk slowly down the path to his carriage, where he turned and smiled an infinitely sad smile and waved at his beloved before climbing up onto his elegant little runabout and clattering off around the corner, past the cathedral, and on up Mott Street.

Lily stayed in the window after he had gone. She imagined Gerald St. Clair at elegant dinner parties and balls, alone in the glittering crowd, desired by all the women but saving himself for A Love That Could Never Be.

Lily and Fran knew about Loves That Could Never Be, for

these were the themes of so many popular songs and poems that from time to time Lily wondered if a love ever happened that could be.

Sister Claudia kept her secret well, and never mentioned Gerald to Lily or anyone else. It was as though his visit had never happened, but Lily knew otherwise, and this great event provided her and Fran hours of thrilling speculation. *They were secretly married! He was ill with a fatal disease, and needed her to comfort his dying hours.*

Now Lily watched Sister Claudia with avid expectation, and read the most significant things into the young nun's smallest gesture. If Sister Claudia was cheerful, it was merely a ruse to mask her bottomless sorrow. If she was pensive, she must be fighting for control, struggling with unmentionable passions. It was partly a game for Lily, this spinning fantasies about the nun, but it was also the first time in her young life that Lily had come to ponder the many shifting shapes of a grown-up's happiness.

Meanwhile, life in St. Paddy's went on. Lily knew how much the orphanage had grown even in the two years she and Fergy had been there; the bishop himself had announced it proudly one day from the pulpit in St. Paddy's, as though it was a fine thing for a parish to be growing orphans at such a productive rate, and not stopping, as Lily thought he should have, to consider what sadness made an orphan and what shame they felt to be thrown homeless and helpless into St. Paddy's. But that would not have been in the fine spirit of progress that Lily detected throughout St. Patrick's. Indeed, and weren't they busy even now with plans for a grand new orphanage up on Fifth Avenue at Fifty-first Street, for the boys only?

If such plans made Matron and Father Gregory happy, then that was fine by Lily. But no new orphanage could dislodge her interest in the romantic life of Sister Claudia, or her concern about Fergy.

One afternoon Lily was summoned to Sister Cathleen's office again.

She wondered, knocking on the matron's office door, what new mischief Fergy might have gotten into this time. The familiar voice asked her to come in. Lily opened the heavy door. Sister Cathleen looked tired. Something about the nun's habits made them look almost ageless to Lily. But this afternoon, and for the first time, Lily could see signs of age on the matron's thin birdlike face. Matron looked tired, Lily thought, and more than a little sad. Fergy must have really put his foot in it this time. Matron smiled and gestured to the chair. Lily sat down, wishing that Matron's smile had more spark to it. Maybe she was sick.

"I'm afraid I have sad news for you, Lily, dear."

Lily, dear. My God in heaven. Fergy was dead! Lily blinked, gulped, said nothing. She waited for the ax to fall.

"Your brother . . ."

Killed someone. Stole the chalice from St. Paddy's. Lily's mind was a dark tangle of possibilities, all of them terrible.

". . . has run away, Lily. I am very sorry, for I know how much you love him. He left you this."

Sister Cathleen handed Lily a folded sheet of paper. Lily took it, then sat back in her chair and unfolded it. Slowly, biting her tongue to keep back the tears, she read the crudely printed note as though it were her own death warrant.

Dear Lil,

By the time you get this I will be at sea. Pleas do not worrie, Lil, for yr. Fergy will be alrite. Soon I'l have gold to spare & will send for you, my sister. I'l write agin from our first port. I must seeke my fortun, Lily, else I'l go mad in this place. Pray for yr. loving brother

Fergy

❧ 6 ❧

Lily sat absolutely still as the certain knowledge of Fergy's betrayal burned into her brain. His note was such a repellent thing to her that she could hardly bear to hold it. His crudely formed words seemed to vibrate on the page as she read them and reread them. The letters wavered as though they were written on water, and Lily realized that her eyes were filled with unshed tears. *"Save your tears, child, for one day you may truly need them."*

There was a moment of silence that seemed to extend through all the long days of her future. The window of Matron's office was open to the bright spring day. One of the gardener's boys was raking a gravel path, scratch, scratch, scratch. A raucous bird cawed.

Lily thought that if she started crying she might never stop. *I will not cry for you, Fergy.* She tried to think of something to say, but it was too great an effort. *So now he's left me too, they've all left me, and now I am completely alone.*

Finally Sister Cathleen spoke, gently. Her words sounded as though they came from far away.

"God," said Matron with the easy intimacy of one who knows him well, "works in mysterious ways, Lily. I know this must be a terrible thing for you, that you may feel Fergus has abandoned you, but we must always try to see things from another's point of view. He was not happy here, Lily, and this may be for the best, it may make a man of him."

And what will it make of me, Sister, can you answer that? But Lily merely nodded and said: "Yes, Sister."

"At the end of his note, Fergus asks you to pray for him. We must all pray for Fergus, Lily, for his safety and for the salvation of his immortal soul. I'll have the bishop himself say a special Mass for the lad."

"Thank you, Sister."

It won't help. None of it will help, any more than St. Jude helped me when I prayed for her to save Ma. He's gone, and left me, and gone forever, is my Fergy, and I'll never set eyes on his green eyes again.

Lily saw a clear and awful vision as she sat there in the pleasant little office. She saw a storm at sea, huge dark waves crashing down on the frail vessel, masts snapping in the wind, and Fergy, swept overboard, thrashing in the churning sea, pale hands clutching, but with nothing to clutch at, going down and down into the green darkness where the patient fishes waited for their prey.

Lily sat as if paralyzed, sure to the bottom of her heart that there weren't now and never would be enough bishops or Masses, not from Mott Street to Rome, never enough to rescue her Fergy from his certain doom. *And what*, she wondered, *would be his chances of getting into heaven when the end did come? Slim as a tinker's donkey, that was for sure. And naturally, being Fergy, he'd walked right into it!*

Lily tried to remember just how she'd felt when her mother died, when the prayer to St. Jude failed her. She could remember nothing, only the loss, only that Fergus had been there.

And now she had lost even Fergus.

Sister Cathleen shifted a paper of her desk. The tiny noise was loud in the quiet room. There was a soft knock on the door.

"Come in."

Father Gregory stood there, tall and solemn, and once again Lily thought of the day her mother died, and how kind the priest had been, and Fat Bessie and the scarf.

"I'm sorry, Lily," he said softly. " 'Tis a terrible unthinking thing he's done."

"Thank you, Father."

"I was wondering, Sister Cathleen," he said, "if I could be taking this young lady for a bit of a stroll?"

"Yes, Father, that might be a good idea." Sister Cathleen smiled brightly, too brightly, Lily thought. *She must be flooded with relief to get me off her hands.*

"May I keep his note, Sister?"

"Of course, child. I'm sure he'll write to you soon, just as he says. And we'll pray for him, Lily."

"Thank you, Sister. I will, too."

Lily folded the note carefully and put it in her sewing bag. Then she stood and followed Father Gregory out of the office and down the hallway.

Lily was halfway down Prince Street, hand in hand with Father Gregory, before it dawned on her that this was a rare treat indeed, a walk outside the orphanage, and practically alone! Sometimes they were taken on special holiday-treat excursions, to a park or a free concert, once even to Barnum's Museum down on Broadway, but always in groups, walking in pairs like so many little ducklings, escorted and formed into lines: it was necessary, of course, and it was surely better than nothing, but there was an air of regimentation about those excursions that made Lily more than usually conscious of the uniforms, of the fundamentally impersonal quality of her life. But this, this was truly special. The price, of course, had been too high. Still, it was a change, another act of kindness from Father Gregory. She wondered where they were headed.

They turned right on Mulberry and headed north past the back of the cathedral with its rusticated stones and brownstone lintels.

Mulberry Street was alive, crammed with merchants and shoppers and people selling vegetables from pushcarts, animals underfoot, straying chickens and wandering pigs and any number of mongrel dogs and dray horses. Now and then a fine carriage would come pushing its proud way through the crowd, once with a lady so haughty and fine Lily gasped aloud at the sight of her: all dressed in dark red velvet she was, even to her rakish hat, the velvet trimmed with rich braiding in black, and a grand black plume. The window of her barouche was open to the bright October afternoon, and as she passed and saw Lily looking up in wonder, the fine lady smiled—a special smile, Lily knew it, meant only for her.

"Who," Lily asked her tall companion, "was that?"

His laugh surprised her. "That, my dear, is a fallen woman."

But she looked so happy and fine, her smile was not a false smile, and there was something in her eyes, not wickedness at all, but a sort of humor, as though she knew a fine secret and nothing could make her tell.

Lily and Fran knew about fallen women, for their romantic speculations were not confined to Sister Claudia. In truth, just before Lily had come there, St. Paddy's had developed its own fallen woman—fallen orphan, more properly—in the person of one Maureen Nesbit, who, at the early-ripening age of thirteen, had contrived to become pregnant by the gardener's boy, Billy Logan, and both of them cast out into the streets, where, official opinion decreed, they belonged. But delicious legends had grown around the sinful saga of Maureen and Billy, and the prevailing opinion among the girls was that what you did for love was well done, wicked as the world might see it. Lily looked at the elegant carriage as it quickly vanished up the street. *And if she had fallen, that woman, sure and there had been someone generous to cushion the fall!*

"Can you guess where we're going, Lily?"

"No. Where?"

"To visit your parents. And that might seem an odd thing to be doing on a day when you've had such bad news, Lily, but there is a reason for it. 'Tis this: I'll wager you're feelin' like you haven't got a friend in the world now, that Fergy abandoned you, and you're right at the end of your tether. Am I right?"

I am hanging by the neck at the end of my tether, and nothing will ever be right for me again, never, not here or anywhere else.

But Lily thought how kind the priest was, and answered gently: "You are, Father. Sure and that's just how I feel."

"Loneliness is a funny thing, Lily. It is quite possible to be lonely even when there's lots of people about—even though they're your own flesh and blood. It's in your head, I guess, is what I'm meaning to say."

That's all very well, Lily thought, *but it won't bring Fergy back.* She could think of no reply to what Father Gregory had said, so she made none. They walked on and on. Soon she could see the brick wall of the graveyard at Twelfth Street looming up just ahead. For a moment Lily was gripped by a new and nameless fear. It had been a little more than three years since Mother died, and in those years Lily and Fergus had been taken to the graveyard only three times, on the anniversary of mother's burial. Lily had gone because it seemed to be expected of her. But whatever she had been meant to feel at the familiar gravesite, it hadn't happened. All Lily had felt on those three occasions was a dull and empty sense of loss. Her memory of Big Fergus was dim— she was only five when he died—but she could see him in Fergy, the shining red hair, the laugh, the bold green eyes. But her mother's image was fading. She tried in earnest to conjure up the gentle voice, the soft brown eyes, the kindness. But all Lily truly had of her mother's memory was the admonition to save her tears for some nameless tragedy yet to come, and the fine, scarcely worn lace-and-linen scarf she'd wrested back from thieving Fat Bessie Sullivan.

And suddenly, as they came upon the black iron gates and Lily felt her feet moving inexorably down the path, she knew the name of her fear. *Oh, and for the love of God let me not displease poor Father Gregory. Isn't he trying as best he can to help me, and aren't I a miserable excuse for gratitude if I let him see how little any of it means, feeling the way I do right now, with the blackness rising up and like to drown me, and wouldn't he think I'm a heartless thing, if he knew?*

In silence they walked into the graveyard, down the neat path past regiments of gravestones in white and gray and black stone, past stone angels with pious folded hands and wings that would never feel the sky again, past willows forever weeping, carved in shallow relief, past urns of stone flowers in cold and permanent bloom.

They turned a corner and found themselves in a poorer section of the burying ground. Her parents were just over there—beyond the big tree. And still Lily felt nothing for them, but only a longing for Fergy so deep there could be no bottom to it, so painful it burned her with a cold fire.

The plain white headstone was as Lily remembered it. The afternoon sun shone through the branches of a nearby willow tree and made long waving shadows on the stone. Lily did not have to read the words, for they had long been carved on her heart. "FERGUS MALONE 1810–1842 / MARY DUGAN MALONE / BELOVED WIFE 1812–1847 / RIP"

Some of the other markers had long flowery epitaphs, but at fifty cents the letter bare names and RIP must do for the Malones. *And who could care for a poem when Death himself stood by you with his scythe all sharp and ready?*

"Do you feel them, Lily?"

"Sometimes."

It was true. She did feel them, now and then, but not here, not now. What Lily felt of her parents was a vague warmth of memory, always followed by the bittersweet pangs of regret.

They knelt, and Father Gregory recited a prayer. He finished and was about to make the Sign of the Cross when Lily spoke.

"Pray for Fergus."

He looked sideways at her, and smiled, and spoke a long prayer in Latin. Lily didn't understand Latin, but the flow of it soothed her, and as she knelt in the soft grass she could imagine Fergus on the blue ocean, hearing these same words, and smiling. The priest finished. They rose.

"Thank you, Father."

"Do you know that prayer?"

"I don't."

" 'Tis St. Christopher's own prayer, the prayer for safe return."

"He'll return, I know it."

"Sure he will, Lily, and who are we to judge the lad, for in truth it may be the making of him. Young America, as the papers call these brave young adventurers, do you know that term?"

Lily had heard the phrase more and more these last two years. Fergy used it himself sometimes, on fire with dreams. "Sure, 'tis the force of destiny, Lil," he'd say. "Young America, they call us, because we hold all the future in our hands." Lily had smiled when she first heard this, and hoped to God the future was in steadier hands than the hands of Fergus Malone Junior.

"Yes," she answered quietly, "I've heard Fergy himself say that."

"Don't be too quick to judge the lad, Lily. Sometimes we do what we must do, and 'twould be wrong if we didn't. There was nothing personal in his leaving, nothing against you, if you take my meaning."

But surely it was against me, who could think else? There's nothing more personal than leaving, Father, you must know that, leaving without so much as a warning, sneaking off, a thief in the night, and sure it was my own poor heart he was stealing, and him not even knowing, much less caring. Oh, leaving is personal, very personal, Father, it may be the most personal thing of all, for could he not know I need him, just to be there, even if it was only once a week? Fergy must have known it, felt it: how in God's blue world could he not? It was a question Lily didn't try to answer, not then or ever.

"Oh," she said, "for sure, Father, I do understand. It was the surprise of it that shook me. Deep down, I knew he'd do something like this one day."

"And did you ever try to stop him?"

"Sure and I did. You might as well stop the wind from blowing."

"He's a strong-willed lad, is Fergus."

"Father, I do wish he hadn't gone."

"Ah, Lily, Lily, if wishes were dollars we'd all be millionaires, now, wouldn't we? True, Fergus ran away, but he'd have been going out into the world soon anyway. And if he must do such a thing, if he must go out and try himself against the luck of the world, why, maybe the sooner he does it, the sooner he'll be back to you. Have you ever thought about that, now?"

"In fact, I haven't. I haven't thought much about it at all, Father, seeing as how it's just come on me, as it were."

"Of course. Well. There'll be time enough for that, my girl. But in the meantime, there's one other thing you might be thinking on. Can you guess what that is?"

"No."

"You must be thinking of yourself, Lily. Of what's to become of you in this world. My opinion is that you've been thinking too much of others, and not enough of yourself. Which is a charming way to be, only it can go too far. How old are you now, Lily?"

"Thirteen, Father."

"Well, then, 'tis never too soon to be planning, now, is it?"

They were walking back down Mulberry Street. The afternoon shadows were longer now, and the sun was losing its warmth. There were fewer people in the street, and even some of the stray animals seemed to have found their way home. Father Gregory's big hand felt good to Lily as he casually held her small hand in his. She felt well-protected, and as they walked, Lily realized for the first time that this was the way she felt about Saint Patrick's orphanage, about Sister Cathleen and Sister Claudia and Frances, and Father Gregory himself. The life wasn't all easy, that was for sure. But they did care for her. This walk to the graveyard proved that, if it needed proving, even though she might not feel what Father Gregory expected her to feel. They walked on in silence for a moment while Lily thought about her future for the first time ever.

If anyone had asked Lily about the future six months ago, when she was in the midst of saving Dreadful Dolan from herself, she might well have answered, "Sure, and I'm going to take the vow, and just maybe become a saint in heaven." Now she wasn't so sure. Because now she knew that any plans she'd had before weren't plans, truly, but more like dreams. It was a dream she could ever be a saint, a mad dream, mad in its own way as anything Fergus had ever come up with.

"I guess," Lily said, thinking out loud, "that I've never truly thought about it. About the future."

"Well, sure and there's no rush. You can stay with us for many a year, Lily, and we'd be glad enough to have you. I know for a fact that Sister Claudia relies on you to keep the new girls in order, and Sister Cathleen, too, is happy with the way you've pitched in and helped poor Bertha Dolan. It's possible you could become a lay teacher one day. We'll be needing teachers aplenty, once we've settled into the new place. Or you could go into service, if you'd like a bit more independence. Sister Cathleen has a fine record for placing our girls in good homes—sometimes very fine homes they are, too—as maids and governesses and the like. That might not be such a bad thing. Or, should you get the calling, should God speak to you as he has to me and to Sister Claudia and the others, you might think of taking the veil. Oh, there's a lot to think of, Lily."

"I see that."

Lily felt her head swimming. She didn't want to decide anything. All she wanted was to get her brother back safe, and soon. They walked on. The air was taking on a definite chill now. A pungent aroma filled the air, riding on woodsmoke. It was an old Italian man with a brazier, roasting chestnuts on the corner.

"Well, now," said Father Gregory, "have you ever tasted roast chestnuts, Lily?"

"I haven't. Are they good?"

"Here's your chance to find out." He gave the old man three pennies and got in return a newspaper cone with perhaps a dozen steaming chestnuts in it. "Try one," he said, offering the cone. "They're just what the doctor ordered to take the chill off an afternoon like this."

Lily took the big blackened shell and at first almost dropped it, it was that hot. Then she pried off the shell and saw the fat yellow nut inside. She bit into it. Here was a taste unlike anything she'd tasted before. Lily chewed the mealy, sweetish, hot, fascinating object in silence for a moment, then quickly ate the rest of it.

"Delicious. Thank you."

He gave her another, took one himself, and before they reached the next corner all the chestnuts were gone.

"Well, now," said Father Gregory, "there's a new adventure waiting round every corner in this life, Lily, and some of them can be fine ones."

"Yes," she said quietly, thinking of Fergy, and that his adventure was not fine at all, only painful, "sure they can."

Lily and the priest walked on in silence for a moment. Her mind was dazzled by all that had happened this day, and the mixture of new sensations was enough to set her head spinning. The shock of Fergy's leaving, Father Gregory's unexpected kindness and the rush of remembrance at the graveside, the feeling of total abandonment, even the strange and wonderful taste of the hot chestnuts were all mixed up into a heady drug.

Lily didn't hear the wild hoofbeats. She didn't heed the shouts of laughter that rode with them. She was about to step off the curbing at the corner of Mulberry Street and Prince when Father Gregory suddenly reached out and stopped her with a firm but gentle grip on the shoulder. She looked up at him, but he was looking at the careless riders. Lily followed his gaze.

Two young men were cantering up Mulberry Street so fast it was almost a gallop. Too fast, Lily realized, but her fear dissolved as she watched them. *What fun that must be, a day like this and fine horses, and them so free!* Lily got only a glimpse of the young men as they swept past: very swell they were, and beautifully dressed, right to the sleek beaver hats, and the horses no less fine, gleaming bays all bedecked in leather that had an almost silken gloss to it, and brass glittering like the rare gilt altar sticks of St. Patrick's. One of the boys was nearly full grown, but a boy for all that, Lily thought, and the other was a smaller, younger edition of the first. *Brothers they must be, and rich, and with never a care in all this world. No one ever left them without a warning, or if someone did leave, they wouldn't care a damn, not those two.* There was no envy in Lily's heart as she watched the boys vanish up the street, but rather a sense of deepening awe that God should have ordained such great differences in the amount of luck a person was born to.

As far as Brooks Chaffee was concerned, this was the best afternoon of his sixteen-year-old life to date. Father's gift of the horse for his birthday had been a true and glorious surprise, for he hadn't known the Old Gentleman was aware that this was Brooks's most urgent desire. Brooks was sure it must be all Neddy's doing, for Neddy did know, but he'd die before admitting such a thing, which might penetrate his carefully built facade of worldly cynicism. *Well, and to hell with all that! Here it was, the finest afternoon in October, an easy errand done for the Old Gentleman, and now off on a run with Neddy himself, rare treat that was. And even though Neddy was frankly using his younger brother to advance his own lecherous schemes, who cared? If the beautiful Sabrina van Vleck had a far less beautiful younger sister, and if Brooks must go for tea, it was little enough to do for Neddy. If only Neddy knew just how much more than this*

*trifling thing I'm prepared to do for him . . . well, better not
to think on it.*

Brooks had named his new horse Wellington. Wellington
had the happy knack of catching his master's spirit, and this
afternoon the beast was high-spirited enough to fairly fly.
Neddy picked up the pace too, as they trotted, then cantered,
then all but galloped up Mulberry Street. Brooks laughed
from the sheer joy of it as they flew past the astonished vendors, some of whom smiled, while others shook their fists in
helpless indignation. There was a chestnut vendor! Brooks
loved chestnuts, but the day seemed too fine and the pace too
deliriously fast to consider stopping. And Neddy, Brooks
guessed, was far too inflamed with his ardor for the fair Sabrina van Vleck to pause for anything short of the Apoca-
lypse. As Brooks flashed past the vendor, he noticed a tall
young priest, and with him a frightened-looking little girl in
the familiar uniform of the Catholic orphanage. Instinctively
his strong young legs tightened around the prancing horse.
The joy still vibrated in the crisp blue afternoon, and Wellington responded with fluency to his master's urging, and
gathered more speed. Brooks flashed by the priest and the orphan in a second, but that second was long enough for his
golden mood to darken.

He wondered what it must be like to be an orphan. Then
Neddy shouted for him to catch up, and Brooks gave the
horse free rein and laughed out loud with the raw joy of
being sixteen in the sunshine and on a true flying horse, galloping head-on into a world of infinite and infinitely delicious
possibilities.

The boisterous riders left the street undamaged, and Father
Gregory took Lily by the hand as they crossed.

They turned the corner of Prince Street again, and suddenly they were back at the orphanage. Lily's day had melted
like butter on a hot bun. She thanked Father Gregory, and
promised him she'd think about the future. He left her on the
walk, and stood watching her as she made her way along the
path and up the stairs to the big front door.

When Lily reached the door, she paused for a moment,
and sensed that he was still there. She turned, and saw him,
and waved, smiling over the sea of black fears that churned
inside her. He waved back, smiling, wondering what in the
world would become of her.

Lily wondered the same thing herself as she opened the big
oaken door.

Frances O'Farrelley could always be counted on for good

cheer and distraction, and Lily was glad of her company as they sat on their neighboring cots in the dormitory, sewing and mending.

"Well," said Frances with a finality that was all but papal, "I think it's very romantic."

"Criminal stupidity, Fran, that's what it is."

"Ah, just think of it, Lil: here we sit in our prison uniforms, sewing our poor fingers to the bone, and Fergus'll be riding the bounding main, having the finest adventures, sporting with naked Injun maidens under the coconut trees, finding treasures maybe, digging for gold in California. Maybe he'll come back to you rich, Lil, then you'll eat your words, won't you?" And she laughed and went on sewing.

Lily looked across the narrow space that separated her from her best friend. "Sure," she said, giggling at last, "and isn't it a wonder you didn't run off with him, now? If I didn't know you better, Fran, I'd say you were daft for the boy."

"Get on with you, now! But I do feel for him, Lil, and isn't it hard enough for a lad with his spirit, bein' an orphan, bein' here and all, and a sister forever naggin' at you?"

"I should have nagged him more."

"It's off he is, then, and I wish him well."

"Matron keeps telling me how God works in mysterious ways, but truly 'tis not such a mystery, for all his ways are the same, and they're all aimed to torment me."

"Lillian Malone, this's blasphemy!"

"Oh, and don't I know it, each new trial is a chance to earn more stars in my crown in heaven. Well, my crown has all the stars in it right now that I'll ever want."

Lily laughed as she said it, but her mind's eye saw some celestial clerk, floating on high with a big ledger, and in it good marks and bad marks for all of them. *How many stars for a father dying? A mother? For taking Fergy? For shaking her faith in the power of the Church and her unanswered prayers?*

In a more somber voice, she continued: "I'd settle for less stars, Fran, and Fergy back, and that's the truth."

Fran sat quietly for a moment, wondering how to lighten her friend's mood. "Shall I tell you a secret," she asked with a dark and foreboding look, "if you swear to carry it to the very grave?"

"Oh, yes, do!"

"And do you swear, Lil, on penalty of eternal damnation and all the fires of hell?"

"Indeed, and heaven denied me, for all that."

Frances stood up then and came very close to Lily and whispered in her ear, even though they were quite alone in the big dormitory. " 'Tis Sister Claudia, Lil, she's had an *assignation!*"

"No!"

"I swear it. The tall young man you met . . ."

"Gerald St. Clair!"

"It must be, him with a new cabriolet, very fine it was."

"With two matched bays?"

"That's it! Well, while you were out gallivantin' with a certain handsome priest, up comes that cabriolet, gallopin' like the divil himself was hard behind, and out jumps the tall young man and runs up the path, and before you know it he's comin' back down the path again with Sister Claudia, and her all in a flurry, and he hands her up and off they go at a gallop. Now, you know 'tis a rule of the sisters that they never go out but in pairs, if at all."

Lily thought hard about her favorite nun, the harder because at this moment Lily herself felt like running away, escaping her doubts, outdistancing her fears for Fergy's safety. *If Sister Claudia broke a rule, she had good reason to.* "Maybe they're eloping!"

"That's what I thought." Fran was flushed with the shared thrill of it, and Lily too felt that in some unstated way they were both conspirators in the romance. If it was a romance.

"Well, there's probably some simple explanation for it all, a family affair of some sort, sickness at home, maybe."

"Or," said Fran in the deep voice she used for her most outrageous comical stories, "it could be a forbidden love."

Lily decided to humor her. Now that Fergy was gone, she felt closer to Fran than anyone except maybe Sister Claudia herself.

"He'll go galloping away to some lonely place . . ."

"Where no one can hear her screams . . ."

"Plies her with whiskey!"

"No, champagne. They always use champagne. And then, when it makes her so dizzy she doesn't know what's happening, he works his evil will on her."

Lily giggled and wondered where Fran got such detailed information on the world's wickedness: the girl was a fountain of lurid tales.

"Still and all," said Lily, "I think it's a family illness."

They sat with their sewing for a while, and Lily thought of all she knew about Sister Claudia and all the rumors she had heard, and it was hard to separate the facts from the speculations. They said she was rich, and for sure there was no denying she was very lovely to see. They said she was one of four beautiful sisters—the Delaneys they were—all the toast of New York, or of Irish New York, for surely the Vanderbilts wouldn't be having them, and that Claudia took the vow to escape from an unhappy love affair. And that had been before Lily or Fergy had come to St. Paddy's. But the rumors had found fertile soil in the enclosed world of the orphanage, and there was never a shortage of romantically inclined little girls to dream about the beautiful young nun and to speculate on the forces that had caused her to give up a rich and worldly life for the Spartan disciplines of St. Patrick's.

If it had occurred to anyone that Sister Claudia might simply have felt the calling, they never mentioned it. This simplest of explanations did not fit into the elaborate framework of romantic fantasy that surrounded Sister Claudia's every move, and was therefore discarded.

It was while they were sitting, sewing busily and busily thinking about the latest episode, that they heard the sound of hooves trotting up Prince Street.

Like two shots from twin cannon, Lily and Fran were at the window.

"It's them!"

Indeed it was. The now familiar cabriolet had stopped at the curb, and even as they watched, a tall, sober-looking Gerald St. Clair was helping Sister Claudia to climb down.

"Whatever they've been up to," Lily whispered, glad that her trust in Sister Claudia's integrity had not been betrayed, "it wasn't champagne and making love!"

"Don't be too sure."

Sister Claudia and St. Clair were oblivious of the fact that their parting was being played out before at least two enthralled spectators whose small, intent faces were pressed hard against the dormitory window four stories above.

The nun and her escort stood for a moment beside the carriage, and Gerald held her hand as though he never intended to let it go.

No words passed between the lovers.

"I wish," said Lily, "that we could hear them."

"He's swearing eternal love."

"I don't think they're saying anything."

"Then he is struck dumb with sorrow at losing her."

"How do you know he's lost her?"

"Just look at him, goose. Is that a happy man?"

"She's not herself, either, that's for sure."

Finally Sister Claudia said something—something short and quick—and turned from Gerald St. Clair and walked up the path to the front steps, never once looking back, her head held high and on her face an expression that neither of the girls had ever seen there before. Sister Claudia looked as though she had seen a ghost, and that the sight of it had frozen her lovely face into an expression of astonishment and terror.

"Just look at her," said Fran. "Surely her heart is breaking."

"So's his."

Gerald St. Clair looked as though he had been struck a sudden and mortal blow. He stood beside his gleaming cabriolet and watched Sister Claudia as she made her way up the path and into the orphanage, and after she was inside he stayed there watching still, as if paralyzed, as if by waiting she might come back to him. Fran reached out and squeezed Lily's hand. The girls looked at each other in silence, sure in their hearts that for once reality had caught up with their romantic games. For there could be no doubt about the sadness, the sense of impending loss and building despair that was gathering like so many storm clouds on the face of the tall, mysterious stranger. Without saying a word, they turned to the window again, and waited until, at last, he climbed into the cabriolet and drove dispiritedly away.

They went back to their sewing in silence, too, and sat there sewing for a long, delicious moment in which both girls tried to savor the unfamiliar, bittersweet delights of this glimpse into an adult world of high feelings and deep loss.

He looks, thought Lily, *about the way I felt when Sister Cathleen showed me Fergy's note.*

Frances was the first to speak. "What," she asked softly, "will we ever say if she comes up here, Lil?"

"We'll say nothing. For we know nothing." *And Sister Claudia's my friend, and you don't betray friends, or do any other thing that might make them leave you.*

"But we saw them."

"And sure, don't we see the moon, and which of us could be saying it's made of green cheese or it isn't? Get on with ye, Fran: it's too much sewing you've had, is what I think, 'tis addling your head."

"He's the one what's addled. Her lover."

"A mortal, mortal sin that would be, and let's not be the ones to say it first. Or ever. She is our friend, after all."

"If you say so."

[71]

They went back to their sewing and saw nothing more of Sister Claudia that day or the next. The routine of St. Patrick's helped to smooth over this incident as it did all the other adventures in their emotional lives, great and small. The regular chiming of St. Patrick's bells defined their life, woke them in the morning, marched them to prayers and to class and to their chores later on. The bells were soothing, constant and immutable, like the routine itself.

The routine helped Lily to think a little less about Fergy, and to think less about her future.

Still, there were times, often late at night, when the last whispers and giggles had died down in the dormitory, when Fergy would come to her more real than any dream, and then the fears would start up in Lily fresh and painful as though she'd never known them before.

Since Ma died, her most fundamental fear was to be abandoned, deserted, left alone in the world with all its dangers and temptations. Now Fergy had certified her fear by leaving St. Paddy's, and even though Lily well knew why he'd left, she couldn't reconcile herself to the fact of his being gone, and gone without telling her, warning her. It was as though the boy were halfway to dead already, and it was only a matter of time, and the waiting in this sure knowledge was part of the pain.

In her waiting, in her fear, and in the sureness of her fate, Lily had invented many a terrible end for her brother. She could summon up fatal storms at sea, attacks by wild savages with spears, dread plagues of the tropics, ambush in the goldfields—if God spared him till he got there—and dozens of other disasters of man and nature.

And although she was cheerful by nature, Lily could not simply be cheerful about this. In time her fears grew to the point where they might lie in wait for her even in the sunniest garden at high noon, or in church, or at a meal. *Quite daft I am getting*, she might tell herself, and did, but even mockery did not drive her fears away for long.

Even God himself must not know of her fears, for they could come sneaking up on her right in the middle of a prayer.

"Our Father who . . . *Fergy just fell overboard* . . . hallowed be . . . *Fergy's being eaten by a whale* . . . thy kingdom come . . . *it's gold, Fergy, you were right* . . . on earth as it is in heaven . . . *those men have guns, watch out, Fergy* . . . amen."

If only I'd hated him.

Lily turned fourteen and saw the summer of 1851 turn into crisp blue autumn.

There was no news of Fergy, and there were no more romantic incidents involving Sister Claudia. The calm everyday routine of Lily's life was vividly punctuated by her concern for Fergy, and slowly she learned to live even with this dreaded thing that was always near her, as though it had been a physical deformity like a humped back. She tried to think of herself, of Lily alone, and Lily's future, and to evolve some sort of plan, for in her heart she knew she might never see Fergus again, be he dead or alive. That was Fergy, and that was life.

But every time Lily began to consider what her future might be, the specter of her runaway brother leaped up to stop her. There was always the enticing prospect of a golden Fergy with all his dreams come true, rich from the goldfields, sending a coach and seven footmen for her, even as he'd promised to do. And while Lily knew that was a fairy tale, the fairy tale had an insidious life of its own, alternating with other, more realistic, more frightening possibilities.

There were plans in the air at St. Patrick's, and they all concerned the grand new orphanage that was a-building even now, that would be ready by next year. Lily was a veteran now. She helped settle in the new arrivals with a sure hand and kind words, remembering vividly the terrors imposed on her by Bertha Dolan. Good old Dreadful herself was gone from St. Patrick's now, gone into service as a cook's assistant in a fine house on Murray Hill.

The rag doll, Hortense, lay almost forgotten in the wicker chest under Lily's bed. She took Hortense out from time to time, not to play with but to help her remember her mother. Even Hortense was unreliable when it came to that. But Lily cherished the doll as a talisman, much as she valued the old linen-and-lace scarf rescued from Fat Bessie. *One day,* Lily told herself, *I'll have kids of my own, and they'll play with old Hortense, and when my daughter gets married—to some fine gentleman like Gerald St. Clair—why, she'll wear the scarf, and lovely she'll look in it, too.*

It was October when Fergy's letter came.

Sister Claudia called Lily out of class, a sure sign of something most unusual.

The pretty young nun smiled, something that happened less often lately. She had a soiled envelope, and handed it to Lily.

"I know how you've been waiting for this, my dear," said Sister Claudia, who then turned and went back to her duties.

Lily stood alone in the big hallway. Her knees trembled. She wanted to sit down. The only place to sit was the deep window ledge at the far end of the hall.

She held the envelope with two fingers, as though it might burn her, and walked gingerly to the window. It was late morning, a gold-and-crystal day with the sky blue and bright leaves dancing in a merry breeze. Lily sat on the edge of the window and looked at the envelope.

She looked on it in wonderment because it was from Fergy, and also because it was the first letter she had ever received. It had once been ivory in color, but now there was a family of smudges and stains on the paper, so varied and intense that the front of the envelope looked very much like the head-cheese marble on the altar at St. Paddy's. There was a big spot of rusty purple that might be dried wine . . . or blood. There were several brown and tan stains, and one of pale blue. A streak of plain dirt, a huge thumbprint in black grease. But the ink was clear and black, and through all the stains and smudges Lily could see at once the unmistakably crude block letters of her erstwhile Fergy.

TO MISS LILLIAN MALONE
THE ORPHANAGE OF ST. PATRICK'S CATHEDRAL
PRINCE STREET, NEW YORK CITY, AMERICA.

The envelope was magical, all by itself, and Lily was almost afraid to open the thing, for fear that opening it might somehow break the spell. *Fergy was alive. Fergy was alive!*

One of the smudges on the envelope was probably a postmark, but Lily couldn't make out what it was, or where the letter might have come from. Slowly, carefully as any surgeon, she opened it.

And for the second time Lily found Fergus' unformed letters swimming before her, seen through a filter of tears. She blinked and paused, and slowly began to be able to make out his words.

LILY DEAR,

I CAN TELL YOU NOW, THE SHIP IS THE INDIAN BELLE, BOUND FOR SAN FRANSISCO. WE'RE NOW IN RIO. I AM WELL, LIL, AND HOPE YOU FORGIV, AND WILL FIND GOLD IN PLENTY IN CALIFORNIA. PLEASE TELL EVERYONE I'M FINE LIL, THE SAILOR LIFE IS NOT AN EASY ONE NOR IS FOOD GOOD BUT IT'S FRISCO

FOR ME, DESTINY CALLS, MY DERE SIS, WILL WRIT
SOON.

YR. LOVING BROTHER,

FERGY

Lily read this twice, and slipped it into her sewing bag and
went back to her class. Every head turned. Sister Hilda, who
was something of a bully, paused in mid-sentence and said:
"Well, Lillian, is something wrong?"

"No, Sister."

"Well, then. Please sit down, girl. I do hope these distur-
bances won't continue."

"No, Sister."

Lily sat down and pretended to pay attention to the arith-
metic lesson. *Fergy's alive. Fergy's alive. Fergy's alive!* Not
only alive, but in Rio. Probably frolicking with naked
maidens under coconut trees, just as Frances said. On his
way to California. On his way to find gold! The very spirit
of Young America, for sure!

She couldn't wait to tell Sister Claudia.

Lily whispered the good news to Frances as they marched
to the noon meal, and Fran was delighted, as Lily knew she
must be. But there was no sign of Sister Claudia, at lunch or
in the dormitory afterward when Lily and Fran went up for
their afternoon's sewing assignment.

They sewed busily for an hour, chattering about Fergy,
mending the blue serge winter uniforms they'd soon all be
wearing. Lily finished the last of her uniforms and asked
Fran if she needed help.

"No, thank ye," said Fran, "but there's a pile of sheets in
the linen closet that'll need patching."

Lily walked out of the dorm and down the hall to the big
cedar-lined linen closet. It was dark in the closet. The only
light came from one small window at the far end, and none
of the orphans were allowed to light the whale-oil lamps that
were the only source of illumination after dark. The sheets,
Lily knew, were kept in the near corner, by the blankets. She
turned to look for them.

At first Lily thought someone had left one of the nuns'
habits to be mended. The sheer black woolen robe hung limp
in the gloom.

Then she saw the shoes hanging under it.

Lily took one step back and felt the wall. Instinctively she
reached back to touch the wall, glad of its solidity, glad to
have something to lean on. She forced her eyes to move up-

ward from the shoes. There was the robe she knew so well, hanging in its graceful folds, belted, with the big wooden-beaded rosary looped at the belt, the wide-cut black sleeve with a pale hand extending from it, a hand Lily knew well, a hand that had touched her often, and gently.

Sister Claudia wasn't beautiful anymore. The starched white collar was the same, but the headdress was all askew. Sister Claudia's head was twisted at an impossible angle, almost resting on her graceful shoulders. And her face. The fair pink and white of it was blotched with purple, and all swollen, and the calm blue eyes that knew how to twinkle were protruding like a fish's eyes, and they would never twinkle anymore.

A wave of dizziness came rushing through Lily's brain. She had never seen a dead person before, except for Dad, for Ma, and the Lord knew they hadn't wanted to die. *To have what Sister Claudia had and end it: why, for the love of God, why?*

Lily sank to the floor.

She never remembered screaming.

❧ 7 ❧

Lily woke up in bed. It was still daylight. She blinked her eyes and tried to convince herself that what she'd seen in the linen closet was a dream.

But it hadn't been a dream.

"There," said a familiar voice that Lily could not quite place, "there. She's coming out of it."

Sister Cathleen's face loomed into view. A cool hand touched Lily's forehead.

"How are you feeling, my dear?"

Yes. It was definitely the matron. Then it hadn't been a dream. Lily's eyes were open now. She looked up at Matron and groped for an answer. She was alive, she could wiggle her toes. Then why couldn't she think of words to answer? At last Lily spoke.

"Is she truly dead?"

"Yes, child, and may God have mercy on her poor soul."

"Sister Claudia hung herself, then?"

"I'm afraid so, Lily. You must try to think of happier things, my child. I know it must have been a terrible shock for you."

"She'll go to hell, then?"

"What she did, Lily, is against all the laws of God and man. Yes. And even be denied the right of burial in holy ground."

"And the angels will weep for her?"

"The angels weep for all sinners, Lily. But, come, child! Can we get you some tea, Lily? Or a little something to eat? When you've had a fright, a nice cup of tea works wonders, I always say."

"No, thank you, Sister Cathleen."

"Well, then, Lily, do try to rest. I'll ask Frances here to look after you. She can bring you a tray for supper if you don't feel like coming down. And, Lily, do try not to think about this dreadful thing too much—can you promise me that?"

"Yes, Sister."

"Thank you, dear. Now, get a nice rest, and we'll talk later."

Lily closed her eyes to see if the vision of Sister Claudia hanging had gone away. It had not. She could hear the tiny bird's-steps of the matron receding, and the door of the dormitory closing softly. The next voice Lily heard was Fran's.

"God in heaven, Lil: just think of it! There you were, flat on the floor, and after that terrible scream you gave out with, sure and I thought there was a murderer loose, and then I saw—"

"I know what you saw."

"Glory be to God, if I live to be five hundred years old, may I never see anything that bad again. And her so young, and so pretty."

"She did it," said Lily with absolute conviction, "for love."

Fran wanted to talk about Sister Claudia's suicide. Lily looked at her friend and for the first time saw a stranger. *She truly doesn't understand, she thinks 'tis still a game, like making up stories for fun, she doesn't understand that Sister Claudia is dead and gone, that she's left me too, like Fergy, and without a good-bye.*

Lily didn't want to talk to anyone, about anything. She asked for tea, just to get Fran out of the room. Then she closed her eyes and tried not to think of what had just happened, for suicide was truly beyond Lily's comprehension. She had watched her mother's hopeless fight for life too closely to do anything but value her own life above all else.

The idea of sending death an invitation, of taking God's will into your own hands, was beyond anything in Lily's experience, worse than her darkest fears. And Sister Claudia, she of anyone!

It was warm in the big room under the eaves of St. Patrick's orphanage, but Lily lay there shivering. If Sister Claudia could be what she was, lovely and rich and smiling and still kill herself, then what hope might there be for a miserable creature like Lily Malone?

Sister Claudia!

Lily searched her brain for an answer, for even the hint of where an answer might lie. It was like counting all the stars in heaven, for there was surely no end to it, only a dark infinity, a cold and empty space. There had always been something safe and comforting about Sister Claudia. Goodness flowed out of her with the directness and generosity of warmth flowing from the sun itself, and in her company Lily had felt the same pleasure she remembered dimly from the old days when both her parents were alive and the world was a happier place.

But this proves there's no sure way to happiness, not even God's way. For hadn't Sister Claudia given up all the pleasures of a rich and happy home for the greater glory of becoming a nun, a Bride of Christ, and still not been happy?

Lily's head swam with the contradiction of it. Just when she had found a pattern for her future, it had been snatched away from her with no reason. It had all seemed so simple. God had rules, and if you obeyed them, you were happy. If you disobeyed, you were a sinner and the angels wept for you and you'd go to hell. *Until this afternoon in that linen closet.*

Maybe Sister Claudia hadn't obeyed the rules! Maybe she had sinned with Gerald St. Clair! It was a tempting idea, but Lily knew Sister Claudia better than that. If Sister Claudia had been sinning, Gerald St. Clair would never have looked the way he did that last time they said good-bye.

Maybe none of it matters. Maybe you're on your own for good or bad, whether you keep the rules or break them.

The door opened. It was Fran with hot tea.

Lily sat up in bed. She felt guilty for sending her friend on a false errand, yet suddenly the tea looked good. She smiled and took the cup and drank thirstily.

"Thanks, Fran."

"You should see downstairs, Lil! Pure commotion it is! The police themselves came, think of that! And lawyers, and the bishop himself. You'd think the world was ending."

Again Lily looked at her friend. She knew Fran to be a decent girl, incapable of doing a mean thing. *But why,* Lily wondered, *why in the world can't she see beneath the surface of the thing? A world did end, for the love of God!*

And as she thought these thoughts, Lily suddenly knew that she must leave St. Paddy's just as fast as she could. For months now, they had played with the idea of joining the novitiate, and Lily felt sure that both she and Fran would be encouraged to do so. But now that seemed empty, just a game, the way making up stories about Sister Claudia had been a game.

And the time had come to stop her games, to get on with the business of growing up and earning a place for herself in this unpredictable world.

Lily looked up from her teacup. Fran sat on her own bed, close by, filled with excitement, waiting for Lily's reply. But Lily said nothing. There was really nothing more to say.

She finished her tea and then got up and walked to the window. The sun shone brilliantly through a clear October sky. Bright leaves danced and twirled as they fell to earth. Lily could see down the familiar backyards between Mott and Mulberry streets, with their animals and fences and a few people, here and there, a late chrysanthemum blooming, someone's wash flapping like the sails of a ragged navy beached half a mile from the sea. In the distance and vividly clear were the church steeples she knew of old, gulls soaring, and far away one small plump white cloud such as might make a fine cushion for one tired little angel. *It's exactly as though Sister Claudia never lived or died.*

Lily somehow got through the next day, and the day after that. The routine helped, and so did Fran's mindless good cheer.

On the third day she went to Matron and asked if she might be considered for a job in service, and leave St. Patrick's orphanage forever.

Sister Cathleen looked at Lily for a long time before she spoke.

"Have you thought about this, Lily?"

"Yes, Sister, indeed I have. I'm fourteen now, you see, and it just seems I'm restless, wanting to be on to the next thing, to make a place for myself."

Sister Cathleen sighed a small and scarcely heard sigh. *Why was it that so many of the best ones were the first to want to leave?* Lily hardly looked fourteen, so thin and pale she was, even with the startling red hair and the deep green eyes. Sister Cathleen liked Lily, and saw a promise of beauty in her, which from the matron's point of view meant the possibility of danger, for didn't she know what temptations might lie in the way of a pretty servant girl in these wicked times?

"Well, my dear, there's no rush, is there? I'll keep my eyes sharp for the right sort of position, and then we'll see, and talk about it some more."

"Yes, Sister. Thank you, Sister."

The first snow came, and Lily wondered when she'd next hear from Fergy, if God had spared him. His letter from Rio hadn't been dated, but she knew it was more than a month's sea voyage to Brazil, with the best luck and fair winds. The sea trip around the Horn to California took three or four months under the best of circumstances. *Which could mean Fergy was there already! Maybe he was rich already. Maybe*—and for Lily this was the dream of dreams, so cherished that she would ration the number of times she'd let herself think of it—*maybe he was even now on his way back to her, rich or not rich, to rescue her, to take her out of St. Paddy's and into a new life forever.*

The nuns always tried their hardest to make Christmas a special time in the orphanage, and there were gifts for all the children donated by well-to-do families in the parish, and by some of the big stores. The food was special, and they had Christmas turkey, and singing of carols, and the older children were allowed to stay up for the glorious candlelit midnight Mass at the cathedral.

Christmas was a sad time for Lily, although she tried to hide it. It didn't seem like Christmas without Fergy. And she was forced to remember, every time she looked at her sewing bag, that only last Christmas Sister Claudia had given her a special thimble, made of white china and painted with copper-colored lilies that were nearly the same color as her own hair. Or so Sister Claudia said when she handed Lily the small box wrapped in red paper. Lily never used the thimble: it was far too precious to her for that. The thimble lay still in its box in her wicker trunk under her bed. The thimble she used every day was old and battered and made of tin. It belonged to St. Patrick's, as did almost everything Lily wore or used or read or wrote with.

Lily had made a present for Fran—a small square of linen beautifully embroidered with her friend's monogram, surrounded by ribbons and flowers and even a bumblebee about to land on one of the flowers.

"Oh, Lil, so fine it is, the fairies must have made it."

Frances held up the embroidery to see it more clearly in the pale light of Christmas Eve afternoon.

"The divil they did, 'tis all me own work, Fran, and in the darkest secrecy."

"Well, I thank you, Lily. It's a lovely thing."

"When you're rich and have a grand house, you can frame it on the wall."

"That I will. But you shame me, Lil, for the thing I have for you is nowhere near so fine."

She handed Lily a little roll of white sheeting tied with a bit of red wool.

Lily undid the tie and unrolled the scrap of white fabric. There, inside, was a length of white linen cut into a ribbon perhaps eighteen inches long, embroidered all along its length with fanciful flowers and green leaves.

"It's to tie your hair with, Lil. You have such nice hair."

Lily sat on her bed and held the ribbon and thought that

maybe Christmas wasn't going to be so bad after all. But as she sat there, Lily made herself a promise. She promised herself that, come what might, this would be her last Christmas in the orphanage.

Then she jumped up and kissed Frances O'Farrelley a great smack on the cheek.

"I may never wear it, that's how beautiful it is, Fran. I may just save it to use as a bell pull to call my butlers and footmen and parlormaids."

"And we'll drink champagne from morning till night."

"And have hundreds of lovers panting for us!"

"Diamonds!"

"Famous millionaires cutting their very throats for the love of us."

And the cold afternoon dissolved in giggles. Before they knew it, the bell rang to summon them to supper.

It was on the way out of the dining hall that Father Gregory called Lily from the line of girls.

"Merry Christmas to you, Father."

"And to you, Lily."

But something in his face was not merry. He put his big hand on her shoulder. Lily felt the warmth of it, and wondered what was up.

"Tell me, Lily," he began softly, casually, "what was the name of the ship Fergus went out on?"

"The *Indian Belle*, Father. Is there news of it?"

"There is, child, and it isn't good news."

Lily had hardly noticed where they were walking. Father Gregory stopped and knocked on a door. It was the door of Matron's office.

"Come in."

He opened the door.

Sister Cathleen sat on her perch, just as Lily had seen her so many times before. There was no smile on her face, but a look of resignation.

"It is," said Father Gregory in a voice so low Lily could barely hear him, "as I feared, Sister."

"The *Indian Belle*?"

"Alas."

Lily looked from one to the other, and her eyes grew wider with apprehension. *What were they trying to tell her?*

Then Lily noticed an unusual object on Sister Cathleen's desk. It was a newspaper. Lily could not remember having seen the matron reading a newspaper before.

"Father Gregory," said the matron, addressing Lily in a

gentle but very precise tone, "was reading the paper, Lily, when he saw this item. I am afraid your brother is lost to us, Lily."

Sister Cathleen handed Lily the paper, neatly folded so that only one feature story was visible. Its black headline would be carved on Lily's brain for as long as she lived:

TRAGEDY AT SEA! "INDIAN BELLE" SHIPWRECKED OFF CHILE. ALL PASSENGERS & CREW FEARED LOST.

gentle that very precise flone ... was reading the paper,Lily,
when to her she said. Then learn your lesson it is to ...

Sister Cathleen bended Lily the bacon. Bially folded an
that entry her feature story was vanfile its black trapping
would be carved on Lily ... drama as she was so strictly as
... ...

SLEEPY AT THAT RELAX, BELL' ... ANYWHERE to our
Child HOLDINGS & CREW INARED LOST
... ... differs

❧ 8 ❧

A darkness came over Lily's soul blacker than any night, and
with the darkness came despair, for hadn't her worst fears
been confirmed? And while part of her brain knew where she
was, her heart was alone in some dark and distant place, beyond the reach of hope, or comforting words, or even God
himself.

*And now I know what Ma meant when she told me to
save my tears, for wasn't poor Fergy the last one in the world
I had left to save them for?*

The tears came at last, and sobbing, and though kind Father Gregory came to comfort her, Lily knew that she was
forever beyond the comfort of a human touch.

Her feeling for Fergy came and went with the inconsis-
tency and violence of fever, bouncing between Lily's outrage
that he'd left her and her sure knowledge that death was his
reward, to a protectiveness in which she recalled his good
points and the happy times they'd had and how he always
believed his wild promises as he made them and—who
knew?—if he'd lived long enough, some of them might even
have come true.

Sometimes, late at night, in the echo of her own weeping,
Lily thought she could hear the angels weeping too, for surely
they must weep for Fergy. For Fergy's sins. For Fergy's sister.

And that dark night that had fallen on her soul would not
see dawn, for hadn't everyone she ever loved betrayed her by
running away, by making that final grim elopment with
Death himself?

She became so unnaturally quiet that Frances got worried
for her, and tried any number of ways to coax her back to
laughter again, but always in vain.

"God forgive me, Fran," Lily said after one of these at-
tempts, in the first week of January, "but the juice is gone
out of me, that's for sure. Too young, I was, when me
mother went, to think on it. But Fergy's done for me, Fran,

and there's the truth of it, and nothing can change that, not praying, nor laughing, nor pretending it never happened. I know, for sure and I've tried all that, and a hundred times."

Her friend looked at her. "If it was God's will, then we must accept it."

"Must we, now? And what, pray, did Fergy ever do to God, that God must go and sink his ship? Tell me that, Fran, and maybe I'll accept God's will."

"Lil, that is blasphemy!"

"I guess. Don't seem to make much of a difference, now, do it? Sometimes it seems like there's just no sense to any of it, Fran, and that's for sure."

"It could have been worse, Lil. You could have been with him."

"If I had a dollar for every time I wished I had been, wouldn't I be rich as old John Jacob Astor, now?"

"Ah, go on with you! Sure, and you don't truly wish that."

"There be times I do, Fran."

"If you're at the bottom of the ocean, then you won't be able to come into my shop with me, and we won't get rich and have servants and champagne and lovers."

Lily smiled then. It was a small, quivering, tentative smile, but as it flickered and fixed itself on her pale face, Fran smiled back, encouraging: it had been three weeks now, and this was the first time Fran had seen so much as a hint of a smile on Lily's face.

"Sure, and it wouldn't be easy to drink champagne under salt water, now, would it?"

And Lily laughed, and laughed the harder for her friend's joining in, and if Lily's laughter had a certain almost hysterical edge to it, well, it was better far than what had come before. They giggled and roared, and Fran thought that finally some of the clouds of grief might be lifting.

The new year started cold and bleak and stayed that way right through March. The plans for the new orphanage at Fifty-first Street and Fifth Avenue pushed ahead, and as the sense of expectation increased, so did Lily's restlessness. The new place would be for the boys' division of the orphanage, that was how much they had been growing. The girls would stay behind, in the Prince Street building, which would soon be filled. Even, Lily thought, if Fergus had stayed behind, the separation would have meant that they'd be seeing less and less of each other. Fifty-first Street was another world: practically out in the country. Lily had never been farther north than the new Croton Reservoir at Forty-second Street and

Fifth, where Father Gregory had taken them one Sunday to see the wonders of progress, source of all the running water in Manhattan. And even that seemed miles and hours away. Still, there was a bustling in the air as spring came grudgingly in on the howling winds of March, and Lily renewed the promise she had made to herself to be gone from St. Patrick's orphanage before the year was out. After all, she was fifteen now, and younger girls than she were supporting themselves in shops and in factories and as servants.

Lily and Fran both wanted to go as servants together, and then save their money to start a dress-goods or millinery shop. And then, if some fine young man came along, well, who was to say? But first they must find a good position in a respectable Catholic household, and for this they counted on Sister Cathleen.

In her grief over Fergy, Lily had all but forgotten this plan. Now, as she slowly regained a sense of herself and of the future, her determination to go into service was renewed. For surely there was nothing now to keep her at St. Paddy's. She had long abandoned any idea of becoming a nun, and there was no hope at all for Fergy's return, if ever there had been.

There was a great to-do when the boys' division of the orphanage moved to their grand new quarters at Fifth Avenue and Fifty-first Street. The press made much of it, and on the great day itself the bishop and the mayor and all manner of bigwigs were on hand. There was to be a formal procession of carriages all the way from Prince Street to Fifty-first, and when the nuns and priests of St. Paddy's discovered that no transportation had been provided for the boys, a ripple of rebellion swept through them and they all climbed down from their assigned carriages and marched with the lads, side by side. Lily and Fran watched from their dormer window, and a fine sight it made: the great line of carriages followed by two hundred and more boys flanked by their own nuns and priests, and all of them marching up Mott Street as if to war.

But Lily viewed all this with detachment, as if she were looking at a picture in a book. For in her heart Lily felt that St. Paddy's was behind her now. Part of her attachment for the place had died with Sister Claudia, and the rest went down with Fergy.

And while Lily did not know just what her future might hold, she did know that what happened to her would not be happening within these sheltering walls, nor within the comforting assurance of the Mother Church.

For, she felt, and felt it to the marrow, *if God loves me, He has strange ways of showing it.*

Surely she had prayed to God that Fergy might have a safe journey, and where had that gotten her—or Fergy? A hard little nugget of skepticism had been forming in Lily's mind for some time now, ever since St. Jude sent her a pear instead of Ma's recovery, and Fergy's shipwreck was all it took to make Lily doubt everything she had ever heard about religion. Doubting itself was a sin—many were the times she had been told that—but Lily could no more control her doubts than she could stop the rain from falling or bring her brother back to life. *And if God wants to punish me, 'tis very clever He'll have to be, to think of worse things than He's sent already!*

In the second week after the boys moved up to the new orphanage, Lily was summoned to the matron's office once again.

There was a stranger with Sister Cathleen. The strange lady sat on the one extra chair in the small office, and more than filled it. She was a big, solid woman, older than the matron, comfortably dressed for the warm weather in gray gingham patterned with small sprigs of flowers, trimmed simply with white ribbon, and a white gingham shawl modestly draped about her ample shoulders. A straw bonnet trimmed in pink sat rather incongruously upon her large graying head, like a butterfly on a rock. Yet her face was the face of a kindly toad, wrinkled but content, and her bright brown eyes danced in her face as she looked intently at Lily. Lily curtsied, first to the matron, then to the stranger.

"Mrs. Groome, this is Lily, Lillian Malone."

"How do you do, Lily?"

"Well, thank you, ma'am."

Mrs. Groome's voice had no airs or graces to it, but Lily felt a warmth there, and honesty. "Matron tells me you think you'd like work as a servant girl. Is that true, Lily?"

"Yes, ma'am, it is."

"And can you sew?"

"I can."

"And you're not afraid to work hard?"

"No, ma'am."

"How old are you, Lily?"

"Fifteen, ma'am."

Lily knew that she was safe, that this imposing stranger could do her no harm, not here, not while the matron was watching. Yet she was nervous, and could hardly look Mrs. Groome in the eyes. Lily stood, facing her inquisitress, and tried not to tremble.

"Do you believe in Our Lord Jesus Christ, Lily?"

"Oh, yes!"

"And you know the fires of hell are waiting for them as disobey His Commandments, as revealed by Christ's Vicar on Earth, His Holiness the Pope in Rome?"

"I do."

"And do you understand, Lily, that if ye should come to work for us, and you're caught in any wickedness, or disobedience, you'll be turned out into the street with nary so much as a crust of bread, nor a reference?"

"Yes, ma'am."

Lily thought of the infamous Maureen Nesbit, caught in the ultimate wickedness of unwedded pregnancy, right here in St. Paddy's, and turned out into the streets to her fate. Mrs. Groome was obviously every bit as stern and religious as St. Paddy's itself. Lily looked at the polished floorboards and wondered if Mrs. Groome ever laughed.

Sister Cathleen's was the next voice Lily heard. "That will be all for now, Lily, thank you."

Lily blushed, and made her curtsies, and fled. She knew she'd failed! Whatever the formidable Mrs. Groome was looking for, Lily Malone was surely lacking. She walked down the long hallway in a kind of trance, wondering where she'd gone wrong, wondering what other kinds of answers might have been expected of her, and how to do better the next time.

Fran was waiting in the dormitory. "How was it? *Who* was it?"

"Scared the very divil out of me, she did, Fran, with all her questions, and do I believe in God, and what's going to happen to me if I'm wicked."

"Sounds grim."

"Grimmer than three Sister Hildas put together. She didn't look all that bad, but, glory, she sure and lit into me."

"Well, you don't have to go there if you don't want to, that's for sure."

Lily looked at her friend, and wondered how Fran would have reacted to Mrs. Groome's questions.

"It definitely ain't," said Lily with new and hard-won wisdom, "going to be all beer and skittles, going into service."

"Never thought it would be, Lil. Still and all, it's a step. It's getting us out of here. One move closer to our shop."

"I guess so." Lily giggled. "You wouldn't be wantin' to reconsider your vocation, now, would ye, Miss O'Farrelley?"

"I guess she truly did scare you, didn't she? But no. Not until it's a case of desperation, Lil."

"Time will tell." Lily took up her sewing and wondered how soon she'd hear from the matron, and whether Matron would be angry with her for such a disgraceful performance.

Lily didn't have long to wait. Within an hour one of the new girls came running up with the dread summons.

There was no Mrs. Groome in Matron's office. Lily felt relief flow through her like hot chocolate on a cold day.

"Well, Lily, tell me what you thought of Mrs. Groome."

If I say she scared the daylights out of me, sure and I'll never get the situation. If I lie, I may go straight to hell.

"She seemed . . . very stern, Sister."

"Did she, now? But I've known Verity Groome for nearly twenty years now, Lily, and I can assure you there isn't a kinder—or more efficient—housekeeper in all New York. Works for the John Wallingford family, and that's about as fine as you can get."

Lily stood there, her eyes firmly fixed on the top of Sister Cathleen's desk. She'd never heard of the Wallingford family, but what did that count for?

"Naturally," Matron went on, "I'd told Mrs. Groome about you, Lily, and she was very favorably impressed. There's a place for you in the Wallingford household, should you like to take it."

Lily looked up quickly. *It can't be true. To have prayed, and have the prayer answered, and such a small prayer, not like the ones I'd prayed for Ma, for Fergy.*

"Would there be a place for Frances, Sister?"

"I'm afraid not, not at the moment anyway. However, Mrs. Groome has promised to consider your friend, should a place come open. It's a fine big house, Lily, on Fifth Avenue, too, at Sixteenth Street. They've three coaches and a couple of traps, and who knows how many horses. Not to mention eight in help, and that doesn't count the gardeners or the stablehands. Solid people they are, Lily, the lot of them."

"What would I do there?"

"You'd start as a tweeny, meaning between-stairs maid. That's as opposed to upstairs maid or kitchen maid, don't you see? So you'd do a bit of almost everything, and some sewing and mending too. Mrs. Groome was very interested in what Sister Mary Agnes had to say about you in that regard."

So Sister Mary Agnes had been asked. Mrs. Groome must

be serious after all. Eight in help! A grand mansion on Fifth Avenue!

"And they'd be paying me a wage?"

Sister Cathleen laughed. "But of course, my dear! There's no slavery in New York, Lily, not in the year of our Lord 1852. It won't be much of a wage, not at first, only two dollars each month, fifty cents a week, but you must remember this: it includes a good warm roof over your head and plenty to eat. The Wallingfords' cook is French, Lily, imagine that! Famous she is, too: even I have heard of that Louise Dulac."

"When might I be starting, Sister?"

"Lily, my dear," said Sister Cathleen softly, "you do realize that you don't have to go unless you want to? We would love to have you stay with us and help with the younger children."

And one day become a nun. Lily had thought about this and little else since Fergy's ship went down, and she knew in her most secret heart that she could never completely trust the Church again.

"Thank you, Sister, for you have been very kind. But I must go."

"I see, Lily, and I wish you luck. We all do. Well, then, first we must make you some new clothes to wear, for only those who wait on the table wear uniforms in the Wallingford mansion. I'd say two weeks ought to be sufficient, if we tell Mrs. Groome today. And you're pleased with all this, Lily?"

"Oh, yes! Thank you, Sister: it sounds fine."

"Then, dear, remember that we love you, and come to visit us, and should things not work out for you, you may always find a home right here at St. Patrick's."

"Thank you again."

Lily ran down the hallway on the wings of her luck, bursting to tell Fran. *Fran! I'll be leaving Fran, as Fergy left me! Only, not without her knowing. And not for good and forever. Maybe there'll be a place soon for Fran.* But Lily's joy had faded as she walked slowly into the dormitory where Fran would be waiting.

"What happened?" Fran's voice had more than questions in it: it held joy and fear and hope, all crazily mixed.

"I got it."

There was a pause then, during which Fran didn't ask, and Lily was too apprehensive to volunteer the obvious. That Lily had gotten the job and there was no place for Fran.

"I guess," said Fran quietly, "that you are surely obliged to take it, Lil, what with Matron going out of her way for you, and all."

"I guess I am."

There was no joy in it anymore. Lily looked at her friend, who was sitting dejectedly on the edge of her bed. How often had they sat just here, each on their adjoining beds, doing their sewing chores all the long afternoon, and gossiping and larking and dreaming such dreams for the future? And who would she joke with now, in that big house on Fifth Avenue, and who would share her dreams?

"Matron said," began Lily with false cheer, "that there might be a place for you soon. In my house, I mean. That the housekeeper promised to let her know. She wouldn't lie, Fran."

"No, I'm sure she wouldn't. Is it a grand house, Lil?"

"Ever so grand! There's coaches, and eight in help—I'll be the ninth—and right up on Fifth Avenue it is, Fran, with all the swells . . ." Lily stopped then, because she had looked up from her sewing and discovered that her friend was crying.

Lily put down her needle and went to Fran, sat next to her on the small bed, and took the other girl in her arms.

"Get on with ye, Frances O'Farrelley! How in the divil are we going to get that shop if you take to carryin' on like this?"

But the sobbing went on and on. Lily had never heard Fran cry, not even when Fergy's boat went down, nor even when Sister Claudia hung herself.

"Oh, Lil," said Fran between sobs, "what in God's name will become of me? I'll be . . . alone!"

"Divil you will. How far away is Fifth Avenue, anyway? Why, you'll be the next one, Fran, Matron good as said so. Or in a house nearby, for that's where all the rich live now. We can still have our talks, and fun, and go out larking. You'll see."

Slowly, but only very slowly, Fran's sobs died away and she wiped her eyes on a scrap of linen from her sewing bag.

"A fine sight I must be," said Fran, sniffling. "'Tis glad I am that no one's interviewing me this day. And I'm sorry, Lil, for carrying on so at your good luck, for who in the world deserves it if not you? It's just that I wish . . ."

"Ah, and don't I know it? I wish it too, Fran, more than anything. And it may happen still. We'll pray for it, and hard."

You are saying a thing you don't believe in your heart, Lily, for how many of your prayers have gone unanswered? Still, you never know when the right saint might be listening, or even Himself.

Fran brightened.

"I'll start this very afternoon, at vespers."

"And me, too." Fran paused then, and gathered her courage. "Just when will you be going, Lil?"

"Oh, not for weeks. There's dresses to make, for they don't abide by uniforms there. We'll have plenty of fun before then, Fran, just the two of us."

"I'll help. And you will be the most elegant servant girl in all New York."

"In a pig's eye I will. But we must think hard on it. What will I need, truly? Matron had no list."

"Well, dresses, of course. And a winter coat for going to church and your afternoon off, and the like. A shawl, I'm thinking. Underthings. You will need at least three dresses, Lil. And maybe one for best, for grand occasions."

"And when, I'd like to know, would I be having grand occasions? Emptying the slops will be the likes of a grand occasion for me, you goose!"

Fran laughed then. "Ah, you never know. Could it be your fairy godmother comes and gets you invited to the ball, where the charming prince falls passionately in love with you?"

"Sure, and I'd hate to be hanging until that happens, Fran. If I get to Barnum's Museum once in six months, it'll be a grand occasion enough."

"Still, you can take walks and things."

"With who?"

"Who knows? Maybe with me, if I'm there or nearby. Or some other girl. If they have eight in help, they'll have other girls."

"They won't be the same as you."

Fran smiled a small wan smile. "Well," she said, "you never know, do you?"

"No. You never do."

The new wardrobe took the full two weeks Matron had predicted. It was a communal enterprise. Sister Mary Agnes had the biggest sewing bag of all, with the most interesting scraps in it, and this treasury was made available to Lily and Fran. They dyed old sheets, one to a soft green, and another to a pale russet, and these became the basis of two simple summer dresses with a "Basque" bodice and separate skirt after the new fashion. Trimmings of plain ribbon appeared from sewing bags, a bolt of flowered calico was unearthed from the storeroom to make a third dress for every day, and one of the dark brown orphanage blankets was cut into a surprisingly becoming winter cape.

"If only," said Fran one afternoon, "you had a bonnet."

Indeed, as Lily well knew, it was virtually unheard of to venture into the streets without some sort of head covering. A shawl might do in an emergency, or even a lace kerchief, but style and expediency called for a close-fitting, ear-covering straw or beaver-felt bonnet trimmed with ribbons and often a veil, and sometimes flowers or feathers too. But there was no such item in St. Paddy's, and no means of making one. At last Sister Mary Agnes came to the rescue with a fringe of old lace edging from an altarcloth that was beyond repair. This, cut into overlapping layers in a ruffled effect, and mounted upon a wide band of stiff muslin and simply trimmed with green ribbon, made a perfectly suitable cap for a young girl. The bonnet—if it ever came—would simply have to wait. Lily could hardly imagine where she'd be wearing such a thing, excepting always to church. Still, she tied on the lace cap with its green ribbon bowed under her small chin and stood on tiptoe to look at herself in the one small mirror in the girls' lavatory.

"I look foolish, and that's a fact."

"You look fine." Frances adjusted the cap.

"It's far and away too fancy."

Lily was unused to seeing her reflection. She looked in the mirror—and casually at that—only when fixing her hair, which took little fixing, since she wore it in braids, and the braids coiled back on her head by Fran. Lily thought the elegant little cap looked incongruous on her young head, but she didn't say so out of consideration for Fran, who obviously considered the thing a work of art.

"You'll see. A proper young lady of fashion you are, Lil, if I do say so."

"Sure, and won't it be lovely as I'm scrubbin' the stable floors, or whatever they'll be having me do."

And they laughed then as they had so often laughed together in the past, and both girls tried to pretend it wasn't almost the last time for shared laughter, that the inevitable time of parting would soon be on them and that there was no predicting when they'd see each other again.

The fatal day was a Saturday late in June.

❦ 9 ❧

The day of her leaving St. Paddy's dawned early and hot,
and stayed hot.

All the windows in the orphanage were opened, but not a
breeze stirred the muggy air. Sister Cathleen had told Lily she
might take with her the wicker trunk that had always lived
underneath her bed. The new clothes were packed in the
trunk now, safe beside her old doll, Hortense, and Ma's
dowry scarf of old lace and linen. And Sister Claudia's
thimble was there too, all unused, and the fine embroidered
hair ribbon Fran had given her.

How Lily had wished for this day, and how she wished
now that it had never come!

For St. Patrick's orphanage had become so much a part of
Lily Malone that she wasn't at all sure how she'd get along
on the outside. *Well, damned if there's not a bit of Fergy in
me too,* she thought, and smiled at herself for thinking it, *for
hadn't Fergy always been crazy to see tomorrow instead of
today, and always thinkin' that what's on the other side of a
fence just has to be better than the side you can see?*

And though she had known for weeks it was coming, this
last day had a special magic for Lily, and a special danger,
filled as it was with both lasts and firsts. The last night she
would ever sleep in her narrow cot in the big dormitory under the eaves. Her last Mass, perhaps, in old St. Patrick's
Cathedral, for surely the Wallingfords would go to St.
Joseph's over on Washington Square. And if it wouldn't truly
be the last time she saw Matron or Father Gregory or—God
forbid!—Fran, surely it would be the last time for a while.

Hard on the heels of the lasts came the firsts. Her first real
job of work! And, with that, her first real wages. Fifty cents a
week was a fortune to Lily, who had never seen so much as a
penny to call her own in all the years she'd been in the orphanage. Oh, and wouldn't she save every bit of it, to go for
the shop she and Fran would have one day. Why, if they
both saved their wages each month, they might have their

shop in three or four years! And in the meantime, she'd be learning about people of quality, for the Wallingfords would be that, beyond any doubt. Fine people, Matron had said, and in a fine mansion, too.

The gray-blue light was slowly gaining an apricot tinge, and Lily could feel the little world of St. Paddy's slowly coming to life around her as she lay in her cot in the dormitory. A rooster crowed in Mott Street, and hundreds of songbirds answered him with their music. Lily could hear the heavy clip-clop of a tired dray horse moving over the cobbles, probably a farm wagon getting an early start to market.

Lily opened her eyes then, and raised herself on one elbow, and looked down the length of the dormitory where she had spent these last several years. And she realized that with the one exception of Frances O'Farrelley, there was nothing and no one left in St. Paddy's that she truly cared for. It was time to move on, to whatever her future might hold. She yawned, and stretched luxuriously in the narrow bed, and smiled.

The wagon came after lunch.

Lily and Fran sat together in the big reception hall. The wicker trunk was waiting by the door. Both girls were unusually quiet, Fran from sadness and Lily from a mixture of melancholy and anticipation so rich her head fairly swam with it. The long-established ease between the two friends seemed to seep away into the darkness of the reception hall. At every sound of hoofbeats Lily would run to the window and pull back the heavy red draperies, only to see the horses pass by.

When the Wallingfords' wagon finally came, they didn't hear it at all. Matron appeared in the doorway, tiny and birdlike as ever. "The wagon is here now, Lily."

Lily looked quickly at Fran and saw a fear come into her friend's eyes that met and matched a sudden fear that Lily felt for herself. She bent and kissed Fran on the cheek.

"Pray for me, Fran?"

"And what else would I be doing? Get on with ye now, Lil, before ye have me in tears again."

"I'll write . . . we can visit."

"Sure. Get on with ye now."

"Good-bye, Fran."

"God go with you, Lil."

And Lily ran from the room, for she felt if she hesitated one second, she might never leave St. Patrick's at all. Matron was standing with a tall, bony, handsome lad with sleepy dark eyes. He looked very bored.

"Lily," said Matron formally, "this is Patrick, from Mrs. Groome, come to fetch you."

"How do you do?"

Patrick favored her with a glance and then winked a large, bawdy wink. "Fine, and yourself, miss?"

Lily blushed. Sister Cathleen took her hand, and Lily turned to the matron.

"Well, Lily, I won't say good-bye, for I expect you'll be coming to visit us. At least, I do hope you will."

"Oh, yes, Sister, sure and I will!"

"Then go with God, Lily, and know that our prayers will go with you all your days."

"Thank you, Sister."

The matron was only a bit taller than Lily. She hardly had to bend to kiss the girl, which she did, and then squeezed Lily's hand for luck, then turned and was gone. And for all her kind words, Lily felt a door close.

"This is your trunk?" Patrick's voice could barely conceal his amusement at the scene he had just witnessed. Lily could guess he was not of a religious persuasion.

"It is."

"I'll be helpin' ye with it, then." Patrick bent and in one smooth movement had the trunk balanced on his shoulder. Standing that way, he bowed low, and ushered Lily out of the door and down the steps. The wagon was waiting at the end of the walk, a utility trap meant for hauling goods and groceries, but clean and with good leather and shiny brasses on the horses. Lily looked at it and realized that she had been secretly expecting some gilded fairy-tale coach to bring her flying into her future. No coach this, and no gallant footman was Patrick. Lily smiled at her folly and climbed up next to Patrick on the bench that served as the driver's seat and the only passenger seat in the trap.

Patrick gave the reins an expert flip, and the two silk-smooth horses started up at a brisk clip. He turned them left at the corner of Mott Street, and as they passed the deserted front of St. Patrick's Cathedral, Lily wondered how long it might be before she'd see the flat, familiar brownstone facade again. The trap turned left again on Houston Street, where the going was slower because of the Saturday throngs. For a few moments they rode in silence. Finally Patrick spoke up.

"So you'll be our new tweeny, then, Lily? Old lady Groome will put the fear of God in you, my girl, you can be sure of that."

Lily felt her stomach drop, as though the wagon had hit a

hole, for this was a basic fear: *God help me, from the frying pan to the fire it is!*

"And is she so terrible, then?"

"Ah, she's not a bad sort, really, but only rough, like, you know, rough-spoken. It's her old man, if you ask me, with all his drinkin' and chasin' after the ladies. Not," he went on with a wicked grin for one so young, "that I'm averse to the company of ladies meself, you understand."

Lily understood.

"Tell me, Patrick, about the house."

"Pat it is, what they calls me. Oh, 'tis a fine house. I'm not allowed in it much, not beyond the kitchens, and the servants' hall, that is, so ye can tell how very fine it may be. I live over the stables, with old Williams, the coachman, and even the stables are highly elegant, if you get my meaning. It's all for show at the Wallingfords', Lily, you may be sure of that."

"What are they like—the Wallingfords?"

"Rich as rich, Lily. Mrs. W. can hardly think of ways to spend it fast enough—try as she may. Mr. W. owns the Wallingford Emporium, as you might have guessed, and it simply rolls in. Opened a branch in Californy, and that's coining it too. Oh, they're rich, all right. Now, the old rich, the Dutchrich in particular, look down their noses at our Wallingfords, you can bet, what with the W.'s bein' fish-eaters and all, instead of proper Episcopalians or Congregationalists. But they're not all bad. Mr. W., you'll hardly ever see, he is that busy. Mrs. W. is everywhere, in and out of the house. Young Miss Marianne, well, she comes and goes, and young Jack's away at school most of the time. It's a rum situation come holidays, though, when they're all there and everything's hoppin' and us runnin' every which way, what with balls an' tea parties and who knows what all. Oh, they spend it, do the Wallingfords."

In the course of this illuminating lecture, Pat had turned the trap north on Broadway. They passed the delicate Gothic spires of Grace Church at Tenth Street, passed the booming stores and restaurants, came into Union Square and rode right around it and down Sixteenth Street toward Fifth Avenue.

And suddenly, well before they reached Fifth, Pat was pointing. "And there it is, my lady, your new home."

The Wallingford mansion rose from the northwest corner of Fifth Avenue and Sixteenth Street like a fortress of kings, shimmering in the heat. It soared, four stories of white limestone excess, a bastard mixture of three styles that somehow managed to incorporate Italianate arches with French Gothic spires and French Baroque mansard roof style. The house faced on the avenue, and seemed to push outward, crowding the sidewalk, too eager for grandeur to spare so much as a strip of green, much less a tree or a bush. On the Sixteenth Street side, the white limestone wall of the house extended itself into a white limestone courtyard wall topped with fierce-looking black iron spearheads and pierced with pointed, grilled Gothic windows and a huge double gate of strangely wrought black iron. These gates stood open in the afternoon sun, revealing a paved courtyard that led to the service entrances of the house, and the Wallingford stables and the Wallingford gardens.

It was a self-contained world, separate as any island or any walled medieval town, and as the smart trap pulled in through the immense arch of the courtyard gates, Lily imagined herself being held prisoner here, never to be seen again.

Pat pulled the trap up to a big service porch at the back of the house. Lily could hear kitchen noises, and a wonderful smell of baking bread rode on the hot afternoon air. Pat jumped down from his seat and came around to Lily's side, where he offered her his hand in a gesture of unexpected gallantry. As she stepped down, her hand in his, Lily could feel the strength of that arm.

"Thank you, Pat. It was a fine ride."

He grinned, and at once Lily knew why she instinctively liked that grin: it was Fergy's grin all over again, reckless, filled with mischief, a cheeky grin to be sure, but never unkind. He swept up her trunk and deposited it on the porch.

" 'Twas nothing, my lady," he said, grinning still, "and I wish you joy of our humble home."

In a twinkling Pat was back on the driver's seat of the trap and moving off to the stables. Lily found herself alone at the back door of paradise.

The first words she heard were very loud and in French. There was a clanging and banging from within, as if someone had thrown down a large metal pot.

"Non, non, non, non! C'est impossible! I-m-p-o-s-s-i-b-l-e!"

A familiar voice responded to this outburst, but the tone of Mrs. Groome's speaking was far different from what Lily remembered. Now she was soothing, cajoling.

"Ah, but Louise, my dear, if anyone can do it, it must be you. Thirty to dinner is a lot, I agree, but surely—"

"With not so much as one day's notice! She is a madwoman. Mad! And in summer, and with everything to be spoiled."

"It is something of an emergency, isn't it? Of course . . ." And Lily heard the voice of Mrs. Groome take on a new and perhaps slightly threatening tone: "Of course, we can always ask Delmonico's to cater for us, if you truly think it is too much for you, Louise."

"Delmonico's? *Mais non*! To stoop to such degradations? For Louise Dulac nothing is impossible. However mad. It will be done. *C'est ça. Sole duglère, salade de homard, poitrine de veau avec champignons, sorbet des fraises de bois, les fromages, mousse au chocolat.*"

"That sounds lovely, dear. I knew you could do it."

"But she is crazeee. Mad."

"Just impulsive, Louise, and so hospitable."

"And so mad!"

There was another crash, then silence. Lily decided it was safe to knock.

The door opened to reveal Mrs. Groome, slightly redfaced, wiping her forehead with a dish towel. "Oh, goodness! It's Lily. Come right in, girl."

She smiled, and Lily smiled too, half-faint with relief that it was possible for the formidable housekeeper to do such a thing. Mrs. Groome touched Lily lightly on the shoulder and guided her into the huge kitchen.

"Louise, this is our new tweeny. Lily Malone, meet Mrs. Louise Dulac."

Lily had never seen such a room, nor such a woman as Louise.

The kitchen was fifty feet long by thirty feet wide, and completely covered in shiny white tiles: floors and walls gleamed with them, and only the high ceiling was untiled. Against one long wall were three immense wood-burning stoves all in a row, black and shining and holding an arsenal of huge copper pots and pans and skillets. Against another wall were the sinks, two gigantic ones, with drying racks and faucets for—wonder of wonders—both hot and cold running water. There were ice chests, and these were perhaps the biggest wonderment of all: Lily had never heard of indoor ice, and in summer, and in a private house at that. But even more imposing than her domain was Louise herself. Tall, taller than most men, thin, and broad of shoulder, Louise had a long, angular face that could hardly be called beautiful. Yet it was a strong face, and her eyes were kind, and when

Louise Dulac smiled, her whole face smiled too. Lily liked her at once, formidable or not.

"How do you do," asked Lily softly.

"Ha! Right now perhaps not so well, but we do not worry, yes? Welcome, Lily. A pretty name, and a pretty child."

Lily blushed. Compliments were not the style of St. Patrick's orphanage.

"Thank you, ma'am."

Mrs. Groome had left the kitchen, and now returned with a girl only slightly older than Lily, but much bigger.

"Lily, this is Tess Reilley, our parlormaid. Tess will help you with your trunk, and show you to your room—which you will share with our Susie. Wherever she is."

Tess answered, a bit sharply Lily thought: "On another errand for Miss Marianne, more likely than not. Leavin' her betters to do her own chores, or so she thinks."

"Well, Tess," said Mrs. Groome evenly, "let's talk about that later. Why don't you help Lily with her trunk, and get her settled in, and then, Lily, if you'll come down to me, I will introduce you to Madame and show you the house."

Lily and Tess took opposite ends of the wicker trunk and headed for the stairs.

There were so many new things for Lily to see in the Wallingford house that at first she thought she might go blind from the dazzle of it all. Even the back staircase was a revelation: all dark walnut and turned balusters and fine little carpets on the landings. There seemed to be a hundred of these as Tess and Lily climbed bumping up the four flights to the servants' garret.

"Just wait," said Tess, puffing, "till you see the grand staircase, all white stone it is, just like the outside walls, and with a fine iron railing that has a genuine gold-plated handrail on top, so's it never needs polishing like all the damned brass does."

Tess Reilley, like Mrs. Groome and Louise, was wearing an everyday dress with a white apron over it. Lily had expected uniforms, in fact looked forward to them, for she was unsure of the dresses she and Fran had stitched together in St. Paddy's.

Finally they reached the top. There was a long hallway that ran all the way down the length of the mansion under the mansard roof, punctured at twenty-foot intervals by small round windows. A dozen doors opened off this hallway, and Lily learned that these were storerooms for linen and old furniture, and the sleeping quarters for all the female servants.

Mr. and Mrs. Groome, as befitted their lofty stature in the servant hierarchy, had their own rooms on the ground floor and, Tess said, hardly ever ventured all the way to the garret. But Louise lived here, and Tess, in a room of her own, and here Lily would share a room with Susie McGlynn, the upstairs maid.

"Well," said Tess flatly, "here it be." She opened the door of a small room halfway down the hall. It might have been fifteen feet wide and a bit longer than its width, but to Lily it seemed like heaven itself after the big crowded dormitory at St. Paddy's. There was one small round window at the back, two cots at opposite sides of the room, under the window a small night table and twin pinewood chests of drawers flanking the cots. On the night table stood an oil lamp. Clean sheets and blankets were neatly folded at the foot of one bed, and Lily assumed that this would be hers.

They set the wicker trunk at the foot of the unmade cot. Brass hooks had been screwed into the wooden wall for hanging clothes. Lily decided she could unpack later. She turned to find Tess staring at her, hands on hips, appraising.

"So it was St. Paddy's they had you in, was it?"

"Nearly five years."

"And tell me, then, is it true they tie you to the beds there and make you fornicate with the priests, and worse?"

Lily looked at Tess, stunned. She had heard coarse language, and plenty of it, as who could not, being about Fergy? And well she knew the stories people told about the nuns and priests, and hadn't she heard the same about the Protestants? But the naked venom in Tess's voice and the hateful look in her eyes were truly frightening. Lily didn't know whether to laugh, or scream, or to strike out at her tormentor. Then it came to her: *She's Dolan, on the first day I came to St. Paddy's.* And Lily's feeling of outrage changed to a kind of pity mixed with not a little scorn.

"No, Tess, that is nothing like the truth."

"Yes, and that's another thing we hear," said Tess, rolling her small eyes toward heaven. "We hear that they also teach you lying from the cradle, and thievin' too, isn't that so, slut?"

Lily could think of only one thing in that moment, and the thought of poor Bertha Dolan was all that saved her from running down those dark stairs and out of the Wallingford house forever. For Tess Reilley, Lily saw at once, was Dreadful Dolan all over again, only possibly worse, more sad, more lost. There was a burning instant when Christian patience and charity warred in Lily's brain with the quick impulse to smash the oil lamp over Tess's thick skull, but Lily's experiences with Dolan had long ago taught her that this was probably exactly what her tormentor would like most. So, instead, Lily smiled.

"The angels will be weeping for ye, Tess," was all she said. "And right now I think Mrs. Groome wants to see me."

Lily turned and walked out of her new room and down the hall. As she had mentioned the angels weeping, something had changed in Tess Reilley's hate-filled eyes. Tess, then, was Catholic. Tess knew about how the angel bands wept for sinners. There might be hope for Tess, then. But Lily was very glad that Tess would not be sharing the room with her.

The dark stairs seemed to go on forever. If they were this dark in the middle of a bright afternoon, Lily could only guess how dark they might be at night. She had passed the third-floor landing when the singing reached her ears.

It was a deep voice, a man's voice, and a pleasant one. And he was singing the popular song by Stephen Foster: "Wa-a-a-y down upon the Swan-e-e-e-e River . . ." Lily didn't really know the music, although the song had caught on so, you could hear snatches of it sung in the streets any day, and it had even crept into the cloistered enclaves of St. Patrick's. The voice went on, a little slurred, but pleasant anyway, growing louder as Lily made her way down past the second-floor landing: ". . . that's where my heart is ye-e-e-e-a-a-rning e-e-e-ver . . ."

She turned the corner of the middle landing between the first floor and the kitchen level, and nearly stepped on him.

An enormously fat man sat on the top step, leaning back, resting on both elbows, a bottle of whiskey in one hand, singing plaintively. He was neatly dressed, obviously a man of some position in life, although not, Lily thought, a true gentleman. He was wearing very clean tan corduroy breeches, boots that might have been made for riding, a white shirt open at the neck, and a dark green linen jacket.

". . . that's where the o-o-ld folks stay."

"Excuse me, sir, if you please," said Lily, thinking that this was most definitely not the orphanage of the Sisters of Charity of St. Patrick's Cathedral parish, nor anything like it.

"Wha? What have we here?" He turned, beaming cheerfully, not focusing. Then, casually, as if by a reflexive action rather than any malevolent intention, the fat man reached out and caught Lily by the ankle and held her tight. She very nearly fell headlong down the stairs, but luckily there was a railing, which she grabbed as if for dear life. And she wondered whether it was time to start screaming for help.

"Why, why, it's a fine little minnow, a very little goldfish minnow, all golden hair, red-gold, if ye take my meaning. So, pray tell me, pretty Miss Minnow, what might be your name?"

Lily froze, unable to speak or to move, sure that she would be raped on the spot and murdered soon after, and who was there to hear her if she screamed, or care for her fate? But she was spared whatever fate might have been about to engulf her by the blessed sound of a now familiar voice.

Verity Groome was on the warpath. "I see, Lily," she said, in tones that would put fear into the heart of a rampaging elephant, "that you've had the pleasure of making Mr. Groome's acquaintance already. Mr. Groome, you are plainly obstructing traffic in your present recumbent posture. It would be vastly more suitable, *not to say prudent,* should you remove yourself to your chambers. You will oblige me by doing that forthwith, Mr. Groome."

Lily looked from one Groome to the other, and thought about what Pat had told her on the ride from St. Paddy's. Groome smiled like any illustration of Father Christmas, corked the half-empty bottle, and rose with surprising agility to his feet.

"Of course, of course, my treasure," he murmured, smiling in several directions as if at an unseen audience, "as 'twas ever the case, you are absolutely correct." Then, nodding to Lily with all the noblesse of a hereditary monarch forced into temporary exile, he tiptoed down the stairs and vanished into the gloom.

Mrs. Groome wasted no time on explaining the obvious. "Come, my dear," she said briskly, "for Mrs. Wallingford is waiting." And she led Lily back up the stairs to the first-floor landing.

There had been a certain amount of gilding and glitter inside of old St. Patrick's Cathedral, and statuary richly carved, and fine woven altarcloths, and sometimes the bishop wore his best surplice, which was splendid indeed, with its threads of gold—real gold, said Sister Mary Agnes, who had reason to know, for it was she who took care of the precious thing—and there were other, smaller splendors to be glimpsed. But nothing in Lily's experience prepared her for the sights and smells that awaited her on the other side of the servants' door to the family quarters in the Wallingford mansion.

Mrs. Groome led Lily up the stairs to the first-floor landing, then on past it to the second floor. She explained the house as she went, although it would be months before Lily completely understood the huge place. The ground floor, it seemed, was all reception rooms, four of them, each more splendid than the last, and the kitchen. The second floor contained the dining room, the library, the ballroom, the billiards room, and the suite of Mr. and Mrs. W. The Wallingford children, Jack Junior and Miss Marianne, had suites of their own, which, along with the guestrooms, filled the whole of the third floor.

By the time the housekeeper had finished this lecture, they had walked down a small, dark-paneled hallway and were faced with a large but in no way unusual door. Mrs. Groome opened it casually.

Lily gasped.

They stood upon an acre of colored marble inlaid in an intricate pattern that seemed to want to be stars and snowflakes all at the same time. They were in a huge hall that led off the main staircase. Lily could see the gold-topped railing glinting far away. The hall was long as a church and nearly that empty, polished like mirror glass, and guarded, or so it seemed, by huge porcelain jars—Chinese and priceless, she later learned—and in the jars, huge palm trees. Lily had never seen such marble, such jars, such trees, or so much space, and all of it unused. She stared at one of the jars in fascination. It frightened her, for clearly depicted on its side was an extremely formidable dragon in bright blue, with a yellow underbelly and enormously long sharp claws, and breathing fire. And no St. George to slay it. The ceiling was so far overhead that it was lost in deep shadows, although Lily caught a glint of gold up there, and colors. Then Mrs. Groome tugged at her arm, and they were off down the hall.

They'll never accept me, Lily thought. *I'll never belong here, this is for kings and princesses, maybe for God Himself.* And for the second time in this dizzying afternoon Lily thought of something Pat had told her: *"Oh, they spend it,"* he'd said, *"they spend it, do the Wallingfords."*

Their shoes clicked like horses' hooves on the cold marble. *If they don't have carpets,* Lily told herself, *it isn't because they can't afford 'em.*

At the end of eternity was a door. The door was huge, a double door, with double handles that curved like snakes and looked like gold, and old gold at that. Mrs. Groome knocked briskly. Lily was learning that almost everything Mrs.

Groome did, she did briskly. A faint voice bade them enter. Lily thought that a lion's roar would probably sound faint through doors like that.

Mrs. Groome opened one of the double doors and ushered Lily in ahead of her. There was a small chamber, empty, completely lined in pale green silk. Flowered ribands were embroidered into the silk, all ivory and roses and blue cornflowers, and all done by hand, and by genius artisans who probably went blind doing it, Lily reckoned, staring at the delicate work in complete awe.

There was more to be awed about. All of the furniture in the green-walled antechamber was old, and ivory-painted, and just touched here and there with gilt. The carpet was woven too, and with greens and blues and roses almost identical to the patterns in the fabric that covered the walls. "French," Mrs. Groome whispered, "said to belong to Madame de Pompadour herself!" Lily didn't know who Madame de Pompadour was, but her taste in antechambers struck the girl as dazzling.

They came to another door, framed in antique ivory-painted wood, and this door stood open. The room beyond it was all done in pale shades of apricot, set off with ivory and a deep rust-colored carpet. There were many tall windows in the bedroom, all hung with apricot-colored silks. The bed was very large and covered in an ivory-and-apricot material that looked like—and was, on Lily's closer examination—old lace re-embroidered with apricot ribbons. One ivory-paneled wall was all closets, and several of these stood open, revealing literally hundreds of gowns in more colors than Lily Malone had ever thought existed. At an ivory dressing table a lady sat, wearing a loose apricot-colored silk wrapper. She held up a rope of diamonds to the afternoon sunlight. Lily stood transfixed. Each of the diamonds was fully as fat as a grape, and there must have been a hundred of them. They caught the sunlight and threw rainbows into every corner of the enormous room. It was as though a star had exploded, silently, without hurting anyone. Mrs. Wallingford sighed, and sent the rope of diamonds clattering down to the table-top.

"Not very summery, are they, Groome?"

"What would you be wearing them with, ma'am?"

"The blue *peau de soie*, I believe, and my new blue Turkey shawl, you know, the one with the gold paillettes all over it."

"The pearls might be refreshing, ma'am."

"But everyone wears pearls."

"The sapphires?"

"Of course! I'd completely forgotten about the sapphires."

There was a large jewel case on the dressing table. Mrs. Wallingford leaped to her feet, inspired now, and ran to the closet, from whose topmost shelf she hauled down another, larger jewel case. She brought this to the dressing table, opened it, rattled through the invisible collection that seemed to fill the chest, and at last, with a small expression of glee, hauled up a sapphire-and-diamond dog collar with all the satisfaction of a fisherman who has just hooked a record-breaking trout.

"What," Mrs. Wallingford asked her reflection in the dressing table's mirror as she held the ten rows of shimmering blue stones, offset with even-more-shimmering diamonds, to her throat, "would I ever do without you, Groome?"

Lily fought to keep from smiling. Her new mistress looked almost precisely like Fat Bessie Sullivan, and all the diamonds in the world could not change that. But, unlike Fat Bessie, who was a bully and a sneak, Mrs. Wallingford had a kind face, a happy smile, and nice eyes. At last she put down the sapphires and turned to Mrs. Groome.

"I'd forgotten!" She stood up then, and Lily forgot about Fat Bessie, for only the plumpness and the shape of this lady's face were similar. "You," she said, coming very close and taking Lily's small chin in one plump hand, "must be the new girl from St. Patrick's. And I have forgotten your name."

"Lily, ma'am. Lily Malone."

"Lily. Lily. That's very nice. And, you are an orphan, Lily?"

"Yes, ma'am."

"Well, Lily, I hope you will consider this your home, and that you will be happy here. How old are you, Lily?"

"Fifteen, ma'am."

"How lovely! Well, then, Lily, I'm sure Mrs. Groome, upon whom we rely for everything, will have many things to show you. Obey everything Mrs. Groome says, and all will go well for you, Lily."

"Yes, ma'am. Thank you, ma'am."

Inwardly, Lily all but collapsed with relief: *She's human, she doesn't wear horns, she knows how to smile, she was nice to Mrs. Groome!*

Mrs. Wallingford dismissed them with a vague smile, and Mrs. Groome guided Lily back through the green antechamber that had belonged to Madame de Pompadour, and down the shimmering marble hallway to the top of the grand staircase. All Lily could see was a dark-paneled wall, although she knew perfectly well that they had walked through that wall not half an hour before. Mrs. Groome walked casually up to the paneling and pressed a corner of it. On silent pivots the entire panel swung back, and once more they were in the sedate and somehow comforting gloom of the servants' quarters. It was only then that Mrs. Groome spoke.

"And what did you think of your mistress, Lily?"

Lily remembered the jewels glinting in sunlight, and something she could not name made her think of the day her mother died in the hovel on Mulberry Street, dead these nearly five years now, and gone in poverty, with only Lily left to remember her. And Lily wondered if it was possible to be rich and be good, both at the same time.

"I think," she said quietly, "that she has a nice face."

This was greeted with silence, and Lily then wondered if somehow she had said the wrong thing, if, perhaps, she wasn't supposed to like Mrs. Wallingford and her diamonds.

"Well, Lily, remember this when you have some hard chore set to you, child: it wasn't all that long ago that Mrs. W. herself was clerking behind a counter, and not a very grand counter at that, in the first store that Mr. John set up, back in 1828."

"Did she, truly?"

"That she did, child, much as she'd like the world to forget it today. But—as you guessed—she is not unkind."

"I'm glad of that," said Lily as they came down the stairs to the kitchen once again.

The Wallingford kitchen, for all its great size and gleaming equipment, had the look and sound of a gigantic battlefield just before the attack. Louise Dulac rose imperial and brave among a sea of pots, a forest of vegetables, a decimated zoo of fowl and fish and veal and Lily knew not what else. The tall Frenchwoman shouted her commands to cowering helpers, darted here and there waving an immense wooden spoon like a sorcerer's wand, pointing, stirring, patting, pushing, ordering fires to be stoked here, banked there, wanting more ice, less dawdling, clear the marble to roll the pastry, is the silver freshly shined, have we claret enough for thirty, and which of four champagnes will be good enough for so impromptu a gathering here on a hot June night in New York, *alors!*

Mrs. Groome took all this in with a glance and motioned Lily aside. "This," she said, "is not the moment for you to begin learning the ways of the kitchen, Lily. Why don't you go up and unpack your things, and Susie will find you soon enough, when she gets back from wherever she's got to. Can you find your way, girl?"

"I think so."

Lily wasn't at all sure this was true. She had the impression you could get lost in this huge stone palace for weeks and months and no one would know where to find you. Resolutely she turned from the clamor of the kitchen and began climbing the hundreds of stairs to the garret.

It was dark and much more quiet on the stairs. There was no sign of the fat Mr. Groome, and for this Lily thanked the Lord. There was no sign of the malevolent Tess, either, and Lily was glad enough for that. It must be late in the afternoon, but there was no way for Lily to know the precise time. Usually a church bell tolled the hour, but there would be new bells to learn now, and new people to know, new rules and new standards.

Lily's head swam with new impressions, images of richness and confusion, of kindness and unexpected cruelty from Tess, of the exotic Louise and her strange, magical empire by the stoves, of Pat the stableboy with his dark good looks and mocking smile and irreverent commentary on the Wallingford ménage. And the mistress with her jewels, just years away from a clerk's job in a store! There was the wonder of this land! There was Fergy's Young America, and in spades. And fat Mr. Groome, what harm might he have done her, had Mrs. Groome not come upon them so quick and knowing?

She thought of the calm and strictly organized world of St. Patrick's, where everyone knew their place, from God in heaven right on down, where rules were rules and the penalties severe, and the road to hell was lined with girls who failed to take heed.

Lily wondered what Fran would make of all this, wondered if she herself would last the day.

Finally, after a climb that seemed like miles, she reached the garret level, recognized the hallway, found her door. The room was just as she'd left it. For some reason this surprised Lily. She remembered Dreadful Dolan all too well, and how Dolan had thrown her doll out the window that first day, and half-expected Tess Reilley to do the same, or something like it. But there was no Tess, no sound at all in the deeply shadowed room. Lily walked to the round window and looked out. Far below, much farther than her view from the orphanage window, lay the back courtyard, with its carriage house and stables, and beyond the stables the big formal garden laid out in designs such as Lily had never seen before except in carpets, great scrolls of hedge bordered with bright flowers, huge copper beech trees in double rows, not full grown yet but threatening to meet when they were, an immense letter W in living roses edged with incredibly precise rows of shorter, bright white flowers. It was dazzling, and for a moment Lily simply stood there taking it all in, her new world, the geography of her future. As she stood, Pat led a fine tall bay horse out of the stables and stood in the sunshine brushing the already gleaming animal to a luster that made her think of satin. Pat had taken his shirt off in the heat, and Lily thought, watching him work, that he was very like the horse itself, with the same offhand grace in his movements, the same lean and rippling muscles, the great dark half-sleepy, half-amused eyes. It occurred to her that she had never seen a grown boy with his shirt off before.

Lily couldn't have said how long she stayed in the window watching Pat curry the horse. A delivery van came rattling through the big gates, and case after case of wine was unloaded at the kitchen door. Pat kept on with his bay horse, oblivious. Even from this distance Lily could see that the boy had a rapport with the horse. The horse nuzzled Pat when it got the chance, and Pat would affectionately stroke the animal behind the ears from time to time. They both looked happy, and Lily was glad, in the confusion of her arrival in this strange and bewildering household, to see any sign of happiness. So she stood there watching, dreaming.

The voice, when it came, was startling. "Oh, he's a fine bit of a lad, is our Pat, have no doubt of that, my girl! Likes 'em young, and likes 'em often, does Pat, and any time you're feeling randy, he'll be happy to oblige, day or night, as he has for others." This announcement was delivered in a lighthearted manner, punctuated by ripples of laughter, in a tone that matched the merry face it came from.

Lily turned, gasping from surprise.

There at her elbow stood a taller girl, round in face and round in body, but nothing of fat on her, with dark blond hair and sparkling blue eyes and cheeks as pink as a sunset and a smile that lit up the room.

"I'm Susie, and you must be the new girl."

"Lily Malone is my name."

Susie put out her hand and Lily shook it.

"Welcome to our humble home. It's a madhouse, of course, but they're not all bad, not the master nor the mistress nor old lady Groome. You could have done worse, Lily."

Susie plopped herself down on her bed and regarded the newcomer. "Skinny little thing, you be. Too skinny for Pat. Now there's a boy-o who likes a bit of meat on his crumpets. How old are you, Lily-child?"

"Fifteen."

"Well, don't let it worry you. One thing's for sure in this rotten world, and that's that we're all getting older by the minute, isn't it the truth, though?"

"Sure, and it is."

"Orphan, be you? Alone in the world?"

"I am that."

"Ahh."

Susie sighed a sigh of regret and understanding. Lily had never met anyone like this bubbling, joking, mocking girl, but there was something about Susie that attracted her. Lily felt at once that Susie would never do anything unkind, and that she could be trusted.

"I haven't unpacked yet."

"Let me help you, then, Lily. The work is lighter, says old lady Groome, and right she is, when the hands are many."

They bent to the wicker trunk and soon Lily's small store of worldly possessions was neatly folded into the drawers of the pine chest or hung from the brass hooks.

Through the unpacking, Susie chattered away, carefree and mischievous, describing the ways of the Wallingfords, which seemed to be diverse and eccentric.

"Miss Marianne's the one, now, the very belle of New York is that one, and the young men's carriages lining up around the block on at-home afternoons, and Miss M. herself playing fast and loose with all of 'em because . . . her heart is set on another."

"No!" The ghost of Sister Claudia was never far from Lily's consciousness.

"Indeed. I have it from the young lady's own lips. In darkest confidence, you may well imagine."

"Of course. Who is he?"

"Her parents would die dead on the spot if they knew."

"He's a pirate? A foreigner? A Jew?"

"Worse even than that." Susie paused for a long pregnant moment and rolled her eyes toward heaven.

"What, then? Do tell me."

"He is . . . an E-p-i-s-c-o-p-a-l-i-a-n!" Susie spelled it out as though there might be young children about whose ears should not be sullied by the dread Protestant sect's name.

"No!"

"Upon my honor. She'd be turned out into the street for it, her parents being nothing if not holy."

"Oh, dear."

"Her heart is breaking by the hour."

"What's he like?"

"Handsome and rich, naturally. I've never seen him. They meet in secret."

"I wonder if . . ."

Lily never finished what she had started to say. Susie raised a finger to her lips and pointed dramatically to the door. As if on cue, someone knocked.

"Come in."

The door opened to reveal Tess, sullen and angry, hands on hips, glowering like all the thunderstorms of summer.

"And what might ye two good-for-nothing sluts be gibbering about while your betters are workin' their fingers to the bone? Come on with ye, now. Mrs. Groome needs help, and fast."

Neither girl spoke, but they both stood up at once and followed the upstairs maid.

⋖ঽ 10 ঽ⋗

Lily woke in the night shivering, and thought at first she must have fever. But then she realized that the little garret bedroom was truly cold. *Well, sure and it's cold, goose, for isn't it October already, going on to four months you've been here, and the days going by so fast, and so much happening, and so much to learn a body can hardly tell day from night, let alone the seasons!*

Lily had come into the Wallingford mansion expecting to learn a new way of life. What she learned was survival. At the first, it was no more than a question of getting through the long days without breaking something, or incurring the terrible wrath of Louise or Mrs. Groome, and avoiding Tess if that were possible. Every morning Lily felt as though she was off to the wars, doing fresh battle with the turbulent currents of physical and emotional activity that flowed and churned through the great limestone palace of old John Wallingford.

The family's plans varied from season to season and often from hour to hour. There were great comings and goings, visits to be paid and received, extra guests without warning, and unexplained absences, crises of needlework like the time Lily was dragged out of her narrow bed to slice the beautiful Miss Marianne Wallingford out of a ballgown she had been sewn into eight hours before, the better to set off her well-known wasp waistline. Lily felt a small twinge of pity for the haughty girl, for she could hardly breathe in all her finery.

There were two great balls, and when they happened all the maids were summoned to wait upon the grand ladies in Mrs. W.'s suite, to be ready with the sewing kit for small repairs, with cologne and smelling salts at hand, and sympathy, not to mention tea and cakes and lemonade and Madeira.

Each day had its own surprises, its own challenges, and its own traps. There was the ever-fascinating question of whether Mr. Groome would show up drunk or sober, and what to do in either case, for Groome sober was altogether different from Groome drunk, and only Mrs. Groome could handle him in either case. There was Pat, the stable charmer, lothario of the hayloft, who represented to Lily a nameless dark temptation, for his smile spoke of secret pleasures and his arrogant eyes were an invitation to bottomless pits of sin. Into those pits, Lily soon learned, her roommate Susie had cheerfully tumbled, and continued to tumble with neither fear nor regret. But Susie was seventeen and a woman of vast experience in many things besides sex, or so it seemed to Lily's very sheltered eyes and ears.

Susie took a certain glee in trying to shock Lily, and her descriptions of how she and Patrick spent their stolen hours in the haylofts indeed made Lily's ears tingle and her soul quiver for fear of Susie's sure damnation. Yet it was a friendly teasing, and Susie was nothing if not generous and warm-hearted and a good companion for Lily's first hard weeks in the house. Still, the stables and Pat himself became infused with a sense of mystery and seduction, a place and a boy to be avoided if possible. For while Lily knew perfectly well how grown-up men and women disported themselves for pleasure, the pleasure they got eluded her, and the sure damnation loomed dark and terrifying, and why Susie took such vast risks for so trifling an amusement was a thing that Lily could simply not understand, however sleek Pat's body might be, however charming his smiles.

Lily and her new friend were exhausted, more often than not, after a working day that might last sixteen hours, up before dawn and working, working, working until after the last silver tray from the Wallingfords' supper had been cleaned and polished and put away in its specially built green-felt-lined rack.

The busier they were, the easier it was to avoid Tess Reilley.

Tess, Lily soon discovered, was a far worse case than poor old Dreadful Dolan at St. Paddy's. Tess seemed to hate everyone and everything with a deep, bitter, burning hatred. She kowtowed to Mrs. Groome, and for all her nastiness Tess was a hard worker, firmly entrenched in the backstairs hierarchy. But never a cheerful word came from her lips, nor a smile. And it seemed that the more Susie and Lily avoided her, the worse she got. They endured Tess in silence, for that seemed to be the only way.

In the confusion, disorder, and wonderment of her first months on the job, Lily found that Susie shone out like a sunbeam.

Shallow she might be, and easily seduced by the likes of Patrick, but Lily found that Susie's good qualities outweighed the bad. Susie was fun, bouncy, an incurable optimist for whom tomorrow was always going to be another day, no matter how badly today might have gone. Susie could make Lily smile ten minutes after Tess Reilley had her on the brink of tears. When Lily was in one of her fits of self-doubt and depression, when she was lost in sad thoughts of Fergy, Susie could bring her out of it, laughing, quick as that.

Susie McGlynn was good fun and good medicine for Lily, and Lily swore that she would not be Susie's judge insofar as her romance with Pat was concerned.

After six weeks' trial, Mrs. Groome took Lily aside and told her she could have Thursday afternoons and evenings off. All week long Lily looked forward to the great day with a heady mixture of anticipation and dread. She had never, since entering St. Paddy's, been out on her own before.

On went her best dress, the one she and Fran had made from sprigged gingham. Lily regarded herself in the little mirror, frowned, put on the little cap. *Fran would be proud of me!* Then she remembered that in all this time she hadn't written to Fran, much less visited St. Paddy's. Well, sure and she would. Someday soon. But not just yet, not today. Today was too special. Today must be kept all by itself, like the flowers Miss Marianne was always pressing into books. Down the back stairs she went, and out the kitchen door, across the big courtyard, casting a sidelong glance at the stables, which looked empty, and out the big wrought-iron gates. *And nobody stopped her!*

Lily turned left at the gates and walked down Sixteenth Street to the corner of Fifth Avenue, and there she stood in the clear light of the bright autumn afternoon feeling for all the world like an escaped prisoner, hardly able to understand her good luck. The broad avenue stretched uptown and downtown into infinity, beckoning. Smart carriages came clip-clopping past, bearing cargoes of elegant humanity on glamorous secret errands. Lily felt the autumn sun pressing on her back like a warm, friendly hand. *I can walk up that street to the ends of the earth,* she thought, *and no one can stop me, nor make me come back, ever, if I don't want to.* The possibilities were dazzling, and so were the perils.

Lily stood there transfixed, a thin, indecisive statue of a girl rooted to the pavement by the enormity of this realization. *Tess Reilley will never scold me again, and I'll never have to carry the damned chamber pots down four flights of dark stairs again, or hear Louise screaming again.* Emboldened, Lily crossed the avenue. Then she turned and looked back at the Wallingford mansion, as if to say goodbye forever.

The huge white pile stood uncaring in the hot light of noon, this great cold white palace guarding its riches and its secrets, kindnesses and cruelties. *If I died right now the house wouldn't care, nor anyone in it.* But even as the gloomy thought crossed her mind, Lily knew it was false, for surely Susie would care, for all her butterfly's attention span. Even Mrs. Groome might care, a little. Pat in his wickedness was at least friendly: he'd care a bit. *Well, then maybe I won't run away just now. I'll save my money and run away with Fran. Or even with Susie.*

Mrs. Groome was their unofficial banker, and she held Lily's small wages in her old blue tin box, safely locked. Lily had asked for twenty-five cents for her holiday, but she knew she'd never come close to spending it. Still it was a luxuriance of money, vast wealth, and all hers, earned by her own sweat, hers to save or squander: thrilling! She felt the burning power of it as though the coin had been heated to glowing. It radiated power and temptation right through the thin cotton twill of her reticule.

The first money in all the world that she'd earned by herself, and a free afternoon in New York to spend it in!

The bazaars of all Araby could be no more tempting.

Lily looked left again, and again to the right, and couldn't make up her mind. For a moment she wished for Susie, or Fran, or even Father Gregory. But this was her special time, and to savor it alone would make it more special still.

She might even go to the Wallingford Emporium! Down on Broadway it was, five stories tall and a whole block long and filled with more things than even Susie's vivid imagination could readily accommodate. Real Persian shawls embroidered with gold, and costing thousands! And cheap things too, bright ribbons and little fans, some things that cost no more than a penny, and it must be true, for didn't Susie have such ribbons, such fans?

Still Lily stood on the corner, and now her indecision began to weigh on her like some guilty secret. She had never tasted ice cream: she could visit Taylor & Thompson's, the finest ice-cream palace, imagine it, where the tables were white marble and there were palms and an orchestra and gilded chairs. She could do any of these things, Lily knew, and no one would dare stop her. If only she weren't so afraid.

Maybe next time Susie would come. Or she'd get Pat to drive her back to St. Paddy's—was Pat allowed to do such favors for the help?—and she could see Fran again, and Sister Cathleen. If they'd want to see her. Lily was still on the corner, drowning in indecision, when Tess Reilley came scurrying around the corner and turned down Fifth Avenue toward Fifteenth Street.

Maybe it was something rushed and furtive in the way Tess moved, or it might have simply been boredom and indecision and a desire not to be alone on her first afternoon outside the house. But for whatever reason, Lily found her footsteps following Tess. She kept her distance and kept to the other side of the avenue. Tess was moving fast, and looking neither right nor left. Down Fifth Avenue she went, past Fifteenth, and right across the wider, busier expanse of Fourteenth Street. On Thirteenth Street Tess turned right. Lily followed, farther behind now, for Tess seemed to move ever faster, bending forward as if walking into a wind. But there was no wind, and Lily wondered why in all the world, and on this bright beautiful day, the older girl could be in such a hurry. Maybe Tess had a lover! That would be a good secret to share with Susie, who shared all of her own secrets with Lily, generous in this to the point where Lily had long since decided that if she, Lily, ever had a real, really-truly secret, then she'd never tell it to her friend, for secrets told to Susie were only one step less public than a thing advertised in the *New York Times*. Still, Tess pushed on, Lily trailing.

In a month of hard work in the Wallingford house, often side by side with the unlovely Tess Reilley, Lily had never seen the older girl move so fast or with such purpose. Tess was a good worker, that was for sure, but never quick the way Louise could be quick, or Lily herself for that matter. Briskly as ever, Tess turned the corner of Sixth Avenue and proceeded downtown. And for the first time Lily began to question the wisdom of trailing her. What fun was it, anyway? Tess was probably late for an appointment with some friend, some other servant girl, and if she was a friend to Tess, God help her, the unknown friend was probably every bit as unpleasant. Lily decided that the block she was on right then would mark the end of her detective work. She hadn't paid much attention to the three gilded balls of the pawnbroker's sign until Tess Reilley turned into the doorway underneath them.

Lily paused in shadow across the street, and watched the small window of the shop, fascinated. It was painted in gold letters edged with black: "A. LEVY & SONS, LOANS, APPRAISALS, GOLD, SILVER."

And what did a girl like Tess have that might be worth the pawning?

Pawnbrokers had been part of the daily life of the Malones and everyone they'd known back on Mulberry Street, feared but respected, a necessary evil attendant on the poverty that stalked their every step. Lily could remember her mother pawning Big Fergus' clothes after he'd died, pawning their own few winter clothes that last desperate summer without the ghost of an idea how she'd ever redeem them before winter got to the Malones. Death had solved that problem for Lily's mother, and the nuns of St. Paddy's had kept Lily and Fergus warm and fed. But for the others, less lucky, if you could call it luck, there were the pawnbrokers.

All Lily could see from her hiding place across the street was shapes moving vaguely behind the glass of A. Levy's window. She decided that Tess would probably murder her right on the spot if the older girl found out that she had been spied upon, and so Lily turned and walked up Sixth Avenue and tried to forget the whole thing. After all, it was none of her business, and going to the pawnbroker's wasn't much of a secret anyway, nothing like having a lover or doing a murder or running away to sea. Lily decided to say nothing about her adventure, and to take Susie with her next Thursday. Susie could make scrubbing floors entertaining, so just imagine what she might do with a whole free afternoon loose on the city, and fifteen cents on top of that!

Lily walked up Sixth Avenue all the way to Twenty-third Street, then turned east and crossed Fifth Avenue to Madison Square, circled the square, then walked back down Fifth to the Wallingford house. The fun had gone out of her afternoon off. Lily looked big-eyed into store windows but lacked the courage to go in. She passed the noisy oyster houses and dodged the drunken men who came reeling out of the ale shops even this early in the day. She gazed with no special interest at the cameos and lockets in a jeweler's shop and thought how even one of Mrs. Wallingford's diamonds would likely buy the whole shop and the jeweler too. Lily saw bands of roving street boys who looked thin and ferret-faced and ran in packs like the very rats they resembled. The street boys frightened Lily and sent a shiver down her back, for they made her think of Fergy and what might have become of him, and that maybe death was better than this, and the sight of these rambling little beggars also reminded Lily of her own good luck, for long as her day might be, hard as the work surely was, still she had a clean warm bed to call her own and decent food to eat.

When she reached the Wallingford mansion, Lily sighed with relief. The huge stone wedding cake lay in shadow now, and the clear fall afternoon had the hint of a chill on it. Lily shivered, half from the chill and half from relief, and thought of the winter coat she and Fran had cut from an old orphanage blanket. She'd go see her old friend next week, and even if she couldn't persuade Patrick to drive her, it wasn't all that far a walk. Smiling with the warmth of her resolution, Lily slipped through the carriage gate and into the Wallingford kitchen.

It was a week before the antique gilt-silver knives were missed.

Lily and Susie and all of the servants, even Patrick and Williams, the coachman, were summoned by a grave-faced and very sober Mr. Groome into the servants' hall one Tuesday evening late in October. It was obvious that something was up, and something serious, but only the Groomes knew what, and they hadn't told anyone. When the entire staff was accounted for, Groome cleared his throat and spoke.

"There seems," said he, in tones that were heavy with impending doom, "to be a criminal in our midst."

Lily caught her breath. *A criminal indeed!* On wings of innocence, her eyes flashed about the room, from servant to servant. She knew some better than others, and Williams, for instance, Lily knew not at all, but still it seemed unlikely that any of them could be a criminal. Drunk, maybe, or, like Pat, lecherous, but were these things crimes?

There was a pause while Groome observed the effect of his words. The effect was considerable. It started with small whispered exclamations, and these grew to full-blown questions, speculations, hissing, and buzzing. Lily thought of the ropes of diamonds stuffed so carelessly into the top of Mrs. Wallingford's closet, wondered if they were always kept there, and who knew, and who had access to them. And Lily thought of Tess scurrying into the pawnshop, then dismissed the thought. Tess might be another version of old Dreadful Dolan, but that didn't make her a thief. Like everyone else, even before she knew what was missing, Lily searched the room as though the culprit might jump up and confess right then and there. That, she thought, repressing a smile, was probably just what Mr. Groome hoped for.

He continued, as if from a pulpit: "I think that it is fair to say we run a kindly establishment here, thanks to the goodness and generosity of the Wallingford family. We pay fair . . . and we play fair. Or, at the very least, ladies and gentlemen, we try to. Mrs. Groome sets a fine Christian example for all of us, and while some"—at this, Groome looked pointedly at Patrick, who was lounging in a corner, scarcely able to hide his boredom—"are more successful at heeding this fine example than others, we try. Yes, we try. And until this week, it is fair to say that Mrs. G. and I were well pleased with our little backstairs family, as it were. But now, now it seems we have been nurturing a viper to our bosom. Six valuable antique table knives of the finest silver gilt are missing. Six. Now, one, possibly, might be lost, thrown out by chance with the garbage. But six? No. Never. Six is deliberate. Six is theft, ladies and gentlemen, and theft, as we all know, is a crime, and crimes must be punished, and the punishment for such a crime is prison, nothing less, and disgrace. Prison and disgrace, ladies and gentlemen. Now, before I continue, let me ask you this, in all honor and fairness. Does any of you know what might have become of these knives? Or who might have taken them? It is always possible, although we doubt it, that this house has been forcibly and illegally entered and robbed. Why do we doubt it? Simply because any burglar would doubtless have taken more, and more valuable things. But, come, now. I hear only silence. Has no one a clue?"

The pause filled the room like smoke from a dangerous fire. Lily shifted on her hard wooden chair, looking from face to face to face, not wanting to confront the suspicions that were welling up in her. Patrick cleared his throat as if to speak, then said nothing. And still Groome waited, silent, eyeing them all, one by one and collectively.

Finally he spoke again. "If those knives were to be returned, I can promise that no legal action will be taken. Now—once again—does anyone in this room have an idea of where they might be? No? I am sorry, then, to say that one of you is lying. Lily Malone, stand up."

Lily stood, blushing, not knowing where to look. She looked at Groome, fascinated, half-paralyzed with fear, a dazed little mouse looking at a very large, very hungry cat. Groome reached into his deep trousers pocket. He pulled out a shining gilt-handled knife and held it aloft like the True Cross itself. Lily stared at it, helpless.

"Can you tell us, then, Lily, what this was doing in your own wicker trunk, found this afternoon?"

It was like being hit by a brick. Lily stammered, tried to speak, failed, tried again. "I . . . never saw it. Never."

She knew they all thought she was lying. Lily saw the jailhouse, the cold iron bars, disgrace, death. She looked at Susie. Susie was staring at the floor as though it represented her only hope of survival. Then Lily heard the whispered hiss from Tess: *"Thieving little slut, that's what she is."* The fear sat in Lily's gut with a cold and paralyzing weight. Yet as Tess spoke, something changed in Lily. She looked at Tess. Suddenly the fear in Lily turned to white-hot rage. She turned to Groome and met his accusing stare. Then she pointed at Tess Reilley, and spoke: "Can ye tell us, Tess, what it was you took to Mr. Levy's pawnshop last Thursday?"

The reaction was even quicker and more dramatic than Lily dreamed. Tess shot to her feet, screaming, clutching at her throat as though she'd just swallowed poison. She made little gasping sounds and her dull round eyes blinked faster and faster. Mr. Groome and his wife looked at Tess in wonderment, not knowing whether her performance amounted to a confession, an accusation, or if the girl was simply having a seizure.

"I . . . I . . . I . . ." But Tess could not form the words.

Lily found words of her own. "Mr. Groome, sir, I surely did not take the knife you have, nor any other. If it was in my trunk, someone put it there. I don't know, to be sure, what it was that Tess brought to the pawnbroker, but by chance I did see her go there, Thursday it was, my first day off, you see. The Levy pawnshop on Sixth Avenue it was, down by Twelfth Street."

"I know the shop. In fact, I know Levy." Mrs. Groome, as was her habit, quickly took charge. Her husband was still staring at Tess as though the girl had just arrived from another planet.

Mrs. Groome continued: "'Tis late, Mr. Groome, but it is Levy's habit to keep late hours. Chances be fair he'll still be in the shop. Go, then, sir, and ask him what Tess brought. Surely, Tess, you can have no objection to that? If it's innocent ye are, there's nothing to fear. Or is there, girl?"

Tess had stopped sputtering and commenced, now, to wail. It was a high, thin, piteous sound that put Lily in mind of the mournful keening of the older women at her own mother's wake. The wailing went on and on, and it seemed to the Wallingford servants that it was going to go on for all eternity. Mr. Groome roused himself to action and left the room, clutching the valuable knife and shaking his huge round head at the inconsistencies of fate.

At last Louise spoke. "This foolishness, *mes amis*, does not mean one should not have some tea, *non*?" And she set about making a big and very welcome potful.

Tess finally stopped her wailing and settled into a kind of rhythmic snuffling. She was sitting down again, and her frazzled head rested on her arms, on the polished oak table from which they all ate their meals. Lily felt sorry for Tess, that this new sorrow should be piled on top of whatever other troubles she must have, to make her so miserable. For surely her behavior amounted to an open confession. To steal knives? What could such knives be worth, and what would a pawnbroker give for them? Lily looked at Tess calmly, knowing that her own innocence was proven. The girl kept her head down, kept on sniffling and snuffling, and the minutes dragged heavy as wetwash. Suddenly Lily felt very tired. She wanted nothing more in all the world than her own quiet pillow, and to close her eyes in darkness.

It was not to be.

Groome came storming into the servants' hall, more angry than Lily had ever seen him, too fat for an avenging angel but on fire with righteousness nonetheless. He paused in the doorway theatrically, savoring his newfound importance in the backstairs world. Then he pointed at the thin, pathetic, quivering back of Tess Reilley, even as Lily had done.

And he spoke with the voice of fate itself. "For shame, Tess Reilley," he boomed, "to so repay our kindness, and the kindness of the Wallingford family!"

The snuffling turned to wailing again, as if a switch had been thrown.

Lily looked at Tess and thought of all the many times Tess had tormented her, needlessly, just for whatever sick pleasure the older girl might get from bullying someone younger, weaker, someone who couldn't really fight back. *I wished—prayed—for bad things to happen to her, and now they have, and why aren't I feeling happy?* But all Lily felt was pity.

Groome spoke again. "You can go now. This is a matter for Mr. Wallingford himself, and for the police."

At the sound of the word "police," Tess screamed outright, then lapsed into silence.

Embarrassed, ashamed, and altogether disconcerted, the

servants began drifting from the room in silence, looking everywhere but at Tess.

Lily stood up and started for the door.

Mr. Groome reached out and touched her gently on the shoulder. For once, she felt kindness in his gesture, and didn't cringe from it. When he spoke to her, there was a new gentleness in his voice, too. "Lily," he said softly, "we are truly sorry. Try not to judge us harshly, child, for we had no way of knowing."

"Oh, sir. Please think no more of it: I understand."

"Then sleep well, Lily. And thank you."

Lily all but ran into the hallway and up the dark stairs. She felt as though she had gone through some terrible and deadly combat, and by a miracle won it. But there was no feeling of triumph or revenge satisfied. To Lily, Tess Reilley was a poor tormented soul, and her howling in the servants' hall was only a small portent of the future, which, Lily was stone-cold certain, the girl would spend howling for all eternity in hell.

They never saw Tess Reilley again. By the time Susie stopped chattering, by the time Lily's nerves calmed down enough to let her sleep, it was well past midnight. She heard the rustle and slam of hasty packing in the room next door, and the bump of a trunk being hauled none too gently down the stairs. The bells of St. Stephen's chimed one. Lily heard Susie's soft, even breathing, and looked up from her thin pillow at the window. The roundness of it stood out blue-gray against the pitch-black wall. Lily could see one small star. It looked cold, that little star, and lonely. One of the girls at St. Patrick's had a theory that all the stars in heaven were actually the souls of dead people who had been unhappy in life, now doomed to roam the cold night skies forever. Lily knew this was madness, but seeing the lone star made her wonder, and she imagined it might be Fergy's soul, wandering the skies forever in search of her, Lily, his long-lost sister. And that was madness, too, and she must sleep, but the more Lily thought on it, the more intriguing the idea became. Unhappy or not, how thrilling to be so brilliant and aloof, to cross the skies in silent majesty, to look down on all the oceans of the earth, on all its citizens, to be so totally removed from all of life's dilemmas! It was a waking dream that Lily had, lying in her garret room and waiting for sleep's late arrival. She closed her eyes, but not to sleep. Instead she imagined what the world must look like, seen from the window of a star. Suddenly Lily was high, high in the night sky, higher than any steeple, higher even than birds flew or the masts of tall ships. And the earth and all its creatures was a small, dark, soft, round thing, a plum that had lain too long in the fruitmonger's basket. The thought thrilled Lily even at the same time that it sent cold waves of terror quivering to her toes.

It was a long time before Lily Malone slept that night.

Lily was the only one of the Wallingford servants who could resist the subject of the late, unlamented Tess Reilley and her shameful depredations.

To Lily, Tess was a sad thing, a Bertha Dolan gone wrong, maybe beyond saving now. They learned the Wallingfords were reluctant to prosecute, having recovered all their knives from the pawnbroker on payment of the fifteen dollars he'd given Tess. Fifteen dollars! Yes, surely that was a small fortune, nearly a year's pay for Lily, but to ruin your life for such a sum? The knives, Groome implied, were worth vastly more than that, although how much more, precisely, remained one of several mysteries surrounding the case. Another mystery was what had become of Tess. There was endless speculation about this, but the Groomes said nothing, and no one else knew for sure.

To Susie McGlynn, Lily had become a heroine. "Ah, and 'twas a fine show you put on, Lil, sure and you turned on the bitch like a scrapper, and gave her what-for, and didn't she go all funny when you did it, and wasn't it grand, a truly grand sight to see?"

Lily found it less than grand, a deed she was hardly proud of. For no matter what the strictures of justice might be, Lily felt that she had done a thing that was somehow dishonorable, playing the informer on one of her own, however guilty Tess had been, however ready to push the blame off on others. *If ever,* thought Lily, *I take up a life of crime, 'twill be on a far grander scale than swiping six old knives!* But she greeted Susie's effusive chatter with silence, and before very long even Susie tired of the subject. It was easy to forget Tess Reilley, for they had done their best to ignore her even while she was in their midst.

October turned to November and the time seemed to slide through Lily's fingers like water, so quickly it went.

There was still no word from Fran. Five months now Lily had been at the Wallingford mansion. She had written once to Fran, sending her love to Sister Cathleen and promising to come and visit, a promise she truly meant to keep, but somehow the visit hadn't happened. Time passed too quickly, and

[123]

there always seemed to be some new and more exciting thing to do. Days off now were mostly spent with Susie. Something about that one fatal afternoon when she'd followed Tess made Lily afraid to go out by herself now. Susie, irrepressible, was afraid of nothing. She was filled with larks and laughter, and if she had no sense of consequences and fewer long-range plans, she was great fun to be with, a walking, skipping tonic, and Lily rejoiced in her company.

It wasn't the same as her friendship with Fran. With Fran Lily had shared dreams, had made plans that seemed possible, so real you could almost reach out and touch them. With Susie, princess of the quicksilver moment, there was no point in even trying to be serious. Yet she was a kind girl, and honest, and implacably jolly. Susie was only half an orphan. Her father was alive, if you could call it that, so far gone he was in drink. She spoke of him only rarely, and always with a mocking air, but Lily thought she could detect a permanent sorrow buried not far beneath Susie's ready laughter.

There were, Lily reminded herself, many things worse than death.

The pace of life in the mansion picked up with the burgeoning winter. It was the Season now in New York, and the Wallingfords were ready and well able to make the most of it. Lily had never seen, nor imagined, such comings and goings, trays so thick with calling cards you could barely see the silver, polished as it was in any case to a mirror shine by Groome himself with white gloves and jeweler's paste. There were teas and oyster suppers and special parties for the men.

Lily had been in the house six weeks before she got so much as a glimpse of Mr. John Frederick Wallingford himself, he of the Wallingford Emporium, with all its cornucopia of the world's dry goods, source of Mrs. John's rope of diamonds and of this mansion and everything in it.

He looked exactly like an old turkey. A scrawny neck protruded from the starched white collar that never quite seemed to fit him, a long, ropy, wattled neck that was colored in a strange and apoplectic shade of red. On top of this unflattering column Mr. John's head rode sharp-nosed and chinless, brows beetling over small gold spectacles, unruly tufts of white hair sprouting in every direction from around his ears, seemingly untamable. A thin, stooped man he was, with the look of having spent far too long hunched up over his ledgers, which, if rumor could be credited, was precisely what the man did. There was none of Mrs. John's softness or good humor about him. He looked capable of biting—quick and sharp and humorless, a turkey, beyond doubt, or maybe even a turkey vulture. The man spoke not a word to Lily as he passed her on the stairs, but he terrified her nonetheless for that.

During Lily's first months with the Wallingfords she saw the family almost not at all. Mrs. Wallingford remained vague and wraithlike among her silks and jewels and the ever-increasing demands of the New York social season. Miss Marianne was, if anything, even busier than her mother, forever coming and going and entirely absorbed in the exhausting business of being young and very fashionable. There was a son, Lily knew, John Junior, called Jack, famous for the hell he raised even at seventeen, now traveling in Europe with a tutor before entering Yale.

The Wallingford family had little reality for Lily. They moved like gods in their world of wealth and gaiety, while Lily's days were spent with chamber pots and dust mops and, increasingly, with her needle. She heard no more of Miss Marianne's secret romance, and saw the famous rope of diamonds only at a distance. Sometimes at evening parties Susie and Lily would be summoned to wait upon the ladies in Mrs. Wallingford's suite, and then they'd hear tantalizing fragments of gossip, slices of mood and merriment, bits of schemes, the small cruelties and aspirations of the newly rich women of the city. These gilded, powdered, scented, whalebone-waisted, jewel-decked, and altogether glorious creatures treated the maids as so much furniture. They would say anything and do anything, and Lily found this fascinating even while she knew it was degrading, too. Their concerns, she decided, were very ordinary ones, given the lofty place most of these ladies occupied in the great world. They, too, were prey to doubts and dreams, to jealousies and love and lust, and all the other sins.

When Mrs. Vanderclift's daughter ran off with the coachman, Lily could plainly see that the protestations of shock and horror that rippled through the retiring rooms were well-laced with sexual envy. And Lily thought of Pat, their own stableboy, he of the lithe muscles and hooded eyes and mocking smile, and she well understood how such a thing might come to be.

And Lily heard fragments of talk she understood not at all, especially from the fine gentlemen, who spoke of debentures and railroad bonds and the paper mysteries of business. It seemed to Lily that there was a price for everything in this strange world, that a paper changing hands could mean the making or the breaking of some great business enterprise, but how it was actually done was like a conjurer's trick to her astonished eyes.

The concerns of the women, however rich they might be, were more direct and human, and Lily thought she understood them well. For weren't they prey to all the emotions she sometimes felt herself, to pride and ambition and a desire to make a place for themselves in the world?

Often, it seemed to Lily, these women lived through their children. She knew for a fact that Mrs. Wallingford gloried in the dazzling popularity of Miss Marianne. *And wouldn't I feel the same, having risen so high, from clerking in a store to livin' in such a palace, and my own flesh and blood waltzing the night away with the likes of the Astors?* The flow of money that supported the Wallingfords' way of life was so vast and unceasing that it was beyond envy: it had the bulk and unreality of the doings of a government. Lily thought of Miss Marianne's latest ball gown, a froth of silk brocade and real pointe-de-Venise lace worth a hundred times what Lily would earn in a year, worn once, and now, mysteriously, torn almost beyond repair. Lily would mend it. Her skill with fine needlework had brought rewards quickly. Both Mrs. Groome and Louise praised Lily and gave her more and more needlework to do.

The incident of the gilt-silver knives had endowed Lily with a kind of presence in the servants' hall that might otherwise have taken her years to achieve. She was aware of the luck in this, and treated her small fame carefully, like a fragile thing that might easily be broken. Only when the question of replacing Tess came up did Lily venture to suggest Fran. And Mrs. Groome did indeed make inquiries at St. Patrick's, only to learn that Frances O'Farrelley was already in service, with a wealthy family in Brooklyn Heights.

If it had been me, Lily thought, *I'd have written, or sent a message somehow.* There was a betrayal in it, after all, for hadn't she and Fran been best friends, and hadn't she made Fran's monogram in her finest needlework, and Fran herself made a hair ribbon all embroidered with flowers? *Maybe they're holding her prisoner, maybe she's locked in the cellar, maybe she's dead.* But Lily remembered her own first months in the service of the Wallingfords, and how queer everything had seemed, what with a hundred different discoveries to make every day, and a whole new world to learn, and the simple fact of being very tired after a long day. Not betrayal, then, but just life, that's what it was, and there was the shame in it, life with all its tricky currents pulling you this way and that, taking from you all of a sudden, and just as suddenly giving you things that you hadn't asked for and maybe didn't want, but there they were anyhow, and what were you going to do about it?

Brooklyn Heights was a world away, far across the harbor, and the only way to get there was by boat; it'd take hours. Fran might just as well have gone to Paris as Brooklyn.

Only when Susie commented on how short her skirts were did Lily notice how much she had grown. Winter had come and gone and the big house on Sixteenth Street and Fifth Avenue was stirring with spring and the expectation of young Mr. Jack Wallingford's return from Europe. Almost a year he'd been gone, making a very grand Grand Tour as Mrs. Groome put it, off with a tutor who was, if you could believe Patrick, more of a keeper. Jack Wallingford's arrival would be a major event for the family, but Lily hardly considered herself part of the family, and so she put this out of her mind, and let down her hems, and thought of other things.

One thing Lily thought of was money. Mrs. Groome was holding eight dollars of Lily's wages, almost a fortune. She lived in thrift, and watched her small hoard grow with a miser's satisfaction. To spend five cents on a day off was to spend a lot. Lily remembered her plan, to set up a dressmaking establishment with Fran. Maybe nothing would come of that now, at least not with Fran, but it hadn't been such a bad plan. The eight dollars wouldn't be enough to set up anything, but it was a beginning. If she could save fifteen dollars in a year, then in five years she'd have nearly a hundred! That was a sum that could do things in the world! Why, you could buy steerage to England for twenty-five! Not that Lily had any desire to go to England, or to go anywhere by steerage. But it was something to dream on, and Lily was never afraid to dream.

One day she woke up and realized that in a few days she'd be sixteen. Susie McGlynn was almost eighteen and considered herself a woman of the world. They still shared the little room in the garret, and Susie was as much of a chatterbox as ever, bubbling over with all the little dramas of seething young womanhood. In Lily, the older girl found a rapt audience for her amorous adventures, real and projected. Susie was such a cheerful girl, and generous in her spirit, that Lily could hardly find it in herself to condemn her friend on moral grounds.

But the fact remained that Susie had long since discovered

the allure of Patrick's hayloft, and of Patrick himself. At first Lily was scandalized, but the romance of it intrigued her, not to mention the danger and the addictive sense of participating, however vicariously, in a great love story while it was actually happening.

"Ah, Lil, a wonderful thing it is, loving a fine strong man like my Patrick!" And Susie would cast up her eyes toward heaven, recalling the strength and the fineness of him. Lily was tempted to ask the obvious: would it last, would he, as the saying went, make an honest woman of her? But these were hard questions and Lily was too careful of her friend's new happiness to risk destroying it. Instead Lily overcame her earlier reservations and became love's willing handmaiden, bearer of messages, deviser of ruses, covering for Susie while Susie and Patrick explored a forbidden continent of lovemaking and self-delusion.

The risk was real, and beneath her joy and merriment Susie knew it. The facade of stern morality was as much a part of the Wallingford establishment as the limestone pillars that framed its iron gates. And while servants as a class were expected to be feckless, if not worse, the more obvious moral lapses were not tolerated by Mrs. John Wallingford. The Wallingfords' position in New York society was tentative at best, their money being new and they being Catholic, and Mrs. Wallingford was well aware that even the smallest chink in her social armor could prove fatal. That was why the scandal of the stolen knives had been so thoroughly hushed up. A guest in the Wallingford household must feel secure in every respect. A servant's immorality might prove contagious and could not be tolerated for that reason.

But love, for Susie McGlynn, transcended all barriers. Her days off were no longer spent with Lily now, although more often than not it would be with Lily that she'd leave the house, only to meet Pat at some predetermined rendezvous. On these long afternoons Pat would invent some business with one or another of the Wallingford carriages, and he and Susie would enjoy long jaunts up into the countryside that lay north of Fifty-ninth Street, out into the meadows and hayfields and orchards where there was no one but an occasional seagull to disturb their idyll.

Watching Susie, Lily learned of the tempestuous heights and depths of feeling that turn love's landscape into an obstacle course for the unwary. Now Pat was a god, golden, untouchable; now a devil, cheating and fickle, despised and forsaken. The truth, Lily was sure, must lie somewhere in between, but it seemed true that, for Susie, whatever pain came with her love, the loving was worth it. Lily had never seen anyone so transported by happiness, and the happiness itself was contagious. They had always laughed and had fun, Susie and Lily Malone, but now their friendship took on a new dimension, welded by secrets, strengthened by the shared confidences of Susie's love.

In a way, Lily was glad that Pat had singled out Susie to love, for Lily had sensed a vague danger in the simple presence of the dashing stableboy. Patrick represented temptation, and even while she considered herself at least half a child still, Lily felt the aura of wickedness and forbidden pleasures every time Pat was nearby. Susie's romance effectively defused the stableboy: Lily could see him clear, and as the air of naughty glamour faded, Pat became more human to her, a rather simple boy, in fact, touched with the luck of his handsome looks and not at all afraid to use them. But there was nothing deep about Patrick. He loved fun, loved horses, girls, and ale, and enjoyed them all as often as possible and with so few scruples and inhibitions that his very passions had a kind of animal innocence about them, a directness and simplicity that had its own special appeal. Especially for Susie McGlynn.

Once cupid's arrow had found its way to Susie's heart, it was quickly followed by all the demons of jealousy, and this, too, became an object lesson for Lily. Pat had a charmer's looks, and magnetism, and there was a directness about his enthusiasm for girls that drew response from many quarters, and with very little effort on his part. He had made Susie no promises, and therefore felt no scruples about going with other girls now and then. This drove her mad, and the second phase of her romance was fraught with dark suspicions, with espionage and tears, with confrontations that had only the effect of confirming her suspicions, because Patrick would never take the trouble to deceive her.

Lily overheard part of such a scene.

"Who was she?" Susie's voice was choked, bitter. "Don't deny it, Pat, for I saw her from my window."

This was happening in the courtyard, in broad daylight, for Susie had grown careless now, and she didn't mind who might see or hear her. Lily, passing by the stables with a jug of milk for the coachman's wife, saw the two of them standing half in and half out of the stable, Susie red of face and damp of eye, Pat stone-faced and cool.

"And do ye own me, then, Susan, and am I a darky slave,

for all that we take a fine tumble now and then? And whose business but mine is it who I see, and when?"

"You don't care for me, not one bit, you're a scoundrel, Pat, just a scoundrel, so there!"

"Am I, then? 'Tis sorry I am to hear it, for I was just beginning to think I'm a fine fellow, after some of the things you've been telling me, and only last night, as I recall it. Was I mishearing ye, then, Susan?"

"That was last night, before you betrayed me!"

"Betrayed? It is a strong word, that, now, isn't it? Well, then, I am sorry if I betrayed you, Susan."

"Ah, what can be done with the likes of you? Nothing. Nothing. Nothing!"

She turned and ran across the courtyard, head bowed, heedless of who might be watching. Patrick stood there and followed Susie with his eyes, and slowly a smile crept onto his lips as she vanished into the kitchen, a soft, curling cat's smile. Lily hurried on with her errand, not sure whether they had seen her. So this was love, what wars were fought for, and suicides died for, and fortunes spent for? Watching Susie's explosion, Lily had suddenly felt sorry for Pat. Was it his fault, after all, that she loved him that much more than he could, or would, return? Here she was, ranting and accusing, and accusing him of what? Of doing a thing that obviously came as natural to Patrick as breathing. Of doing a thing he felt no guilt for, as why should he—the guilt was all on Susie's part, her invention, a new device to torture herself with, for Lily was coming to realize that for Susie this torment was a part of the pleasure, strange as that might be. Puzzled but loyal, Lily took Susie's part automatically, unthinking, as befitted her role of confidante and friend. How sad it was to see the grand affair curdling right here before her eyes! For as she moved briskly into the carriage house with her jug, Lily realized that for Pat the affair had been just an incident, a brief exchange of pleasure for pleasure, and that it was over now, or soon would be over, and what had her friend gained for losing her honor to a stableboy? Unimaginable delights, to be sure. An adventure, even if it ended sadly, might be better than no adventure at all. It was most confusing, this new wisdom that had come so fast, and uninvited, to Lily Malone.

She hadn't asked for the burden of Susie's love, and having been given that burden, Lily wasn't at all sure what to do with it. How could she, a virgin, advise a girl like Susie? Lily wished for Sister Cathleen, who always knew what to do. But even Sister Cathleen might be unapproachable on such a subject as this one. Mrs. Groome, whom Lily often asked for advice on other matters, was precisely the last person in the world to tell about this. If any telling was to be done, Lily decided, she most surely would not be the teller. She left the milk with Mrs. Williams and walked slowly back to the big house. Susie, she knew, would be upstairs in their room dissolved in tears. Lily resolved not to go there, not just yet. For what would she say, and what could she do? To imagine being able to change Pat was like thinking you could stop the tide from running, or the sun from coming up tomorrow morning.

Lily thought these things without quite realizing she had just made the first mature decision of her life.

While Susie worried about Pat, and Lily worried about Susie, grand doings were afoot in the Wallingford mansion.

Mr. Jack was coming home.

"Ah, Lily, he's the wild one, is Master Jack, a real divil, just eighteen he is, and the fine young ladies can't stay away from him, nor he from them."

Susie was enthralled.

"Near onto a year he's been away, and they say he damn near had to flee the country, for wasn't he caught climbing up the wisteria vine on the way to a young lady's bedroom, and that more than a year ago, and him not quite seventeen at the time!"

Lily reserved her judgment on Master Jack, but she couldn't fail to be caught up in the bustle and excitement of the preparations for his return. His third-floor suite of three rooms was aired and polished and freshened, and Louise was filled with plans for the grand homecoming banquet, for Master Jack was the apple of her sharp French eye and nothing but the best would do for the young man. Mrs. Wallingford seethed with plans too, eager to make sure the banquet would be worthy of young Jack and of the Wallingfords' ever-loftier position in New York society.

And what a stirring and clanging and whisking it made! For three days before the big event the kitchen bubbled and steamed and echoed with the clash and chime of spoon against pot, the thunder of oven doors opening and closing, of ice being crushed and berries squashed in the big tin strainer, flour sifted, cakes baked, eggs magically transformed into fluted swirls of meringues so light they could almost float. There would be eleven separate courses, each one with its own rare wine, and only Louise and God himself knew how many separate dishes made up each course. Nine desserts were created, from spun-sugar castles, frozen custard garnished with fresh peaches in brandy, to a simple old-fashioned rice pudding with raisins that Master Jack had loved as a child.

A hundred guests there would be for the supper, and more in for dancing afterward! Extra waiters would come from Delmonico's on Twenty-sixth Street. The ballroom was turned into an enchanted forest: Lily's eyes all but popped from her head when she spied the florist's men struggling to haul tub after tub of live six-foot orange trees fat with real fruit up the marble stairs to the ballroom. These—and there were fifty of them, no less—were supplemented with living rosebushes and regiments of cut flowers for the small round tables that ringed the dance floor. Two orchestras they'd be having, the one to spell the other so there'd be continuous music through the night.

Lily couldn't think what it all must cost, or who could be worth it, except that he must be like a prince, this son of the house of Wallingford. Mrs. Wallingford kept daguerreotype portraits of both children on her dressing table, taken by the famous and fashionable Mr. Mathew Brady in his studio down on Broadway. They stood, Miss Marianne on the left and Master Jack on the right, framed in heavy silver and staring right at the viewer with faces that might have been made of marble. Two minutes they'd had to hold the pose, so Mrs. Wallingford told her, and no wonder, then, that they looked like statues. But handsome statues, there was no denying it, Marianne all pride and grace and the hint of deviltry in her great dark eyes. Master Jack looked solemn, but from Susie's tales his actions belied his portrait.

Susie put Lily up to hiding behind one of the huge urns in the second-floor hallway on the day of Master Jack's return, the better to get a peek at this young man of mystery, this conquering hero for whose pleasure such grand preparations had been made. But hiding proved not to be necessary, for all of the staff were summoned into the front hallway to greet Master Jack formally. This was Mrs. Wallingford's idea. She had read about such a thing in one of the Walter Scott novels she devoured like candy, of how they behaved in some old British castle, and damned she'd be if the Wallingfords put on any less of a show for Master Jack.

They waited and waited in the echoing polished marble reception hall. Old Mr. Wallingford, as ever, was away at his business. But Mrs. W. stood like a fat expectant hen, her head twitching nervously from left to right, as she checked and rechecked on the smallest details of the hall's decor. *It's as though she were on trial for some crime*, thought Lily, *and her not at all sure she's going to get away with it.*

A coach came clattering up to the door at full speed and Mr. Groome ceremoniously opened the great door. Jack Wallingford stood there for a moment, taking in the scene. Then he began roaring with laughter. Still laughing, he went to his mother and kissed her.

"Still the same informal little cottage, I see, nothing altered."

He kissed his sister, smiled and nodded at the servants, shook Groome's hand and kissed both Mrs. Groome and Louise, who shrieked with pleasure, and vanished up the stairs.

All this time Lily could not take her eyes off Jack Wallingford.

He was so exactly unlike anything she had expected. His sister, Marianne, whom Lily knew but little, was a proud, moody girl given to fits of temperament alternating with other fits of silliness, none of it mixed with any noticeable kindness or good manners.

Lily liked Jack for laughing so readily at his mother's pretensions. He looked very grown-up for eighteen, two years her senior and just the same age as Patrick, but worlds removed from either of them in the ease with which he moved, the grace with which he wore his fine clothes, the careless good nature that seemed to flow from him naturally.

Susie had told her that there was another, darker side to Jack's nature, but surely his arrival gave no hint of this.

"I've seen him with thunder in his eyes, make no mistake, Lil, it ain't all beer and skittles for our Master Jack, not by a long shot. Three fine schools they've had him in, and him asked to leave—given the boot would be more like it. He seems almost desperate, like, sometimes, the way he'll ride a horse till the poor beast's near dropping, and then leaving the creature for Pat to clean up. And there's his drinking. Now, mind you, I've nothing against a friendly drop or even two, but this lad-o can truly pour it down, and when that's mixed with one of his black moods . . . beware."

Lily took this in, but said nothing, for she felt it was not her place. On the night of the great ball she and Susie stood by to help the ladies in Mrs. Wallingford's suite, and it was impossible to avoid hearing the impression Master Jack was making on the female guests. Opinions were mixed. The younger ladies, especially the single ones, were captivated by the mischief in him, and a sense of mystery. Their mothers were not so sure.

"There's a wild look to him, Cornelia, you mark my words," said one overstuffed dowager to another as they panted and fanned themselves and sipped lemonade from the tiny cups that Lily offered on a silver tray. "Breeding tells, my dear, and we know how little of that there is in this case."

"He is rather common, my dear, but there's nothing common about the Wallingford fortune."

They think I'm deaf, or part of the furniture, Lily thought with mounting anger. *If they think the Wallingfords are so common, then why do they come here? They'd be all smiles and graciousness if Jack courted one of their daughters, damn hypocrites!*

Lily decided that when she was rich and had maids of her own she'd be very careful what she said in front of them. Rich, indeed! And then she smiled at her folly. *Servants, indeed, and her with life savings of just under twenty-five dollars!*

Lily saw little of Master Jack in the next few months. He came and went on mysterious timetables of his own devising, often out until dawn, often sleeping until noon. Then one day as Lily sat at a small deal table in a corner of the servants' hall, mending a tablecloth, the door flew open and there stood Master Jack, red-faced and sleepy-eyed, though it was nearly noon, and shouting.

"Louise! Louise! Where the devil has she got to? You could starve around here!"

Lily blinked at this unexpected apparition. *Who does he think he is, carrying on so?* But she realized instantly that for Master Jack it was not a question of thinking he was this or that. Being Master Jack Wallingford was quite enough, and it should be enough for Lily, too. She put down her sewing and stood up.

"Louise is marketing, sir. Can I help you?"

He looked at her, squinted, then smiled. Lily had the familiar feeling of being part of the furniture.

"Well, maybe you can, miss. I am starving, it's as simple as that. Slept right through breakfast. I'll eat anything. The table. Have you any coffee?"

"That we have, sir; I'll get some."

Lily got coffee, which was kept in its big enamel pot warming all afternoon on the back of the wood stove. She poured him a cup, then went to the larder. There was Louise's orange pound cake, and some fruit, and a bit of leftover pie. Lily arranged these things on a plate with a knife and fork and a napkin, and brought them to Master Jack. He smiled again, a big wide grin it was, friendly.

"Thank you . . . I don't know your name."

"Lily, sir. Lily Malone."

"Thank you, then, Lily Malone, for you have saved my life."

"You're welcome, I'm sure."

Lily turned, to hide the blushing. A fine young man he was, and that's for sure, no matter what Susie says, or Pat. Down from Yale for the Christmas holidays just now, although from what Lily could see, Master Jack spent more of his time in New York than New Haven, even when it wasn't holiday time. And, indulgent as she was in all things, his mother seemed not to mind. And as for Mr. Wallingford Senior, he cared not a fig for education, not he!

"Ejjakashun!" That was how old turkey-faced Mr. John Wallingford described the process, hooting derisively all the while, for what was the profit in books? There had been little enough *ejjakashun* for Mr. John, and he had his Emporium and his millions to prove how little any of it mattered.

The debates among the servants regarding the future of Master Jack and his sister were long and lively, but Lily took no part in them. It was Susie's opinion, firmly held, that Miss Marianne would end up miserable in a palace and Master Jack would find himself happy in a gutter.

"For many a heart has been broken by that boy-o, and him no more than eighteen, and more's to come, and with that and the drinkin' and the tempers, what's to become of him?" Susie delivered her speculations with a merry giggle as the two girls prepared for bed. "Or," she went on, "don't you care, Miss Lily?"

"I would care more," said Lily softly, "if there were anything I could do to help the matter, one way or the other."

There were other things for Lily to think about these days more compelling than the fate of this proud young man she barely knew.

After she had turned fourteen, the physical changes that are part of becoming a woman had been of great concern to Lily, but now other, more important changes were happening in her mind. For the first time, she found herself contemplating herself, her life now, and her future.

It had been a year since the last of the dresses she'd made for herself from the sheets of St. Patrick's orphanage had been consigned to the dust-rag bin. Lily was still a small creature, but there was more flesh on her now, and the legs that had been like sparrow's legs, sticks almost, had curves to them now. There were other curves—a rounding of breast and a swelling of hip. Only her hair remained the same, red as polished copper, and her eyes, green as jade.

Lily had her friend Susie instead of a looking glass, and Susie was quick to mark every new development. There was one small glass, in fact, just big enough to do your hair in, hanging behind the door of the garret room they still shared.

They still laughed and dreamed and made mad plans. Susie had done with Patrick now, and thanked every star she had managed not to get pregnant by him, for that would surely be the end. And Pat went his merry way, casual as ever, treating Susie with the same half-friendly, half-mocking banter, making it clear that she had been no more to him than a cool glass of ale on a warm day, that easily taken, that easily forgotten.

The romance had aged Susie McGlynn, made her quiet, more thoughtful. Lily herself had always been a listener more than a talker, observing as much as doing, for all her dreams and all her planning. There was nearly thirty dollars in Lily's treasure-trove by now, secure with Mrs. Groome. And Lily herself had risen in the household. She was Mrs. Wallingford's personal maid now, a familiar of Madame Pompadour's green salon and the apricot silk boudoir beyond. From Mrs. Groome Lily learned a sorcerer's bag of tricks for keeping Mrs. Wallingford's fine wardrobe looking its best. She learned how to make an unlikely paste from gin and honey and French soap and water to clean unwashable silks like new, and how to steam gossamer crepe over a teakettle, and the wonders that could be worked from fuller's earth and rectified spirits on all the spots a fine lady's gowns and table linens were heir to. Lily learned how to pack the flowing dresses in crisp tissue paper, how to dress her hair in the latest styles, which oils she preferred for her bath, how to iron the most elaborate pleats and ruffles.

And as her life grew busier and her duties in the Wallingford household more responsible, Lily found that she thought less about Fergy, although when she did think of her brother it was with a sharp and irresistible pang of sorrow. Her old friend Fran from the orphanage had receded into the dim past, even though their last fervent parting had been less than two years ago. Nor had Lily returned to see Sister Cathleen, or Father Gregory. St. Paddy's was as distant from today as Ma's dying had been, and if the pain of remembering those years was less now, so much the better. Tomorrow began to mean more for Lily now than it had ever done, and as she saw her small savings grow, the idea that she might actually have a future, that life was more than living just for the moment, began to take root in Lily's mind and to grow.

Lily found Mrs. Wallingford to be a rather silly woman, vain and selfish, but kind for all that, in the way that one might be kind to a small and helpless pet. In Lily, Mrs. Wallingford seemed to find a kind of instinctive good taste. She complimented Lily on the small details of arranging a hairstyle or a bouquet of flowers, and soon Lily found that her mistress relied upon her for more basic suggestions regarding wardrobe, colors, accessories, jewels. It was an education, and Lily absorbed all she could.

Groome was a dedicated reader of the daily newspapers, and Lily tried to improve her small skill at reading by borrowing these when he was done. In this way she became aware of the greater world, the world of wars and chicaneries, of great natural disasters, promises made and broken, of wondrous inventions and outright frauds. The papers were filled with Mr. Phineas T. Barnum and his wonderful museum, of the simmering politics of Spain and Cuba, of the legendary temptress Lola Montez and someone deemed half-mad who wore men's trousers and kept giving speeches about the rights of women: Amelia Bloomer.

But mostly what the papers were filled with was Fergy's old dream, and reading about it brought all her memories of Fergy tumbling back in a painful cascade.

For the gold was still flowing out of the mountains in California and the rush of people eager for it was still moving west. Young America! Fergy's old battle cry was still echoing loudly in the land and Lily found herself less deaf to its siren appeal than she had been when first she heard Fergy's schemes.

If only I were a man!

Lily felt vague stirrings, a restlessness. Big as they were, the marble walls of the Wallingford mansion sometimes seemed to be closing in on her, a trap. And yet there was such comfort here now, now that she had become Mrs. Wallingford's own maid, with Susie as a friend, liked by the Groomes and Louise, warm and well-fed. Part of Lily wanted to fly, to seek adventure, a new life. The other, greater part remembered the treacherously insecure past all too vividly. *Wait, then,*

*bide your time, learn, save your money, get yourself ready
. . . for what?*

And still Lily was restless. She was almost seventeen. Girls
were women at seventeen. Many were married and mothers
by then. Lily hadn't met a man she'd feel like wedding. Nor
had she set up her shop, nor put half a hundred other fantasy
schemes into effect. There were days now when Lily wished
that more of Fergy's blood flowed in her veins. She could
think of Fergy now and not be reduced to tears. What energy
he'd had! What dreams, and the guts to go chase them. There
had been fires in her brother that it had taken an entire ocean
to put out. The heritage of Big Fergus Malone, that would
be, and she must have at least a bit of it herself, or so it
seemed.

But what fires lived in Lily had yet to be ignited.

The summer of 1854 was quiet in the Wallingford mansion, for Mrs. Wallingford took both children abroad with
her, and only the old man remained behind. He seldom ate
in, but for his breakfast, which Groome brought to him on a
tray. Lily tended to Madame's wardrobe, cleaning and brushing and making sure there was camphor out against the
moths, ironing what needed to be ironed, straightening the six
long closets and making room for the bundles of new gowns
that would be arriving from Paris and London and Vienna. It
was growing ever harder to keep ahead of fashion, and Lily
knew that Madame would be spending more time with the
dressmakers of Europe than in the museums.

The season grew hot, the pace grew slower. Peaches and
pears ripened in the orchard behind the carriage house. Once
Patrick tried to kiss her in the stables, and Lily gave him a
great smack, half-playful but with force enough behind it to
show him what-for. Let him not think of *her* as another of
his playthings, to be toyed with and discarded and likely ruined, too, in the bargain!

"Get on with you, then, Pat!" Lily said, laughing. "For
what manner of hussy do you fancy I am?"

"Fancy you is just what I'm doing, Lily, for sure you're
blossomin' like the very roses in the garden."

He reached out and caught her wrist then, and pulled her
close. Lily could feel the warmth of him in the warm stable,
and she smelled the man-smells of him, tobacco and sweat
and something else, dark and compelling. He smiled the slow
mocking smile and drew her closer still. Sweat gleamed on
his broad smooth chest, seen beneath the coarse shirt unbuttoned against the heat.

"No, Patrick."

"Too good for me, are ye, then?" He pulled a clown's sad face, then laughed and let her go.

"Not too good, Pat, but not a toy, either."

"Fair's fair, then, Lily, you cannot blame a poor lonely lad for trying."

She ran from the stable to the sound of his laughter, mocking.

All at once it was October and the Wallingfords were back in an avalanche of crates and trunks and hand valises. Mrs. Wallingford's suite looked like high tide in an ocean of silk and velvet and lace. *There mustn't be a dress left in all Europe,* thought Lily as she gazed in awe at the richness of this hoard.

Miss Marianne had arrived with nearly as much, and something better. Miss Marianne was to be married, and this winter, and to an English lord!

Her mother was bubbling over with the news, and Marianne herself could hardly wait. The *Times* put the announcement in headlines, and on its front page, for in New York, Lily realized, titles were worshiped on an altar only just below hard cash, and here was an irresistible combination of wealth and aristocracy.

Lily wasn't really sure what a baron was, but from childhood she had loved all fairy stories to do with princesses locked in towers, and gallant knights and kings and great deeds. *And if this isn't a fairy story come alive, may I never see another!* The Baroness Marianne! In truth, Lily had never been overly fond of the girl, but the glamour of the engagement was not to be denied. It seemed to reflect its glory all over the great house, and on everyone in it.

The wedding, by Mrs. Wallingford's decree, would be the social event of the year 1855, and quite possibly of the decade. All the glitter that had so bedazzled Lily's poor eyes in the last two years seemed to pale by contrast with the preparations that began immediately.

And Lily saw it all from first-hand, close as she now was to Mrs. Wallingford. Lily saw, and she helped, and her help was gratefully accepted. There was a whirlwind of parties and balls. The magic in Marianne's conquest of the British aristocracy was instantly evident, for calling cards appeared on the silver tray in the front hall that had never appeared there before. The most haughty Vanderbilts and Astors became accessible, eager, even, to be a part of the great event. Mrs. Wallingford became a general of the ballroom, empress of petits fours, sovereign of florists, caterers, stationers. And Lily was her trusted lieutenant.

Brooks Chaffee looked up at the stone wedding-cake facade of his best friend's house and took a deep breath, as though he were going into battle. Then, typically, he grinned. Much a Chaffee had to fear from the suddenly formidable Wallingfords!

What, the young man wondered, would Jack's mother not give for an invitation to his family's simple Greek Revival townhouse on Washington Square? Still, Brooks liked Mrs. Wallingford. For all her aspirations—and what, when you thought about it, was wrong with aspirations?—she was a jolly old trout, and God knew she let Jack raise merry hell in six directions at once, and never complained or grudged his gaming debts, or the champagne nights spent chasing after showgirls, or any of it.

Brooks stood hatless in the December afternoon, and a cutting breeze tossed his long dark blond hair. Everyone was expected to wear a hat, but Brooks hated hats. He rang the bell and heard it echo down the miles of polished marble. It seemed odd to be going to tea at Jack's house. Usually he was there at night, for some dinner or ball, or to collect Jack en route elsewhere, or to drop his college roommate off after the evening's revels. How many times had he dragged Jack Wallingford up those marble stairs at three A.M., Jack sloshed with wine or whiskey or both, and himself none too sober either, if the truth were known, although usually not quite so bad as the unstoppable young mercantile crown prince and amateur debauchee Jack Wallingford. And both of them singing and laughing and comically trying to hush each other to avoid alarming the household! Well, it was expected. As so many things were expected, especially if your name was Brooks Chaffee, of the Washington Square Chaffees, and your mother a Van den Hoven, which only meant that the entire Dutch-colonial social establishment of New York were blood relatives and, on your father's side, more than half of the quietly gilt-edged old Yankees. For wasn't Hiram Chaffee one of the most respected lawyers in America, his head packed with all kinds of knowledge, including several complete family trees, whose purity he counted on his sons Neddy and Brooks to preserve and nurture.

Brooks wished a familiar wish. He wished he saw more of Neddy these days. Neddy didn't approve of Jack Wallingford, either. Common, he called him. Well, common he was,

Brooks couldn't argue the point. But Jack was also great good fun, a true friend, and loyal, and with a fascinating edge of danger about him.

Jack Wallingford was ever willing to take the wild risk, to dance on the thinnest ice, to go just that bit faster, come what may. And for Brooks, who was naturally conservative, the contrast was thrilling.

The Wallingfords, he knew, liked the fact of his friendship with Jack, and their hospitality, without reciprocation from Washington Square, was so lavish as to be almost embarrassing. The Wallingfords considered, rightly, that Brooks was a good influence on Jack, a balance wheel. For himself, Brooks found his larks and sprees with Jack a true revelation. It was more than the wine and the girls and the music, although the good Lord knew Brooks loved all those things.

What Brooks loved in Jack was his total freedom from convention, his outright mockery of the standards that society held so dear. And while Brooks was far from ready to overthrow the establishment that had been so kind to him all his life, it was good fun to watch Jack try. And try he did, with cost as no object.

Jack had an immense allowance, and still managed to owe everyone in New Haven. And you'd lend Jack any amount in a flash, because you knew he was good for it, and you knew you'd get it back in the form of Jack's own largess the minute he was flush again. Which was never long in coming, because dear Mama would send a draft by messenger, if necessary, all the way from this vast monument to the Wallingford money on Fifth Avenue. Brooks himself was on a tight allowance by comparison, and every cent of it had to be accounted for in writing, every quarter, before the next quarter was advanced.

To Brooks, the Wallingfords were a permanent circus-in-residence, and he found their somewhat simpleminded devotion to spending the Wallingford fortune upon every possible frivolity curiously endearing. If there was harm in it, the harm would not be for Brooks Chaffee. So he basked in the warmth of his friendship with Jack, and the generosity of Jack's family, just as a frog might sit in the sun on a bright day, more than a little drunk with the mindless pleasure of the act.

At Yale, Brooks knew men who had far better minds than Jack's, men of more serious scholarly interests, men who would, beyond doubt, make something significant of themselves in the greater world.

It was hard to imagine Jack Wallingford at forty. But Brooks and Jack were twenty, and forty was an eternity away, and in any event, who cared?

Brooks stood waiting for the door to be opened. He wondered idly what new mischief Jack would have cooked up for tonight. Already he had a small, delicious sense of guilt, for he was skipping Aunt Theodora's dinner party, a family occasion that ranked right up there with christenings and funerals, and was every bit as much fun. To hell with Aunt Theodora. She served terrible food and undrinkable wine, and little enough of that. An evening with Aunt Theodora was the social equivalent, as far as Brooks was concerned, of a month becalmed, in steerage, on a leaky ship.

Whatever he and Jack got up to, it would be miles ahead of Aunt Theodora's gruesome festivities.

The huge door opened. The fat butler, Groome, smiled. It was as though two hams were trying to dance across his flushed face. Fond of the claret, was old Groome, or at least that was what Jack said.

"Mr. Jack is in the library, sir."

"Thank you, Groome."

Brooks was enough of a familiar in the Wallingford household to be left on his own to find the library. But the minute he got to the landing on the second floor of the mansion, he realized he wasn't quite sure where the damned place was. Down there, he thought, about half a mile past that potted tree, turn right at the marble centaur, down there someplace. God, but you could get lost in this place! He thought of the simple foursquare plan of his parents' house, and how much more sense it made. Brooks liked things simple, if the truth were to be known. He walked down the empty, polished, gleaming hallway and turned right at the statue. There were three large walnut doors, and any one of them might be the library. He chose the first, knocked briskly, and opened it.

Damn! It was the dining room—now he remembered. But for the life of him he couldn't remember where the library was. Then he felt the girl's eyes on him. He hadn't seen her at first. Brooks Chaffee blinked in the half-light of the big room, touched his cravat to feel if it was tied properly, for she was staring at him rather intensely; then he thought, what the hell, a maid, helping with the table flowers it looked like.

"Excuse me," he said quietly, "but I seem to be lost. Could you direct me to the library?"

It was a small, pale face, with extraordinary hair, a red

that might almost be gold. Immediately she dropped her eyes, blushed, then answered, "Surely, sir. If you will follow me."

The maid led him to the door, and down the hallway, and stopped before the third door. Damn and damn! He knew— should have known—it was that one.

It had been a grand day when Lily was first allowed to arrange the table flowers. And still, although that had been months ago, she took a special pride in doing it. For who knew, after all, what eyes might be looking on these very arrangements when supper was presented.

The flowers came from Arrigo's, Manhattan's finest florist, in stiff paperboard boxes lined with fresh straw. And the flowers themselves were miraculous. Mr. Arrigo could grow roses in midwinter, irises when no right-thinking native iris would dream of blooming, branches of pale shy quince blossoms, and narcissus whose very scent could break your heart. Had his own glass houses, had Mr. Arrigo, kept warm as summer all season long, and here the miracles happened, and for the wonders he produced Mr. Arrigo also produced equally wondrous bills. These, the hostesses of New York paid gladly, for there was rivalry in flowers as in many other things. It was no light question, Lily knew, who set the finest table, served the rarest, most out-of-season delicacies, or found the most interesting musicians to play.

Mrs. Wallingford had decided upon an all-white banquet this evening, and the flowers, too, were to be entirely white. There were white roses, proud on unimaginably long, straight stems, and white French lilac branches, white-on-white narcissus, and, in separate small white porcelain tubs, lilies of the valley actually growing and in bloom!

Lily worked on the large central bouquet, the box from Arrigo's on a side table behind her. It was nearly done, and a fine thing, if she did say so herself. She had started with the biggest flowers, the lilacs. Too big, they proved, and in need of trimming. That done, the sweet-smelling branches tamed and shaped, she added the roses, first trimming the stems, then singeing them over a candle flame as Louise had taught her, then trimming them again, which prevented their drooping. Last, Lily added the smallest of the flowers, the narcissus. There!

She stepped back a bit, surveyed her work, frowned, walked slowly around the huge table, frowned again, changed three roses, and was at last satisfied. Lily was standing thus, in the shadows halfway down the long room, when the knock came gently on the door.

Saying nothing, she stood there watching as it opened.

Oh, my. A young man's head poked in, followed by the young man himself. Fair he was, and handsome, more than handsome: these were the features of a knight in the old stories, a fine pure warrior knight riding out of legends. Or even an angel, Lily thought, yes, and did the angels themselves look so fine?

She said nothing, transfixed, waiting. He might not be real, she might be dreaming such a man. But Lily's dreams had never dared so much.

She held her breath, and felt a flush building on her neck, her cheeks. He might disappear in a puff of smoke! He might be the devil himself, cleverly disguised, sent to earth for the temptation of poor young virgins. For Lily was poor, and young, and surely a virgin, and just as surely tempted. And why? she wondered. There were men around and plenty, and some of them good to look on, Pat for one—the girls chased him like bees after a flower. Why had no man ever caused her to feel like this? She felt her knees going all weak on her. Maybe he'd go away, and never see her, and she'd forget all about him.

But even in that instant, sure as death, Lily knew she might live to be a hundred years old and never forget the mere sight of him. When his words came, one part of Lily's head told her it was just a young man's voice, good enough, to be sure, educated beyond a doubt, but not all that heavenly-inspired special. All the same, she trembled. Lily Malone found sweet music in his words, heard trumpets calling in the everyday request: "Excuse me," said the voice, called the trumpets, "but I seem to be lost. Could you direct me to the library?"

Oh, fine sir, if you think you are lost, it's glad you should be you're not me.

She stood there like a deaf-mute, and only after a terrible effort did Lily find her tongue. "Surely, sir. If you will follow me."

She made her legs move, and thanked God and all his angels that she managed to get down the length of the room without actually falling, fainting, or otherwise making a fool of herself. She'd have to pass by him! So close. Close enough to touch him. The strange young man held the door open for her, and stepped back a bit as he did this, smiling vaguely.

He doesn't see me at all, and that's a fact. And thank God for it.

If she touched him, passing, her dress would burst into flames sure as Victoria ruled England. Lily passed the young man, close enough to touch, but not touching, and as she passed, Lily could smell a familiar scent. The young man used the same cologne as Master Jack. Somehow the spicy, faintly floral aroma of Roger & Gallet reassured Lily that the man was real, not an emissary from the darker powers. She led him down the hall to the library, and bowed and hurried back as though all the demons in hell itself were hot on her trail. And maybe they were. For surely she was lusting after the poor man, if this yearning could properly be called lust. Properly, indeed! Thoughts like these were very far from proper, there was no doubt at all of that.

Lily smiled then, for she remembered her own impatience with Susie McGlynn, when Susie was all mad about Patrick. Girlish nonsense, that was how Lily felt about that, and here she was drowning in the very same nonsense!

But it wasn't nonsense. It was completely real, foolish and sad, and altogether hopeless. *At least Susie had her little dream come true, for all that it never came to much, and ended quickly. At least she had the memory of it.* But for Lily Malone and the young and golden stranger who had just touched her heart, there could be no hope at all in this world. There were things you shouldn't want, or even be thinking of, not if you were poor, and Irish, and a servant.

Lily walked back into the dining room and looked at her flowers. They were every bit as lovely as they had been five minutes ago, but now they held no magic for her.

In these few devastating minutes Lily's whole life changed. She would never be the same girl again, or dream the same dreams.

She knew with shattering finality that the young man, who in a few minutes would barely recall that he'd seen her, moved in a world so far from hers that it was a kind of miracle she had ever seen him at all. A miracle it was, for sure, and a sad one.

Lily gathered up Mr. Arrigo's straw-filled box, and with it the trimmings of her flower arrangement, and walked slowly down the back stairs to the kitchen.

Lily might have known that Susie McGlynn could tell her all about the strange and wonderful and disturbing visitor.

"That's Mr. Brooks Chaffee, who's the college friend of

Master Jack, and a fine old New York family they are, the Chaffees, Lil, finer by miles than you-can-guess-who."

"I thought him fine to look on."

Lily was reluctant to bare her feelings about the young man, but she felt the need to know more about him as an almost physical thirst or hunger.

"Well, you're not alone, then, for sure and Mrs. W. thinks him a fine catch, and if a certain young lady hadn't gone and caught herself a royalty, it wouldn't surprise most people to find Mrs. W. aimin' Miss Marianne in his direction."

Lily thought about that. *Of course, it would be natural, a step up the social ladder, no doubt, if what Susie said was true, but not so fine as catching an English baron. I hope I live to see the baron who's a finer sight than that lad!*

"Did she love him? Miss Marianne?"

"Ha! That one loved dozens. But I have heard speculations. Mostly wishful thinkin', I'm more like to call it."

Susie laughed, and Lily made herself laugh too. And with a twinkle in her eyes, Susie went on: "I think, Miss Lillian, that you've been hatching randy thoughts about Brooks Chaffee. Could that be the truth? You can tell your old pal Susie, who's had many a randy thought herself, and done randy deeds, too, may God forgive me for a sinner."

"I thought him handsome." *I would die for him, here and now.*

"Aye, and so do all the girls, rich and poor. You're not alone in that, Lil, more's the pity. And he's taken up with young Master Jack, and you know what deviltries that can lead to. Between the pair of them, well, I'd be surprised if there's a virgin left in all New York by springtime."

"Are they that bad?"

"Who's to say what's bad, my fine lady? They're busy, that's for sure and gone!"

And Susie laughed again, pleased with her woman-of-the-world tolerance.

Lily smiled, and turned back to her sewing. Well she could imagine the young master and his friend cutting through the ballrooms of New York like hot knives through butter, leaving trails of tears and palpitations and broken maidenheads. And laughing, and maybe not remembering in the light of harsh dawn what the poor girl's name was. She sighed, and smiled at the sighing, for wasn't she becoming the very spit and image of a Lovelorn Maiden? For her, for Lily Malone, whose heart had hardly been flexed yet, to have it all of a sudden smashed and broken all beyond repair, all in one quick moment, in daylight, and by a stranger, a man she'd never meet upon any equal plane. It was a thing to make you laugh, or weep. And Lily had never been a weeper, and she wasn't going to start now, not for Master Brooks Chaffee, nor any man, however strange and beautiful.

Then why could she not clear her damned head of him? Why must she keep seeing him, and seeing him again in the first wondering surprise of him, seeing that fine and noble-looking head come suddenly around the dark edge of the dining-room door, filling her empty heart with this unfamiliar, terrible sweet burning?

She stabbed her thumb with the needle, and swore, and thought how it had been years, she couldn't remember how long, since she'd made such a stupid mistake sewing, and knowing why, and hating herself for not having better control than that, and wondering where, if ever, this would end.

Brooks Chaffee looked at the room, and at the girl, and laughed for no reason. A violin played gypsy music three flights below, and the music wound its plaintive way up the carpeted stairs and down the hall. It even seemed to fill the big back bedroom, as the girl did herself, and her perfume, and her promise of pleasure. Brooks looked at her and smiled, and wished he hadn't drunk quite so much of the widow Clicquot's champagne.

Rose, her name was, and truly she looked like a rose, pink-skinned and soft, a bit on the plump side, older, he thought, than his age, but not so very old. Only her eyes were old, and they were merry too. A girl who liked her work. Jack, good old Jack, always knew where to find them. This was a new place, discreet, just another house in a row of fine town houses off Sixth Avenue, nothing but the number 16 to advertise its presence. Inside, the discretion continued. Luxury, to be sure, but understated; nothing was loud, or ever would be. Madame Duveen ran a top-drawer house. The only danger, Jack had said with a chuckle, was running into your own father on the stairs.

Then Jack had disappeared with two of Madame Duveen's finest girls, laughing still in his pleasure over Brooks's protests of how much the night must cost: "Consider it your Christmas present, old man, underwritten by the New York and New Haven Society for Moral Rearmament."

The NYNHSMR was Jack's invention, and its activities could have kept an army of reformers very busy for years. He even had cards printed, naming himself as director. There was never a dull moment when you were with old Jack, not by day, not by night. Brooks was a New Yorker born and bred, but Jack had shown him a New York the Chaffees never imagined. It was Jack who took him to the Louvre, Manhattan's gaudiest dance hall and concert saloon, where the waitresses were much more than waitresses and the revelry never stopped. With borrowed pistols, disguised in rags, they'd cruised the murderous dives from Five Points to the docks, heard the lurid tales of characters like Sadie the Goat and her Charlton Street Gang, river pirates complete with Jolly Roger and a plank to walk, and Gallus Mag, the six-foot cockney barkeep whose skirts were hoisted by her man's suspenders, whose favorite trick was to bite a man's ear off and hand it to him with the bar chit.

Brooks looked at his Christmas present. She stood before him, pink and fragrant and ready. Rose helped him undress. Then she stood back and regarded him solemnly. For an instant Brooks wondered if he met her standards—whatever they might be. Then she grinned, and came to him, and enfolded him in her soft perfumed arms. Rose kissed him full on the lips, still standing there near the wide bed, and all the quick hot blood in him began churning and throbbing with desire.

She threw her head back then, and laughed, and said: "Aye, lad, and it's sure I don't know why you're paying for it, but to say the least, you're well-equipped to get your money's worth!"

She took his hand then, and led him to her bed. *Merry Christmas, Jack*, he thought. And then he abandoned thinking altogether.

⤜ᵍ 11 ℰ⤛

MISS MARIANNE WALLINGFORD

TO MARRY CLARENCE, BARON WEST

British nobleman arrives on HMS "Brunswick"

New York, January 7, 1855. Baron West arrived here
today with a retinue of servants to claim the hand of his
betrothed, the lovely Miss Marianne Wallingford, daughter of Mr. & Mrs. John Frederick Wallingford of Fifth
Avenue in this city. Mr. Wallingford is the owner of the
Wallingford Emporium, and is prominent in other business ventures in Manhattan and elsewhere.

Baron West, who will be residing amidst the well-
known splendors of the St. Nicholas Hotel on Broadway,
is the seventeenth Baron West of Castle Westover, in
Hertfordshire. The ancestral demesne consists of some
17,300 acres of land and the fabled castle itself, which
was bestowed upon the first Baron West by Henry V in
1419. Baron West is a fifth cousin, once removed, of her
Majesty, Queen Victoria. The nuptials will be celebrated
at St. Joseph's Roman Catholic Church on Saturday,
February 17. The newlywed couple will then set sail on
a honeymoon cruise to the Mediterranean, after which
they will reside at Castle Westover and at the Westover
Square home of Baron West in London.

Lily was happy for Marianne, and all the servants basked
in reflected glory. The article came as no news to the Wallingfords' servants, but it was read and reread in the servants'
hall nevertheless. The intensity of Mrs. Wallingford's preparation for this marriage had been building ever since her arrival
from Europe in October. Marianne Wallingford would be the
first American girl in decades to catch herself a bona fide
British nobleman, and her mother intended to make the very

most of it. Sure, there were penny-plentiful—and often dubious—Italian titles and French titles and German titles by the score. But an authentic British barony! To be a shopkeeper's daughter and become Marianne, Baroness West, of Westover Castle! It was almost too good to be borne, yet Mrs. Wallingford blossomed under the strain. Dear Clarence must not be disappointed in his choice, and dear Clarence had very high standards, indeed.

Mrs. Wallingford's first household change was to insist upon uniforms for one and for all, just as they did things in the great houses of England. Patrick and old Williams, grumbling, were made into proper coachmen. Groome became even more flushed and stately in a frock coat and white gloves. The maids were fitted out with dark blue gowns and white frilly aprons and tiny white butterfly caps. Two young footmen were hired to man the great front door at all hours, for the door began swinging now at a rate that Lily feared might melt its hinges. Nearly every day now there were supper parties and luncheons and teas to be given or gone to, and in the meantime, plans and plans and more plans to be hatched and followed through in thousands of complicated details.

On the day of the Mass, for instance, it would not do to use the regular everyday candles in St. Joseph's. Lily was sent with her measuring tape to take the size of every candlestick, so that colored, perfumed candles could be especially ordered from Paris for the great day. The invitations were anguished over, not only for the question of whom to invite and, more importantly, whom not to invite, but the very size and design and color of ink. Should they be gilt-edged or just plain? Or possibly edged in a color, royal purple perhaps? Was it a done thing to use the bridegroom's crest? Should they cook up a Wallingford crest for the occasion?

Lily had never seen such a fuss, and she was glad of it, partly because the preparations were exciting, and even more because the extra work helped take her mind off Brooks Chaffee.

She had never seen him again after that one unsettling afternoon in the dining room. Oh, and sure, she knew he and Mr. Jack were thick as thieves together. But Lily saw even Mr. Jack himself very seldom now, busy as she was with his mother and the wedding plans, isolated as she was with the ladies in the ladies' retiring rooms when the Wallingfords entertained on a big scale in the evenings. Maybe it was the not seeing him that intensified her memories of that golden head, the clear blue of his eyes, the tone of his voice, the way he stood, tall and proud he was, straight as a soldier but not in any way threatening. Except to her sanity, for truly there were moments now when Lily thought she might be going mad. *Sure, and I'll end my days raving in the madhouse,* she thought, as the head of Brooks Chaffee popped uninvited out of some dark pantry, out of her sewing basket, out of a dark alley. *Poor girl, she went mad for love, she did, turned into a right lunatic from just one sight of him.* And Lily would smile then, quietly, to herself, but it would be a bitter smile, for her secret was a sad secret.

No more did she ask Susie McGlynn about the Chaffee lad. Once, bringing Mrs. Wallingford some tea late in the afternoon, Lily caught a glimpse of Mr. Jack and his friend just as they were going down the great marble stairway, Jack with his arm on Chaffee's shoulder and both of them laughing, not one care between the two of them, Mr. Jack's dark, mocking laughter making a noticeable counterpoint to his friend's lighter, more even tone. Lily had paused then, her silver tea tray growing heavier as she stood there, and she caught a glimpse, just a flash of the dark gold head in the sudden light as one of the new footmen opened the great front doors. A flash of sunlight on gold, that's all it was, and the two young men were gone on a ripple of laughter. And Lily wondered what fine young girls might be waiting, for surely there must be girls, surely that laughter, those looks, those eyes were not to be wasted. Then she started, as if from a dream, and walked down the hallway to her mistress's bedroom.

Clarence, Baron West, had only one failing, but in the eyes of Susie McGlynn it was a major flaw. Her eyes widened as she told Lily what Pat had just revealed. Lily blushed. She knew such things existed, but, good heavens, he was royalty, he was betrothed to Miss Marianne.

"You don't mean it! Patrick's joking."

Susie nodded wisely, sure in her knowledge of the wickedness of the world. "Never, Lil, not about something like this. Pat went there, don't you see, went right up to the baron's suite in the St. Nicholas Hotel, with a message from Mrs. W., in the morning it was, just yesterday, and in he goes to the suite, and hears funny sounds, laughing and sportin' and carryin' on, and naturally he's thinking the sly baron's got a fancy woman in there, havin' his will of her and all, and he's just about to leave the note, except he can't, because the mistress is expecting a reply by hand, and all of a sudden who should leap out but the baron himself, naked as Peter's goat he was, and in a passionate condition at that, says Pat, and what should he be doin' but havin' his sport, all right, but with one of those footmen he's brought all the way from his old castle."

"God in heaven! And what did Pat do then?"

"Well, Patrick's no angel, as well I know, but even he was shocked, for he's all man is my Pat, and what should the baron do but invite Patrick to join in with their filthy games."

Susie had to stop then, because she fair to died of laughing at the spectacle of the great lover, Pat, being confronted with such a distasteful invitation.

"No!"

"Ha! That's not the end of it, Lil. He offered Patrick money."

"God. How much?"

"Five dollars, Lil—now what do ye make of that?"

Lily stood silent for a moment, chilled to the bone. Then she spoke.

"I think," said Lily gravely, "that someone ought to tell Miss Marianne. Or her parents. Lord Almighty, Susie, think what's waiting for her back at that castle."

"Unspeakable perversions!" Susie spoke with a kind of glee that shocked Lily even more than this unexpected bit of information about the baron. Lily felt no special affection for Miss Marianne, in fact she knew the girl very little. From a distance, Marianne Wallingford seemed as empty-headed as most of the other young ladies Lily saw at such close range in the ladies' retiring room at the Wallingfords' parties. They all seemed more concerned with the sweep of a train or the cut of a bodice than any of life's real problems. Yet Lily felt a great reluctance to judge these girls, her betters, and so ordained by fate.

At last she spoke. "What did Patrick say then? Did they fight?"

"Not Pat, the sly fox that he is. He put on his finest manner, did Pat, and smiled, and bowed, and said, 'Thank you, your Lordship, but I am otherwise engaged!' Can you imagine?"

"I can. What then?"

"Cool as ice cream, the baron, who's still Adam-naked, mind you, and still in a condition of lust, goes to the desk and writes a fine reply to his future mother-in-law, hands it to Patrick without so much as a smile, winks at Pat as if to say, 'Well, lad, if not this time, maybe some other time,' bows, and goes back to his buggery."

"Patrick should tell Mr. Groome. And Mr. Groome should tell Mr. Wallingford."

"That's what I told Pat. He won't do it."

"Why not, for the love of God? Miss Marianne's whole future happiness might be at stake."

"It's as simple as this, Lil, and maybe he's right: who would believe an ignorant stable lad against a fine English baron? People would think Pat was just setting up for blackmailing the baron—or the Wallingfords—or anyhow, that he'd be up to some kind of mischief. At least that's how Pat sees it, and I've got to admit he might have a point there."

Lily sat on the edge of her little bed, as she had been sitting through all this recital, and then stood up and walked to the small round window. It was dark out. She could see the lights from the stables and from the carriage house across the courtyard. Of course Pat was right. Who, when it came right down to it, would ever believe a servant—any servant—against the word of a gentleman? Or gentlewoman? She looked at her friend.

"What you say is true. It may be we can do nothing at all, and there's the pity of it."

"I feel," said Susie with a sigh, "sorry for Miss Marianne, with all her gowns and jewels and her baron."

"Fancy us, Susie, feeling sorry for the likes of her."

"Better we look to our own advancement, and forget the telling of tales like that one."

"Could she know?"

"Never. I mean, she'd never go through with it if she did."

"Are you sure? There's some who'd say the Wallingfords are very strong after his title, to make 'em more respectable, and you can't deny that it's worked. We've all seen what's happened since the announcement: Astors all over the place, where never a one set foot before."

"Ah, then, Lil, what kind of a mother would sell her daughter to a pervert just for the sake of some old title?"

"There's them as would. There's them as have sold their daughters—and, yes, their sons too—for much less than that, I fear."

This was true. Lily had heard too many stories of the brothels that festered and flourished in New York's teeming underworld, places where the wicked could buy just about anything, however lewd, girls, boys, even, some said, animals, and in every combination, too. Lily thought of these strange things, and of Mrs. John Wallingford, and wondered what lengths that lady would go to to elevate her daughter into the highest circles of titled European society. It was a question fraught with danger, and Lily decided not to think on it too deeply, for what was bought and what was sold and the prices paid that had nothing to do with gold or money were no concern of hers, nor should they be. Instead Lily thought of happier things. She thought of her nest egg, safe with Mrs. Groome, safe and growing now, thirty-six dollars she had, and if her wages went up a bit, that would soon enough be fifty. Fifty dollars! That was a sum to conjure with. And to think that nasty baron offered Patrick five for . . . what? A moment's dissipation. She shuddered. It all came down to nothing more than buying and selling, and glad she was that Pat decided not to sell. But still and all, Lily wondered, with a nagging, abrasive wonder, how strong she'd be in such a situation, faced with such temptations.

The days raced on, and there was no more talk of the Baron West and his strange tastes in love. The great house on Fifth Avenue seemed to vibrate with the growing excitement of Miss Marianne's wedding. All day long carriages came and went at both entrances: to the front, with an endless variety of wedding gifts, with invitations and notes and flowers; and to the service entrance came rare wines, rich foods, more flowers. Special tables had to be set up in the ballroom to hold the glittering trove as all of New York society and all who aspired to that society entered into a kind of golden competition to see whose offering would most impress the future Baroness West of Castle Westover.

Wattled dowagers with ancient names and predatory eyes, women who six months ago would have sneered openly at the nouveau-riche Wallingfords, entered smiling and traded little jokes and larger secrets with the triumphant Mrs. W., the shop clerk that was, the arriviste who had now very definitely arrived.

Lily watched it all unfolding, and if she smiled in secret at the schemes and antics of the rich and the mighty, she could not help but be mightily impressed by the sheer mass of their wealth. Great mounds of wedding silver overflowed the display tables in the ballroom, huge trays encrusted with swags of flowers and cupids and burnished silver fruit, punch bowls big enough to bathe in, armies of candlesticks there were, sufficient to light six churches, Lily thought, and thought, too, of who would have the sore arms from all the polishing. There was gold, too, among the silver; vermeil dishes gleamed like some old king's treasure, as well they might, for surely a baron was much like a king, was he not, or at the least a step in that direction?

Not all the gifts were gold or silver. There was china too, cups so fine you could read the paper through them, an old French mirror Mrs. Wallingford said had once belonged to Louis himself. Lily wasn't sure who Louis was, but his mirror was a fine thing, going a little smoky now with age, but splendid nevertheless in its carved gilt frame.

Lily paused, one afternoon late in January, in front of old Louis's mirror. It stood behind one of the tables in the ballroom, reflecting a priceless array of gifts and the table on the other side of the long room, piled even higher. Soon they'd have to put the things on the floor, or build more tables. Five shafts of golden afternoon light cut the dense gloom. Lily looked at the mirror, and at her reflection. It was like looking at another girl, from another time. Lily wore her new uniform, dark blue woolen, with a little white cap and touches of white at the neck and the cuffs of the sleeves. The Lily in the old mirror seemed to float across a forgotten legend: there was a power in the mirror. It knew secrets. Slowly, hypnotized, Lily lifted a hand to touch her hair, which made a spot of brightness in the gray, silvery image on the old glass. It was reassuring, somehow, that as Lily raised her hand, the reflection also raised its hand. It was proof the thing was just a mirror after all, not magical—and stop daydreaming, girl, she told herself sternly, you're going off your head for sure, that's all there is to it! But still she paused, fascinated not so much by her reflection as by the sense of magic in the glass. The voice, when it came, shocked her.

"It's quite a hoard, isn't it, Lily? The spoils of war, you might say."

Jack Wallingford had come up behind her, unseen. Lily started, and turned to him, frightened. She vividly recalled the incident of Tess Reilley and the stolen knives, and prayed young Mr. Jack had no such ideas about her.

"Oh! Forgive me, sir. You startled me."

"I'm sorry, then, Lily, for I didn't mean to." He looked at her, and smiled a small but friendly smile. His dark eyes seemed to look right through her, and beyond her, but maybe that was just a trick of the light.

"Well," he continued, "it seems the sweet young newlyweds will not have to face the cruel world empty-handed, doesn't it? Have you ever seen so much junk?"

Lily frowned. The bitterness in his voice was unmistakable. She had never sensed any enmity between Mr. Jack and his sister, nor had she heard of any in the backstairs gossip. But the bitterness was there; it, surely, was no trick of the light. Something was bothering Mr. Jack. Lily felt helpless, for whatever might be his trouble, sure and there was no way in all the world for her to help him out of it.

"It makes a fine show, though, doesn't it, sir?"

"That's just what it does. It makes a show. At any given moment, Lily, half of New York is giving a performance for the other half, which pretends not to notice, because it, in its turn, is also performing. They just never take their masks off even for a moment."

"If you say so, sir. And if you'll excuse me, it's too long I've tarried, admiring Miss Marianne's presents."

"Lily?"

"Yes, sir?"

"You're getting to be a very pretty girl."

No man ever said that before, and sure I am that Jack doesn't mean it. "Oh! Thank you, sir, I'm sure." Still, Lily blushed, and cast down her eyes from his. She turned then and walked out of the enormous ballroom as fast as her feet could carry her. Mr. Jack was a devil with the girls, there was no secret about that! But what had made him say she was pretty? Lily never thought of herself as ugly or pretty or anything but Lily Malone. Susie was pretty. You could see that in the way men looked after her, even the fickle Patrick. Well, and hadn't Pat tried to kiss her, kiss Lily, just a few weeks ago? Still, that signified nothing, for Pat would kiss a horse if there was nothing better at hand.

Lily's head was whirling as she made her way back to Mrs. Wallingford's rooms, trying to sort out what might be disturbing young Jack, trying to forget that he'd called her pretty. And an unfamiliar sensation went tingling through her: the lovely, dangerous possibility that it might be true. It would be a fine thing, she decided, to be pretty. Lily thought that beauty must be a gift from the gods, a thing you were born with or not, like being born rich or poor, Irish or Dutch, a baron or a beggar. You could not, surely, go and buy beauty in a shop, or learn it the way you might learn to cook, or to speak French, or to sew. *I'll ask Susie,* she thought. *Susie will know what I truly look like, whether Mr. Jack was making a joke of me.*

Lily did ask her friend, and that very night. Susie McGlynn regarded her gravely.

"Stand up."

Lily stood, trembling a little in her nightdress, for the

drafts of January found their way through the pretty round window, mansion or no. Susie walked slowly around the younger girl, one finger thoughtfully in her mouth, frowning, angling her head, poking here, pulling there. For a moment Susie said nothing. Lily's worst fears were coming true: she wasn't pretty, not at all, and her friend was too kind to tell her. At last Susie spoke.

"I think there is hope, Lil." Then she burst out laughing, scooped up a feather pillow, and gave Lily a great whack over the head.

"By all the saints in heaven, you silly goose, can't you see it, Lil? Pretty? Sure as the Lord made angels you're pretty, my girl. And more than that, maybe much more. Most women would kill for hair like yours, Lily Malone, and don't you forget it. Why, just the other day Patrick was saying how you're fair to blooming just like your name says, into our own lovely Lily, says he, rogue that he is, and were I you, girl, I'd stay away from his stables, for he'd be glad to work his lustful will on you, that he would."

Lily shuddered: whether from fear or from pleasure, she could not tell. "Do you mean it, Sue?"

"About Pat? I know it!"

"No, goose. About me. I'm not ugly, then?"

The answer was laughter, but Susie's laughter held no mockery and no hurt. "I wouldn't lie, Lil, you know that."

"I never thought of it before. About being pretty."

"And you're better for that, make no mistake. Who wants a woman who's forever fussing and regarding herself in mirrors, and primping and all? No real man, I'm sure of that."

"Not even Pat?"

"Especially not Pat. You should hear him carrying on about Miss Marianne and her pals, especially now that she's about to become a baroness and all that. But aren't you the sly one, Lil? Who's the lucky gentleman who put you up to all this thinking about how pretty you are or aren't? For don't try to tell old Sue there ain't one. Is it that Chaffee lad, now? Sure and he's a fine one!"

Lily's heart froze. *No one, not even Sue, will learn my secret, not if I die.* "No. It isn't that. I just wondered."

"Ah, you're no fun, then, Lil. Keep your secret if you will. You'll never fool me that there isn't some fine Irish root sproutin' all hot and passionate for you, to make you go on so."

"And what may that be, an Irish root?"

More laughter. "Get on with you, Lil, there's no use pretending. I'll make it a riddle, then: it don't grow in the ground, but it do grow, and mightily, and whenever you see it, there's surely a man not far behind!" And Susie laughed more at her cleverness, and left her friend to blush.

Lily sighed and turned off the lamp, for her very innocence embarrassed her. And as she climbed into the narrow bed, her mind was churning with many conflicting emotions, with doubts and with fears. *Maybe Sue's right, maybe I should be having a fling with some lad. Am I not almost eighteen, and a young woman already, and aren't plenty of girls younger than me married already, and with kids?* But Lily's memories of her own mother and her terrible losing battles with poverty and sickness were too recent and too bitter for the idea of marrying some boy of her own class to be an appealing one. *Yet what else lay in store for her? To be the maid for some rich lady all her life, or to end up like Mrs. Groome? You'd eat, it wouldn't rain on you, but what was there besides that? No freedom, surely, all but a slave you were, if the truth was told. A shop! That would be an answer. Her old dream might not be such a bad one, after all. And weren't the Wallingfords themselves shopkeepers, when it came to that?*

Thinking of a shop made Lily think of her little nest egg, carefully saved through all these years at the Wallingford house, nearly fifty dollars it was now. Maybe her dream of a little shop could come true after all! Lily had never confided this dream to Susie, or to anyone since Fran had up and gone to work in Brooklyn Heights. Fran! How long ago that seemed. Well, sure and it was long ago. Three years now, come June, she'd been in the Wallingfords' employ.

Lily drifted off to sleep in a haze of doubts and hopes that seemed to advance and recede, shimmering, all silvery, as if reflected in that old French mirror that someone had given Miss Marianne as a wedding present. And her last thought before sleeping was a warm and happy one: *Master Jack thinks I'm pretty!*

Mrs. Wallingford smiled the smile of a tired but victorious general.

"My dear," she said to Lily, who knelt pinning the train of the mauve satin gown her mistress would wear at the reception, "if we survive this wedding, we can survive anything."

"Surely, madame, it will be a grand day for the Wallingfords."

"I hope so, Lily. I surely hope so."

The great day was only a week away now, and it seemed

to Lily that no anthill or hive of bees could have been busier than the Wallingford mansion, both above and below stairs. For months the plans had fluctuated on a wild scale that ranged from merely lavish to downright imperial. Finally the guest list had been frozen at one hundred, the maximum number that Louise calculated could be fed a truly deluxe eleven-course supper following the reception. The limited number appealed to Mrs. Wallingford's newly heightened sense of exclusivity. Let all of New York wonder who'd be asked! Let them dream of invitations to the most celebrated wedding of the year! Mrs. W. frankly gloried in it, drank it like some nectar of the gods. How little had she dreamed, waiting upon some of the very dowagers who now sought her company, helping John Wallingford build the Emporium to its present state of physical and financial splendor, that her wildest dreams of social achievement would be realized and—yes!—even surpassed. For this day, this wedding was her achievement, solid and real as any marble building a man might erect, negotiable as gold and diamonds, a landmark clear as anything printed on a map.

Tonight, Lily knew, was a grand ball given by young Mrs. Astor for the betrothed couple. A ball given in Marianne Wallingford's honor, and by an Astor! They'd all be there, and in their newest and most impressive finery. Miss Marianne would wear her new gown of emerald-green silk moiré with its breathtakingly low-cut bodice specially designed to set off the ancestral emerald-and-diamond necklace Baron West had presented, as an engagement gift, eighteen flawless round-cut emeralds drowning in diamonds, and the green stones big as robins' eggs, priceless, as Mrs. W. herself said, who surely had reason to know about such things. There'd be diamonds in Miss Marianne's hair, too, for Lily herself would arrange it, and more diamonds upon her wrists and fingers. And her mother would glitter only slightly less, for Marianne was to be the star attraction of the ball, even though the triumph was rightly accorded to Mrs. John Wallingford, barons being prized only a whisper less than dukes of the realm. All the family would be out, then, and in an extra burst of generosity Mrs. W. had decreed it would be a servants' holiday too, they'd all been working so hard lately. For three weeks now, special guards had been engaged to protect the wedding gifts. The event had gotten so much publicity the Wallingfords feared for robbers. So the guards would remain, and the footmen, and all the rest of the staff were free to do as they liked.

Lily found herself with nothing to do, and nothing she wanted to do. Susie had a new lover, a footman who worked three blocks away. She took advantage of this unexpected holiday to go sparking and larking with Freddie, for that was the boy's name. Lily had never met the estimable Freddie, but from the sound of him, he was Patrick all over again, a dashing lad with a roving eye and a gift for useful promises. Still, he lit a glow in Susie's eye that Lily hadn't seen there for almost a year now, and who was to begrudge the girl her fling? Surely not Lily Malone. But the novelty of the event had worn off now, and for Lily the wedding was but another great chore to get over and done with as best she could.

Lily fixed herself a cold supper from Louise's amply stocked larder, read Mr. Groome's newspaper, and decided to finish up a gown she was letting out for Mrs. Wallingford, who seemed to grow ever more plump as her social horizons expanded. The kitchen clock read nine. The gown was in Mrs. W.'s room. Lily climbed the back stairs and opened the door in the paneling that led to the great marble hallway.

The hall was silent, dimly lit, an occasional gas light flickering off the highly polished marble, dancing on the gilt of the railings. For an instant Lily thought the dark figure standing at the railing was one of the statues. But no! There was no statue there. The figure moved. He was coming toward her. Lily froze, all set to scream. A robber. Just as they'd feared. Knowing the house would be empty. They'd kill her for sure! She stood stiff and quiet as the marble statues themselves, praying to all the saints he wouldn't see her, trying with every atom of her being to make herself invisible. The words came at her out of the darkness.

"It's only me, Lily. Don't be frightened." Jack Wallingford walked up to her, silent in his carpet slippers. He was wearing everyday clothes, an open shirt with no tie, and a heavily embroidered smoking jacket of wine-colored silk with red and blue Chinese dragons chasing each other across his chest and right around his back.

"Thank goodness, sir!" Lily almost fainted with relief, for truly she had thought her time had come. "I thought it was robbers."

He laughed. "Well, God knows there's enough to rob, isn't there?"

"Sure and there is, sir. Are ye not going to the ball, then?"

He looked at her across the shadows with a look of bottomless despair. When his voice came, it was more like a gasp, like something ripped out of him by force.

"No, Lily, I didn't feel up to it."

"Are you not well, sir? Can I be getting anything for you?"

"Ah, that's kind of you. No . . . yes! There is something. Come with me, Lily."

Obediently, and not really thinking about it, she followed him up the marble stairs, stairs she hardly used day in and day out, to the third floor, where his rooms were, and his sister's rooms. Lily knew the rooms, although her new duties as Mrs. Wallingford's personal maid no longer required her to clean them. Jack had a small sitting room with a fire, a bedroom, and a dressing room that included a real bathroom, with heated running water and a genuine toilet! That was a marvel to Lily, for backstairs they all used washstands and chamber pots, and many had been the chamber pots that Lily had emptied in her first year at the Wallingfords'.

The house seemed to grow more quiet as they climbed the stairs. Jack said nothing, but merely opened the door to his rooms and stood politely aside as she entered.

There was a small coal fire glowing in the hearth. The brass fender gleamed from continuous polishing. There was a small leather Chesterfield sofa, deeply tufted and inviting, and two wing chairs covered in old green tapestry, all leaves and birds and flowers. A small mahogany table held a decanter that was cut like diamonds, and an amber fluid, and several small glasses. He motioned to a chair.

"Sit down, Lily."

She said nothing, but only sat, primly, on the edge of the big soft wing chair, poised for flight. Jack picked up the decanter and poured two glasses full. He handed one to Lily. She looked up at him doubtfully. No member of the family had ever offered her a drink before.

"Oh, sir, I couldn't, thank you very much."

"Don't be silly. You could and you shall. After all, Lily, it's the old gent's finest cognac."

He grinned, and something in her responded to the deviltry in him. There was Fergy's grin, to the life. Well, what harm was there, really? Lily didn't like strong spirits, nor beer either. Still, she lifted the glass.

"Cheers. Tonight we celebrate a great and noble event, Lily."

"And what would that be, sir?"

"Aha! What every New York mother dreams of. Tonight, Lily, we celebrate the grand and solemn launching of my sister's career as a certified prostitute."

"Sir! You can't mean it."

Lily looked at him, deeply shocked. *He must be joking!* But there was a dangerous look to him that told her he was deadly serious.

"If only I didn't. If only and only and only." He lifted his glass so that the firelight danced through the amber-colored brandy. Then he drank the whole glass off in one swallow.

"You know, of course, what a prostitute is, Lily?"

"Yes, sir, and more's the pity."

"Sells herself, that's what. Well, that's just what we seem to have here, a very fancy whorehouse, and Miss Marianne Wallingford the star attraction."

"That's not true, sir. I can't hear you say it."

Lily stood and put down her glass, untouched, and turned to the door. Crazy, that's what he was, downright loony. Suddenly her hand was caught and held by his hand, and she was surprised at the strength in him.

"No, Lily. Stay. Hear me out. I'll fair go mad if I don't have someone to talk to. Will you do that for me?"

It was a plea more than a command, the voice of a small boy lost without hope of finding himself, and something in that little boy's voice struck an immediate response in Lily. Slowly she sat down again, sat a little farther back in the chair now, and picked up the glass and drank a tiny sip. The cognac first burned, then numbed her tongue, then warmed her throat, hurting and pleasing all at once. She waited.

"It's a business arrangement, pure and simple. His title for Marianne's money. There's no love in it, Lily, only surface and show and good old-fashioned hypocrisy. Why, the buggering baron doesn't even like girls, did you know that? Little boys are his style, the bastard."

Lily sat there as if in a dream, warmed by the fire on the outside, and by the cognac inside. *He truly loves his sister,* she thought, *or else he wouldn't care so very much. And maybe what he says is true, after all. Maybe she is no better than a common hooker.* The thought was so entirely new to Lily that it shocked her as much as it pleased her. In God's eyes, after all, what would be the difference? Selling yourself was selling yourself, and if there was a marriage ceremony involved, did that truly make a difference? Pieces of paper changed hands between common street girls and their clients too. Maybe it was different if a fine girl like Miss Marianne had only one customer, and was married to him. Still and all, to marry without love, wasn't that a sin? Or shouldn't it be? She thought of Susie, generous with her love and with her body. And was Susie sinning, and who made one set of rules for fine folk and another for the rest of us?

It was confusing, intoxicating, delicious. She took another cautious sip of the brandy.

"Does she know that, sir? Miss Marianne, I mean."

"Ha! She knew it from the first. A very cool number is our little Marianne. Not going to let a small thing like perversion stand in her way, not when there's a barony at stake. They have it all worked out between them, don't you see? There's the horror of it. Little baronets will appear from time to time, and no one's going to question too closely who's the proud papa, if you take my meaning. And dear Clarence will find his usual consolations with the footmen and the stable lads. A perfect marriage, that one. With the bloody queen smiling benignly down on all of it. I thought of killing her, Lily."

"You wouldn't!"

"No, you're right. I wouldn't. A stronger man might, but not me, not good old Jack Wallingford, amateur black sheep and certified bounder!"

He filled his glass again, and again he drained it. Yet Jack didn't look drunk or act it. Lily said nothing, and looked down at her own glass, and turned it nervously, wishing that she had an answer for his unanswerable problem. She could feel the resentment in him, the sense of hopelessness. So this was why he hadn't gone to Mrs. Astor's ball! She thought of how they'd talked about the possibility of telling Patrick's tale about the baron to Groome, or someone, and how they'd decided not to. A good decision, or so it seemed. Fat lot of help that would have been, with the deal already being made, so to speak.

Lily felt his eyes on her, burning. She looked at him, into his eyes, and it was like looking down the black and deadly barrels of twin dueling pistols.

"Have you ever been in love, Lily?"

"No, sir."

"You will, though, one day. You'll make someone very happy."

She shivered a little then, although there was no draft. He stood up then, smiling, and walked to her chair, and stood behind it, and put his hands upon her shoulders. She didn't want him to be touching her, but there was nothing threatening in this. This was gentle. His hands moved slowly on her shoulders. She felt herself relaxing, felt the warmth of the fire, and the cognac, and another, subtler warmth, unaccustomed, growing.

"Love," he said very slowly, softer than she ever remembered hearing his voice, "should be a question of sharing."

Lily closed her eyes and thought of Brooks Chaffee. Jack Wallingford's friend. If this were Brooks Chaffee! Somehow, in ways she could never quite analyze, being so close to Jack had become a way of being closer to his friend. These hands, which had touched Chaffee's hands, these hands moving upon her shoulders, touching her neck, comforting, making her feel softer, somehow, making her very head spin with the wonder of it: what was happening, and should she let it go on?

For a moment the silence continued, and only the hiss and sputter of coal in the hearth interrupted a quiet so dense it seemed to reach from the stars in heaven all the way down through the center of the earth. She was used to his hands on her shoulder now, and when they stopped their gentle stroking, Lily was glad of the weight and warmth of them, just resting there, quiet as the night.

Then he kissed her neck, and she shivered to her toes.

Lily moved, half from surprise, half from the urge to run away. And he kissed her again, covered her throat with kisses. Jack moved around to the front of the big chair then, and Lily felt herself rising, being lifted from the chair, his arms around her, and his lips still kissing, finding her own lips now, holding her tight and lifting and stroking her too, all at once, and still kissing, and carrying her out of the sitting room. She tried to speak and could not, his mouth on her mouth.

Lily squirmed under his touch, relaxed, began to struggle, and could not. She feared the violence in him, sensed danger building, and felt pleasure too, strange pleasures she had not known before, nor dared think of, and it seemed as though she were being swept away down some great dark river against which it was useless to struggle, and that the river, this mighty dark secret force, was her fate, and although the place it was taking her might be wild and mysterious, it was a better place than she had been, and she would find her destiny on its forbidden shores.

His bedroom was dark, and darkly furnished. One small gas jet flickered behind a frosted globe. She looked up at him, frightened. The urgency in him was hot and real as a blast from a furnace door. Gently he set her on the feather bed. His fingers found the row of buttons at the back of her dress.

"Sir!"

Lily intended to scream, but the word came out softly.

"Help me, Lily, I'll fair go mad if you don't."

Help him! She sensed the desperation in him, the wild animal trying to claw its way out of a cage. Help him, indeed! It was happening so fast. Jack knelt, unfastened her shoes, gently lifted her, and she felt no more able to resist him than a rag doll, and hated herself for it, for the weakness. And if she screamed, who was to hear her? He could say she'd up and seduced him, if he liked, and who'd take her word against his, heir to the Wallingfords, the young master? But even in her panic, and even in the sure knowledge that he was using her, Lily felt something else; new and unsettling emotions followed close behind her fear, and these emotions were something very like pleasure and anticipation. So this was what all the fuss was for! Jack said nothing now, and she could hear his breathing, coming louder. The bedroom was warm, and for an instant Lily hardly realized he'd got her shift off too, and she was baby-naked now and helpless. Again she wanted to scream, opened her mouth, only to have it instantly covered by his mouth, rougher now, more urgent, and his hands seemed to be everywhere now, stroking, soothing, telling her in ways he had no words to describe that no harm would come of this adventure. He held her very close now, and Lily could feel her shallow breasts tight against the embroidery of his Chinese robe. And all at once the robe was gone and his other clothes too, and her skin was touching his skin and Lily felt, more than she could see in the darkness, how his smooth skin was riding the hard muscles underneath, and more hair on him than she would have thought, and the strength in him surprised her too, he not being a working lad, after all. Jack lifted her, and she hardly noticed that, too much else was happening, and now Lily felt the heavy silk of the bedcover underneath her, and his hands, still busy, and his mouth, busier still, and finally in one quick sharp moment it was done, he was inside her, stroking still, still urgent, with pain and sudden joy mingling unforgettably.

Lily felt herself trembling as though she had been dropped naked in a snowbank, and her whole body seemed to contract, jolted, wrapped itself around him as her breath escaped in one long sharp sigh. It was only then, and for the first time, that she kissed him.

For a moment that may have been an hour they lay still, entwined, at peace. He said her name, and it came to her like a stranger's name, for he said it almost like a prayer.

"Lily . . . Lily . . . Lily . . . I truly did not know that . . . oh, God! you were a virgin!"

She lay in silence before answering, her body a blending of

pleasure and pain, and confusion in her heart. Lily spoke softly:

"It's all right, sir."

"Jack is my name, Lily."

"Yes, sir."

"Can you forgive me, Lily? I meant no harm. It's just that suddenly I felt so lonely tonight, as though I were the last man in the world, and only you could make me feel human again."

No, she thought, *you're not the last man, not by far, nor the first, either, it's a sure thing you're not Brooks Chaffee, but you're not a stableboy, either.* She looked at him, saying nothing, and their eyes met in the shadowed room. *It could have been worse*, she thought in the backwash of her passion. *It could have been worse.*

Lily smiled then, a small and secret smile. *So I am not to be struck dead! The angels are probably weeping for me right now, for my sins, sins of the flesh they are, maybe that's the noise I hear, that faint whisper, the sound of angels' tears falling softly on clouds.* But the sound was only Jack stirring on the silk bedcover, touching her with all the length of his body, raising himself on one elbow now, looking close in her eyes.

"You're a fine girl, Lily. Say you don't hate me."

She did not answer him at once, for this was a new thought to Lily, that she could even entertain the possibility of hating one so rich and so great in the world as Master Jack, that he would care was a shock to her. Finally she spoke.

"A lie it would be if I said I loved you, sir. But no, nor do I hate. It happened . . . between us. I could have screamed, or run, and did not. You never forced me."

There was a heavy pause, and he said nothing to fill it. Lily went on. "It may be better, truly, 'twas you, sir, than some others I could think of."

He kissed her then, and the loving began again. This time for Lily, it was more discovery than shock, more pleasure than pain. Two hours passed quickly. Three times more they made love. She found Jack gentle and strong in near-equal measure, now ruthless, desperate, now weak, pleading. It was a strange and heady mixture, like some mysterious but delectable sauce Louise might make. And always there was the thrill of danger, the wild breath of wickedness, the stimulating fear of discovery. Twenty, he was, not much more than two years older than she, but in lovemaking far older still. A distant church struck twelve. She sat up.

"I must go."

"Stay, Lily."

"Oh, please, sir . . . for I'll be ruined!"

"Not while I live."

Yes, she thought, *how easy the promises come to your lips, Mr. Jack.* But Lily smiled to herself as she dressed quickly in the dark, thinking of where those lips had been, of how she'd felt. A devil he might be, but a fine devil was Mr. Jack Wallingford. She buttoned the last button and looked in a glass to fix her hair. He appeared in the glass behind her, naked as one of his father's marble statues. Lily stood still as his arms reached out from behind and circled her. The dark head came down, and one last time he kissed her throat.

"You'll come to me again, Lily?"

He wants me! No one ever wanted me before. Lily thought of Brooks Chaffee. And she paused a moment before answering: "If you'd have me, sir."

"I could ask no greater honor."

You could tell no bigger lies, she thought, unable to ignore the comical aspects of her situation even while she wanted to believe him as much as she ever wanted to believe anything. She turned, and looked up at him, and smiled gently, as if to say good-bye forever.

"Thank you, dear Lily."

"Good night, sir."

"Jack."

"Mr. Jack, then."

He laughed, and kissed her hard, and she was gone.

The marble hall was just as empty now, after midnight, as it had been three hours earlier, a lifetime earlier. Lily retraced her steps, down the hall and down the stairs, through the secret door in the paneling, and back to the servants' quarters.

Her little room looked exactly as it always had looked. Susie was still out somewhere with her footman. Lily took her clothes off and washed herself and slipped into her cotton nightgown. Before she went to bed, Lily paused in front of the small round looking glass that was nailed to the back of the bedroom door. All she could see was her head, but that was enough.

The same green eyes she had always known looked back at her from the slightly rippled glass. Her hair was just as red as it had been that morning, and there were no telltale signs of sin and corruption on the pale smooth skin of her face. *Had God ignored her, then? Were so many servant girls being ruined this night that one more was not to be counted?* As she stood there gravely contemplating her face in the mirror, Lily learned a great secret. *If she told no one, no one would know.* Susie, irrepressible, could never be told, for to tell a thing to Susie McGlynn was to tell it to the world. And who else was there? Not a soul.

So here I am, she thought, *a fallen woman. So this is how it happens, and this is how it feels afterward. No wonder there were so many fallen women, and no wonder so many of them seemed to enjoy it!*

She climbed into her narrow little bed then, and closed her eyes, and could not sleep. Lily thought of this night, of Jack, of how he looked and what he did, and why she liked it, even though she knew perfectly well she did not love the boy, barely knew him, hadn't even liked him much, not until tonight, not until he'd told her how he felt about his sister's marriage to the baron. There was something in Mr. Jack, for all his deviltry. He did care, he did have a sense of honor, more or less, he was well and deeply shocked by the hypocrisy he found even within his very own family, right here in this mansion. And what did he care for her, for Lily? Had he even said, lying, that he loved her? No. He never had said that. Well, maybe there was a strange kind of honor even there, in the fact that he hadn't lied. *"Help me, Lily,"* he'd asked, as though she could give him some rare kind of medicine that might ease the dreadful pain within him.

Lily turned, sleepless, on the bed. She felt tired, a good kind of tiredness, and there was a lingering glow, a warmth that was not from Jack's fire or his brandy, maybe even not from his lovemaking. She fell asleep smiling.

She woke the next morning to discover that God had continued to spare her. Getting dressed, Lily heard of Susie's adventures in greater detail than perhaps was necessary, but Lily smiled and encouraged her friend in the telling, and so learned the delicious and hitherto unknown pleasures of having a real secret, something that, were it known, would cause no end of excitement, consternation, and . . . what?

For Lily hadn't thought out the logical end of her adventure with Jack Wallingford. The thing had come too fast, and the surprise and excitement, the shock and revelation of it had drugged her, had slowed her usually quick wits. And where would it lead her, after all?

Stories of ruined servant girls were common as dirt. Lily

knew any number of them herself, and anyone who'd been in service could add dozens more. Slender might be the rewards of virtue, and yet the swift hand of retribution for straying could seldom be stayed. Time and again, girls who'd earned a bad name—Tess of the stolen knives, for instance—were turned into the streets with no more than the clothes on their back, and lucky they'd be not to have the police set on them. And what lay ahead for a girl turned out with no reference? Dark thoughts filled Lily's head as she went about her duties that day.

Mrs. Wallingford was filled with gossip about the Astors' ball, and Lily counted herself lucky that there were a thousand things for her to attend to, the wedding being next week and coming at them like a runaway fire engine too. She didn't see Mr. Jack that day, or the next, but Lily thought about him often, and how strange it had been, how very like an accident, a tree falling in a storm maybe, a bolt from the sky. For surely he hadn't planned the thing, no more had she. Well she could have gone out gadding that night, and him too, well they might never have met in the lonely hallway, or him inviting her to hear his troubles. Or any of it.

So Lily couldn't blame Jack Wallingford any more than she blamed herself. There was fatalism enough in her to accept what happened as a fact and go on from there.

It was the question of going on that drove her all but mad.

Would there be any going on, or was it all done and finished already? And what had the fine young master felt, waking up that next morning? Disgusted, maybe, to have showed himself so plain, and to his mother's own serving maid. Or maybe—worse—he'd forgotten her already. Maybe Jack had so many girls he could hardly tell one from the other, maybe it was all a fine sport for him, one here, there another, and after a time you don't even keep the score. On the third day she decided he was having no more to do with her, and Lily couldn't find it in herself to blame him.

When Mrs. Wallingford herself asked Lily to go up to her son's rooms, the girl almost fainted dead away.

"The silly boy has torn something, Lily, maybe you can fix it for him."

She curtsied and turned and fairly flew up the marble staircase.

It was late afternoon on the Thursday before the Saturday on which Miss Marianne would become the Baroness West of Westover. Lily knocked on the big walnut door. He opened it, smiling, wearing the Chinese robe.

"Ah, Lily." Jack looked to the left and the right, and ushered her in. Then he closed the door and bolted it. He turned and came close to her, but made no move to touch her or kiss her.

"It's damned awkward, you see, Lily, because there's hardly a way I can get a message to you without people catching on. We'll have to work something out. I've done nothing but think of you since the other night. Do you hate me, Lily?"

"No, sir."

So he had remembered. She did mean something to him, however shameful. Lily blushed and looked at the floor. He reached out then with one hand and lifted her chin until she was looking into his eyes. They were dark as ever, but not so dangerous now. And he smiled, and kissed her.

"I will count it a happy day when you stop calling me 'sir.'"

Then his arms were around her again, and she was being carried into his bedroom again, and the loving began again. This time she couldn't stay. She dressed, and straightened her hair, and turned to him. Jack lay where she'd left him, on his bed, naked and smiling.

"It isn't easy to share you, Lily, not even with my own mother."

"Who'll be wondering where I am."

"Is there a clock in the servants' hall?"

"There is."

"Can you come to me tonight at nine?"

Lily closed her eyes for an instant. She could hear the angels weeping. Then she looked at him: "I can try."

"I'll be a desperate fellow if you don't."

"Your mother said you'd torn something."

He got up, smiling still, and picked up the Chinese robe from where he'd let it slide to the floor. Then Jack took one of its fine shimmering silken sleeves and tore it half away from the shoulder. It was a fine robe, well-sewn, and it had him straining like a common bricklayer before it tore. Jack handed the damaged robe to Lily.

"If you deliver it in person, Lily, you will not regret it."

She looked at him and thought how he'd described his own sister. *He thinks we're all alike, that we're all for sale, hookers every one.* Lily flushed with the insult of it. *He thinks I'd sell myself.*

"I ask for nothing, sir."

"Well do I know that, Lily. It's part of your charm."

He laughed then, and she could not be angry with him. And he kissed her, and Lily could feel the passion stirring in him, and thought of Susie's words: "in a passionate condition." Sure and Mr. Jack was getting himself into a passionate condition, and the fact of it partly amused Lily and also frightened her, for here were forces at work which she little understood, forces she might never be able to control, that could easily destroy them both.

She turned from him and walked quickly to the door. Jack's parting words rang in her head with the lasting resonance of a clarion: *"You're beautiful, Lily, my Lily."*

Lily delivered his robe, in person, a few minutes after nine that night.

⊸⊰ 12 ⊱⊷

Lily was surprised at how little she felt the excitement of Marianne Wallingford's wedding day when at last it came. She went to the church with Susie, for all of the servants had been invited, and the church was so filled with flowers they could hardly see the bride and her bridegroom, except as tiny figures far away. And as she heard the lovely music and smelled the fine flowers, and as the muted echo of Marianne's marriage vows came floating through the hallowed air to her ears, Lily found herself thinking of Jack, and his bitterness about the great event.

Yet, if you could believe the New York newspapers, this was the grandest thing to happen since who could say when. It seemed a public event, for Marianne's wedding burst upon the New York social scene like all the fireworks of a dozen Fourths of July, sudden and spectacular and, Lily guessed, as quickly forgotten.

On the day after the wedding, Jack went back to Yale.

There was no way for him to write her, no way for her to visit him in New Haven, even had he asked her to, which he did not. Lily went about her normal duties in the normal way, joked with Susie, helped Miss Marianne pack for her wedding trip to Italy. The routine of the great house protected Lily, for it kept her busy, gave her less time to think.

When she did think of Jack, it was not with love or hatred. She thought of him as an event, an act of nature and unavoidable, like a great summer storm. She thought of Jack's lovemaking, and recalled it warmly. And Lily thought of Brooks Chaffee, too, and in a way that was so laden with admiration and wonder that in the vision in her heart Brooks was on some exalted plane far above and beyond the everyday grappling and tumbling and the joys and juices of making love. Brooks was less a man to Lily than a golden and unapproachable deity, and the fact that she knew him not at all, but to look at, amplified her estimation of his virtues while concealing any human failings he might have.

The winter of 1855 was bitterly cold, and spring crept in tentatively. March arrived unobserved, for all the change it wrought in the icy cold: there was nary a warm breeze nor a crocus. The bitter winds of winter touched Lily whenever she left the house, and they seemed to have invaded her very soul too, for Jack Wallingford had slipped out of her life with the quickness and skill of a practiced thief. Sometimes Lily thought she had dreamed their few times together, that his touch and his kisses and the fine words he spoke were no more than the result of some fever on her brain.

Then one day at the end of March Jack Wallingford came home.

Lily was fixing Mrs. Wallingford's hair, and she was just about to insert a diamond pin into the heaps of lacquered curls when the news dropped on her like a hurled stone, stunning and without warning: "Yes, he'll be with us for a few weeks, dear boy. He's all I have left, Lily, now that Marianne's off and away."

Lily smothered a gasp and nearly stabbed her mistress through the skull with the point of the big diamond brooch, a bouquet of diamond flowers in the French style, each stone set on springs, to quiver with any movement. Lily concentrated on the pin, in silence: the diamonds danced before her eyes, shimmering, coming into focus and then turning all blurred. Lily realized that she was blinking back tears, and could hardly explain why.

For her to weep over Jack Wallingford! Ma would be spinning in her grave.

She decided right then to make no move, to communicate not at all. Maybe he had forgotten her, and maybe that would be for the best. It had been a temporary madness, like a sudden fever, and she had been cautious and calm as any millpond ever since the lad had taken himself back to college, where, after all, he belonged. And with Brooks Chaffee.

Lily put Chaffee out of her mind and tried to imagine Jack's life at New Haven. As if there'd be a serving wench or a girl of the town quick enough to escape his hot hands! But thinking of Jack made her think of his roommate, and to do that suddenly became unbearable.

Automatically, glad that she had been nearly finished with Mrs. W.'s hair when the news came, Lily completed the job and let her mistress admire the results in her triple-faced dressing-table mirror. To Lily's eye she looked ridiculous, something between a Christmas tree and one of Louise's French whipped-cream desserts, but it was the fashion, no

[173]

one could say it was not, and Lily had grown skillful at copying the latest hairstyles from the illustrated Paris fashion papers that arrived by clipper ship every week.

Mrs. John Wallingford might be nearly as wide as she was high, she might move with a kind of swaying, waddling motion like a duck out of water, but when she swayed, a hundred thousand dollars' worth of jewels swayed with her, signaling that here went Mrs. John Frederick Wallingford of the Fifth Avenue Wallingfords, mother of the Baroness West.

Mrs. Wallingford stood up, smiled at herself in the mirror, then turned and smiled at Lily. Her eyes were bright and hard as small black buttons, and no one would ever call her a beauty. Her son had as much as called her a procuress.

She reached for her maribou fan, which had been specially dyed in Paris to match the peacock blue of the heavily reembroidered brocade of her gown, a blue so violent Lily herself would have shied away from it, a blue that seemed to almost burn the eyes. Mrs. Wallingford waved the fan with something like a graceful motion, and turned to the enormous gilt-framed mirror that filled the wall at the foot of her bed, and struck a pose that reminded Lily of some of the posters she had seen outside the theaters where some grand tragedy might be playing: Mrs. Wallingford's plump and powdered elbow angled up, a shallow angle, true, for she was so plump now that it was getting to be an effort to raise her arms at all. But up went the elbow, and the fan half-hid her face. What was left were cascades of sapphires on her neck, a tiara above, and the explosion of blue brocade that was the gown itself.

"Oh, Lily," she said in the voice of a naughty little girl, "spring is in the air tonight, can't you just feel it all around us?"

"Yes, madame, it does promise to be a fine night."

"Whatever would I do without you, Lily?"

"I'm sure you'd find someone else, ma'am."

"But not like my Lily." She giggled.

Lily curtsied then, and turned, and left the room.

Brooks Chaffee stood still as a hunter stalking deer, sheltered by one of the huge potted palms that divided the dancing area of old Mrs. Vanderbilt's ballroom from the saloon, transfixed by the sound of a girl's laughter.

Caroline Ledoux stood on the other side of the palm-tree forest, gaily juggling the earnest attentions of four young men.

Brooks was glad, after all, that he'd come tonight. There had been four invitations on his dressing table, all for this evening, and he'd chosen Mrs. Vanderbilt's, not for the glitter of her name, for the Chaffees were sought after, not seekers, and not because Mrs. Vanderbilt was some sort of distant cousin on his mother's side—Brooks could never remember the exact connection—and surely not for the food or the music, which were dubious at best. Brooks had come to the great Italian Gothic pile of a mansion on Fifth Avenue tonight simply because Jack Wallingford was coming too.

And Jack had introduced him to Caroline Ledoux.

And meeting Caroline was like taking a high dive into a sea of ice-cold champagne. Brooks knew in his bones that this astonishingly beautiful stranger would change his life permanently and unalterably.

Brooks knew girls, and loved them, and relished the adventure of being loved back, often to a degree that became irritating. He knew whores and heiresses, girls of great beauty and wit, and girls who were just plain fun to be with. But he'd never known anyone like Caroline. *You're twenty already, Chaffee, and face up to it, you have never truly been in love.* Brooks had often reprimanded himself for that. It was fashionable to be in love. Most young men he knew were constantly traversing the heights—and depths—of romance, scampering gypsies of the heart, swearing eternal passion five times a month, always to a new girl, always for the last time. It was comical, to be sure, and all the more so because the lovers took themselves so seriously, quite lost their sense of humor on the subject, would look at Chaffee or Jack Wallingford with great tragic eyes and tell the laughing cynics they would never understand. Brooks had tried to fall in love, had learned to give a very convincing imitation of being in love, and elicited all the right responses from any number of desirable girls. But he never fooled himself. To be in love! To be totally, deeply, damn-all in love, in love with all the strings cut, dancing on a high wire without a net, riding the runaway horses of love, scaling heights of passion from which the view was rare and dazzling and visible to nobody else—all of these things had been denied Brooks Chaffee, and he wished for them as a child longs for Christmas in July. He wanted the dazzle and risk of it, the losing of self in someone else, the exhausting climb of it, the dizzying plunge. Brooks wanted sex at its most rhapsodic, gilt and certified and framed by love, a glory to cherish for all the world to see.

And tonight it had happened!

He was afraid to examine this sudden miracle for fear it would vanish, perfect and fragile as a snowflake on your fingertip, elusive, unforgettable, and gone as you gasp at the wonder of it.

Caroline had walked into the Vanderbilt drawing room alone, dressed all in white, her long raven-dark hair combed simply, unadorned, as a child might wear it. The white dress, modestly cut, white gloves, and her only jewels simple pearl studs at each ear.

The sound and rhythm of the great drawing room changed instantly: the girl had such power in her. There was a sudden pause in the chatter, then a ripple of whispered questions, comments, suppositions. Who in the world was she? Brooks himself had contributed to the effect. Jack, luckily, was at his elbow by the punch bowl. You could count on Jack to know everything about everybody, especially everybody feminine.

Jack laughed at his chum, and for the first time in months Brooks felt annoyed because of the ribbing. And even this was a new and welcome experience, for it was the girl who caused his anger, not Jack.

"That my dear simpleton, is the notorious Caroline Ledoux."

"Why notorious? And who are the Ledouxes?"

Jack laughed again. "Notorious, sport, because New York is a tiny little small town whose old wives have not much better to do than sit around the fire gossiping. Caroline's a perfectly respectable little piece—a right dazzler, my sainted brother-in-law might call her—and the Ledouxes are very, very rich and respectable New Orleans cotton brokers. Caroline is considered quite racy in certain circles because she has been known from time to time to go out in the afternoons unattended, quite often to the old man's store, I've been told, and you know what a scarlet adventuress that makes a girl."

Now Brooks shared his friend's laughter. The standards of their parents' generation were as restrictive as the whalebone cages that gripped their middles. You'd have to be dead in your box with a lily before you met their expectations.

Jack Wallingford brought his friend right across the room to her. Brooks took her hand, and even through the fine kidskin glove he felt a shock of emotion. Her voice was like the look of her, dark and velvet soft and rippling with the distant music of someplace warmer, somewhere where it was always midnight, where gaiety and danger performed ancient dances in the moonlight, a place where a man could easily lose his heart, or his mind, or both.

"It's a right pleasure, Mr. Chaffee."

"Will you be in New York long, Miss Ledoux?"

"I'm not sure."

Mrs. Vanderbilt came up to them then, and claimed Caroline, and took her away. Brooks could cheerfully have shot the old lady dead. It had been the most conventional of greetings. Simple to banality. *Then why are you sweating, you dunce? What's that roaring in your ears? Do we notice a certain commotion in the loins, Chaffee, or do you carry a mouse in your pocket? And in Mrs. Vanderbilt's bloody drawing room, for shame!* He turned, blushing still, and followed her with his eyes. As did half the room, the masculine half, while most of the ladies pretended to ignore the new arrival. Well they might try. Caroline made even the prettiest of them look cheap, overdressed, too fussy. Jack was right. New York was a small town. Brooks surveyed the big room with new awareness. He'd known most of the people here, or their families, all his life. He was related to half of them by blood, and to all of them by position. The girls and their mothers were look-alike editions who slavishly read the same Paris magazines, who copied the same elaborate gowns and hairstyles, who draped themselves in ropes of jewels like Christmas trees, whose main occupation was cementing the thick and unyielding walls of the social fortress they had built for themselves.

Like all fortresses, Brooks suddenly realized, it was also a prison for the people inside.

Only when Jack touched his arm did Brooks Chaffee drift back to reality.

"You're making a spectacle of yourself, old chap," said Jack quietly. "The Moral Rearmament Society would most decidedly not approve."

Jack took his friend's arm and led him to a quiet corner of the huge room. Finally Brooks was able to speak. He felt as though he'd been kicked by a horse, dazed, not sure of himself.

"Tell me about her."

It was the plea of a dying man.

"In truth, there's not a whole lot I know. She's about our age—possibly a shade older. Only child. Staying with her aunt. Mrs. Farragut's her name. It's probably a fair guess that Caroline's husband-hunting, but what girl isn't?"

"How well do you know her?" Brooks asked this hesitantly,

for well he knew that Jack would swive a snake if it would hold still for him, and if Caroline had indulged in any amours with Wallingford, Brooks wasn't sure he wanted to know about it.

Again Jack laughed. "You really flatter me, Brooksie. As far as I know—and that's pretty far—the lady is a pillar of virtue, more's the pity. Why? Are you planning a spot of debauchery and defloration?"

Once again Brooks felt the anger rising in him. But he smiled; this was too childish, the girl probably hadn't given him a second thought, there were dozens of young men in the room, including at least five Vanderbilts, who had far more to offer of money and charm than he.

"I think she's splendid, that's all."

"Well, you've got good taste. Splendid's just what she is. Makes you think a little Southern tour might not be altogether unrewarding, if Caroline's a sample of what they grow down among the magnolias and cotton blossoms."

Brooks drifted through the remainder of the evening like a man drugged. He coasted on his charm and on the good manners that were bred into him so thoroughly they had long since become automatic. A stranger might never have noticed a difference in his behavior. Jack Wallingford noticed, and grinned, and immediately forgot about it. Brooks hoped Caroline might notice him, changed or not, but he had no way of knowing what effect, if any, their meeting had caused in her.

All through the evening, through supper and the dancing afterward, and the midnight buffet, Caroline was surrounded by men. There were other very attractive women in the house, other centers of attention, but Caroline had a magnetism that would not be denied. *No wonder she likes to go out alone sometimes*, Brooks thought; *it's probably the only chance the poor creature gets!*

He stood now, behind the palm, lurking like a cutpurse, feeling an unaccustomed sense of guilt, as though he truly was up to some dark deed. There was nothing rational in this, no clever plan. He simply wanted to be near her, by any means, fair or foul. Eavesdropping from behind the shrubbery was definitely foul, by Brooks's own private code of conduct, yet there he was shamelessly doing it, and for all the world to see!

And wasn't this what he'd wanted, dreamed of, prayed for? This sweet pain, this happy dread, this unfamiliar sense of being quite ready to risk everything he owned or ever hoped to own on one toss of the dice with no markers? Brooks learned many things at Mrs. Vanderbilt's ball that night. He learned that there is such a thing as happiness, that happiness is a solid physical thing, an accountable treasure that waits for anyone who has the key, and that the key, for him, was a girl in white with bottomless dark eyes and a laugh that flowed and rippled through the night like all the moon-gilt Southern rivers of a poet's dreaming.

It had become a habit with Brooks Chaffee to do a thing expertly or not at all, and now that moment seemed ripe to fall in love, he expected nothing less than that the love would be total, true, and forever, and that it would be returned in the spirit that gave it wings.

Fool, and all you've done is shake her by the hand, and once, for a minute!

Her voice curled around him, the laughter spiced with unspoken promises, the way good claret reminded him of any number of fruits and flowers more desirable than the homely grape. *You could bait traps with that laugh,* he thought, *and catch some very big game.*

It now seemed to Brooks that he'd wasted all of his twenty years. They had been spent without Caroline Ledoux and were therefore empty, worthless, to be discarded and forgotten. He sighed. The ball would soon be over, he'd be obliged to go out into the cold and inhospitable night, a night that surely would be darker because it contained no glimpse of Caroline.

He had never thought of himself as having any special fate, any all-consuming hopes or fears or urgent destiny. And she had changed this part of him too, had Caroline, and with one gaze from those eyes, one hint of a smile. Chaffee had a destiny now, and its name was Caroline. Brooks knew, every atom of his mind and body told him, commanded him, compelled him to dedicate his entire being, from this moment and forever, to the pursuit and capture of Caroline Ledoux.

Once again Jack's voice came to him as a shock, interrupting the dream. "Damn shame I'm not a pickpocket, Brooksie my lad, because you are prime material tonight. Is it the wine, or the lady, or have you just gone off your head altogether?"

"Hello. You're perfectly right, Jack. I've taken leave of my moorings. And I think you're to blame."

"For introducing you to the fair Ledoux? A pleasure, old chap, I'd do it anytime."

"Once was quite enough, thanks."

"I do believe she's got you."

"The question is, how do I get her?"

"I truly might be able to help you there, sport. My old gentleman is acquainted with her old gentleman, in trade, don't you know, terribly vulgar and all that, but I have heard Dad mention Mr. Ledoux. I'm fairly sure an introduction could be fixed up, if you're really going to be serious about it."

"Serious is the word for it. You'd do that? You are a friend, Jack. That would be splendid."

"It's as nothing, sport. Hell, and haven't I performed the introductions at Madame Duveen's? It's only fair an innocent lad like you should meet some of the gentry too, from time to time, so long as it doesn't go to your head, and that sort of thing."

Brooks laughed. Jack could always make him laugh, even when the object of the joke was Jack himself. Jack often blasted his family's social pretensions, and Brooks found that refreshing in this sea of social climbers who seemed to do nothing all day and all night but elbow each other aside in an eternal struggle to crowd into the right drawing rooms, like so many salmon fighting their way upstream to spawn and die.

They left Mrs. Vanderbilt's together, but this night Brooks turned down his friend's invitation to further adventures. Meeting Caroline had been adventure enough for Brooks, for that night and forever. Jack went rattling off in a cab, but Brooks walked the fifteen blocks down Fifth Avenue to Washington Square. It was after midnight, and the night was just as he'd feared: dark and inhospitable and empty of Caroline. As his bed would be empty of Caroline, and his breakfast table, and possibly even his life. But that was a prospect too terrible to contemplate, he mustn't think that way, for that way would be fatal to his dream, and maybe even to his life, for surely no life would be conceivable if it lacked her warmth, her beauty, and her laughter.

Brooks walked with long strides, his gloved hands thrust deep into the pockets of his greatcoat, looking neither right nor left, dreaming the dreams that only an untried heart can know, painting a future in shades that were richer and brighter and more sensuously alive than any pigment that ever touched palette or canvas.

Washington Square was a black hole in the night, ringed by gas lanterns whose points of yellow light only emphasized the greater darkness in the park, a darkness that Brooks knew would be echoed in his heart forever if he didn't win the affections of Caroline Ledoux, and quickly.

The Chaffee town house was usually a reassuring sight to Brooks, the soft brick of its walls and the simple white Grecian pillars of the portico quietly mocking the vulgarity of the nouveau-riche châteaux and palazzi and schlossen that were sprouting up the avenue like bloated mushrooms after a particularly long rain.

The house had a dignity all its own, and Brooks liked that, respected it, savored the understatement of the building and the family who lived there, who never felt they had to shout who they were or what they owned because everyone who mattered already knew these things, and everybody who didn't matter was best forgotten.

It was a small, snug, smug world, and Brooks had always found it very comfortable. Until tonight, when every part of his world had been shaken to its foundations and below. And the arriviste Wallingfords might be the means to his meeting the girl on a more familiar basis! How that would scandalize his mother. How that would delight him. He smiled then, climbing the nine white limestone steps to the white front door.

The gas light still glowed in the foyer. That meant Neddy must still be out. His older brother hadn't been at the Vanderbilts' tonight: vaguely, and only for a moment, Brooks wondered where Ned Chaffee had been. Now that Ned was graduated from New Haven, they hadn't been seeing each other as often as Brooks would have liked, for he fairly worshiped the older boy. Two years wasn't so much of a difference now that they were grown up, but as boys it had been vast, and Neddy had always been the hero, bigger and bolder and quicker and the apple of everyone's eye, for good reason. Brooks had always felt that he lived in Ned's shadow, but there was no tinge of jealousy in this; he accepted it as part of the natural order of things, and the boys had a special kind of friendship.

Maybe Neddy would know how to approach the courtship of Caroline. Brooks turned the key in the big brass lock. Tomorrow the campaign would begin in earnest. Tomorrow would be the start of a new life, a new Brooks Chaffee. Tomorrow! And Caroline. Caroline. Caroline. He rolled the word on his tongue like some fine confection. The name sang to him. Caroline! Everything that was rare, perfect, eternal, was Caroline. Love was Caroline. Dawn washing a Venetian canal with gold was Caroline, and the songs of birds and the music wind makes dancing through groves of spring blossoms. Caroline was light itself, and hope, and love. And Caroline would be his, or he'd die trying.

Brooks opened the door, locked it behind him, and climbed the familiar stairs to his room on the third floor. There he lit a candle and undressed, washed, and climbed into his bed. The last thing he thought of before sleep came, the first thing he'd know on waking, was the name, the look, the sound and the hope of her. Caroline!

Fate was named Caroline, and now he'd found her.

❧ 13 ❧

Lily looked at Jack Wallingford and wondered how to end it. Nearly a year had passed since that first night, just before Miss Marianne's wedding. And for all the charm in him, and the passion too, and the need he had for her, the affair had brought Lily nothing more than doubts and fears, for hadn't she refused all his gifts, and offers of money, and other, less specific hints of greater, more dangerous generosities to come? Lily hated the sly parts of it, the sneaking up back stairs at odd hours, the invented errands, the stolen moments, the grave risk to her position in the household.

And now he had invited her here! To this little suite of rooms in the small, comfortable hotel on West Sixteenth Street. At a glance, Lily knew what the rooms were for. *Here's where he takes his fancy women, and here am I, no better than they are, maybe worse!*

It was obviously more than a transient apartment, well-furnished with things Lily recognized from the Fifth Avenue mansion, and with small personal touches to make the hotel's furniture more homelike. A coal fire hissed and crackled in the little black marble hearth. There was a tray set with cut-crystal decanters and glasses. Jack wore the familiar Chinese silk dressing gown. He smiled a smile that could melt ice.

"And how do you like it, Lily?"

"It's very fine, I'm sure."

"Are you frightened, dear? I did it for you, Lily, to spare you creeping about the house."

"For me?"

"You don't want to be a servant all your life, do you, Lily?"

"No, but I don't want to be a fancy woman, either!"

He laughed softly and took her hand. "Why must we put labels on such things? Isn't it enough that I love you?"

She looked into his dark eyes and wondered how much brandy he'd drunk this afternoon. Lily thought long before she spoke.

"The world loves its labels for better or for worse, and I must make my way in the world."

He stood up and walked to the window. "I had hoped you might consider . . ."

"Living here? Oh, never! Never!" *And give up my place in the world, small though it be? And sit here, a sinner, waiting for the time when I begin to bore him, when he leaves me, as all the others have left me?*

"I mean that little to you, then?"

"You mean a great deal, Jack, but not so much as my reputation, my place in the world, for that is all I have, and little enough it is."

"You are incredible, Lily, and that may be why I love you. Any other girl in your situation would jump at the chance."

"Then you must find one of them."

Again he laughed, but it was different from his earlier laughter; this was short and edged with bitterness. "And haven't I? Oh, my, but have I not! And not a one of them is a patch on you, Lily Malone."

"I must go."

"But you'll come on Thursday? Don't break my heart so cruelly, Lily. At the least, give me a chance."

"I . . . I'll come."

She walked out of the suite, down the red-carpeted stairs, and out into the cold, cold February afternoon. She turned up the collar of her coat and pulled down the deep brim of the hat she'd bought, more from shame than fashion, because it hid all her hair and most of her face. The weather matched her mood: cold and bleak. The new year had come sulking in, creeping behind a veil of snowflakes and sleet, howling in the courtyards, painting the gutters with ice; 1856 looked to be a cheerless year for Lily, for she felt trapped by Jack's affection, and knew no sure way to get herself out of that trap.

Not that he wasn't in earnest, or as earnest as he could make himself be. *Why doesn't he go away again, across the sea or somewhere!* Lily clung to her dream of setting up a shop, and she watched her small savings grow with an almost miserly affection. Jack, she knew, would set her up in a shop in a trice, for the asking, but then it would not be her shop, and Lily would have none of it, nor his other gifts either. Just last week he had thrust a jeweler's box at her, only to have it handed back unopened.

"Lily, Lily, when will you learn? Why, 'tis you who have made me a priceless gift. You gave me your virginity, after all."

"It was all I had to give, and it was not for sale."

He set the box down then, and kissed her, and that was the end of all their discussion. She was used to his lovemaking now, used to all of Jack's tempestuous ways. He was a mystery, was Jack Wallingford, now all flash and surface and gaiety, now roaring drunk, now in moods of despair so black that even Lily could not pull him out of them.

"You see before you," he'd said once, swirling some cognac in a big balloon glass, sprawling naked, but for his Chinese robe, before the fire, "a rare creature, Lily. The true cynic is often talked about but seldom captured. Rather like the unicorn."

"What is a unicorn?"

He laughed without humor. "A mythological creature, very beautiful, all white, like a fine white horse, but with one long corkscrew horn rising from the middle of his forehead. It was said that the only way to capture a unicorn was to set a snare and have the bait be a pure and virginal maiden. Needless to say, there are very few unicorns captured these days."

"And is it a true story?"

He smiled into his glass, sipped the amber liquid, then sipped again. "It is a true myth, Lily. The best kind."

"You mock me."

"No, no, Lily, not you. Perhaps it is the world I mock, but not my fair Lily."

"But what has the world done to you, Mr. Jack, that you should mock it?"

"What has it not done! It's ruined me, girl. It has given me eyes to see with, and set me loose exploring this garbage dump that is New York society, given me a chance to see my own dear parents sell my sister into an unspeakable kind of prostitution with that limey pervert Clarence—yes, I've seen the fair Marianne Wallingford sell herself more eagerly than any Five Points hooker, seen half the fine young maidens of the town putting themselves up for auction, shameless as any nigger slave was ever sold on the block, seen knaves and crooks and even killers deified because they got themselves some money, bought themselves some respectability, which is also for sale in this lovely marketplace, like the girls, and the titles, and the rest. That's what I've seen, Lily, and that has made me cynical."

"And you never see the good things?"

"Ah, the good things. Well, I am told that they exist, like the unicorn, and I am willing to accept that as theory. In practice, it waits the proving."

Lily turned away from him, disturbed. She could understand why he might feel this way, or parts of it, but the depths of Jack's scorn yawned deep and terrifying before her. Lily was doubly afraid then, afraid for Jack, afraid that she might be drawn into his ways of thinking.

" 'Tis a sad thing, then."

"Sad? For me? Why do you say that?"

She took a deep breath. Lily had never challenged him on his own ground before. "It is sad because what you talk of is no more than death. If all there is in life is rotten as you say, what's the point of it?"

"A good question, Lily, you're learning fast. It is a question I have asked myself over and over, and never found the answer. What, indeed, is the point?"

Suddenly Lily was back at St. Patrick's orphanage, and the words of Sister Cathleen came floating back to her across the years.

"The angels will weep for you if you think such things."

"Ah, Lily, my sweet Lily! The angels have long since shed their last tear in my direction. Did you not know that we, all of us, even the angels, have just so many tears to shed, and that once they're gone, there is no more weeping left to us, not ever?"

"You're joking!"

" 'Tis God's own truth!" And again he laughed, but it was black laughter, the laugh of a doomed man.

Lily looked at him and saw not Jack Wallingford, but her mother, dying. *"Save your tears, child, for one day you may truly need them."* Then maybe it was true! Lily had trained herself not to be a weeper. Tears she had shed for Fergus, when the ship went down, and once or twice on other occasions. But for a girl her age, she knew she had scarcely tapped her allotment of tears. And it suddenly came upon her in a rush of dread that maybe she would, indeed, have need of them.

She looked at Jack, whose glass was nearly empty now. Lily hated to see him drink, and one of the good things about her affair with him was that he seemed to drink much less when they were together. But these last few months the drinking had been getting worse. Jack had been spending less and less time in New Haven, more and more time in New York, and not all of it, Lily was sure, with her. *"Hell-bent for ruination!"* That was how Patrick the stable lad described Master Jack, and Lily was half-inclined to agree. Still and all, there was a dark fascination to him, and to her relationship with him. Jack did need her, Lily was sure of that. He needed her, and admitted it, because she, at least, was honest. There were no schemes in Lily Malone. She steadfastly refused even the smallest trinkets from him, for to accept them would be to become a paid, kept, dishonored girl. She was dishonored, naturally, in any case, but there was a difference, and Lily clung to that difference as a drowning person might grasp at a straw.

And what would become of her when this adventure was over, as most certainly it must be over, and maybe soon?

Lily couldn't make herself think about such a time. Instead she thought of the moment, of her work, of her next meeting with Jack. If it ended, then it ended, and she'd worry about that when the time came.

And in the meantime, her nest egg was growing, more than sixty dollars now, safe with Mrs. Groome, waiting. There was some hope in that.

Still, Lily felt clouds gathering. Maybe it was a reflection of Jack's darkening moods, or her own uncertainty about the future.

The year 1856 had dawned ominously, although for the life of her Lily couldn't have named one concrete reason why it was different from any other year. Oh, to be sure, the air was filled with the ever-angrier politics of slavery, and men had endless debates pro and con, and tempers flared. The word "secession" had been hinted at, although it was only a hint. The new territories, Kansas and Nebraska, were alive with the conflict, for their laws were just being formed and partisans of both slavery and abolition pulled mightily in the direction that best suited their ideals.

To Lily it all seemed remote and slightly absurd, for surely slavery was against the law of God, and therefore why should there be any question at all? But the dissension was in the air, poisoning the air, and the general mood was a dark one. Publicly and privately, in the great world and in the small private world of Lily Malone.

Jack finally let himself be talked into going back to Yale College at the end of the month. Lily heard him mention his friend Brooks Chaffee from time to time, but her fear of her own emotions was too deep to let her even try to draw him out on that subject.

Brooks would remain what he had always been for Lily, a mythical creature, like Jack's unicorn. It was a fine thing to think on, to dream of Brooks Chaffee in the way you might dream of some tropical paradise where there was always sunshine and plenty to eat and everyone went about with smiles on their faces. The truth of the matter, she knew too well, was that the Lily Malones of the world had no business dreaming of the Chaffees. They were lucky enough to take what they got, if it was a slightly tarnished affair with someone like Jack, or less, much less.

So Lily went about her business, and the time passed quickly after Jack went back to New Haven, for when Jack was about, the conflict in Lily's heart focused on him, festering, tempting her and damning her at the same time, filling her with the promise of joy and the certainty of eternal damnation.

The sickness in the morning was, at first, a mystery to Lily. She woke feeling dizzy one morning in early March, and barely made it to the chamber pot to be sick. And Lily was never sick.

She felt a little better after vomiting, and got herself dressed and went down to eat breakfast. She found herself fighting the waves of nausea at the crowded, noisy servants' table, felt dizzy while sewing for Mrs. Wallingford, had to lie down in the afternoon, trying to sleep but not sleeping. The next day was much the same: her nausea seemed to fade away as the day wore on. Lily put it down to some mild stomach complaint, perhaps even a touch of the dread influenza. In a week the nausea left her, to be replaced by a vague torpor, a sense of being tired much of the time. This was a new and unwelcome feeling for Lily. She had always been a fountain of energy, eager to get on with a thing, and then on to the next thing.

Now it was a chore to lift a teacup.

Lily sensed something seriously wrong, and plain refused to let herself think on it. If she didn't think about being sick, then maybe she wouldn't be sick.

The time for her monthly bleeding came and went, and there was no bleeding. Oh, she told herself, sure it's sometimes a few days late, or early. A week went by, then ten days. The dread grew in her, a slow and awful thing, the seed of doom. She knew in her heart what was happening, knew that Jack's child was growing inside her, that her disgrace must now be known, that she would surely be punished, and the child too.

Lily had sinned, after all, and now the wages of sin would be paid, and in the fullest measure, just as was promised in the Scriptures.

Lily Malone, fallen woman!

✺ 14 ✺

Lily lay awake in the blackness of three o'clock in the morning, her eyes closed as if to shut out the truth.

I'll go down to the docks and throw myself in, it will be over quickly, and there'll be no one to know or to care.

But while she might have the strength to do herself in, Lily knew even while the dark thoughts were forming in her fear-stricken brain that she would never, never be able to murder the child within her.

Despair filled the little room until it seemed like to smother her, and drown her heart forever.

Never had she felt so lonely, or this far beyond help of man or God.

Lily thought of Jack, and how to tell him, and what his reaction might be. *Laughter and scorn, like as not, and a quick denial too, and who'd ever take her words over his, him being the heir to all the Wallingford fortune and a fine gentleman too.*

For many long hours she lay there tossing on the narrow cot, tormented by wild thoughts and forming desperate plans that were as quickly rejected as formed.

One thing was immediately clear, through all her fears and doubts: she must take some action, and soon. Write Jack. See a doctor. All night long she lay there, silent, too sad even for tears, hearing the even, thoughtless breathing of Susie McGlynn just across the little room, Susie who sinned and sinned and never seemed to get caught, cheerful, empty-headed Susie, Susie who must never, never know of Lily's shame.

She'd leave the Wallingford house, then, with her savings, without a word. She'd vanish! Go to Boston, maybe, or some-place farther. Sixty-three dollars could take her a long way. Maybe to the frontier! She'd call herself a widow, find some good farmer to marry her, make him a good wife, too, better than he deserved, maybe, and he'd be proud of her then, and there'd be no question of disgrace, and the child would have a name.

The child! Already Lily thought of this seed, this wave of illness, this faint month-old swelling, as a child. Him! Her! The child. Her child!

Suddenly, and against all logic, Lily wanted the child. Even if it was begotten in sin and shame. Even if it was Jack's child, the child of lust and not love, the child of darkness. At least it was hers.

Her child. The thought haunted Lily. It opened before her, huge and dark, inviting and threatening, with just a string of hope running through the black mystery of it like a clear path through a magic forest where you might find un-dreamed-of treasures or unthought-of doom.

How very little she had ever had to call her own. And this would be hers, and entirely hers, this child, no matter where or how it came to be. Lily swore on all the saints and angels that she'd make the child hers, make it glad it was hers, glad it was born. The angels wouldn't weep for Lily's child, what-ever they might think of its mother.

Lily's child! And what would be its name? Baby Wal-lingford? Not likely! Baby Malone! Baby Malone. Yes, Lily's child, and with Lily's name on it, and a fine name too, the name of Big Fergus. If it was a boy, she'd call it Fergus, and then Fergy would come back to her, and her father too, and there'd be a Fergy Malone again. And if it was a girl? Clau-dia. She'd call it Claudia. Then Lily remembered the end of Sister Claudia. Cathleen, then, after the matron. Cathleen Malone! That had a fine ring to it. Cathleen she would be, then, or Fergus.

Then, in the darkness, Lily smiled.

She woke smiling, resolved, ready to meet whatever the world was going to offer her. Or try to take from her.

Mrs. Wallingford held up a new bracelet, three inches of blazing emeralds. "He is so very thoughtful, isn't he, Lily?"

"Oh, indeed he is, ma'am. They're lovely." *I'm carrying your grandchild, Mrs. Wallingford, what do you think of that?*

"I think they'll set off the lavender gown. Or possibly the mauve?"

"They'll be splendid with anything, and that's a fact." *My child will be the grandchild of a procuress. Mrs. Fine-and-dandy Wallingford, do ye think the poor little creature will get over the shame of it?*

"Of course, now I don't have any earrings to go with it."

"Perhaps the plain diamond studs, ma'am."

"Yes! Of course, or even the pearls. It's nice not to have everything match, for a change."

I make my child a promise, Mrs. W. I promise I'll never sell her, or him, for a title, nor for anything else. "Have you tried them against your blue gown?" *You'd sell your only daughter to a pervert for a title, and you'd turn me into the gutter for a slut because your son ruined me, and never once would it dawn upon you that there is such a thing in the world as two standards, one for the rich and another for everybody else.*

Lily smiled gently and held up the peacock-blue ballgown.

On her next day off she went to Mr. Levy's pawnshop and bought a simple gold wedding ring for three dollars. He had it engraved, that same day, with her initials and Fergy's, to make it look truly like a wedding band.

Lily took the ring and hid it in her trunk next to her other treasures, the old linen scarf that had been in her mother's trousseau, her rag doll, Hortense, Sister Claudia's china thimble, and the hair ribbon Fran had embroidered a thousand years ago at St. Patrick's orphanage. And on the next week's afternoon off, Lily went to the doctor.

The Wallingfords had a family doctor who was used for servants' emergencies, but naturally Lily avoided him like death itself. But Lily knew where there was a doctor. She had seen his shingle almost directly across the street from the hotel on Sixteenth Street. "DR. SAMUEL ELLIOT, M.D." His sign was neatly painted in gold against black, and it hung from a respectable-looking house. Lily walked down the familiar street, the deep brim of her bonnet offering scant protection from the doubts and fears that walked with her.

Oh, and it was all fine and well-intentioned to want the child, to be prepared for the worst, to fight for her child. But suppose there was no child! Suppose it was some other kind of sickness! She thought of Jack then, happily carousing around New Haven, beyond doubt, unaware of what he'd started, blissfully ignorant of the fact that he'd torn a girl's life all to shreds. Such a life as it was.

The walk was only four blocks, but it might have been that many miles. Lily had learned many things about herself in these past few weeks. She had learned that all her dreams had been just that: dreams, and intangible, prone to melting away like the dew in the morning sun. The baby—if it was going to truly be a baby—was at least a fact, something different, something to be acted on. What, after all, had she been going to do with her little nest egg, with her life's savings? A shop, she had thought. And hadn't old Mr. Wallingford started life poor and with a shop? Well, the dreams would have to wait, at least until she learned the truth. Lily stood for a moment on the pavement outside of the doctor's neat brownstone house, gathering her courage. The ring felt strange on her finger, a golden lie. It was the only jewelry she'd ever owned, and sad it was to put it to such a wicked use. Lily took a deep breath and walked up the stone steps and rang the bell.

The doctor was kind. He seemed to take it perfectly for granted that Lily was what she said she was: namely, Mrs. Fergus Malone. She shivered when he touched her, for no man had ever touched Lily but Jack, and you could hardly call a lover a man, at least not in the sense that Dr. Elliot was a man, a stranger after all, doctor or not. He questioned her, and poked her here and there, and felt her pulse, and looked into her eyes. For a moment Lily feared he was going to be romantic, the way he looked into her eyes, but then he explained there was a sign to be read there, a certain dilation that almost always meant pregnancy. Lily tried to control her trembling. *If he could tell just by looking into her eyes, then so could anyone else who knew what to look for!*

"I think," he said, smiling gently, "that you can tell your husband the good news tonight."

"It's a fact, then, Doctor? I truly will be having a baby?"

"It's as certain as anything can be, Mrs. Malone, and I'd say that with reasonable care you have nothing to worry about. You seem strong and healthy to me."

"Thank you. He will be very pleased, I'm sure." *Like as not, he'll kill me, that's what he'll do! Pleased, is he?* Lily tried to imagine Jack's reaction and could not. Yet she had determined to tell him. And just as soon as she got the chance.

The doctor gave her a tonic to take, and charged her a dollar, and Lily found herself smiling at him as she left. *Of course, you fool, of course you'll be smiling, for are you not the well-known Mrs. Fergus Malone, respectable as churches, and won't your dear husband just love this happy news? And aren't the angels weeping their eyes out for you, liar and slut that you are?* But underneath all her fears, and running side by side with her doubts, Lily was glad of it. The life inside of her might have started in sin and carelessness, but there was surely a power in it, and something sacred, too, for sinners could be redeemed; look at Mary Magdalene, after all. The power was that for the first time in her life Lily was in control of something, of her fate. It had been her decision to keep the baby, for she well knew there were ways enough to get rid of unborn babies. And it was her decision to tell Mr. Jack, too, whatever the outcome might be. Lily knew him, and knew the world better than to expect much thanks, or any other kind of support from Jack Wallingford. Likely as not he'd throw her into the street, and it was lucky enough she had a little put by in case that happened. On the other hand, the child was half his, and he'd want to know that. There were bad sides to Jack's character, but Lily thought she had seen good in the boy too, and it would be cruel not to tell him. And there was the possibility he might help, at least find her a place to live, or help her get some sort of work she could do and still raise the child. Lily, who had never accepted so much as a flower from Jack, would indeed accept help for Jack's child. If he offered such help.

It was now almost six weeks since Lily had discovered her pregnancy. She determined that if Jack didn't come back to New York in a week's time, she'd have to write to him in New Haven. This prospect frightened Lily, for although the good nuns had taught her to write, and her hand was legible, she had never composed a letter in her life. She imagined Jack Wallingford in his fine college, laughing over her attempt, scorning her news, damning her for an adventuress.

The letter was never written. Jack came back to the city that very week, and asked her to meet him in the hotel the day after his return.

It was a cold day, windy, with gray clouds scudding past a pale and cheerless sun. Lily walked down Sixteenth Street as a condemned prisoner might walk to the gallows. She passed the doctor's house, clinging to the opposite side of the street, her face burning with unaccustomed shame. *Mrs. Fergus Malone, en route to tell her husband the good news!*

She had never been more frightened in her life, yet still she must go to him, and tell him, and pray for his help. Lily had a key, but she knocked at the door of Jack's suite in the little hotel. And her hand trembled. The door was open.

Jack looked healthier than she remembered him. Yale College must be good for him. He stood by the fire in an open-necked shirt, sipping cognac. At once he came to her and kissed her hot and full on the lips. Trembling still, Lily pulled back.

"I have news."

"Save it for later."

*You fool! Why don't you lead him into the thing gently,
for you'll get more kindness that way, and soften the blow.*
But she could only say what she must, in the most direct way
she knew. "I am to have a baby."

The flat unalterable statement hung between them final as
death, but without death's merciful release.

"You are . . . what?"

"Pregnant. With your child."

He held her still, and Lily could see the changes in his
face: from shock, to despair, to a kind of wry amusement.
Then, it seemed to soften.

A sigh came out of Jack Wallingford then that was like no
sound Lily had ever heard. It started low and soft and built
like the wind in a gathering storm until it became a banshee's
howling, then faded again to a kind of a moaning. It was a
wounded-animal sound, a sound of rage mixed with mourning, the music of doom.

"A baby."

"I'm sorry. But I will have the child. I will not kill it."

Lily gathered all of her courage to say this, for she had
been sure, in some secret corner of her soul, that he would
suggest just such a way out. That would be like Jack. That
would be easy, obvious, and painless—to Jack. So it surprised
Lily when he turned to her, truly angry now.

"Dammit, Lily, what do you take me for? Do you really
think I'd let you—or anyone else—do such a thing?"

The wave of relief rushed through her so fast she was almost speechless. "I didn't know."

"Well, girl, you know now."

"Yes. I am sorry."

"Stop being so damn sorry. It took two. It's bad, that's for
sure. But not the end of the world."

"Not for you."

"You really hate me, then, is that it, Lily?"

"No. Not hate. I never hated you."

"Nor loved me, either, I daresay. Well, fair's fair, Lily.
You realize, of course, that I cannot marry you."

Lily knew this well, but it pierced her heart all the same,
to hear him say it plain. "Of course."

"We'll make some arrangement."

*Of course. Arrangement. The rich were so very good at
making arrangements. Arrange for your daughter to marry
a buggering baron. Arrange the seating at a truffle-and-
champagne supper party. Arrange the ruination of a servant
girl. They could probably arrange their way right into heaven*

[194]

or hell, could the Wallingfords. Lily trembled as she thought of what arrangements Jack had in mind, for he was a lad capable of anything.

"I was going to go away."

"Where?"

"I hadn't thought."

"I'll do the thinking, Lily, if you please."

"Yes, sir." *How easily she fell back into calling him "sir"!*

He laughed then, not a humorous laugh, but the laugh of Jack-the-cynic. "Well, Lily, I daresay if you're having my child, you might call me Jack."

"Jack, then." She said it and didn't drop dead. It was the first time she had called him that, an unpardonable familiarity. Jack. Jack! Lily rolled the name around on her tongue. It hadn't been so terrible, after all, calling him by his name. Jack.

They did not make love that afternoon. Lily went back to the Wallingford house and stayed in her room for the rest of the afternoon. While Jack made his arrangements, Lily wondered, and then stopped wondering, for the matter was so far out of her hands that she might as well try to control the sun's rising, or the turn of the tides. *And what if he made an arrangement so terrible she couldn't agree to it? Had she any rights at all? What would the police say?* But Lily knew, even as the fear welled up in her, that she had no more rights than a flea on the back of a galloping horse. A dishonored servant girl making a complaint against the heir of the Wallingfords? So she waited, and waited, and saw the day turn into the longest night of her life.

The next day dawned brighter in every way. The chill had gone out of the air, the sky was clear, cloudless blue, and Lily could hear a bird singing as she dressed. All during the sleepless night she had taken what stock she could of her situation.

At least he hadn't murdered her on the spot, which had been one of the dreaded possibilities. Nor had he tried to force her into an abortion. Nor had he beaten her, nor turned her out naked and disgraced into the streets.

Lily dressed slowly, thinking on these things. Susie had gone down to breakfast. The brightness of the day seemed to confirm Lily's unexpected optimism. She thought of Jack's arrangements. And of Jack's formidable father, a right turkey buzzard he looked, the old man, with whom Lily had exchanged hardly a word in all her four years in the Wallingford house. How would he react to the news of his first grandchild's being born on the wrong side of the blanket?

The knock on her bedroom door was loud and unexpected.

"Come in."

The door opened and Lily all but fainted. There stood Jack, smiling. She was surprised to discover he knew where the servants' quarters were. Jack said nothing, but only motioned her to follow him. He led her down the stairs and through the paneled wall to his suite. Then he turned and kissed her.

"Arrangements," he said rather grandly, "have been made."

They're going to kill me dead. They're going to turn me out without a good word, or a good-bye. Can you be pregnant and a nun?

Jack smiled, calm, benevolent. "I think you'll be pleased, Lily."

Lily gathered what strength was left in her. "I don't understand you."

"I can't say it was easy, don't think the old man let me get away without some very harsh warnings. But the upshot is, my dear girl, that a draft for one thousand dollars will be written to your name—"

"One thousand dollars!" Lily gasped. Never had she dreamed of such a sum.

"Surely it will be enough?"

"Oh, yes, yes . . . and thank you."

"That's not all, Lily. The details are being worked out on the other end, at the Emporium. Passage is booked on a cracking new clipper."

"What are you telling me?"

"Simply that you'll have a new life, Lily. A position in the Wallingford Emporium, some respectable clerical sort of thing, not bad, you know, my mother did it."

"But the clipper?"

"California, Lily. You're going to California. To San Francisco, and next week!"

₰ 15 ₰

Jack left her then, and all Lily could do was to sit down on her bed in mute amazement.

California!

It was startling, unexpected, and absolutely right. *To make a new life in the new golden land! To share a small part of Fergy's dream at last, and to escape her shame, and to make a good life for the little creature inside her!* Surely these were good things, great things, even.

Yet there were dangers too, both in the voyage and in the steps she must take to be sure her shame did not pursue her. *So far, at the least, no one knows. And no one shall know. Jack will keep his secrets, and so will the old man. But what can I tell to Susie, to the Groomes? Well they know all I've got in the world, and it's far, far less than a thousand dollars.*

Suddenly the hard fact of it came up and hit Lily with the unwelcome violence of a thrown rock. *I am going to have to invent a lie, many lies!* To have sinned, to have even enjoyed the sinning, with Jack Wallingford was one thing, and maybe a bad thing, but somehow not like deliberately inventing a lie. How to explain her departure in some logical way that wouldn't set all their tongues to wagging? Or should she go about her arrangements in secret, and leave this house like a thief in the night, suddenly, and let them think what they might? Lily sat thus for some time, and slowly it occurred to her that she would never be a truly successful liar. *I'll tell part of the truth!* For wasn't it God's own truth that Mr. Wallingford Senior had offered her a position in the San Francisco store? Surely she could say that, and let them think what they might. At ease for the moment, Lily stood up then, and smiled, and thought of California.

California meant more to Lily than just a new start.

California was all the hopes of her generation, wrapped in gold and glittering with promise. California was freedom and hope, a chance to make of yourself what you could in a free land without prejudices, without chains, without limits. No one in California would care that a girl was Irish and Catholic and barely literate. No one in California would scorn her for a hussy, for no one would know her secret.

Lily was smiling as she opened the door of her little bedroom and went down the stairs to seek out Mrs. Groome.

Mrs. Groome offered Lily tea, rather formally, Lily thought, and sat in silence while Lily told her story. Lily was brief, and unsure of herself, but what she said was pure truth, so far as it went.

Finally the housekeeper spoke. "This is a great surprise to me, Lily. I'd always thought you were happy with us here."

"Indeed I have been. But to have so great an opportunity . . ."

"I wish you'd told me sooner. It won't be so easy to replace you, my dear."

"It happened all of a sudden, like."

Lily looked into Mrs. Groome's eyes and could read nothing there. *Does she believe me? Is she sad to see the last of me? Does she care at all?* Lily thought of the almost four years she'd been in this house, working under Mrs. Groome every day, and of all that had happened to her in that time. Already, the time of her servitude in the Wallingford mansion seemed to be receding behind her.

Mrs. Groome replied, and smiled a little, and grew more friendly. "I see. Well, child, we will miss you. You have always been a good girl, Lily, and I'm sure you will go on being one. There are many temptations in a place like California, and you must be ever vigilant against them. Keep all your wits about you, Lily. You'll be wanting your savings, and I have them all for you in Mr. Wallingford's safe, and you can have them tonight."

"Oh, yes, please. And thank you."

"Very generous, Mr. Wallingford."

"Indeed he is that."

She suspects, but she daren't say a thing. Lily felt herself blushing, made an excuse, and left. Her next parting was going to be even more difficult, for she must see Jack and thank him. And find out about such details as the letter of credit, or whatever he had said it would be, and the sailing, and what she'd need to take.

Lily made her way up the familiar stairs and down the hall she knew so well. *They've always had the leaving of me, everyone I ever cared for in the world, and now the tables are turned. Now I'm leaving them, and to hell with them, too!* There should have been a sort of victory in it, but all Lily felt was emptiness, a sinking sort of feeling, and, in spite of the baby she knew was thriving inside her, a sense of being very much alone.

When Lily got to Jack's bedroom door at last, she paused for a moment and thought of all the changes that had come to her since the first time he'd invited her inside, innocent and a virgin, and little more than a year ago, and look at her now, ruined and saved all at the same time!

Ruined. No better than she should be. Fallen woman. Soiled dove. How well she knew those phrases, and how poorly they described what had happened to her and to so many thousands of helpless girls every year! *Well, if I've fallen, it's damned I'll be if I don't rise again, and higher by far, or die trying!* Lily felt the pride of the Malones bubbling in her blood, and she thought of her father for the first time in months, and his joy and the power in him. *What could Big Fergus not have done, had God only spared him? And Fergy, too, for that matter.* Well, things were going to be different now. Fate had dealt Lily a new hand, and she would play it for whatever it was worth, with all the strength and wit in her.

She knocked on Jack's door and opened it without waiting for his reply. Something told her he'd be there, and she was right. There he stood by the fire in the familiar Chinese robe, his strong hands thrust deep into the robe's pockets. Lily remembered sewing that robe, and why he'd torn it, and many other things both painful and sweet. *He'll be wanting me,* she thought with an intuition far older than her years: *he'll want me for his pleasuring this one last time.* Lily stood silent and watched this young man who was the father of her child, the manipulator of her fate. And she felt an enormous wave of gratitude that he had seen fit to pity her in her ruin, that he hadn't merely cast her out into the streets as she had heard of many other disgraced servant girls being so treated, and without recourse.

Jack turned to her and smiled a slow, easy smile. "Everything is done. You sail a week from today, on the clipper *Eurydice*. First-class cabin and all paid for, and she's a spanking-new ship. You have shopping to do, Lily, and plans to make. I think it's best if you'd move to the hotel today. The fewer questions asked about the house, the better, don't you agree?"

Lily would have agreed to almost anything, so deep was her gratitude. "Of course."

"Do you hate me, Lily?"

His question startled her, even though Jack was given to saying startling things: he often did it in fun. But now there was an edge on his voice, a cutting edge, that told Lily this was deadly in earnest.

"Never. Surely not. You have been . . . most kind."

"Lily, sweet Lily, do you know what you are?"

"Ruined, is what I would be, but for you."

"You are an angel. You're beautiful, Lily."

This was a new game. Lily didn't understand what he was getting at.

"A fallen angel, then."

"Not in California. You'll be good as gold out there, Lily, and you'll get yourself a fine decent husband, a better man than I'll ever be, for I don't deserve a girl like you."

Never had it occurred to Lily that a man of Jack's station in life was even remotely available to a girl of her background on any terms of equality. The gap between them had ever seemed impassably deep and wide, and his passion for her no different from the passing affection a man might have had for his dog. Lily paused, and considered her reply, then spoke gently, for she could see that he was in some pain.

"That's as it may be. Still, I thank you."

He came to her then, and took her in his arms. Lily said nothing. She felt his arms closing around her, warm under the richness of the silk robe, and she thought: *Well, he is human after all, a strong young man with a man's needs, and maybe not truly bad, he is honest with me anyway, and his honesty sometimes touches bottom when he thinks about himself.* Lily felt the lust rising in him, and his need for her—for anyone—and she smiled a small regretful smile as he fumbled with the buttons on her dress. She'd been right, after all, then: he would be wanting her this one last time.

Later, in the deep quiet of Jack's bed, she looked up at him where he lay at her side. Jack was staring at her, must have been staring even before she looked at him, and his face, slack with the backwash of their lovemaking, was troubled. And then he spoke, a hoarse whisper edged with desperation. "A man loses the world, Lily, when he loses you."

She looked at him, said nothing, smiled. *What nonsense they talk when the heat of lust is on them, boiling in their brains!*

Jack reached for her, gently now, and buried his face in the curve of her neck. He trembled, and the trembling went all through him; Lily felt herself shaking with it, not the convulsions of love, but something strange and troubling. He made a sound like no sound she had ever heard, a deep sighing sort of gasp, and then the trembling stopped and Jack simply lay there quiet as death. Finally he turned his head and reached out to touch her cheek, and it was only then that Lily felt the dampness on her neck, and she knew that Jack Wallingford had spent the final moment of their lovemaking in tears.

Lily smiled at him, not knowing why he cried, wanting to comfort him as she might have comforted some small child. But Jack was lost to her then: he had gone to a place where Lily could not follow. *Maybe*, she thought, as her smile faded away, *maybe he's always been lost.*

Lily never saw Jack's mother again. Mrs. Wallingford had gone out in the morning, stayed out for luncheon, and hadn't returned in the afternoon. This was unusual enough for Lily to realize it must be on account of her. *The old lady probably thinks I've seduced her precious little boy. Or maybe she simply can't face the possibility of a scandal.* Somehow, as she packed her few clothes into the old wicker trunk that had come with her from the convent, Lily found herself smiling at Mrs. Wallingford's delicate sensibilities. For a woman who could scheme and pander and prostitute the future of her only daughter to entertain such fine sentiments about a serving maid was comical indeed. *I won't be sad to see the last of her, or this house either*, Lily thought, packing ever faster. She had felt a moment's sadness for Jack, poor, lost, embittered Jack. But poor Jack could take very good care of himself, Lily was sure of that, and she had other things to think on, happier things, things like the entire future of Mrs. Fergus Malone, soon to be of California.

Her deft fingers moved among the contents of the trunk. Here was her mother's linen scarf with its fine lace edging, the trousseau scarf, the scarf that Fat Bessie had tried in vain to steal. And here was the rag doll, Hortense, none the worse for wear. *My baby will play with that doll in California*, Lily thought, *and be happy, and I'll be happy because of it.* There was Sister Claudia's gift thimble, never used, too pretty to use. *I will put it on a shelf in my new house in San Francisco, just to look at, and to remember her by.* And there was the hair ribbon Fran had made so long ago, and that never used either. *I will wear it on my wedding day when I marry some fine good man, a shopkeeper maybe, or a clerk at Wallingford's, or did it matter?* It was hard for Lily to imagine that any stranger could ever be interested in her. Why? Thin and frightened and of no background as she was, as her position in St. Paddy's and in the Wallingford house had so thoroughly educated her to believe, why then should anyone care, much less notice her in the first place?

The pain and torment of inventing a lie, and the knowledge that she might have to act it out on the long voyage of the clipper ship drove Lily half mad with fear. How much would her pregnancy show on the voyage? Maybe by the grace of God she could avoid the whole issue. Still, it was better to be traveling as "Mrs." if she were traveling alone. It was fear that made her choose the obvious name: she would be Mrs. Fergus Malone. At least she did love Fergus Malone—both of them. At least it was a name she'd never, never forget. And when the time came to announce his death, she could make herself sad by remembering the real deaths of the real Fergus Malones.

How many of her fears in the past had come to nothing. And how many more had proven themselves deadly accurate! Lily had no way at all of knowing what fate awaited her in California, but she continually reassured herself that it would be better. It simply had to be better. The terrible questions might never be asked. The dread unmasking and its subsequent shame might never happen.

She thought of all her yesterdays, and everyone who had left her, and how all that would turn into something better in this new place beyond the sunset.

✦ 16 ✦

The *Eurydice* seemed to be flying even as she rode at her mooring in Pier Nine on the East River near South Street.

Lily had never thought much of ships, never gone down to Battery Park to watch the sailings and hear the bawdy chanties the seamen sang at the top of their very healthy lungs as they raised anchor and set sails. But here was the *Eurydice*, one of the newest of the brand-new clipper class of long-distance cargo ships, paint-fresh from New Bedford and hungry for the high seas.

Lily shivered at the sight of her. Long and white and slender with a carved, painted, gilded lady on her bowsprit, the great clipper was shaped almost like a fish, sleek, quick-looking, truly beautiful. Her three great masts were raked backward at such an angle the sea wind seemed to be pressing against them even now, even as the ship rode at the short end of her hawsers, tamed and docile, but only for the moment, restless, pulling at the arm-thick ropes, lusting for the sea. South Street was a parliament of ships, ships of all kinds and all nations, fishing boats that announced their presence half a mile off when the wind was right, fat schooners, an occasional man-of-war, small tenders, pleasure craft, tugboats, some of them fitted with the newfangled steam engines that belched smoke like the keyhole of hell itself. But the unchallenged queens of this and every harbor were the clippers, and of all the clippers, the *Eurydice* was the newest and possibly the fastest. The *Flying Cloud* had the record, eighty-nine days round the Horn to San Francisco, but the *Flying Cloud* might not have it for long if Jack Wallingford could be believed.

"Only the best for my Lily," he'd said, handing her the voucher that guaranteed her passage in a cabin all her own, a rare privilege on a ship that was more interested in setting speed records than taking travelers. There would be, Lily knew, only a few first-class cabins, and no steerage at all. The *Eurydice* carried thirty-something able seamen plus the captain and his wife and the first and second mates. Cooks and cabin boys. No doctor.

Lily looked at the ship that would carry her to her fate.

Then she smiled. All the fears and doubts of the last few months seemed to fly away from her. The *Eurydice* had that power, for the *Eurydice* was beyond any doubt a marvelous thing, gallant and swift and unconquerable.

Lily could never erase the terrible image of her lost brother and the fate of the *Indian Belle* so long ago. Ships did go down, and well she knew it, and the good Lord knew Lily couldn't swim a stroke. Well, that was in God's hands, and if God was going to do her in, so be it.

She looked at the proud ship and saw California. Not California as it might truly be—for who knew about that?—but the California of her imagining, a sweet, warm and gilded place filled with laughter and music and rivers of gold, a place where it was always dawn, the dawn of a fine new day, a place where you could dream and build on the dream and find the dream still there in all its shimmering grandeur tomorrow and the next day and the day after that. This was California as Lily saw it, the journalist's California, the California that had lured Fergy and hundreds of thousands of other adventurers. Somehow the ship itself became California for Lily: all fresh and gleaming with hope, eager, pure and lovely. It was California. And it was hers!

Lily had come to South Street especially to look at the ship. This was a luxury, for her shopping was only half-done. The climate, she knew, was mild in San Francisco, but for the voyage she'd need warm clothing for the Horn, where it was always winter, and light stuff for the tropics, for they'd cross the equator twice, once in the Atlantic and again in the vast Pacific. The railroad across Panama had just been finished, but it was plagued with wrecks and foul weather and bandits and fever. Jack had talked her into the clipper voyage, long as it was, on grounds of comfort. The Wallingfords always shipped with the North Star line, owners of the *Eurydice*, and it was an absolutely reliable outfit. This was Jack's first indication of fatherly feeling, and it came and went in a moment.

He'd left her very much to herself in the hotel these last two days. Lily was grateful for that, even as she wondered about it. Maybe that last time in his room at the Fifth Avenue house would be truly the last time they made love. Forever. Lily was fond of Jack, but she did not regret him, either. Close as he was, Jack seemed already a part of her past.

Jack, she was sure, had many sources of consolation if what he wanted was a tumble in the hay. *"A man loses the world when he loses you, Lily."* Sure and he'd said that, but what had he meant? He'd also made it very clear there was no question—none in the world—of his marrying her. Absolutely unsuitable. Lily was the first to realize that, and she had always realized it. But knowing a thing was different from being told it to your face, and the hurt of that was with her still, even though he'd also said those other things, even though he was surely treating her generously. Lily walked up Broadway, too thrifty still to take a cab. She had purchases to make at the Wallingford Emporium, for her sense of fair play told her if she was being the beneficiary of Wallingford largess, she might at the very least spend some of it in their store.

The Emporium was huge. It filled an entire block, a five-story white limestone mercantile palace all columns and arches on the outside, brilliant with gas chandeliers within, and sparkling mirrors, polished walnut display cases set with glass that had been cut and beveled like diamonds, potted palms sprouting in this eternal June, gilding and brass and wine-red carpeting on all the corridors.

But the splendors of the building took second place to the treasures it contained. Here were bolts of fabric from France and England, and Oriental silks, lace from Belgium and Venice, cretonnes and taffetas, tweeds and gauzy fairy fabrics such as Lily had scarcely imagined. Here you could buy a spool of thread for a penny, or a gold-embroidered Persian shawl for a thousand dollars. Here were ready-made gowns based on the very latest Paris styles, hats by the score that seemed to have depleted entire jungles of all their finest feathers, gardens of silk flowers, rare porcelains, jewels, preserved delicacies to eat, and here, too, were humbler things, simple cotton dresses such as a Mrs. Groome or even Lily herself might wear. All under the one glorious roof, and all for sale, and bringing the crowds in every day by the thousands.

No wonder the Wallingfords were rich as kings and emperors! The people were as various as the things they'd come to buy, and for a few minutes Lily simply stood quietly in a corner, half-hidden by a palm tree, at ease with herself and enjoying the free social circus that was the steady parade of shoppers. She saw servants and shopgirls, dowagers that she recognized from having served them in Mrs. Wallingford's green-walled boudoir, idle young men in pairs, come to leer at the young women and possibly to make acquaintance of them, beggars, street boys who were likely as not out to grab and run, to snatch some resalable bauble from the open counters. There was a smattering of foreign visitors, French and English and German, for this was one of New York's great attractions and everybody came.

Lily stayed five minutes near her palm.

Then a well-remembered voice curled around her like a noose. It was Brooks Chaffee's.

Lily froze, shrank into her coat, cringed beneath her wide-brimmed bonnet, hoped against every hope he wouldn't see her.

But Brooks Chaffee had no eyes for Lily, nor for anyone else in all the world but the girl who walked beside him, her fawn-gloved hand resting lightly upon his arm with the imperial grace of one born to rule the hearts of men forever.

Caroline Ledoux was shopping for a reticule.

At first Lily hardly noticed the girl. She saw Brooks, and it was the first time in more than a year that she'd seen him. He looked older, less a boy, more a man, taller perhaps, more beautiful than ever. *No man has a right to look like that: it's a pure danger.* He wore a light overcoat of dark blue, and the dark gold hair gleamed with a dull radiance in the lamp-light of Wallingford's Emporium. As usual, Brooks went hatless. Lily heard the laugh, saw his light head bend close to the girl's dark head, heard them both laugh, and then they were gone in a flutter of shoppers, gone around a mirrored pillar, gone from Lily's sight but forever fixed in her memory.

She turned quickly and walked to the street exit of the great store just as fast as she could without actually running. Lily's loyalty to the Wallingfords' generosity did not extend so far as having her heart broken right there in their store. She'd buy her yard goods elsewhere.

Brooks felt the touch of Caroline's hand on his arm. It was a small hand, her touch was light as a butterfly's touch, but nevertheless it warmed him all through, from the flush mounting on his cheeks to the toes wrapped in stout English leather. Caroline had more moods than the wind, more currents than all the rivers on earth. It was the mystery and the changes in her that held his attention, almost as much as her beauty and his very fundamental physical desire for her.

Today she was being playful. Tonight she might be a philosopher, tomorrow a child, the next day a hussy. It was all done with a light touch, for Caroline's mind was a quick skimming thing, elusive as rainbows, and the brightness of it was always edged in a kind of warm darkness that Brooks did not truly understand except for the fact that it made him love her even more, and more urgently.

". . . but, Mr. Chaffee," she continued, "you must perceive that buyin' a reticule is a matter of the highest importance. Why, when the Democratic party nominates Mr. James Buchanan for President, as my daddy insists they must do, I do daresay less thought will have gone into that selection than I give to a reticule."

"I'm perfectly sure of it." He laughed then, and she with him, and they swept past a potted palm tree and around a corner to the section of the store where the best reticules were displayed.

Was it just three months since he'd met her? It seemed to Brooks that he had only just been born that winter night in old Mrs. Vanderbilt's house, the night he'd first set eyes on Caroline Ledoux. And all the other girls he'd known, and liked, and tried to love, all those girls faded gently into some misty half-forgotten time, the time he now thought of as his childhood, the time before life became worth living. The time before Caroline.

His life, Brooks knew all too well, had always been a very safe, well-insulated life. And what struck him instantly in Caroline was that she was absolutely fearless. If there was a chance to be taken, this sweet girl would take it, laughing, just for the fun to be had. Harmless fun, of course, but fun and in plenty.

Many were the dowagers whose long disapproving noses had been twitted out of joint because the mischievous Caroline would not dance to their pompous tunes. Caroline was frankly a flirt, and she said that in New Orleans flirting was an ancient and respected art, even old grandmothers did it, if they could carry the thing off, and many could.

"Now, you wouldn't want me sitting all plain and prune-faced in some corner, pretendin' life's no fun, would you, Mr. Chaffee?"

And Brooks had to admit that was the very last thing he would want.

"You Yankees are charmin' in many ways, but this is a cold, cold place, your old Northern states, and what you need, if I do say so myself, is a little flirtin' and a bit of moonshine and violins playin' someplace yonder, hearts beatin' faster than they should . . . and the flowers. The perfume of flow-ers. These Yankee flowers have no soul to them, they spend all their lives in some glass house and they just don't smell right, leastways not to this simple Southern girl."

Brooks looked at her, enchanted. He had never seen a girl like Caroline, nor heard such talk. This elusive little crea-ture could make his soul jump through hoops, make his pulse dance on the high wire, make his yearning heart pound like galloping hoofbeats. Brooks felt young, shy, cold, hot, afraid, and fearless in turn. For the first time in his life he felt ill-at-ease, worried about doing or saying the wrong thing, and what he did manage to say sounded coarse and stupid to his ears by contrast to the capricious and altogether dazzling wit that came bubbling so effortlessly out of Caroline.

"You think," he said, grinning like a fool, "of yourself as simple?"

"Why, I hardly think of myself at all, and that's the truth."

"All New York is thinking of you, Caroline."

"Just goes to show how very little is on your old Yankee minds, then, if a bitty thing like me can make an im-pression."

Brooks's mind raced and turned and darted this way and that as he desperately sought the magic formula that would bind her to him forever. For, lovely as she undeniably was, and yearn for her as he did, with his body in eager partner-ship with his heart and soul, there remained something wild and ephemeral about Caroline, as though she were some ex-otic bird who might, at the slightest provocation, fly away to the mysterious land that had bred her, leaving only a memory and a legend.

"Down home," she replied with a ripple of laughter, "I come by the dozens, like spoons!"

"Then I am emigrating tomorrow."

"Ah, no, Mr. Chaffee: stay where you are. Some fine plants just wither and die when you transplant 'em."

"I'll only stay, Caroline, if you'd stay with me."

Brooks took a deep breath as he said these words, for they were a commitment, and although he hadn't devised a formal strategy about the time and place of his proposal, he was sure in his heart that the proposal would come in its own time, and if that time was now, so much the better, to have stumbled into the dangerous, uncharted forest all at once, without formal preparations.

Caroline Ledoux looked up at him then, and something flickered across her immense brown eyes. It was a fleeting thing, the reflection of windblown clouds on the surface of a dark pool, a brief restless shimmering that gave no clue to what caused it, nor to what might lie in the depths of that pool. She spoke softly. "I declare, Mr. Chaffee, now you are simply flirtin', too. It must be contagious, like the fever."

She laughed, and her laugh held a challenge.

Brooks took her hand and prayed to God she wouldn't laugh at what he was about to say. "The fact is, Caroline, that I love you."

She took his hand then, and gave it a little squeeze, but the laughter stopped. "Lordy, this shoppin' for a reticule surely is a serious business. You take me quite aback, Mr. Chaffee."

"Brooks."

"Brooks, then. You aren't triflin' with my affections, Brooks Chaffee?"

"I would die first."

"I do think you would."

"Can you give me hope?"

"Hope is a very portable commodity, Brooks Chaffee. The question seems to be, can I give you the heart of Miss Caroline Ledoux?"

"I would be happier than any man on earth if you could."

"I do flirt, Mr. Chaffee, as you know, and I mean no harm by it, it's one of our native customs, you see, like the changin' of the guard at Buckingham Palace. I take it you are askin' me to marry you?"

"Will you . . . could you?"

"Right here in Wallingford's? Don't you think that would be a trifle public?"

She laughed again, ripples and ripples of it. Brooks thought that he had never heard a more painful sound. The light inflections of her laughter seemed to be ripping his guts out, and slowly, as with a dull knife.

"Refuse me if you must, Caroline, but please don't mock me."

Again he felt the pressure of her hand, the lightest pressure, but as effective as any blow with a hammer. And he looked into her eyes and found them fixed on his, and the laughter died then. They stayed like that for a moment, people swirling and jostling all around them, stayed transfixed like statues before the best reticule counter at Wallingford's, and then her expression changed from something solemn to a slow warming smile. And Brooks knew in that instant that he had won this strange and exotic creature, this beautiful Caroline who was so many different Carolines, all in one and—now—all his.

They said nothing, for there was nothing to say.

Slowly, still hand in hand, they turned and made their way through the throngs of shoppers and out onto the street, all thought of the reticule vanished in the wonder of this discovery of each other.

Lily's head was full of lists, and she recited them to herself now, hurrying up Broadway away from Wallingford's Emporium, to keep herself from crying in her embarrassment, to keep herself from going mad. The voyage would be a long one, and tedious. The eighty-nine-day record of the *Flying Cloud* had been accomplished under the best of weather and with no passengers. Four months was the standard reckoning for the trip under reasonably good conditions. Four months away from cities, away from shops, away from everything but the sea and the sky and the other passengers, whoever they might be! And away from her past, and away from Brooks Chaffee.

Lily was bringing books, a grammar and some novels and a Bible, for she meant to study and improve her reading on the voyage. And she was bringing the materials of a new wardrobe, too, on top of the ready-made clothes she'd bought already. Everything cost the earth in San Francisco, she'd heard, and Lily intended to make Jack's thousand dollars last just as long as it could out there. So she would have dressmaking materials for herself and for the baby. Louise had taught her to knit and crochet, and Lily intended to do that, too. And aside from work materials and books, there were extra provisions to buy. Jack had been firm about that. The clipper provided all meals, and they were supposed to be good meals at that. But unexpected delays might occur, and it never hurt to have things like potted meats and raisins and other dried fruits, pickles and candied orange peel and ginger root, sassafras and spices, herbal wines, balms and lotions. There seemed no end to it, but the end was indeed in four days, for today was Saturday and they were sailing on Wednesday!

Well, then. It was nearly all done. The foodstuffs and medicines were bought and crated, her clothing packed, the books bought. All Lily needed was cloth to sew and patterns to cut from. She'd bought a fine new sewing kit at Wallingford's, fitted with scissors and pinking shears and a hundred needles, twin thimbles, and many kinds of thread.

So Lily's mind was busy as she made her way up the

crowded street. She'd stop at Stewart's then, the Wallingford store being temporarily out of the question. The bright April afternoon suddenly seemed to have a chill on it. Lily had been feeling much better in this, the second month of her pregnancy. The morning sickness had left her, and she went about the hundred chores of packing with new energy.

Lily's life had changed so fast it made her dizzy.

She alternated between making long, thoughtful plans for the future and impetuous moments when she decided there was no controlling fate, and why bother, since her plans and dreams had such a fatal habit of turning out differently from her expectations?

She found herself pausing on the street now and again, in the late afternoon, and looking at the sun as it slowly rolled toward the west, thinking that where the sun was going she soon would be, and all her hopes and dreams, whatever they amounted to. The shock and shame of her pregnancy had slowly evolved into something close to happiness. It might not be the kind of change she would have wished for first, if by some magic she were given her choice of all the wishes in the world, but surely it was a change, a fresh start, and she was glad of it. And Lily was glad of the baby too, for the baby would give a shape to her life, and around the baby she would build a better life than she or Fergy had ever known, or she'd die trying.

Suddenly, it was Tuesday afternoon. Lily finished her packing and stood up to make some tea. There was a scuffling sound outside the door, which caused her to look up in some alarm, for it sounded as though someone was trying to force his way in. Then the door was flung open and Jack Wallingford came stumbling, lurching in, obviously very drunk. Lily looked at her benefactor calmly, for hadn't she seen him this way many times, though never so early in the day? *How sad it is, for now I won't be able to thank him properly, he'd barely hear me.*

Jack stumbled into the room, looked about in wonderment as if he didn't know where he was. He smiled, a loose, slippery smile that soon faded.

In the short time that Lily had known Jack intimately and been his lover, she had come to recognize his many fleeting moods the way a good sailor gets to know shifting sandbars or a tricky current. For Jack was never the same man two days—or two hours—in a row. He could be all charm and thoughtfulness in one moment and wildly gay in the next, and skid from these golden heights to the very pit of despair in a swoop so sudden and so completely without warning that it was a frightening thing to behold. And the drinking only made his depressions that much worse.

Sure and he'd been drinking that first night, the night he'd taken her to bed for the first time, drinking and despondent over Miss Marianne's betrothal to the baron. Jack sometimes drank in festive moods, too, but not like this. Not to lose control.

"Sorry," he said, lurching past her to the love seat.

He sat down heavily, not having so much as taken off his greatcoat, and stared at his boots.

"Sorry," he repeated, as though he'd never said it to begin with. "Sorry, sorry, sorry."

"What are you so sorry for, Jack? Surely not for me. I'm fine."

He looked at her then for the first time. His dark hair, uncombed, fell in tatters across his forehead. His eyes, dark at their brightest, had gone coal-black, black as graves, black as the door of hell. A kind of grin found its way to his lips. He closed his eyes, then opened them again. It was as though he were trying to shut out some terrible vision that would not go away.

"Fine," he said softly, sighing as he muttered the words, "fine is what you are, Lily, and truly so. One of the few fine sights upon a very dark horizon, you are, and always will be."

"What's wrong, then?"

"Ah. The rub. What . . . is . . . wrong?" He stood up quite suddenly and looked about the room as though he'd never seen it before. "The first thing that's wrong is that Jack's got nothing to drink. Could you, pray, obtain for me a tot of brandy, fair lady, angel of mercy, balm of my soul?"

Lily poured him a small amount of brandy, for surely he'd had more than his share, and filled the rest of the glass with water. She handed it to him.

"You are kindness itself, Lily, and ever have been. Thank you, my dear. What's wrong, you ask, as well you might, seeing me in this wretched condition, and in the afternoon, too, more's the shame. What's wrong, Lily, is that I've lost my best friend."

He stopped then, and sipped the brandy and water. Lily felt the world come shuddering to a stop. *Brooks Chaffee, dead!* That had to be it. Surely Brooks was Jack's best friend. To be lost surely must mean he's dead. *And Jack doesn't*

*even know I've seen him, or loved the sight of that golden
head, that smile, that gentle manner.* She stood absolutely still
and wished the earth would open up and swallow her right
then and there, wondered what to do, what to say, how to
keep from weeping, or worse. Lily said nothing, but only
paused, and soon enough Jack filled the silence between
them.

"I guess you don't know poor Chaffee. He was a fine lad,
Lily, believe me, the best. They don't make them like Brooks
Chaffee. And now . . ."

"What happened? Is he ill?" *Maybe it's that. He's ill. Not
dead.*

"Sick in the head, he is, gone right off his senses. Fallen in
love, has Chaffee, and for a strumpet out of hell, the devil's
own little ambassadress on earth, Lily, a real bad 'un, and
take it from me I know a bad 'un when I see her."

"Who is she?" *You know who she is, fool: she's the girl
from the Wallingford Emporium, the girl who had him so
curled around her little finger he couldn't see to the right nor
the left of him, and glad you were of it at the time.*

"The hussy is called Miss Caroline Ledoux, and she will
poison Brooks Chaffee and probably ruin his life for him, and
laugh all the time she's doing it. Whom the gods would
destroy, Lily, they first make mad. And Brooksie's mad as a
hatter, blind-mad, bewitched, and by an authentic witch at
that. She's got him all tied up and stowed away in her little
perfumed reticule, and not all his armies of old Dutch aunties
nor his chaste Calvinist soul can save him from her. He's
doomed, my girl, just as surely as if he'd done bloody murder
on Fifth Avenue in broad daylight. The gates of hell yawn
open before him, and there is not one damned thing I can do
to stop it, and that's what's wrong. Wrong, wrong, wrong-o-
wrong."

"How do you know she's as bad as you think?"

"Fair question. Because it takes a thief. Because we're two
of a kind, and bad to the core, mischief-makers, nose-thumb-
ers in the face of all that's good and cherishable, mockers
and scorners. Only, in my own wicked way, at the least I am
honest about it. I make no bones about my attitudes, and to
hell with anyone who takes exception. They may look at me
and sneer, but even while they're curling their well-bred lips,
they are also thinking: 'There goes the Wallingford heir,
surely he can't be as bad as all that.' If I were poor tomorrow
morning, Lily, there'd hardly be a drawing room in New
York that would welcome me for myself. They welcome me,

surely, but only because I come to them perfumed with the delicious aroma of the old gent's millions. Can't bear to face the idea that their daughters might miss a chance at all that pelf. The fact that I would make any decent girl the most miserable husband on earth fails to deter them one inch, even as it failed to deter my sainted mother. It's a hunting expedition, don't you know, and whoever comes back with the biggest trophies is immediately superior to everyone who doesn't fare so well."

To Lily, for whom one dollar was a sum to be reckoned with, Jack's attitude was shocking. "Is she rich, this girl?"

"Oh, yes indeedy. Bags of it. Not that old Brooksie is particularly in need. Fortune hunting is not Caroline's game. She plays for different stakes, more dangerous ones."

"And what may those be?"

"She plays a desperate game, Lily. She plays a gambler's game, always close to the edge, always pushing her luck, never afraid to take enormous chances, even when by doing that she might break the heart of a man like my friend, for Brooks Chaffee—even though he may not know it—has a heart that is so very good and so lacking in even the perception of evil that it is a terribly fragile commodity. Caroline will smash his heart and not even hear the crash, much less stoop to pick up the fragments later on."

"You make her sound dangerous."

Lily looked at Jack, and her heart warmed to him, for it was good of him to be so concerned about his friend. And a sad, sad thing it would be if what Jack said were true. Yet how could he know, for sure? Jack's estimate of himself was so very low that it dragged others down with it, and surely Brooks Chaffee was not stupid, to be so taken in by a girl of bad character.

Jack drank off his brandy in one long draft and rose to make himself another. This new drink was darker than tea, nearly straight cognac. Jack sat down again, sprawling, his long legs stretched out in front of him, warming at the fire. Lily remained as she had been, standing.

"She's as dangerous as any viper that a Cleopatra ever dreamed of. She's dangerous as a lightning bolt's dangerous, because it is her nature to be that way, she can't help it, and there is no such thing in her as a conscience, nor a regret, nor a thought for someone else's happiness."

"You know her very well, then."

"Hardly at all, as I said. Like recognizing like. Naturally, Caroline hates me, and Brooks wants us to be friends, and she knows I know what her dirty game is. It's a bad show, Lily. A very bad show. If I try—even mildly—to warn Chaffee off, I lose a friend. If I don't, I also lose a friend, and the friend loses his soul, maybe his mind, maybe the entire remainder of his life.

Jack held the brandy to his lips and merely sipped it. He stared into the glass as though he hoped to find some message of hope written there. Lily felt helpless. She looked at her baggage and once again felt an enormous sense of relief that tomorrow she'd be leaving all this behind her. *Let Brooks Chaffee marry whom he would. Much she could do about that!* Lily knew she had no more influence on that situation than she had on the wind in the trees. Still, a warning came to her lips, and she decided there was nothing to lose in saying it out loud.

"I think," she began quietly, "that you should not say anything against the girl. For if you do, he will remember it forever. If you say nothing, and he later finds out that she is . . . as you say, he cannot blame you for having been fooled also. And you might end up with his friendship where otherwise Mr. Chaffee might have lost both his fondness for the girl and for you, poor man."

"Ah, you're right, as ever, Lily. I'll say not a word."

Lily looked at him, and in her heart was a strange, sad mixture of gratitude and pity. *He isn't half so bad as he paints himself. If only there could be a way of showing him that, he might yet be saved.* The time of their parting was on them, and Lily could not find the right words.

"I'll be taking a cab to the docks, then?"

"I think it's best. Patrick could come, but you don't want that, do you?"

"No. If it's to be a new beginning, I'd sooner have it completely new. Right from the start."

"Will you think of me sometimes?"

"What do you take me for? Think of you? And me carrying your baby! I will think of you, Jack, every time the baby moves inside me, and every time he cries or smiles—he or she!—I will think of you and be grateful for your kindness."

"It is a small kindness, Lily."

"Not to me, it isn't, for couldn't you have flung me into the gutter without a penny, and there'd be little I could do about it."

"I may be a cynic, Lily, but I'd never do that."

"No, and yet there's gentlemen who would, and do, and 'tis the poor girl who gets blamed for their wickedness."

"Well, wickedness is a two-way street, Lily, and I shall probably know every mile of it, and all its gutters, too, before I die. But now I think it's time I should be going home, and trying to sober up, and change for the ball tonight where the engagement will be announced between Mr. Brooks Chaffee and the fair Caroline Ledoux."

Jack came to her and took her hands in his. He kissed her lightly on the cheek, a brotherly kiss.

"Good-bye, then, my Lily. I wish that things had been different, that . . ."

"Good-bye," she said quickly, not wanting to prolong the moment. "Good-bye, and wish me luck."

"I wish you all the luck there is, and more."

"Then good-bye, and thanks."

"You haunt me already."

"Good-bye, Jack."

He turned quickly and left her. Lily stood by the door for a moment, listening to his footsteps upon the stairs until the footsteps faded away and mingled with the muffled sounds from Sixteenth Street outside. Then she turned back to the little parlor that she'd be leaving, tomorrow, forever. Then Lily walked to the mantelpiece and picked up her teacup, untouched since Jack's arrival. Good. The tea was still warm enough to drink.

You will be calm. You won't cry or do anything silly. Save your tears, Lily, for one day you may truly need them. Lily sat on the love seat in the silent aftermath of Jack's leaving and thought: *Of course, it would be just that way with a man as fine and good and beautiful as Brooks Chaffee. But maybe Jack was wrong. The girl might not be as black as he'd painted her. Jack tended to be overcynical, to despise himself and anyone he thought was like himself.* Lily found herself hoping the girl was good, that she would make a fine happy life for the boy.

Wednesday dawned gray. There was plenty of time, for the *Eurydice* sailed on the afternoon tide. Still and all, Lily was eager to be off, to begin this strange and thrilling new life. She drank some tea and rang for the porter.

This in itself was momentous: the first time in her life that Lily had summoned a servant for her own use. Having rung, she watched the door anxiously, wondering what she'd do if the man refused to help her, if he saw through her flimsy disguise into all the secrets of her heart. *For what right do you*

*have to be in this hotel, with these new trunks, to be sailing
on a fine new clipper?*

It burned in her heart with the intensity of live coals that
her new life must be launched with a lie.

*You are Mrs. Fergus Malone, wife of a decent striving
young man, sailing to join him in San Francisco, where he is
a clerk in the Wallingford Emporium.*

Lily looked into the mirror and said these things out loud,
as if by saying them they might become true. Her lie might
be a small one, compared to all of the lies that had ever been
told in the history of the world, but to Lily on this April
morning of 1856 it loomed bigger and darker and more
threatening than any storm cloud. She was sure that the eyes
of God and all his angels were upon her, knowing, disapproving, and planning for her punishment.

A knock sounded at the door, discreet but clearly audible.
The porter! Facing up to him was the first test of her new in-
carnation as Mrs. Fergus Malone, and Lily faced it with a
martyr's courage.

"You rang, madame?

He was a big man, neither young nor old, with a face expressionless as unrisen dough. He meant her no harm and his
eyes held no doubt or malice.

Lily smiled from sheer relief. "Yes. Can you bring down
my trunks and fetch me a cab? I'm going to the docks."

"Surely, madame."

He immediately lifted her biggest trunk, wafting it to his
burly shoulder with a sudden grace, as if it were no heavier
than a flower. Trumpets sounded in Lily's heart, and a feeling
of unlimited power flowed through her with the intoxicating
warmth of good brandy. *It had worked! He hadn't laughed,
or scorned her, hadn't refused!* The porter came and went,
and soon all of her luggage was waiting at the curb and he
vanished to find a cab.

He would never know, this silent lumbering man, that in
Lily's eyes he was more glorious than all the shining knights
in the old fairy stories, that he had been her escort into a
magical place where dreams came true and the future beckoned with a generous hand. A hand that pointed west.

The porter came back with a cab and helped the cab man
load it. Lily tipped him then, and thanked him, and he
wished her a good trip.

Then Lily climbed into the passenger's compartment like a
queen, and smiled through the polished glass window. The
whip cracked and the cab rumbled off toward the docks. Lily

[217]

had never ridden by herself in a cab before. Down the familiar street they drove, turned right on Fifth Avenue, moving briskly on the fine spring morning. Lily felt her past slipping by and scarcely looked at it.

For the cab was heading into tomorrow, and all the rest of her tomorrows, and it couldn't get there soon enough to suit Mrs. Fergus Malone, of San Francisco, California, USA.

◦§ 17 §◦

South Street was teeming, quivering, pulsing with all the life of the busiest port in the New World.

Lily's cab rattled over the wet cobblestones, threaded its way in and out among lorries and hand barrows and push-carts and stevedores bent double under heavy burdens. Here was the nesting place of the great clippers. Their arrogant bowsprits thrust into the low brick houses of the waterfront, sleek pointed lances of New England's crusade against an implacable sea. The huge bowsprits made a dark arbor under which the cab moved, slower now for all the waterfront activity. There was the famous clipper *Hurricane*, and the old *Half Moon*, and the *Niobe* and the *Sea Witch*, and now, just ahead, at Pier Nine, the *Eurydice!*

Eurydice! Strange name. A girl in the old Greek tales, Jack had told her, a lovely romantic girl, a girl who'd gone to hell itself, and her lover came right after her to bring her back. Something like that. And who, Lily wondered, who would be coming to bring her back from whatever unknown hells or heavens she might be getting into? Surely not Jack! The cab jolted to a halt and Lily put aside all her doubts and hesitations. The sun had managed to break through the scurrying clouds, and now its clear light bounced off the fresh-painted flanks of the clipper *Eurydice*. White she was, with touches of gilt, a fine sleek vessel, a speed-maker, you could tell that in every line of her hull and the raked-back masts, three of them, and huge they were; Lily had never seen a tree so tall as the trees that had been cut to make those masts. *Eurydice*. New and beckoning and eager to be off again. Maybe as eager as Lily herself.

They were loading her, had been loading her for days, day and night, for every hour's delay was money lost to her owners. The driver set Lily's trunks on the wet cobbles near the *Eurydice*'s gangway. She paid the man and tipped him, and he, too, smiled and was gone. *It is a small thing to draw courage from, my girl, but it's the only thing you have, so don't be putting up your nose at it*. Another test passed. Another question not asked. Lily looked around her and wondered where Captain Endicott might be.

Everyone on the dock and on the ship itself seemed to have an assigned task and to be busily carrying it forth. Sailormen swarmed over the ship, scampered through its rigging like fleas in an old dog's coat, dashed up and down the trembling gangway, swung a huge cargo net from a tall wooden crane that looked like construction equipment Lily had seen in the city. They yelled and chattered in many tongues, and some of them sang. The five sailors in charge of the great cargo net sang as they rolled enormous barrels into it, then hoisted the bulging hempen web into the sky:

> In eighteen hundred and forty-six,
> I found myself in the hell of a fix,
> A-working on the railway, the railway, the railway,
> Oh, poor Paddy works on the railway.

Poor Paddy, indeed. Lily smiled at their song, but she wondered if the hatred would sail with her to California. Poor Paddy sounded all fine and jolly as the sailors sang it, no harm in the ditty, but there was harm enough in the fact that the poor Paddies of New York were a race apart, mocked and reviled for it, for their poverty and their ignorance and their willingness to do the dirty jobs: Paddies and bog-hoppers and Micks they were. Dirt they were, and lower than dirt.

> In eighteen hundred and forty-seven,
> When Dan O'Connolly went to heaven,
> He worked upon the railway, the railway, the railway,
> Poor Paddy works on the railway, the railway.

Yes, she thought, on the railway and in the scullery and in the ditches: you'd have to think a piece before you could think of a job too dirty or too mean for the Irish.

> In eighteen hundred and forty-eight,
> I found myself bound for the Golden Gate . . .

Their singing trailed off now, for the men had finished with the net. Lily gathered her courage and asked one of them where the captain might be. She wondered if all the rest of her life would be a series of such tests, and decided, a little grimly, that it probably would be.

"He'll be below, ma'am," said an enormous seaman in a filthy jersey striped with red. "The gent you'll be wanting is Mr. Parker, the first mate. And here he be."

Parker was a tiny man, built like a seagull, with a soft plump chest and narrow pipestem legs and a nervous tendency to hop about. He was pale for a seagoing man, and wore small steel-rimmed spectacles. Parker looked as though he would be far more at home in a clerk's office than on a clipper as dashing as the *Eurydice*. But Lily soon learned that Parker's stock in trade was efficiency. He smiled and shook her hand and had her trunks moving in seconds. Then Mr. Parker gently took Lily's elbow and escorted her on board the clipper. His manner was calm, polite, precise, and orderly. The man looked anything but a hero, but still and all he inspired confidence in her. And any amount of confidence was very welcome to Lily Malone at this crucial moment.

The deck was surprisingly neat, considering all the hustle of loading. The *Eurydice* was less than a year old, with only two Cape Horn voyages behind her, and there was still an aura of freshness about her. Lily knew nothing of ships, but she did understand housekeeping, and one glance was enough to tell that here was an extremely well-kept vessel. The brass glowed. The deck railings were polished, and even the oaken planks of the deck itself seemed to have been scrubbed recently. Ropes not in use were neatly coiled, sails furled tight as an Englishman's umbrella, and even the glass in the small round porthole in Lily's cabin looked lately shined. Captain Endicott, Lily decided, knew his job very well.

Her cabin was tiny, but it delighted her. *Her cabin!* How lovely that sounded. What a ring there was to it: *Mrs. Malone's cabin.* The little space was about twelve feet long by eight feet wide, and once two of her trunks were stowed there, and the hand valise, plus the bed and a small armoire and a little table, it was all a person could do to turn around. Still, it was hers. Her first home. A place where, for the first time in her life, Lily ruled. However small, however temporary, however much the result of sinning. Come in. Don't come in. Stay. Go. All these commands, all this authority was hers to exercise. At whim. It was delicious. A person could get drunk with it! The walls were wood and not painted. They curved, of course, being the outer side of the ship's hull, and the low ceiling of the cabin was the deck. Lily could hear footsteps, heard them vividly, felt the thumping as trunks and boxes were deposited none too gently on the deck. And every footstep held a promise. Who might the other passengers be? What friends might she find among them? Naturally, she'd be very discreet. A young married woman couldn't be too careful, that much she knew; her reputation, however false, was a thing to be cherished.

Suddenly Lily felt tired. She had done no real work this day, but the anticipation, the meeting of tests and passing them, the finality of it all, these things took their toll of her. She sat down on the narrow cot and thought about all the things she was leaving this day, and all that might come to her in the new place on the far side of the world. There. That was better. Maybe a bit of a nap. She relaxed, lay back, swung her feet up, being careful that they dangled over the edge of the bed a little, for she was the last girl in the world to soil someone's good coverlet. Then Lily closed her eyes and drifted into a dream.

In Lily's dream the sun shone hot and clear on the land, all golden and pure, warming and gentle as love and, like love, if it burned, she did not feel it. The land in Lily's dream was gentle too, rolling hills covered in grain, and the grain itself was golden, ripening. The hills flowed in their gentle rounded way to the horizon, gold meeting blue, and now and again on a hill there would be one huge tree, strong and deeply green, a tree for the fairy folk to dance under by moonlight. And Lily was not alone in her dream. She walked through the fields, which she somehow knew were her fields, hand in hand with a tall, gentle, golden man. They said nothing. They had no need for words. Who was this man? The land seemed to belong to Lily in the dream, and he, too, was hers. In the dream. In the new golden land. In the clear warming sunshine. In her dream Lily smiled, then frowned just slightly. There must be a child in the dream! But there was no child, not there, not in this part. Maybe the child was at home, or with its nurse, for surely in such a golden place there must be a house, and servants. Of course. She lay there in the shadowed ship's cabin and dreamed this dream, a slow and silent dream, no words in it, and no sounds. Not a bird sang in Lily's dream, and even the wind was still in the wheatfield. She moved in the dream and never felt the earth beneath her, held his hand and didn't feel the strength in it, or the warmth either, like a ghost she moved, that's what it must be, a ghost dream, and everyone in it dead. *It was a lovely dream, too bad it died. Died and must go to the place where dreams got buried.* Lily wondered, half in her dream and half analyzing the magic of it, wondered if the angels wept when a dream died, and how you buried hopes, what the prayers might be to whisper at the crypt of expectations.

Slowly Lily raised one hand to her cheek and wiped away a tear.

Still she lay there in the ship's cabin and drew a kind of sad nourishment from her golden dream. If she could think of Brooks as truly dead, this would be a help for her. Dead as Fergy he must be, and if not forgotten, then surely put aside to the place where memories of dead people lie. Nice to think on, but do not think too long or too hard about a thing so very far beyond control. Think, instead, about tomorrow morning, and all the other tomorrows, chains and chains of them stretching from New York to California from this year of our Lord 1856 into who knew what distant time.

Suddenly the ship moved. Instinctively Lily reached out and clutched the sides of her bed as if to keep herself from falling out of it. The ship was alive now, creaking and groaning and making a hundred unfamiliar noises. They must be putting out to sea! And she'd almost dozed through the greatest event of her life! Lily sat up, shook the dregs of her dream out of her head, stood, rearranged her dress, caught a glimpse of her hair in the porthole, straightened it, and left the little cabin to go up on deck.

Lily's cabin was amidships, and the steep, narrow, brass-edged stairway was just two cabins away. Her wide skirts filled the narrow hallway and engulfed the tiny stairwell. Soon she was on deck, and it was a sight worth waking for.

The huge iron anchor lay dripping in its housing below the bow. A longboat manned by fourteen crack oarsmen was towing the big clipper out into the East River and around the tip of the island to a place just off Battery Park. Lily found herself a quiet nook back from the railing and stood shyly by herself, unashamedly awed by the spectacle.

She had never seen Manhattan from the water. It seemed to have more church steeples than her pincushion had pins, each one beckoning to God, some more aggressively than others, Catholic steeples and Episcopalian steeples and Methodist steeples. All pointing to God, armies of steeples. And would God point back? The tallest tower was not a steeple at all, but the immense shot tower where they made cannon-balls. Lily wondered what God might make of that, the closest thing to him being an instrument of death? Still, it was a fine sight, and the bustling on board was fine too, all the raggle-taggle seamen working as a team now, rather as many small teams all doing different things. They climbed in the rigging so high and so fast it took Lily's breath away, the sheer height, and what could save them if they fell? They were off the Battery Park now, and Lily could see the fine ladies and gentlemen who had nothing better to do than come down to hear the chanties and see the clippers set sail. The chanties were part of the routine just as much as coiling a line in a certain way, or shining up the brass. Each little knot of men had its own chanter, and its own special chanties. They were setting the sails now. And a new chant began:

> Then up aloft that yard must go,
> Whiskey for my Johnny.
> Oh, whiskey is the life of man,
> Whiskey, Johnny!
> I thought I heard the old man say,
> Whiskey for my Johnny.
> We're bound away this very day,
> Whiskey, Johnny!
> A dollar a day is a white man's pay,
> Whiskey for my Johnny.
> Oh, whiskey killed my sister Sue,
> Whiskey, Johnny!
> And whiskey killed my old man, too . . .

It was endless. And every time the beat came around, the men hauled on the long ropes in unison. It became a kind of a dance, and the rhythms in the chant were echoed in the rippling sails, which rose with great slaps and popping sounds, loud as pistol shots but with a deep resonance, as if the wind god himself were applauding the seamen's singing. And Lily felt that she was a part of it all, too, that somehow just by being there she was speeding the great clipper on its way.

The sun itself seemed to be on the move now, darting in and out of the clouds, giving and taking its light and adding to the pace and drama of the scene. The afternoon air had suddenly taken on a chill. The crowds on shore were thinning. The main topsails went snapping up, the topgallants, royals, and skysails. Suddenly, at no signal that Lily could discern, the clipper strained forward.

The sails were all up now, startling in their enormity, pregnant with the freshening wind, eager on the turning tide. The raked-back masts groaned like thrashing lovers with the force of it. The gilded lady on the bow gazed resolutely seaward.

Lily found herself at the rail without remembering how she got there.

The *Eurydice* seemed to glide, to soar as a gull soars. But one look at the river rushing past the rail showed Lily the force and speed of her. The Battery was receding, the trees and steeples and people were toys in the distance now. They raced past Staten Island, past the Heights of Brooklyn, and Lily had a moment's pang as she thought of her old friend Fran, gone into service there these four years, and not a word in all that time. Was Fran living, even, and living still in Brooklyn?

Lily smiled a rueful smile then, for sure and no one had to tell her how very much could happen to a girl, even a servant girl, in four years. *Why, Fran might be married and a mother. She might be rich, or a fallen woman, or dead. Or she might be scrubbing floors, dulled by drudgery, persecuted. She might own a gold mine in California!* Brooklyn Heights slipped past, and vanished, silent, dim as Lily's memory of Fran from the orphanage. She turned, and looked back. You could hardly see Manhattan anymore. Lily wondered if she would ever see it again, or if she'd want to. They were in the Narrows now and the sea was coming at them headlong. Soon the calm and current of the Hudson River would be behind them. Soon they'd be at the mercy of God and his oceans. It was getting quite chilly. Lily had forgotten her shawl. She covered her left hand with her right hand and instinctively twisted the narrow golden wedding band on her third finger. A golden lie, false as her golden dream. And yet it was a kind of passport into the new world she would create for herself, for her child.

New York was now nothing more than a few dark bumps on the horizon. They passed another clipper coming toward the harbor, passed quite close, heard the cheering of the merry crew, home and safe at last after who knew how many months and what perils on the seas.

Months and perils. *Well,* Lily told herself, *if you aren't ready now, my fine Mrs. Fergus Malone, you never will be.*

"I hope you will forgive my presumption," said a quiet voice at Lily's elbow, "but since we two seem to be the only unescorted ladies on board, I thought it might be useful to make your acquaintance, my dear. I am Sophie Delage. Mrs. Sophie Delage."

Lily turned, startled. There stood a most imposing lady, of middle height and ample build, an older lady whose brown hair was touched with gray, dressed simply but expensively in black, almost in mourning, adorned with a fine cameo brooch set in gold at her bosom, wearing a black mohair shawl and, like Lily, hatless in the breeze. The woman's face was unusual: neither pretty nor ugly, it had a definite and very resolved character about it. She looked like a person of some consequence, a woman of decision. Then, remembering her manners, Lily smiled and offered her hand.

"I," she said softly, "am Mrs. Fergus Malone." The words came out of Lily's mouth so easily that it frightened her. To tell such a lie and not be struck dead for it! To inflict an unsuspecting stranger, a kind stranger at that, with the bold deception that must become the foundation of her new life.

Sophie Delage smiled. Lily smiled back, suddenly shy, feeling much younger than her years. How old must Mrs. Delage be? Surely no older than Jack's mother. Surely the woman was well into her fifties. And very prosperous, by the look of her. And sailing alone for San Francisco. Lily wondered about her new acquaintance, where Mr. Delage might be, and in what line of work, did she have children, why was she on the clipper? But the questions and their answers would keep. Four months, likely, they'd have in these close quarters. Lily wondered if they'd become friends, if she could afford to have a friend, if it would be possible to maintain a friendship and yet keep her secret—the living, forming, growing little secret that she literally carried within her.

The two women stood together at the rail as the last glimpse of land slipped out of sight behind the wake of the *Eurydice*. This would be her world now, this little wooden platform with its three huge raked masts, its acres of bulging canvas, polished brass, rough-looking sailors. And, somewhere, Captain Endicott and the occupants of the four other cabins. What adventures might they not share! What thrills and perils! Lily's basic fear of the deep, greedy ocean had all fallen away in the excitement of leaving New York, of leaving her past unalterably behind. But now, as she stood at the rail with Mrs. Delage, staring into the darkening sea as the ship strained forward, the fears came back. The sea that got Fergy might get her, too. It might get all of them.

Mrs. Delage's voice startled Lily. "You look rather pensive, my dear. Are you thinking sad thoughts, perhaps regretting loved ones left behind? I always feel happy and sad when I sail, both emotions at the same time. Is it that way for you, Mrs. Malone?"

"Oh," said Lily too quickly, hoping she hadn't been rude, "I'm afraid I was thinking a sad thought. Which is foolish, for sure and I'm happy to be sailing. It is a great adventure for me, my first voyage."

"Better, far, I am told, than the overland route, or cutting across Panama. One day, they say, the railroad will be safe. Until then, we all must become sailors."

"Yes. Do you live in San Francisco, then?"

"I do, my dear, although I daresay I won't recognize the place when we get there, it does change that fast."

"Growing like weeds, they say."

"Exactly like weeds, with as little plan. It is a rough place, you'll discover, but lively. It is a town, if I do say so, of many opportunities."

"Oh," said Lily, more fervently than her new friend could possibly know: "I hope so."

They traded small pleasantries as the sun set. Then Mrs. Delage went below to unpack, promising to join Lily at supper. Lily went down herself a few minutes later, her head filled with thoughts of her new acquaintance. It was hard to put Mrs. Delage into a category. Her appearance and dress indicated prosperity. But something about her, a certain brusqueness, a businesslike quality, made Lily think that she was not simply a rich man's wife. Well, time would tell about Mrs. Delage and her occupations. Lily was grateful for the older woman's offer of friendship, however tentative. Sophie Delage was right, of course: it made sense for the two lone women on the ship to stick together if that would be possible. Lily wondered if the captain had brought his wife, if he had a wife. Clipper-ship captains often took their families on voyages, particularly to the Far East, for a trip out there and back might well last years. It would be pleasant to have still another woman among all these men. But in any event, one more test had been passed. Mrs. Delage had been kind, had accepted Lily at face value.

The next test would be the evening meal. Lily dreaded that, and her doubts and fears were only a little eased by the thought that Mrs. Delage would be there too, that she wouldn't be quite alone. Still, it was terrifying.

Suppose there might be someone on board who knew her story! Could they put a paid-in-full passenger off for misrepresentation? What would happen if they laughed at her? Was it a crime to have a man's baby and not be married to him? Lily's head began spinning. She held onto the cabin wall, sat down on the bed, tried to force herself to be more cheerful. But the cheerfulness would not come. *This isn't like you, Lillian Malone, hop to it!*

She tried to think of something funny, but all Lily could summon up out of the depths of her mind was the image of Fergy the last time she'd seen him, there in the big dark reception room of the orphanage, seen the fire in his eyes, the eagerness to be off, the do-or-die resolution in his young face. Well, he did, and he also died. Do or die. And here she was, pregnant, too, following the same watery path. Maybe to the same watery grave! To be reunited with Fergy again! And would it be worth the dying?

Lily had a vision of herself, dead, still pregnant, forever pregnant, which would be God's punishment on her, her special hell, yes, herself dead and passing by Fergy at the front door of hell and him not even recognizing her. Did people talk to each other when they were dead? Did they kiss and laugh and make love? She thought of her parents, side by side in the black earth of the Twelfth Street cemetery. She hadn't even gone to say good-bye or to put a flower on that grave. And now there was no one to do that, or even think of doing it. She could write, maybe, but to whom? Lily closed her eyes then, and lay down as she had earlier, when the beautiful golden dream had come to her. But there was no golden dream this time. Only darkness filled Lily's head, and dark thoughts too. The motion of the clipper was soothing to her. It rocked and rocked, up and then down with a steady falling rhythm. A huge wooden cradle it was, the *Eurydice*, specially made for the unborn child of Lily Malone and Jack Wallingford.

And there was another she'd likely never set eyes on again. Jack, too, was slipping away from her as the shoreline had slipped away. Careless, moody, dangerous Jack. Jack, who was bursting with passion one moment and with despair the next. Jack, who obviously hated himself and his life, but hadn't the courage to chuck it all and make a new life. Jack, who had planted his seed in her, wild and thoughtless as the wind, paid her off and sent her packing. Jack was probably setting about ruining some other innocent right this minute in his snug little hotel suite on Sixteenth Street. Lily squeezed her eyes tighter as if by doing this she could squeeze out the image of Jack Wallingford. She'd concentrate on the motion of the ship. She'd rehearse what she'd be saying tonight at supper, what she'd say to the captain and the other passengers. What could she do to cement her new friendship with Mrs. Delage? Finally, mercifully, she dozed into forgetfulness.

It was dark when the ship's bell woke Lily. Seven times it

chimed. She sat up, blinking, wondering for a moment where she was, then remembering, feeling the fear and the adventure of the sailing come rushing back at her with a force so strong it was almost physical. There had been a candle on the little chest of drawers by the bed. Lily fumbled for a match, struck it, lit the candle. The orange flame sputtered and caught, brightening the small cabin. One candle surely would do for such a space. The candlestick was ingenious, a brass saucer and two curving arms coming up out of it, with the candle itself cunningly suspended between the arms on a pronged pivot so it remained upright no matter how the ship rolled. The candlestick pleased Lily: someone had thought about the problem of steadying a flame, and solved it handsomely. The *Eurydice* continued its rhythmic plunge through the Atlantic Ocean, but Lily's candle flame glowed straight and proud against the night. *And I will be steady as that flame, no matter what the weather*, she thought, and smiled on the strength of it, fixing her hair and finding her shawl.

My, but wasn't she hungry? Used as she was to the beautiful food of Louise Dulac at the Wallingford mansion, Lily was prepared for the worst on board ship. That would be another regret: Louise's food, and the fact that Lily hadn't learned more about how to duplicate those wondrous soups and sauces and magical desserts. Well, there might be time enough for all that in California. In the meantime, the mission of the moment was to get to San Francisco alive and healthy and with her reputation intact, false as that reputation might be. She caught a glimpse of herself in the mirror just before she left the cabin: the new Lily, a matron, pregnant in the bargain. Well, at least the other passengers didn't have to learn that most secret part of her deception. If the clipper made decent time, her full skirts could easily hide the bulge when it became a real bulge. She blew out the candle and closed the door of her cabin, locked it, and climbed the narrow stairs.

Sophie Delage was already in the captain's wardroom when Lily got there, and had been thoughtful enough to save Lily a place at the long common dining table. Mrs. Delage seemed to know all of the passengers, and she introduced Lily deftly, but it would be days before Lily got them all sorted out.

They were as mixed a lot as you could ask for. There were Mr. and Mrs. Peabody from Gloucester, Massachusetts, and their small daughter, Dorothea. Mrs. Peabody had prematurely graying hair and a face like a winter apple in springtime, shriveled-looking, as though she were drying up from within for reasons best known to herself and her God. The Good Lord, as Mrs. Peabody liked to call him, was seldom far from her thoughts or her conversation. If the Good Lord permitted, they might be able to have something to eat soon. Mr. Peabody said very little. The child, Dorothea, was as fat as her mother was wizened, and showed every promise of becoming a little monster. Dorothea whined. Dorothea hated the soup when it came. Dorothea, Lily decided, would be lucky if she didn't find herself floating alone in the wake of the *Eurydice* some dark night. Then there were the two foreigners—Herr Grundig, a traveling hat salesman from Munich, with scant English but much enthusiasm; and Mr. Gordon, an Englishman of implacable snobbery; and Mr. Harold Perkins, American from New Haven, Connecticut, nonstop talker and relentlessly boring. Lily wondered if by any remote chance Perkins might have run into Jack Wallingford at New Haven, but she quickly decided they would have nothing in common. Jack might be many things, but boring he was not, nor would he tolerate a man like Perkins for more than a few minutes.

So there they were, and not a sign of Captain Endicott. Lily wondered if, indeed, there was such a person. She also wondered how all three Peabodys fit into one cabin, if theirs was as small as her own cabin. And she decided that in Sophie Delage she had already discovered the most promising of the passengers. She hoped Mrs. Delage felt likewise. Mr. Parker poked his head in to see how they were doing. They were doing quite well. The food was simple but adequate: a vegetable soup followed by chops of mutton, carrots cooked in plain water, potatoes, also boiled, and a sweet custard with raisins in it for dessert.

Lily ate heartily. The sea air seemed to have improved her appetite, and the fact was, she had eaten very lightly these last few days, in all her excitement about sailing.

Sophie Delage set the pace of the conversation, led it easily at their corner of the table, which was, luckily, as far as it was possible to be from the garrulous Harold Perkins. The Peabodys said little except to each other and to the deity. Herr Grundig beamed and cheerfully fractured the language. The Englishman had obviously decided that all of the other passengers were beneath consideration. His conversation was limited to remarks like "Please pass the salt."

Lily was glad of Mrs. Delage's company. She was also glad she'd brought several books and plenty of sewing. When dinner was finished, Harold Perkins lit up a foul-smelling cigar.

As if by a prearranged signal, Lily and Mrs. Delage got up and left the table.

The night was black as the devil, with only the thinnest slice of a crescent moon and a light dusting of stars. Lily and Mrs. Delage paused by the railing.

"I often think," said Mrs. Delage, "that being on a ship is a bit like being on a star, that lonely, that much removed from the rest of the world."

"A sailor's life must be lonely, unless he is the captain and brings his family."

"Captain Endicott, I am told, did not bring his lady on this voyage. He is closeted with his charts, plotting our little journey through the night."

"I knew a girl once," Lily said thoughtfully, looking not at Mrs. Delage but up into the star-sparked night, "who believed that each little star was the soul of a dead person, condemned to wander forever in the night and the cold. It always seemed to be a sad thought."

"It is, at that. Are you feeling better, Mrs. Malone?"

"Much better, thank you."

"I was worried this afternoon."

"Thank you. I will be the better for your company."

"It's kind of you to say that, my dear. I do feel we will be thrown much together on this voyage, judging by our fellow passengers. Who do not, to put it mildly, strike me as being an especially promising lot."

Suddenly Lily found herself laughing, and for the first time in weeks. There had really been very little to laugh about in Jack's secret hotel rooms on Sixteenth Street. The laughter started as a small ripple and built, and might have gone on a bit longer than the joke warranted. It was the laughter of emotional release as much as amusement. But Mrs. Delage joined in, and in some small way this episode seemed to put the seal on their growing friendship. To share a secret, however tiny, to be partners in fun, however inconsequential— these things were new to Lily in her new role as Respectable Married Matron. And she was carrying it off, here was hard evidence of it.

They said little more, but remained at the rail for perhaps ten minutes longer, just enjoying the dark beauty of the night, and the quiet, and the comforting feeling of shared companionship. Finally Mrs. Delage said she must retire. Lily followed her down the stairs.

"I'm nothing like unpacked, my dear, or I would invite you for a sweet. Perhaps tomorrow."

"Thank you anyway. And for saving me a place at the table, for it's bashful I am with strangers."

"Well, my dear, we won't be strangers with each other now, will we?"

"No, and thank heaven for that."

"Good night, then, Mrs. Malone, and sleep well."

"Thank you, and the same to you."

Lily closed the door of her cabin and found the match box. Once again the orange flame filled the little space with warmth and brightness. It was tiny, it looked like the inside of a violin, but it was hers. Home! A floating, rocking home, but Lily's own. Undressing slowly, quietly luxuriating in the fact that here at last was a room of her own, no orphanage dormitory, no garret at the Wallingfords' to share with Susie, no lover's couch on which to quench the fire of Jack's passions. She must do something with the room. Suddenly, on impulse, Lily opened her big trunk, burrowed into it, down deep, trying to remember.

And she found it. Out of the bottom of the trunk, wrapped in tissue paper and looking quite the worse for wear, was the rag doll, Hortense. *If Mrs. Delage sees Hortense, she will think I've gone mad.* Still and all, Lily placed Hortense on top of the chest of drawers, as reverently as any priest ever set the chalice on the altar. And there sat Hortense, resurrected from the past, surveying the tiny cabin with button eyes and a slightly crooked smile. Hortense would sail around the Horn, and keep her company, and be a friend. Lily looked at the doll, then reached slowly out and touched Hortense's cheek. She undressed then, blew out her candle, and climbed into the narrow bed.

The ship's bell struck eleven. No light at all came through the small round porthole. Lily's last thought, as she drifted down into sleep, was that she must set about making a set of curtains for the porthole. Yes, and for Mrs. Delage, too. That would be a good thing to do, friendly but not presuming. Then Lily closed her eyes and let the ship's rocking motion soothe her into sleep.

❦ 18 ❧

Lily had expected, and feared, many things from the voyage of the *Eurydice*. But she had not anticipated the dominant feature of the journey, which was boredom.

Except for changes in the weather, which generally held fair, one day was very like the next, with no real work to do and little entertainment beyond what the passengers and crew might devise for themselves.

The men took to playing cards all day long: spinado or euchre or whist. Dominoes were much in evidence too, and their syncopated clicking could be heard most afternoons on deck. And there was singing. The sailors had their chanties, as much a part of the great clipper as her ropes or canvas, and it was a rare hour that did not include one of the rhythmic chants. And often at night some sailor's voice would overflow with song, to the tinkling strains of a banjo or the mournful wail of a mouth organ. The rousing stanzas of Stephen Foster rode south with the *Eurydice*, and so did the older favorites, sea songs and river songs so ancient no one could say where they came from.

Lily's mood changed as often and as unexpectedly as the shifting wind. Now she'd be brave, now timid. In one frame of mind she wanted nothing to do with any man, ever again. In another mood, she turned all soft and romantic. There was a young sailor on board, a Norwegian no older than herself, who had hair exactly the color of Brooks Chaffee's hair. Every time Lily saw him she felt her knees go weak, and she forced herself to look at the boy with no sign of emotion. *Sure and if the color of a lad's hair can do that to me, then it's trouble I am heading for unless I do something about it right this minute, and let what can never be go to rest.* Still her moods came and went, and her struggles to control them were only intermittently successful.

Once, on deck in the moonlight, Lily found herself on the verge of tears because somewhere in the stern a young sailor's voice rose clear and sorrowful as he sang the ballad

[233]

of a trapper who loved the Indian chief's daughter: *"Oh, Shenandoah, I love your daughter! Away, you rolling river: for her I've crossed the rolling water. Away! I'm bound away! Across the wide Missouri . . ."*

Well, thought Lily, glad for once that she was alone, that Sophie had gone below earlier, *and aren't I crossing the rolling water, too, and a lot more of it than that old trapper.* But not for love, she couldn't claim it was for love, even though that was part of her lie, part of the tale she'd told Sophie, that she was prepared now to tell anyone who might ask, even knowing as the false words crossed her lips that she'd be damned to hell for it.

And why was a simple song from an unknown sailor bringing her so close to tears? She, who had saved her tears so long, and through so much sadness.

Lily turned to the rail and gazed out through misted eyes at the moon. It was so near to full as made no difference, and it turned the sea to polished pewter capped with foam, with a shimmering path of moonlight that seemed to stretch all the way to the end of the world. Lily watched, dazzled, and as she stood there a school of five big dolphins came leaping and dancing by, jumping high in the moonlight as though they had no purpose in life but to entertain Mrs. Fergus Malone on her long, dull voyage. She could not help but smile at these delightful creatures, and her sadness disappeared to whatever dark place had bred it. Suddenly tired, she went below.

Weeks went by. They crossed the equator, with much fuss and festivity, and the most dignified officers made themselves ridiculous, all dressed up as King Neptune and his court. Occasionally they passed another ship, and traded news, and this was a big event in their otherwise uneventful day. Once someone sighted a whale, but Lily was below, and she missed it.

Lily was very glad of Sophie Delage's continuing interest in her, for with Sophie she could relax a little from the rigid decorum she imposed upon herself in her public performance as Mrs. Fergus Malone. They had long been on a first-name basis, and for the first time in her life Lily found herself sharing the company of a grown-up, worldly and obviously quite prosperous woman on something like an equal basis. It was an uneasy but delicious sensation.

The *Eurydice* skimmed down the coast of South America past exotic lands where paintbox birds and snakes big around as a man lived in emerald jungles; but all Lily saw was an immense circle of water that they seemed to drag with them wherever they went. To hear they'd gone nearly two thousand miles now, that they were off the coast of Brazil, that they'd see no more land until they'd rounded the Horn and put in to Valparaiso—all of this interesting information made little impression on Lily, for one ocean wave looked much like another, and she was by now so familiar with the ship and its occupants that there seemed to be no surprises left in it.

The food deteriorated, and the water supply was now meted out by the first mate, one quart per person per day. They did their laundry by dragging it behind the ship in nets, and the results, while better than no washing at all, were far from satisfactory, for there was always a stiff residue of salt in everything. Lily sewed and read and practiced her still-unfinished handwriting in the secrecy of her little cabin.

And she talked to Sophie Delage. They talked of many things, and Lily found her new friend to be both humorous and perceptive and altogether amused by the follies and pretensions of the world in general, and certain of the other passengers in particular. Lily was flattered by the older woman's attention, and tried to learn what she could from her. Yet there was always a reserve about Sophie, a certain guarded quality when the conversation approached anything to do with her private life. Lily never heard Sophie speak of friends or family, husband or children, church or business. That, of course, was her privilege, and Lily thought this reticence becoming, and in fact used Mrs. Delage's discretion as a model for her own.

It was somewhere off Rio that they ran into the great calm.

The calm came sneaking on them in the night, and when Lily woke she sensed something was very wrong, although at first it was impossible to tell just what. Then she realized they weren't moving, and there was no sound at all. Gone was the flap of sail, the straining of hemp, the rhythmic pounding of the clipper's bow cutting through the waves. For there were no waves.

Lily made her way on deck and saw a sea flat as glass. The sails drooped with the dispirited lassitude of wilted flowers, and a strange silence hung over the *Eurydice* like a portent of doom. Lily had heard sailors talk of calms that lasted for weeks. She stood on the deck and slowly turned so that she could see the full circumference of the horizon. It stretched out around them, miles away, a thin flat line curving as slick and precise as the rim of a China plate, remote and unattainable as the moon, charged with danger and undisturbed by even the smallest ripple. Suddenly Lily felt the fear rising in her, for if they were to be delayed, what would happen to her baby?

The long day dragged on, and the sea stayed flat. In the afternoon, Captain Endicott had a longboat lowered, and himself in it, standing in the stern as a crew of husky sailors rowed three times around the ship, chanting at the top of their lungs.

"Why, pray," Lily asked the mate, "are they doing that?"

" 'Tis a custom, Mrs. Malone, old as the sea. To break the spell."

"And does it work?"

He smiled. "Let me ask you this: can it do any harm?" He bowed slightly and turned from her. Lily went below to find her sewing, and to calm the fear that gnawed at her insides like some cruel fish of prey.

Caroline Ledoux looked at Brooks with the full intensity of her great dark eyes. "You are a silly boy," she said softly, "if you don't take the slave states seriously. You Yankees seem to derive all your political knowledge from the speeches of the Reverend Mr. Henry Ward Beecher, and you all think that right and justice will just automatically prevail. And you are wrong, Brooks, wrong as wrong can be! It will surely be at the peril of everyone if we don't take these people—my people—seriously. They will fight and they will kill to keep hold of their way of living. If they become desperate, and I believe they are desperate, every one of us may be in danger."

Brooks looked at her and smiled. He loved his fiancée when she was serious—loved her frivolous, calm, angry, and at every way station in between. And he knew her observations were shrewd ones, and in some distant corner of his mind Brooks did take heed of them. For wasn't she a New Orleans girl born and bred, all but a hostage here in New York, about to risk all by marrying a bonded, blooded, deeply connected Yankee?

"If I haven't been thinking enough about politics," he said, taking her hand, "you know what I have been thinking about instead." He leaned forward playfully and kissed her cheek.

"Hush now!" She laughed, but there was an edge to the laughter. "You are like a tiny child, if I do say so, always wantin' to be kissing and having larks. Down home, boys your age and younger are out drilling, that's for sure. And when the war comes, they aim to have a good head start. And the war will come, Brooks, mark my words."

"A war wouldn't dare happen now, not on the eve of our wedding."

"It may please you to think so."

"Oh, they'll grumble and make speeches, but it's all talk, darling. Secession's just a dream. Anyone who thinks about it knows the South couldn't exist as a separate country."

"You're off bein' logical again. Logic is the least of it, Brooks. It's what folks feel, in their hearts, that makes wars. And what my people feel is fighting mad."

"You may be right, though I devoutly hope not. Anyway, we're safe. By this time next month you'll be Mrs. Chaffee and a certified Yankee. And I shall be the happiest man in the world."

A new light crossed her face then, and she reached up and touched his face. As ever, Brooks melted to her lightest touch. On the slender hand that so affected him was his engagement ring: a large cushion-cut ruby framed in seed pearls and diamonds, the ruby red and fiery as her lips, pearls perfect as her skin, the diamonds pure and hot as his need for her. Next month, in New Orleans, this extraordinary girl would become his wife, and to Brooks this was a true miracle whose cataclysmic power erased the fact that his brother, Neddy, seemed a little cool about the match, that Jack Wallingford seemed to be drunk more or less constantly now, and that a big war might well be brewing. In the pink light of his newfound joy, the world looked perfect to Brooks, and everyone in it reflected his happiness. He kissed her.

Lily paced the deck, sometimes alone, often with Sophie, always fighting the fear that they would be becalmed here forever, that they'd starve, that she'd give birth to the baby on board and her shame would be known to everyone, that she'd go mad.

The calm had lasted ten days now, and going mad seemed to be a real possibility. The tensions on board multiplied with every new day.

The captain threw a corked bottle overboard to mark their progress, if any, and for three days the bottle stayed exactly where he'd flung it, a few dozen yards off portside, hanging almost motionless in the slick green sea like an accusing finger. Not a breeze stirred nor a fish jumped. It was as though the *Eurydice* and everyone on it had been visited by some strange curse. The forces of nature were all asleep, and this

[237]

was more terrifying than a violent storm, for at least in a storm there was action, a sense of having some control over the furies of fate.

Now came a time of make-work and petty squabbling among the crew. All the brass had been polished until it shone like gold, every rope was coiled into new perfections of geometry, the deck stoned and oiled, paint renewed. A canvas screen was improvised in the stern, the better to preserve the modesty of the female passengers, and some of the crew and a few of the male passengers went swimming noisily from rope ladders.

Lily read and sewed and talked lazily with Sophie. Sometimes Lily had a sense that Sophie was observing her with a strange intensity.

Lily might look up from her sewing and find the older woman's eyes fixed on her with an appraising stare that Lily found disconcerting. *Ah, surely she means no harm, and isn't it natural for her to be a bit curious, for the Lord knows I am, too.* And Lily would put aside her doubts, for the practical side of her nature told her she must keep her fears under the tightest rein, or they'd run away with her for sure.

And for all the strangeness and privation of this voyage, Lily found herself enjoying it, for wasn't it the first step in her new life? And wasn't it a good thing to have this time to gather her wits and practice her new role?

And, thus far, the new role seemed to be working. No one had challenged her, or even questioned her identity. *Well, it's because I'm of too little account to be worth questioning, that's why, and lucky I am for it.*

Lily cherished each small particle of respectability like a miser, and every time one of the crew or a fellow passenger called her "Mrs. Malone," this added to her small and precious hoard; a frail and stolen foundation it might be for the new life she hoped to find, and yet it was all the foundation Lily had, and she was glad of it. She could see herself in San Francisco, the baby fat and healthy and under the care of some inexpensive but loving housekeeper, and herself off to work at the Emporium, neat in her hand-sewn dresses, and getting ahead, and maybe, one day, even finding a good man to marry her, and why not, her being a respectable young widow and a great scarcity of women in California, or so she'd heard.

It was with thoughts like these that Lily passed the endless hours while the *Eurydice* lay becalmed off Rio.

On the last day of the second week of the great calm, the cook went mad.

Lily was on deck in the stillness of the afternoon, sewing with Sophie in the scant shade of a furled sail. All of a sudden there came a terrible, incoherent yell, a clatter and a crashing, heavy footsteps running, and over it all the shrill, piercing, wounded-animal screaming of a soul writhing in the very fires of hell.

The cook came charging around the corner of the captain's cabin, wild of eye and red of face, screaming louder, blood streaming from a gash on his forehead, waving a huge cleaver in death-dealing arcs over his head, so that none of the crewmen who followed him dared come close.

He raced to the ship's rail and vaulted over, still yelling all the long way down to the glass-smooth sea. They all raced to the rail and looked down. Still yelling, the screams mixed with splashing and sputtering, clutching his cleaver like Neptune's very scepter, the crazed man lit out for the farthest horizon.

Captain Endicott had the longboat half-lowered when the sharks came. The cook had been screaming so steadily that Lily was astonished to find Sophie screaming too. She turned to her friend, then back to the bloody spectacle below. There was the quick black triangle of a shark's fin, then another. The foam turned red. The cook gave one last unforgettable howl of pain and madness. The sharks made another pass and then it was over. The last they saw of the wretched man was his arm waving spasmodically in hideous parody of a salutation, still clutching the cleaver. Then there was only silence and the smooth, smooth sea stretching uninterrupted to eternity.

Unconsciously Lily found herself making the sign of the cross. *And I didn't even know his name!* The passengers and crew stood crowded at the rail long after the last trace of the cook had vanished from sight. *One moment of screaming, and a life is gone. It's that cheap, that accidental. Well, come what may, I will never do myself in; no matter what, I'll fight and go on fighting and go down to death fighting, too, if I must.*

Lily felt the baby within her, and a strange new sense of well-being came over her, strange, because in some way she could not understand, it was connected to the sad death of the cook. Suddenly she felt tired, and went below to sleep.

❦ 19 ❧

Brooks Chaffee slid the shining brass bolt shut and sealed the world outside. Then he turned to his bride. The world could well stay outside their opulent suite on board the *Corsair*, and forever!

Caroline was gazing out of the brassbound porthole, still wearing the cocoa-colored traveling gown she'd put on directly after the ceremony at the old Ledoux plantation, Belles Heures. What a well-named house! Many were the lovely hours they'd spent there this last week, and would again. Brooks fairly glowed, for he knew the lovely hours were really just beginning for Caroline and for him, and that with even the smallest bit of luck they would go on forever.

It seemed he'd been waiting for this moment all the days of his life. Twenty-one years was a long time to wait, and now he would wait no longer.

He went to Caroline, smiling, and thought of what she was giving up to marry him. This last week had been a whirl of the merriest, most elegant parties Brooks had ever seen. The scale of life on these great river plantations frankly astounded him. It was all so vast, so easy, so very heavily populated with armies of black servants—slaves, of course. If, beneath the lovely veneer of charm and soft accents and gentle manners that almost everyone he met seemed to come by naturally, there seethed a caldron that might soon bubble over, none of this intruded—or would be allowed to intrude—on his happiness. He saw Caroline, and only Caroline, and the world and its problems could wait, maybe forever.

Even this suite on the *Corsair* was perfect: large and paneled in mahogany, three rooms and a real bath, the owner's suite, and why not, since old Ledoux himself was the owner! There were ivory-colored roses in a big old silver bowl, champagne chilling in a gilt-silver tub, and in the next room a wide low bed covered in silk and filled with the promise of love.

He walked up to Caroline, and standing close behind her, encircled her with his arms.

She was crying.

"My darling darling," he said softly, "what can be the matter?"

Caroline, a sad wraith and lovely enough to break his heart, spun around in his arms and nestled close on his chest. He had never seen her like this, weeping, vulnerable as a wounded sparrow.

"I'm so afraid!"

Brooks felt himself growing as he stood there, growing stronger, more brave, the better to defend his Caroline from all the winds of fear that might be pursuing her, real or imagined. *The poor thing, she's afraid of the lovemaking, afraid I'll hurt her!* Brooks would have cheerfully died on the rack rather than hurt Caroline. He smiled again, indulgent, protective.

"Afraid of what, my dearest? There is nothing in all the world to harm you, dear Caroline, not while I live."

"You're so sweet." But still she shuddered, and still she sobbed.

"What is wrong, my darling?"

"I'm afraid . . . that you'll think . . ."

"Think what, my love? I think only of you, and only beautiful thoughts."

"Once, when I was twelve, climbing in the peach tree at Belles Heures . . ."

"Yes?"

"I fell and . . . I did something to my insides, Brooks. I tore myself up."

"Well, that's too bad, dear, but surely you're all right now. There's nothing to worry about."

"I was afraid you'd think . . . you see, I tore whatever you call it, I was afraid you'd think I'm not . . . pure."

And she dissolved into sobbing again, and buried her small dark head in his shirtfront.

"How little you know me!" Brooks reached out and touched her cheek and gently lifted her face until at last she was looking into his eyes.

"You must understand," he went on, "that I love you, Caroline, more than I have ever loved anything. I love you completely, insanely, perhaps stupidly, but totally and irrevocably. When first I saw your face—your beautiful face that should never shed a tear, ever again!—it was like falling off a cliff, that sudden, that shocking. Never doubt me, darling, nor that I love you as much as it is possible for me to love."

For a moment she said nothing, but simply looked up at him, blinking her tears away. Then slowly a smile formed on her face, a smile that held all the magic of dawn lighting a field of wildflowers. And she spoke.

"You are a beautiful man, Mr. Chaffee, and you say the most beautiful things. And I love you, I do!"

She kissed him then, and he held her tighter so that she would never feel frightened again, not of him, nor of anything or anyone else in the world. And, still kissing her, Brooks lifted his bride of three hours and carried her into the waiting bedroom.

They never opened the wine that afternoon, nor that evening, either.

There was no timepiece in Lily's cabin. Only by the light and the ship's bells could she gauge the passing hours. Now she lay in the heat of late afternoon, thinking about the poor dead cook, and about many other things besides.

The voice, when it came, seemed to come from a great distance, and indeed it did, from the top of the tallest mast, from the crow's nest, where a lookout was ever posted, looking for sails.

"Sail ho!"

A dozen voices took up the cry, louder, nearer. "Sail ho! Sail ho!"

Lily well knew what magic lived in that brief cry. *If there's a sail, then there must be wind to fill it, and this damned calm may soon be over.* Quick as she could, Lily got up and went on deck. The excitement was vibrating in the still air. Faces that had been expressionless or frowning just this morning now wore grins. The captain was lowering two longboats, the better to tow them into the breeze. And there, there far to the starboard horizon, was a tiny white fleck that could only be a sail!

They looked at it in wonderment, like a sign from heaven. The air itself seemed to change now. It was brighter, less damp. The stranger ship passed them some fifteen miles away, a big clipper, regal as any swan. Then came a sound they'd thought they might never hear again—the crack of wind against canvas!

The great sails came alive again, swelling and straining, and looking, Lily thought, quite pregnant with wind. *Preg-*

[242]

nant, indeed! But at least she could smile at herself for entertaining such an irreverent thought.

Slowly at first, the ship began moving.

And as it moved, and gained speed, a great cheer went up from passengers and crew alike. It was as if the poor mad cook had been some kind of necessary sacrifice to the sea gods, who were now appeased and would let them go on their way again.

The ship seemed to fly now. A new and happy mood pervaded the *Eurydice*. Once, walking the deck alone, Lily found herself face to face with the blond Norwegian sailor, and found that she could look at the lad, and smile, and that it meant no more to her than seeing any other member of the crew. In that moment a vast weight lifted from her soul, for Lily felt that she had somehow exorcised the ghost of Brooks Chaffee at last.

They sighted the coastline of Brazil on the second day after the calm ended. The captain sent two longboats ashore, heavily armed, fearing the natives, and all of the passengers were made to stay on board. Back came the boats laden with fresh drinking water and all manner of exotic fruits and vegetables: sweet green coconuts, bitter little oranges, limes, small fat bananas, breadfruit, and papaya. For days they feasted like natives, and only when the fresh food was gone did they realize how much they were going to miss the dead cook.

The flour had turned moldy weeks ago, and their only bread was the tough, dry hardtack that had all the flavor of an oak board. The dead cook had turned out surprisingly varied and edible meals, considering the small size of the galley and the limitations of his larder. Now his helpers took over, and the results were dubious at best. Gone were the tasty "ship's pies" the old cook had made so well with chunks of pork and chicken and vegetables all sealed in flaky crust, perfect to eat when the ship was rolling. Now they got floury gruels with scraps of unidentifiable meat, and even the fresh fish they caught suffered in the preparation.

But at least they were moving. The clipper raced south. They could all feel the urgency in their pace, for full sails were flying and the captain pressed on relentlessly in his eagerness to make up for lost time.

The air grew colder, the coastline more mountainous, less green. Before long they'd be rounding the Horn! The voyage was nearly half done!

Having smiled on the *Eurydice* once again, the wind gods blew hard and fair, and the air vibrated with expectation.

It was Lily herself who first saw the albatross.

At first she could scarcely credit such a bird. His wings seemed to fill the sky. Huge he was, and pale gray, with webbed feet wide enough to shovel coal with. He hovered far above the ship, almost motionless, with never a beat of his great wide wings nor a nod of his cruel-beaked head. Nor did he make any sound. *If the albatross sings*, thought Lily, in the grip of a sudden and irrational fear, *then it must be a dirge*. For this was a ghost bird, the spirit of everyone lost at sea, a bad omen. *Why was I on deck at this moment? Why did I look up? He might have passed unseen, for surely, by all the laws of God, only seeing the thing made it real*.

Two days after Lily saw the albatross, the *Eurydice* sailed within sight of Tierra del Fuego. The land of fire. It certainly didn't look very fiery, cruel gray mountains pasted against a cold gray sky. It was not a reassuring spectacle. Lily stood at the rail, her woolen shawl drawn tight around her, for the air was cold as winter now, and thought about being halfway to California.

The world on board the *Eurydice* was not a perfect world, but by now Lily felt at home there, whereas the San Francisco of her imagining held as many problems as it did possibilities. *Suppose I get sick? Suppose the baby's sick or a monster—God's justice!—and suppose I can't do the work they ask of me at the Wallingford store? Maybe it's all a hoax, just to get me away from Jack, as if I'd want him in the first place!* Well, his letter of credit was no hoax. Lily knew that, for hadn't she cashed half of it already, the gold coins sewn into her waistband, and the other half, full five hundred untouched dollars, due in San Francisco? And didn't she have the manager's name and address, Mr. Charles Linton, the store's chief executive? Old John Wallingford had even written a letter to Linton, which Lily carried, unopened, in her trunk. Every time the fears welled up in her, Lily sternly reminded herself that they were unfounded, that all had been done to assure her secure employment in California that could be done. This did not make the doubts go away forever, but only temporarily, and they would come creeping back to torment her when she least expected them.

When they sailed around it two days later, Cape Horn proved to be an anticlimax, a shapeless gray lump of an island barely visible in the pale gray mist. Still, the event itself was charged with meaning. To have sailed straight into another ocean! To be on the other side of the world, with nothing between you and China! Lily expected to hear trumpets playing, or a chorus of angels singing, but all she heard was the familiar slap of the *Eurydice*'s prow against the waves, the straining sails, and the crew chanting.

Three days passed in which it was impossible to tell the Pacific from the Atlantic. The ship's routine was precisely the same, and only the wind turned fickle. The old sailors frowned, sensing trouble.

The ship plowed onward up the coast of Chile.

Lily sensed a new mood on board, a deepening tension, and especially in the crew, but there seemed nothing to be done about it. She minded her business as ever, sewed, read, talked some to Sophie, and went early to bed.

She woke in a mad dream of violence. The world in her dream had gone all topsy-turvy, shaking and tumbling and taking great unexpected leaps. It sounded the way Lily had always imagined a war must sound, with loud crashing noises, shouting, alarms. Something bumped violently against her head in the dark cabin. *God in heaven, we've been invaded by pirates, they'll kill us and rape us and this is the end!* Not knowing whether to scream or to pray, Lily started to do both, and failed. The cabin took another violent lurch, and she was thrown hard against the wall. Then she reached out and gripped the oaken frame of her bunk. *It wasn't a dream, then. In dreams, your head didn't throb like this, from where you'd bumped it.* She clutched at the sides of her bunk for dear life, and listened, and wondered what to do next. And she thought of Fergy, and Fergy's ship going down in a storm in these very waters, off the coast of Chile. Maybe the albatross was Fergy's soul, doomed to roam the skies forever, until he found his sister and brought her home to rest, in a grave made of coral and sand and walled with water.

I'll die right here in the cabin and never see the sun again, nor my baby, nor California, either!

Shouts came from the upper deck, but Lily could not hear what they said. There was nothing solid in her world now. Only by clutching with all of her strength to the sides of the bunk did she prevent herself from being tossed about the cabin like a bit of dandelion fluff blown by a wanton child. She wondered how long she could hang on, and if it mattered.

The wind screamed in the rigging, and this screaming was punctuated by huge cracking sounds that were almost like cannon fire. *The sails,* Lily guessed, *flapping loose, or maybe it was truly a cannon, maybe the captain was signaling their distress. And who would hear, far away as they were on the edge of the earth?*

There seemed nothing to do but hold on. Lily doubted she could walk even the short distance to her cabin door and hope to remain upright. And she dreaded what a hard fall might do to her baby. The noise level grew, although that seemed hardly possible. Now the howling wind and the thunderclap of the flapping sails were joined by the mad clanging of the ship's bell—summoning whom? To do what? Lily determined that if she was going to perish, she'd perish right here in bed. She closed her eyes then, and prepared to die.

The preparation lasted no more than half a minute, for it was quickly followed by outrage. *Die, indeed! She'd swim like a fish if she had to! Whoever thought they were going to get Lily Malone's life so cheap, had best think again. And her pregnant. If this was a trick of Fergy's, she'd get her own back on that score, yes, and others too.*

Lily sat up then, even though the *Eurydice* was still bucking and heaving like a wild beast gone mad. She staggered out of bed, splashing in nearly an inch of brackish seawater, fumbled until she located her rubber storm boots and heavy coat and a scarf, then made her way out into the corridor to meet her fate.

❧ 20 ❧

Lily fought her way to the door, lurching, staggering, groping, and all the way thinking about her own life and the life of the child within her. *If Fergy wants me to join him down at the bottom of the ocean, by God, he'll have to fight for me then, for 'tis a sure thing I'll not go willingly!*

The distance was only a few feet, but in the tossing, heaving, plunging blackness it seemed like miles.

Lily thought of all the good people she had known and lost, some to chance and some to death, and she wondered if by dying she'd see Ma again, or Big Fergus, Fergy, Sister Claudia. *And are they all up there watching, waiting, calling me so soon?* Lily wondered who'd miss her if the *Eurydice* went down, who'd say a prayer, weep a tear, or remember her at all. The list was not a long one.

Taking the greatest care for fear of damaging the baby, Lily moved across her well-known cabin with the stealth of a common burglar, feeling, holding on to any support as though her life depended on it, for in truth she felt it did. She had no real plan but to get out of the cabin. Somehow it must be safer up on deck, or in the corridor, even. Clutching, sliding, bracing herself for each new jolt, every inch that Lily gained was a small victory.

But here's the cabin door, and haven't I crawled through hell's own fiery battlefield to get here! The nausea welling up inside her couldn't diminish her joy at having made it safely this far. Lily reached for the brass door handle and turned it, bracing herself against the doorframe to steady herself as she opened it.

Just then, quick as prearrangement, the *Eurydice* gave a mighty lurch, plunging like a dropped stone. The bow struck the raging sea with an impact that set every beam and timber vibrating. Lily was flung hard against the opposite wall of the narrow corridor. She heard several crashing noises, and the loudest of these was her own bruised shoulder striking the mahogany wall.

Quivering, half bent over from the pain and surprise of it, Lily reached out with one leg and braced herself for the next jolt. And she wondered if it was such a fine idea after all, to leave her little cabin.

The hall was pitch-black, and nothing could be seen at either end of it. *They must have sealed the hatches against the waves.* Lily knew those hatches could be bolted from above and from below, and a new fear came rushing at her: *We could be trapped down here with no way out, should the ship go down.* Lily had never swum a stroke in her life, but now she swore she'd die trying, if only she could make it to the deck. And there were the longboats, for whatever good they'd be.

She inched her way down the hall.

Suddenly she stopped. There was a dancing, uncertain shaft of light. Sophie! Sophie's door had opened just a crack. It was as though the sun had come out after a long cold winter. For there stood Sophie, somehow majestic even in the shared terror of the ship's mad gyrations, wrapped in a green kimono of scintillating Chinese silk, richly embroidered with green and blue and gold flowers. She held up a whale-oil lamp, high and steady for all the bouncing of the ship.

"Lily? Come in, child, for I've been worried about you."

Trembling, half in fear and half in gratitude, Lily inched her way into Sophie's cabin. It was bigger than her own, and in some disarray. But Sophie made a place for her in an upholstered armchair, and carefully set down the lamp on a low table and braced it with two fat books, one of which, Lily was pleased to notice, was a Bible.

For a moment they sat there in silence, listening to the awesome noises from above and all around them.

Finally, in a small voice, Lily spoke: "I have never been so frightened: is this a very bad storm, Sophie? It being my first sea voyage, there's no way for me to measure it."

Sophie laughed, an astonishingly light and youthful ripple, considering the crashing violence all around them. "Yes, my dear, you may rest assured this is a very bad storm, far and away the worst I've been through."

"How can you be so calm?"

"I'm not, Lily, if the truth were known. But here we are, aren't we? If I thought that by screaming and tearing my hair I could stop the wind, then there I'd be, screaming and tearing. As it is . . . well, I am far from brave, Lily. Life often deals us strange cards, and we must play them as best we can. As for tonight, I am glad of your company."

The noises got louder, and now there was a dreadful scraping sound from the main deck above them, as though some giant were dragging his foot slowly across the tortured boards.

"I believe," said Sophie gently, "that the loudest crash was one of the masts breaking off, and what we hear now is the same mast rubbing across the deck. Usually they try to cut it free."

There was knocking on Sophie's door. She rose, clutching furniture, and opened it. There stood Mr. Parker, the first mate, dripping in oilskins, holding a storm lantern, and peering into the cabin. There was something almost comical in the little man's appearance, but his voice held assurance.

"I am glad to find you ladies safe and well," he said quietly, as though someone might possibly be asleep on the rampaging clipper. "The worst of it seems to be over, and a fearsome storm it was. We lost our mainmast, and four good lads were swept overboard, and many small leaks have been sprung. But the pumps are working, there's no other major damage, and thanks be to God, the winds are diminishing. There's water in your cabin now, Mrs. Malone, but I'll have the men pump it out within the hour. If you could rest here until then . . ."

"Of course she can, and spend the night, too, if it's necessary."

Sophie's voice seemed used to authority, nearly as much as any officer of the ship. Lily sat back then, and for the first time in hours felt a little relaxed. *Then maybe we won't go straight to the bottom. Maybe I've cheated the albatross, or Fergy, or whatever it was wanted to get me.* Just faintly, for she still felt queasy, and still the ship rolled and shuddered, Lily felt herself smiling. Mr. Parker told them about the emergency measures the captain had put into effect, how there would be no regular meals topside, but rather covered dishes delivered to their cabins when and how they could, and how the passengers were to stay below until summoned, for some of the ship's safety railings had been broken, and there was danger of falling overboard. Then he wished them good night and left.

"Good night, Mr. Parker."

He left, but Sophie paused in the doorway for a moment looking after him, the lamplight flickering on her flowered robe until the blossoms almost seemed alive.

"As good as his word, is Parker. Here they come now, to

pump you out. I've been in fine hotels, Lily, where you don't get such service."

"It was kind of him to come in the middle of the storm. I do feel better now."

"Storms are no fun," she said, closing the door at last, "but the very worst is fire. Which we've been having regular as clockwork in San Francisco, especially in the old board-and-tent days. Decimated, we were, in 1850, Lily. Who would believe one little shantytown could rebuild itself so fast there'd be time for three major fires? But three there were, in May, again in June, and again in September. But we just all pitched in and put her back together again, and now we've got fine brick and stone buildings, good as anywhere, fire-proof too, the shells anyway, and some of the most dashing gentlemen's fire brigades you'll find in any city in the land."

"My father died with a volunteer company, putting out the great fire of 1842, in New York. The Red Rovers, they were, and a fine outfit."

"A sad but gallant end, I'm sure. Well, San Francisco's like that, Lily, up and at 'em, pastes itself back together somehow and gets on with it."

"I like that. I'm sure I'll like San Francisco."

"I'm sure you will. Now, what say we see if those lads have you dry enough to get a few winks of sleep, if there's any sleep left in this godforsaken night."

Sophie led the way down the bouncing hallway with her lamp. The sailors had done their work quickly, but well. All of the water was gone, although the cabin still smelled of damp. Sophie showed her friend how to make a barrier sop of rolled bed linen, then stayed while Lily lit her own oil lamp.

"Good night, my dear," said Sophie, smiling. "Don't worry about the storm, or anything else. Our luck has beaten your old albatross, at least for the moment."

Indeed, it had leveled off, although the motion of the ship was still very rough.

Lily, too, managed a smile. "Thank you, Sophie, for taking me in. It was foolish of me to venture out at all."

"Sleep well, Lily. Tomorrow's another day."

"Good night."

Lily closed the door and turned to her bunk, feeling as though she had been scrubbing floors for a month without rest.

She turned out the lamp and set it on the little chest by her bunk, then climbed into the bunk and pulled the blankets right up to her chin. They were clammy at first, from the damp that pervaded everything in the cabin. But soon they got warmer, and Lily drifted off into an uneasy sleep.

Daylight seeped through Lily's porthole, wet and gray and discouraging. She stirred and opened her eyes and wondered if it had all been a dream. One look at the disorder in her cabin told her it had been all too true.

It took Lily longer to dress than she could ever remember taking, but finally she was ready to go out and inspect the damage.

The minute she got on deck Lily wished she had stayed below.

The deck of the clipper *Eurydice* looked like a war had been lost there: the sleek, quick vessel that had been was no more. It's great thrusting mainmast, more than a hundred feet high, had been splintered off twenty feet above the deck. She could see the crude ax marks where the dragging mast had been hacked away to prevent the *Eurydice* from capsizing. The deck itself, usually immaculate and precisely ordered, was strewn with debris that might have been left behind by an army in fast retreat. There were unrecognizable fragments of wood everywhere, bits of rope, rags of canvas, splayed kegs, one empty boot, half a Bible, and innumerable dead fish, their glassy eyes staring dumbly at Lily as if in supplication, as if she could forestall the sad irrational fate that had already befallen them.

Only the forward mast was fully operational. The mainmast was gone, and the stern mast broken too, she now realized, but broken higher up, leaving the two bottommost cross braces intact. They had furled all but the skysails, for the storm was far from over.

And the proud *Eurydice*, built to fly, now limped awkwardly toward the indifferent refuge of the Chilean coastline.

A few dispirited sailors were listlessly cleaning up the deck. These same men, Lily well knew, could move like monkeys up the ropes, balance on a high boom like jugglers at P.T. Barnum's museum, furl or unfurl a giant sail in seconds. But now they moved heavily, like drudges, even as the ship moved. Without purpose.

"*Valparaiso.*" Everywhere, she heard it: Valparaiso was the only place equipped to make such extensive repairs, Valparaiso, where they'd planned to put in in any event, for fresh water and provisions, Valparaiso, a thousand miles up the inhospitable coastline of rocky, wretched Chile. And they would creep those thousand miles, down at heart, dismasted.

Lily stood at the rail and clutched it until her knuckles turned white, and tried to see the coastline. It was hidden behind a wall of huge gray rollers.

She felt dizzy again. She'd seen enough; she should have waited below. Mr. Parker said they'd be having meals in their cabins for the time being, anyway. Cabin. She must get back to the cabin. And rest a little. But not just yet. Lily stood gripping the rail as if her very life depended on it. Could she move at all? What was this dizziness, this fuzzy-headed feeling, the burning at her temples?

She stood at the rail feeling almost a part of it. Lily looked into the forbidding gray sky, half-expecting to meet her albatross once again. But the sky was empty, sullen, heavy with menace. And suddenly, instead of looking for a bird, Lily felt she was one, light and free, such a lightness, floating! She let go of the railing and floated toward the deck.

The voices came through a filter, came from far away, ghost voices.

"Mrs. Malone's fainted."

"Get Erikson. Take her below. The lady's ill."

But I'm not ill, I am flying. Soaring. Now I see the funny little ship, broken, with its broken-off masts, its funny people, down there, white ship in the gray sea, so this is how it feels to be an albatross!

Then Lily went soaring into silence, and darkness, and forgot about being an albatross.

It was warmer now. Very warm on her forehead. Burning, nearly, and there was something someone—Sophie!—had said about fires, about many fires. There were many fires now, and within her. Yes, fires, in, down, on her skin, in her belly. Lily could feel the sweat on her forehead, and the deep soreness in her arms and legs, an aching in the joints as though she'd been working too hard, scrubbing floors, maybe, a thing like that. Her lips were very dry. Where was she?

Suddenly there was a coolness, blessed, comforting, and a special smell. A lovely springtime smell. Flowers. She was dead, then, and they'd sent flowers? But who would send Lily Malone flowers, alive or dead? She wasn't dead, then. But . . . what? Another of Fergy's tricks, to get her off her guard, to lure her into a place where he could do for her well and truly. Him and his damned albatross.

Her eyes fluttered.

Sophie! Lily tried to form the word. "Sophie?"

She wasn't dead, then, or mad.

The vision answered. "My dear child. Poor Lily, we've

been so worried. You have quite frightened us out of our wits, Lily."

"Where am I?"

"Still on the *Eurydice*, my dear, but you have been very ill. Jungle fever, Lily: the captain thinks you'll be well soon, but it is a very serious thing."

"Fever."

"Lily, you must tell me something."

"Of course."

"When is the baby due?"

Lily closed her eyes. The baby. She'd forgotten about the baby.

She felt a great shudder run the length of her body, and it was sudden and uncontrollable as the ship pitching in the great storm. *So the secret is known now, and my other secrets with it!* Here was the worst thing Lily could imagine, worse even than death itself, and somehow, in ways she could not understand, having it known was a relief to her. Lily sensed that the secret would be safe with Sophie Delage. When she answered Sophie at last, her voice was small and seemed to come from some lonely place far away.

"I think . . . the end of October." She couldn't tell how much time had gone by. She could only hope.

"Then we should be in time. We're in Valparaiso now, Lily, and the ship is being repaired. It will be some time, maybe two months. But we should make it. You must rest now, child. Get lots of rest, and think happy thoughts."

The coolness came again. Cologne! It was Sophie's cologne. Lily would buy her a bottle, a huge bottle of it, when they got to San Francisco, even if it cost the earth!

"Thank you, Sophie . . . very much."

"Sleep well, Lily, and don't worry about anything."

"Good night."

Lily's "good night" came drifting out of some dark distant place, barely audible.

Sophie touched the young girl's forehead with her handkerchief, soaked in the finest French cologne, and smiled. Lily would get better now. The baby would be born well. The two weeks of nursing would not have been in vain. Or however many weeks more might be necessary.

She stood up then and smoothed down her rich black challis dress, and left Lily's cabin. *It was just as she'd suspected, then. A love child!* You had to get up pretty early in the morning to have a head start on Sophie Delage. Life had taught Sophie to spot even the earliest of pregnancies almost as they happened. There was something about the eyes, a gentle swelling, an infinitesimal dilation, a certain extra glow to the skin. Oh, surely she'd known the child was pregnant the minute she laid eyes on her.

Well, still and all, Lily was a sweet little thing, pregnant or not. Her secret would be safe as houses with Sophie. Up to a point.

Sophie climbed the narrow stairs now and walked on deck. The repairs were coming along well, if not speedily. Nothing, she had been assured, happened speedily in lazy Valparaiso. And, God knew, there was little enough to do in the wretched town. It was almost a blessing to have Lily to nurse. Almost. Sophie smiled, and walked on.

Brooks Chaffee looked across the room at his hostess and smiled. For a shopkeeper's daughter, Marianne Wallingford had come a very long way.

There she stood, the Baroness West of Westover, at the head of her marble stairway, decked in the Westover diamonds, greeting the *crème de la crème* of London society as though she had been born to do no less.

Marianne smiled, Marianne glittered, Marianne was charming, but there was something disturbing about Jack's sister, a new hardness, a sharp edge of desperation that hadn't been a part of the girl Brooks remembered from less than two years ago in New York.

Of course, time, he reflected, thinking on his own happiness, *can make all the difference in the world.* And it couldn't be easy, being married to Clarence. Brooks had never liked the baron, even before the Baron's sexual predilection for stableboys became common knowledge. What Clarence possessed in titles and land and money was hardly matched in his own charm or character: he seemed to Brooks effete, overbred, thinned out, infinitely weary of the world. There was a waspish, feminine, petty-gossiping side to Clarence that made Brooks uncomfortable.

Clarence was always ready with a bad word about someone, a new scandal, a nasty bit of tale-telling, told, to be fair, with a certain wit and style. But still, Marianne remained Jack's sister, and it would have been rude not to visit.

And Caroline loved the idea of staying with a real live nobleman. From Caroline's point of view, Marianne was the perfect hostess, taking her to all the best shops, to tea parties with other titled ladies, a garden party at Buckingham Palace itself, and cheerfully enrolling Caroline's assistance as confidante and courier in Marianne's latest love affair.

This only amused Caroline, but it outraged Brooks, and their first harsh words were exchanged on the subject.

"You mean to say," Brooks asked his wife late one night in

Westover-House as they were getting ready for bed, "that she just came right out with it, with no shame, no sense of honor?"

"My darling, where lies honor when you are dealing with a degenerate like Clarence? I feel sorry for the poor girl. After all, she is young, and . . . healthy in her womanly needs."

"I think it's disgusting. Has she no sense of propriety?"

"Perhaps . . ." said Caroline softly, turning her back to Brooks so that he could unhook her elaborate ball gown, "perhaps she did. But, my dearest, they must have children, and he is not—or cannot—"

"Caroline, you do shock me."

"It's life, darling, why be shocked so? Are you shocked by the rain, or thunderstorms, or the nakedness of a flower? In a way, she is behaving very sensibly. This is a different world from ours, Brooks, and they hardly think about such things so long as they are carried on with some discretion. The way Clarence is—his fondness for boys—this is far from uncommon here. And yet the babies appear, and the titles are passed on, and everyone is happy. Or appears to be happy, which is perhaps the same thing."

"Not for me, it isn't, and I truly hope not for you! How can they live with themselves?"

Caroline turned to him, her dark eyes flashing in the soft candlelight.

"That, dear husband, is a question you must ask them, isn't it? How do any of us live with ourselves? How do I live with the fact that I married a Yankee and many of my own kin feel I am a traitress?"

"I didn't mean that. You know what I mean. I mean the inner morality of anyone's life. To be hypocritical on such a grand and public scale—that is what astounds me. And shocks me."

She walked the few paces that had separated them, barefoot on the fine old carpet, and stood on her tiptoes to kiss him. "Moral perfection," she whispered in the flickering light, "must be a heavy, heavy burden, my darling."

He looked at her then, startled, and kept his arms wound tight around her for fear that this lovely creature might turn to smoke as he held her, and vanish forever up the cold white marble chimneys of Westover House.

Sophie's was not a beautiful face, but in the long course of her fever, Lily Malone came to love it dearly. Now, in the steamy morning of their third week in the harbor of Valparaiso for repairs, Sophie bent over her patient and smiled.

"There's such good news, my dear: we sail on the morning tide! We'll be home in five or six weeks."

The mere fact of it made Lily feel better. The trap was sprung now, and now they'd be on their way. A month and more she had been struck with fever, going on to five weeks. Well, at least it hadn't killed her. Not yet. People died of the fever all the time; Sophie said that. Two of the seamen had it, and one of them was not expected to live. And now that her patient was truly feeling stronger, Sophie confided in her that there had been moments when they'd despaired of Lily's life too.

"You're far stronger than you look, child, to have been so sick, and with child, too, it's enough to kill a horse."

"You haven't . . ."

"No, dear, of course not. I've told no one, nor shall I. Your business is your business, Lily."

"There is no way that I can thank you. You've done so much, Sophie, dear. I do believe I would have died but for you."

"Fiddlesticks! It gave me something to do. Might well have kept me from murdering dear Dorothea, Lily, so you've saved me from a sure trip to hell's hot gates, not that I won't be going that way in any event."

Lily laughed then, for the first time in weeks. And it was only then that she truly believed in the fact of her recovery. They spoke for a while, then Sophie left her.

Lily was alone, and dozing, when the magical cry came floating in at her open porthole: "Anchor . . . aweigh!"

And the answer: "Anchor . . . aweigh!"

Freedom! It was a wonderful thing, release, escape! Lily knew she was getting better. The *Eurydice* was sailing. No storm would dare touch them. San Francisco was waiting, and its streets were paved with gold and its rivers ran bright with hope.

Lily slept then, and went off to sleep smiling.

The *Eurydice* cut through the blue Pacific like a knife. The long weeks of repair now justified themselves as the clipper put out every sail and fairly flew up the South American coast, the wind holding steady, the skies clear, the mood optimistic. They had been through the crucible now, and nothing dared harm them.

Lily sat up in her bed and began to recover her appetite.

On the second week after they left Valparaiso, she dressed

herself with great care, and with Sophie at her elbow as a human crutch, made her way up to the deck.

It was like being born all over again.

Lily looked at the sky as though it had been made fresh that morning, especially for her. She walked to the rail, and held it firmly, both for physical support and moral affirmation: *It was real!* It was real, then so was she. This wasn't another one of the fever dreams. This was mahogany, round and warm and solid. Hope, quick and irrepressible, came flowing through her. *Maybe, just maybe, everything would be all right!*

Lily's fever came and went, but it never went away entirely. Once, just after the ship passed the Mexican border, she fainted again. Sophie nursed her dutifully, and one afternoon invited Lily to stay with her in San Francisco until the baby was born. Weak with fever and gratitude, for truly she realized it might be impossible for her to fend on her own, Lily accepted.

"You're sure," said Lily in a faint voice, "that there is room enough, that I won't be a burden?"

"There is room aplenty, Lily, and it will give an old woman pleasure to have you for so long as you care to stay."

"You are a true friend, Sophie."

Lily drifted off to sleep now, happy that the end of the journey would not mean the end of her friendship with Sophie Delage. Somehow Lily felt tired almost all the time now, even though she spent the greater part of her days in bed. She measured out her energy with a miser's spoon now, saving herself for the ordeal of giving birth, and for settling herself in this wild new country called California.

The *Eurydice* cleaved its quick proud way up the coastline, past the ever-higher coastal mountains, past schools of immense blue whales, through gray clouds of gulls and sleek encampments of brown seals on rocks as smooth and as brown as the seals themselves. They were sighting other ships regularly now, drawn to the magnet that was San Francisco, the greatest gold port of the world.

It was early morning when the ship sailed through the Golden Gate, a warm Thursday in September. They were all on deck for the big event. The coastline had been getting more dramatic every day: great hills that obviously wanted to become mountains, rising steep and proud from the white fringe of surf, purple at dawn, green at noon, and touched with gold fire when the last rays came reaching out over the water all the way from China. Now the *Eurydice* was sailing right into the hills, through the narrow cut they called the Golden Gate. *This should be a glorious moment for me, I should be singing, cheering, but all I feel is tired.* Lily sat on a bulkhead and watched the hills roll by. The great harbor was thronged. There were scores of clippers, some even bigger than the *Eurydice*, and fat cargo carriers, a few steam-powered ships huffing and puffing and belching black smoke. There were rowboats and small sailboats and barges, and all the water traffic was coming or going from a thicket of masts and a sprawl of low buildings in the distance.

San Francisco!

Lily looked at her future home and soon felt faint again. It was a raw place, surely, she'd expected that. The buildings had no consistency of size or style: some were quite grand, brick or limestone or granite; others were nothing more than shacks. There were great sandy gashes in the hills that looked like wounds slowly healing. As they sailed ever closer, Lily could see beached hulks of ships rotting on the shore. Sophie had told her how, in the first days of the gold rush, entire crews would jump ship and head for the mines, that at one point there had been hundreds of such hulks waiting to be cut up for lumber or simply disintegrating where they berthed.

The packing and organizing for arrival had been too much; Sophie had warned her to take it slowly, that she was overdoing, and now, too late, Lily felt the truth of it in her heavy eyelids, in her aching limbs. She wanted to share the excitement and could not. She wanted to feel release and did not. All Lily Malone felt as the clipper sailed into San Francisco harbor was a deep desire to sleep, and sleep, and maybe never wake up. She'd just go below and take a little nap. Then she'd feel better. Lily rose from the bulkhead slowly and made her way back to the stairway.

She stood at the open door for a moment to get some strength back. There was a loud command shouted at a sailor, and an equally loud answer. Lily couldn't quite make out the words. Then, as she stood there, the *Eurydice* swerved sharply to the left.

It was just enough to throw Lily off balance. She gasped, blinked, reached for the rope stair railing, and missed it. Then she fell headlong down the fourteen steep wooden stairs.

It was a burning pain, and it tore through the darkness in Lily's mind with the intensity of a razor cut. All she knew, her entire world, was darkness and pain, pain and darkness. The pain had a pattern. It came, then it went. Came and went. There was no getting used to the pain; it was too sharp, a bitter pain, every time a cruel surprise. When it went, she lay trembling, gathering what small strength she had left for its next onslaught. When it came, the pain took over everything; every corner of Lily's heart and brain and body seemed filled with it, to the exclusion of hope or fear or even praying. On and off it went, the pain, on and off, on and off. She was beyond screaming. From time to time a voice could be heard, several voices, whispering, far away, on the far side of pain.

"Has the bleeding stopped?"

A friendly voice, Sophie's voice, friendly. Frightened.

"I'm afraid not. It's bad, Mrs. Delage, very bad."

A man's voice. Whose? Not the captain. Very bad, says he. That is understating matters, my good man. The pain came again, urgent, hot, sharp. Lily twisted on the bed. The pain got sharper. Then she lost consciousness altogether.

It was dark still.

Lily's eyes were closed, and it seemed that to open them would be the hardest job in the world, that it would take far more strength than she could muster. She lay absolutely still. This wasn't her cabin. She could feel a difference—what? The bed was wider, to begin with, and the sheets much softer, very fine sheets they were, almost like silk. Maybe she was in Sophie's cabin. That would be like Sophie, kindness itself was Sophie. Lily lay in the quiet and the darkness, and it slowly dawned on her that the pain was gone. Oh, and sure, she felt sore and wretched, and her head ached. But these things were nothing compared to that other, dreadful stabbing, jolting pain.

Her ears began to pick up sounds. Somewhere, far away, there was music, piano music, faintly tinkling a popular tune. Doors opened and closed, not slammed, but unmistakably doors. *Music and doors. This was not the* Eurydice! A door opened. Footsteps entered the room, and a dim light. A light touch as someone's hand smoothed the blanket. Lily's eyes fluttered open.

There was Sophie! But this was a different Sophie from the Sophie on shipboard. This was Sophie Delage dressed for the opera or some fancy ball. Sophie resplendent in yellow satin and diamonds, Sophie carrying a golden reticule and a small ivory fan! Lily tried to smile, and almost made it.

"Lily! Thank all the gods! We despaired of you, child, indeed we did."

"Sophie. What happened?"

"You fell, my dear, you took the most terrible fall down the stairs on the *Eurydice,* just as we were mooring. And lucky it was, we were close to home, and doctors. But you're safe now, Lily. You're with Sophie now, and you have a fine little girl."

Lily blinked back her disbelief. *Truly I must be dreaming.* Slowly, fearfully her hand slid down the blanket, touched the place where the bulge of her pregnancy had been. *Nothing! So it was true, then.* She tried to find words great enough to hold all her wonder, and could not.

"A girl." The words seemed to stick on her tongue, and she repeated them: "A girl."

"Oh, she's a lovely little thing, Lily, quite perfect and lively and screaming for your milk. One of the maids is looking after her, a sweet little Mexican girl, and we'll send for her presently. But first, first we must get some nourishment into you, for you've hardly eaten a thing, and the doctor was very concerned. Could you take a bit of broth?"

"I'll try." *One of the maids. Sophie was rich, then.* Lily accepted this as just one more wonder on this day of wonderments. *A little girl! Why did I always think it would be a boy?* Sophie kissed her and left, and quickly returned, bearing a silver tray, and on the tray a bowl of clear steaming broth, and buttered bread, and good hot tea.

Lily sipped at the tea but found she had no stomach for the broth.

Someone knocked and was bidden to enter. A small dark girl stood shyly in the doorway, framed by the light of the hall, carrying the baby. The maid was young, probably not more than thirteen or fourteen, Lily thought. Shyly, smiling, she came close to the bed.

"Lily, this is Dolores. Dolores, Mrs. Malone."

"How do you do, Dolores?"

"Buenos días, señora."

"She speaks," said Sophie quietly, "very little English."

Lily looked down at her baby. The child was fast asleep, pale, its face a little puckered, a light red fuzz of hair just beginning to cover its little round head. The baby's face looked like the face of a little old woman. The child frowned in its sleep, moved its head, then smiled. Lily could hear the angels singing. *The baby had smiled for her!*

She reached out for the infant, and Dolores handed it to her. Gently, tentatively at first, Lily drew her daughter to her. Still, the child slept on.

"When was she born?"

"Five days ago, my dear. You were completely unconscious."

"She is lovely. You saved my life, Sophie, and the baby's too."

"Nonsense! Good luck and good doctors did it, and if you ask me, it was more luck than doctoring. But now I must be off, my dear. Duty calls, as it were. We'll have a nice talk in the morning, Lily. In the meantime, I want you to eat as much as you can, and get some rest. The child is fine with Dolores—for the moment."

"Good night, Sophie. And thank you."

Lily held the baby for a while longer, then sent Dolores away. She'd have plenty of time with the child—her child! How fine that sounded, how good it made her feel. Her child. Her baby. And how much better the child's life was going to be than hers had been.

Lily's brain swarmed with plans. Oh, she'd get well fast now, she'd get herself to the Wallingford Emporium, get that job, a little house, or a flat, whichever was easier, a maid for the baby, maybe this same Mexican girl if Sophie could be persuaded to part with her, but anyway someone. The things her baby would learn! The school learning she'd have, and the books and pictures! And a good church education too, never forget that.

Her baby. Her child. Why, it didn't even have a name! You can't go on calling the child "it," Lily, get moving, girl, there's no time to be lost.

The names came marching through Lily's head, a great long parade of names, some grand, some silly, some ordinary. She'd ask Sophie. They'd talk about it tomorrow. Maybe Sophie could be the baby's middle name. Something Sophie Malone. Lily smiled. She was very tired, she could feel the weight of her fatigue as though it were a physical thing. But Lily could feel that a weight had been lifted from her, too.

For here she was, alive and a mother, and in San Francisco. And if it had been a rough voyage, at least she'd survived it. Stretching her luck thin, maybe, but at least there was luck to stretch. Finding such a friend as Sophie was luck, sure as there are leaves on apple trees. Living through the fever and the tumble downstairs was luck, and having a fine perfect little girl baby, that was the greatest luck in the whole world. *You are a lucky girl, Lily Malone, and thank God for it.*

Sleep came to Lily and found her smiling.

⊸§ 22 §⊸

It was three days before Lily discovered that she was a guest in a whorehouse.

She woke on the second day to discover Sophie at her bedside, smiling, holding the baby.

"Did you sleep well, my dear?"

"Very well. She's a pretty thing, isn't she?" Lily could still not quite believe that she had made this child, this strange and perfect little creature whose tiny hands, soft and sweet and all unknowing, held the secret of her mother's past and her future.

"She has a pretty mother, Lily."

"Half-dead, is what her poor mother is, and thanks be to God for you, Sophie, for the other half."

"Here. Take her." Sophie handed Lily the baby. The child was wearing a little gown of the finest handkerchief linen, banded with rows of white lace. *A princess might have worn that gown*, Lily thought, and then remembered that she had never seen the dress before.

"There, now," said Lily as the child's small eyes fluttered open and it gazed gravely at its mother, "you'll be tired after that long sea voyage, won't you, little lady? All the way round the Horn you went, and never knew it. You're in California, baby, and in Sophie's house. Yes, your Aunt Sophie has been very kind to us, baby, and we won't soon be forgetting it, that's a fact."

"Her eyes are nearly as green as yours, Lily, and the hair will be the same golden red, like a San Francisco sunset."

"If she grows healthy, and smarter than her old mother, that's all I ask."

Lily nursed the baby then and found her daughter hungry. Sophie left, and after a while the nursemaid, Dolores, came in, and Lily drifted back to sleep.

When she woke it was afternoon, and she thought the fever had got her again.

It was like a dream.

There stood three girls, half-naked they were, all wearing one kind or another of gaudy silk Chinese robes, loosely tied or not tied at all. One of the girls was dark and tall and very beautiful. Another was plump and wore a dull, almost drunken expression. The third was small and blond and hard-looking, with a face like a mink's, a sharp predatory face and little black eyes that glittered.

"She's coming awake."

"Thinks she owns the place, like as not, queening it up in Sophie's rooms and all."

"Hush, now! The poor girl's sick, can't you tell?"

"We're all sick, Lola, and that's for sure."

"Stuff it up your crumpet, slut! And speak for yourself when it comes to the sickness."

"She said demurely, like the fine lady she is, la-di-da."

"Stuff it, Ruby, or I'll stuff it for you."

"I'd be the last to doubt you could, dearie, what with your odd tastes."

Lily closed her eyes then, and the strange vision dissolved in laughter and the shuffling of slippered feet, and the closing of doors. *What a peculiar dream. But nearly all of her dreams were peculiar, or so it seemed. Very peculiar indeed, she was getting. It must be the fever.*

When she woke again, it was dark. Lily realized she hadn't been out of bed for a week. Even thinking of it made her shiver with doubts of her ability to do that. There was a tray beside her bed, with a teapot on it, and sandwiches, and cookies. Lily wondered how long the tray had been there. She reached out and touched one of the sandwiches, a fancy thing, all its crusts trimmed away, prettily arranged. The bread was dry. It had been here for hours, then, and herself sleeping like the dead. Well and truly, how far was she from death? She reached for the sandwich and brought it to her lips. Ham, it was, very thinly sliced, with mustard and butter. She ate it all, and then another. Lily sat up, poured some tea, and found herself ravenous. She ate the other sandwich—three in all!—and then drank some more tea, then ate two of the cookies. What lovely cookies they were, fine and thin and crispy!

Lily smiled in the darkness, thinking of the child. The music was playing again. Someone in Sophie's house, or in a house nearby, must be very fond of piano music. How good the sandwiches had tasted, stale or not! And the cookies. She decided to get up. Slowly, as if she were still pregnant, Lily slid first one leg to the floor, then the other. There. Standing.

It was like learning to walk all over again. She made her way to the door, a tall mahogany door set between two white columns. Lily opened it and saw a long, wide hallway, richly carpeted and lit by flickering gas lights in etched crystal globes. There were five doors on each side of the hallway, ten in all.

The hallway was empty, but the sound of music was louder now, music and laughter and all the familiar noises of a party. Very swell, was her hostess. Sophie must enjoy herself here in San Francisco, for all the rather reserved appearance she had made on the *Eurydice*. Well, then, Lily knew she was in no condition—and no costume!—to join the party below. She turned and walked back into the big bedroom and closed the door behind her. Lily felt as though she had been on a great adventure, just by getting up out of bed. To be no more a prisoner of that bed! She looked around the room, and suddenly felt tired again. She climbed back into the big bed and soon fell asleep.

Sophie laughed when Lily told her about the vision of three girls looking at her yesterday. Sophie threw her head back and fairly roared. Then she looked a bit stern, the way she had looked that first day on the *Eurydice*, formidable, a lady of great character.

"I must tell you sometime, my dear, and now's as good as any. That was not a dream. Those girls are real. And it was most impertinent of them to sneak in here like that: I'd expressly told them not to, but you know how girls are when they're bored."

"They live here, then?"

"They work here, to be precise."

"They're servant girls, then?"

"Lily, you are truly sweet. And what I am about to say may shock you. I beg you to hear me out. They're whores, Lily. And this is a whorehouse. Not to put too fine a point on it."

Lily looked at her friend Sophie, who had comforted her all through the long, terrible voyage, who had taken her in, who had saved her life. *Sophie a madam!* If Sophie had come at her with a bloody hatchet in one hand and the severed head of the baby in the other, Lily could have hardly been more shocked. It was like a cruel physical blow, and all of Lily's training in the church, in the orphanage, and in service recoiled from this news as from a deadly serpent. *And yet, it was Sophie. How could Sophie be Sophie, and still be a whore? Whores were wicked, low women, and they went right straight to hell, and the angels wept for them. Everyone knew that.* Lily regarded her friend with astonished eyes and a tongue too numb to speak.

Finally it was Sophie herself who broke the dense silence. "I meant to warn you, my dear, but in the condition you were in, it seemed dangerous, for I knew you'd want friends on landing, and had none."

She saw through my little story, then. "I can't believe it."

"Ah, you've been taught that prostitutes are evil women, Lily, and maybe we are: I'll not judge. But surely we've all known fine married ladies with no better morals than a gila monster in heat. It's a business, Lily, like any other. I run it right, I make a profit, and a fair one at that."

"My baby was born . . ."

"Say it, Lily. Say it straight out. In a whorehouse, that's where, and but for me she'd have been born in the gutter, like as not, and she might be an orphan by now."

"Sophie, stop! Don't think I'm not grateful. It's the surprise, is all. I don't care what you do, for you are as good a friend as ever I had, or hope to have."

Timidly Lily looked at her friend and managed a smile.

Sophie forgot her anger and returned that smile. To Lily it looked as though all the stars in heaven had come out all at once.

"Ah, Lily, my poor sweet Lily! You are a delightful child. I won't try to justify myself, Lily, not to you, nor to anyone living. I have done what I've done for reasons we need not go into. I run an honest house, a clean house, and if I can help it, no one ever gets robbed here or cheated here or diseased here. Delage's El Dorado Hotel is the cleanest sporting house in town, and with the best-looking girls and the finest wines. And the highest prices. The only harm I do, Lily, is to the sanctimonious married ladies of the town, so stiff in their whalebone and their psalm-singing and their noses so high in the air they couldn't see love if it climbed in the carriage with 'em, and their husbands running to Sophie every chance they get. Drives 'em mad, does Sophie's place, and I can't say I mind."

Lily suddenly felt very tired again. When she replied, her voice was weak. "I feel better now, thanks to you."

"You must take it easy, my dear. It was doing too much too quickly that made you fall down those stairs."

"Oh, indeed I will. But, Sophie, I would like to pay for what you've spent, the doctor, things for the baby, all of that."

"Fiddlesticks! You'd deprive poor old Sophie of her few remaining pleasures, would you? How often do you think I get the chance to do a good deed, Lily Malone? Hell's bells, girl, I've got to at least try to offset my terrible wickedness somehow, don't you think? So I can at least have a bit of a conversation with that old St. Peter, when the time comes, instead of just being sent directly to hell."

"We'll be there together, then, you and me, in hell. You won't lack for a friend there, Sophie."

"It's the other place I'd be lacking, my child. Out of my mind with loneliness, I'd be, on the right side of the pearly gates."

Lily looked at her friend, at her only friend in California, maybe her only friend in the world. The shock of Sophie's revelation was still on her. It hadn't truly registered yet, not in its fullest meaning. *That you have known this woman, and liked her, and been befriended by her, yes, and even had your very life saved by her, and her a brothel keeper, a scarlet woman!* Inwardly Lily found herself mocking her own astonishment. *And who are you, my fine girl, to judge the morality of others?* Still and all, it was one thing to have been seduced, however willingly, and quite another thing to embark on an entire career of seducing others, and for money! *Then what's that in your money belt, Lily? If it isn't money, and the very wages of sin, it surely is the color of money, and sure enough, it buys what money buys. And didn't you get it from a man, for the pleasures of your sinful flesh?*

Lily started to say something, then stopped.

"You are shocked, aren't you, Lily?"

"Only surprised. It seemed . . ."

"That I was a fine upstanding lady? Many appearances are deceiving, child. You seemed to me exactly what you claimed to be, for example."

"Yes, and it was a lie, too, wasn't it? I do not blame you, Sophie, nor will I ever. It's just that I don't know anyone else who . . ."

"Who runs a whorehouse? Give the thing its proper name, my dear! We're very outspoken here in California, it's all the fashion."

". . . who runs a whorehouse, then. You will help me find a place to live, Sophie? As soon as I'm well enough?"

"Of course. And you do look better. I'm glad we've had this little chat, Lily, however painful it might be to you at first, for it has been weighing on my mind."

"Please, think nothing of it. I could not be more grateful."

"That is kind of you, Lily. I must go now. I'll send Dolores with the child."

"Sophie?"

"Yes, dear?"

"What was your mother's name?"

"Kate. Katharine. What an odd question."

"That's what I'll call her. I love that name. Kate. Katharine. Kate it will be, then."

"In honor of me? Lily, you astonish me. And I thought I was beyond astonishment. You'd name your child after a madam's mother?"

"I would and I shall."

And as she said those words, Lily felt a rush of happiness. *Maybe 'tis a small thing I've done, but if it helps make Sophie feel better, then I count it a good thing.*

Sophie smiled, a little too brightly, and turned away. "Thank you, my dear," she said quickly, "thank you very much."

Then she left the room and closed the door softly behind her.

Lily lay there trying to sort out what Sophie had told her. The bed was soft as any bed, and surely the sheets were of the finest. But it was a whore's bed and a whore's sheets, and she, Lily Malone, was eating a whore's food and drinking a whore's tea. Lily turned the word over and over in her brain: *whore, whore, whore, whore.* The bed stayed as soft, the sheets as smooth, the food did not poison her. *This was the way it went, then, and here lay the road to damnation.* Lily knew all about damnation, and had, since earliest childhood. Damnation was what happened to bad people, people who sinned against the church, liars and whores and fallen women, and they'd all roast in the fires of hell, and devils with pointy tails would stick hot forks into them for all eternity. *Oh, and how the angels must be weeping for Lily Malone on this black day!* Sophie a sinner, and Sophie damned for all eternity did not alter the fact that Sophie had saved her life.

Dolores came in with the baby Kate then, and Lily had only to take one look at her child's smile in order to forget about Sophie and Sophie's house and her profession. For in Kate's smile lay all the happiness in the world, a free gift for anyone who cared to reach for it. Lily knew that she cared more than anyone, and would keep on caring all the days of her life.

September turned to October before Lily felt well enough to go out and inquire about her promised position at the Wallingford Emporium. Kate was three weeks old now, lively and radiant with health, and Lily herself had put back a few of the pounds she had lost. Her strength came back more every day, though she was still prone to spells of dizziness when she tried to do too much. Lily paced her room and looked out of its windows at this strange new world called California.

The city Lily saw from her window teemed and vibrated with life. All day long and halfway through the night, the hills resounded to the bang of hammers on nails, the rasp of saws, the rumble of wagonloads of bricks and building stones being unloaded at last after their long journey around the Horn and even from Europe as ballast for the restless clippers. And night, in Sophie's house, brought its own special symphony of sin. The piano was as much a part of Lily's life now as the luxury of Sophie's bedroom or the flower smile on Kate's sweet face.

On dry days the streets smoked with dust and windblown sand. When it was wet, San Francisco turned into a swamp, for only Market Street was paved, and with rough boards at that. Mud and dust and horse dung were taken for granted underfoot everywhere else.

The city seethed with people, and nearly all of them were men. Lily could sit in her window and watch knots of gibbering yellow Chinese thin as wires moving with quick, choppy steps like puppets. There were huge lumbering Russians in furs head to toe, so heavily bearded it was hard to tell where the beard stopped and the fur coat started. There were miners rampaging in from the gold and silver fields, filthy as beggars but with fat leather sacks of pure gold dust and nuggets, their eyes red with greed and cheap whiskey and lust. Highly tailored gamblers moved among the crowds with the supple and somehow faintly evil grace of a snake rippling through tall grass. Every nation in Europe was well-represented, and places beyond: all the wide-brimmed, black-haired, two-gunned amateur banditos from Mexico and points south, Australians who had started out as convicts and had nothing more to lose, half-breed American Indians, an occasional Polynesian carved from amber and out of place, Scandinavians tall and fair as birches, fat Germans, weedy men from nameless places with the look of whipped mongrels, shifty-eyed and smiling too quickly, the schemers and wheedlers who would prey only on the weak, jackals of the gold rush, the takers of leavings.

The animals were as mixed as their owners. Fine horseflesh

was priceless, and the streets ran with compromises: mules and burros and oxen and now and then even a dog cart. From time to time a proud Castilian would deign to be seen in town, glistening on the sort of horse legends are built on, sleek and dark, the man like his mount, both decked in the supplest of leathers and the brightest of silver. These were the old race, owners of the immense Spanish crown land grants that sometimes ran to hundreds of thousands of acres, feudal baronies they were, said Sophie, whose owners held absolute power over all the peons and anyone else who presumed to set foot there. But that was all changing, for these proud men never thought of their wealth, and often lost it. The great baronies were slowly being chipped away. It was sad, said Sophie, but inevitable. Lily wondered why.

On the day she gathered her courage to set out for Wallingford's, Lily felt that a whole new chapter was beginning in her life. It was much the way she had felt on setting sail from New York Harbor in April. April! It seemed a lifetime ago! How carefully she dressed, putting on her New York-bought dress of plain but well-cut gray challis and the green cape she had made on board the *Eurydice*. Her black bonnet added the right note, she felt, conservative yet becoming. It was ten in the morning when she walked boldly out the side door of the El Dorado Hotel.

Sophie had built her house on the corner of Broadway and Montgomery Street, just four blocks from the wharves. Lily stepped carefully across the dust and filth of Montgomery and paused on the planked sidewalk on the other side.

She looked up at the notorious house that had been her hospital, her refuge, her sanatorium of recovery for nearly a month now.

The El Dorado Hotel was four stories tall, solidly built of gray stone, with six rows of arched windows on every floor, and every window framed in some other, lighter-colored stone. It could have been a bank, or a fine shop, or almost anything. Instead, as well she knew, it was the fanciest sporting house in town.

And if anyone sees you coming out its door, there goes your reputation, Lily Malone. What reputation? Lily had heard many voices, whispering many things inside her bewildered brain, ever since Sophie had revealed what the business of the El Dorado truly was. Well, whatever tempting whispers the voices put in her ear, and however confusing it all was, she'd soon be free and clear of the wicked El Dorado. *I will never, never forget Sophie's kindness*, Lily told herself over and over again, as though it were a prayer, *but surely even she can see I must be gone, and soon, with Kate to think of.* Lily could feel the thick, reassuring square of Jack Wallingford's letter of introduction where it lay in the soft pouch of her reticule. *Mr. Charles Linton, Esquire. Manager, The Wallingford Emporium, 117 Market Street, San Francisco, California.* Lily felt as though her whole future was sealed inside that envelope. Soon she'd know all about it, for Market Street was just ten blocks west, and 117 a block or two down toward the Embarcadero.

Lily had walked one block, deep in thought, her head alive with hopes and plans, before she realized what a sensation she was causing, just by the simple fact of being a woman, alone, on the narrow boardwalk.

"Can you believe it?"

The man's voice was not loud, yet Lily could hear it across the street. She looked back, startled, and saw six well-dressed men, all in a tight little group, pointing at her and frankly staring. *They saw me come out of Sophie's, and they think I'm a whore.* But they hadn't seen her come out of Sophie's, and their looks were respectful, if staring can be respectful. There were no lewd remarks, no catcalls, no provocation was offered. Confused and embarrassed, Lily looked down, and quickly walked toward Market Street.

And everywhere she went, the stares followed.

Sophie had suggested the carriage, but Lily had decided against that well-meant offer. Sophie's carriage, she was sure, would be easily recognized, for San Francisco was more a small town than a city, gold or no gold. And Lily would be damned if she arrived for a clerk's job at Wallingford's in the equipage of the fanciest bawdyhouse in town.

When she found the courage to look up and around her, Lily realized that a woman on these streets was probably perfectly safe, for surely she was a rarity worthy of continuing astonishment on the part of every man in the town. Soon her embarrassment disappeared, and she found herself able to smile at the fundamental silliness of it all. Nothing was going to pull her spirits down on this great day! For here, in truth, was the beginning of her new life, and a fine life it would surely be. She walked on down Montgomery Street and practiced ignoring the naked stares of virtually every man she passed.

I am the only woman on this street, and if trouble came, who would come to my rescue?

Only four more blocks to Market Street. Market, Lily

knew, was the main commercial thoroughfare of the new city. Paved with boards it was, and proud of it. *Think, Lily, how you took Fifth Avenue for granted, and the fine marble mansion of the Wallingfords, where here they are grateful for a few old boards as frosting on the mud!*

Montgomery Street was a crazed mixture of buildings and people and animals. The buildings were sometimes shabby and primitive, knocked together of canvas and boards, and sometimes they were very grand. There was marble to be seen, and gilt-bronze, and gas lamps twinkling inside the bars and banks. Death lived in San Francisco along with gold and sin and hope: Lily shuddered as she passed "GRAY'S COFFIN WAREHOUSE" and recalled how very close she had come to being one of Mr. Gray's customers, just a few weeks ago. The photography craze had made its way west, and here was a fine four-story brick house sporting a large painted sign announcing "VANCE'S DAGUERREAN ROOMS." There were assaying offices and three banks and any number of small merchants. The time was late morning, but the sidewalk was bustling, and everyone on it but Lily was male. Just before the corner of Market Street Lily saw another woman. She was small and plump and her skin was the color of a walnut, her eyes flat and pointed, almost Chinese she looked, but not exactly: *An Indian,* Lily thought—*I'm seeing my first Indian.* The other woman passed, expressionless, dressed in greasy layers of skirts and shawls that showed faint traces of the bright colors that must once have adorned them. The woman smelled like a dirty kitchen. Lily wrinkled her nose as the Indian woman passed, and thought how lucky she had been, to be at least this far above such filth, however tenuous her hold on cleanliness and respectability.

Well, Mr. Charles Linton would certainly help with that.

Market Street ran straight down from the hills, cutting the young city nearly in two, struggling like the town itself under the weight of its aspirations.

Carriages and wagons and mounted horses thundered on the echoing pavement of dirty boards.

The width of the street diminished the size of the buildings that lined it, although they were taller, for sure, and more grandly decorated than any that Lily had seen thus far. Left, she must turn, and toward the water. At the bottom of Market, as at the end of nearly every street she had crossed, Lily could see the dark fingers of masts pointing to the sky. There was no escaping the water here, nor the ships that made their own highways on the great trackless seas. For herself, Lily would just as soon forget the ocean, and the *Eury-dice*, and all that had happened on the long voyage. The sea had taken enough from her: her strength, it had taken, and Fergy's life, and very nearly her own. And Kate's life too, worst of all. Well, here was the three-hundred block. She must find number 117.

Lily was learning to ignore the stares now. They came so thick and so often that a girl could either ignore them or fall dead beneath the weight of them. When she had imagined San Francisco, back in New York, or on the long voyage around the Horn, Lily had never dreamed of a city without women. Yet this was just what seemed to be the case here. She looked up at the raw, sandy, scrubby hills. Here and there were little cottages that must be homes. Now and then she could see a washline flapping in the morning breeze. Surely there must be some decent women somewhere!

Lily noticed, too, that there were almost no children to be seen.

She recalled New York, and the ferret-faced street gangs, and the fine young children walking with their nurses along Fifth Avenue, dressed like little princes, they were, the girls sometimes even wearing furs, tiny versions of their mothers' seal and beaver and mink. In San Francisco, it seemed, children were hidden away, or Mexican-looking. What a strange town this was, half-exciting, half-bewildering!

Lily walked briskly, lifting her skirts when she crossed the unpaved side streets, passing the two-hundred block now, hurrying to meet her future. And there! There, halfway down the next block, she could see it. A grand four-story building in new red brick, with a fine big sign on it, gilt letters against black, gilt-framed, beckoning: THE WALLINGFORD EMPORIUM. Strange, and yet not so strange, was the shudder that went through Lily then. She felt part of it all, even though she had no real right to feel that way. And hadn't Jack Wallingford come panting for her love, and hadn't she held him close in the dark and wanton nights? And hadn't she carried Jack's bastard through hell and high water both, and almost to the gates of death itself, and back, and didn't she deserve something for all that?

Wallingford's must be having a fine sale, to draw such a crowd outside. Sure, and maybe I'll pick up some things for the baby.

As Lily got closer to the big store, she realized that something was wrong. This was not a happy, bustling, sale-going crowd. *Maybe someone's dead.* She thought of Jack's father, then, and all Jack stood to inherit should the old man have gone to his reward. With a slow buildup of dread that seemed to numb her very toes, Lily made her way through the muttering crowd. The men instinctively made a path for her. Now she could see the front door.

Suddenly Lily felt faint. A wave of heat rushed to her head. She seemed to feel the ground shake. Lily blinked, trembled, and looked again, not believing what her eyes plainly told her was fact.

The door to the Wallingford Emporium was chained and padlocked. The notice in the window was an auction notice. The Emporium was closed until further notice, and all of its contents were to be sold up for taxes, by order of the marshal of San Francisco!

Lily stood like one paralyzed, unable to move or think. How long she stood thus, she could never remember. It seemed like days. There was an undercurrent of anger and concern in the crowd. Some of their grumblings penetrated through the icy walls of shock and panic that were forming around Lily's ruined expectations.

"They say," said one tall man who carried an official-looking leather document case, "that it's the start of a real panic back in New York, that half a dozen businesses are going under."

"But Wallingford's? They were solid as anything!"

"Overextended in the stock market, that's what I heard, put the big New York store up as collateral, and they grabbed it away from him just like that."

"Is it true the old man killed himself?"

"That's what I heard tell."

"Never! Old buzzard like that?"

"I heard tell."

"Sixty dozen pair of French gloves of mine, they've got, and never paid for, and where the hell are they?"

"Where's Linton?"

"Is it true the old man killed himself?"

"Sold all her jools, that's what he did."

"The very house they lived in, that too?"

"Hear tell."

Lily turned and moved through the crowd without quite knowing how or why she did it. *It isn't true, it's the fever come again, I got up too soon, it is another one of those bad dreams!*

But the chain and the padlock were true, and the sign in the window was real, and if the mutterings and questions of the crowd weren't real they must have some nugget of truth to them—great stores just don't close for nothing. She felt the square of the envelope in her reticule. It felt sharp as daggers, deadly, mocking, cold. *How could anyone rich as the Wallingfords lose their money?* Lily had heard, but only vaguely, of panics and great risings and fallings of the stock market. She had only the most hazy idea of what the stock market might be. For years she had supposed it to be a place where cattle were traded.

As usual in a crisis, Lily thought of the immediate problems first. *Get through the minutes, Lily, and the hours will take care of themselves.* The Wallingford Emporium was closed tight, and where, then, was Charles Linton?

There was something else in Lily's purse besides the letter to Linton. There was Jack Wallingford's draft for five hundred dollars on the Merchant's Bank of New York, which had a branch here in San Francisco, and on Market Street, too.

Lily had to ask directions, and gladly did so. It gave her something real to do.

The Merchant's Bank of San Francisco was a grandiose white limestone fortress of a building on the corner of Market and Front streets, just a block away from the ruin of Wallingford's. A uniformed attendant ushered Lily into a small but elegantly furnished office.

"Mr. Harrison, this is Mrs. Malone." The attendant bowed and withdrew. Mr. Harrison was a thin gray man who looked as though the last time he'd smiled might have been back around the War of 1812. He had rimless spectacles through which he regarded Lily with the dry clinical interest of a bird inspecting a not very promising worm. Lily felt uneasy, as though she were somehow trespassing. He spoke.

"Yes, yes, Mrs. Malone, it's always a pleasure to meet a new customer. May I be of some service?"

His voice had no pleasure in it. Lily had to think about her hand to stop it from trembling as she fumbled with the clasp of her reticule.

"I have a draft on your New York branch," she said quietly, "and I hoped you might cash it for me."

"Of course, of course. If you'd just let me have a look at it."

She found the draft and handed it to Mr. Harrison.

He held it up, at some distance from the rimless glasses and the nearly colorless eyes behind them, held it out with two long skinny fingers as though it might in some way contaminate him.

Silence filled the little room until Lily felt it must choke her.

Finally Harrison made a small noise. He cleared his throat. It was like dry leaves rustling in the wind.

"You are a friend of the Wallingford family?"

"I know them."

"Then you will be distressed to hear that a rather serious misfortune has befallen them."

"And what is that, sir?"

"They have, Mrs. Malone, lost all their money."

In the brief moment before the full impact of this hit her, Lily found herself thinking of Jack Wallingford, of how helpless he'd be without money. For herself, who never had more than a few dollars in all her life, the loss of a great fortune was unreal, impersonal—but for the baby. But for Jack, Lily feared, it would be the breaking of him, and while Lily knew very well that she had never loved the boy, she remembered his kindnesses and was sad.

The banker cleared his throat, a signal.

Why, God, why are my worst fears always coming true?

Lily looked at him, and at the draft, which was now resting on Mr. Harrison's desk like a dead thing. She said nothing. Once more silence crept up on them.

Then he spoke. "When this draft was written, in . . ."

"In late March or early April, I believe."

"Of course, of course. March. Well, in March it was good as gold—heh-heh—and gold is very good indeed. It is a shame, Mrs. Malone, that you waited so long to cash it."

"I was sailing around the Horn. It seemed a risk to carry that much cash."

"Yes, yes, well, everything is a risk, isn't it? In any event, it will be impossible for us to honor this paper now, as things stand."

Lily took a breath and gathered what strength was left in her. "How do they stand, Mr. Harrison?" Lily heard the words forming in her throat, and could not believe she was truly saying them. Bold as brass, she must sound, an old hand at trying to cash in false drafts on New York banks. But it isn't—wasn't—a false draft, dammit!

"A merchant of old Wallingford's magnitude rarely goes under for long. But at the moment, all of the Wallingford funds—such as are left of them, that is—are frozen, Mrs. Malone. Frozen assets, we call them. Pending the bankruptcy, don't you know? Don't, don't by any means throw the thing away. Given a bit of time, a recovery period, it may be worth its full value someday. But for the moment, impossible. There is the beginning of quite a bad panic back East, Mrs. Malone, as possibly you hadn't heard."

"No," she said flatly, "I hadn't heard that."

"Yes, yes, quite a panic. Many businesses going under. Some quite big ones. Wallingford's won't be the last, mark my words."

"Very sad it must be for them, rich as they were." *And sadder, far, for me, for Kate.* Lily choked on her words, for she felt like a hypocrite saying them to this cold little man.

"Sad, sad. Exactly, very sad indeed. Well!" Harrison stood up then, rubbing his thin, lifeless hands together as though he expected to strike sparks from them. "I am sorry, very sorry, to be the bearer of such sad news, Mrs. Malone. Do hold onto this"—he handed her the draft, and she folded it carefully and returned it to her reticule—"and do let me know, yes, let me know if there is any possible way I can be of service to you."

"Thank you. There is one thing."

"Yes? Yes?"

"Do you by any chance know where I might find Mr. Charles Linton? The manager of Wallingford's?"

He looked at her quizzically, suspecting God-knew-what. "The fact is, I do, I do. Look for him at number 328 California Street. He'll be there still, by all accounts."

"Thank you, sir, you have been most kind."

"Think nothing of it, Mrs. Malone, nothing of it."

Harrison smiled his death's-head smile and grandly opened his office door. Lily walked out of the bank with her chin held high, looking for all who cared to see—and there were many who did care—as though her world had not just come crashing down all around her in sharp and hurtful pieces. She knew where California Street was: she'd crossed it on the way from Sophie's this very morning. *Not an hour ago, and all the world changed in that small time!* Lily walked up Market Street and used every ounce of the strength that was left in her just to keep from crying, or breaking into a mad run and throwing herself into the harbor. *There was less than a hundred dollars of Jack's money now.*

And how far would that go, with prices what they were in San Francisco? How far would that go, when a cabbage alone could cost two dollars, and meat twice as dear, and who knew what for rent, for a nurse, for firewood? And how long could she presume on Sophie's good nature?

Lily thought of Harrison and of all the men like him, and how smug they were, how far removed from panics, from fear, from the gutter, the very grave!

And who would Mr. Charles Linton be, and what might he have to offer?

You must try, Lily. You must not give up; he may have something, he may be a good enough friend of the Wallingfords to honor their note, to get some kind of work for you, anything, anything!

She walked up Market Street to Montgomery and turned right. The stares still followed her, but all Lily could see now was a future that had been filled with promise an hour ago, and was now filled with terror, with fear for herself, and for the baby, for life itself. For what could she do, here in this strange wild place, this city without women?

Still in a trance, she came to California Street and turned up the hill. She climbed up the street in a daze. She looked neither left nor right except to glance at the house numbers. Three-twenty-eight. It was a tall stone house not unlike Sophie's, solid and elegant. It was an apartment house and the name LINTON was indicated as resident in apartment 2B.

The marble-floored foyer was empty. Lily climbed the stairs directly, there being no bell to announce her.

Two-B had a tall, polished wooden door with a large lion's-head knocker in sparkling brass. She lifted her small fist to knock, then quickly withdrew it as if from a flame. Then Lily's courage came back to her and she knocked twice, boldly.

The sharp resonance of brass striking on brass echoed in the empty hall.

Lily waited, alone with the echo and the mocking silence that followed.

Then his voice came, loud and careless. "Come in, come in, for heaven's sake: it's taken you long enough. The damned door's open."

Trembling, she opened the big door. It moved silently on well-oiled hinges. The door opened inward to reveal a big many-windowed room. It was absolutely empty. There was not a stick of furniture, not a rug or a plant or a curtain at the big arch-topped windows. The sun poured in through the windows. At the far side of the room was another door, nearly as big as the first. Slowly, growing more and more concerned, Lily made her way to it. And the voice urged her on. "Well, well, get on with it, then!"

She came to the second door and stood in its opening.

The next room was not quite so big as the first, but it was big enough for what was in it.

This room, too, was empty but for one large and fancifully carved mahogany bed on the far side, piled with pillows and paisley shawls and splendidly colored fabrics that might have been draperies or parts of ball gowns, or almost anything but bedsheets.

Under this pile was a great lump of heaving flesh. Lily's disgust was nearly as strong as her fear. *Who—what—was this creature? And why in the world had the Wallingfords sent her to him—it?*

The naked torso of a very fat man emerged from the tangle of bright silks and challis and cotton prints. On top of the torso was a stack of chins, and above that a round red mouth, great jowly cheeks, small dark eyes that regarded Lily with more curiosity than surprise. His head was round as a pumpkin and nearly that big, draped in fat, cushioned by rolls of plump flesh, pink in color, the flesh itself striving to hide the features that God, many plum puddings ago, had put on the face of Mr. Charles Linton.

"You," said the querulous voice, "aren't Jackson."

"No, sir. I am Lillian Malone, if you please."

"I would be the last to doubt it, my dear. Yes, the very last. How charming of you to come."

"I come from New York."

"Even more charming, then, charminger and charminger."

"From Mr. Wallingford."

Lily handed him the note, and quickly drew back, as if he might bite her. Linton's arm, which resembled nothing more than a fine Easter ham, reached out, all pink and round and edible-looking. Each finger was a kind of fat little sausage: there seemed to be no bones to the man at all. He picked up the letter carefully, between two fat fingers, as if it were some rare species of butterfly, and he a collector. The button eyes danced over Jack's father's words on the heavy paper. Then Charles Linton carefully tucked the letter back into its envelope and extended his arm in Lily's direction, not bothering to look at her.

He sighed a deep and terrible sigh. "You may be sure, Mrs. Malone," he said softly, as though speaking to someone very old, "yes, you may be quite, quite sure you've come to the right place. The cloven hoof, you see, is much in evidence here, yes, yes, the Old Nick has a rather free hand in our fair city, so he does. Aided and abetted by the likes of young Jack-o Wallingford and his endless, or so it seems, chain of castoff hussies. Oh, you blush! Oh! For shame! Fair coveys of soiled doves has Mr. Jack-o sent my way, Miss, Mrs., whatever you call yourself. Fair coveys. And right useful some of 'em. Very consoling to the needs of the flesh, so to speak."

Lily stood silent, shuddering, too shocked and angry to speak.

He roused himself now, and rose up on one elbow, and turned to look at her, his small eyes burning. Lily watched him as a rabbit is said to watch a serpent, in silence, frozen, hypnotized, utterly fascinated.

"Since I seem to be occupying half of the connubial couch, so to speak, Mrs. whatever-your-name-is, mayhap you would see fit to join me? We can discuss your possibilities at—hee-hee—some length!"

A flash of rage inflamed Lily's mind in that moment, and she found herself glad her reticule contained no deadly weapon. For, surely, this would have been a time for guns or knives. If Linton hadn't been such a comical figure, fat as he was, crazy as he might be, Lily couldn't have answered for her behavior.

As it was, she could think of nothing to say in her surprise and outrage, so she said nothing. She turned on her heels and walked out of the room.

Charles Linton seemed not to notice her hasty departure. His voice went on.

"Yes, possibilities, oh, the possibilities, you are a lady of many, many possibilities, Mrs. . . . Miss . . . oh, yes, the hair of copper and gold, oh, the eyes, aha! the flower flesh, yes, the joy of it all, the cloven hoof dances at the thought of it, of the many, many possibilities, yes . . ."

Lily walked out of Linton's bedroom and across the emptiness of the front room and into the hall and down the stairs, shock piling up on shock, insult on insult, until she thought she could bear it no longer. *He's insane, of course, the failure of the Emporium drove him right off his head, saying things like that. Mr. Wallingford never would have put such a thing in a letter, nor Jack, either, not ever.* Mr. Charles Linton might be crazy, but Lily's hurt was real and deep, and by the time she reached the sidewalk on California Street she was filled with it to the point of fainting.

She looked up and down the street. There they were. Men. All men. All thinking the kind of thoughts that Mr. Charles

Linton thought, all knowing—or guessing—her secret, all wanting her flesh, all conspiring against whatever might be left of her self-respect or her good name.

The good name she'd hoped—prayed!—to make here in the new golden land. New golden land! And that was the final bitter joke.

The streets of San Francisco were paved with mud and broken dreams, and the gutters were just waiting, hungrily, yawning and gaping for the likes of Lily Malone!

Lily couldn't fight back the bitterness, and at last she stopped even trying. For hadn't they all left her, everyone she had ever loved, or belonged to, or even cared about? Hadn't her parents gone and died on her, and Fergy run off too, and dead like the rest of them, and Jack wanting her body, and getting it and casting her off like his torn Chinese robe, throwing her across the continent to the likes of Charles Linton?

Only Sophie cared for her, and Sophie was in partnership with the devil himself. In the end, there was Kate, only Kate, Kate, who was hers and hers completely and forever, Kate, who'd have no recriminations, Kate, who'd never leave her or betray her.

Kate: her baby born in a whorehouse.

Lily walked down California Street blinking back the tears, determined to hold her head proud, high, if it broke her neck to do it. She'd take her baby out of Sophie's place this very day!

Well, tomorrow, at the latest; she'd have to find a new place, a cheap place, somewhere to shelter them until she found the job that had to be waiting for her in this raw and frightening city.

The first thing Lily did when she got back to Sophie's was go straight to her room and read Mr. Wallingford's letter. It was just as she'd thought: stiff and formal, polite to the point of diplomacy. Well, at least that was a relief. At least it proved Linton was mad, that the Wallingfords hadn't been setting her up for some kind of white slavery, for some devil's practical joke. If you could call playing with a girl's life and, yes, a baby's life anything like joking.

Some of the bitterness left her then, but none of the regret, and not much of the humiliation. For Lily hadn't known herself until that moment how very desperately she had relied on Jack's bank draft, on the promise of a job in the store.

What in the world was she to do now? Alone, with the baby, the money running low, an Irish girl who could only just read a little and write not much more, who could sew a bit, take care of a fine lady's clothes. But no one wanted a ladies' maid with a baby—she knew that from her days in the Wallingford mansion; none of the maids had babies, they weren't even supposed to be married, unless it was a situation like Mr. and Mrs. Groome.

She sat on the bed, then lay back, exhausted. Lily closed her eyes, but sleep would not come.

Dolores came and went with the baby, and Lily could hardly bear to look at her child. In some way she couldn't quite comprehend, Lily felt she had betrayed her daughter. It was as if Lily herself had caused the Wallingfords' ruin, caused Charles Linton to go mad, caused there to be no women on the streets of San Francisco and few enough women's jobs, and fewer still the places she could go for sympathy.

Except right here, here in Sophie Delage's brothel.

You've gotten too well used to the comfort of it, Lily, and to Sophie's kind words and thoughtfulness. She's made it too easy for you, with the fine food always ready, and the maid coming and going for you, and the rest of it. And the resolve came back to Lily, stronger and more clear now, for she saw the trap for what it was.

How easy it would be to get used to this life. How hard she'd fight not to get used to it or the wickedness that created it. Sophie might be a good person, but surely she was the devil's agent on earth for all that. *I must get out of here, and tomorrow is none too soon!*

⤜§ 23 §⤛

Lily knew just what she wanted as a place to live. A clean suite of rooms in a well-kept house, kitchen privileges, and a kindly landlady who might be persuaded to take care of the baby while Lily went out working.

All the next day she looked, walking the length and breadth of San Francisco from the steamy waterfront to the top of Russian Hill, crossing and recrossing Market Street, sore of foot and heavy of heart, walking, walking, daring not to spend even the ten cents for a horse-drawn omnibus, much less hire a cab.

Again, Sophie had offered her barouche. And again, Lily refused. A fine thing, to look for cheap rooms—*cheap, Lily, but respectable*—in Sophie's carriage.

Lily walked. She walked on the muddy sidewalks and out where there were no sidewalks. She walked almost to Rincon Point, past the rotting hulks of ships abandoned in the first hot fervor of the gold rush eight years earlier, past the squatters' cabins, and always, always past the silent, lonely eyes of men.

The longing in their eyes was almost more to endure than mockery would have been, or lewdness, or propositions.

Lily knocked on many doors and got many different kinds of answers, but never the right one. Yes, there were rooms to let, said a harridan who smelled of gin, thirty dollars the week, payable in advance. Lily swallowed her repugnance and followed the woman up a dark and reeking flight of stairs. The thirty-dollar room was dim and filthy, with one small window looking over a chicken yard. Lily walked on.

Finally, at the end of a day that seemed to last forever, she found a place. For sure, it wasn't what she'd hoped for, but then, what ever was?

What Lily found was the second-floor front of a clean house far out on Broadway at the foot of Russian Hill. The woman who owned the place wasn't old, but she looked older than time, gray-faced and thin of lip, a face that might never have known a smile. She looked at Lily unblinking, in a way that made Lily wonder if something was wrong in her dress. But no. The woman looked at the whole world thus, in the certain knowledge that no good would come of it. A room and a half it was, but sunny, with a nook for Kate, almost her own little room, kitchen privileges, but watch you don't cook up any of those smelly foreign messes, and be sure you scrub up proper afterward, and no pets, and does the child cry? Mrs. Moss was cut from the same unyielding fabric as Mrs. Peabody, scourge of the *Eurydice*, and Lily could see that she'd get no sympathy from that quarter. But Mrs. Moss kept a clean house, Mrs. Moss would look after Kate for five dollars a week, and there seemed to be no other alternative in all of San Francisco. Lily had promised herself and her little daughter that she'd spend not one more night under Sophie's roof. So she smiled and thanked the grim chatelaine of number 2014 Broadway, and said that she and the child and her belongings would return that very evening.

Sophie laughed when she heard the name.

"Louisa Moss? If it's respectability you want, my dear, old Louisa'll give you a bucketful! He left her, did Jerry Moss. Ran quite away, and can you blame him? What a dried-up prune of a woman that is, not a drop of juice in her, mark my words, and mean, Lily, mean as the day is long. If blood could be got from a stone, Lily, it's Louisa Moss who'd be there straightaway drinking it."

"She seemed quite grim, it's a fact."

"Grim, next to Louisa, is a barrel of laughs, Lily. But she's honest enough, I suppose."

"She'll help look after Kate, and that's a help."

"Lily, you know it isn't going to be easy out there? There aren't many jobs for a woman here, and such as there are don't pay well. The respectable ones, I mean. It's a man's town, and women are either married or fancy, and not much between."

Lily looked at her friend. *She's trying to persuade me to take up whoring. She's trying to make a scarlet woman of me. Well, she won't.*

"I couldn't sell myself, Sophie."

"You don't think we all sell ourselves, one way or the other? That it's putting too fine a point on it by half, to call me a whore, and the girl who marries the rich man she doesn't love fine and proper? Where's the difference, I ask you?"

"God knows the difference."

[284]

"That's as may be, but I'm not God and neither are you. Think of it, Lily. I'm not trying to lure you into wickedness, if that's what you're thinking. But you could make a fortune—I mean a real fortune—in just a few years. And then retire into something else, set up a shop, who knows what? Believe me, it happens, and no one would think the worse of you."

"I know you mean to help, Sophie, but I couldn't."

"Well, dear. Perhaps not. In any event, the carriage will be ready now. I'll have someone load your things. You will come and see me, Lily? You won't forget old Sophie?"

"How could I forget? Never! Never think I'm ungrateful, dear Sophie. But I have to make my own way as best I can. For Kate's sake. For my own sake."

"I understand, darling. Now. Before I start weeping and carrying on like a fool. Go. But keep in touch, dear."

"I will. Always. And thank you, thank you, Sophie. For everything. For being a true friend."

Lily stood up then, and kissed Sophie. Then they both went downstairs, where Dolores was waiting with the baby. The riage, and a hamper of food, milk for the baby, extra little towels and sheets and blankets, for the nights were often luggage had already been loaded onto Sophie's glittering car-chilly. There were more kisses, more promises, and then Lily and Kate went clattering off up the dusty street toward the dubious comforts of Mrs. Moss and her second-floor front and her pursed lips and respectability. Lily found herself sighing as they drove off, for the hopes that had vanished for-ever, for the comfort and companionship of Sophie, for the luxury of the maid Dolores.

Yes, you're on your own now, well and truly, and may you find what you are seeking, my girl, and find it damned quickly, for Jack Wallingford's money can't last you a month, and there is surely no more where that came from! The sun had nearly set when the Delage carriage pulled up in front of Mrs. Moss's narrow gray front door.

Lily thought it a good omen that her new landlady seemed not to know Sophie's fine carriage, bought with the wages of sin.

The first day Lily spent at Mrs. Moss's house dawned bright, and the very intensity of the sunshine made Lily feel better. The baby had slept peacefully and was sleeping still as Lily got up and washed and put on a plain rust-colored cot-ton dress, her walking boots, and a simple ribbon in her hair. This would be a day of discovery, of arranging the little apartment, of finding places to shop. She smiled at the promise of it. Her first home, the first place in all the world, but for the tiny cabin on the *Eurydice*, that she could call her own!

As long as she had money. The thought of how terribly vital that question had become stabbed into Lily at once, deep and sharp, and took the pleasure out of her fair morning. *Well, then, I'll just do what I have to do quickly, in the morning, there's lots of time, and find a job in the afternoon.*

Lily was afraid to mention her quest to Mrs. Moss, afraid the older woman would consider her unreliable and ask her to leave. She went out onto Broadway to do errands, and was appalled by what things cost. Milk, thirty cents the quart, and Kate needed nearly a quart of it fresh every day! One not very handsome cabbage, two dollars. Beef, four dollars the pound, when you could find it. She had heard that there were Chinese stores where things were cheaper, where they had fish for not too much money, but these were far away from Mrs. Moss's practically suburban end of Broadway. Looking dubiously about the small greengrocer's shop, Lily realized it would cost her and Kate at the least nearly a dollar a day merely to survive. And that was without clothes, medicine, if, God forfend, they should need it, or anything else.

A handsome young farmer will ask me to marry him, and I'll fall in love and he'll take me to his beautiful farm in the country and we will have five fine baby boys to play with Kate, and we will live happily ever after. Lily smiled sadly at her daydream, bought the milk and a little cheese, and walked back to Mrs. Moss's.

The best weekly newspaper was the *Alta California*, and it was filled with advertisements, including many for help wanted. But there was nothing for Lily, and the ten cents she had spent were all wasted. Two rich ladies over in South Park, near Rincon Hill, where she had been apartment-hunting just yesterday, had advertised for maids. Twenty-four dollars a month, room and board included, only single girls with good references need apply. *Well, single I'm not, and references I have none, unless you count old Wallingford's letter, but that doesn't say about me being a maid.* There were situations open for cooks in restaurants near the docks, and Lily wondered if she could talk herself into a job like that. Or if, in fact, she could do that job if she got it.

Interspersed among the help-wanted ads were notices proclaiming the arrival of clipper ships and their luxurious cargoes, which apparently were as newsworthy as any political development or natural disaster. The Maison de Ville, which

Sophie had told her was the town's fanciest ladies' store, was offering High Quality Kidskin Gloves à la mode, six dollars the pair, lately arrived on the clipper *Eclipse*, not to mention Farina Colognes in raffia baskets, candied violets, *Godey's Ladies' Book*, and yard goods from Siam. Just reading the exotic list made Lily realize what a fairyland this town could be, for them as didn't have to worry where their next cabbage was coming from. She sat on the edge of her bed, with Kate in her lap gurgling happily, and slowly reread every page of the *Alta California* just in case there was some advertisement, some clue, that she'd missed. Several of the town's fashionable gambling parlors proclaimed that they featured "PRETTY WAITER GIRLS," and that made Lily wonder exactly what the duties were of a pretty waiter girl, and what she might earn. One such place, the Golconda, announced with a typically Californian lack of modesty that it served San Francisco's finest cuisine, had pretty waiter girls, gaming, and entertainment. And it was right on Broadway, down by the docks! Lily left Kate with the ever-unsmiling Louisa Moss and set out on foot.

I'm not pretty enough, and I've never been a waiter. They'll hate me because I am Irish. They won't want a girl with a baby.

It was late afternoon by the time Lily reached the Golconda. The gaming house filled the bottom floor of a big building just one block from the Broadway wharf, and its main entrance was at the corner of Front Street. *Convenient,* Lily thought, passing by her former refuge, *to Sophie's place.* Indeed, they were only a block apart.

The bar of the Golconda was crowded even in the afternoon. Inside, the fading light outside was totally obscured and gas lights sparkled from huge gilt mirrors, glasses, bottles, brass, and silver. A piano was being flogged with more persistence than grace, somewhere in a room Lily could not see. The air was filled with cigar smoke and exclamations. There were "pretty waiter girls," all wearing sleazy low-cut gowns, too much face paint, and expressions of sullen boredom. *Whores,* Lily thought, *the pretty waiter girls are whores, and nothing more!* She stood near the door wondering what to do next, when one of the waiter girls approached her.

"Sorry, lady, but unescorted women aren't allowed here. Better you take your wares down the street, honey."

Lily gathered up all the courage that was left in her and spoke. "I'm looking for a job."

The girl's laugh was quick and cruel. "As what?"

"As . . . a waitress."

Lily looked at the girl. *She's no older than I am, but tough as nails already. God spare me from ever getting like that.*

"Well . . . maybe." The girl looked Lily up and down with exactly the same expression of doubt that Lily herself had used on the two-dollar cabbage not long ago. At last the girl made a little shrugging gesture and spoke again. "Follow me."

Lily followed her into the back room, and then into still another room to the left of that. The back room was filled with green-topped gaming tables and noisy men at play. The waiter girls lounged about, sometimes actually bringing a drink or a sandwich, but for the most part teasing the gamblers, egging them on, receiving their roving hands and drunken propositions with the bland acceptance of long practice.

The girl led Lily to the door of an office. "The kid wants a job, Lucy," she said quickly, and left.

Lily squinted a bit, for the office was big and dimly lit. At the far end of the room was a huge oaken desk, a desk that might have served for all the business of a large bank, a desk of almost monstrous proportions, fitted with dozens of pigeonholes and tiny drawers and compartments. At the big desk sat a woman. Lily had never seen such a figure. She was tall, very tall, one foot taller than Lily at the least, and slender as a stalk of wheat. And as sallow. She seemed to be all of one color, this Lucy, pale ivory, no makeup, and pale ivory hair that might have been blond or white with age. Her face had a masklike quality, expressionless, with half-mast eyelids that looked as though they had seen everything and paid only the most minimal attention.

"Come here, girl." Her voice was smooth and as expressionless as her face, and like her face, it hinted of hidden dangers in some subtle way Lily could not quite define. "You're looking for a job."

"Yes, ma'am."

"Your name?"

"Lily. Lillian Malone. Mrs. Lillian Malone." Lily was very close to the desk now. She saw the woman's hand come floating out toward her, supple and threatening as some pale snake. The hand just barely touched Lily, but it touched nearly all of her, passing down her breast, down the curve of her hip, down the top of her thighs with no more force than a breeze. Lily shuddered at the touch, and froze with fear.

She prepared herself to run, to fight, to scream. And who would hear?

"Yes. Possibly, just possibly you might do."

"What would . . ."

"Be a waiter girl. Be kind to our respected customers. Indulge them in their little whims. Be nice to me."

Again, uncontrollably, Lily shuddered.

"Do I frighten you, dearie? You'd rather have one of our fine brave *hombres* working you over, hasn't had a bath in six months, pockets filled with gold dust, up there in the hills fucking the goats and the little Mexican boys too? Is that what you want, little Lily?"

Lily blinked in disbelief. *I am going to be sick right here and now!* "I didn't understand . . ."

"No, of course not, they never do. You're an attractive little creature, do you know that? Probably not. Don't know very much, do you, girl? But there is a certain . . . freshness."

Again the pale hand came floating in her direction. Lily turned then and ran from the dark office. A pale echo of laughter followed her departure.

Lily stumbled through the crowded gaming room, and paused, looking this way and that, desperate for the quickest route out of this terrible place. She felt a hand on her shoulder, and turned, ready to scream. It was the waiter girl who had shown her in, and underneath the paint, and the habitual sneer, the girl's face had softened.

"Look, honey," she said in a hoarse tone, "you don't want to work here, this here's a rough place. Go up the street and try Sophie's. They treat a girl right at Sophie's. If I could get in there, you can bet that's where I'd be, *comprende*?"

Lily was so thoroughly frightened that she could only nod her thanks and run. And run she did, no matter who might be looking.

It was dark in the street now. Lily came hurtling out of the Golconda and turned right, up Broadway toward home.

The street was filled with men, as usual. She walked a block, and then passed Sophie Delage's El Dorado Hotel.

The El Dorado glowed in the darkness.

Lily looked up at Sophie's house as she passed, and quickly looked away. There was all the temptation of a thousand devils, bright and beckoning. She thought of the strange woman, of Lucy, and her flesh crawled. And for the first time Lily felt pity for the poor waiter girls of the Golconda, and what they must put up with.

[289]

Kate was crying when Lily got back to the Moss house. She could hear the child's lusty wailing half a block away. Lily let herself in and went to the gloomy front parlor. Mrs. Moss stood up at once, plucked Kate from where she lay wet and wriggling on a torn sheet on the floor, and handed the infant to her mother.

"Thank you," said Lily. "I hope the child was not a bother for you."

"Everything is a bother to me, Mrs. Malone, and one more or less hardly matters."

"Yes. Well, good evening, then."

Sophie, Lily thought as she climbed the narrow stairs, was right: Louisa Moss was about as far from cheerful as a body could get, this side of the grave.

"But we don't mind, do we, Kate, Katharine, Katie? We won't let that old wet blanket bother the likes of us, Kate, not us, for the sun is going to shine on us, Kate, and all the angels will be singing for us, and you'll grow up fine and strong and smarter than your old lady, yes, that's what's going to happen, little Kate, and you can bet your bottom dollar on it."

Only when the words "bottom dollar" slipped out did Lily realize that the damp on her cheek came not from kissing Kate's anger away, but from her own tears of weariness and frustration. She flung open the apartment door and changed Kate's diaper, washed the child, and put her to bed. Lily's supper that night was a little cheese, a slice of hard roll (the remainder being saved for breakfast), and one glass of Kate's milk.

The manager of the Maison de Ville was charming. *He thinks I'm a customer*, Lily thought. *Little does he know!* But even when she told him she was looking for work, that she could sew a fine hem, and even do embroidery, his good manners remained undiminished.

"Alas, the Chinese have ruined all that, I fear, at least from your point of view, Mrs. Malone. They work, you see, for practically nothing, and we simply can't afford not to use them, since everyone else does."

"I see."

Lily saw the problem only vaguely. There were throngs of Chinese men in the street, odd-colored, quick-moving, jabbering people, always busy, always en route somewhere, always moving faster than the white men. And they did all of the most menial tasks, did the Chinese. Laundry was their specialty, for Lily had considered even that; she knew how to care for fine ladies' clothing, but the Chinese, again, knew as much and did it for remarkably little. As they sewed, and cooked, and dug ditches, and did the donkey work in the mines. They had no babies to care for, these Chinese, they were single men who lived in hovels, six or more to a room.

By the end of the second week, with more than half of her money gone, Lily began to realize the full extent of what she was up against.

The normal jobs that might have been available to a young girl in any other big city simply did not exist here. The overwhelming predominance of men meant that men often took jobs traditionally worked by women. There were many—too many—male shop clerks, waiters, cooks. Even the Chinese men who sewed were usurping women's work. In two weeks Lily had all but worn out her walking boots. Her feet were sore and blistered, for she would not spend what it cost for an omnibus. She knew all the byways of the raw new city now, and its main streets too, and all of them, to Lily, seemed to lead nowhere.

Lily saw her small reserve of cash melting away in the face of the astounding prices the merchants asked, and got, for even the simplest food. It seemed that every hour, every bite of bread or sip of milk, brought her closer to some terrible day of reckoning, a day on which she would have to beg, or steal, or do only God knows what, simply to survive.

All day, for as long as her strength and her will would carry her, Lily walked the streets in search of work. The rejection that she met at every turn had long ceased to surprise her. It seemed to be part of her life now, like a spell of the worst weather. It would have been easy to hate the Chinese, who took the menial jobs that might otherwise have saved her, but she could not, for didn't they need to eat too, and didn't they have problems of their own? Every afternoon Lily dragged herself back to Mrs. Moss's house, wondering how long her everyday shoes would last, thin as they were getting. Only Kate could cheer her, but what a cheer this was! The baby seemed happy and looked well, and her smile could charm even the prune-faced Mrs. Moss. But even this joy was mixed with sadness, for Lily would look down at her daughter and think: *One day soon, Kate, you are going to want new clothes, and where they'll come from is a mystery.* And Kate would smile and make small gurgling noises that drove Lily half-mad with doubt and fear for the child's future.

She would not give up hope. Her luck had carried her this

far. It must carry her farther still: *It simply is not possible that there are no jobs at all for me in San Francisco.* Lily knocked on so many doors that she began to feel like a beggar. *And I would beg, and steal, too, for my Katie.*

Mrs. Stanford Dickinson had a rich husband, an old name, and no chin. She had advertised for someone who could do fine mending. Now Lily stood nervously in the front hallway of the big Dickinson house in Spring Park, twisting her worn reticule in anticipation of the interview. The little Mexican maid came back and gestured for Lily to follow. The house was large and had a fine view. Even by the ostentatious standards Lily was used to from her days in the Wallingford mansion, this place was almost grotesquely overfurnished. Mrs. Dickinson sat on a heavily carved sofa, her back stiff as a board, holding an opulent red damask ball gown on her lap. Even from halfway across the room Lily could tell that the gown was all but ruined. A huge jagged tear extended nearly twelve inches across the front panel of the gown, from the hem almost to the knee.

Mrs. Dickinson nodded icily as Lily introduced herself. "Yes, yes young lady. Now. What might you be able to do with this?"

She held up the tattered gown. Lily wondered how in the world the rip had got there, for the silk damask was heavy, very strong, and new.

"Have you any more of the material, ma'am?"

"No, no, of course not! It's from Paris."

"Then I would disguise it with a fringe, here, and another, for the balance, here."

"And how long might that take?"

"Three days, perhaps, maybe four. After finding the fringe, that is. There is much fine work to be done on it."

"And what might you charge?"

"Perhaps . . . fifteen dollars."

"Outrage! Do you think money grows on trees, girl? Why, I can get any chink to do it for five. And in a day. And beautifully, too."

Lily looked at the woman and ceased to see her clearly. Lily saw, instead, Kate's little face. She saw Kate's face smiling, happy, not wondering where her next meal would come from, for sure and she had a good mother to get it. Sure. Lily sighed.

"Five dollars, then. And carfare."

The curl of triumph on Mamie Dickinson's lips was not a

pretty thing to see. "I am willing to try you, girl, out of charity."

Lily's heart shrank at the word "charity." It wasn't charity at all. It was damnable thievery, and well Mrs. Dickinson knew it.

But it was also her only chance to earn a few days' grace to buy a bit of food for herself and the baby. Maybe, if she did the work very well, and quickly, maybe then Mrs. Dickinson would give her more to do, and at more reasonable prices.

Lily spoke softly when she replied. "Where," she asked in measured tones, burying her anger deep, "would I find the fringe, ma'am?"

"At the City of Paris, of course, they have the best: I'll give them a note, and you can have them bill it to my account. And I shall expect a detailed receipt, not an inch more than you need, don't try any sly tricks on me, girl!"

"I shall need thread, too, Mrs. Dickinson."

"Well, if you insist."

Mrs. Dickinson rose and walked stiffly to a little desk that gleamed with gilt-bronze hardware. She opened a drawer and pulled out some creamy notepaper and quickly scrawled a message.

"There," she said, handing the note to Lily. "Take this to the manager at the City of Paris. And I'll expect the dress back tomorrow, and not a moment after five."

Lily's mind raced. It was easily two days' work. Mrs. Dickinson reached into a little beaded reticule with fingers that seemed like claws, so bony they were, and so grasping. She fetched out a fifty-cent piece and gave it to Lily.

"Carfare," she said. "I don't want my Paris silks trailing in the mud of San Francisco."

"Yes, ma'am," said Lily, thinking murder.

"Tomorrow before five, then?"

"Yes, ma'am."

Lily folded the ball gown carefully, slipped the note into her worn purse, and left. The rage in her heart had subsided into sorrow. Mrs. Dickinson's attitude went beyond unfairness. It went all the way to cruelty. Lily wondered what life had done to the woman, that made her enjoy taking such brutal advantage of a stranger. Still, it was a chance. The fifty cents glowed in Lily's mind as though it were some treasure out of a fairy story. Mrs. Dickinson's gown would not trail in the mud, but only because Lily would take great care of it. The carfare would buy milk for Katie, and a few loaves of bread, stale of course, but that didn't matter much if you soaked it in milk.

Lily hurried down the hill and across the bustling streets to the heart of town. Before long she was smiling again. *That mean old woman was going to get a surprise! She'd have her gown back before she expected, and so perfectly sewn that she'd melt, and give Lily more work, and tell all her friends, too. If a woman that mean had any friends to tell.*

All the City of Paris had to hear was the name Dickinson. Clerks were sent running, eight kinds of fringe were produced, and Lily found exactly the right one—a perfect color match—in minutes. Luck was with her, and not a moment too soon!

All that night, she sewed.

It was incredibly difficult. The tear was more than a tear. It looked as though some ravening lion had slashed the heavy satin with his claw—jagged, frayed, with parts of the skirt hanging almost in ribbons.

First Lily sewed the ragged tear back into a semblance of what it had been, using the finest French stitching. And wouldn't Sister Mary Agnes be proud of her pupil! Lily sewed in the last of the daylight, then lit the kerosene lamp and drew it close to her hard straight-backed chair. The baby played and gurgled happily. Lily sewed until her fingers ached. The only relief from it was rising from time to time to pick up Kate, crooning and talking to the infant, murmuring words of hope. Kate smiled, and seemed to understand.

Finally the great rip was sewn. Lily draped the gown over the back of the chair and scrutinized her work. The pattern of the tear was visible, but only barely, and her stitches were so fine that they all but vanished into the heavy satin. And the skirt draped well. When the fringe was applied, the repair should be undetectable. She rubbed her cramped fingers and began basting the fringe in an attractive sweep. Then she matched the concealing fringe with another sweep on the opposite side of the skirt. There! It was really almost an improvement, considering the gaudy nature of the gown, which was nearly as overfurnished with draperies and decorations as Mrs. Dickinson's drawing room.

Lily sat and began sewing the fringe into place with careful, undetectable little stitches. She squinted. Her fingers passed the point of aching and became numb extensions of an indefatigable will. The dress would be done and delivered by noon. Mrs. Dickinson would learn what skill and dedication could do. Lily pricked a finger, swore silently, for the baby was sleeping, and managed to catch the drop of blood before it soiled the satin.

The black night was fading into pale dawn when Lily cut the last thread, tied the last knot, and finally draped the gown over the chair again. She was almost too sleepy to see, but the gown was finished and it looked splendid. Yawning, Lily splashed a little water on her face and dragged herself to bed.

Lily woke to a bright, clear day. Her fingers ached and her eyes felt sore, but in her heart was the warm glow of achievement. *How many girls in San Francisco could have done the job so well, and so quickly?* It was worth much more than five dollars. Lily knew that, and so must Mrs. Dickinson. Maybe the woman would see reason. Surely she'd see that the job was expertly done, and Lily worthy of more work.

If she could earn just ten dollars a day, she and Kate could survive!

Lily half-sang, half-hummed a little tune as she dressed and refolded the gown. She fed the baby, took a sip of milk for herself, and half a stale roll, and set out briskly on foot for the mansion on Rincon Hill.

The walk took nearly an hour. Once again Lily rang the bell, and was admitted by a servant. Mamie Dickinson was wearing an afternoon gown only slightly less elaborate than the ball gown that Lily had spent the night mending. Lily found herself greeted with a glare.

"Your gown, ma'am. And a bit of the fringe that was left over, and the thread, should it ever need mending again."

Without so much as glancing at the gown, Mamie Dickinson spoke in a voice that was very like a snarl. "You sly little thief! To have the brass to demand carfare from me, and get it, and steal it!"

Lily was shocked to her toes. For a moment she stood, dumbstruck.

"I . . ."

"Did you or did you not take money from me in this very room, yesterday, and then keep it for yourself?"

Lily felt her head spinning. What could she say? It was true. She had kept the carfare for herself—for Kate. How did the woman know? And why did she care? Fifty cents to her, a millionairess?

The rasping voice went on. "Don't try to worm out of it. You were followed, sly vixen that you are. You don't suppose I'd let a stranger walk away with a gown worth thousands of dollars? Well, it's lucky for you, Miss whatever-your-name-is, that you got yourself back here with the gown, or I'd have you jailed. I may do that yet."

Rage flowed through Lily like a flood tide. "All night I stayed up sewing your gown, Mrs. Dickinson. If you want your carfare back, I'll give it to you, out of my pay. I am not a thief."

Mamie Dickinson laughed. The wattled turkey's throat stretched back and the chinless mouth opened wide. Her laugh was jagged, the sound of cheap glass breaking.

"You don't imagine I intend to pay you, thief that you are? And a liar to boot. Better you take yourself out of here, you wicked girl, and thank the good Lord that I don't have the police on you, for I easily could."

Lily felt hot very suddenly, then cold. She actually shivered, standing before Mamie Dickinson, trembling, desolated beyond words. Beyond anger. *This must be what dying feels like.*

Slowly, still trembling, Lily turned. It was like learning to walk all over again. She put one foot in front of the other and made her way across the rich carpet, hardly able to comprehend what was happening.

If a mule had kicked her in the head, Lily could hardly have been more stunned, more profoundly hurt. Without a word, but with Mamie Dickinson's horrible laugh echoing in her heart, Lily somehow got herself out of the house and down the wide front steps to the street.

Back inside, Mamie Dickinson unfolded the dress, spread it out on a settee, and smiled. You'd have to get up pretty early to put one over on Mamie Dickinson.

✿§ 24 §✿

Of all the many and luxurious wedding presents that had come to the newlywed Mr. and Mrs. Brooks Chaffee, Brooks best liked the simple Greek Revival brick house his father had bought for them on West Eleventh Street, just off Fifth Avenue. It wasn't as big or as elaborate as the senior Chaffees' establishment on Washington Square, but the clean lines of the house and its beautiful proportions from within were pleasing: chaste black marble fireplaces in the twin parlors, tall windows framed in flat pilasters, gleaming walnut doors, ceilings high but unadorned.

Caroline, of course, wanted to add an iron balcony in the Gothic style that was suddenly so fashionable, and on that issue Brooks refused her for the first time in their short marriage. She took it in good grace, as Caroline took everything, and contented herself with redoing the interior in the height of style, using influences she'd picked up on their honeymoon in Europe.

How Brooks wished that lovely adventure could go on forever and ever!

But they were back now, three months away was quite long enough, and Brooks was eager as any sapling tree to settle in and put down roots. He had always known his future would be here, in New York, in his father's law firm or his uncle's bank. There had always been such a depth of comfort in the Chaffee household, and so little talk about money—for to talk about money was considered vulgar—that Brooks was only vaguely aware of the world of finance. And the more he found out, the more it fascinated him. By the time they'd landed in New York again, Brooks was determined to seek a position in his uncle's investment-banking firm. And now, three months later, in the bright blue of October, Brooks was the most industrious young clerk in the well-known firm of Chaffee, Hudner & Zuydam.

Caroline, to her husband's surprise, had been opposed to his taking a job of any kind.

"In the South, a young man in your circumstances would not dream of workin' in some tacky old office every day. He'd be out with his horses, or shootin', or things like that."

Brooks laughed. "Yes, my love, and look at the South, the condition it's in. Your young man would also have hundreds of slaves, I'm sure, and a vast inherited fortune, or a great plantation."

"You have a fortune."

"Only grandmother's trust, and the generosity of my father. I'm not truly rich, not yet anyway."

"Well, Brooks Chaffee, I must declare I do not understand you Northerners. You are positively fanatical."

"I am," he said kissing her, laughing still, "fanatical about one thing, darling, and that is my beautiful bride." And the discussion ended in their big old mahogany four-poster bed, where more and more of such discussions seemed to end these days. Brooks could find nothing to complain about in that. Caroline's healthy response to his lovemaking was a source of deep pleasure and infinite delight to him. If more women were as warm and loving to their husbands, he often thought, there would be far fewer husbands sneaking off to the sporting palaces of Manhattan.

Yet as Brooks became more and more involved with the burgeoning affairs of Chaffee, Hudner, it became increasingly obvious that Caroline's primary interest was the pursuit of pleasure: not only sexual gratification, but social pleasures of all kinds. Caroline quickly became one of the more popular young hostesses of the city. With her beauty and charm and breeding, combined with the hitherto unapproachable cachet of the ancient Chaffee name and connections, an invitation to dine with Brooks and Caroline was very close to irresistible.

And the entertainment she provided to those who accepted was remarkable.

In a city noted for its vulgarity and excesses, Caroline Ledoux Chaffee had the wit and imagination to be different. While other hostesses in her set might fill a room with a thousand dollars' worth of flowers, Caroline made people gasp by floating one perfect gardenia in one small crystal bowl in front of each guest's plate. She was the first to give an Oriental banquet, the first to have a Spanish gypsy guitarist instead of the usual stuffy string ensemble playing at supper, the first to give a midnight picnic on a chartered sailing boat that ghosted up the Hudson propelled by champagne and laughter.

Life with Caroline became a gilded whirl, and when the

money he gave her as a household allowance ran out, Caroline simply used her own and never mentioned it. The important thing was to keep the carousel turning, and while Brooks had never found the social life either very amusing or very necessary, she did, and therefore he indulged her. After all, it kept her busy, it gave many people pleasure, and so why question it?

In the meantime, the year ground remorselessly on, with the slavery issue growing ever more flammable. The newly settled Midwestern states were tearing themselves virtually to shreds over the issue. Kansas, after months of bloody debate, voted Free. Minnesota, which no one had even heard of five years earlier, suddenly had a population of more than 150,000 and was agitating for statehood and against slavery. Brooks could see the tension building, the relations with the Deep South growing more strained every day until, sure as sunrise, someday soon, the strain would reach the breaking point.

He remembered the soft days and long nights of his wedding celebrations in New Orleans, and wondered if that style of almost ducal splendor could sustain itself much longer. He thought not.

Caroline, meanwhile, was entrenching herself as the belle of New York. Precisely how she spent her daytime hours, Brooks never knew, nor did he bother to ask. She was a wonder, forever in motion, organizing parties or going to them, shopping, decorating, doing the thousand sweet female things that her sex and position in the world made her heiress to, and doing these things so very well that to many of the bored postdebutante set in Manhattan, life without Caroline Chaffee began to seem boring, insupportable, unthinkable. Their little argument in London, over Marianne Wallingford's lover, had faded so completely that it might never have happened.

Brooks, to whom preeminence in society had arrived with his first diaper, was less aware of the speed and scope of her triumph than more distant observers. As ever, Caroline caused a wagging of tongues, a looking-down of noses, for Caroline was irreverent, very sure of what Caroline wanted and to hell with everyone else, and not afraid to show it or say it. It was a matter of months before she had the brightest and most decorative members of the fast young set in town all but eating out of her small, white, fine-skinned hand.

Brooks knew that his older brother, Neddy, was one of the frowners and disapprovers, and this disturbed him, for he loved Neddy. They never talked about Caroline these days, because Brooks sensed that to do that might create an open unpleasantness between them, and there was a great deal that Brooks Chaffee would do to avoid that.

So Neddy became less and less a part of their lives. The elder Chaffees, too, were less and less in evidence at West Eleventh Street. The social duties were well and regularly performed, but beyond that there was little communication. Brooks's mother, always a quiet woman, grew even more inward in the glowing, bubbling presence of the dynamic Caroline. And his father simply didn't care for parties.

As October danced and sparkled toward deep fall, and the New York social scene cranked itself up for yet another merry winter, Brooks sometimes wondered if he'd had a life at all before Caroline. Maybe, but it had been a nursery kind of life, only dimly remembered.

One person still much in evidence from that past life was Jack Wallingford.

It was terrible to see what the Wallingfords' bankruptcy had done to Jack. Jack, who had always been such a good sport, unfailingly generous, always ready to laugh, to set up some fun, had become a kind of dark memory of his former self. He had always been a drinker. Now the drinking had a desperate edge on it, as if Jack could see his death in every glass, and didn't care. His laughter had an unwelcome edge to it these days, too. Jack mocked everything, including himself. Leaving New Haven, as he'd been forced to do, was no sacrifice for Jack. But the shabby boardinghouse he shared with his parents, just off Lexington Avenue in the Twenties, was an insistent reminder of how far and how suddenly they had fallen.

In the past, Jack's inconsistencies had seemed charming whims. Now he merely appeared unreliable. Jack might or might not respond to a written invitation, and, having accepted, he might or might not show up. And if he showed up, he might or might not be sober. Brooks and Caroline fed him, joked with him, tolerated him. After all, Brooks often reminded himself, hadn't it been Jack who first introduced him to Caroline?

One night Brooks came home late from the office and found his house glittering with light and ringing with laughter. Blushing, he hung up his coat and entered the drawing room. He had forgotten that Caroline was having another of her little supper parties. He looked around the pretty room and wished she had chosen some other night. Then he saw Caroline and, as always, melted. There were women in the room, but she was surrounded by three men. One of them was Jack, and from long experience Brooks could tell that his old friend was far from sober. He kissed his wife, shook hands with the men, clapped Jack on the shoulder.

"It's good to see you, Jack."

Wallingford grinned, and in the flash of his smile Brooks could almost imagine they were boys again, and about to set off on some grand adventure. But then, quick as it came, his friend's mood changed and darkened. Jack's hot, dark eyes burned into his own eyes, and their intensity was such that Brooks soon looked away. There was a plea in Jack's gaze, and a kind of desperation. He was far out on some bleak edge of despair, maybe beyond reach. Brooks thought of the old days, and determined to try. He led Jack out of the little group and up the stairs to the library.

"Is something the matter, old friend?" Jack's reply was a harsh laugh. Then he spoke, slowly, as if from some faraway place.

"It does my heart good to see you and the lady, indeed it does, for seldom in this vale of tears does one get the chance to glimpse perfection."

"We are far from perfect, as well you know."

"Ah, say it not! To the world's eyes, you are perfection. You glitter with it, inside and out. So young, so fair, so brimming with luck. Say, you don't keep any brandy up here, by any chance?"

"I'll ring for some."

"No, don't bother. I've had more than my share, as you may have noticed. I shall just bask in the reflected glow of your happiness, then slink off to my usual low haunts."

Brooks looked at his friend and felt a sense of helplessness choking the very breath out of him.

"If there is anything I can do, just tell me."

"Ever kind. Ever considerate, a compendium of all the virtues. I love you, Brooks, truly I do. But no, the only help that could be given me is long past the reach of God or man, for it would mean inserting a new heart, new soul . . . new hope. And it's too late in the game for that, I fear."

"You don't mean it."

"But I do. Now . . . shall we rejoin the ladies?" They walked down the blue-carpeted staircase into a hall filled with light and laughter.

Lily made her way down Rincon Hill, past the opulent houses of the rich, past fanciful iron fences and elaborately planted flower gardens struggling to take root in what just a few years ago had been sand dunes.

She felt like a ghost, so remote was she from this world of wealth and servants and never a care about whether you'd have enough to eat tomorrow. Or today.

Lily's mind was hardly able to accept what Mrs. Dickinson had said and done. Maybe it had been wrong not to take the tram. But surely buying food for her baby counted more than that small scruple.

Lily felt as though something dirty, something contaminating had happened to her in that house. She breathed deeply, and tried to organize her thoughts. She could feel a pang of hunger deep in her belly, for it was well past noon now, and she'd had only a sip and a bite for breakfast.

At the bottom of the hill was a small greengrocer's. Lily paused, tempted. *Thirty cents for one apple, and not a very fine one at that!* She looked at the apple, unimaginable luxury. A quart of milk could be bought for that much: enough to last Kate one day. What a fine thing it must be, to be a farmer. With peace and quiet and green all around you, and always, always enough to eat.

Lily stared at the display of fruits and vegetables like a woman obsessed. It was a meager showing. She felt herself sinking. *And maybe it would have been all for the best if the* Eurydice *had sunk in that gale!*

Lily turned quickly from the counter and walked on, unseeing, beyond tears.

The first street she came to was named Folsom, first of some twenty blocks she'd have to walk, and many of those uphill.

Lily stepped into the dry dirt road, lost in the depths of her troubles and only vaguely aware of a building thunder coming closer and louder. She never saw the stampeding carriage.

Suddenly there was a shout and a roaring and a clatter of hooves. Strong arms locked around Lily and dragged her back and downward.

"Whoa, there, lady!"

She was sitting in the dust and a tall stranger knelt in the road beside her, fanning her with a clean handkerchief, offering her water from a copper ladle.

"You must have fainted, ma'am. Are you feeling better?"

Lily blinked, realized she wasn't dreaming, looked up.

The sun was behind him, and it made a bright halo all around the pale gold of his hair. She could see firm white teeth in his smile, but the face was shaded.

"I'm fine, thank you. What happened?"

"Damn fool—begging your pardon—nearly ran you down, stampeding his carriage like the world's on fire. I grabbed you just in time."

He offered his hand and pulled Lily to her feet. She could see him clearly now. He had a nice face, but it wasn't the face that was forever associated with that kind of hair in Lily's dreams. She smiled at the same time as she quickly dusted off her long skirt.

"Well, I surely thank you, sir. I must have been fast asleep, not to see him coming. You may have saved my life."

"My name's Luke Ransome, ma'am, and you still—if you'll forgive me—look pretty pale. Could I fetch you some tea, maybe, or something to eat?"

Lily looked quickly down into the dust of Folsom Street, unable to credit her luck. *Something to eat!* The words could hardly have held more magic to her if he had offered her all of Rincon Hill, Mrs. Stanford Dickinson included! *No, he'll think you're being forward, God knows what else he'll think!* But then Lily thought of all the lost-sheep looks in the eyes of all the lonely men on the streets of San Francisco: they meant no harm, those looks, those eyes. Simply sad, as sad they were, for women lost or left behind. They were alone, those men, this man, and felt it deeply. *And you're alone, Lily, never forget that, and what's the harm in it?*

She felt herself blushing even as she answered. "My name is Mrs. Fergus Malone, sir, and I would be delighted to take tea with you."

He walked her to a small Italian coffee shop on Market Street not far from where she'd had her strange interview with Charles Linton. They had dark bittersweet coffee and very sweet pastries. Lily liked her rescuer at once. Luke was twenty, had survived the terrible overland journey from St. Louis that had killed off both his parents and one sister. He was clerking in a law firm now, but what Luke really wanted to do was buy a farm.

"Nobody values the land, yet, Lily: they're all in gold or in trade, and you can still buy big old ranches from the land-grant Mexicans for a few dollars an acre. And look what produce costs."

Lily smiled and nodded. *A handsome farmer will ask you to marry him, you'll fall in love and have five sons for Kate to play with, and live happily ever after.* Luke Ransome was handsome enough, tall and straight and with a built-in kind of honesty about him that was direct and reassuring. Not smooth, not elegant as a Brooks Chaffee, but who could be? A decent young man, thinking right. They finished, she thanked him, and he asked if he could walk her home.

"It'll be a long walk, Mr. Ransome."

"My pleasure."

Why did I ask him to call me Lily so early on? He'll think I'm a loose woman. She told him a sketchy version of her made-up story, about sailing the Horn to meet her husband, only to find him dead, and her with the new baby. *Don't mention that you've got less than a week's worth of money to live on, Lily, pride is pride after all, and something is sure to turn up.* The strong coffee and the sweetness of the pastries warmed her, and her good luck warmed her too. It was luck to meet such a fine young man, and to have him like her enough to want to walk her home.

The walk home took most of the afternoon, for Luke insisted on showing her all the sights, pointing out landmarks that Lily had passed many times without knowing—or caring—what they were.

Lily told him about Kate, what a fine happy infant she was, how she smiled. And Lily found herself smiling, laughing even, for the first time in weeks.

How very good it felt to have a friend, someone who seemed truly to be interested in her, and without the dark edge of temptation that Sophie's friendship held for Lily now. Luke was gentle for a San Franciscan, and while he was the first to admit his family had been simple people, farmers, uneducated, he seemed to have natural good manners, and that, surely, was what counted most. He took her arm as they crossed the many streets, and that felt good too, reassuring, steady, warming.

Finally they were in front of Mrs. Moss's gray, grim residence. Lily turned to her rescuer, and smiled, and held out her hand.

"It has been delightful, Mr. Ransome."

"Please, Luke."

"Luke, then. Thank you very much."

"I thank you, Lily, and I hope, maybe, that . . . sometime—"

Lily cut him off quickly then, afraid to continue in this delicious but possibly dangerous vein. "We'll see, won't we? Again, Luke, I thank you. Good day."

"Adios, Lily."

The next morning a large basket of groceries was delivered to a frowning Mrs. Moss. It contained a card addressed to

Lily. The card said simply: "Dear Lily, these are for your baby. Maybe we could have supper tonight? I will call for you at seven. Your friend, Luke Ransome." Lily looked at the basket, dumbfounded. If it had been heaped with rubies, it could hardly have been more welcome. A glimmer of happiness flickered on someplace deep inside her, and grew, glowing, warming the damp morning. *He cared. He remembered her—and the baby. How very kind. How very promising.* Lily accepted the basket with a smile, ignoring Mrs. Moss's sniff of disdain, for Mrs. Moss was forever sniffing disdainfully. It was her normal way of expressing herself. Let her sniff! Lily was sure she'd read Luke's message, for the note was not sealed. Well, just let her read, then: nothing and no one was going to deprive Lily of the fullest enjoyment of this unexpected treasure. A gift from heaven itself, nothing less!

Lily arranged for Mrs. Moss to look in on the baby, and then dressed carefully for the occasion. She reminded herself that in the story she had invented, she was a widow, and a recent one at that. She chose a simple dark blue dress figured with small white flowers, dressed her hair simply in a bun, and took a green shawl against the night's chill. Then she kissed the baby and went down to the parlor.

Luke appeared promptly at seven, dressed in his best dark suit, looking handsome, wearing a smile that could have lit up the whole California sky. Lily introduced him to Mrs. Moss, who sniffed noncommittally, and they left.

"Luke," Lily whispered as they walked down the stairs, "truly, you should not have been so generous, with that basket. But it was kind, and Kate and I thank you."

"My pleasure. It's a better use, Lily, than where my money usually goes in this wicked town."

"You, wicked? I can't believe that."

"Good. I don't believe most people are either good or wicked, really. We are what we have to be."

They walked for a few blocks, and then Luke hailed a passing hansom cab.

"The Golden Rooster, please."

"What's the Golden Rooster?"

"Oh, it's a fine place to eat, Lily. You'll see."

The Golden Rooster was both fine and golden. It had walls of wine-red silk and dark wood paneling. There was a profusion of brass and mirrors and potted palm trees. The headwaiter led them up a wide flight of carpeted stairs and into a private room that contained a fireplace, a small round table set for two, discreet candlesticks here and there, a wide chaise longue upholstered in dark blue velvet, and a silver ice bucket with a bottle of champagne cooling in it. The waiter took Lily's shawl, then uncorked the wine and poured it. Luke handed her a glass, which was not merely glass, but the finest crystal, etched with scrolls and flowers. Lily blinked at the contrast between this opulence and her small gray room in Mrs. Moss's small gray house. And here she was drinking champagne in a room with walls of silk while all there was between her and Kate and starvation was one basket of groceries donated by this amazing stranger!

He lifted his glass to hers. "To the most beautiful girl in California."

Lily quickly looked over her shoulder to see who that might be. What she saw was a thin startled face in the dark mirror, and Luke's big golden head behind her.

"You're mad!"

"No, very lucky. But for that reckless driver, I might never have found you."

His glass touched hers with a small silvery chiming sound. They sipped the bubbling wine. Maybe it was the sudden warmth of the fire, or the small amount of champagne in that one sip, but Lily could feel a gentle glow slowly spreading through her. For a moment she panicked, and could think of nothing at all to say.

There was a discreet knock on the door, Luke said "Come in," and the waiter appeared with a cart on wheels covered by a dome of pure silver. He whisked two bowls of clear brown soup onto the table, bowed, and indicated a discreet bell pull hanging next to the fireplace.

"Ring, sir, should you need anything more."

"Thank you," said Luke as he helped Lily into her chair.

The soup was turtle, laced with Madeira, and it was followed by venison ragout, buttered noodles, and small green peas the like of which Lily hadn't seen or thought of since Louise's kitchen in the Wallingford mansion in the old days. There was a salad, too, and a tray of petits four for dessert. And more champagne.

Luke looked at the luxurious spread, happy as a pig in new mud. He grinned a small boy's grin, and laughed out loud before he spoke.

"If you're wondering how a law clerk can pay for all this, Lily, let me tell you that you've already brought me luck. For on the very day I met you, I won near to three thousand dollars in a poker game."

"But that's a fortune!"

"In San Francisco, Lily, it's play money. I could tell you of broken-down bums who made millions overnight, and lost 'em just as quick as that. It's a crazy place, this town. Anything can happen here."

Lily looked at him and said nothing. But she was coming to feel that his words were true ones.

Luke did most of the talking. He spoke of his Missouri boyhood, how they'd decided to join up with a wagon train over the southern route, through Utah territory to California, the slow, dragging oxen, the broken axles, bad water, dysentery, furniture abandoned by the trailside, animals rotting, stinking, vultures circling, people dying, and dying.

"The signposts on that trail are gravemarkers, Lily. Sometimes you'll see a whole family, spread out over a thousand miles, the kids go first, most times, and nearly always the women go last, they've got the most fight in 'em, I guess. But not Ma. She was always sickly, and she went first. Then Sally. Then Pa."

"And you were the only one left?"

"Sixty-three of us started out. When we got over the Sierras, there were nineteen, and three of them died later on, from things they'd caught on the trail."

"I'm glad I sailed, then, bad as that seemed at the time."

"I am, too, Lily, for there were things I've seen on that trail I'll tell to no man, much less to a lady."

He got up then, and came around and stood next to her chair. His hand rested lightly on her shoulder. Suddenly Lily was reminded of another rich, dark room, and another young man whose hand had rested on her shoulder. Luke knelt beside her and reached out with one hand and touched Lily's chin. She turned and looked into his wide-set brown eyes.

"Sometimes, out in the desert, on those cold clear nights, when all you could see for a hundred miles was the white sand stretching out in the moonlight, and the coyotes would be howling for blood, banshee howls they called 'em, and you knew there were Indians somewheres not far away, and so many of us had died there was no betting on whether any of us'd see the next sunrise, much less the next moon, well, at those times I'd think of a woman, of a perfect, beautiful woman, Lily, and she was always slender and delicate-like, and she always had hair like a mountain sunset, and eyes green as jade."

He buried his face in her neck then, and kissed her, and

then he was kissing her lips, and the warmth of him touched her and she was kissing him back.

And Lily thought: *This isn't how I wanted it to happen; if he loves me so, I should make him marry me first, except that's just like what Sophie said, selling myself on the altar.* Her mind swam, and logic drifted away from her on waves of pleasure. It had been a very long time since anyone had needed her so. Jack Wallingford, surely, had never truly needed her, Jack, who could have any woman, anywhere. This was something different, a rare and special thing. When Luke stood up slowly, lifting her as though she had no more weight than his need for her, Lily floated up with him, locked in his arms, and still he kissed her, and still he whispered her name.

He carried her slowly to the waiting chaise longue.

His hands were gentle, undressing her, and his lips were warm too. Lily gave herself to him, and gave herself up to the pleasure in it, to his deep need for her. He was strong, and urgent, and yet gentle too, kissing her and whispering her name like a prayer. She took pleasure in his pleasure, for Luke fairly glowed with it. *And when did Jack Wallingford spend some long desert night dreaming of redheads with green eyes?* The candles were still lit and she could see their glint reflected in the gold of his hair, feel the warmth of the fire reflected on his smooth flesh and hers, feel the warmth of his loving set her on fire as his need exploded inside her with a gentle violence she had never known before. And through all of it, Lily was comforted by the echo of her name, whispered gently through the half-light of the room, through the urgency of his lovemaking, down all the distance of his lonely dream.

Finally she slept.

It was the chill that woke her.

Lily blinked, sat up, saw that the fire had burned down, though the candles still flickered against the red walls of the room. And she saw that the room was empty. And the chill of the room was nothing compared with the chill that spread in Lily's heart and in her mind. *He'd left her. He'd used her and bought her and left her like a common whore! And where were all his fine words now, or his dreams?*

Slowly, trying against heavy odds not to panic, she got up and pulled on her clothes. The remains of their meal had vanished. Someone had thrown her own green shawl over her nakedness. The waiter, then, had seen her like this, naked on the chaise! She could never forgive Luke for that. It was only when she approached the mirror that hung over the fireplace that Lily saw the bag.

It was a soft leather pouch about six inches deep, cut round and tied with a leather thong. The pouch sat on the pink marble of the mantelpiece next to a torn bit of paper. On that paper, in Luke's handwriting, was one word: "LILY."

She opened the thong, knowing and dreading what might be inside. The little pouch was heavy, heavier far than it looked. And it gave a faint metallic clink when she moved it. Slowly, dully, as though she were in a dream, Lily poured the contents of the pouch onto the shining pink marble. *Gold!* A stream of bright nuggets came rolling out, a small avalanche of riches, nuggets of all sizes with that odd, soft-edged burnished quality of things that have been tumbled in mountain streams for years and years.

Lily looked at the gold in disbelief. It hypnotized her. She had only the vaguest idea what it might weigh, or what gold was worth per ounce these days.

But well she knew what it meant.

Lily looked up over the pile of gold nuggets then, looked herself straight in the eye in the gilt, expensive, wicked mirror of this sinful room in this house of assignation.

The harlot and her gold!

It might have been the title of some allegorical painting in a child's textbook, meant to warn the innocent young away from the temptations of the flesh. *His flesh was tempting, Lily, don't be a hypocrite, and so was that basket of groceries, and the fine supper.*

And where were all Luke's dreams that he'd told her about so gently? Were they lies, to be bought and sold as he obviously thought her body could be bought? A small desperate voice somewhere in her shock-struck brain kept insisting: No! But Lily wasn't sure of that, or anything else beyond the very obvious fact that a decent young man had thought her a whore, and treated her like one.

She thought of these last weeks, of all the doors she'd knocked on, of all the answers she'd received, of Mrs. Stanford Dickinson, of Mrs. Moss's constant disapproval, of the six dollars and change that stood between her and Kate and starvation, the gutter.

Until Luke came along, and his gold.

A handsome young farmer will fall in love with me. I'll have five strong sons to play with Kate, and live happily ever after.

Lily's image in the mirror blurred through her tears. Automatically her hands began scooping up the nuggets and replacing them in the pouch. At last the pouch was filled, and the tears stopped. *"Save your tears, child, for one day you may truly need them."* Still she looked at herself in the mirror, facing facts.

And as she looked, Lily saw her chin rise just a little, saw her green eyes blink away the final tear, saw the small beginning of a smile start to form on her pale lips. *Well, then, my fine young lady: you are going to be used by them in any event, let's see how much we can make them pay for the privilege! The favors of Lily Malone aren't going to be scattered to the winds of California, not when there's bags of gold to be had, and who knows what else!*

Suddenly Lily thought of Luke Ransome with a strange gratitude. He was only the latest in the long line of men who had left her, beginning with her own father. No more would she pin her high hopes on a man. Well they might love her or leave her, or she them, but they'd pay now, and pay well, she'd see to that. Lily slipped on her shawl, adjusted it in the mirror, slipped the small sack of gold into her pocket, and smiled. For all at once she knew just how to make them pay, and pay they would!

❧ 25 ❧

Lily woke the next morning with her head in a whirl of conflicting emotions. Almost without realizing why, she found her hand reaching up slowly, dreamily, to the place under her pillow where she'd hidden the leather sack of gold nuggets.

And there they were. Her small hand closed around them, she could feel the hardness of them, and in that moment all the pain came back, the remembrance of Luke's fine words, and how she'd sold herself without even knowing it. *To be such a fool, such a silly little goose*. She got up then, and fed Kate, and dressed with care. Lily had an apple from Luke's fine basket, and nearly choked on it when she thought where it came from. She sipped a little milk, kissed the baby, carried her downstairs to Mrs. Moss, and went out.

The old man at the assayer's office never questioned where Lily got her gold, and that was the saving of her, for she knew she'd die if anyone demanded an explanation. *I sold myself for a hundred and twenty-two dollars and a basket of food*. The assayer took her gold and paid her in crisp new bills. Then Lily walked out the door and down the street to Sophie Delage's El Dorado Hotel.

The El Dorado had never been quite real to Lily before. It had been an accident of fate, an unexpected way station en route to her dream.

Now she walked up those gleaming limestone steps with her eyes wide open, her head held high to hide the numb, cold terror in her heart. *How the mahogany doors gleamed, how the brass glittered, just as though this were anything but the devil's own residence in this city forsaken by God!* Shuddering, she rang the bell.

Sophie looked up, only mildly surprised. She was having her usual light breakfast of tea and toast, still relaxing in the big soft bed Lily knew so well from the long fever-struck days she had spent in it herself.

"Well, Lily dear, how nice to see you. Will you take some tea?"

Lily crossed to the bed and bent to kiss her friend. She didn't know how to make fine speeches, so she came right out with it.

"I came," said Lily with the beginning of a tremor in her voice, "to ask for work, if you'll have me."

There was the smallest possible click as Sophie set her cup down on its saucer and put them on the tray. Then she looked up. "Whoring, you mean?"

"Yes. Whoring. Anything that gets me a lot of money. There is no work for me in this town, Sophie, there isn't a thing I can do a coolie can't—and won't—do cheaper. Except one."

"There's plenty and plenty who'd marry you, my girl, young and pretty as you are."

"That's another kind of whoring. To marry a man without love? I've come too far for that, Sophie. If I'm to be a man's chattel, then let him pay, and pay."

There was something shocking in Sophie's laughter, although it was the lightest ripple of mirth.

"I didn't want to be the one to suggest it, Lily. But if you are sure, I'll be glad to help. But don't think this is going to be easy. It isn't easy, and particularly not if you are to be something special. And I want you to be special, my Lily, for I have no doubt at all that you can be."

"If you say so." *Hypocrite! You'll be the best or die trying, just as you were the best maid at the Wallingfords'.* Then Lily asked the question that had doubled her torment ever since she'd resolved to come and work for Sophie. "But," she said softly, "before I can do anything, I must find someplace for the child. It fair breaks my heart, Sophie, and I pray 'tis only for a short time, but we cannot have her here, then, can we?"

"That wouldn't be fair to her, dear. What Kate needs is a fine clean home, maybe a bit out of town, where there's love, and other children to play with, and good fresh food to eat. And . . ." She paused dramatically. "I think I know just the place."

For the first time this day, a gleam of real hope found its way to Lily's stricken heart.

"Oh, Sophie! It would be the saving of me. She's all I care for, that little thing. Who are they?"

"She's Mary Baker, a good woman if ever there was such, married to a fine man, too, a farmer, Fred Baker, and they've a good little spread just out in San Mateo, and two—no, three!—little ones of their own. We can go see them this very day, if you like, and bring the baby, for I am sure they'll agree. We go back a long way, Mary and I, and she's good as gold."

The afternoon was bright with promise. Sophie's carriage made light work of the rutted road to San Mateo, and the trip took less than two hours. The Bakers' farm was just as Sophie had said—small but neat—and the Bakers themselves were obviously a decent and happy little family. Mary Baker radiated her love of children, and when she scooped up little Kate, the baby smiled, and Lily suddenly felt some of the torment of leaving the child slipping away from her. *It's only for a little while*, she thought, *just until I save enough money to set up my own shop, or even buy a little farm like this one*. The Bakers agreed to board Katie for fifty dollars a month. Lily paid two months' advance and agreed to bring the child back in a few days. Mary held the baby to her ample bosom, rocking Kate gently, and looked at Lily with understanding eyes, eyes that did not judge. Lily met her gaze, liking the woman for her honesty, for the way she kept her house and loved the children.

"What," asked Mary Baker softly, "will Kate call me?"

Suddenly a new and unexpected terror pierced Lily to the heart. But she held her gaze and did not flinch. "I think," she said in a voice that faltered only just a little, "that it would be easier if Katie calls you 'Mother.'"

Sophie and Lily rode in silence for several minutes as they headed back to town, Kate happily asleep between them. It was Sophie who broke the silence.

"From the first moment I set eyes on you, Lily, I knew you were special."

"Ah, get on with you, Sophie, kind as you are. I'm about as special as a lost left shoe."

"You are very beautiful, my dear, more beautiful by far than you know, and very much more beautiful than any whore I've ever seen in this town. That alone makes you special. You can have men by the hundreds fighting in the streets for you, Lily, if you work it right. And I intend to see that you do work it right."

"Thank heaven for that, because 'tis little enough I know about . . . the business."

Sophie laughed, but it was a kindly laugh. "You haven't had many men, have you, dear?"

"The boy at the Golden Rooster was only the second."

"Well, dear, innocence has its possibilities, just like any other condition. You think too clearly about some things,

Lily, not to think as clearly about men, and what they want from us, and all the reasons there are to make them pay for it. You should have known, Lily, that no one ever went upstairs in a place like the Golden Rooster to say her prayers."

"He seemed so kind . . . and so young, at that."

"And he bought you like a sack of oats."

"He said . . . I thought . . . he might love me." Lily tried to remember just what it had been about Luke, but she knew it was not one specific thing that had weakened her will. It had been many things: first, his kindness in a place where no one had been kind. Then the simple fact that he had been young and good to look on, and seemed so true when he told her how much he longed for her love. And his hair, the color, almost, of Brooks Chaffee's hair.

"Well, Lily," said Sophie in her gentlest voice, "no one's saying he didn't mean it—at the time. They always mean it at the time. And then they're gone, aren't they? That's why they must pay. Gold lasts longer than promises, Lily. Never forget that. You can't feed little Kate, here, on promises."

"I know that now. That's why I came to you."

"I'll try to see you never regret it, Lily. Now, then, tomorrow you must rest, maybe do a bit of shopping. On the day after, I'll send the carriage for you and Kate at ten in the morning to take you to the Bakers'. And after that, you'll come back here, to the El Dorado. And what Sophie will make of you will take your breath away, mark my words!"

Lily looked at her friend with a mixture of gratitude and despair.

The step had been taken now, there could be no turning back. She looked at the sleeping baby. Kate smiled faintly, happy in some infant dream, as the beautifully sprung carriage gently rocked along the road back to San Francisco.

Then Lily looked away, for she thought that if she gazed upon her baby thus for one more instant, her heart would break into a thousand pieces.

They spoke little more on the remainder of the trip back to town. Lily was lost in her own thoughts, and Sophie was content to plan and to dream.

Finally the carriage drew up at Mrs. Moss's house. Lily picked up the baby, who was sleeping still, and kissed her friend. "Thank you, Sophie. You'll see me the day after tomorrow, in the evening."

"I'll see that you won't regret this decision, Lily."

Lily stood in the road as the carriage moved off down the hill and wondered how many thousand regrets she would have every day, and every night. Only the warmth and the peace of little Katie in her arms kept the tears back. *Whatever the future brings, I will make it bring good things to you, my Katie. You may rest sure on that.*

Lily went alone in the big carriage on the day she brought little Kate down to the Bakers' farm in San Mateo.

The Mexican driver, Juan, came for her at ten in the morning. She had been ready for hours; all of the baby's clothing and a few small toys Lily had made for Kate were packed in one wicker trunk. The day was cool. Kate rode in her mother's lap, wrapped in a small blanket against the chill. The baby's hair was a wisp of pale red, and her eyes were dark brown, more Jack Wallingford's eyes than hers, Lily thought. Kate smiled and laughed; this was a new adventure. And she slept after a time, lulled by the well-sprung carriage's gently bouncing motion.

Lily spoke to her daughter as they rode, and knowing that the six-week-old child understood not a word of what her mother said made no difference.

"You'll have fine times down there, Kate, with the little lambs and the other children—why, there's a tiny girl only a little older than you, two years, I believe, sure and you'll be like sisters soon, and you'll like Mrs. Baker, she's a sweet kind woman, Kate, the sort a baby might choose for a mother, if babies had their choice . . ."

Kate dozed, smiling. Lily looked out the window through eyes misty with unborn tears.

". . . and there's a big green meadow with all kinds of flowers growing in it, and such things to eat, Kate! There's fresh milk all the time, even goat's milk, and cheese, and fruit, vegetables, you'll be a fine healthy child, you'll probably grow so fast we'll hardly know you when we come down next week, your Aunt Sophie and me, for we'll be coming every week, regular as clockwork, maybe more often if we can. Sure, you'll see a lot of your old silly mother, Kate, we'll play such games, sing such songs, and the presents you'll have! Fine presents, for I'll be rich. No old rag dolls for my Katie. Fine French dolls with china heads and real hair, that's what you'll have, and they'll wear silk and lace . . ."

The carriage joggled on, and with every curve in the road and at the crest of every hill Lily felt the bottom draining out of her world. She looked at the tiny sleeping child and could think of no more words to say. Softly then, Lily sang:

Come all you fair and tender ladies,
Be careful how you court young men,
They're like a star of a summer's morning:
They'll first appear and then they're gone.
They'll tell to you some loving story,
They'll declare to you their love is true;
Straightaway they'll go and court some other,
And that's the love they have for you.
I wish I was some little sparrow,
That I had wings, could fly so high;
I'd fly away to my false true lover,
And when he's talkin' . . . I'd be by.
But I am not a little sparrow,
And neither have I wings to fly;
I'll sit down here in grief and sorrow,
To weep and pass my troubles by.
If I'd a-known before I courted,
I never would have courted none;
I'd have locked my heart in a box of golden,
And pinned it with a silver pin.

By the time she finished her mournful ballad Lily was smiling again. Her story was an old one, so old and so common they made songs of it, and somehow the sorrow shared with the sad writer of that song diminished the pain in her own ravaged heart.

The steady rhythm of the carriage soothed Lily. The baby kept on sleeping. Soon they'd reach the small valley that held the Baker farm. Fifty dollars for the month's board was what the Bakers asked, fair enough at that, considering the terribly high cost of things out here. Only Luke's gold enabled her to pay the Bakers in advance. Lily looked at the small sweet face of her sleeping daughter, and suddenly bent and kissed it.

Kate stirred, smiled in the warmth and security of an unknown dream, and kept on sleeping. *And may she always smile, and be unafraid, and never know what it is to have nothing to be at the end of your rope, to be at the point where death or dishonor is a very real question.*

Lily could see the white farmhouse now, gleaming at the far end of the rich green meadow. There was a great peace here in the Bakers' little valley. It seemed to be a magical kingdom, protected by unseen wizards from all the strife and bitterness of the world outside. Lily prayed that it would always be so, that she would find such a place of her own one day, a place of quiet and peace, a place where small dreams might grow into big ones.

But as the carriage drew closer to the farmhouse, Lily felt her resolve melting like butter on a hot griddle. *I can't leave her! I won't! Kind as they are, she's my own flesh, she's the only thing in all this world I care about.*

"Juan!"

Lily's call to the driver was so urgent he imagined she was sick.

"Sí, señora?"

The carriage slowed.

Lily looked at the baby. Kate smiled. A new game was being played. Then Lily looked at the Baker farm. They were very close now. Mary Baker stood in the kitchen yard, smiling, waving, immaculate in a crisp new apron. Her four-year-old boy was beside her, and a little dog. Lily thought of the El Dorado, of Mrs. Moss's house, of the last few desperate months.

The driver's voice reached her through a cloud of doubt. "You called, lady?"

Lily sank back against the fine mohair upholstery of Sophie's carriage and sighed. "It was nothing, Juan. Please drive on."

Lily stayed at the farm only as long as decency required, for the danger of snatching up her baby and galloping back to town was not yet over for her. Finally she said her good-byes, and kissed the baby, and left. The last things she heard were Mary Baker's soft endearments to Kate, and Katie's responding gurgles. Happy gurgles. They stabbed Lily's heart with the force of a sword thrust.

She rode home in silence as dark and as empty as her abandoned dreams.

Lily moved into Sophie's house that very night.

Her actual career wouldn't start for several days, but the thought of one more minute spent under the roof of the forbidding Mrs. Moss was more than Lily cared to contemplate. Leaving Kate with the Bakers had been more painful than she had imagined anything could be after all she'd been through. So Lily held the shining carriage and paid the rest of her week's rent, and the driver helped her load her possessions onto the carriage. And as he worked, Lily stood outside the mournful gray house where she had never been happy, and hummed a small refrain: *"If I'd a-known before I courted, I never would have courted none; I'd have locked my heart in a box of golden, and pinned it with a silver pin."*

Let them try to get her heart now, all those lonely, lusty men. They could try with gold and they could try with smiles and promises, but all they would buy would be her body, and that at the highest price on the market.

I will put myself where no man can touch me, not now, not ever. Not even if he has golden hair and a face like an angel from heaven.

Juan finished his packing and helped Lily into the carriage. She rode off, never looking back at the small gray house or the pinch-faced gray woman who stood unsmiling behind its fraying curtain.

The carriage moved briskly down Broadway to the corner of Montgomery Street. The distance was less than a mile, but in that short time Lily moved from one world into another, from the past into the future. She was solemn as she climbed down to the pavement outside of Sophie's El Dorado Hotel. Lily looked up at the impressive facade of the big house, so like the Wells Fargo Bank in its newness and grandeur, and by all accounts very nearly as prosperous. She didn't know how long she'd be there, or what success she might have, and there was a nervous trembling in her stomach at the thought of all the dangers Sophie's house might hold for her, now and hereafter.

Then Lily noticed that a group of men had stopped their strolling and were staring at her. Demurely she turned to the driver, Juan, and asked him to take care of her baggage.

Smiling just slightly, and with her flaming head held high, Lily Malone walked gracefully down the gauntlet of their stares and into the best-known whorehouse in California.

◄§ 26 §►

Sophie Delage's El Dorado Hotel was more opulent than most millionaires' mansions, and cleaner too, if Sophie could be believed, and Lily was sure that she could be. The prevailing color was a deep burgundy red, and what wasn't red was lustrous mahogany and walnut, and what wasn't fine wood was glittering brass and crystal. The air was filled with a combination of sounds and aromas that amounted to a narcotic in itself: good French perfume—for Sophie selected every fragrance herself, for all her girls—and fresh flowers, rare Havana tobaccos, and fine cognacs, whiskeys, and the occasional fruity whiff of freshly opened champagne.

From late afternoon until the early hours of the following day, the rooms on the parlor floor were filled with clients, with the tinkling of Sophie's rosewood grand piano, with laughter and good talk. For the El Dorado was a club and a restaurant and a gaming house as much as it was a house of pleasure, although in the minds of most clients the pleasure part of the establishment was its soul, and they could have done without the rest.

Yet the luxury and festivity had its reasons, as Sophie was quick to tell her newest protégée.

"It all adds up, Lily," she said. "A man will pay double the price for the selfsame girl if she's wearing silk instead of muslin, if she's clean and smells of lilacs instead of slatternly and maybe diseased, if she smiles and sweet-talks him instead of haggling and using foul words."

Sophie had given Lily the best room on the third floor of the four-story building, a big corner room that was flooded with sunlight all day, just down the long carpeted hallway from Sophie's own suite.

Ten girls worked there besides Lily. They were as different as Sophie could make them, for the El Dorado was famous for the range and variety of its girls as well as their good looks, talents, and high price.

The parlor floor opened onto the street and was used for

receiving clients, for selling them food and drink, for gaming and music, and for the selection of girls.

The girls, richly gowned, were encouraged to mingle with the clients in these parlor rooms when not otherwise engaged, but there was another, more discreet means of a man selecting his companion for the night. This was a handsome leather-bound photographic album in which every girl was pictured in a demure or seductive pose, as directed by Sophie's estimate of her attractions. Lily was photographed in virginal white, sitting on a gilded ballroom chair, holding a silk calla lily.

The second floor was for gambling, but it also contained a special little room for the viewing of sexual exhibitions. This was no more than an elegant bedroom, its walls and ceiling lined with gilt-framed mirrors. Between these mirrors was gilt grillwork, and behind these grilles sat men and sometimes women who were sufficiently jaded to pay fifty dollars apiece to witness the delights that went on within the mirrored room, which was named "The Chamber of Venus."

The third and fourth floors were given over to the girls' bedrooms, and it was there that they took their clients.

Sophie was adamant about not trafficking in boys, even though many of the other houses did, but aside from that the El Dorado was entirely geared to offer the maximum variety both in the physical and ethnic types of its girls, and in their sexual specialties. If there was a nation or a type not represented here, Lily was hard put to imagine what it might be.

She met all the girls on her first day, but it was weeks before she could put the right names with the right faces.

There was Ruby, tall and dark and beautiful, who said almost nothing, and Lola, her exact opposite, small, blond and plump, with a face like an elegant little weasel's and a sailor's vocabulary. There was Luana, from Tahiti, café-au-lait in color and famous for the numbers of men she delighted in entertaining with no sign of tiring—Sophie said this was a custom in those islands—and others whose attractions were less obvious to Lily. Jude, fat and Polish and a bit of a slattern, who told lies long as your arm and never batted an eye for it, kept on by Sophie because some of her European customers liked their women fat. There was a jolly American girl named Polly, all smiles and gold-framed teeth, who sang and played the piano, a sloe-eyed Chinese woman, Ah Toy, and a haughty Englishwoman known only as the Duchess, who had the slender throat of a swan and gave herself airs to match, and floated night and day in an opium haze, barely aware of her surroundings. There was a girl so black she might have been carved from jet, a torrid Mexican named the Serpent, La Serpentina, and others. How Sophie kept them all straight, and kept the peace among them, was a continuous amazement to Lily. For there were jealousies, there was petty theft, and the calling of names. Lily determined early on that she would be very slow to choose friends from among these girls. Lily watched, and learned, and waited.

Every afternoon for an hour or two Sophie instructed Lily in the fine points of whoring.

For Lily, whose knowledge of the sexual world was a hodgepodge of rumors and old wives' tales and superstitions, Sophie's command of hygiene, physiology, and the art of salesmanship was nothing less than amazing.

Lily learned how to check each client for the telltale chancres that meant disease, how to wash them, how to use Sophie's famous douching preparation that was surefire against pregnancy, how to handle drunks, where the hidden bell pull was that would summon Juan, the coachman, who also served as bouncer. She learned that every week, without fail, old Doc Maloney came and checked every girl for infection or pregnancy.

"I run the cleanest house in town," said Sophie proudly. "No one can ever claim he got poxed at Sophie's, and that alone is worth its weight in gold. They keep coming back, see, and they pay Sophie's prices, which aren't cheap, not at all."

Lily worked up her courage: other than Luke's bag of nuggets, she had no idea what she might be worth.

"How much," asked Lily, "might I earn?"

"The sky's the limit, Lily. I'll start you at one-fifty. Then, we'll see."

"That'll take forever." Lily was trying to think how many men she'd have to serve at a dollar and a half each to pay for Kate's board.

"One hundred and fifty dollars is no small sum, my dear," said Sophie, with an edge in her voice. "Polish Jude gets but twenty-five."

Lily laughed from sheer relief. "I truly thought you meant one and a half dollars!"

Sophie's chuckle mingled with the sound of Lily's laughing. "Oh, that's a rare one! Lily, the poor Chinese crib girls get more than that from coolies."

"How much do I keep?"

"Half. But for my half, Lily, I keep up this place, and all its staff, and feed you handsomely, and take care of you if you're ill. It isn't a bad bargain, my dear, and if you save, and your price goes up—as I am sure it will do—who knows?"

Lily learned about the tokens. These were shining brass disks about the size of a fifty-cent piece, and on each one was stamped "EL DORADO HOTEL . . . $25.00" For to prevent theft among the girls, cash changed hands during the night only between Sophie and the clients. They bought tokens according to the price of the girl in question, and gave the tokens to the girl on finishing with their pleasure. The next day, the girl exchanged them for her share of the fee. There was no fixed number of clients that a girl was expected to take in a given evening: this might be one, for a special price, and the house record was held by the Tahitian girl, who had once entertained thirty-three. Lily heard of this and shuddered.

Sophie invited her to see what went on in the Chamber of Venus.

"Now, this may seem shocking, my dear," she said as they walked down the red-carpeted stairs, "but you must think of it as part of your education. It's amazing what people will pay to see, rather than do."

The Chamber of Venus was encircled by one narrow aisle that held small upholstered stools fixed to the carpeted floor so that whoever sat on the stool would have a good view through the gilt grillwork. The many mirrors did the rest.

It was like looking into a gilt box filled with rubies and diamonds, for the mirrors glittered in their frames of gold, and the floor was carpeted in deep ruby red, and the bed was covered in gleaming silk brocade of the same shade.

There was a girl in the room, a girl Lily had never seen before. She was tall and had lustrous black hair that fell in cascades, a midnight waterfall, almost to her waist. Her skin was supernaturally white, the eyes dark and wide-set and bottomless, eyes that seemed to absorb the light rather than reflect it. She wore a silk robe of the exact same color as the carpet and the bedcover, and she was smoking a slender brown cigar.

"La Serpentina!" Sophie whispered.

Lily and Sophie were alone in the small viewing chamber. There was a hush, an anticipation. Lily felt herself at the same time eager to see whatever might happen, and also afraid, as though she had been given a preferred seat at the very gate of hell itself.

They didn't have to wait long.

Soundlessly, one of the big mirrors slid aside. A man stepped into the chamber. The mirror slid shut behind him. The man was tall, very tall, nearly a giant. His hair was dark. There was a Mexican look to him. His skin was olive-toned and his features were handsome but at the same time brutal. He radiated a kind of elegant cruelty. The man was dressed like a wealthy Mexican rancher, in a loose-fitting white shirt open at the neck, tight black trousers tucked into silver-studded black leather boots, and a black leather vest. He carried a black bullwhip.

The man looked at La Serpentina with a mixture of scorn and anticipation. *"Puta,"* he whispered. *"Querida puta."*

Lily hardly saw his arm move.

She was only aware of the whistling of the bullwhip, and the effect it had on the girl. The whip cracked and coiled itself around her. She stood still as any statue, while he undressed her with his whip. The silk robe slid to the floor, and it seemed that her slender pearl-white body was rising out of it like a growing thing. The whip coiled around her like a snake.

He drew her to him. She moved in a kind of trance, floating. The whip seemed to leave no mark. She was very close to him now. She knelt, like a servant, and slowly drew off his boots. Then she stood, all in silence, and began unbuttoning his shirt. He wore nothing under the shirt, or under the trousers. Soon his clothes lay in a careless heap. Lily gasped. The man was truly a giant. With one arm he reached for the girl and casually, disdainfully flung her to the bed. She lay there in silence, waiting, a small smile flickering at the corners of her bloodred lips.

He was on her then, and thrust inside her, and the combat of love began in earnest. He plunged, she writhed, her arms and legs wrapped around him like some jungle vine, as they moaned and grunted in their pleasure, wild and lost in the storm of their own dark needs and gratifications. They rolled to the floor. She straddled him like a horse, still fused sex to sex, threw her head back, and screamed with pleasure. Then he tossed her off, laughing, and she coiled against him and Lily could see how the girl got the name La Serpentina, the Serpent, for she moved as though there were no bones in her at all, one flowing undulation of lust incarnate. She kissed him on his lips, bit his ear, kissed his throat, and then began a voyage of discovery with her lips, her tongue, her stroking fingers, that led her down his heavily muscled torso to his navel and below, where she easily roused the beast between his legs from its temporary slumber, and the passion began all over again.

After ten minutes of such variations on the arts of love, Sophie touched her arm and signaled that they should leave. Lily found herself trembling. *Please God, Sophie doesn't expect me to perform like that.* They were in the hallway then, and finally Lily got the strength to speak.

"Does she know she's being watched?"

"Not only does she know it, my dear, she prefers it that way. So does he. It's amazing how many people do, they get more fun when someone's watching, you see. And then there's the other kind, who never do anything, but just pay to look on. Sad loss, it seems to me, but that's their business. Fifty dollars a head for sitting in the dark watching two monkeys like that going at it is money wasted, if you ask me."

"I could never . . . do that. In public, I mean."

"Of course not, most of us couldn't, and I'd never ask it. I just wanted you to see the Serpent. That girl truly enjoys her work, and it shows. You've got to make them feel you're interested, Lily, that's the secret of success, make 'em feel they're important to you, that you've never had such a good time before, even if it isn't strictly true."

Lily walked in silence, not knowing how to reply. Sophie took her upstairs, and they had a cup of tea.

"That picture in the album is working, my dear. I've already had one firm request for you, and tonight is the time for it."

"What sort of request?"

"One of my best customers, just as I'd hoped. Oh, others have asked, but I wanted to make sure it was the right one, a gentleman of stature."

"Who is he?"

"One whose name you know—in fact, it might give you a laugh or two, thinking on it. He is none other than Stanford Dickinson."

"No!" Lily laughed, and was afraid at the same time.

"A fine jolly gent is Stanny D. Loves a good time and a good lay. Get him as a regular, and your fortune's made, for he's one of the richest men in town."

"And when is my appointment?"

"Tonight, Lily, this very night, at nine-thirty!"

If Lily had been the bride of a prince, she could hardly have given more thought to the occasion than she did to her imminent appointment with Stanford Dickinson.

For two hours in the afternoon Sophie coached her, reassured her, described the man and his tastes and how the evening would be likely to go.

"The secret's a simple one, dearie," she said. "Just think of it from the man's point of view. Here he is, rich as old Croesus, wanting nothing more than a few laughs and a little fun, and he's married to that chinless old prune up on Rincon Hill, temper like a shrew she has, has Mamie Dickinson. So be fun, be lighthearted, nothing too sentimental, but not giddy either, if you take my meaning. One thing stands much in your stead, Lily, and that's your looks, for if there's one thing Stanny D. prides himself on, it's his judgment of horseflesh and womanly beauty."

"I'll never live up to his expectations."

"But you already have. He chose you from the album, and that hardly does justice to you, my dear, nice as it is."

"Does he have any . . . odd tastes?"

"Not our Stanny D., quite the contrary, he's a bit old-fashioned underneath all the blustering and laughter. You'll like him, Lily, I swear you will. I wouldn't fix it up if I didn't truly think so."

"You're very kind, Sophie, and I appreciate it."

"Fiddlesticks! Good business, that's all it is: we make him happy, he makes us happy, and happiness reigns, if you take my meaning, as well it should in the temple of Venus."

Lily knew what the routine would be: she would be called by the bell in her room, the ingenious two-way bell system that allowed her to summon a maid or be summoned downstairs should a client request her. She'd go down then, and greet her guest, and take a drink with him in the main parlor. Then they'd come back to her bedroom, where a small table would be set for supper *à deux. Just like the Golden Rooster,* she thought with a rueful smile, *except that this time I am a little more in control, not quite the silliest goose west of the Mississippi.*

The hours crawled.

Lily laid out her gown, of the simplest ivory satin, girlish it was, with a demure neckline and narrower hoops than were the height of fashion. It was absolutely plain but for a moss-green satin sash at the waist, whose wide ribbons trailed to the floor at her side. With it she would wear white gloves, and in her hair a ribbon of the same satin as the sash. And no jewelry whatsoever but for her wedding ring. For Kate's sake Lily still kept up the fiction that she was the widow Malone.

She had tea and some biscuits in her room around five o'clock, took a bath, did her hair, and tried to read a book of European travels. Lily felt inadequate in dozens of ways, and the state of her education was one of the most important items on her mental list of drawbacks to be corrected. She was already a young woman, but her reading ability was still that of a child. She had bought a small dictionary with part of Luke's gold, and now she found herself referring to it so often as she tried to read any new book that the dictionary was never far from her hand. *When I get a bit ahead of the game,* she told herself earnestly, *I will hire a teacher and learn to speak proper, and to read and write like a lady. My Kate isn't going to have more of an idiot for a mother than I can help.* In the meantime, the dictionary saw a great deal of action.

When the clock on Lily's dressing table showed seven, she began to get dressed. She was ready well before eight, and sat down and tried to concentrate on the travel book. But the attractions of Budapest kept slipping away from Lily, pursued by nameless fears about the night to come.

Smile, what's so hard about that? That's what Sophie had said, be lighthearted, he likes to laugh. *Suppose I can't think of anything funny? Suppose he thinks I'm ugly? Suppose he's drunk and wants me to do disgusting things? Suppose he hates the color green?* Lily wondered if La Serpentina was available for emergency duty.

I'll be out on the street tomorrow, he'll hate me.

She stood up, paced the room three times, examined herself in the tall mirror with the merciless scrutiny of a surgeon, decided she was hopeless, sat down again, picked up the book, read the same sentence three times, put the book down, looked out the window, prayed for a quick and merciful death.

Sophie says you're pretty: why would she lie? Lily stood up again, looked in the mirror again. It was the same old face she'd always had, too thin, pale, with the great green eyes peering out in terror. The clock said quarter to nine.

A maid appeared to set up the table. It was a smallish round table, covered with a deep cloth of ivory lace, set with two places, nestling into the corner between two windows. *How pretty it looks,* Lily thought, seeing the silver candlestick and the flower-trimmed plates and the cut-crystal wineglasses. *He may not like me, but he'll have to like this. But maybe he's not the kind of man who notices things like that, for most men don't. All he'll be thinking of is bed, and how can I possibly please him there, man-about-town as he is?*

Then she thought of that chinless, mean-spirited woman sitting alone in her overdecorated drawing room on Rincon Hill, and suddenly Lily began to feel a bit better. *Young I may be, and stupid, and inexperienced in bed, but it would be very hard to be less attractive than that one.*

It was a small enough consolation, but the only one she had.

The bell startled Lily. Nine-thirty on the button! Up she stood, and quickly checked her appearance in the mirror, straightened a lock of hair that was not out of place, brushed the gleaming satin of her skirt, and reached out for the great embossed brass knob of her door. Then she squared her slender shoulders and walked down the wide red carpet to what fate she knew not.

Even in the third-floor hallway Lily could hear the festive sounds from below. Music and laughter, a bustling, tinkling symphony of merriment filled the warm air that smelled, as always, intoxicating in its odd mixture of flowers, perfume, cigar smoke, and lust. Lily walked slowly, for it was the first time she had worn the new gown. Her left hand glided down the smooth rounded top of the mahogany stair rail. Her feet seemed to float in the deep red carpet that flowed down the stairs from the top of the house to the parlor like love's own warm welcome mat.

She heard his rich laughter even before she entered the parlor, a deep polished sound that seemed to vibrate through the whole house with quick hot waves of enjoyment. Lily would never understand how she knew it was Dickinson's voice, but at that moment she would have bet her life on it.

And she would have won.

Suddenly she was standing alone at the entrance of the main parlor.

There were only two other women in the room: Polly, sitting at the piano, playing and singing a new bawdy ballad, and Sophie, regal in black satin embroidered all over with jet, a glass of champagne in one hand and a man's hand in the other. Sophie's quick button eyes roved the big room even as they smiled at her guests. It was only a matter of seconds before she saw Lily hesitating at the door.

"But here she is now, my blooming Lily!"

There were five men in the room, all richly dressed. Five heads turned to stare at the new arrival in frank curiosity. Lily blushed, tried to smile, and only half-succeeded. Sophie sensed the girl's embarrassment and walked smoothly to her side and took her hand.

"Just smile, dear, that's all!" The words came out in a barely audible hiss through Sophie's fixed smile. Lily had never seen Sophie in her public role before. She found herself being propelled toward the small knot of men, and felt their eyes on her with an almost physical impact. Then the miracle happened. Lily found herself smiling. If she was going to actually die, she might as well make a good show of it!

"Mrs. Lily Malone, may I present Mr. Stanford Dickinson, Mr. Hector Coit, Mr. Sean Donahue, Mr. Bobby Leyland?"

Lily nodded, smiled, blushed in response to their chorus of "Charmed," "Delighted," "How do you do." Only Dickinson remained silent, watching her with bright dark eyes.

At last, after a second's pause that seemed to last a week, he spoke. "Hello, Lily," he said, "and welcome to San Francisco."

She accepted a glass of champagne and lifted it in a salutation before she sipped. Lily's eyes met the eyes of Stanford Dickinson over the rim of her crystal wineglass. *He's not bad at all. Quite handsome, in an outdoors kind of way, a fine figure of a man is Stanny D.*

Dickinson, she decided, must be nearly forty, quite middle-aged by Lily's standards, but well-preserved at that. Tall he was, and with broad shoulders that hinted at a sporting kind of life. He was square-built, but nothing fat, solid as a tree, with a ruddy complexion, dark brown hair worn in big sideburns, but beardless, and dancing dark eyes and a mouth that seemed eager to laugh. A man, obviously, who enjoyed life to the hilt, and who should not? And nobody's fool, either, from what Sophie had told her of the Dickinson fortune, made by this very man, not inherited. *Smooth he is, too,* she thought, as Dickinson quickly cut her off from the other men and eased her into a corner at the far side of the big room from the piano. *Very smooth indeed.*

"Do I frighten you, Lily?"

"Oh, no, sir! It's just that, well, you see, this is my first night here, working, I mean."

"And, naturally, you are frightened. Sophie said you might be. You don't have to be frightened of me, Lily."

"Oh, Mr. Dickinson, I'm not. Truly." Even as she said the words, Lily cursed herself for a liar.

"Stanford is my name, Lily."

"Stanford, then. 'Tis a fine name. I never knew anyone called Stanford before."

"Nor I. It's my grandfather's name, so I guess I'm stuck with it."

Lily noticed that his glass was empty. "Would you be having more wine, Stanford?"

"Thank you."

She went to the ice bucket and came back with the bottle, all the time desperate to think of some amusing thing to say, something to make him laugh. Lily had never been a teller of jokes, though, and she could think of none now, not if her life depended on it. She poured his wine and returned the bottle to its silver bucket. At least, down here, there was music to fill the silences, and other people talking. Whatever would happen when they were alone?

Stanford Dickinson himself came to Lily's rescue.

"I must," he began, "tell you a thing that happened on the way over here this evening . . ."

His words continued, a complicated story about his horse, a drunken Chinese, and a member of the vigilante police. It was far from being the funniest story Lily had ever heard, but it was quite funny enough, and soon she found herself laughing naturally. It was then, beaming, that he suggested they go upstairs for some supper.

He offered her his beautifully tailored arm, and she took it, feeling the strength in him, and the assurance. Lily smiled and held her head high. Sophie's eyes were on her, speculating. *And well might she worry,* thought Lily, quelling a tremor of fear, *for here she's been kind enough to introduce me to this fine gentleman, and who's to say if I'll please him?* With every stair they mounted, Lily's apprehensions mounted, too. *Suppose he expects me to do things I don't know about? Or can't do, or wouldn't? Suppose he has unspeakable tastes?* Lily had heard about unspeakable tastes, but she wasn't quite positive what they were. She gritted her teeth and remembered Sophie's advice: *"Make him feel important, make him feel this is the best time you have ever had."* But how? There was the terrible, unanswerable question. How?

Lily opened the door of her room, wondering if it would still be there. He followed her inside and closed the door softly behind them. She could tell from the smooth way he did this that the gesture must be the result of long practice. There was more champagne in a silver ice bucket on the table, and a silver tray containing small cheese-filled pastries to nibble on. A fire had been lit in the little iron stove that nestled against the far wall, deep black iron trimmed with brass so highly polished it shone like gold. He tasted one of the crisp pastries.

"Signor Cucci," he said, "never fails. Along with the loveliest girls in town, our Sophie has snagged the city's best chef."

"The food is delicious, isn't it? Shall I ring?"

Lily took his silence for affirmation and pulled the embroidered bell pull. Stanford Dickinson busied himself with the fresh bottle of wine. He extracted the cork with only the softest hissing sound, filled two glasses, and handed one to Lily.

"Cheers, Lily."

"Cheers, yourself."

He sat down on the settee near the stove and stretched out his long legs. For a moment there was silence, and only the noise of the stove's fire interrupted them, its crackling and rushing of air making a miniature storm in the quiet bedroom. Lily cringed inwardly, wanting to shine, wanting to be witty and charming, unable to think of a single thing to say. *He'll hate me for sure,* she thought. *He'll think I'm the village idiot. He won't pay, he'll say he's been cheated, and he'll be right!*

Desperate, she asked, "Have you ever been to Budapest?"

Somehow he found that funny. "No," he replied, laughing the deep, rich, far-reaching laugh she had heard from the stairs, "I can't say I have."

"Why do you find that funny?"

"I find almost everything funny, Lily. Everything, that is, that I don't find sad."

"I was reading about Budapest."

"Good for you. That's more reading than I've done lately. And what did you learn?"

Lily had to laugh at herself then. "Nary a thing. Between looking words up in the dictionary, so many of them I didn't know, you see, and being nervous about this night, and reading the same sentence over and over again, I got no further than half a page into the story."

"But you tried, and that's what matters."

"Tomorrow I will try harder."

"I'm sure you will, Lily."

There was a soft knock on the door, and Lily opened it. The maid carried a large tray that held all their supper. A simple, light supper it was, by Dickinson's request, just turtle broth followed by lobsters, asparagus, and rice, and a little chocolate *gâteau* for dessert.

During supper he spoke most of the time, and told Lily colorful tales of San Francisco, of the early days when there was just a city of tents here and no law to speak of, of Mexican bandits and claim jumpers and convicts shipped in from Australia by the boatload.

"We're a temple of civilization now by comparison, Lily, believe me, even if most of our streets are paved with mud and horse manure instead of the widely advertised gold."

"San Francisco will be a grand place one day, it'll be New York all over again, but more beautiful, for the land is more beautiful, don't you agree?"

"I sure do, Lily, but not everyone does."

"Then they surely are fools, for the views from the hills fair take my breath away."

"Ah!" he said, smiling. "If eyes so fair to look at can also see beauty elsewhere, you are blessed indeed, Lily Malone."

He told her a bit about his business, which involved land, land and timber, one feeding the other, for his timber built the houses on his land. And now he was building kilns, for bricks were much in fashion, and the burgeoning city needed more than the clippers could carry as ballast. It was fascinating to Lily, and she made no attempt to disguise her interest. The thirst for knowledge had been growing in her ever since she set foot in the Wallingford mansion and discovered how very much there was to learn. Stanford Dickinson was obviously able and willing to help her learn, and she was grateful for that.

"Nobody makes lobster Fra Diavolo like Cucci." Stanford refilled her champagne glass, and his own. This would be her third glass of wine, more than she'd ever drunk at one time in all her life. *What wicked ways you're learning, my girl, best you watch yourself, or who knows where you'll end?*

"What," she asked, "does 'Fra Diavolo' mean?"

"It is a kind of joke, meaning 'Brother Devil,' as though the devil joined an order of monks."

"He's come to the right house, that's for sure."

He laughed again, and Lily smiled at the success of her little joke.

They finished the entrée, and Lily cut the small chocolate cake.

He took one bite, put down his fork, and leaned back in the delicate chair that threatened to crack under the bulk of him. He lifted his half-full wineglass and sipped slowly, thoughtfully. The candle fluttered in reaction to some unfelt breeze.

"Sophie," said Dickinson, "was absolutely right when she told me you are special."

Lily could think of no clever reply, so she blushed and kept silent. He smiled and put down his glass and stood up.

Gently he reached for her hand, bent and kissed it like a courtier in some old engraving, then lifted her easily as a feather to her feet. In the same gentle motion Stanford Dickinson drew her close and kissed Lily full on the lips. Already his hands were busy with the buttons and ribbons of her gown. She smiled, not knowing what else to do, and helped him as best she could.

He kept repeating her name, and kissing her, and soon they were together on the soft feather bed, flesh against flesh, his desire filling the darkness, his need for her sweeping them both along on the swift hot riptide of passion. His was a gentle violence, a soft destruction: he smiled in the darkness and held her as a drowning man might grasp at driftwood.

Finally they lay exhausted.

He said nothing. Lily wondered, terrified, if he had been pleased.

They lay for an unmeasured time, very close, and Lily feared to move, that she might displease him. When she heard her name, Lily had to think where it came from, so soft were his whispered words.

"Lily," he said, so low it might have been the distant sea breaking upon the sand, "Lily, Lily, Lily . . ." And he moved then, kissing her shoulder, her neck, stroking her, and his passion came surging back then, stronger, wilder than ever.

This time, when they finished, he left her. He stood beside her bed, bent to kiss her, said nothing.

"Did I do something wrong?" The fear was like a flame in the night.

"Wrong?" His laugh was muted, for it was very late. "No, my dearest Lily, you did nothing wrong at all, except perhaps come into my life too late. But rest now, Lily Malone. We'll talk later on." He kissed her again and was gone. When, she wondered, drifting off to sleep at last, would "later on" be?

Lily slept late and woke to find six brass El Dorado twenty-five-dollar tokens neatly stacked on top of a hundred-dollar gold piece. She rubbed her eyes, not believing what she saw. She had heard about tips, and tips were hers to keep. But this? A hundred dollars on top of one-fifty?

She thought of last night, of Stanford Dickinson and what a bad bargain his wife had made, to treat him so meanly he was forced out to Sophie's. Lily thought of Kate, too, and how she might well be risking hellfire and damnation to keep the child in comfort. Yet, whatever the world might think or say about such transactions as last night's, there was a basic honesty in it: a simple sale and a simple payment. And judging by the tip, the customer had been satisfied.

Lily got up and put the gold piece in her reticule. She'd exchange the tokens for half their value later on. She knew that all her customers couldn't be as fine and as gentle as Dickinson. Still and all, the first dreaded hurdle was over. She had knowingly sinned and been paid for it. God hadn't struck her dead, and if the angels were weeping for her, Lily could not hear them. Kate was out in the valley, well fed and cared for, and in this one night Lily had earned enough to secure that care for three whole months!

The room danced with morning sunlight. Lily walked up to the big mirror and studied her reflection critically. "You," she whispered to the mirror, and smiled a faint, faintly bitter smile, "are a whore."

Then she rang for her breakfast.

ᶾ 27 ᶾ

Brooks felt the weight of the small blue leather jeweler's box
as he surreptitiously slid his hand into his evening-coat pocket
and drew it slowly out.

He looked at Caroline, sitting across the small round dining table they set up in the library for one of their increasingly rare dinners alone. Light from twin silver candlesticks
bathed her creamy skin in a most seductive glow. The simple
burgundy gown was cut low, low enough for Brooks to be
glad they were alone, although if Caroline wore a thing, one
could be perfectly sure it was the coming style. As always
when he looked at his wife, Brooks forgot whatever might
have been troubling him during the day, or even five minutes
ago.

He reached out and took her hand in his, and put the box
in it. "Happy anniversary, my darling."

Her eyes flashed. She opened it. She let out a child's sigh
of wonderment and held the glittering gift up to the nearest
candle. One large ruby pendant, framed by small pearls and
smaller rubies, dangling from a rope of twisted gold. She
jumped up from the table and kissed him.

"Oh, my darlin' thoughtful Brooks! You know I just love
and adore rubies."

Quickly, with deft fingers, she clasped it around her neck.
It set off the burgundy gown to perfection, gleaming with
dark, mysterious lights against her flawless skin, the stone
dancing with unexpected fires. *Just like Caroline herself,*
Brooks thought with a slightly ironic smile, *mysterious, with
unexpected fires.*

"Rubies," he said softly, "become you, my dear."

She bent over and kissed him. "Love becomes me, Mr.
Chaffee. That is why I sometimes get impatient when you
stay downtown with your old ledgers and debentures and
things."

"That," he said, laughing, refilling her wineglass and his
own, "is where the rubies come from. I'm glad we have this

[334]

evening together, Caroline: it seems, lately, I'm forever sharing you with a crowd."

"But," she said with a parody of a small child's pout, "it is perfectly dandy for me to share you with all your old stuffy banker friends?"

But then she smiled, and when Caroline smiled at Brooks, he could feel the icebergs melting in the faraway sea. She went on, her passion building: "It just drives me crazy, the time we're wasting, when there's fun to be had, when the world's on fire, and who knows—"

"The world may be smoldering, darling, but it isn't quite yet on fire."

"Wait. Just wait till we have your Mr. Honest Abe Lincoln in the White House, then see what happens, what's on fire!"

Brooks looked at her patiently, understanding her concern. They had this discussion several times a week, and they both knew there was no real answer to it, for the events that threatened to grind one-half of the Union against the other were far, far beyond their control—or anyone else's control either, for all of that. And Brooks didn't want to talk about war in the abstract. He wanted to express his love for her, and in very physical terms, and right now. He laughed and went to her.

"The biggest fire I know about, my love, is right here in this room."

She came to his arms and he clasped her tightly, kissed her soft mouth, and felt the ruby pendant burning into his chest. He slid an arm around her and lifted her in one smooth surge of desire. Brooks carried Caroline through the sleeping household and up the stairs. And the night dissolved in loving.

Lily sat tall in the sleek green landau and enjoyed the day for what it was: one of her better days. The fresh air delighted her after the perfumed confines of the El Dorado, and she loved the feel of the sun on her face and the wind rushing by, and just to watch the perfectly matched bays was a joy, for they trotted with such pride and pleasure it seemed they knew this was the finest and fastest new carriage in town, and who owned it. Lily turned to her companion and tried to make herself heard over the wind and the sound of the horses' brisk hooves.

"If they do build the coast road to San Mateo, it'll cut an hour from the trip both ways. I could see Kate nearly every day, then."

Stanford Dickinson nodded, adjusted the cigar in his

mouth, and replied, "They'll build it, Lily-o, or all my information's worthless. How old's the child now?"

"A year and a half, though it hardly seems so, and fit as a fiddle, thinking Mrs. Baker's her mother, which is just as well."

"Her mother is the most beautiful woman west of the Mississippi, and maybe east of it too, for all I know."

"Her mother," said Lily matter-of-factly, "is a whore."

He made no reply to this, although many were the times during the past year when Stanford had offered to make her his full-time mistress, to set her up in a little house of her own somewhere, or a fine apartment.

And Lily would have none of it, hating whoring as she did, liking Stanford as she also did.

The last year had been one of discovery and sorrow for Lily, of success and self-loathing. Many of the things she had learned were things she would rather not have known.

She learned how to smile when she felt more like screaming in anger, how to use charm as though it were a honed and polished weapon, how to handle men who were drunk or savage or both. For not all of her customers were like Stanford, not by miles.

She remembered the meek, bespectacled, almost clerical-looking man who followed her upstairs and locked the door behind her and pulled out a deadly-looking razor. Lily froze.

"Now, what," she said quickly, keeping her voice light, praying it was some kind of joke, "would you be doing with that, Mr. Williams? For surely you have shaved already."

He advanced toward her, his eyes glittering. His mouth hung open. His pale, thin tongue slowly traveled the full distance around his gaping lips. A drop of spit hung trembling from his tongue, then fell to the carpet. He grinned. Then his face became a mask of righteousness, and he spoke slowly in a flat low tone that increased its intensity until it was something like a scream. "Daughter of Satan! Despoiler of youth! Corrupter of the innocent!"

The razor glittered in the candlelight. Lily slowly backed away from him. The emergency bell was behind her, near the bed. She must keep him away from her until she rang it, until Juan could get up here. She tried to think what might be a weapon. She decided to try words, for they were nearest at hand.

"Surely, sir, you knew what kind of house this was before coming here. No one forced you."

He stopped and lifted both hands toward the ceiling, threw

his head back and laughed a terrible laugh. Lily backed against the wall and leaned on the bell, hard. She rang it again and again, praying there was someone to hear, that the bell worked, for she had never had an occasion to use the thing before. The man's mad laughter died down, and he looked at her again, his eyes more baleful than before.

"I am the avenging angel of the Lord Jesus!"

"Surely the Lord Jesus forgives sinners," said Lily breathlessly. "Think of Mary Magdalene!"

"Magdalene! Jezebel! Filth. Corruption. It must go. It must be eliminated!"

He was ranting now, and there was actually a pale froth at the corner of his mouth. He waved the razor wildly about his head, then seemed to realize where Lily was and to focus his attention again. He took another step toward her. She darted sideways. He lunged. She ducked. The razor tore a wide gash in the drapery. Lily dived over the bed, rolled, landed on her feet on the other side, and ran for the door just as Juan's strong fists began pounding on the other side.

Juan quickly subdued the maniac, and soon the police were taking him away for questioning. It turned out that he had murdered three prostitutes in as many weeks, in different sections of San Francisco and Oakland.

The next day Lily asked Stanford Dickinson to teach her how to use a gun. He did that, and presented her with a small, beautifully cased revolving pistol that she kept in her night table, fully loaded, from that time on.

Lily had other adventures, for even Sophie's house was far from immune from violence. Compared to coarser places, the El Dorado was a palace, but the men still had quick tempers and guns at hand, and some were so rough that to them a slap was hardly different from a caress. There were good nights and bad nights, and nights so humiliating that only the thought of Kate kept Lily sane. During this year, two things grew steadily: one was Lily's bank account at Wells Fargo, and the other was her respect for her own ability to survive. She was more determined every day to quit the business of selling her body, and to become respectable in her own eyes, the eyes of the world. To this end Lily devoted all her energies, and sometimes she surprised even herself.

Lily studied the other girls and learned from them. She was friendly but made no friends, for there wasn't a girl in the place she truly cared for. As a lot, Lily found them dull, selfish, and lacking in imagination. They drank and they drugged, some stole, most of them fought, and nearly all of them were whoring to support idle lovers. None of this had an ounce of appeal for Lily. When she wasn't with Kate or with Sophie, Lily tried to improve her reading. She still sewed constantly, and she made most of the alluring gowns that life in the El Dorado required. From Sophie Lily learned all she could about running the house, about the management of the kitchen, and all the thousand details that went into making the El Dorado the showplace it unquestionably was. Always reserved in private, Lily slowly learned to be more free in public.

This did not go unnoticed. Her price rose from a hundred and fifty to two-fifty, and then to five hundred and finally to a thousand dollars for the night, and Sophie promoted her to the undreamed-of honor of being the only girl in the house who took all-night customers exclusively.

It was during this first year, too, that Lily got the name "Lily Cigar." The name came to her almost by accident, one night in Sophie's parlor when Lily lit a cigarillo for Stanford Dickinson and teasingly took a puff first. The sight of such a slender, white-gowned sprite of a girl smoking teased good-natured Polly, who immediately played a dramatic chord on the piano and giggled: "Lily Cigar!" The name stuck, although in fact Lily smoked but seldom. At first she hated the name, but in time she began to feel more comfortable with it. There were other girls named Lily: there was only one Lily Cigar. The name set her off, and the name plus her price, plus her beauty, began to make her a legend.

Stanford was her most frequent client, and the thousand-a-night aspect of this only amused him, although he groaned comically every time he paid. Lily was fond of the man, but fondness was not loving, and this was a distinction that never escaped Lily. Stanford took her for drives in his fine landau, caring not a whit that he be seen in company with the town's most famous prostitute. Stanford repeated his offers to make her his mistress, and each time he offered, Lily politely, gently, yet firmly turned him down. For to be Stanford Dickinson's mistress was neither more respectable nor more profitable than plain whoring, and when Lily stopped whoring, she intended that it would be for good and forever, and for an entirely new and respectable life.

On a fine afternoon in March, Stanford took her driving out to see Kate in San Mateo. The welcome, as ever, was warm. Lily, as always, brought presents, and not just for Kate, but for all the Baker children, two boys and a girl. Kate was toddling about on plump little legs, wearing hair of the same red-gold as Lily's and an almost perpetual smile, and every time the child called Mary Baker "Mama," something inside "Aunt" Lily cringed and seemed to wither.

She was quiet on the ride back, thinking that the time was none too soon to start making real plans for her future, instead of the formless dreams that had been teasing her ever since she had set foot on the *Eurydice* two years ago. There was nearly twelve thousand dollars in her account at Wells Fargo now, and growing fast. Her long-ago dream had been for a shop, and maybe that was still not such a bad idea, for good shops flourished here, there was a shortage of nearly everything, and everything fine commanded the highest prices. Yet Lily loved the countryside too, and often found herself dreaming of a little farm someplace. *Silly goose! And what do you know about farming?* Well, she'd decide on something soon—before the year was out!

The landau pulled up before the El Dorado. Lily thanked Stanford, invited him for tea, but he declined. She kissed him lightly on the cheek and climbed down. Heads turned on both sides of the street, but Lily had long since stopped noticing such things.

Lily had tea, bathed, took a short nap, and then got dressed for the evening. Pale lavender she wore, trimmed with ivory lace, a color Sophie had thought of, that worked surprisingly well with the copper hair and the pale skin. She looked at the small gilt-bronze clock on the mantel: eight-fifteen. Soon the bell would summon her down to Sophie's parlor. There would be a half-hour or so of mingling with the assembled clients, a glass of wine, some laughter, a quiet introduction to the man of the evening if she didn't know him already.

She inspected herself in the mirror. *Not bad*, thought Lily. *It is a becoming color, after all.* This was the first time she'd worn the lavender gown, after many misgivings in buying the thing, for it came from the City of Paris and was far from cheap. She twirled a bit and smiled at the girl in the mirror. It had taken Lily many months to accept the fact of her good looks, to learn a touch of vanity about her appearance, but this was a thing she would always have to force herself to remember, because none of the primping and fussing and posing came naturally to her. Sophie's taste, thank God, was excellent, and Sophie took an interest. *"If we're asking a high price for the merchandise, Lily my dear, then we must display it most attractively, however tedious that may seem to you. For it's the cologne and the lace they're buying as well as the loving. It's the smiles and the wine they'll remember as much as whatever happens between the sheets. Clean sheets in themselves are a new and exotic thing for some poor man who's been up in the camps for months at a time."* There was no doubt about it: working for Sophie Delage was many kinds of an education.

The bell rang. Lily put down her month-old copy of *Godey's Ladies' Book,* which had arrived just today via the overland route from Kansas City, and walked down the stairs.

Sophie's parlor was far more than a marketplace for the girls and gamblers and drinkers of San Francisco. The El Dorado attracted the cream of the fast set, men of business and politics, clipper captains and visiting dignitaries; it had evolved into a jovial and rather exclusive club where men could meet as if by chance, where deals could be sealed with a handshake and a glass of Sophie's excellent French wine, where political careers could be furthered or destroyed. The El Dorado had cachet. It did a man good to let the world know he had the taste—and the hard cash—to spend a night at Sophie's place with the fabulous Lily Cigar.

And Lily herself found it fascinating. If she had a choice, she would have spent all her time in this parlor, smiling, and listening, and learning.

The parlor was well-filled this early October night in 1858.

The talk was, as always, half of politics and half of business. The big news was about the supposedly bottomless gold strike at Fraser, in British Columbia, which just last April had men leaving town by the thousands, plunging the city into a temporary panic, abandoning perfectly good gold claims, some of them rushing north as they had earlier rushed to California, chasing the elusive dream and finding that the dream eluded them still in the far, frozen north. There was indeed gold at Fraser, but not very much of it, and now the men were trickling back, beaten, to make a start again. Lily had never given much thought to Fraser Fever, as it was called. This town was hers now, and for as far ahead as she could imagine. Frazer Fever or not, the El Dorado had remained busy, her price went up and up, and in San Mateo Kate thrived. Let who would chase after gold, as long as enough of it found its way back to San Francisco, to the El Dorado, and into Lily's account at Wells Fargo.

Lily took the smallest possible sip of her champagne and listened attentively to an old man in hot debate with a younger man about the prospects of the proposed transcontinental railroad.

Suddenly the door opened and a hush fell on the parlor. Lily noticed this and turned toward the door.

A man stood there, a tall, good-looking young man who seemed at the same time fierce and expectant. There was an air of danger about him, of recklessness. For a moment Lily wondered if they were going to be robbed or otherwise assaulted.

Then she looked closer. Slowly, as if being drawn on strings, she moved toward the stranger.

His hair was dark red. His eyes blazed green across the big room.

He was Fergus Malone, Junior.

Lily closed her eyes, sure that when she opened them again the apparition would be gone, for surely he was dead, surely this was a ghost, or some cruel trick!

She came up to him, and for a moment they both stood speechless, staring, hardly breathing, hardly daring to blink an eye.

In the end it was Lily who broke the reverberating silence. "Fergy?"

Her question hung on the air like a drifting feather, unsure of itself, vulnerable to every current of fate's wind.

There was no way to measure the time it took for him to reply.

Lily looked deep in his eyes, and it was like looking in the mirror. But his eyes had a hardness to them that was not in hers, and she knew without being told that those eyes had seen terrible things. Yet he was beautifully dressed, expensively, perhaps a bit flashily. Lily looked up at this stranger who must be her brother, and thought: *He's come to me, he's come back all the way from the dead, all the way from the bottom of the ocean.*

And still he said nothing, eating her with those eyes, as if speaking might make her vanish into the night.

"Fergy?" Lily's question was more of an answer now, for she was convinced of the truth in it.

When he spoke, it was like a faraway sigh. "Lily, oh, my Lily! It's fair to being a miracle, Lil, for I'd long given up ever seeing you again."

Then he wrapped his long arms around her and squeezed her to him and laughed loud and happy.

For a moment she simply rested in his arms, and felt safe, truly safe, for the first time she could remember.

Lily held him tight, and closed her eyes, and felt his arms around her, as though those strong arms were part of her—and they were part of her, sure, for this was Fergy, flesh and blood of the Malones, her own Fergy, come to rescue her just like he always said he would, and give her a coach and seven footmen. *Well, brother, it doesn't matter about the footmen, what matters is that you're here, not at the bottom of the ocean, and I shall never feel alone again!*

Then she pulled back and smiled and led him to Sophie. "A miracle's happened, Sophie. My brother has returned from the dead."

Sophie took it in good part, and kissed Fergy herself, and bought champagne for everyone in the room. They laughed and talked for a few moments longer; then Lily felt herself growing shy with this stranger, her brother. She whispered her excuses to Sophie, canceled the night's appointment, and took Fergy upstairs.

Lily had more champagne sent up, and a supper table for two was already laid out in her room. She motioned him into the big chair by the wood stove, filled his glass, and sat on a padded footstool at his feet.

"Now," she said, brimming with pure joy, "tell me all of it. From the minute you left St. Paddy's."

He waited for a short time that seemed to Lily like hours. Fergus sipped the golden bubbly wine and began talking. His voice was low, and while it had changed very much from the street boy's chatter she could only vaguely recall, Lily could still hear the echoes of Dublin in it, small fragments of their father's merry brogue, a touch of their mother's softness.

"I never believed in miracles, Lil, until five minutes ago. I thought I'd had all the rotten luck a fellow could have, divil take it, and then I saw one of those pictures of you they're selling, and even in the black and white of it, there was something. I asked, and they told me where to find Lily Cigar, and here I am."

"Here *we* are, Fergy. But tell me about you, about the *Indian Belle*. Seven years just disappeared, Fergy. Where were you?"

"Where was I not? The *Belle* went down off Valparaiso some ways out at sea, a terrible storm it was, Lil, all hands lost but for three of us, drifting on a spar for four days. Only God knows how we got out of that one. Tied ourselves to the damned spar, there was just enough rope. And after four days of blazing sun and freezing nights, a New Bedford

[342]

whaler picked us up, just at the start of their voyage they were, outward bound for cruising all the far South Pacific. If I never see a whale monster again, it'll be too soon. Three long years we sailed with the *Sandra Manne*. At first we were glad to be alive, and maybe I still should be. But what a stinking, rotten job it was, and cold, and lonely, flensing the poor great beasts, boiling down the blubber for whale oil, blood everywhere all the time, the decks slimy with it, clothes stained red, stinking. Well . . ." He paused, drank, and continued. "Three years they had us out. That was the price of our rescue. Early in 1855 we got back to New Bedford, and you can bet I kissed the dirt of good old America, Lil, and thanked all the stars in heaven."

"You never wrote."

"There was no place to write from, Lil, for all we ever got in the way of ports was some nigger island where you couldn't be sure of anything, let alone a mail drop. I did write, from New Bedford. Didn't you get it?"

"No. No, I didn't."

Lily spoke softly, and touched his arm as she rose to refill their glasses. *And what might not have been different if, in 1855, I knew you were alive, Fergy, if I'd known I wasn't altogether alone?* But it was too late for recriminations. Luck was a wild thing, wild as any storm at sea, and if it tossed up a treasure or a curse, what was the point in questioning the thing, the force of it, of shaking an impotent fist at the gods of fortune?

"I wrote to St. Paddy's. I meant to come down and look for you, Lil, but . . . well, to make a long story short, I got in trouble."

"What kind of trouble?"

"Bad trouble. I had to run away." He looked into the glowing red windows of the iron stove as he spoke, avoiding her eyes, guessing what she'd be thinking.

Lily said nothing. *Of course,* she thought, *that's how we solve a problem, isn't it, Fergy? We run away, we just pack up and leave and hope we can run faster than trouble. Only, trouble has wings, Fergy dear: trouble moves quicker than thinking.* Lily thought of many things to say, and said none of them.

"I'm sorry."

"I couldn't help it, Lil, believe me."

"Of course you couldn't. Where did you go?"

"Well, I'd done a lot of growing up on that whaler, Lil. I wasn't a kid anymore. I could do a man's work. I knew about women. And I knew how to play cards. So when I ran, I ran with a wagon train, going West."

"In fifty-five, this was?"

"Summertime. We gathered in Pittsburgh, went west from there. It was tough going. Dangerous. We got to St. Louis finally, and I stopped there awhile. Better part of a year. Then . . . I moved on."

"More trouble?"

"I moved on to Kansas City. Not much of a town, Kansas City. Didn't stay there long, just enough to get a stake together. Ended up in Denver. By then it was 1857. Last year. Denver's quite a town, Lil. High up. Clean. Booming. I liked Denver."

"But you moved on."

"I moved on. And here I am."

There was a pause while Lily considered what to say next, for her head was dancing with questions, and her memories of Fergy in the old days warned her to proceed with caution. Still, there was a thing she must ask, and she did so.

"Fergy, my dear, how did you live? How did you get money?"

She could tell in an instant it was the wrong question. The smile poured across his handsome face like spilled honey, announcing the lies even before they formed on his lips.

"Oh, you know how it is, Lil, I did this and that—some gambling here and there, a touch of clerking in a store, a few little ventures . . . none of it came to much, I'll be the first to admit."

Lily looked at her brother and smiled. He hadn't changed one bit, for all his getting tall, and the broad shoulders and the fine clothes. He was still Fergy, her Fergy, a bundle of mischief and dreams and a wild itch to run from trouble. Yet, there was something about him: oh, fine to look at, sure. But that wasn't what made the heads turn when he walked into Sophie's parlor tonight. No, it was more than that: it was the sense of danger building in him, and the whiff of brimstone. She rang for supper and told him her own story quickly, quietly, before the maid came.

"That was tough, Lil, about the kid, I mean."

"She's a beautiful kid. She needs all the family she can get, Fergy. I'll take you to see her one day soon."

"I'd like that."

They seated themselves at the table and enjoyed Sophie's chef's oyster bisque, roast quail, late-summer squash, and pecan pie. And there was more wine. It was a fine meal,

Fergy was charming, but still there was a tension in him that was new to Lily. Even the wine failed to soften that. She toyed with her dessert.

"The question is, my big brother, what now?"

"What do you mean, what now?"

"What do we do? Together? You don't think that now I've found you I'll let you drift away again."

"My eye is a rover, Lil, and my heart wanders, and my feet always want to find out what's around the next bend in the road, over the next mountain. You might as well try to chain the wind."

"I need you, Fergy. I need you bad."

"Hitch your wagon to me, Lil, and you're hitching it to a typhoon. It might be a pretty rough ride."

He reached for the champagne bottle and refilled his glass.

Lily looked at her brother and was suddenly, vividly reminded of Jack Wallingford. Here was that same driven look, the wild glint in his eye, the self-scorn mixed with self-pity, the gambler's terrible love affair with losing. She smiled her sweetest smile.

"I've been on rough trips before, Fergy. Do you think this place is some ivory tower? Your long-lost sister's a whore, Fergy, in case that hadn't dawned on you."

He laughed. The laugh, too, was like Jack's laugh, self-mocking, meant to tell whoever heard it that however little they might think of him, his own estimate was lower.

"I didn't imagine Madam Sophie was running a convent, Lil. By the look of you, you're doing right well."

"I am doing well, and I'm going to do better. I'm saving every penny, Fergy, and I'm right on the lookout to do something with my savings. Some new business. Something that's going to get me out of here, out of this life, something that'll make us rich. That's one more reason I need you. I need a partner I can trust."

"And what business would this be? I'm a gambling man, Lil, not a businessman."

"I don't know. I'm not sure yet. It's only the last few months that I've even been able to think about it."

"You're pretty famous, do you know that? I mean, with the pictures and all. People talk about you. I heard the name Lily Cigar just about as soon as I hit town. A fine green carriage went flashing by, and you in it, and someone said: 'There she goes! There goes Lily Cigar.' By the time I looked, you were gone. But they know you. Your name means something. If a man'll pay . . ."

"A thousand dollars a night, Fergy. Say it."

"A thousand dollars a night, that means something. And you get to keep . . ."

"Half."

"Suppose you got to keep it all?"

"My own place? You don't get my meaning, Fergus Malone. I want to get out of this. The sooner the better. Maybe you enjoy gambling, but I don't like whoring one bit."

"How much do you have saved?"

"A little more than twenty thousand."

"How long did it take you to earn that?"

"A year. But I started low. Lower, anyway."

"And just suppose you got it all, plus half of what some other girls brought in, plus the profits on the wine and the food? You'd be rich in a year. Maybe very rich. Sure and you'd be rich enough to get into something else—in a big way."

"Sophie might not agree."

"Sophie doesn't own you, Lil. You've done as much for her as she has for you."

"Sophie saved my life. I'll not soon forget that."

"Think about it. You know the business now. You'd probably do it better than she does. Have fancier girls. Charge fancier prices. This place is fine, but the city's growing, changing. There's room for someplace even finer. Think, Lil. One hundred percent instead of fifty. You're in this for the money, you say, so why not be in it for all of the money you can get?"

"I'll sleep on it. Now let's talk about something else, because if Sophie heard us, she'd probably murder me in my bed."

They drank a little more wine, far more on Lily's part than she was used to, and Fergy left just after midnight. Lily went to bed alone, and she was a long time falling asleep.

Lily's blood churned, racing through her head, and her pulse beat fast from the thrill of discovering him again. Fergy, back from the dead! Who said there weren't miracles? Fergy, charming as of old, filled with dreams and forever dancing with danger. Ah, but wasn't it a fine thing to have him, for he made her feel safe, made her feel almost the way Kate made her feel, as though, at last, she belonged to someone. Someone who would not leave her, ever again. Lily smiled at her folly even as she thought this, for Fergy was Fergy, and you could not sooner put a net around the moon than tie him to one spot. Yet, maybe . . . maybe!

A funny little tune kept running through her head, a bit of an old ballad he'd sung just before leaving, laughing, flushed with Sophie's good wine:

Her golden hair in ringlets hung,
Her dress was spangled o'er,
She had rings upon her fingers,
Brought from a foreign shore,
She'd entice both kings and princes,
So costly was she dressed,
She far exceeds Diana bright . . .
She's the Lily of the West.

And Lily felt a bit tipsy herself, but not from wine. *Ah, Fergy, my Fergy, you're a blessing even if a mixed one. And you wouldn't ask me to go on whoring if you knew what it cost me.* But this was no night to think about whoring. This was a golden night. Sleep found Lily smiling, for Fergy was back, and nothing could harm her.

⊷ 28 ⊶

Lily looked at her brother critically as they walked up the hill. *Well I might have known he'd talk me into it. Fergy can talk a stone into flying, and always could.*

Ever since he'd suggested the idea of going into business for herself, the thought had buzzed about in Lily's head with the noisy insistence of a bumblebee. Try as she might, it would not go away. Lily analyzed her situation with all the logic she could summon, and she had to agree that, as far as logic went, there was much to be said for Fergy's proposition.

"Why make money for Sophie, when you could be banking all of it? You may command a thousand a night, Lily Cigar, but you only get five hundred. And that's what it boils down to, not counting the take on the other girls, and the profits on the gaming and the drinks."

She sighed. He'd stated and restated his arguments a dozen times over, and she knew them all by heart. When Fergy got hold of an idea, he was like a terrier with a bone, playing with the thing, gnawing at it, getting the last possible ounce of meat and marrow.

"So you'd sell your own sister, would you, my fine brother, my protector?"

He laughed, assuming, wrongly, that she was joking. "But you're already sold, my Lily, my Lily of the West! Not only sold, but famous too, and that's worth hard cash, Lil, never forget it. Look, Lil, I know it's no life for you. This way you'll get out twice as fast—because you'll earn twice the money."

She looked at him and nodded her agreement, for there seemed nothing else to do.

Now Lily smiled as she smoothed down her walking coat. It was the latest style, if you could believe *Godey's Ladies' Book*, which was one of her few sources of fashion news. The coat was a deep green tartan plaid, in wool, edged with black braiding, a great sweep of green and black and deep blue that matched the afternoon dress beneath it. The hoops were growing fatter by the week, like pumpkins in summer, and Lily found them inconvenient to the point of absurdity, and therefore had her Chinese dressmaker keep them to the minimum.

Lily had dressed with special care this morning, for it was to be a special day.

She and Fergy were going shopping. And what they were shopping for was nothing less than the real estate on which they firmly intended to build a whorehouse such as the West had never seen.

They had laughed and debated and come close to fighting about the name. In the end it was Stanford Dickinson who had solved it, smiling, his eyes mischievous and kind at the same time.

"Elegance is all, my love," said he, "and nothing's more elegant to the unwashed nouveaux riches than a touch of the French. I think you should simply call the place Fleur de Lis."

"Flower-of-what?" Lily was still busy teaching herself proper English. French was on her list, but for later.

"Skunk cabbage, you goose. It's French for 'lily,' and not only that, but the royal symbol of the kings of France."

"Fleur de Lis. I like it. We can have a little sign."

"Small and brass and very discreet, like its owner."

"You find me brassy, do you, then?" She kissed him playfully on the cheek.

"Never, Lily. I find you more precious than gold."

Lily looked at him sharply, decided this was more of his usual banter. "Gold," she said, laughing, "is quite precious enough. At least for the moment. But I thank you for your name."

Fergy had liked it too. "It has class, Lil," he said. "A name like that makes you think everything's going to be that much fancier, a bit more expensive, maybe . . ."

"A lot more expensive, and well worth it."

"You bet."

"Until you-know-who finds out, and then it'll be lilies at my funeral, for sure as God made apples, she'll murder me."

"Sophie's not the murdering kind. But she might not be too happy about it."

They had left it at that, but every day Lily dreaded the inevitable confrontation more and more, the terrible moment when she must pay back Sophie's uncountable kindness with treachery.

Whoring had taught Lily one lesson that came in handy

[349]

now. It had taught her to keep her mind in many watertight compartments, so that what she did with one part of herself had almost nothing to do with the rest. Thus she could be charming to a stranger for his money, even if it was essentially a false charm. She discovered how easy it was to manipulate these men, how hungry they were for a kind word, a smile even, a bit of coquetry. For all their size and strength and rough language, these men were essentially children, Lily discovered, spoiled children screaming for their toys. So she learned to soothe them, to make them feel strong and admired and attractive.

Lily never looked on this as deception. It was part of the service. It was what they paid for as much as the more physical aspect of love, although they surely wanted that too.

So it happened that after almost two years in Sophie's house Lily could look at Sophie and smile as she passed her on the stairs, and walk out into the bright November sunshine of San Francisco to meet Fergy and go shopping for the land on which they'd build a house that would outclass Sophie's, Lily profoundly hoped, in every way.

It took Fergy and Lily two weeks to find the site. What they found was a corner high on Nob Hill at the corner of Sacramento Street and Powell. It wasn't the biggest lot they'd seen, only one hundred and fifty feet by two hundred, but the situation was ideal, at the top of the growth district but not yet fully developed, and very nearly at the top of the hill. The land had four neglected shacks on it now, and a price of fifteen thousand dollars.

"We'll need a mortgage," Fergy said with the air of a solid old-school businessman, "and an architect, and decorators."

"Now, who'd lend money to the likes of us?"

"Leave that to me, Lil. I'm not a gambler for nothing. Besides, we have the blessing of your pal Stanford Dickinson, and that must count in these parts."

"Not a penny of his will I touch, Fergy. Not a penny, and don't you forget it. What I do—what we do—we'll do on our own, and be beholden to no man."

"As you say. In any event, if I'm to be your partner, Lil, you must leave the business end of things to me. You'll have your hands full just running the girls and the kitchen and the bar service. I'll take care of the financing and the police and all that."

Lily had many a doubt about Fergy's capacity to handle this business or any other for more than a few weeks steady. But she buried her doubts, and for a reason. His eyes sparkled. Fergy had a new dream, and she was sharing it! This was a thing Lily had wished for since they were small children. And somehow it didn't matter what the dream was, exactly, for what counted most was the sharing. The Fleur de Lis would tie Fergy to her in a way that would keep him with her forever. As far as forever went in San Francisco in 1858.

Two days later Lily was handed an envelope on her breakfast tray. She recognized Fergy's writing, still nearly as crude as it had been in his cabin boy's letter to her in St. Patrick's orphanage. But the message was unmistakable and it sent a thrill shuddering through her to her toes. There was no greeting to the letter, and no signature. He must have been afraid Sophie'd open the thing, as though she'd stoop to spying! All the note said was "We're in!" That was all it had to say. Lily closed her eyes and saw the Fleur de Lis rising brick by brick. But no! Maybe it should be marble! They hadn't found an architect as yet. That would be next, and the decorations, and the staff. And the bad part, telling Sophie.

The day soon came when Lily knew she could put it off no longer. It was morning, a gray and foggy morning in early December. Just yesterday she and Fergy had spent two hours with the architect, looking at drawings, discussing materials, a timetable, costs. The Fleur de Lis was going to be very grand indeed, far grander than Sophie's place, which thus far was the standard of luxury for San Francisco's parlor houses. Near onto a quarter of a million dollars it would cost! At first the size of that sum terrified Lily, still used to counting her pennies.

"If you're jumping off the cliff, Lil," Fergy said with the now familiar gleam in his eyes, "it might as well be a tall one, the best and the biggest, right?"

"I guess so. But the payments will be huge, Fergy."

"And so will the profits! Are you not Lily Cigar? Will it not be the finest house in town? With the highest prices, the best wines, the greatest gaming?"

Fergy could talk the moon out of the sky, and Lily went along with his plans in a kind of hypnotic daze. His optimism might be far from rational, but it was infectious in the extreme. You could hardly be close to Fergy without sharing his moods, and his moods these days were expansive.

Although the sources of Fergy's income were cloudy, he was never short of money, and never asked Lily for cash. He spent freely, mostly on women. Fergy had become a regular at Sophie's place, and the girls all loved him. At first this embarrassed Lily, even as her profession embarrassed her in the most secret corner of her heart. But then she began to take a kind of pride in Fergy's easy triumphs with the girls at Sophie's. The more attractive he was to them, the easier it might be to recruit them, and she had every intention of trying that, and soon. These were her hopes, mingled with guilt and fear, as she went to knock on Sophie's door. How often had she put off this dreadful moment, the moment of telling Sophie of her plans? Sophie, who had saved her life. Sophie, who had made her a whore. *No, Lily, don't turn hypocrite this late in the game: no one made you a whore. There weren't any guns at your head. Sophie never even suggested it, and she had a million chances, especially when you were weak and sick and your money running out.*

Lily knocked, feeling like Judas himself, and was bidden to enter.

Sophie was lying abed late, finishing her tea and toast.

"Will you have tea, Lily?"

"No, thanks."

"Foul day, is it not?"

"Gray as gray. Sophie . . ."

"Yes, my dear?"

I'll never be able to say the words. I will stand here forever, tongue-tied. "Once you said, if I came to work here, that in time I might be able to . . ."

"Start a business of your own. Exactly. Is that what's been bothering you, my dear?"

She noticed. I'll never be able to keep a secret, and I don't know why I even try. "Yes. Now that Fergy's come . . ."

"He can help, naturally. What could be simpler? Not that it'll be easy without you, Lily, for what I predicted truly happened, didn't it? You did become my star attraction."

She thinks I'm going to open a little dress shop. Lily took a deep breath and blurted it out. "We're starting a house, Sophie."

There seemed to be no way to soften these words or of making them easier for Sophie to digest. There was a pause. Sophie Delage looked up from her teacup and stared at Lily. Lily felt those dark eyes drilling into her with all the force of two knives. Sophie's expression changed not at all, and for some reason this was more ominous than rage or tears.

The silence grew heavier as it lengthened. Lily felt it crushing her with an almost physical force. Finally she could stand it no longer.

"It'll only be for a little while, Sophie," she began, too

quickly. "Just until I can save enough to get out of whoring forever, just as we planned. The town's growing so fast, I won't be taking your business, I promise. I'll help you if I can, just as you've helped me."

Still the silence filled the space between them, solid as cement.

Breathless now, Lily went on. "We won't even be nearby! We'll be 'way on the other side of town, far from the docks."

The silence deepened, and suddenly Lily felt a mortal fear creeping up her spine. Sophie, she knew, kept a small derringer in her bedside table. *I wouldn't be surprised if she shot me dead, and don't I deserve it?*

"Sophie, please, say something. I mean no harm, truly, I'm doing it only for Kate, for I must make a proper home for the child soon. Say you understand that. Say . . . something!"

When the sound came from the woman on the bed, it was a long and joyless sigh. It was so deep, this sighing, and so long-drawn-out that to Lily the noise might have been some distant autumn wind mourning the loss of springtime. Finally Sophie spoke.

"Once," she began slowly, softly, with a quiet dignity that Lily found more fearful than a scream, "once I met a girl, a shy little mouse of a thing she was, small and frail-looking, but with something about her, a kind of delicacy you might call it, the promise of beauty. And nice she was, in her way, ignorant of course, unformed, terrified of the great world, not knowing what to do with herself. Well, I took her in, that child, and protected her, offered her what I seldom offer anyone—man, woman, or child. Took her in, that's what I did, nursed her when she was sick, helped her in childbirth, gave her food, shelter, gave her hope, gave her a way of earning a living when she asked me, and—"

"Oh, Sophie, please don't go on so. I can't bear it!"

"You can't bear it? Can't bear it? You can bear it enough to do the thing that drives me to say such words, though, can't you, Lily Malone? You can do that easy enough. Do it with a smile, you can. I expected better of you, Lily. I expected more of a reward than this."

"Sophie, I am sorry. I don't mean to harm you, or to take any business away, or to offend you. Can't we still be friends? Can't you understand why I must do this?"

"Of course I understand, child. That is precisely what makes me so very sad. Understand greed? Understand disloyalty? And am I not Sophie Delage, who has seen things that

[353]

would make even you blush, my proud Lily, my fine Lily, my thousand-dollar-a-night Lily, my Lily whom I nourished and tended and set in a special place, only to discover I have been nurturing a poison weed? I understand you all too well, Lily, and I am the sadder for it."

In that moment Lily felt the gates of hell itself closing behind her. *It would have been kinder if she had shot me.* "Then there is nothing more for me to say." Lily turned from the bedside. She would pack this very day, and go to a hotel, and never see Sophie again. But the voice called her back.

"There may come a time when I'll forgive you, Lily. But you can't expect me not to be hurt, can you?"

"I guess not. But I thought you might understand that I do everything I do only for the child, Sophie, only for Kate. Do you imagine I enjoy letting your customers have me for cash? That I like the smiling and pretending, and being gracious and all? I never told a lie, Sophie, until I began to lie with my body, and may God forgive me for it. You know I tried everything to get honest work, and failed. And as soon as I get enough by whoring, you may be sure I'll get out, and for good, and you'll have nothing to fear from Lily Cigar. Including the sight of her."

Choking back her sobs, blinking back her tears, and stumbling like a drunk, Lily walked to the door and opened it.

"Stop."

She turned. Sophie was sitting up now, and her face had gone pale. Her lip quivered. Lily realized the woman was on the verge of tears.

"I couldn't help what I said, Lily, for in all these years you are the only girl I ever cared about as a friend. I never had a child. I never had much luck with the men. Delage left me a month after we got together, never even married me, the beast. I've made myself into what I am, Lily, built walls around me, worked and schemed and done things so terrible no one will ever know them, not even you. And now I have it all, and it is nothing. For I have no one to share it with. Remember that, Lily, as you go out into the world. Don't let the world make you into a lonely old woman, for that is more painful than any wound, and more sorrowful than any loss. Of course I understand, Lily, and I forgive you. Let us remain friends, as best we can."

Lily ran to the bed and kissed her. Tears mingled with tears, and Sophie hugged her so tightly the teacup overturned. They laughed then.

"Oh, Sophie! Thank you. Thank you."

"I wish you the best, Lily, and I always have. It won't be easy, but you'll do fine."

"I hope so."

"With Fergy to help you."

"With all you've taught me."

"Don't go, Lily, don't move out just yet. You can stay here as long as you like, it's a comfort to me. I'm nearly sixty, Lily, and rich enough to retire if I want. That's the real reason I went back to New York, to look into some investments. In a year or so I'll be out of the business too. I get so tired some of the time, you wouldn't credit it. That may be why the thought of losing you upset me so. For watching you blossom, my Lily, has been a great pleasure these last two years."

"I'll never forget you, Sophie."

"Nor I you, my dear. Now! Tell me all about it."

And Lily did, smiling, and in detail.

⊸§ 29 §⊸

The fact that it was an unexpectedly glorious afternoon in March did nothing to relieve Brooks Chaffee's mood as his one-horse cab made its way up Fifth Avenue to the meeting at Delmonico's. The year 1859 did not promise happy things for America, even though it had begun well enough for the bank. No more did Brooks dismiss Caroline's predictions of war as a kind of womanly homesickness, a sort of reverse patriotism. Every week brought more news of bitter developments on the slavery question, and these items were always followed hotly by debates on states' rights, about the fatally imprecise borderline between the national government's authority and the power of the individual states to govern themselves. Ironically, maddeningly, Brooks found himself humming the silly minstrel-show tune that was suddenly the rage. *"I wish I was in the land of cotton . . ."* Caroline assured him that this slender musical thread was practically the only thing the South had in common with the North these days, that it was every bit as well-loved down home as it was in New York. *". . . old times there are not forgotten: look away! Look away!"* The name of the silly damned tune was "Dixie's Land," and Dixie's Land was going to be drenched in blood if things didn't take a dramatic turn for the better, and very soon.

Brooks and all his friends bitterly resented the concept of slavery. The Chaffees had never owned slaves and never would. For Caroline, who had grown up in a big New Orleans house filled with black slaves—very well-treated black slaves, she was ever quick to remind anyone who questioned her—it was not such an easy decision. She could readily see the underlying evils of the system, but Caroline could also see huge injustices in the aggressive Northern economy. And Brooks admitted that working conditions and wages weren't always fair, even right here in New York. But factories could be improved, and wages could be raised. Slavery was another thing altogether, a basic moral question. If slavery were to be lawful, then why not murder, or bigamy, or any number of other crimes against humanity? The problem had never been resolved between them. They dealt with the question by skimming over it.

Brooks began thinking about the British banker he was about to meet, and the terms of a mortgage the Britisher wanted to effect for a big block of real estate north of Fiftieth Street off Fifth Avenue. The cab swung around the corner and Brooks was startled to see his wife walking briskly out of Delmonico's and into a waiting cab. She was too far away to hail, but unmistakably Caroline. He'd know that flower-stalk carriage, that elegant head, the imperious mask she sometimes wore in public, whose intimate smiles were reserved only for him. God, but what a beauty she was! And how lucky he was to have her. He grinned as heads turned to stare at Caroline, who, typically, looked neither left nor right but marched about her business. A smasher, positively a smasher, to use one of old Jack's favorite expressions. Probably coming from tea, or a late lunch. He'd ask her later. Then his mind slid back into the intricate complex of international real-estate financing as the cab pulled smartly to a stop at the granite curbstone in front of the glamorous hotel.

The meeting dragged on, as meetings with Britishers tended to do. Brooks was late getting home, and Caroline was already dressed for the dinner party they'd promised to attend. He kissed her, quickly bathed, and was dressed in twenty minutes.

"I nearly bumped into you this afternoon," he said when they were snugly in the passenger compartment of their carriage, being driven up Fifth Avenue. "Coming out of Delmonico's."

"Oh, indeed, yes, I had tea with Miss Sally Patterson."

Caroline smiled and took his hand. "It was a typical day in the life of Mrs. Brooks Chaffee," she went on, happily. "We went shopping at Lord and Taylor and then I entered into—and handily won—a debate with your Mr. Honest Abe Lincoln on the subject of states' rights. You will be sad to know he has left politics forever as a result of my little efforts."

Something clicked in Brooks's mind: *Wasn't Sally out of town?* He could swear she'd gone to Paris with her father. But maybe they'd decided not to go, or maybe he was thinking of someone else. Too silly to go into in any case. Caroline ought to know whom she'd taken tea with. He'd never met a girl so positive in all her opinions. He turned to his wife, whose delicate profile was at that moment framed by a halo of gas light as they passed a lamppost.

"You," he whispered, although there was no one else to hear him, "are the most beautiful woman in America."

"And you," she said, laughing her husky and infinitely tempting laugh, "are the most shameless flatterer in America!"

She leaned across the tiny distance between them and kissed him in a soft cloud of jasmine perfume. The carriage moved discreetly up the avenue to the huge limestone palace wherein a Vanderbilt dowager kept looking nervously at the door because her evening's social triumph would be incomplete unless it included the dazzling young Caroline Chaffee.

On the night of March 20, 1859, you could have shot a cannonball through any of the fanciest parlor houses in San Francisco and injured no one. It was Lily Cigar's twenty-second birthday.

It was also the official opening of the Fleur de Lis.

The rumors had been building along with the limestone structure itself. For several months the demimonde of San Francisco had been hearing tales, hints, and speculations. The Fleur de Lis was to be the definitive pleasure palace of the West, perhaps of all the world. Five stories tall and glittering it rose, filling half the block, looking down on most of the city and all of the other parlor houses, gambling halls, barrooms, and cribs.

Lily fed the rumors, and so did Fergy. But mostly the myths created themselves, for there was nothing the San Franciscans liked more than a spectacle, especially when it was a success story, and more especially when it involved wine and women and pleasure.

There were carpets from Brussels, tapestries from France, marble from Italy and an imported crew of Italians to carve it. There was a genuine pipe organ in the main parlor, and a rosewood bar seventy feet long. Paintings of naked ladies and nearly naked gentlemen cavorted up the soaring walls. The gas chandeliers dripped real crystal, the main stairway had a balustrade plated in real gold. Or so it was said, and no one denied it. The chef and the wines would be French, the musicians from Vienna, the girls from every corner of the world. And it was all the more wonderful because Lily and her dashing brother had put it together in just a little more than four months.

Lily had used her time at Sophie's well, and her memories

of the Wallingford mansion on Fifth Avenue were deep and clear. The Fleur de Lis was a fusion of all that was best in Sophie's place with the gaudy display that had so delighted the Wallingfords.

"You've made it," said Stanford Dickinson when she took him through the nearly completed rooms, "a true palace of love, Lily."

Lily looked at him fondly. She knew she could never love the man, but she hoped he would remain her friend.

"I'm delighted to hear you say so, for that is just what we intend it will be."

"There's nothing to touch it from here to Chicago, I can personally swear to that!"

"Very personally, no doubt, you villain." But Lily laughed as she took his arm and led him down the grand staircase.

The invitations had gone out two weeks in advance of the occasion—engraved, they were, on Shreve's finest cream paper; the governor himself sent no better. *"The Fleur de Lis requests the pleasure of your company at a small supper dance on Wednesday evening, March 20, 1859."*

There was a traffic jam on Nob Hill that night. Extra police had been hired for the occasion, directing the carriages, keeping the gaping crowds at bay. The mayor was there, and the chief of police, and the cream of the fast set. Five prominent madams came in varying degrees of jealousy, all except Sophie, who had made her peace with the situation now and was actually glad to see her protégée doing so well by the profession. Fergy, well-versed in such matters, had gone to Chicago on the Wells Fargo coach to recruit new girls, and on to St. Louis and Denver. He personally investigated the qualifications of every candidate and returned, exhausted but very happy, with an even dozen of the prettiest and (Fergy assured her) most accomplished girls Lily had ever seen. This added a rare piquancy to the festivities, for San Francisco was a small town still, for all its pretensions, and all too soon the men who could afford the very best knew the merchandise of every top-flight parlor house by heart.

The Fleur de Lis had the shimmer of novelty, then, on top of its very obvious luxuries. A new house in town, with new girls, a new chef, and more gambling and drinking accommodations than anywhere else! It was a spectacle, and a most welcome spectacle.

Lily stood at the top of the great curving staircase and received all her guests personally. Fergy presided over the gaming rooms below. The string quartet from Vienna played all the latest tunes, gliding waltzes, merry polkas, passionate gypsy tunes, and even the well-loved melodies of Mr. Stephen Foster and others. Once Lily caught the familiar strains of "Dixie's Land" bouncing and tumbling up the densely carpeted stairs. She smiled at the merry tune. The South and all its problems seemed far away even on a normal day. Tonight they might not have existed at all.

Two hundred and fifty invitations had gone out, and no one counted the number of people who actually came. The rooms were so tall and so spacious that they never seemed truly crowded, although the sound of laughter and the tinkle of champagne glasses testified that there were guests aplenty, and every one of them a potential customer.

At last all the guests seemed to have arrived. Lily stood alone for a moment at the top of the stairs, then felt a gentle hand on her arm. Stanford Dickinson. She turned and smiled.

"It's beautiful, Lily."

Lily paused for just a moment then, and put her small white hand over his, strong and tanned and near to twice her size. It was good to have him here this night, of all nights. He might try to be her lover, but he would always be a friend, she was sure of that now. Lily looked down at the glittering rooms and the glittering people who filled them. *Oh, and for sure 'tis a triumph. Then why aren't you feeling triumphant, Lily, and on your birthday, too, and all of this yours?* The spectacle below her blurred for a moment, and suddenly Lily saw, not the gilt and dazzle of the Fleur de Lis, but her daughter's face, radiant with health and with innocence. Lily sighed softly, and softly she replied to Stanford Dickinson.

"It's a whorehouse."

"It's the best."

"Yes. It is that. Do you think we'll do well?"

"I'd bet anything on it. Have I told you how lovely you look?"

"Many times. But thank you."

"How about buying a good customer a glass of champagne?"

"It's my pleasure."

Lily led him into the reception rooms, where space had been cleared for dancing. There were six bars scattered through the huge house, including the gigantic one downstairs. They got their champagne. He lifted his glass.

"To the Fleur de Lis and its lovely owner."

"To the future, Stanford, for that's what this place is all about."

"To the future, then, Lily—yours and mine."

"Cheers."

The room was lined with mirrors, a fairy palace it looked like, or so Lily thought. She caught their reflection in one of the looking glasses: Stanford, tall and broad-shouldered and handsome in his black evening tailcoat and white starched shirt and tie, and herself, all in deep green velvet, hair piled high and caught with a green velvet ribbon, and—as usual— no jewelry whatever. The long white kidskin gloves were her only ornament. Lily smiled at her admirer and thought of Kate. Sleeping, by now out there in the valley, in the Baker farmhouse at San Mateo. *Believe me, child, I would give every bit of this to be with you this instant, singing a little lullaby. And I will be, soon. It shouldn't take long, my darling Kate, a year or two at best. And please God that may not be too late!*

She tasted the wine: golden, bubbling, dry and faintly sweet at the same time. Oh, it was excellent champagne, the best. Her green eyes scanned the room: it was all the best, and the best of the best. The richly furnished rooms, the food on the huge buffet table, even the music, this very spot high on the hillside. *They'll have to go some to outclass the Fleur de Lis.*

Then Lily spotted Sophie across the room, alone, and went to have a word with her. Stanford Dickinson watched her in silence, smiling, then finished his wine and went downstairs to find Fergy.

The Fleur de Lis was an instant success. Lily had no way of telling how much business—if any—she actually took away from Sophie, for Sophie would never tell her. But men flocked up Sacramento Street every evening as if racing the setting sun. The wine and the gaming and the laughter started at five and went on until the dawn came creeping over the far Sierras. And the gold flowed in. Fergy's girls were all he claimed. The atmosphere was more like a fine hotel than a bawdyhouse, and Lily exerted herself to keep it that way. As news of her innovations spread, more and more men throughout the West felt no visit to San Francisco was complete without a night at Lily's. The Fleur de Lis was as famous for its food as its girls, and famous, too, for being the only parlor house in the West where every girl had her own private bathroom, complete with tub and hot running water! This was a revelation. Not only could a client bathe himself, but for the price of a night at Lily's he could also have his clothes completely laundered and even his boots shined at the

Fleur de Lis's own self-contained laundry. The Chinese who had once done Lily out of a job now made niceties like this possible, and she took every advantage of that fact.

It often happened that a man would come to town for a week or more and simply check into Lily's place as though it were a hotel. The fact was, the Fleur de Lis was far superior in all its services to any hotel in town. And it had something more: it had *cachet*. Men would say they'd been at Lily's even if they'd actually been to one of the lesser, cheaper houses. Fergy once figured out that if all the men who claimed to have been at Lily's truly had been, the house would need a hundred bedrooms and that many girls, instead of the very choice dozen who were actually in residence.

Lily herself took only old, favored clients now, and for twenty-five hundred dollars the night. She thought her new price was outrageous, and did it for the publicity value and also in hopes that it would slow down the demands on her. The result was just the opposite. The higher her price, the more they wanted her.

Stanford Dickinson groaned. "It's a goddamned plot, Lily, you're conspiring with my wife! You'll drive me to chastity if this goes on."

"That would be quite a long trip, now, wouldn't it, my friend?"

"Long and highly uncomfortable." He kissed her. They were in bed. Even Lily's bed was extraordinary, all rosewood and gilt-bronze, sinuous curves topped by a pale green silk canopy pulled back by huge braided cords of deep green silk entwined with gold. The foot of the bed ended in swans' heads, also gilded, and the headboard was a bower of carved wooden flowers.

It was rare, these days, for Stanford to mention his wife, although the image of that unfortunate lady had never left Lily's mind after their painful interview. And it had been months since he'd asked her to marry him.

She rested her head against his deep furry chest and sighed. "You were right, Stanford, right as rain. The Fleur de Lis is coining money. Soon I'll need your advice again."

"You have it, my love, or any other part of me you might be needing."

"Get on with you! I really mean advice. About land."

"No better investment. Buy every inch you can."

"I'm going to be . . . a farmer."

He roared like a lion in the mating season.

"Don't laugh. I'm serious."

"I'd be the very last to deny that, Lily. But I had a picture of you in one of your low-cut silk gowns, white gloves, champagne, hoeing a row of early cabbage. It is a comical thought."

"That would be more nearly what I'm like than any of this folderol."

"You hate it that much, then?"

"How would you like it, Stanford, if our situations were reversed, if you had to put yourself up for sale like any black slave?"

"You're hardly a black slave, Lily."

"You haven't answered me."

"I'd hate it."

"Then why should I not hate it too?"

"I don't know why not. I'd just thought . . ."

"You thought what all men think. That we don't know any better, that we like to be pawed and jumped on and treated like dirt. Maybe there's some who do. I'm not one of 'em."

"You're even prettier when you're angry."

"If you were buying farmland, now, in a few months anyway, where would you buy it?"

". . . and so romantic. I'd buy in two places, in the San Mateo area for relatively quick return, convenience, because that road is going to get built one day soon, and across the bay for the future. Land's cheaper up the coast, you can still get some pretty big spreads reasonably, and the transportation's getting better every year, if you're really talking about serious farming."

"Indeed I am. Have you priced food lately? Outrageous. Always has been."

"I never thought much about that."

"Hardly anyone's doing farming. The Bakers are good farmers, but they don't have enough land. I'd hire Baker in a minute, if he'd come."

He turned to her, smiling, and kissed her cheek. "My little farmer. Tell me about the pleasures of the countryside. Better yet, show me."

"You are a rogue, Stanford!" But Lily laughed with him, and kissed him, and showed him rare pleasures.

Kate was nearly three now. She had grown to be a bright and lively child who played happily with the Bakers' own three children and called Mrs. Baker "Mama." Lily had never tried to change this. It was natural, and she wasn't sure just when she could take the child away, or just how she'd go about it when the time came. Surely the Fleur de Lis, grand as it was, was no place for a baby. And Lily's long-range plan might well include the Bakers.

Now the drives down to San Mateo took on an extra meaning. She looked long and hard at the landscape as she passed, and sometimes didn't pass but rather stopped and talked to the farm folk or the occasional Mexican. The farms were few and unevenly tended. The Bakers had by far the best and most productive of the smaller spreads, but a smaller spread had nothing to do with Lily's plans.

Building the Fleur de Lis and seeing it prosper beyond even Fergy's wildest dreams had taught her the advantages of thinking on a grand scale. And that was just what she intended to do with her dream of farming. Stanford was already keeping an eye out for likely properties. And so did Lily, in person or through discreet questioning among the well-placed clients of the Fleur de Lis. The quickest way to get a lot of land at one fell swoop was to acquire one of the old Mexican land grants. These were seldom available, but when they were, they were huge. Ten thousand acres and more, some of them, and some of them went for per-acre prices that were surprisingly cheap. Many of the old royal grants had never been worked as farms, but maintained for hunting or horse breeding, so the land was all but unimproved. And for reasons nobody really knew, the old aristocratic families were thinning out, retreating into their pride, paying less and less attention, gambling away huge inheritances, selling out and going back to Spain.

So Lily watched, and waited.

In the meantime, she played hostess at the Fleur de Lis, and her legend grew apace with the fame of her pleasure palace. And everyone's list of San Francisco attractions put the Fleur de Lis right up there with the Mission Dolores, the Mechanics Institute, and the Ocean House. In the end, the Fleur de Lis had cost nearly half a million dollars to build, and Fergy told his sister they'd have it all paid back inside of a year. This sounded incredible to Lily, but no more incredible than some of the other get-rich-quick stories she'd heard, and from reliable sources. That meant that, with luck, they'd clear half a million next year—1860. And half a million meant there'd be no stopping her.

Lily smiled, and waited, and thought of doubling her price. In the grand game that her affair with Stanford Dickinson had become, it amused Lily to see just how far she could press him—indeed, could press any man—to pay her ever-escalating price.

[364]

In September, on a whim, she priced herself at five thousand dollars cash the night. No one blinked an eye. It was the sort of thing they expected of Lily Cigar.

Lily was learning what the world expected of Lily Cigar, and this was a lesson that sometimes amused her and sometimes frightened her nearly to death.

She was so used to her exclusivity now, to picking and choosing, and very often taking no client at all, despite her five-thousand-dollar fee, that she actually smiled one afternoon at the Fleur de Lis when Fergy told her a gentleman wanted an appointment with her.

"What gentleman, Fergy?"

The look in Fergy's eyes told her something was wrong, for her brother looked everywhere in the room but at her.

"It's O'Meara, the chief of police."

Lily had seen O'Meara, bug-eyed and obese, and she knew that the ugliness of his person was nothing when compared to a catalog of his vices and corruptions.

"But you've taken care of the police."

"And handsomely. Yet he wants to see you."

"As . . . a client?"

"He didn't say, Lil, and I didn't ask. He is a government official, after all."

"Send him in. And stay by me, Fergy, for I may be needing a strong arm or two."

Chief O'Meara oozed into the room, two hundred and eighty pounds of walking corruption, fattened by every fancy house and gaming den in town. Greedy little button eyes glowed dully from a face as pale and pink and puffy as a newborn pig's.

"Madam Lily," he said, bowing slightly, "what a pleasure."

Lily smiled and gestured to the delicate love seat, fearing he'd break it. "What can we do for you, Chief?"

His answer was a laugh that redefined coarseness. Lily shuddered. It was what she feared: naturally, he'd heard about the famous Lily Cigar, and he wanted free samples. She looked at Fergy. Fergy was staring out the window. Lily felt the trap closing in on her. Anyone else might be talked out of it. Anyone else might be thrown bodily into the street. But this load of blubber could close the Fleur de Lis in five minutes flat, and where would her fine dreams be then? She looked at him and suppressed a shudder. When she spoke, her voice was level.

"I think you'd better leave, now, Fergy. The chief has something he wants to say in private."

Fergy left to the sound of O'Meara's laughter getting louder and louder.

Lily turned to the man. She rose, and walked to him, smiling. She reached out and touched his three chins softly. And she made herself a solemn promise. *If a year goes by and I'm not out of this business, I will throw myself into the bay, as God is my witness!*

In Lily Cigar, she had created a gold mine. But she had also created an uncontrollable monster that would stalk her down all the days of her life. Smiling still, Lily slowly reached for the top button on her dress, and unfastened it, and the next and all the rest.

She had created herself as a fancy woman with the intention of being unique, an unforgettable experience for her customers, a drawing card for the Fleur de Lis. When the nickname "Lily Cigar" was given to her, almost by chance, back at Sophie's house, Lily played with it, decided she liked it—memorable it was, and therefore useful—and kept the name. Now, every evening in the Fleur de Lis, Lily would be found in the biggest parlor, standing in the middle of the room like any proud Fifth Avenue hostess, draped in some rich fabric, low-cut, revealing the supple curve of her breasts, making the most of the slim waist and the pearlescent glow of skin, the flame-red hair. She would be smoking a cigar in the long jade holder Stanford had given her, deep green as her eyes it was, and tipped in gold, and specially made for the slim Cuban cigars she puffed gently, never inhaling. In time Lily got to rather like the smelly things.

Being a celebrity was a new and uncomfortable role for her. From the earliest days Lily had forced herself to ignore men's stares when she went out in public. Now the stares were bolder, now they called her name, some of them even dared to run after her carriage or gallop beside her on their horses. Her name was public property now. It appeared, and the Fleur de Lis with it, in the local newspapers, usually as the object of revilement. The moral outrage of the pulp-paper press was always good for a few extra sales, and periodic drives to "clean up" San Francisco met with cynical amusement on the part of the police and city government, many of whose officials were friends and cash customers. San Francisco had ever been a wide-open town, and very tolerant, and no amount of muckraking seemed likely to change it. Still, as the proprietress of the town's fanciest parlor house, Lily was a natural target. "Satan's Handmaiden" they called her, and worse. The Fleur de Lis was a "gilded dovecote for soiled doves" or an "emporium of painted pleasures." Fergy merely laughed and kept the books and said it was good for business.

But Lily saw further than her own cashbox.

Lily could see a time when the fame of Lily Cigar might live to haunt her, and—worse—to bedevil Kate. This was why Lily remained ambivalent when little Katie called Mrs. Baker "Mama." The child called Lily "Aunt Lil," and loved her, but every time Lily looked down at Kate's small radiant face, nearly always smiling and filled with the wondrous discoveries that come every hour to a three-year-old, she could imagine a time when an older, unsmiling Kate learned the truth. And that was a moment that Lily feared more than death itself, a moment when the lurid fame of Lily Cigar might destroy all her happiness and maybe Kate's too.

So for the time being Lily was unable to face the thought of educating little Katie to the fact that she was her mother.

And Lily smiled in her red-damasked, gilt-mirrored parlor, and took her five-thousand-dollar clients upstairs and counted the hours until the beautiful, dangerous time when she could leave it all behind.

She fostered the legend even as she feared it, feared that it might grow of its own momentum, and keep on growing, that it might not be easy for Lily Malone to leave Lily Cigar behind.

Stanford Dickinson was a comfort. Her enormous price bothered him not at all, even though he continually made jokes about it, groaning as he peeled off the crisp five-hundred-dollar bills that his bank kept in ten-bill envelopes just for this purpose, always at the ready.

"You might," he said one morning, "at least let me run up an account here. Fergy does."

"You don't—I truly hope—go to bed with Fergy. In this department, Stanford, it's strictly cash-and-carry."

When he replied, there was an edge of desperation in his voice. "I love you, Lily Cigar. I loved you poor and I love you rich. And if it takes my last penny, I'll still need you, and if it were to be my last penny, I'd spend it on my Lily."

She looked at him to see if he was joking. But it was no joke. Their affair had leveled off these past few months. Lily was never quite sure he meant it when he'd asked her to marry him. And Stanford was still thoroughly married, however he carried on outside of his opulent house on Rincon Hill.

She turned to him, and reached out and touched his cheek. As always, after five in the afternoon, he needed a shave.

"You've been good to me, and you've been good for me, Stanford. I'll never forget that. Besides Sophie and Fergy, I truly have no friends."

"Have you ever been in love?"

"Once, long ago, I thought so. But nothing . . . nothing happened."

"He left you?"

Lily managed a small laugh. "I was a moon-struck girl then. It seems the devil of a time ago, truly a lifetime. I never really knew the lad. He was, maybe, a sort of idea of love."

"Could you love me?"

"I like you, Stanford. Is that not enough?"

"It's a long way from love."

"I'm a whore. I sell love. 'Tis not a fair question to ask of Lily Cigar, the notorious madam."

"And it's not a fair answer. You say you sell love. It isn't love you sell, Lily, it's a dream. They come here drunk on the myth of you, intoxicated by this famous beauty, this past mistress of all the arts of love. The town's filled with men who claim to know you—in every sense—who in fact have never set foot in the Fleur de Lis."

"More power to them, then: they know a bad bargain when they see it! What I give a man for five thousand he can get in five minutes for a dollar from any Chinese crib girl."

"Why must you slander yourself, my darling, when there are so many experts prepared to do it for you, and in print? If you think for one instant that what you're selling in the Fleur de Lis is simply your body—or anyone else's—you are badly mistaken. I think I said you're selling dreams here. Can you know what it means to a man—a man who's never known real love, except in the most brutal, animal sense? A man who has no woman of his own, or who finds himself married to some puritanical harpy who won't give him the time of day in bed, who lies stiff and dry as a sack of raisins, who resents his healthy desires, who literally drives him out of the bed, out of the house, and right up the hill to the Fleur de Lis? Can you begin to imagine what that man feels like when he walks into your fine rooms, and hears the music playing, and the laughter, sees the beautiful girls and knows that it's all for him, all for his pleasure? In a way, his is a very innocent dream, Lily. Making it come true is what you're selling, not some quick, dirty little transaction between the sheets."

"I know a bit about dreaming."

"I guess you do."

"The Fleur de Lis is only the doorway to my dream. When my dream truly begins, the Fleur de Lis—and all I have done here, and before—will end."

"And me? Will I end too, Lily, my Lily, my darling?"

He kissed her and she closed her eyes so that she would not have to look at him when she answered. "We will have to see about that, my dear, when the time comes. Won't we?"

Lily knew that she would never be able to give a true, fair answer to Stanford Dickinson, or to any other man, until she felt herself free, free of the Fleur de Lis, free of this hateful whoring, free from the blackmailing of odious bullies like Chief O'Meara. That day was coming, and soon, for now Lily felt her very life depended upon it, let alone her happiness. *If there ever will be happiness for me in this world.* There it lay, shining in the far distance, her freedom! But what she would be in that magical place, or how she would feel, Lily could not and would not say. And if that caused sorrow for Stanny D., he would have to bear it, for it was nothing to the sorrows she had borne for years, and still bore, every day and every night.

Lily slowly began to feel that her real life hadn't happened yet, that everything she had done and all that had happened to her were only a prologue, a catalog of events that had happened to someone else, another girl, and in another time. The orphan, the servant girl, Jack's mistress, whore—these were other people. The glamorous, wicked Lily Cigar was not the real Lily either. The real Lily had yet to be born, and the years up to now were only a preparation.

By thinking thus, Lily insulated herself from the reality of what she was doing, of how she appeared to the unsmiling eyes of the world. In the meantime, there was the Fleur de Lis to keep going, and Kate to love, and her growing concern about Fergus.

In the excitement of finding him again, Lily managed to forget what Fergy's character had been in the past, and to overlook some quite obvious failings that had grown into his personality as a man.

The first thing Lily saw in Fergy was his charm. If the devil was in him—and she often sensed that Fergy did give house room in his soul to dark forces—then they were devils of delight, devils who could charm the apples down from the tree. He'd grown into a fine-looking figure of a man, had her Fergy. Tall he was, and lean, and wide of shoulder and quick to smile. That smile could ever melt Lily's heart, and her brother seemed to know this instinctively. He used the smile like a weapon, and he used her love for him as a ticket on one long free ride to hell.

Fergy did what pleased Fergy, and all other considerations took second place, be they the business, his sister, or the laws of God, man, or nature.

Only slowly did Lily learn how much her brother was drinking. Fergy's capacity for whiskey and brandy and wine stretched far beyond Lily's comprehension. He almost never looked drunk or acted drunk. Yet Fergy put away glass after glass of straight bourbon whiskey, or champagne if the mood was on him, or brandy. Once Lily watched him drink half a bottle of whiskey before supper, the other half afterward, and two bottles of good French red wine in between, and never slur a word or stagger a step. His eyes would glaze a bit, and his words would come out slower. And in this condition, often as not, Fergus Malone ran the biggest gambling operation in California, the gaming parlors of the Fleur de Lis.

Drinking was a man's business, or so Lily saw it. For herself, she choked at the taste of anything stronger than wine, and she drank even wine sparingly, by sips, to be companionable. San Francisco was a hard-drinking town, and many a time had Lily seen grown men roaring drunk in the gutter at ten in the morning, in from the mining camps and on a spree, shooting and shouting and falling-down, sloppy drunk and not caring who knew or what became of them.

But Fergy's drinking was a quieter thing, more subtle, more poisonous in its effects. It affected his temper. Fergy was like sunshine itself most of the time, when sober. But when the whiskey got in him, he could turn nasty fast, and against anyone, even Lily herself.

She feared his anger, for anger might drive him away from her, and Lily felt she could not bear to have that happen, not now, not after the miracle of finding him alive and well again after all those years.

But the miracle had holes in it, and one of them was the whiskey. Lily smiled and chose not to mention his drinking, out of fear that, by mentioning it, she might inspire his temper, or even make him drink more out of spite.

For Fergus Malone was capable of spite.

In some ways, Lily discovered, he was exactly the same boy who'd run away from St. Patrick's orphanage. Fergy of the short-fused temper, Fergy who felt that the world owed him favors, Fergy whose attention span lasted for only as long as his own gratification could be fed by a situation.

How fine he'd been when they were first setting up the

Fleur de Lis! How quick his mind, what great leaps his imagination could take when a thing appealed to him the way the Fleur de Lis had.

And how very quickly he grew bored and restless again.

Lily soon realized why he had been such a wanderer, making trouble for himself and moving on.

She soon discovered that no misfortune was ever to be considered Fergy's fault. Fergy might have bad luck, the gods might conspire against him, but never, never did Fergy make a mistake or a miscalculation.

The strangest thing about the wild success of the Fleur de Lis was that Fergy couldn't deal with it. He was, Lily sometimes felt, too well used to failing.

When he was on top, and in a situation of his own devising, Fergy must find a way to stir the muck a little, to make things tough for himself. Like so many gamblers, Fergy wanted to discover new ways to lose.

There were many, and he tried them all.

It was in November that Lily first noticed something wrong with the books. Every month, like clockwork, they went over all their expenses, income, mortgage payments, salaries, the girls' share, everything that could affect the fiscal progress of the house.

Neither Lily nor Fergus took anything like a regular salary: they merely drew pocket money from the cashier, and little enough of that at first, since food, drink, and shelter all were provided, and extravagantly, by the Fleur de Lis.

When Fergy began dipping into the till, he didn't even think to hide it.

"Something's wrong here." Lily spoke half to herself as she looked at the ledger for October. "Last month we cleared eighty-two thousand six hundred and fifty-three dollars and change, and the month before that a bit more, and this month we're only ahead fifty-eight thousand and two hundred and something."

He answered too quickly. "Beats flensing whales, I can tell you."

"Fergy, we're off nearly thirty thousand. Something's wrong."

"So, it was a slow month."

"It was our busiest month ever."

She looked at him then. There was something in his voice that rang oddly in her ears. His back was turned to her. He stared out the office window. Lily felt the tension gathering in him. *Go softly, Lily, or you must surely lose him again.*

"Tell me, Fergy, for I'll find out anyway."

He turned, grinning. The grin melted as he saw its lack of effect. "Caught red-handed. I confess, my sweet Lily. I had a bad day at the tables."

"You took that much money—and lost it? Here? How could you lose to yourself?" Lily gasped, and paused for a moment, sickened, fearing for what she might say.

"Would that I had. Then at least it'd show up as profit. It was a private game, Lil. I'm sorry."

"Sorry be damned. You'll replace every penny of it. Fergy, that's cheating my little girl, and I won't have it. It's one thing to enjoy yourself. If you want to take money out of the business, for some good reason, then you have my blessing. But this! This is madness, Fergy. It must stop."

"Ah, Lily, you're a fair sight when the Irish comes bubblin' up in you. And can you not take pity on your poor idiot of a brother, who lost his head and is truly sorry for it? Sorrier, too, because he has made his Lily angry."

"This is a business, Fergy, and if we don't run it as a business, we'll end in the gutter. I've fought too hard, and sold myself too dear, to have you throw it all away with a toss of the damned dice or the turn of a damned card."

"Well, now, aren't we high and mighty? It's my business too, you know."

There was an edge to his voice now, and Lily could feel the anger in him. It was exactly the kind of scene she'd prayed to avoid. And still she would not back down. Lily had anger of her own, and if it came to the surface only seldom, it was no less the strong for that.

"This business is founded on my body, on my shame. That's what we sell here, Fergus Malone, don't ever forget it. You sell your own sister as though she were a black slave for the taking. There is no way to put a price on what I do or have done, and if you don't understand that, we had best part company now. The one hope and the one consolation I have is that someday soon I'll be able to put all this behind me, Fergy, and every penny you toss away postpones that day a bit longer. I won't have it, Fergy. I just . . . won't . . ."

Lily's words choked off in rage and suppressed tears.

Fergy came to her, and took her in his arms, and kissed her cheek. "Ah, there, there, Lil. This is your Fergy you're talkin' to, not some rascal off the streets. This is your Fergy who loves you, Lil, who wants all the best for you. I'm a poor excuse for a brother, Lil, well I know it, and an even poorer excuse for an uncle of that dear little girl out there.

[372]

But I do try, Lil, and I will try to be good, to be worthy of bein' your brother. And I'm sick with the shame of it, of taking your money and throwing it away. 'Twas plain criminal of me, I'm just good for nothing, nothing at all. Sometimes it gets so bad I just feel like going down to the harbor and . . . I don't know what all."

"Don't! Don't even think such a thing." There was panic in Lily's voice now, overriding her anger. He couldn't leave her! Not now and not ever. She clutched him like a drowning woman. "I understand, Fergy, really I do. It's just that I've got to get myself out of this life, and soon, and that means saving every last penny."

"We'll do that, Lil, and I will replace what I lost. You'll see. I'll be a whole new Fergy for you, if that's what you want."

Lily smiled, knowing he believed this, knowing it could never be true, and knowing too that an unreliable Fergy was much to be preferred over no Fergy at all.

"The old Fergy is just fine, thanks."

"I'll do better, as God is my witness."

"Let's not talk about it anymore."

"You'll see." He kissed her again, and left.

Lily sat looking at the door for a moment after Fergy passed through it, and it seemed as though every limestone block of the Fleur de Lis was bearing down on her with a crushing weight, a destructive pressure that she could never escape, twist though she may, scream though she might.

Fergy, dear brother, you'd sell me and gamble away the profits, and smile and do it all over again, knowing I'll love you anyway, and indeed I shall. But how long, how long, how long?

∞§ 30 §∞

The bitterness of the bleak December afternoon seemed to seep into the elegant drawing room on West Eleventh Street. A fire glowed and crackled in the black marble fireplace and the gas chandelier had been lit to ward off the early dusk. But Brooks Chaffee felt a chill deeper than winter as he read the article in the *Times*. Caroline, strangely silent, sat on a low bench near the fire holding a flower-painted teacup as if she had forgotten why it was in her hand.

Brooks began to read aloud. " 'I, John Brown, am not quite certain that the crimes of this guilty land will ever be purged away but with blood. I had, as I now think, mainly flattered myself that without very much bloodshed it might be done.' "

He sighed and folded the paper. Brown's desperate raid on the arsenal at Harpers Ferry, Virginia, in October had ignited all the worst suspicions in the fearful, hostile South. Brown's mad scheme to lead a slave revolt had failed, instantly suppressed by Robert E. Lee. In fact, only four men died in all of it. But the ripples spread, intensifying the fear, building the hatred, consolidating positions.

"His last words, the monster?" Caroline spoke softly, as one whose thoughts are far away.

"His last written words, found after they hanged him."

"After *we* hanged him."

"Yes, of course, we. Any word from your father?"

There was a gentle clink as Caroline Chaffee set down her untasted tea. "He won't do it, the fool. He won't sell out and come north. I guess I never really thought he would."

"But at the least, my darling, you tried."

"The news is worse and worse. The boys are coming home from college, the ones at Yale and Harvard and Dartmouth. They're even leaving West Point. They're getting themselves ready, Brooks. They are getting ready for blood."

"We all are."

"Well, I am not. I will never be ready for such a thing,

[374]

however inevitable it may be. To see the whole country calmly preparing to destroy itself over such nonsense, pretending it just has to happen, the way a rainstorm happens, I cannot credit such stupidity."

"War is always stupid, my darling."

"Then why, why must it happen? When we could all be living in peace, having a good time, being happy?"

"Are the slaves happy, Caroline?"

"I declare, there's more happy slaves than the wage slaves in your mills and factories!"

"Those wage slaves can come and go as they please, they can educate themselves, and no one sells them away from their wives, or children away from their parents."

She looked up at him and smiled. It was a small, thin smile but better than the gloom and tension it replaced. "I am a selfish old creature, forever thinking of myself and my loved ones, not clever and a philosopher like you men all seem to be, knowing all the answers as you do."

"I never claimed to know all the answers, my love."

"What I see when I read the newspapers is this: I see our old house in New Orleans in flames, my daddy ruined, bloodshed, and wickedness. I see my husband going off to the war, maybe not coming back. And for what? For what?"

"For a just cause. To preserve the Constitution. To free those slaves."

"All mischief is done in a just cause. The Confederacy is perfectly sure their cause is just, they are ready to die for it. And so's the Union, right as rain they are, all God's angels on their side. And I am in the middle, a simple woman, neither one nor the other. I hate it, Brooks, I hate it truly and deeply and with all my heart. It is destroying my life, this stupid war."

"We will survive this and worse. If it truly comes to fighting, it can't last, my dear. That's the plain sad fact of the matter. Those wicked mills you mentioned will keep right on working, long after the Confederacy has used up its last ounce of gunpowder, its last stitch of thread, its last length of railroad track."

"And in the meantime?"

"In the meantime life goes on." He came to her, bent, and kissed her cheek. "Love goes on."

She tossed her head impatiently, brushing off his kiss with it. "You men are so damned sure, aren't you? You have every little bit of it all worked out, as though life were some clockwork machine that only needs to be wound now and then, and oiled a little, and everything's just fine."

She stood up, and her dark eyes flashed with dangerous fire. "One day you may have reason to remember, dear Brooks, what I've said today. Life isn't as simple as you pretend to think: not politics nor love nor any of it."

She turned away from him and stormed out of the room. Brooks followed her with his eyes and with his heart but made no move in pursuit of her body. *How very right she is: life isn't simple, not at all, and especially not the parts that involve Caroline.* Such scenes as this one had been growing more frequent lately, and Brooks had no idea why. He could feel the sands of his life shifting underneath him, and felt helpless to make them more solid, try as he might. The coming war had made the poor girl nearly frantic with fear for her family and friends in the South—that was plain to see—but there was more to this new, restless mood in Caroline than mere politics. Brooks would have given his life to make her happy if only he knew how. He sighed and turned back to the newspaper, wondering for the hundredth time that week what he could do to bring back the girl he married.

The sea breeze felt delicious on Lily's face. She eased herself back against the bright blue-and-white-striped canvas pillows in the cockpit of Stanford Dickinson's new racing sloop and tried to clear her mind of all troublesome thoughts as they skimmed across San Francisco Bay in the bright sunlight of mid-April 1860. The sun caressed her, the wind was cool and clean, and Lily's mind danced like the waves, filled with excitement and bubbling with change. It was in the very air: all America seemed to be on edge as the presidential nominating conventions swung into action. And all San Francisco was thrilled with the success of the brand-new pony-express run, just ten days from St. Joseph, Missouri, to Sacramento! And Lily's private life was churning too. Stanford's sloop was whisking her across the bay to San Rafael to inspect a huge Mexican land-grant plantation that Stanford had located for her.

The old Velasquez hacienda it was, more than six thousand neglected acres rolling up from Tiburon to the hills, land gone to seed like the ancient family that owned it. The proud Velasquez clan had deteriorated to the point where the eldest, Tiberio, was a much-dreaded bandit with a price on his head—ten thousand dollars gold, dead or alive, for this killer, rapist, thief. Lily shuddered at the thought. The old place was in the hands of an aged uncle now, nearly senile, so Stanford said, whose only wish was to sell out and return to his beloved Seville to die. Lily thought of the land, and a new warmth filled her, for the land was what she wanted, with a deep and almost primitive longing. Even the neglect appealed to her, for there would be so much to do!

It had always been in Lily's mind to quit whoring the instant she had earned enough to support herself and little Katie. Now that time had come. In her brief career as the madam and mistress and half-owner of the Fleur de Lis, the Fleur de Lis had coined money. Lily had banked nearly every penny of her own fees, plus half of the earnings of the other girls. Now more than half a million dollars sat in her account at Wells Fargo, earning enough interest to keep them in comfort. And when they sold the place, it would bring big money—millions, probably. And the farm itself would generate a living after a time, for Lily intended to do the most serious and up-to-date kind of farming, and fresh produce ever brought a premium price in San Francisco.

I will come here away from the scorn of the town, thought Lily as the Tiburon shore drew nearer. *I will come here away from the dangerous looks in the eyes of men and the revulsion in the eyes of their women. I'll come here with Katie, and we'll make a whole new world, all our own, where we will be happy all our days and all our nights forever.*

The slender bow of Stanford's new plaything headed directly north across the choppy bay, cutting the waves like butter.

The wind defied the encircling hills, and Lily had the feel of adventure again. It was almost like being back on board the *Eurydice*. Almost, but what a difference! What a poor, thin, frightened creature she'd been then, Jack Wallingford's hush money burning a hole in her pocket and in her soul, a girl filled with subtle dreads and unformed hopes.

She could look back on that other Lily now and smile indulgently.

But it had been dicey. It had been a very narrow thing, the fine sharp-honed edge between life and death, between good luck and bad. *I had so little to lose, and gained so much.*

It was a big sloop, and Stanford had two crewmen to help him sail her. He'd wanted to name her the *Lily,* but Lily would have none of that.

She looked back over her shoulder to the seven hills of San Francisco. The nearest was Rincon Hill, and on it, squatting proudly like some fat king, was the big gray-shingled, white-trimmed mansion that Stanford had built for his wife. *Mamie Dickinson's probably up there right now with a spyglass or— more likely!—a mortar or a cannon.* Mamie Dickinson, self-appointed doyenne of San Francisco society, moral avenger of all the affronted matrons whose dignity was threatened by Lily and her kind. Mamie Dickinson, whose lofty moral position would not earn her the love of the man she married, nor grow the missing chin. Lily had long since left off fretting about the Mamie Dickinsons of the world, for nothing they could say or do could make her feel more shame or regret than she felt already.

The sloop edged in past Sausalito and entered the small harbor at Tiburon. A horse-drawn trap, she knew, would meet them there and drive them the eight or so miles north to the hacienda where Diego Velasquez waited.

It was scrubby land for the main part, hills laced with sand and low bushes, just like the San Francisco side of the bay. But once the rickety trap hauled them up over the first low hills, the character of the landscape changed, and for the better.

The land here was uncultivated still, as Lily knew it would be. But the richness of it was obvious in the green of the wild grasses and the luxuriance of the live oaks and pines and eucalyptus groves with their strange spicy aroma. How empty it all was, and wild. And how very promising.

They trotted past a rude stone marker. "The hacienda," Stanford said, pointing to the marker, "starts about here."

Lily said nothing, but felt a quickening in her pulse, a flush on her cheek. *Sure, it's not much to look at the way it is, but what it can be!*

They drove for two hours on a dirt track through emptiness before the first decaying outbuildings announced the existence of the ranch itself. It took Lily's breath away, first for the splendor of the setting, then for the sad state of ruin that had come on the beautiful old buildings.

Adobe lasts almost forever if it is properly kept up and continually whitewashed and mended. What Lily saw at the old Velasquez place was a near-ruin. Roofless sheds might once have held chickens or small animals. A very large stable, a long colonnade of big arches, all but three of them in ruins now, and stalls for fifty horses.

"Pure Arabians, they were," said Stanford. "They moved like the wind itself, Lily, and were priceless. Or, at any rate, the old man would never sell them, just kept them for his own pleasure."

"How did he lose it?"

"The same old story. A fine proud man, but never a businessman. Never had to be. Thought the money would just go on forever, as it always had done. But then everything went bad for the Velasquez family. The old man's brother—older brother—who was the rightful heir, got himself killed in a duel. The son ran off and came to no good, worse than no good—Tiberio's a menace, a real killer, not just another wild kid. And it all fell to old Tio Diego, who wasn't ready to handle the situation. So it's mortgaged now, and in bad repair, just look around you, and he's sold off the Arabians, what few were left, and some of the furniture, and now all he wants is to go back to Spain and forget all this."

"As if you could have all this and just forget it. Poor man."

"He may not be so poor after he gets finished with you, my dear."

"I'll pay fair."

"I'm sure you will, and in gold."

"Is it his to sell? Doesn't the son—the bandit—have some right to the place?"

"Tiberio Velasquez is wanted for five murders at the very least, Lily. He has no rights whatsoever, under Mexican law or our own. And now that we're a state, officially, there can be no problem about that."

Lily had too much Irish in her, and too intimate an acquaintance with the fickleness of luck, to believe that this land and all it represented could ever truly be hers. She would try, and make a fair offer, but to own these hills, this house, that piece of sky? Heaven itself could offer no better, for truly the Velasquez place was a heaven on earth, or could be. She paused for a moment, soaking up the stillness, letting her eyes wander over the hills with a building desire, a need so intense it scared her. *I look at these hills as though they were Brooks Chaffee himself, for aren't they a dream, too, just as much as he was?* But even as she thought it, Lily knew that this part of her dream was attainable, to own this land or some land like it, whereas her feeling for Brooks had no more reality than a sunbeam, to warm her heart in the flash of an instant, then vanish forever with the first passing cloud.

When she spoke, it was in a reverent whisper. "The land is very beautiful."

The Velasquez hacienda's main house was in slightly better condition than its outbuildings, but the house was still a pathetic ghost of what it must once have been. Just looking at the missing roof tiles, the sagging balconies, the door that didn't hang quite straight, and the windows carelessly patched with wood where glass had once been made Lily sad for the old man who'd struggled for years to keep the place together.

Nothing stirred in the dusty courtyard as they climbed down from the trap.

Stanford knocked with the huge black iron knocker that made the ancient door rattle on its hinges.

There was total silence for a few minutes. A dog barked, high on the hill behind the main house. They could hear the wind conversing with the trees. There was a shuffling sound, then a grating, creaking noise as a rusty bolt slid painfully out of its hole. The door opened slowly, by fractions of inches, to reveal a tiny white-haired man, beautifully dressed in a style that Lily had seen once or twice in old pictures. The man bowed graciously, smiled a vague, unfocused smile, and beckoned them to come in. They followed him in silence. The front door opened onto a large reception hall that stood absolutely empty, two stories tall, flanked by a double staircase in heavily turned dark wood. The floor was pale terracotta tiles, their edges softened by time, still faintly gleaming in the shaded light. It was a mournful sight, but beautiful. Lily could instantly see what might be made of such a fine space, given some new paint and sunlight and the proper furnishings. Immediately she imagined little Kate playing here. It would be a palace to Kate after the tiny Baker farmhouse. Indeed, it seemed a palace to Lily herself.

The tiny man led them down a dark hallway paved with the same soft tiles. Then he stopped, bowed, and directed them toward a library whose door stood open.

It was a large, high-ceilinged room lined with dark bookshelves. The shelves were all empty, and so was the room, but for one huge trestle table that obviously served as a desk. Behind this desk was a great high-backed chair covered in fraying brocade. In the chair was a man. He was every bit as small as his servant, and equally distinguished-looking. In fact, Lily thought with a sudden irrepressible mirth, they could have been brothers. The little man nodded and gestured for them to sit down in the two primitive chairs that were the room's only other furniture.

"*Buenas tardes, Señor Dickinson, señora.*" His voice was like a whisper from the past, a ghost's voice.

Stanford carried on the conversation in fluent Spanish, for Lily herself had only a few words of that soft tongue. They talked, and Stanford nodded wisely, and the old man produced a document that was both a map and a deed, very old it was, hundreds of years old, and drawn on yellowed parchment, sealed with deep green wax, tied with a ribbon that must once have been red. It was the original land grant, signed by the king of Spain! There was more talk, more nodding and smiling, more questions. After about forty-five minutes that seemed like a week, Lily found herself agreeing to purchase 6,783 acres, all of the original Velasquez grant, for one hundred thousand dollars. Subject, naturally, to certification by the proper authorities in the county and in San Francisco.

It was over in an instant, this great, enormous deed that would change Lily's life forever. Stanford wrote a few words in Spanish, the old man signed underneath them, and then Lily. A letter of agreement, prior to signing the actual transfer of deed. But Lily knew that this was the crucial document, for the old man's word was implacably good. She signed effortlessly, then looked down at the little paper and felt herself trembling. It was happening, then! No angels sang, nor devils appeared in puffs of smoke. Yet with this simple stroke of her pen Lily certified all the dreams that had carried her through the pain and inner shame of the last few years. She could never erase the Fleur de Lis, nor Sophie's house, nor Jack Wallingford's bedroom in the mansion on Fifth Avenue. But somehow, with this paper, on this great ranch, Lily felt for the first time in all her life that her fate was in her own hands at last. It was a feeling so new and awesome that she had no concept of how to deal with it.

She looked at Stanford as if seeing him for the first time, and smiled. He reached out and squeezed her hand. She turned her eyes to the old man; he, too, nodded slightly, a nobleman's gesture of recognition, and he smiled.

There was a slithering noise behind them then, and the old servant glided into the room with a small silver tray. On the tray were three glasses of rare old sherry. None of the glasses matched, but each was very fine.

The old man lifted his glass. *"Salud. Y buena suerte, Señora Lily."*

"Gracias," she replied, smiling, for Lily caught the twinkle in the old man's eye, and thought: *Why, the old devil knows precisely who I am, and thinks it's funny. And I'll bet anything he was quite the ladies' man in his day.* She sipped her sherry, which was soft and mellow as old satin.

As they drove back to Tiburon, Lily could scarcely believe her luck. She had left the old man a bank draft for a deposit, and he had given her the land-grant deed. There would be weeks of detail work before the thing was truly official, but Stanford had assured her that Diego was absolutely a man of his word, and everything she had seen at the hacienda led her to agree.

"Look," said Stanford, pointing to the far hills. "It's all yours, Lily. Lily's hills, Lily's valleys, trees, house . . ."

"Don't, pray, forget Lily's sky and God and all his angels, Stanford. After all, I don't own the place yet."

"But aren't you pleased?"

"Pleased hardly covers it. 'Overjoyed,' that might do. It's what I have wanted all these years, to the bottom of my heart. It's a new life for me, and I count the hours until it begins for real."

≈§ 31 §≈

Lily's life dissolved into a frenzy of planning. It was only the good counsel of Stanford Dickinson that kept her from selling out of the Fleur de Lis at once and moving onto the ranch. He reasoned with her, and she saw the sense in what he said: the ranch buildings must first be restored, an overseer found, workers hired, land cleared, plantings considered. It would be at least a year before the place was even habitable. And perhaps another year before the ranch was a going concern. Stanford advised her to wait until then.

Still, Lily burned for it and rushed as best she could to speed the day when she could leave the Fleur de Lis forever. Lily went out to the Baker farm and made Fred and Mary a handsome offer, for she liked them well, and having Fred as her overseer would make the transition easier for Katie. Lily offered Fred a generous salary and five percent of all profits. He accepted on the spot, and Lily felt the world could hardly contain her happiness.

Lily looked at the Fleur de Lis as her prison now, and if it was a prison of her own devising, knowing this diminished her desire to escape it not one whit. She took no customers now, but for Stanford, and this from gratitude, and at Stanford's suggestion found an accountant named Rufus Holden to manage the books of the Fleur de Lis and to keep an eye on Fergy. Subtle feelers were put out regarding the possibility of selling the Fleur de Lis, and here, too, Lily accepted Stanford's advice, to bide her time and hold out for the best price. Still, she paced the floors and counted the hours. Stanford's sloop was put into such regular service, ferrying Lily back and forth across the bay, that he jokingly called it "Lily's Navy," and Lily herself began considering the purchase of some sort of boat. Malone Produce, Incorporated, was now a fact, all properly drawn up and witnessed. Fergy laughed at her suggestion that he come in as a partner, but Lily made one in any case, for blood was blood and Fergy was all she had in this world besides Kate.

Her visits with Katie were touched with a special poignance now. The girl was four, bright as a penny, and convinced the Bakers were her parents. Katie was happy, and healthy, and seemed to love Aunt Lily, and this was enough for the moment. *God in heaven knows I did what I could, and soon will do more,* Lily told herself, watching the child, *but it won't be an easy thing, telling her the truth, when the time comes, and if she ever finds out what I have been, that may be the end of it.*

Lily's withdrawal from active whoring only served to feed the growing legend of the fabulous Lily Cigar. A silver king offered her fifty thousand dollars for one night, and she refused, and before dawn the fifty had grown in rumor to a hundred, and another facet had been added to the glittering myth, unasked for, unwanted, but always present, looming like a thundercloud over all her plans. For some time now Lily had gone out into the town only seldom, hating as she did the unabashed desire in the stares of the men and the open scorn of the respectable ladies. Shopkeepers sent things to her at the Fleur de Lis, dressmakers came, and she still sewed for herself from time to time. She went out with Stanford and to see Katie, and now, to the ranch. But the simple pleasure of stepping out of her own front door for a breath of air was all but unknown to Lily, and she longed for the freedom she knew she must find on her own little kingdom across the bay.

In the meantime, the Bakers and Katie were living on the new ranch, and work was going forward quickly. *Soon,* Lily prayed with every passing day, *please, God, let it be soon!*

The smile came hard to Brooks Chaffee's handsome face. It wasn't his style to fake emotions, but he did it now as he walked down the blue-carpeted, mahogany-railed stairs of his town house on West Eleventh Street in New York. At the bottom of the stairs was the drawing room, and in it was a large and brilliantly decorated Christmas tree. And Caroline. Caroline would be there, gowned in the very height of fashion, her skin glowing, her eyes sparkling, the ruby pendant he'd given her for their anniversary making a spot of fire against the creamy skin of her bosom. As if more fire were needed, when it came to him and Caroline!

But something was wrong this Christmas of 1860, and Brooks wasn't sure what it was, or how to make it better.

So he fixed a smile on his face and entered the drawing room and kissed Caroline as she stood by the fire, rearranging an ornament on the black marble mantelpiece.

"You are looking very damn beautiful, Caroline."

She half-turned her fine dark head, laughing. "It's the company I keep."

"How many are we expecting?"

Caroline was giving one of her famous little suppers, sparkling, witty, glamorous occasions at which her husband sometimes felt a bit like part of the furniture, so little did he have in common with her fast-living artistic crowd.

"An even dozen. So many people must be with their families this time of year."

"Speaking of this time of year, Merry Christmas, my darling."

He handed her the little box, plain blue leather, unwrapped. Caroline said nothing, but took the thing and opened it. Her eyes said it all. It was a dull gold ring set with one large cabochon ruby surrounded by small pavé diamonds, a drop of blood on a lake of ice. She slipped it onto her finger, smiled, and kissed him again.

"You are too kind, Mr. Rich Banker, husband of my heart."

"Impossible to be too kind to the likes of you, my angel!"

Caroline held the jewel out, turning her slender white hand this way and that to make the ruby and its attendant diamonds catch the light. "It's lovely, Brooks. Just lovely."

Still, there was a distance in her voice. Her thoughts were not in this room, Brooks realized, and why should they be? Abraham Lincoln had been elected just over one month ago, and already the country was in flames. Just as Caroline had been among the first to predict. Deep in Carolina, Fort Sumter and Fort Moultrie were in imminent peril from the secessionist troops of South Carolina. And the news from Caroline's own family, what was left of it, in New Orleans, was spotty, for the mails had suffered along with every other form of communication. There was talk—and maybe more than just talk—of blockades soon to come. Suddenly the sound of drumbeats was being heard in the land, and young men were appearing in uniforms that shocked the peaceful eye with their quick splendor, their air of instant gallantry.

And still there were complacent voices, the droning of men who refused to take any of it seriously, who were comfortably oblivious of the fact that the Union, less than one hundred years old, was in immediate and deadly peril. *They'll never dare.* That was part of the conventional wisdom, and the other part was: *It could never last; even if they do declare war, it'll all be over in a few weeks.*

Sometimes Brooks thought he might be losing his mind, to see what he saw, and feel what he felt, the abyss gaping just underfoot, and to be alone in seeing it.

Caroline had changed.

Caroline spoke of politics no more. Caroline was merry, Caroline entered upon a round of social activity that left all New York gasping, such was its energy, such was her sparkle. But it was a desperate, feverish sparkle, and Brooks sensed this without knowing what to do to ease her worry. How could he placate Caroline, when he was so deeply plagued by his own doubts and fears? To the world, Caroline was the star in an especially lovely firmament, beautiful and witty and clever in all she did. To Brooks, there was a growing sense of loss, a feeling that he was somehow failing the girl, losing touch. The ruby in the ring was bigger than it needed to be, and the very size and richness of it was a kind of admission of failure on his part. It was a strange, haunting failure, made all the sadder by the fact that there was no one fact or incident that he could put his hand on and say: "This is where I went wrong, that's what I must do to make it all right again."

For it had been all right, Brooks was sure of that. And very lately, too. He took her hand in the dim, rich room, and for just that moment Brooks Chaffee felt like a little boy once more, lost and afraid of whatever might happen next, terrified that the bottom of this world might drop out from underneath him the way the trap is sprung for a hanged man. The warmth of her hand comforted him, and the dark unfathomable secrets in Caroline's eyes seemed to be retreating now.

They stood like that, in companionable silence.

The fire crackled, and the big old clock that Grandmother Chaffee had brought from London in 1762 ticked eloquently in the twilight.

Then the doorbell rang, and Brooks could hear a muffled sound of laughter.

For Lily, all the best hours of her life were the ones that she enjoyed at the ranch. The new year came, and the war was coming with it. But while Lily hated the very thought of war—any war, no matter who was wrong or right—her thoughts and her energy and the very considerable force of her bank account were now all focused on Malone Produce, Inc., and the dramatic changes she was working on the former Velasquez grant in San Rafael in the hills across the bay.

And dramatic they were.

Fred Baker was working out better than Lily had dared hope. Already, despite a severe shortage of skilled farm labor, Fred had put together a good working crew, fifteen men, some skilled, some willing to learn. They were clearing some of the land now, and in early spring they'd plant. And the restoration of the main house was moving forward too, although quite slowly, for the place was truly a ruin and Lily wanted it perfect, this fine old house that would soon become her only home. The whitewash must sparkle, and the dark wood gleam. The crumbling stables must be recreated, with new stalls for dozens of horses, and pipes for water, and a huge new water tank high on the nearest hill so that the whole ranch might have running water, even the bunkhouse and the stables themselves. A right showplace it would be, but above all a working farm, horse breeding and cattle grazing and hundreds upon hundreds of acres of vegetables for the growing San Francisco market.

Lily and Fred Baker became addicted to the seed catalogs that came with nearly every pony-express delivery. Carrots they'd have, and lettuce, beans and tomatoes and cauliflower. And orchards! Apples. Maybe lemons. Pears, surely.

Lily looked at her scrubby hills and saw clouds of fruit-tree blossoms, looked down her valleys and envisioned neat rows of cabbage, lettuce, possibly asparagus. The earth itself seemed to thank her, and the sun, for everything in these golden hills was pregnant with the possibility of growth. Lily learned to ride, and with Fred she'd spend long afternoons exploring the huge place, riding for miles and miles, seeing no living thing but for the odd startled jackrabbit, soaring hawk, shy deer. She learned to love the silence of it, the wind murmuring, the resonant percussion of their horses' hooves, a neighing, deep intake of stallion breath. Fred, blessedly, spoke only when he had a thing to say.

Lily came to realize that the ranch meant a new and happier future for Fred Baker, almost as much as it did for her. He had done well, the best one man could, with his little place in San Mateo. But not so well that he was above taking in a foster child, nor so well that he could afford to buy more land or hire more hands.

Lily had made all of these things possible to Fred, and in one fell act, on the wings of her ill-gotten gains, the wages of sin. *Well*, she told herself, *let who will call it sin, it's wages all the same, and I'm going to make the most of them or die doing it!*

The parlors of the Fleur de Lis were often half-filled with

tense young men in dark blue uniforms now, dripping gold braid and gallantry, talking in half-poetic terms about the great conflict to come, and how they'd carry the noble Union cause into the very mouth of hell itself if necessary, right to the front door of that devil incarnate, old Jeff Davis. And hang him from that sour-apple tree, as the song went. And Lily would smile and agree, but her mind would be twenty miles away, across the cold swift currents of the bay, high in her golden hills, thinking about turnips. The contrast often made her laugh: to behold a gilded whore in satin, sipping French wine and smoking a slim cigar in Stanny D.'s jade holder, while her most lustful thoughts dwelt upon the subtle differences between McIntosh and Northern Spy apples, or a new French hybrid grape she'd read about in a British journal.

One day, and for no special reason, Stanford brought her flowers, always a great luxury in San Francisco, and Lily found herself thinking even as she thanked him: *Surely flowers could become a fine cash crop for us, and easier in some ways to raise than vegetables, with less digging.* She put them in a vase and made a mental note to discuss the prospect with Fred tomorrow.

The weeks passed. Spring this year meant more to Lily than any spring she could remember. The new leaves and the sudden astonishing deep yellow flags of the wild poppies dancing over the hills—her hills!—were a signal to Lily more urgent and more profound than the mere passing of time.

She learned just after her twenty-fourth birthday that the Confederacy had declared the existence of a state of war between it and the United States. But another, more significant event happened at almost exactly the same time.

Fred Baker and his men began a small spring planting. The war was a distant rumbling and showed every sign of remaining so, for surely the actual fighting could never come this far west, surely California was well and firmly committed to the Union cause, there was no need or desire for slaves here! And some of the young men enlisted, for the patriotic fever was contagious. There were California brigades, and the color and dash of uniforms, and now and again a parade, with brass and drums and bunting. But it all seemed a showpiece. It was hard to believe that those gleaming sabers, so proudly worn, would ever draw blood, or the rifles kill, or the gallant young men in blue fail to come home again.

The ports of all the South might be blockaded, but the way around the Horn was free and clear, and no one seemed about to stop the trade routes overland. Lily's seeds from England would come on schedule, and go into the land on schedule, and if God smiled, there would be a harvest, and maybe two, before this year was out.

So Lily watched her new-plowed fields begin to sprout and grow under the careful hands of Fred Baker. And she watched Kate grow too, nearing five now, and still in happy ignorance of her birth.

Somehow the war brought on a new burst of romantic ardor in Stanford Dickinson.

He had talked of joining, of taking command of some regiment or other, but Lily sensed his heart wasn't in it. At forty-two, the man was simply restless. Stanford was ever a very physical man, roaring with unspent energy, always wanting to be in the place he was not, pacing floors, urging his fastest horses even faster toward no goal in particular, and giving off sparks of an almost electric force even when sitting still.

They were on horseback, high on a hill overlooking the soft brown of Lily's new-plowed fields, fields just beginning to be dappled with the gentle green of tender new carrot tops and the darker thrust of bean vines.

Stanford reached for her hand: they were that close. "Lily's kingdom. It's beautiful, Lil, nearly as beautiful as its owner."

"Go on with you," she said, pleased that he saw progress, brushing back a vagrant strand of red-gold hair that had tumbled out from under the black wide-brimmed Mexican horseman's hat she wore to shield her eyes from the brilliant June sunshine. "Lily the whore is exchanging all her finery for a fine new threshing machine from England, and then we'll have wheat, Stanny. I'm a simple farming woman more and more, and don't forget it."

"Marry me."

He said it rather than asked it, and the words came out so smooth and sudden that Lily thought she'd misheard him.

"Do what?"

"Marry me. Become my wife."

"That's not funny."

"I don't mean it funny. I mean to say I love you, Lily. I guess I always have loved you."

He had talked of marriage before, but Lily had never taken it seriously. She sat for a moment in silence, thinking how she might have reacted only a few years ago, had he—or anyone else as rich and respectable and passionate as Stanford—asked her such a question, meaning it. The hill they were riding on was high enough to see the length of Lily's ranch, the hills growing gentler and diminishing in size as they spread out and down toward the bay. Just one flash of white against the rich greens of the land signaled the stables, freshly whitewashed, waiting for the shipment of purebred horses that Fred told her was due any moment now. And beyond the stables, more land reached for the restless blue bay, much of it her land. And beyond the bay, the city struggled up its seven hills. On one of those hills, invisible in the distance but solid as any rock in the hard reality of Lily's brain, was another woman, sad perhaps and bitter, but very real and wearing the name "Mrs. Stanford Dickinson" along with her expression of almost perpetual disapproval.

Lily extracted her hand from his and gestured toward the city. "And her?"

Stanford's eyes followed Lily's hand. She did not have to tell him who "her" was. "I'll ask for a divorce. It doesn't take so very long."

Lily laughed then, and hoped it didn't sound too cruel. "One reason I'm so fond of you, Stanny D., is that there's not a drop of bitterness in all your body or soul."

"What is that supposed to mean?"

"It means that she'd die first. Before giving you your freedom. I'd bet anything on that—this ranch even."

"She would be very well-off."

"As well-off as she is now? What has she to gain but the burden of having been rejected? It isn't easy to be left, Stanford. And no matter how just it might or might not be from where you sit, the pain's none the less. To be cast off, tossed aside—money can't buy the cure for that hurt, for it cuts too deep. Deep as a woman's heart."

"You're too young, Lily, and far too lovely to know that much about being cast off. Who in their right mind could ever leave you?"

She closed her eyes for just a moment, but it was a moment long enough to remember everyone who had ever meant something to her, and then left. The list was a long one and heartbreaking, for it included both her parents, and Fergy as a child—and for all she knew, Fergy as a man, too. For wasn't he always in danger of slipping away from her yet again? And Lily's list went on, for Jack Wallingford was on it, who had left her by sending her away, and Brooks Chaffee, although the poor lad could never know it. And Luke had left her maybe at the worst time of all, Luke with his golden hair and his promises. And his bag of gold nuggets on the table in the empty room.

Lily opened her eyes quickly, and soothed the horse, which had begun to paw the earth. She looked at her friend—and lover, mentor, protector—and smiled a thin sad smile.

"Ah, Stanny, thank you, but I couldn't. Even if it were possible, it would not be fair, not to either of us. For you deserve better, and I . . . well, I don't know what I deserve. Eternal damnation for my sins, more likely than not."

"You are the only woman I have ever loved."

Lily's eyes met his. *How well I know these eyes,* she thought, *and yet 'tis little enough I know of the man behind them, for haven't I accepted his help and his kindness and his money all these years, and given him—what?—in return.* In the deepest and most private recesses of her soul Lily felt that she had forfeited the right to love, to being loved by a man, and the words fell strangely on her ears, and stranger still was the recognition that Stanford Dickinson meant exactly what he said. Lily felt a great sadnes then, an overwhelming sense of loss, not for losing the love of this particular man, but for trading the right to love any man for her daughter's future security, and her own.

She reached out to him and touched his arm. "Oh, Stanford!"

He repeated himself, in a low steady tone, looking out beyond her now, out over the hills to the sea. It was as though he were talking to himself, and sadly. "You are the only woman I have ever loved."

There was a dull edge on his voice as he said this, and somehow Lily knew that this moment was a very important one for Stanford, a moment that might never come again, for usually he was all hearty good cheer, not at all a man to reveal the secret depths of his soul, not even to the woman he so convincingly claimed to love. The years of whoring had taught Lily many things about maneuvering the emotions of men. It was so very easy that she disdained to do it. Yet surely it could be done: the well-timed smile, the half-hidden tear, the lightest touch, the gentlest whisper of a suggestion—all had more force than bullets or screaming. She thought, instantly and instinctively: *Right now, right in this moment and on this hill, I could make him do anything, anything at all. If Mamie won't give him a divorce, he'd probably even kill her for me. The things people do for love!* Just thinking such thoughts frightened her profoundly. Lily reached out and touched his cheek. "I would give anything I have to be able to say the same thing to you, Stanford, but I cannot, and no more could I deceive you. Will you not have me for a friend?"

He laughed, a sudden startling laugh that might have been half a sob. "I'd have you any way I could get you, Lily, don't you know that? Do you think it's been easy for me all these years, paying your price, knowing when I wasn't with you someone else was?"

"I'm sorry, then. Surely I never pretended to be a nun. Men who use whores, Stanford, must accept that they *are* whores, and accept who helped them get that way. It does take two."

He sighed so softly that it might have been the wind making love to the pine trees nearby. "At least you're dead-honest, Lil, and ever have been."

"Which is not easy."

"I guess not. There's women in plenty who'd kill to get an offer like that from Stanford Dickinson."

"He said modestly."

"Don't mock me, Lily."

"Ah, Stanny, I'd never do that, not really. If life were fair, all donkeys would fly, and isn't that the truth?"

"You won't consider me at all, then?"

"Not as a husband. You said I'm honest. Well, at the least I try to be. And that would not be an honest thing, Stanford, not by any measure."

He laughed for sure then, deep and hearty and loud enough to startle up a fat mother quail from some brush nearby. "I am high on a hill in the bawdiest state in the wickedest country in the world, being lectured on truthfulness by a whore!"

"And well you should be, since it seems to be news to you."

The laughter died the death it deserved, a quick one. "I love you, Lily Cigar," he said flatly, "and I will probably always love you. But never again will I pay your price. Some things are too expensive."

Lily turned to him as she might turn to a wounded animal. "Some things," she said gently, "can never be bought."

Then she kicked her spirited horse to a sudden gallop and rode off down the hill ahead of him.

And as she galloped and felt the horse surging to the challenge of it, and the wind rippling past her, losing herself in the thunder of hooves and the sheer excitement of the ride, Lily knew that something had changed on that hill, permanently and irrevocably. Whatever Stanford had been to her—and he had been many things, important things—he would now be cast in a different role, and by her own choosing. *Is it because I don't truly need him, because his money means so little to me now I've got money of my own, and land, and plans for it?* But Lily knew that her quick decision had been based on something deeper and more solid than that. *If I don't love him, then whom could I love?* She thought of a time long ago, many lifetimes ago, or so it seemed, and she saw a fine golden head and a face that matched it, and a smile that would make the sun itself go into hiding. And all this seemed a dream. Maybe it had been a dream, and maybe she ought to forget it, as most dreams are best forgotten lest they shatter against the unyielding surfaces of life in the real world. But Lily's dream was a persistent one, and she knew that however seldom it might come and however small the chances of its ever coming true, it would never go away completely.

She urged her horse to run faster, and thrilled to the sound of Stanford's mount receding into the distance.

And what was love anyway, that people made such a fuss about it?

For a man to pay five thousand dollars for one night with Lily Cigar, for another man to offer ten times that and be refused! That was real madness, and they called it *selling love*. But no, it most certainly was not love that demanded and received such prices. Sophie Delage had named the thing, defined it, and time had proved her right: *"It's the idea of love you're selling, the dream of a thing that maybe never happened."* Well enough. But for herself, Lily had another kind of dream, another kind of love. And that love was for this very earth flying under the horse's hooves, and what would grow out of it, and the life it would bring them all: to Kate, to the Baker family, and to Lily herself. And in that moment Lily realized the time had come for her to leave the Fleur de Lis forever. She smiled a welcoming smile at that thought, and urged the horse on ever faster.

≈§ 32 §≈

The tissue paper crinkled merrily as Brooks Chaffee opened the paperboard boxes lately come from his tailor. But the mood in the house on West Eleventh Street was anything but merry.

Caroline stood in the window of their bedroom on the third floor, gazing pointedly at nothing in particular. Brooks often came upon her thus, these days, looking into the far distance as though she expected a message that the horror they were living through was all some practical joke that had gone too far.

But the message had never come, and the tension in their marriage had deepened as the war careened down its gruesome course toward what outcome they could only guess.

Brooks was ashamed at being so late to enlist. It had been his own damned indecisiveness, his sensitivity to the pain Caroline must feel, the isolation of a Southern girl trapped here in New York, her soul wounded with every anti-Confederate headline, for all her many Northern friends, for all the splendor of her marriage to a Chaffee. Brooks sighed, slipped off his suit coat of bankerly gray, and pulled on the custom-made British broadcloth of his second lieutenant's deep blue jacket trimmed with gold.

He stepped up behind his wife and put his arms around her. Caroline shuddered, as if a sudden chill had forced its way into the cozy apple-green and pink and ivory room.

Finally she regained control of herself, turned in his arms, looked up, and made herself smile.

He could see the effort in it but thanked her in his heart at least for trying.

"It has always been a good color on you, Brooks, dark blue."

"I'm glad, at least, they've cut out that Zouave nonsense, with the baggy red trousers and all."

"The rebels loved them, I hear: they made such fine targets."

"It was all a game then, and just a year ago."

"Centuries ago, my darling, aeons."

"At least I'll be with Neddy."

"Yes. I daresay you'll see more of him in the army than you ever did in town."

"If the good general can spare his brightest aide."

"The good general's a moron, Brooks, unpatriotic though it may be for me to suggest it."

Her eyes glittered with a faint unfocused mockery. Brooks knew it wasn't directed at him particularly, but rather at the massive ironies fate had been throwing at his bride these last few years. Still and all, the bitterness was not a pretty thing to see, nor to live with. He held her tighter, as though by doing this he might squeeze the sweet poisons right out of her.

"Neddy wrote Dad—in great secrecy—that McClellan's sure to be replaced."

She laughed, but it was not a happy sound. "Y'all just betta be keerful, Yankee boy," she said, deepening her gentle drawl into something out of a minstrel performance, "for y'all's talkin' to a Confed'rate gal shonuff, an' honey, you just never can tell who I might tittle-tattle to."

He kissed her cheek, and she instinctively turned away from his lips.

"Please, Brooks."

"Please what?"

"Please don't remind me of how lonely I'm going to be this time tomorrow."

"My darling. I know how terrible it is, and that it must be even worse for you than . . . most people we know. But I must do what I must do. I've waited too long as it is. If we can't please ourselves, my darling, then how can we please anyone else?"

"Ah, you've finally said it! To *please* yourself. As though this were some matter of which dessert to order at Delmonico's, or whether to go to this play or that opera. You don't have to go, Brooks, and well you know it. You could just buy out like Jack Wallingford did."

"Jack's a good fellow in many ways, my dear, and Jack has to live with himself the rest of his life. Just as I must live all my life with my conscience. Can't you see that?"

"I can see you dead. Which means I might as well be in the grave with you, I guess, just like that. Two birds with one stone."

"If I don't do what my heart knows is right, then just as

[395]

well might I be dead, even though I'd be walking around, for it's dead I would be inside, and that's where it counts."

He released her then, and slipped off the uniform and hung it in his closet. Tomorrow he'd be wearing the damned thing in earnest. Tomorrow they marched off to join McClellan's army somewhere in Maryland. *Maryland, by God!* That was inches away from Pennsylvania. The rebs were really giving them what-for. And this was the three-week war!

Caroline's voice reached him softly, almost a whisper. "Do you hate me so?"

He looked at her and felt her beauty cut into his soul. Caroline seemed to ripple and change as he held her in his glance, reflecting her quicksilver moods. It was like trying to hold water in your cupped hands, and Brooks felt a deep and poignant longing for that lovely time not so long ago when he was absolutely sure of himself and of her and the durability of their love. What exactly had changed between them, or when, or why, he could not have answered if his life depended on it. The change was there, uninvited, a sea change, unpredictable and sly, and under the dancing ripples of the surface there lurked, he feared, sleeping monsters.

"You know that's not true, darling."

"Sometimes it's hard to tell. A man who leaves a woman usually is in disagreement with her."

"Caroline, let's not torture the thing. I'm not leaving you. I'm joining a cause I believe in."

"Ah. Not leaving, but joining. I see. And the fact that I will be alone in this big house is only an incidental little result of that . . . your joining?"

"I'm afraid so. It isn't my war, darling."

"Not your war. No, I guess it isn't. But it will be, by this time tomorrow, won't it?"

"I just want to see the damn thing over!"

She walked up to him and took his big hand in her tiny one. "You are taking more of a chance than you know, Brooks Chaffee."

And Caroline smiled a strange and bitter smile, stood up on tiptoe, and kissed his cheek. Then, suddenly, she was gone.

Brooks stood alone in the bedroom for a moment, pondering the deep and inexplicable mysteries of beautiful women. Then he unpacked the rest of his crisp new uniforms and hung them in neat regimental rows in his closet.

Lily looked at her brother and couldn't help but smile.

Fergy was in his element, for sure! He'd arranged this last party at the Fleur de Lis, at Stanford's suggestion. Lily's own instinct had been to simply slip away to the ranch and never come back, and leave the explaining to Fergy. But Stanford said they'd never forgive her if she did a trick like that: the press and her old customers would count it mean and deceitful, and at last Lily agreed. The arrangements had been left to Fergy, and Fergy had done her proud.

It was still a secret that they'd sold out of the Fleur de Lis, that a syndicate had bought the building and its reputation for an astonishing four million, six hundred thousand dollars. And tomorrow she'd see the last of it, and not a moment too soon.

The main parlor was crammed with newspapermen, with old friends and curious tourists, with the mayor and the disgusting chief of police, O'Meara, with half of the richest men of the town and, of course, with Stanford. If there was anything San Francisco liked, it was a party, and if there was anything Fergy excelled at, it was giving parties. Drinks flowed and laughter followed. Popular songs came rollicking out of the big pipe organ they'd installed last winter. Finally Fergy took his sister's hand and led her to the first landing of the staircase, a natural platform for speech-making. He gestured to the organist, and the notes swelled to a thundering climax.

Fergy broke the silence that followed the last organ notes.

"Gentlemen, there is news today that will alter the history of our fair city, a tale so astonishing that you might not credit it from me. So here, to give you that news, is our own beloved Lily Cigar!"

Lily bit her lip, knew a moment of sudden fear, then began enjoying herself, buoyed by the thought that this would be her last appearance, anywhere, as the notorious Lily Cigar. She smiled and spoke in a low, clear voice.

"Boys," she began, and the room was more quiet than any church, "Lily Cigar is quitting. This is my retirement party. You've all been good to me, and I've tried to run an honest house. But now that's over, and Lily Cigar is moving up to San Rafael to become a farmer."

There was a chorus of groans and protests, howls of disbelief, rumblings of consternation. Lily waved her hand for silence, and silence came.

"Believe it or not, all my life I've wanted to be a farmer, and a farmer's what I'm going to be. So you can say good-bye to Lily Cigar, boys, and say hello to Mrs. Lillian Malone, of Malone Produce. I'm trading my cigars for cabbages and beans, and I couldn't leave without saying a proper good-bye—if anything in the Fleur de Lis could be called proper. Now, the drinks are on the house, folks, so let's all have a fine time on Lily!"

Her slender white hand on Fergy's arm, Lily descended the stairs with a gracious smile on her lips but a heart that was already in residence in the hills of San Rafael. She turned to her brother and kissed him on the cheek.

"And now, Fergy," she said happily, "could I have a glass of that champagne?"

Their dark blue uniforms spread over the red plush train carriage like spilled ink. The first-class carriage of the Philadelphia, Wilmington, and Baltimore Railroad made a strange contrast to the sober dress and deadly intentions of its passengers. The carriage was carpeted and upholstered in burgundy-colored fabrics, paneled in rich wood, fitted with fringed window shades that were all raised now, as the windows were opened to the blistering heat of late August to take in the air and to offer a view of the Pennsylvania land-scape as it rumbled past their window.

Brooks Chaffee was tired. He hadn't slept the last night, nor the night before that, partly from worry and partly from loving, from fear of leaving Caroline and fear of his conscience if he stayed behind. It was all mixed up in his brain, and seething. This was a more terrible feeling for being unfamiliar. Brooks had always prided himself on being able to think quickly and clearly, to know the difference between good and bad, be the question a business deal or a choice of wines, or the love that smoldered incorrigibly inside him, the love of Caroline Ledoux.

She had kissed him, and smiled when they parted, and pledged her love forever. But this did not make him rest easy, nor forget her strange, impulsive behavior these last few months, her bitterness, her gallant tries at gaiety, her rather desperate mockery of the entire political situation, both sides attacked unsparingly, North and South. *Well*, Brooks thought, *she's young yet. I forget that sometimes in her beauty and her cleverness. We've plenty of time, Caroline and I, to solve whatever it is that's bothering her. But first there's a job to do, a cause to serve, a war to win.*

And what a cause! The new uniform felt good on Brooks's young body. It fit superbly and the very fabric itself seemed invincible, the tightly-woven, richly lustrous broadcloth, the glint of gold braiding, the sparkle of new brass buttons, the sweep of his saber. Brooks could sense the enthusiasm bubbling and rising in the other men on the train. A few he knew slightly, but most were strangers, and a very mixed lot at that, mixed in their ages, in their physical types, in the towns and farms that bred them.

There were boys who looked almost like children, and some few men who must be past fifty, with graying hair or no hair at all. Fat and thin, loud and pensive, scholarly and bawdy, louts and gentlemen: how grand it all was, to have such a human stew so tightly bonded together by one just cause.

Until this very train ride Brooks Chaffee had never stopped to think about the huge and invincible fortress of privilege inside whose shining towers he had lived all his life, cheerfully unaware that outside was another world entirely.

Brooks had quite naturally taken the ease and gentle manners and education of his family and friends and schoolmates all for granted, for these things came to him as naturally as the air he breathed, and always had. Brooks had ever been a happy boy, and he was now a happy man, especially in his love for Caroline.

Brooks had never been forced to strive or scheme, to manipulate people or to knock on doors and know the silent shame of an advance rebuffed. In this sense he was an innocent; in being kind to Brooks Chaffee, life had paved the way for disillusionment.

The train clattered, rumbled, and jolted its way through a countryside so green and peaceful, it might have served as the illustration of a child's book. This was farmland, and pregnant with the coming harvest. Tall cornstalks saluted them as they passed, branches of fruit trees bent languorously under the weight of fat green apples just beginning their final blush of ripeness. Wheat rippled. Cows grazed. Barefoot farmgirls scattered grain for snow-white geese and motley chickens. There was no cloud in the sky, no hint of thunder; a perfect late summer's day stretched the length and breadth of the Union state of Pennsylvania.

Mercifully, the fat Bostonian sitting next to Brooks had fallen asleep. Brooks, too, closed his eyes and dreamed, awake, of the girl he had left behind in the house on West Eleventh Street.

How infinitely lovely Caroline had looked that morning! And how sad. What sweetness could match that kiss, what marble from the masters of ancient Greece could compare to that slim, yet deliciously rounded body?

Caroline had worn blue for his leaving, a morning dress of soft blue calico, sprigged with tiny white flowers, hooped and trimmed with deep blue ribbon. And she had smiled, fighting tears; Brooks could understand that, for hadn't he been fighting back the tears himself?

And hadn't she been brave, then, as she kissed him and held him with more strength than he could imagine in those slender arms! In the quick sweet urgency of her good-bye kiss Brooks could feel all his doubts and confusion of the last few months slipping away as though they had never existed at all, for in that wild magical place that was the kingdom of their love there could be no doubt or disagreement; only pure bright things lived there, joy and hope and the highest exaltation of love.

Brooks stretched luxuriously on the stiff plush train seat and his lips floated into a slow and appreciative smile at the memory of Caroline and her kiss. He thought himself the luckiest man in the world just then, for who of all the other men on this train, in this country, in all of God's creation, for that matter, who among them all had a woman like his Caroline?

He imagined Caroline as she must be right this minute, late afternoon; probably she'd go out to try to shake off her despair, shopping maybe, or to take tea with a friend. Tea at Delmonico's, with music in the background and the merry chatter of female voices stirring the great potted palm trees. At least she had plenty of friends, a busy life; there would be parties—she'd promised to overcome her shyness about going alone, and she'd promised, too, to have people in, just as always, as though he were still there. And his own friends would rally round, Brooks was sure of that. Jack Wallingford would cheer her up, no doubt, and there were his parents, although Caroline was still not quite at ease with the Old Gentleman as yet. Well, that too could be remedied, when all this was over. In a few weeks, with luck, or a few months at the very latest.

Brooks kept his eyes closed, feigning sleep, not wanting to let some casual stranger break the spell he was weaving around Caroline's day. Just thinking of her made him feel better. The time would pass, he knew this intellectually, but even now, even on the first day of their separation, the minutes dragged painfully across his brain.

Caroline! Even the separation might be beneficial, in the

long run, for surely it magnified his longing for her, surely it would make him cherish her more deeply, if that would be possible. Suddenly Brooks understood why men sometimes betrayed family and flag and honor for the love of a woman. Caroline was a cause all in herself. Caroline could make the war shrink to insignificance. Well, nearly. Caroline was the future. Caroline was why he was going to this terrible war. He must believe that, must keep telling himself it was all for her, even if Caroline herself could not be made to believe that.

The train rumbled on through the gentle green hills of Pennsylvania.

❧ 33 ❧

Lily grinned.

The sight of her trunks and baskets and valises made her as happy as anything she'd seen in months, not counting Kate's smiling face or the hills of the ranch across the bay.

The trunks were filled to bursting with finery Lily might never wear again. Maybe she was wrong even to bring the damned gowns and shoes and hats and feathers. But still and all, she would come into town now and then, once things were more settled on the ranch, once she had gotten the routine established. And she might even do some quiet entertaining in the big ranch house, eventually. God knew, there was room enough. And in any event the stuff could be cut down into little dresses for Kate, for the Baker girl.

But even as she looked at the luggage, Lily felt a small shudder of apprehension. The finery of San Francisco's most famous whore had no place in her new life, none at all. In that instant Lily made a decision that went contrary to all her thrifty instincts. No daughter of hers was going to wear a whore's cut-down ball gown! And if she herself were to visit town, it would be in different clothes altogether! Impulsively Lily called the maid who had just now finished helping her pack.

"All these," she said, pointing to seven of the nine trunks, "go to the public orphanage, as the donation of Malone Produce, Incorporated." The maid blushed and stammered, nodded and disappeared. And Lily smiled again. A weight had lifted from her heart. She walked out of the room and down the grand staircase of the Fleur de Lis, and gloried in the fact that she was doing this for the last time.

The landau was waiting.

She looked at the sleek little carriage, so much like Stanford's green one, but pale blue, the blue of a winter sky. Lily loved the landau, but it was far too delicate for the ranch. She'd given it to Fergy, who loved fast driving nearly as much as he loved fast women.

[402]

On Stanford's advice, Fergus Malone Junior had no voting stock in Malone Produce. He was accorded a salary, at the discretion of the board of directors, which consisted of Lily herself and Stanford and the lawyer.

The price for the Fleur de Lis had been paid in cash, and Lily had immediately settled half of the total on her brother. He'd be rich now, completely independent, a substantial member of the community. If he worked at it. For herself, Lily had the profits in the sale of her business discreetly invested in railroad bonds and bank stocks until such time as she could prudently add to her farming ventures.

She walked out the front door of the Fleur de Lis: another last, as the carriage ride to the harbor would be the last in this particular landau, as her restless sleep last night had been a farewell to the big carved bed that was too crowded with memories Lily would rather forget.

Her bed at the ranch was more than a place to sleep—and alone. It was symbolic of a new life, a new direction, with the past where it should be: buried. Lily stepped into the elegant little landau and softly told the driver to move on, looking straight ahead, a trace of a smile on her lips, head held high, oblivious of the small crowd that had gathered in silence on the paved walk outside of the fanciest parlor house in the West.

The exhilaration was intense, better than champagne, fresh and clean as some wildflower, more heady than the breeze dancing in off the ocean. Lily felt like singing aloud, felt like dancing a jig and letting out an Indian war whoop. How she had planned and sweated and prayed and wept for this moment! To be free! If ever a man touched her again, and she doubted that one would, it must be from the deepest devotion, the purest love. For in the Fleur de Lis, Lily knew, she had sold more than her body. She had traded her good name for gold, mortgaged her illusions and put her scruples at the very back of her safe-deposit vault at Wells Fargo. And if any of these things would come back to her, it could only be in time, and after a penance, and after working so hard for them that it would prove to all the world, and to herself, that she deserved hope, or love, or respectability. *Yes, and they well may laugh and scorn me, but I'll do it or die trying!* It might be impossible, making a good new life, but Lily had seen many impossible things come to be in her twenty-five years. She owed it to Katie, and to herself, that she must try with all the strength and wit that was in her.

Lily drove away from the Fleur de Lis on this bright September morning, drove straight down Sacramento Street to the docks, and never looked back.

There had been no rain in Brooks Chaffee's dream of glory. In his mind's picture, the sun shone clear on well-scrubbed troops who marched in orderly phalanxes to sure victory over the rebels, for surely all the force of right was on their side.

For three days now Brooks and four-hundred-some relief troops had slogged through mud on country lanes and trackless pastures, enduring a cold and relentless rain that was never quite a downpour and never quite a mist.

The fine broadcloth of his uniform soaked up the rain with the voracity of a sponge, doubled its weight, and hung on him like an ancestral curse. Boots and saddles mildewed while he looked at them in disbelief, and the simplest walk became a nightmare of mud and confusion. Tempers eroded with the cart track they marched on, rifles rusted if they were left uncovered for five minutes, maps that were inadequate to begin with dissolved from the wetness into soggy indecipherable lumps, and cooking became impossible. Brooks cursed every god whose name he could remember and wondered if it rained on Johnny Reb with the same murderous persistency.

The rain followed them like an enemy scout. It crept into their thin tents when night came, ambushed them at dawn, marched with them all the way from Baltimore to this place no one had ever heard of but Lee and McClellan, this god-forsaken corner of Maryland somewhere between Frederick and Harpers Ferry, Sharpsburg.

At least Neddy would be there. The thought of seeing Neddy again and the warm memory of Caroline were all Brooks had to sustain himself on the long wet march. The men squished and slid and stumbled, grumbling and short-tempered before they'd heard even a single shot fired in anger.

The food was terrible, and seemed worse, because for the most part these were green troops, lately from clean beds and happy hearthsides. There was no place to wash properly, and the only reason Brooks could sleep at all at night was simply because he was bone-tired, spent, exhausted beyond anything he could recall.

And they were supposed to be the fresh troops, the reviving influence on McClellan's weary corps!

It was amazing, how fast a man's spirit could melt in the rotten weather, how the juices could drain out of your very soul when you were hungry and cold and everything smelled of wet wool and mildewed leather and unwashed bodies.

Brooks had never really considered the question of physical comfort before; he had both time and reason to think deeply about it now. Was courage a matter of clean sheets and a hot joint of beef? He devoutly hoped not, yet this damnable march through the mud was raising that very question.

There had been no pessimists in Brooks's dream of glory. Now, as the irresistible red-clay mud of Maryland seeped into every pore of his body, rumors of impending doom fell around him with the dampening persistence of the rain itself.

He could hear the men grumbling through the thin, clammy canvas of his tent, heard them on the march, heard them over the clatter of tin spoons on canteen bowls of barely edible slop-stew at mealtime.

"I'll tell you, Sam Miller, the man's a coward, pure and simple, got a yaller streak down 'is backside a mile wide."

"Naw, you've got it wrong, Bill, man can't noways be a coward when he's dead, now, can he? That ol' Mac, why he's so slow, he just *has* to be dead, hear?"

And they laughed, but it was gallows laughter, and, like his men, Brooks half-believed the rumors. All armies, Brooks knew, were marching rumor machines. Yet the tales about McClellan were too many and too consistent to be entirely off the target. At first Brooks had tried to stop the grumbling, but these were fiercely independent soldiers and it was like trying to stop the rain. By the third day Brooks fell silent. Getting to the general's camp would be enough, for getting to McClellan meant getting to Neddy. Neddy! That was worth the rain and the mud and the grub and the grumbling.

The march was spiked with rumors that went unconfirmed, with gossip about McClellan's famous ability to hesitate his way out of nearly any victory, his deeply ingrained knack for failure, his seemingly mad refusal to press the advantage when he had one. Robert E. Lee, on the other hand, was a mythical hero to these raw Union replacements.

Lee was invincible, gallant, a legend out of the court of King Arthur himself, shrewd yet just, braver than lions, elusive as smoke, a man to inspire courage in the lowliest toad of a coward.

Lee, in the tales and legends, was everything McClellan was not. And Lee was the enemy.

Brooks pitied Neddy, knowing the quickness of Neddy's mind, the firmness of his convictions, the unalterably noble standards by which he lived every aspect of his life.

Neddy, wonderful Neddy, bright and burning to win this damned war single-handed, chained to a cowardly vacillating fool like McClellan!

Was there no justice whatsoever in this world?

Still, he'd be seeing Neddy, talking to his brother for the first time in nearly six months. It would be a chance, Brooks hoped, to get close to his brother again. Neddy had always been a kind of god to his younger brother, and with good reason. Yet, just these last few years, almost from the moment Brooks had fallen so deeply in love with Caroline, Neddy had seemed to drift out of his life. Maybe that was part of growing up. Maybe it was a reflection on Brooks's all-consuming love for Caroline.

But whatever the reason, it would be better now. They'd talk, just like they used to, halfway through the night. What plans they'd planned! What impossible dreams had seemed right upon the edge of coming true!

Neddy had always been magical to Brooks. Neddy had hung the moon. Neddy could make the impossible happen, and quickly, and make it all look easy. And smile and be fun. And be the kind of brother you'd hand your life to, on a silver server, or your deepest fears and secrets. Neddy could probably even make the rain stop.

If anyone could win this war fast, it was Edward Hudner Chaffee. Brooks knew this as surely as he knew his name.

And he'd be seeing Neddy, soon, maybe tomorrow.

The joy of it made him forget the rain and the moldy biscuits and the raw blister that burned like fire with every sliding, stumbling step he took.

Many were the times when Brooks had tried to analyze the distance that had slowly come between Neddy and himself of late.

Brooks tried to do this, and failed. Surely, part of it must be Caroline. After all, a man could only give so much of himself to one person at a time, and in Brooks's case he had given himself to Caroline so totally and irreversibly, more than one hundred percent of his heart and mind and body, that it might well be there simply wasn't enough emotional energy left in him to sustain his friendship with Neddy on the level where it had been.

Maybe it was just that they'd both grown up these last few years, and, in growing up, they'd grown apart.

Somehow, his thoughts of Neddy always ended tangled up with thoughts of Caroline. That might be natural, since these were the two people in all the world that Brooks loved most; yet, natural as it might be, it was also confusing.

He marched and thought of Caroline.

Her smile danced in the dripping treetops. Her eyes shone darkly from otherwise undistinguished puddles at the roadside, and somewhere in the depths of those dark and liquid eyes was hidden all the sweet unfathomable mystery of a Southern girlhood.

He might kill some blood relative of hers; Brooks knew this, and trembled at the thought, at the smallness of the world and the terrible ironies it bred for all of them. Yet at least he wasn't on opposite sides of the barricade from his brother, a not uncommon thing in this most heartrending of all wars. Hell, hadn't Lee himself been the commandant at West Point until just lately? And didn't Lee's own white-pillared mansion gaze serenely down from the heights of Arlington, Virginia, onto the seething Union Capitol at Washington?

He marched and thought of Caroline, of her smile and her eyes and of other, more secret parts of her, and how a whole night could melt away on the deep, surging tide of his love for her. It wasn't blood and gunfire at the end of this bitter march, but Caroline. For wasn't she at the end of everything in his life, and the beginning, and always would be?

The rain fell indiscriminately on lovers and heroes and frightened men.

This, Lily thought, *must be exactly how a prisoner feels the day they let her out.*

The sense of release was a drug for her. The landau clattered down Sacramento Street and Lily cherished every bump, for every rotation of those costly slender wheels was taking her that much farther away from the Fleur de Lis, from her past, from the lurid fame of Lily Cigar.

Even the day itself seemed to join in her liberation. It was a bright blue day filled with sun and expectation. There was so much to do, and all of it challenging! Running the Fleur de Lis had made a planner of Lily. Details fascinated her, and well she knew that a smooth and glittering result was only the sum of many small things properly attended to, done right and on time. This, she vowed, would be the story at the ranch.

Oh, sure and there'd be trial and error, but the weather was reliable, and so was Fred Baker. Farming was so irregular in these parts, even now, that no one had formed a proper system for doing it on a large scale.

Malone Produce was going to change all that, and as fast as was practical. The climate here in San Francisco might be ideal for some things, but Lily had no intention of limiting herself to the immediate neighborhood. The talk of a great Union Pacific Railroad was shaping up into much more than talk. It would come, and when that happened, vast new areas would become available for every kind of farming. Down in southern California, near the Bay of Angels, tropical vegetables and fruits flourished uninhibitedly, whereas in the north they required special care. Fred Baker said he heard experiments were starting farther north, up Sonoma way, in the growing of wine grapes. Now, there was a thought. At the rate of wine consumption in the Fleur de Lis, anyone who came up with a decent local vintage would be rich overnight. And they were doing this back East, growing their own wine grapes high up in the Finger Lakes district of New York. Lily had never tasted the stuff they made, but it was being done—that she knew from one of her many farming journals.

There was the planting to consider, then the furnishing of the big ranch house. The restoration work was done now, and well done too, but the place was still largely as bare as she and Stanford had come to it the first time. This too would be a pleasure.

And best of all, there would be Kate. Kate near at hand, Kate to see every day. Kate to become a real mother to, at long last. *What do I know about being a mother? How will I tell the child—and when? And suppose in the telling, she decides to hate me, not to forgive, not to understand?* Lily did not consider herself anything like a coward, and yet the prospect of confronting a six-year-old with the hard facts of her parentage decimated her. Lily could face many things, and had. She had overcome huge obstacles, striven and buried the shame of her whoring, and pulled herself out of it by pure will and the raw force of her determination and her love for Kate. To be rejected now would present a reversal so frightening that Lily could not bring herself to think about it. Several times lately she had nearly worked up her courage to tell the girl, and always she had backed down, found some excuse to postpone the dreaded confrontation.

The trim blue landau pulled up at the dock and the driver handed Lily down. Her sloop was waiting.

The boat itself was a part of her dream, and as Lily walked lightly up its gangplank, the sense of freedom she had felt in leaving the Fleur de Lis doubled and tripled and made her almost dizzy with pleasure. The captain bowed and greeted her. She smiled and told him to set sail.

Set sail! Wasn't there magic in those simple words? *Yes, and it's a new life I'm sailing to, newer even than the life I found when I left New York, for this is mine, my own doing, earned by my sweat and my shame, my own magic kingdom, Katie's and mine, where the world cannot harm us.* The sloop was not as big or as elaborate as Stanford's, but it was a fine, jaunty boat all the same, dark green it was, and with the name *Katie* in neat gold letters on the stern. Malone Produce owned the sloop, and that, too, added to Lily's sense of pride as she sailed across the bay to her new home.

It hardly seemed over two years since she'd bought the ranch. Now, all of the hard work—all the delays in restoring the main house and outbuildings; the shortage of supplies; the sea-borne deliveries that were unaccountably late; the scant yield of their first little harvest—seemed to melt away like some half-forgotten dream. It was happening at last, and that was all Lily cared about!

It was all happening, just as she'd dreamed it! No conquistador of old ever sailed more proudly to his destiny than Lily Malone on this bright September day in 1862.

Ned Chaffee looked up from the map, blinked, squinted in the flickering light of a badly trimmed kerosene lantern. "Yes?"

Brooks stood dripping in the insistent rain, gaping in disbelief at the changes six months of combat had wrought on his brother's handsome face. Neddy was thirty, two years older than Brooks. Now he looked fifty. Too thin he was, and all the muscles and cords in his face and neck stood out like rope stretched to the point of breaking, as if they were straining against each other in some demented effort to tear that familiar face apart. Still, it was Neddy, and in one piece.

Brooks walked into the little tent, crossing the barrier of his brother's irritation at the unannounced interruption. "Lieutenant Chaffee reporting for duty, sir."

Again the blink, the straining, the questioning, slightly feral expression on Ned's face betrayed six months of tension, fatigue, suspicion. Brooks thought of Neddy's smile, his easy laughter echoing down all the years of their shared boyhood.

Then George McClellan's aide-de-camp recognized his visitor. Instantly Ned became another person. The grin came quick as ever, and quick as ever he was on his feet, around the trestle table, embracing Brooks, laughing, questioning, cheering all at once.

"You devil! Nobody told me! I knew you'd enlisted, but this . . . How's everyone? Mother? The old gent? And your Caroline? Quick, tell me everything, old sot, I want all of it! How's the bank? I can't believe you. My little brother. Here. Sit. Have you eaten, not that it'll be fit to eat, but we can roust up something."

"Whoa, there, Neddy. One item at a time. Don't forget, you're dealing with a raw recruit. I'm hoping you'll be the one to tell me things."

It felt good to sit down. It felt even better to see Neddy smiling again, laughing even. It made Brooks think his first impression of a new and strained-taut Neddy had been a false one.

"We'll tell each other. God, but it's good to see you, Brooks."

They sat for nearly an hour, a stolen hour, Brooks was quick to learn, snatched from frenzy, embezzled from the all-consuming effort of the Grand Army of the Potomac to regroup, and rest, and gather their energies for a massive and hopefully fatal blow against Lee's Virginia Army now holed up at Sharpsburg, just across a little creek named Antietam.

Brooks soon learned the chaos that lurked very close to the surface of this campaign, and all of the other Union campaigns Neddy told him about.

"The famous victories, so-called, are pure dumb luck, Brooks, and often as not we lose as many as we kill. It's a losing game for both sides, and even when we win—and we will win—we lose."

"What about Little Mac? The old gent said—"

"Shhh!" Ned's face showed fear for the first time Brooks could remember.

"Canvas," Ned murmured nonchalantly, too late to cover his apprehension, "is not the most solid building material you're likely to find, old bean, it has a nasty tendency to carry sound."

"I thought—"

"That's one of the more popular rumors, and a persistent one. One day it'll be true, I think. In the meantime, the gentleman in question is a man, Brooks, like all of us. He's not been known to walk on water, but on the other hand, nor is he all that bad. War makes legends, destroys reputations. Lee's a saint already, even though I view that with a certain skepticism. We need our myths, little brother, and unfortunately, at the moment this side of the fence is suffering under the wrong kind of a myth. Take Pope. Pope was going to be our savior, loudmouth bully that he is. Well, General Longstreet disabused us of that happy notion in one hell of a hurry. And suddenly Pope is off in exile in the West somewhere, doubtless shooting up the passenger pigeons and chasing the odd Indian through the woods. War is a most delicious concert of tiny, exquisite ironies, Brooks. It could be very amusing if there weren't all that blood."

Brooks felt his head swimming. His delight at seeing Neddy mixed with concern for the way Neddy looked and the new, unwelcome cynicism in Neddy's voice. *This isn't the real Ned Chaffee, he's just playing at being a soldier, he can't really have become this hard, this unfeeling, in just six months.* But Brooks watched his brother closely, and saw the cold awareness glittering in Neddy's eyes with the arctic brilliance of some distant, unreachable star, and he wondered. He wondered, too, at the rush of names and rumors, for here was Neddy, his Neddy, on first-name terms with famous generals whose deeds Brooks knew only from the press, or from soldiers' gossip.

Brooks paused for a moment after his brother's torrent of information had stilled, and when he spoke, it was softly, and in the hope that what he said might somehow become true just by the bare physical fact of being spoken.

"But surely our cause is a just one." The sound of his brother's laughter cut Brooks Chaffee like a knife.

"You are perfect, Brooks, you always were. Do your tired old brother a favor, my boy, and don't change, not ever."

Ned turned toward the tent flap, hyper-alert, as if he'd heard some enemy approaching. Then he turned back, and smiled a thin and bitter smile, a mockery of the happy face Brooks held in his memory like a talisman against evil.

"Oh, indeed ours is a just cause. One-half of all the murders in the history of the world have been done in some just cause. One often forgets precisely what the cause is, or was, but most assuredly it is a just one. We die to free the souls of all those poor black wretches we dragged screaming from their jungles a hundred or more years ago, is that it? Sometimes I forget. Or is it a fine legal point we're defending, whether this or that number of angels can dance upon the head of a pin, and for how long . . . how long?"

His voice trailed off, and Ned brought both hands up to his eyes and rubbed them vigorously. "Ah, then, to hell with it.

I'm sorry, Brooks, don't think I mock you. It's just that I'm so very tired."

Brooks looked at his brother and felt as though they'd both just stepped off the edge of the earth, falling in limitless darkness. "Can't you take a few days, and get away?"

"No. That's just it. None of us can. Not even a few minutes. I've hours of work left tonight, and the information's not always reliable, we make plans based on guesses, and so does Lee. It boils down to who's the best guesser. Now there's a new plan."

Ned looked around the little tent as though it might be filling up with unseen Confederate informers.

"There's this Professor such-and-so, forget his name, doesn't matter, and guess what he does?"

"He has a crystal ball?"

"Nearly that. He has one of those Montgolfier balloons, Brooks, and up he goes with his spyglass, high in the sky, spying away to beat the band, and also—here's the wonder of it—he has a telegraph up there with him, so the news comes flashing into headquarters on wings of lightning. It is the very latest thing, sure to put the fear of God into the wicked foe."

"Does it work?"

"Nobody knows yet. It works on paper. It works in Little Mac's dreams, and that's enough for the moment. I'm sorry, brother mine, but I really must get back to all this . . ." He indicated the maps, the papers, the daybook that littered the table.

"I'm sorry too, but at the least of it, we're together. When's the strike?"

"Don't know. No one knows. It's a question of luck, and guessing, and the damnable rain stopping."

"I'll see you tomorrow, then?"

"You bet, Lieutenant Chaffee. It's very good to see you, Brooks."

Brooks walked the few steps to where Ned was already sitting at the table rustling through the heaps of paper. Brooks put his hand on that familiar, too-thin shoulder, and spoke quietly. "It'll take more than some war to keep us apart, old bean."

He was going to add ". . . or some woman, either," but could not. He turned and walked out of the tent into the constant drizzling rain.

❧ 34 ❧

Lily looked at Fred Baker and frowned. "You truly think it's necessary?"

"You know I wouldn't ask you if I didn't." That was irrefutable, but it didn't cure Lily's lifelong distaste for firearms, for loud noises or violence of any kind.

Lily owned a gun, the revolver Stanford had given her after that terrible incident with the razor-wielding religious fanatic at Sophie's. But she had never practiced enough to truly master the thing. Lily was capable of feeling fear, but her fears were all emotional ones: guilt and shame were frequent visitors to Lily's mind, and she often wondered if the time would ever come when she could walk down a city street without dreading the scorn of respectable men and women. But physical fear was all but unknown to her.

Fred was worried about bandits, and while Lily's keen mind told her there might be something in his fears, her heart refused to accept the possibility. She had come too far, and at too great a cost, to be put off by the distant scent of danger.

Nevertheless, here they stood, she and Fred and an even more reluctant Mary Baker, at the edge of a new-plowed field, trying to master both their misgivings and the heavy blued-steel Colt repeating pistols Fred was insisting each woman keep at hand, each in her own house.

"There's times I'll be away, or so far out in the grazing lands I might as well be in China. And you never know. Not only bandits might come snooping around, there's rattlers too, and maybe a bear or a mountain lion."

"God help us, then, if it would depend on my shooting."

Lily said it lightly, laughing, but these were real dangers. The land was wild still, wilder than she cared to admit. The wildness was one reason she loved this place, for wild meant quiet, being alone with only the enormous sky overhead, and the wandering wind, and hearing no sound at all but the birds making plans in the pine groves. Three weeks she'd been living on the ranch now, and had returned to town only once, and then just to see Fergy, for she worried about her brother, and Fergy never visited the ranch.

Young Stephen Baker, thirteen, was mad for bandits and wildlife of all sorts, and it was from Stephen that Lily heard the most bloodcurdling tales of bandit adventures.

". . . and they say Joaquin Murietta still lives in the high Sierra, him and his white horse, and the whole troop, and there was Three-Fingered Jack and Rattlesnake Dick, and Tiberio, Lily, who was born right in this house . . ."

Lily looked at the boy and smiled, although in fact she would have preferred some other line of talk. But the pleasure it gave Stephen was obvious, and, the good Lord knew the pleasures were few enough for a boy his age in this isolated ranch. She took a tray of fresh-baked cookies out of the big wood-burning stove and deftly scooped them onto a wire rack to cool.

"Yes," she said lightly, "he was very naughty, wasn't he? Would you like another cookie, Stephen?"

"Thank you, yes. Oh, he may be the worst yet, Tiberio may, for wouldn't he slit you from head to toe just for looking at him the wrong way, and wouldn't he be laughing all the time. They say his laugh would peel the bark right off a eucalyptus, Lily, and didn't he have a gang when he was only my age, or nearly?"

"Darling, let's not talk about Tiberio, please? Tell me about the new chicken house instead."

The conversation drifted on, and Kate came scampering in for cookies and milk, perfectly oblivious of the fact that Tiberio Velasquez was not a legend like the other bandits who roamed through Stephen Baker's lurid imagination. Tiberio was very much alive, at large, and sworn to avenge himself on the woman who had, he insisted, stolen his birthright.

Brooks woke in the night and instantly wondered why. God knew he was tired enough to sleep for a week.

There was something about the quality of the noise. The lack of noise. Then he knew. The rain had stopped. The rain he had been praying would go away had finally got his message.

He lay still on his cot drinking in the silence with his fears. Nothing about McClellan's army was as he'd imagined it, not even Neddy.

Especially not Neddy. This was Neddy changed, grown suddenly bitter, a Ned Chaffee visibly plagued with doubts and questions and a kind of cynical resignation to his fate that wasn't like him at all.

And if Neddy could change so, then anything could change. Anything at all. In the sudden quiet of the great camp, in the blackness of his tent and the even greater blackness that seemed to be filling up his heart, Brooks felt his world shivering, slipping, changing. It was as though all the solid granite structures of his boyhood had suddenly been revealed as cardboard cleverly painted, a stage setting for a not particularly entertaining play. His own fear surprised him, for he had never been afraid.

Somewhere down the creek, just a few miles away, forty-some thousand Confederate troops had gathered for their first invasion of the North.

And Little Mac McClellan had nearly double that, seventy-five thousand prime soldiers waiting to crush them.

The fact that they waited in confusion and disorder among conflicting rumors and orders that often seemed impossible hardly altered the fact of their immense superiority of numbers.

But it was not death that frightened Brooks Chaffee. It was rather another, subtler kind of destruction, the moral blight that seemed to have taken hold of Neddy, that could therefore as easily take hold in his own heart and spirit. Even before hearing one shot from a rebel gun, Brooks knew the true and ultimate horror of war: it seethed in his dark tent, coiled and ready to strike, evil, poisonous; inescapable: the possibility that it was all for nothing, that none of it really mattered.

He had no idea how long he lay thus, eyes closed, thinking thoughts more black than the night.

Finally the normal sounds of a huge camp awakening seeped into his tent with the first gray shards of dawn. One day soon, maybe even today, little Antietam Creek was going to run with blood, and some of it might well be his.

It had been one of the best days Lily could remember, a blazing October day almost warm enough for summer, but still with a welcome crispness to it, the promise of apples ripening and, at sunset, the cozy need for gathering around a crackling fire.

Fred was away, hot on the scent of an unimaginable treasure: twelve prime milk cows, if the reports could be believed. Even the news from the far-off war was encouraging, coming by telegraph from St. Louis now, in hours instead of days, on the pony express. There had been a great Union victory somewhere in Maryland, Antietam, they called it, Lee defeated and fled, the reports said, his invasion of the North stopped cold. The war would be over in a few weeks, they were saying.

She wished, not for the first time, that she cared more.

But what Lily cared for in this world was here, in the ranch, here in the hills of San Rafael, three thousand miles in distance and removed even further than that emotionally, from the terrors of Union versus rebel that were spilling blood all over the East.

For what did she know of politics? Or care?

Lily looked about the great kitchen, where she and Kate sat by the fire, Lily with her tea, Kate with milk and cookies, Lily trying to teach the child some of the fine needlework the good nuns at St. Paddy's had taught her an eternity ago in New York. They worked quietly, companionably, each with her embroidery hoop and needle, Kate struggling with clumsy determination and goodwill. *Soon,* Lily thought, *it'll be like this always, Kate with me all the time, my daughter in her rightful role, in her rightful place, by my side, and happy.* Soon, but not yet. Lily was still timid with the girl, courting her like an unattainable lover. But Kate seemed to like her, Kate always came when invited, Kate smiled and got on well with the Baker children and the other people in her small world here on the ranch.

Lily thought of the Baker house, far on the other side of the stables, and how well her arrangement with Fred Baker was working out, better even than she'd expected. He'd been gone for two days now, which was a good sign. If the cows had been sickly or otherwise undesirable, he and the three hands he'd taken with him would have been back today. As it was, they must be driving the herd with them, a two-day job at best. And twelve new cows plus the seven they already owned would mean a goodly amount of milk to sell, to make cheese from, and cows to breed. In a few years, with the birthing and buying new stock, they'd have a fair herd for sure.

She looked around the big old kitchen, bright as it was with new whitewash and gleaming Mexican tiles and polished wood. A cook was what she needed, one of the many details yet to be attended to. The girl who came in to clean was only just adequate; a live-in maid would have to be found, too. The novelty of being alone in the big manor house was wearing thin for Lily. At first it had been a blessed relief after the bustle and tinsel of the Fleur de Lis and her life there. Then had come the days of high-pitched working just after she'd moved in, with so much to be done that there was never a moment to think about luxuries like servants. But now, yes, there was no doubt about it: a cook and a maid to live in. And a nursemaid for Kate, when the time came.

Lily looked at her daughter, and saw how gently the glow from the fire caught the little girl's red-gold hair. Suddenly, impulsively, she bent and kissed Kate on the cheek. The girl giggled and squirmed away.

It was then that Lily heard the hoofbeats. And the gunshots.

For one heartbeat that seemed to last for hours, Lily froze. These were not friends, and she was very much alone. She thought of the faraway war. And she thought of bandits.

There was a sudden thundering, the sound of many horses, galloping horses. Not, definitely not, the horses of Fred Baker and his men. And there were gunshots, roaring, a scream, and high-pitched madmen's yells cutting the evening air like so many knives.

Instantly, without thinking, Lily stood and hustled Kate into the little pantry that was almost completely hidden behind the big fireplace.

"Quick, Katie, hide. Hide in here, and don't come out until I say so. This isn't a game, Kate. You must make never a sound. Do you understand? Not a peep!"

The girl nodded dumbly, her pink cheeks going white with apprehension.

Lily wondered where she'd put the damned pistol. Of course. In her bedroom. She reached for a cleaver, then put it down again. They might mean no harm, after all, it might simply be some noisy strangers passing by, or even some of Fergy's drunken friends. It wouldn't do to greet your guests waving a kitchen knife. The shots had stopped now. There came a pounding at the door.

Lily walked slowly down the great hall, feeling more alone than she ever had.

She paused before the big door, wondering what it would take to break it down, wondering how long she could hold them off, armed with a pistol and very few bullets, armed with a kitchen knife and her own dark fears for Kate's safety.

The door trembled, quivered on its old iron hinges, the big iron ring knocker jangling insistently.

With no plan and no weapon, Lily drew back the bolt and opened the door. The smell hit her first, sweat and brimstone, unclean stables, garlic and death.

The monster stood in front of her, laughing a madman's laugh.

Tiberio Velasquez was known to Lily only in legend; she had never seen a picture of the bandit nor heard him described. But somehow she would have known him anywhere.

Lily looked at him and beyond him, saying nothing. The courtyard was a shambles. Six riders, still mounted, were grouped defensively against the corral. In front of them, in the dust, was the bloodied corpse of Stephen Baker, a deer rifle still in his pale hand.

A wave of nausea rose in Lily, choking her, riding over her dread and loathing: *May God take his soul, the poor lad, trying a deer rifle against this lot. Stephen had gotten his wish at last. He'd met a real bandit.*

Tiberio's laughter drew Lily's eyes from the pathetic corpse to his dreadful face. She looked at him dumbly, unable to form even the simplest greeting or the most basic curse.

The most frightening thing about Tiberio's face was that you could still see in it some trace of curdled aristocracy, of gentle breeding thinned out and twisted. He was a big man, wide-shouldered but wiry, dark-skinned and dark-haired and dressed all in black. His eyes glowed with a strange dark fire, eyes that had seen every signpost on the road to hell, eyes in which any hint of human compassion had long since hardened into steel. Lily knew he was beyond desperation, that only death itself could stop him.

A beard covered the lower half of Tiberio's face, and from his forehead to his left ear ran a deep and livid scar. His hair was wild under the wide-brimmed vaquero's hat. He wore two revolving pistols in a black leather belt tooled in silver.

And he laughed.

Finally Tiberio spoke, and Lily was astonished to hear his voice. It was a quiet voice, educated, with all the quiet menace of coiled snakes and bad things lurking under rocks. *"Buenas tardes, Señorita Lily Cigar,"* he said softly, mocking, bowing as his men laughed in the background. "It is only fitting, is it not, that my ancestral home should be dwelt in by a whore? May I come in, if you please?"

Lily stepped aside, and stood in silence while he marched into the hallway.

"Yes. It is as I heard. You have done well by my heritage, Señorita Lily Cigar."

Finally she found words. And even as she spoke them, Lily knew they were the wrong ones.

"I bought the ranch fairly, from your uncle, as the public records show."

"As the public records show!" He laughed, a high-pitched, almost feminine giggle. "It is my ranch. My hills. My house. And you . . . you are my woman."

Lily felt her blood chill, and suddenly she seemed incapable of thought or movement. Tiberio grabbed her then, and pulled her to him and kissed her violently while one hand fumbled with the buttons on her simple calico dress. Lily's first impulse was to vomit. The stench of the man, his greasy hands pawing her, the Baker boy dead in her courtyard, and Kate . . . Kate! *You must buy time, Lily, you must delay the monster, for Fred will be coming soon, Mary may have gone for help somehow.* She was sure he'd rape her then and there, and kill her too, all the time laughing. And it was the thought of the rape that gave her the beginning of a plan.

She twisted in his arms as though overcome by passion. She pulled her face away from his and smiled a slow seductive smile. Then, choking back her nausea, Lily lifted his greasy hand to her lips and kissed it.

"*Por favor . . .*" she murmured, and took his hand and led him up the great stairway.

Tiberio smiled and went with her. It was as he suspected: the famous bandit was irresistible to the famous whore. Still holding his hand, Lily led him down the hallway to her bedroom. He looked around and laughed, and held her tighter. He would have his fun before turning her over to the others. Why, they might stay for weeks!

There was a decanter of sherry on a low chest of drawers. Lily poured him a glass, and one for herself. She lifted the delicately etched crystal to her lips. "*Salud, Señor Tiberio.*"

"*Salud.*"

Then Lily put her glass down and slowly unbuttoned her dress. She stepped out of it where it fell, and unlaced the chaste white camisole she wore underneath, pulled off her shoes and stockings and all the rest.

Tiberio's eyes glittered, never leaving the amazing creature before him. *The snake,* Lily thought, *watching the rabbit.* Still, she continued the performance, smiling sweetly in anticipation of the pleasures to come.

He watched, smiling, curling his tongue around the bottom rim of the wineglass.

Finally, naked and glowing, she came to him. Again he clutched at her, violently, as if to crush her then and there. But Lily only smiled, put her finger to her lips, and whispered

[419]

in her halting Spanish: *"Quiero todo un hombre, Tiberio mio."*

She reached up and began unbuttoning his vest, then his shirt. Graceful as a dancer, she knelt and eased off his muddy boots, struggling not to gag as she noticed the fresh bloodstains. Then she stood and pressed her face into the reeking black mat of his chest, and began unbuckling his belt, her breath growing heavier, her motions quicker. Gently, now, his arms encircled her again, stroking her back.

This was the moment. Quick as thought, Lily jerked the pistol out of its holster and shot him three times through the chest.

She reeled back from the explosion, trembling.

In all her life Lily would never forget the expression on his face.

Tiberio smiled. His eyes widened as he looked down at the gaping holes in his chest, as the blood poured out of him.

Then his eyes seemed to glaze, to go all blurry.

He spoke softly, and not in anger: "It is fitting . . . *puta . . .*"

Tiberio seemed to float down to the floor. He sank in a slow, boneless flow of movement, curiously graceful, drifting into death. It was over in seconds, but to Lily, awestruck, his was a lingering death. She watched him for a moment, too shocked to fully realize what she'd done, then pulled on the dress over her nakedness, reloaded the pistol, and went to the door.

She was just in time. The six bandits were on the stairs, so close together that Lily's first shot got two of them, who fell screaming back on the rest. Two shots drilled into the fresh plaster behind her head, then three more. Lily began to feel faint. She ducked behind the bedroom door, only to be greeted by a thundering volley from the bottom of the stairs, a mad concert of anguished screaming, then a deep and smoky silence.

At last a voice reached Lily and sank into her consciousness. It was a woman's voice, faintly familiar, but changed somehow, a voice drained of all emotion. Mary Baker's voice, Stephen's mother. "It's all right, Lily. They're dead. All dead."

Silently, wondering if this was some terrible dream, Lily walked down the stairs. She stepped over the twisted, bloodied corpses of Tiberio's bandits, trailing her skirts in their blood, hardly seeing them. Mary stood limp, holding a smoking shotgun. Lily embraced the woman, yet still she could find no words of comfort. Together they walked into the kitchen, and all at once Lily came to her senses. She put down the pistol and ran to the little cupboard and pulled open the door. There sat Katie, terrified, the tears half-dried on her little cheeks. Lily scooped her up and covered her face with kisses.

"It's all right, my darling," said Lily softly, "the bad men can't harm us anymore."

Brooks Chaffee lay still in his little tent, awake, as usual, before dawn. He looked up at the dirty canvas and tried to guess the time. A faint wash of gray was seeping through the blackness. It must be nearly four. *September 17, 1862.* Neddy had whispered that this might be the day. Little Mac might finally be going to move it. Brooks's head whirled. He felt that inside of his brain was nothing less than a complete Government Survey map of the Sharpsburg area, with special emphasis on the sleepy little creek with the unlikely name of Antietam. It was such a miserable excuse for a river! Why, any athletic boy could skip stones across Antietam Creek. And now two great armies were making it their own private Rubicon, Lee to the west and McClellan to the east, and three little bridges would tell the tale: Upper Bridge, Middle Bridge, Lower Bridge. Brooks saw the boldness of Robert E. Lee's plan, a wild thrust into the North, crossing the Potomac itself with a weary, understrength army, betting on reinforcements that might not come, riding his own legend and his own unshakable conviction in the justice of the Confederate cause. It might be a madman's gesture, it might be suicidal, but Brooks admired Lee for all that, the boldness of his moves and the unflagging devotion he inspired in his men. And the good Lord knew the Union forces could use a bit of inspiration just now!

He felt a small ironic smile forming on his lips and thought: *A few more days of this and I'll be cynical as Neddy.* His men—all the men—were spoiling for action, seething with boredom.

A sentry came and roused Brooks then, and from the new tension in the trooper's whisper Brooks sensed that Neddy was right, this was the day! He fairly leaped out of the narrow cot and into his uniform. Brooks shaved carefully by the light of a small kerosene lamp, checked his pistol, and went out into the camp to help ready his men. The camp seethed with anticipation. Here were nearly seventy-five thousand Federal troops, regular and reserves, from every part of the Union, from every conceivable background, bustling and cursing and working up their courage for the big thrust to come. By God, and wouldn't they drive Robert E. Lee right back over the Potomac and right into the ground, for that matter?

Brooks was second in command of a reserve platoon. Now, in the half-light before dawn, he went to his men and helped them check their gear. Ammunition was counted, rifles oiled, dry socks that might never be worn were tucked into knapsacks, hostages to an uncertain future. And then, in the light of guttering candles, letters were written to lovers and family and friends. Brooks watched a young Vermont farm lad painfully struggling with a broken-off quill and blotted paper. What was the boy's name? There were so many names to learn, and so little time to do it in. Patterson. Bill Patterson. "Snowville," they called him, for that was his home town. Snowville. Brooks stepped up to the boy. Big as he was, Snowville couldn't have been more than seventeen. They would be missing those shoulders, that strong back, from the harvest this fall.

Brooks spoke softly. "Can I help you, Bill?"

The boy blushed, looked away quickly, and as quickly met Brooks's eyes, and when he spoke, it was with the trace of a stammer. "I . . . just don't know how to finish the darn thing. It's to Vivie, see? She's a girl."

Brooks postponed the smile that wanted to form on his lips. When he spoke, it was with measured gravity. "Well, when I write to young ladies, I often end with 'Affectionately yours.' Assuming, that is, that I feel affectionate toward them."

"Oh, I do that. That'll be just dandy, and I thank you. Lieutenant . . . ?"

"Yes, Bill?"

"How do you spell 'Affectionately'?"

They formed ranks in darkness, and in darkness they marched. Brooks could feel the awesome power of Little Mac's massed cannon and mortars banked on the hills at his back, on the heights east of the creek, silent, waiting. Four abreast they marched, for the little path would take no more, it being a road for farm wagons at best. There was a shuffling, creaking, rustling sound to it, try as they did for silence. It seemed to Brooks as if some old stiff-scaled dragon was painfully pulling itself through the woods, across the cornfields, rustling, scaly, hate in its heart, ready to breathe fire on whomsoever might be so bold as to offer opposition. Brooks knew, too, that there was virtually no chance at all of their movements going undetected by Lee's spies. The creek was so small, the woods were such a perfect hiding place for the spies of both camps. Brooks wondered what General Hooker was like. His platoon was backing up Hooker, crossing the Antietam creek at Upper Bridge to attack Lee's flank. But Brooks had never met the general. They crossed Upper Bridge just as dawn broke, and their footsteps made a muffled drumming on the worn boards.

The cart track led through woods and past a cornfield. Brooks could smell the late-cut corn, a good rich smell. He wondered who'd cut the corn next year.

Then the earth began rippling like a flag in a windstorm, and a roaring grew in his head that had the crashing density of a hundred thunderstorms reverberating inside a big tin drum. His ears hurt but there was no time to feel the pain. They broke formation without an order, scattered and dived for cover, and Brooks could feel the pent-up tension in him breaking too, as the silence of the Antietam dawn was blasted away along with half of the opposing hillside. *That'll wake up Johnny Reb good and proper*, thought Brooks as he yelled an order for his men to regroup, shouldered his rifle, and shot at he knew not what. Brooks wondered why his men weren't obeying him, for they were good men, and only then did he realize that the noise was so overwhelming no one could hear his shouted commands. And he was hoarse already with the yelling. Running, stooping, darting this way and that, he made the perilous cover of the woods at the end of the cornfield. The battle roared around him. It was nothing at all like textbook battles, and bore no resemblance to the map in his head. Everything was roaring and smoke, confusion punctuated with screams, a swirling, dodging, turning whirlpool of a skirmish that seemed no part of a larger plan.

Brooks made it to the woods but felt no gain in it, nor safety either. For the woods were thin, and exploding around him. Brooks couldn't tell whether the artillery blasts were coming from Lee or McClellan, and it seemed not to matter in this awful new world of smoke and screaming. The woods thinned out into another field filled with burning haystacks, and at the far end, the blackened shell of someone's farmhouse.

Someone ran past him, close, and Brooks turned. It was the boy Snowville, running low, crouched. As Brooks watched, the boy clutched at his throat and fell, silently, not even whispering, a pantomime of death. Brooks rushed to his side, knelt, looked, and as quickly looked away. The boy hadn't cried out because his throat had been blown open, leaving a gaping red crater big enough to put your fist in. There was a horrible gurgling sound. Brooks fought down a quick, hot wave of nausea, and remembered the boy's letter to Vivie. He unbuttoned the lad's tunic, reached into the pocket, and withdrew the letter. He looked at it: cheap white paper, crudely addressed by a hand that would never move again: *Miss Vivian Macdonald, Ledges Farm, Snowville, Vermont.* Poor Vivie. Brooks carefully pocketed the letter, vowing that if he got out of this hell alive, the first thing he'd do would be to post it with a covering letter to the girl and Snowville's parents. And he thought of Caroline. How right he'd been not to send any eve-of-battle maunderings to Caroline. It would only add to her fears and worries, and goodness knew she had more than her share of those. He wrote regularly, and at leisure. Not that any written words could sum up what he felt for Caroline. Then a new volley of artillery hit the hayfield and shook Brooks from his reverie. He leaped up and ran for the far side of the field, past the burnt-out farmhouse, beyond fear, beyond thinking. He had yet to see a Confederate soldier.

Brooks lost all track of time. The sun rose hot at his back, made pale by battle smoke, by the haze of peaceful things burning. The smoke seared his throat, burned into his lungs, made his eyes run red with rage and sorrow. He had started this black day with two hundred rounds of ammunition. He ran out well before the sun climbed to its noontime heights, and stooped, running, and almost without thinking liberated an ammunition round from an armless Federal corpse. The fields grew bodies now, and his eyes had seen so much death, such oceans of blood, that it all became one death, one wound, and his heart was numb with the force of it. There was only so much horror a mind could hold without overflowing. Brooks could feel his fear slipping away with his sanity in this world without logic or direction. He had no idea where he was, or where he was supposed to be. It had been hours since he'd seen one of his own men, or anyone else he recognized.

Noon found him on a little rise with a knot of ragged Federals, and someone said Hooker's line was that way, and when Brooks looked that way, all he could see was a fringe of woods and puffs of smoke, nothing like a line or a formation of any kind. Madness. They crouched on their rise, embracing tree trunks. Suddenly, from the woods where Hooker's line was supposed to be, there emerged a screaming rabble of Confederates, the first enemy Brooks had actually seen this day. He felt strangely calm as he raised his rifle and fired. One of the Confederates fell down. He aimed again, fired, missed. Aimed again. Another gray-clad figure fell. The line was wavering now. And now a mortar came whistling out of heaven and did the rest, roaring death, exploding in a burst of fire and smoke, leaving a crater and no grays at all. And the little knot of Federals dissolved as mysteriously as it had come together. Brooks ran for the left of the woods, not knowing whether it was the right direction, not caring. *This will go on forever. I am trapped for eternity in this roaring hell.* He was tired beyond exhaustion, tormented beyond the edge of fear, running on pure gut instinct now, and it was a wild new instinct, the urge to kill, to get through the next five minutes alive at any cost, just to reload and fire one more shot.

He was in a plowed field now. The neat furrows had grown a nightmare crop of corpses. Brooks had stopped trying to help them now: in a world where death was the standard, surely it was madness to try and prevent it.

A familiar shape appeared at the far edge of the field. Almost idly, between shots, he wondered what it was.

How like Neddy to ride into my nightmare on a big black horse. But there he was, in the flesh, Captain Edward Hudner Chaffee, fresh as a daisy and galloping. *Of course. Little Mac's aide with a message. Is the message that we can stop playacting now, Neddy? Tell me it is, tell me it's all a dream. Please.*

Brooks watched his brother rein in the stallion. The huge horse reared up. Just like all those equestrian statues in the town squares of Europe. *Very good, Neddy. Play your cards right and we'll have you on a coin.* Neddy was looking for someone—Hooker, beyond a doubt. Neddy must have some vital scrap of news, the entire secret of warfare, no doubt. Brooks wondered why he didn't care. Ned was maybe fifty yards away. Was it etiquette, in full battle rig, to exchange a few idle pleasantries with one's only brother? He thought not. The roaring was so constant now that it had become something beyond noise, a physical thing, insistent and terrible, punctuated only by some very close shellfire and rare, eerie moments of silence.

The horse came down on all fours, but not for long. *Skittish, like certain women,* Brooks thought, as the graceful animal stamped his feet in the blood-soaked earth. There was still no sense of time passing. He might have watched Neddy for seconds or for half an hour.

This is silly. I'll just go ask him what he's looking for. Maybe I can help him. Hell, we're all in this together.

Brooks stood up then, clutching his rifle lightly in one hand, and loped across the field toward Neddy. Neddy was looking every way but in the direction he'd come from, which was also the direction Brooks was coming from.

He didn't see Brooks.

He didn't see the mortar round that blew him into a thousand unfindable fragments.

Brooks froze. He couldn't move, not a foot, not a muscle. His eyes stared at the spot where Neddy had been, where Neddy's big black horse had been.

There was nothing. No corpse, no horse, only a little crater. Brooks stood transfixed, forcing himself with all the will left in him not to acknowledge in his mind what his eyes had seen. It couldn't be. *It was a dream, then, seeing Neddy. Neddy wasn't there, nor the horse, either. If Neddy wasn't here, then he can't be dead. Of course not. He's probably back there right this minute with Little Mac, laughing. Neddy laughing. Of course. You could imagine the strangest things in battle, everyone said so. Everyone.*

There was an odd, wet noise nearby, on top of the roaring, a sort of plopping noise. Brooks found his head could move after all. Slowly, drifting down an ocean of time, he turned to his right and looked down. A horse's foreleg had fallen to earth, the foreleg of a big black horse. Severed neatly above the knee. It had landed hoof-down in the fresh-plowed earth, the hoof firmly planted, waiting for its owner.

Brooks Chaffee was already screaming when the rebel bullet shattered his kneecap.

Lily looked at her brother and tried to hide her concern. He was too young, surely, to have such a bloated face, and eyes so red, and with little pouches forming under them. All the signs of constant carousing were making themselves evident on the handsome face of Fergus Malone, and Lily's worry was all the deeper for her certainty that there was not one blessed thing in the world she could do to stop it. Turning Fergy loose on San Francisco with more than two million dollars hadn't worked out the way she'd hoped. Oh, for sure he was filled with plans, but they were mad schemes for the main part, and it was just like the old days: Fergy lacked follow-through. All of his great charm and energy and enthusiasm were right up front, right on the surface. He had no staying power, and he never had.

It was a characteristic that doomed him to a never-ending series of disappointments, and he had a loser's ingrained ability to place the blame on someone else, every time.

Still, he was her brother, and she was glad to see him.

But Lily was less than glad at the news he brought. "If it's in headlines, Fergy, I don't want to see them. Can't they leave a body alone, even for a minute?"

"Not," he said, laughing, "when 'tis such a famous and beautiful one as belongs to Lily Cigar. Anyhow, my dear, you're a heroine, that's for sure."

"Go on with you. They'll be saying I was entertaining the creature."

"Ten thousand dollars blood money, that's quite a sum, Lil, even for one rich as you."

"I gave it to poor Mary Baker, not that it'll bring Stephen back to her, God bless him."

"I'm proud of you, Lil, and so's the whole town. The whole state of California, for that matter, is fair to bursting with gratitude. Tiberio Velasquez was the most wanted villain since Murietta got his."

"I don't really want anyone's thanks, all the same, Fergy. All I want is a bit of peace and quiet."

"Not a night goes by at the Fleur de Lis but they're askin' for you."

"I'm a simple farm lady now, and well you know it."

"You're a myth, Lil, and killing Velasquez crowns it well and truly, and myths don't die, not in this town. If ever there was a town that loves a legend, 'tis San Francisco, USA."

"You seem so proud of it. Do you think I liked whoring? I counted every minute."

"And every dollar."

"Damned right I did, and look what it's got me. A fair chance at a new life. I'm only twenty-five Fergy, there's still time, or anyway I hope so."

He grinned then, and when Fergy grinned like that, Lily would have given him anything she owned or could borrow. Here was the Fergy of old, the Fergy who ran off to sea, Fergy whose dreams were bigger and brighter than anyone else's dreams. *"A coach and seven footmen, you'll have, Lil, just you wait."* And how many lifetimes ago had that been? She smiled, wondering.

Fergy bent and kissed her. "Ah," he said, beaming, "Lily, my Lily, whatever would become of your poor devil of a

[427]

brother if he didn't have this beautiful guardian angel lookin' after him betimes?"

"It's only fair, Fergy dear, that your guardian angel would be a whore."

"I've got a plan, Lil. A real plan!"

She looked up, alarmed. The only thing more dangerous than an idle Fergy was a Fergy under the influence of pipe dreams.

"And what," she asked softly, "might that be?"

"Hawaii!"

"What about Hawaii?"

"Well, there it is, Lil, and for the taking. Rich, rich land, and lots of it, and gold, maybe, in the hills, and nothing but a few fuzzy-wuzzies. Ours for the asking, Lil."

"Get on with you, Fergus Malone. You? My city-loving brother who never even comes out to San Rafael except when I'm half-murdered by bandits? What would the likes of you be doing in Hawaii?"

"Breadfruits and pineapples drop into your hands for the asking. A fair paradise it is."

"Fergy, when will you learn that nothing on this good earth simply falls into your hand? It takes planning, and hard work, and plenty of cash, believe me."

"We could get rich, Lil."

"We are rich—or on the way there. If we watch ourselves, Fergy, if we don't throw it away on wild schemes."

Lily looked away from her brother and out the bedroom window. She could see her own good green hills rolling away to the sea. As always, the mere sight of them made her feel good, for they were real, and here, and hers. But the real and the here had little appeal for Fergy. For him the unknown ever held magic, and the promise that lay over the far horizon was the sweetest promise. Lily felt the old fear again, rising in her, the fear of being left behind. When she spoke again, she spoke softly.

"Tell me more."

"Sugar. There's big money in sugar, Lil."

"Sure there is. And in wheat, and in carrots, and sheep and cows too. And gold and oil and big fisheries. There's even money in trees and grass, Fergy. But the gold won't come leaping out of the hills, and running a sugar refinery must be hard, demanding work. Do you know anything about it? If you hate my farm here, Fergy, what makes you think you'd like it in Hawaii?"

"I didn't say that . . . that I'd be a farmer."

"How are you going to feed your sugar mill?"

"We'd hire farmers."

"But you've told me it's all jungle and fuzzy-wuzzies. Are they farmers?"

"We'd get farmers. Bring them in."

"Dear brother. I can't get farmers enough right here on the mainland. How in God's name do you imagine you'll persuade them to go way out there? 'Tis a far, far distance, Fergy."

"You always find fault, Lil, it's like a curse with you."

"It is known as being realistic. Fergy, you know I love you. You're all I have, besides Kate. But I've worked too hard, and counted too many pennies, to finance wild schemes. Of course there's money in sugar, for them as know how to refine it. But I don't think it's the sugar you want, Fergy. I think you have feet that are permanently itchy, that you simply want to be off again, somewhere, anywhere."

Fergy stood up then, and his ruddy face went pale. "Someday," he said in a low, dull voice, "someone will believe in me."

Then he turned from her and walked out, and closed the door behind him.

Lily closed her eyes. *Oh Fergy! If you knew how I have tried and tried to believe in you.* Then she opened her eyes and got out of bed and walked to the window.

Lily looked out over the ranch, across the fields to the hills and the sea. Her eyes misted over, and the long-ago words came floating back to her across time and a continent: *"Save your tears, child, for one day you may truly need them."* She heard Fergy's hoofbeats receding as he galloped down the driveway. But her eyes came clear again, and her hills were still there, and her fields, and she felt the future all around her.

ᵈᵍ 35 ᵍᵉ

Brooks kept his eyes shut against the horrors that might confront him if he dared to open them. This was a child's trick, and it didn't really work, because the horrors were with him day and night no matter what he did with his damned eyes, night folding into day and day into night in a grim and funereal procession. And still he could see Neddy on that horse. He could hear the roaring; the roaring had never left his ears, nor the echoes of screams, men screaming, and horses, and the thunder, and his own voice screaming.

Now other, softer voices intruded gently on his dark hell. Brooks could feel the clean sheets. There were three voices, not his battle-screaming voices but quiet tones, tones of concern. Doctors they must be, and talking about him. Let them talk, then. It wouldn't bring back Neddy.

"How long has he been thus?"

A new voice, that, an old man's voice, impatient. Brooks was imposing on the gentleman's time. Pity.

"Going onto two months, and that's counting a week after the battle. He spent some time in field hospitals, then they brought him to us."

"And he never speaks?"

"Only when the fever took him, when we nearly had to amputate. He kept saying one thing, over and over again. *'It was one of ours, Neddy . . . it was one of ours!'* It's a mystery, Doctor. This war does terrible things to our lads."

"And we don't know who he is, or this Neddy?"

"There were no papers on him. There is, I am afraid, a great deal of looting, and it isn't always the rebels doing it."

"No wedding ring, or locket . . . a pocket watch?"

"Nothing. Stripped clean. He was very lucky to live at all. Hours away from gangrene, by the look of it."

"You've done good work with his knee, at least."

"We saved the leg. It'll be stiff, always. But he must get up, try walking, exercise the limbs, or I fear we may lose it to atrophy."

"Quite right. And him so young. Fine-looking specimen he was."

"It's a pity. He may be beyond help. And he's far from the only case of the kind. We have dozens, and so does every base hospital."

"And Honest Abe calls Antietam a victory."

Their voices drifted away. *So they've written me off, have they?* Brooks clenched his fists under the crisp linen sheets. Overhearing the doctors brought some of the anger back, replacing the dull pain, the moral numbness, the refusal to think or even move. *It was one of ours!* And so it had been, horror on top of horror. That mortar round had come right from the heights by Upper Bridge. Right from Little Mac's own artillery. And they didn't know that. Hell, they didn't even know who he was. *If they don't know who I am, then they don't know about Neddy.* Brooks thought of his parents. Six weeks. He and Neddy must both be listed as missing in action. Which everyone would translate as dead. Now, for the first time, he thought of Neddy more in sorrow than in outrage. How very terrible it must be for his parents, sitting up there in Washington Square, waiting, thinking both of their boys dead. And Caroline! Of course, she must think the same. And here he had lain, monster of selfishness, licking his wounds, too horror-struck by Ned's death and his own reactions to it to think of how anyone else must feel.

Brooks sat up then, and opened his eyes, and saw both the hospital ward in Baltimore and what he must do to get out of it, quickly. No papers. They'd even taken his wedding ring! How could he prove he was who he was? They'd believe him, because he'd make them believe him. When his voice came, it was a hoarse croaking, the sound of a carrion bird.

"Doctor! Doctor!"

He smiled as the sound of their footsteps reached him, hastening down the long hallway.

Lily looked at her daughter and tried to master the worst fear she'd known since that day two months ago when Tiberio Velasquez came calling. It was now or never. How could Kate, at six, hate her? *Easily, all too easily!* They were in the kitchen of the big house, slicing apples for a pie. Malone Produce apples, at that, and fine ones. The old man had a few apple trees, pears, too, and Fred was planting more, just as soon as spring came. *How carefully I've watched the child, these six years, and how little I know her.*

[431]

"Katy Katharine, I think you are old enough to know a great secret. What do you say to that?"

Kate's eyes sparkled, dancing with green fires. "Sure I am. Tell me, please."

Now or never. "Well, once upon a time . . ."

"Is this a story, or a secret?"

"Both. Now, hush, or you'll have to wait before I tell it. Once upon a time, before you were born, a young girl sailed all the way from New York to San Francisco, just to have the most beautiful little baby in all the world. This girl was very sad, because the baby's father was dead. But she was also glad, Katy, because she knew the baby would be wonderful."

"How did she know that?"

"She knew. Sometimes you just know these things. But there was trouble brewing. The clipper ship ran into a great storm and almost sank. They had to put into a wild tropical place in South America to get it all fixed, and there the girl—the mother of this baby—got very ill. With fever. She almost died."

"Did she say her prayers?"

"Oh, indeed she did, and very often. Well, the angels didn't want her to die, because they, too, knew that this beautiful baby was going to be born. At last the big ship got to San Francisco. The baby was born . . . and guess what her name was?"

"Hortense."

Kate had been given Lily's old rag doll to play with, and was enamored of the name.

"Guess again."

"Is this the secret?"

Lily put her arm around the child and squeezed her tight. Kate squirmed.

"It is. That baby was named Katharine. Katharine Malone."

Kate's eyes widened. She looked at Lily very thoughtfully. "It's me."

"It is you. And the baby's mother . . ."

"Is you!"

"That's the secret, Katy. For a long time, I had to work in the city. But now, now that we're all together out here on the ranch, now I'd like you to come and live here, with me, in the big house, and be my own little girl, just as I always . . . prayed . . . you would. Do you think you'd like that?"

The girl turned, and blushed pink. She twisted the corners

of her apron nervously with both chubby little hands. Her eyes found the floor. Finally she spoke, almost in a whisper. "Is this true, Lily?"

"It is very true, my darling, you know I would never lie to you."

"Then Bill and Mary aren't my brother and sister?"

"No, darling, but they will always be your friends, you'll always have them close by, you can see them anytime you want, they can come here, you can go there."

"It is true." Kate said this to herself, testing the words, as though she were learning a new language.

"I've wanted to tell you for some time, Kate, wanted you here with me." Lily couldn't tell how the news was affecting the child. She wondered what more there was to say, or to do. "Come, then, Katie-Kate, and I will show you another secret."

Lily took her daughter's hand and led her out of the kitchen and down the great hall to the stairway. Up they went, in silence, suspense building in both of them, in Kate for a glimpse of the secret, in Lily for fear of how the child might react to two astonishing developments all at one time.

Down the upstairs hall they went, past Lily's room to a closed door of heavily carved dark wood. Lily took the handle and turned to the child.

"And here," she said, trying for lightness in her tone, "is the rest of the secret."

Then Lily swung the big door open.

Kate gasped.

For three months Lily had been secretly furnishing her daughter's nursery. It was a spacious room made to seem more spacious by being painted entirely in white, the moldings and trim in palest pink edged with leaf green. There was a white four-poster bed with a curving canopy of white lace, a white silk coverlet embroidered with pink flowers and green leaves. Tall white bookshelves held some books, but more dolls, toys, and stuffed animals. There was a Kate-sized white desk with its own small lamp in flower-sprigged white porcelain. Hortense occupied a place of honor on the bed, flanked by Kate's two other favorite dolls, smuggled from the Baker house in a basket of eggs this very afternoon.

Kate walked slowly into the room. She might have been walking into a dream. Lily smiled, for it was a dream, her own dream cherished all these years. Kate moved with the natural delicacy of some forest animal, a baby deer maybe, who can roam the woodland without ever bending a leaf. The little girl would put out her hand to touch something, then quickly withdraw it, as though by touching a thing she might cause the dream to disappear.

"These are your things now, Kate darling. 'Tis perfectly proper you should touch them."

"This is my room?"

"All yours, and everything in it."

Including your mother's heart and soul, now and forever, at whatever the cost.

"Open the closet, Katie."

The closet held all of Kate's old clothes and many new ones. The room was finer than the clothes in the closet; this was still a working ranch after all, and yet Lily could see that to Kate, so well used to living simply with the Bakers, sharing a small back room with young Mary Baker, it must be like a fairy tale. Good, well it should, that was exactly what Lily had hoped for.

Then Kate turned from the closet. Her lip was quivering. She was going to cry. Lily smiled and tried to think what to say. It was all too much, too many secrets in one helping.

"Thank you," said Kate softly, "thank you." Then she ran to Lily and threw her arms around her, sobbing.

"What is wrong, my darling?"

"I . . . don't want to leave them. Don't want to be different."

For a moment Lily just held the trembling little creature. This was nothing more than a case of overexcitement. Kate would get over it, and soon. She'd have to.

"You aren't leaving anyone, my darling. That's the best part. You'll have all this, and the Bakers too. Anytime at all—you'll see. Soon you'll all be having lessons together, too, won't that be fun? And you can play here, and have Mary here, or go there, any way you like. It's only a few feet away, after all, goodness, Katie-Kate, think how I had to sail halfway around the world."

The sobbing stopped. Kate sniffed, shook her head like a wet dog, and spoke. "It's a beautiful room, Lily."

"Can you call me 'Mother'? For sure that's what I am, darling."

"Mother," said Kate softly. "Mother."

The angels sang. And now it was Lily fighting tears, all for a word she had feared might never be spoken.

Brooks Chaffee wished the kindly old lady would sink right into the earth, that she'd vanish from the train carriage and never be heard from again. It was bad enough that he was wearing an ill-fitting uniform of the wrong regiment and the wrong rank, bad enough that he didn't know whether the letters he'd scribbled yesterday would get home before he did, that his leg throbbed as though devils were tearing it apart with hot tongs, that he missed Caroline with every fiber of his brain and body, that he had no words to tell his parents what had really happened to Neddy in the horror of Antietam.

Still, there she was, eighty if a day, spry and smiling, offering him platitudes and home-baked shortbread.

There was such a reservoir of grace and good manners in him that Brooks could not bring himself to be rude to such a person. He simply wished she'd shut up, go away, vanish. But her voice droned on, and her eyes twinkled with unrelenting cheer behind the gold-rimmed spectacles.

". . . all our gallant lads, gathered in this noblest of causes, it does my old heart good, Lieutenant, to know that there is such nobility left among us . . . have some more shortbread, you're looking peaked, if I do say so . . . and the glorious victory at Antietam was just one such . . ."

I'll kill her. I will simply kill her. No jury in the land would convict me. Of all the people on all the trains north, I had to get this animated recruiting poster. He prayed to whatever gods were left that she'd get off at Philadelphia.

It was not to be. On she went, relentless, all the way to Jersey City. By then, mercifully, Brooks had fallen into a kind of hypnotic doze. What a fool he'd been to travel in uniform. Even that was a farce; he'd be mustered out the minute he showed up at regimental headquarters, that was for sure; the medical papers they'd given him proclaimed his complete inability to walk unassisted by crutches at any time well into the indefinite future.

Yes. He should have taken the time to get some decent civilian clothes. But time was what he had none of; he'd been in the depths of his own private madness too long, and at what cost to his parents and his wife, he knew not.

And all the unanswerable questions clawed at his mind like maddened animals in a trap. *If it had to be one of us, why Neddy? Will Caroline love me as a cripple? Will there ever be any kind of sanity in the world, ever again?* And the unspeakable fact. *It was one of ours, Neddy.*

The train's wheels clicked and rattled northward. Well, at the very least he'd be home, surrounded by quiet and comfort and love, home to lick his wounds, home where his attention could be diverted by Caroline, by the bank, by old friends and familiar sights and tried values. *They don't shoot you from behind on West Eleventh Street.*

Surely he'd get straightened out at home. Surely now if he woke up sweating ice water from the nightmare, at least Caroline would be there to comfort him.

It was late afternoon when they pulled in to Jersey City. The dreadful old lady took his hand when they parted.

"Dear gallant boy, I feel I've known you all my life. Keep up the good work, Lieutenant, it's boys like you who make the Union what it is."

"Good-bye, Mrs. Briggs."

If it's boys like me who make the Union what it is, Mrs. Briggs, then God help the Union. And for the first time on the long and painful journey north, Brooks smiled.

Sophie Delage came out to the ranch just before Christmas, trailing laughter and presents, and looking happier than Lily remembered. Lily heard the carriage and ran to the front door, flung it open, and embraced her old friend. "Dear Sophie! How good of you to come all this way."

Sophie beamed. "I wouldn't have missed it for anything, my dear. Come. Let me look at you. Why, Lily, you are brown as a wild Indian. You'll never catch a husband that way."

Lily smiled and took Sophie by the hand, leading her into the library. Soon they were settled by the fire and Gloria brought tea. And only then did Lily reply.

"Sophie, dear, if the only men I ever see again are Fred Baker's farm workers, it may be just as well."

Sophie looked at her hostess. Brown she might be, but there was definitely a glow to the girl. Farm life obviously agreed with her.

"Are you bitter, then? You don't think I lured you into a life of wickedness?"

Lily's laughter was an answer in itself. "Dear Sophie. Once, for sure you saved my life, and probably twice, and Katie's too, by taking me in. If there's any blame, it falls on me, and when St. Peter asks me, should I get that chance, that is exactly what I'll say."

"Just seeing you look so well makes me feel better, dear. To have all this . . ." Sophie gestured at the handsome room, its bookshelves only a quarter filled as yet, and mostly with farming journals. "You truly have made a life for yourself, just as you planned. Tell me. How's the baby?"

[436]

"Not such a baby. Kate's six, and she's with me now, and she knows the story, more or less."

Sophie sipped her tea, nibbled a lace cookie, leaned back in her chair and sighed. It seemed to Lily that there was a world of regret in that sigh, and this made Lily feel in one quick rush of happiness how lucky she had been to escape the bawdy life after only six years of it, and with her health intact, and a good nest egg.

"I have come," said Sophie with a portentous air, "to tell you some news."

"Oh, tell me! All the news we get out here is how the crops are sprouting and is the henhouse finished yet."

"Well. I am following your good example, Lily. I have sold the El Dorado. I'll be sailing for New York in two weeks, and when next you see me I shall be Mrs. Sophie Pritchard, The Elms, White Plains, New York, and a most respectable widow. Actually, that is my real name."

Lily looked at her friend, amazed. Suddenly it occurred to Lily how much there was about Sophie that she didn't know and had never asked. Impulsively, Lily jumped up and ran to Sophie and kissed her.

"I'm very happy for you, Sophie, and I know you will be happy, too, in your new life."

"I never thought I'd do it. Truly, it was your good example that set me off." Sophie dropped her bright eyes to the tea table. "You are everything I could have been, Lily, here, on this fine ranch, with your child. But I was too greedy. I waited too long, and suddenly my youth was gone, and with it all the chance I ever had of real happiness."

"But surely you've had friends . . . had fun?"

Sophie hesitated before she replied, and when she spoke, her voice was so low, she might have been speaking only to herself. "The only friend I ever made in this business is you, Lily, and your scorn for the business showed me my life for what it is, and, worse, for what it might have been."

"My scorn was never for you, dear Sophie."

"But you, Lily, you could be anything . . . still can be. You could be a queen."

"I'll be happy if our squash vines grow well, and if Kate blooms strong and fair."

"You know yourself better than ever I did at your age, my dear. But don't be too harsh on the world just because you had a bit of bad luck. The right man might still come along."

"Get on with you! Sure, and he'd have to be far off the path to find me here, and you can bet I'll not go hunting. I'm through with all that Sophie—I guess we both are. I'll take tea over champagne anytime, and a day riding in my hills to all the balls and parties that ever were."

"The saddest thing in all the world, Lily, is a door shut tight, for who can ever know what great joys are locked out forever on the other side?"

"Or what great sorrows."

"Maybe they go hand in hand. Well, perhaps that is enough of philosophy for the moment. I really came to say good-bye, and to tell you, Lily dear, that you will live forever in my heart, even if I'm on one side of this big country and you on the other."

They both stood, and again Lily embraced her friend. They kissed warmly, and promised to write often.

"I won't forget you, either, Mrs. Sophie Pritchard, The Elms, White Plains, New York!"

"My dear farm lady! Remember my words, Lily, and don't lock yourself away from the world. You aren't a nun, you know."

"That fact," said Lily with a laugh, "has come to my attention. Bon voyage, Sophie, and I thank you for everything."

"Good-bye, my darling."

As she watched Sophie's carriage disappearing down the long driveway, Lily thought: *There goes my last real connection with the old life, but for Fergy, but for Stanford, and the Lord knows it's little enough of those two I'm seeing these days.* Then she heard Katie's voice, laughing at play with little Mary Baker, and went to invite them in for milk and cookies.

Brooks drew the oversized military coat tight around him as he stood on the deck of the ferry. It was a cold gray day in early December, but still he stayed on deck. The ferry's progress was so smooth and so slow that the skyline of New York seemed to be moving toward them, an army of steeples and row houses; shops, factories, and water towers; and trees. New York at last!

He surveyed the place where he'd been born and lived nearly all of his life. If anyone had asked him, even now, how he felt about New York, Brooks would have readily sworn he loved it. But now the sight of these familiar streets and spires, the bustling wharves, even the smells and sounds of home were reaching him, but with a disconcerting difference. He felt, even as he swung himself down the gangplank on his borrowed hospital crutches, a sense of detachment, as though none of this were real. It was like looking at pictures in a stranger's album.

He hailed a cab and gave the address on West Eleventh Street.

Oh, there might be those who'd say he owed it to his parents to go first to them. But they'd waited this long, and he was uncomfortable in the borrowed uniform—a dead man's uniform, he was sure, for there had been no mention of his giving it back—and he had closets filled with good clothes. And Caroline! All the excuses he might make up led straight and simply to the real reason he urged the cab on faster. Just to see her again would be a balm to him. To hold her, to love her, to be bathed in her warmth and all the sweet reciprocities of loving: that was what Brooks wanted, perhaps more than life itself. And all the rest of it could wait, the tragedy and the telling of it, the bottomless horror of his own doubts and fears.

It hadn't changed at all, but for the leaves being gone from the trees. They had just been about to turn when he'd left this dear street, this lovely house. Three months?

It hadn't changed. Here were the brownstone stairs, here the acanthus leaves wrought forever in the iron of the rail, there the brass oval gleaming with the scrolled number plate, the doorframe all chastely white, twin columns framing twin strips of glass, the door itself deep green, in fine contrast to the warm brick, lights gleaming from within. Home!

She might not be there.

She had no reason to be, unless his letter had arrived, which it well might not have done, mails being what they were in these confusing times. He paid off the cab and swung himself down on his good right leg. The left leg was so painful now that it had moved almost beyond pain. It seemed like a permanent hereditary curse burning into his brain. He fitted the wooden crutches under his arms and lurched across the sidewalk. *I must look like the devil. They'll think I'm one of the begging wounded. Well, in a way, I am.*

He had no key. As he reached for the polished brass lion's head with the steel ring in its mouth, Brooks wondered where all those things were now: the locket of Caroline, painted on ivory, charming but not a patch on the original, his wedding ring, keys, letters, all the fine uniforms in the best British broadcloth. Neddy's things too—who had them? Maybe they, at the least, had been salvaged; you wouldn't expect looting in a headquarters company. But then you wouldn't expect any of it, not the looting, nor the confusion, nor the horror. He knocked and heard it echo in the empty hall.

It was a quiet time on West Eleventh Street, just before sundown. Here and there a gas lamp flickered in the gathering dusk. Lights were on in his house, too, and surely even if Caroline wasn't at home there must be a servant. Was that the sound of someone laughing? It was vague, if he had truly heard it at all, and it might as well have come from across the street, or another house. How long it had been since he had heard a carefree laugh, or even imagined one, if that was what he was doing at this moment. Again he reached for the lion's head. It was damned cold on these steps. If no one came this time, he'd go to his parents' after all. The thought of doing that chilled him even more than the brisk December wind.

The door opened a few inches. A woman he'd never seen before stood there in a disheveled maid's uniform, greasy apron, a lock of her mouse-brown hair tumbling neglected over her forehead.

"Whacherwant?"

There were so many answers to this that for a moment Brooks stood at the door gaping. He really must speak to Caroline about having so slatternly and ill-spoken a servant, in any capacity. His mother would probably faint, greeted by such a mannerless hussy. She stared at him with the fixed intensity known only to madmen and the very stupid.

"I want to come in. I live here, my woman. I am Brooks Chaffee."

Her reaction to this was as unexpected as the woman herself: she screamed at the top of her lungs and tried to slam the door in his face. But Brooks had seen it coming, and wedged one of his crutches into the small gap, and leaned on the door with all his weight. The girl retreated, still screaming, as the master of the house came tumbling into his own front hallway. Brooks was enraged, but not so thoroughly that he couldn't see the comedy of it. How he and Caroline would laugh, later on, when all was known! For the moment, he hoped none of his conservative neighbors had witnessed the undignified scene.

Brooks righted himself and slid out of his coat. The servant had vanished into the depths of the house, undoubtedly to arm herself or bring reinforcements.

A door opened upstairs. There was laughter; then the door slammed. A man's laughter. Footsteps, seeming to stumble, on the stairs.

"Caroline?"

Her voice was slurred. "Whoever you are, I am not receivin'."

"Caroline, it's me. Brooks."

"That, sir, is not funny. Not funny at all."

He hobbled to the stairs and began pulling himself up. It was more work than he expected. Brooks heard the sound of his own heavy breathing fill the stairwell, punctuated by the thumping, bumping of his awkward crutches. She heard it too.

"Don't you come any further, hear?" There was something strange in the voice he loved so well. Brooks kept on climbing.

"If this is another one of your jokes, Jack Wallingford, it is in very poor taste."

"Caroline. It is me."

"I will scream. I will get the police."

Women who say they'll scream never do it. Where had he heard that? From old Jack himself, most likely.

"I warn you, I am not alone."

He pulled at the handrail and pushed with his crutch. The bedroom door slammed, a lock clicked. There. The landing. He paused, got his breath. Their bedroom was only halfway down the hall. The well-remembered blue carpet stretched in front of him, beckoning, a mine field. Slowly, painfully, propelled by crutches and willpower and the power of all the love for her he'd been storing up these several months, Brooks swung his way down the hallway. *Where were the old servants? What was this mad laughter in the afternoon? Was this really his house after all?* The sinking feeling in his gut struggled with the burning desperation of his love, of all the hope that was left in him, and the fragrant memory of last year's dreams.

Like a demented crab, Brooks pulled himself to her door, knocked, and knocked again. The sound of it seemed to rattle the big house to its foundations.

Then came that laughter. A man's laughter. A sound like scuffling. And Caroline's voice, slurred, drunken, mocking. "Do go away. You—all are intrudin' upon the grief of a poor war widow lady."

And the man in there laughed.

Brooks looked at his bedroom door, gateway to the dearest pleasures he had ever known or ever wanted to know. His brain went mercifully numb then, or he might have found a gun and shot them both, or burned the place down. *They don't shoot you in the back on West Eleventh Street!*

He lifted his crutch, feeling the weight of it. Good solid maple, by the look of the thing. He wondered if it would serve to break the door down. He wondered if seeing her would finally drive him over the edge of sanity. He looked at the door, at the fine-edged moldings and gleaming hardware of it, at its immaculate white paint.

He didn't want to see what was behind that door, or hear it explained. He'd heard too much already.

Brooks turned then, pivoting on his crutch, and made his way back to the head of the staircase, leaving small round tracks in the deep Axminster wool of the carpeting. He gripped the smooth round mahogany railing and lowered himself, tread by tread. He might as well have been lowering himself into his own grave.

Brooks noticed, as he let himself out, that she'd changed the lock. Then he was on the street again, hailing a cab for the short ride to Washington Square. The borrowed officer's overcoat lay where he'd dropped it in the hallway. Brooks was beyond pain now, past feeling cold. The chill that was settling on his heart had no end: a kind of infinite numbness was settling over his feelings now, an emotional frost that could keep all the glaciers of the Alps in perfect, unmelting form forever.

The little maid at his parents' house squealed with pleasure, forgot herself, jumped up, and kissed him. Brooks smiled, but it was a thin and chilly smile. The welcome had come too late. He'd picked the wrong house to come home to first. His parents were at tea in the back parlor. The Old Gent looked very old indeed in the flickering firelight, paper-thin he looked, and brittle, as if made of some rare and fragile blown glass. His mother, unchanged, pink-cheeked and vigorous, rose with a shout.

"Oh, Brooks, thank God," she said, and fairly flew across the room to him. "We just got your letter, and we've been counting every minute."

His father rose, and they embraced. All the Old Gent said was: "Welcome home, son."

But that was enough. Brooks sat by the fire and was soon being plied with tea and little cakes and the ginger cookies he'd loved since childhood. Brooks felt all the warmth and tradition of his family home closing around him, comforting in its permanence. Some things, at least, didn't change.

And when he had to tell them about Neddy, his parents

gallantly made it easy for him. Having expected the very worst, they were quick to assure him his survival counted as the best and biggest of miracles. And never once did they mention Caroline.

Finally, after dinner, he brought up the subject himself. They were back in the parlor, the men sipping port, Mrs. Chaffee quietly sewing.

"I won't," Brooks said quietly, looking at neither of his parents but into the flames, "be going back to Eleventh Street."

"You've seen her, then?" His mother's voice was restrained as ever, picking up the words with silver tongs.

"I stopped by this afternoon."

"We're very sorry, Brooks."

"Who is he?"

Mr. Chaffee had said nothing until Brooks asked this question.

He poked a log viciously, unnecessarily. "That," he said bitterly, "would be one thing. I am afraid, son, that it isn't just a case of 'he,' but rather, of 'they.'"

Brooks had no way to reply. He sat silently looking at the fire, wishing with all his heart that Neddy's mortarball had come to Antietam with Brooks Chaffee's name on it. "I had no idea. None at all."

"There were," his mother said softly, going right on with her needlework, "rumors, even before you left, but we do not traffic in rumors."

No, Brooks thought, that was true: the Edward Hudner Chaffees were far above gossip, although obviously not beyond the reach of its insidious whispers. Brooks remembered Caroline coming out of Delmonico's Hotel, her tale that she'd taken tea with a girl he was sure had been in Europe at the time. He thought of Caroline's soft skin, and her smile, and the eyes so dark and filled with secrets. Secrets, indeed.

"I have only the clothes I'm wearing. Tomorrow we can send Perkins for what I left at Eleventh Street."

"What," asked his mother, "will you do?"

"About Caroline? I don't know. Divorce her, I suppose, messy as that might be. I don't want her dragging our name any deeper into the mud than she's done already. But, as for this minute, all I can say is, I'm very glad to be home, here, in this house. And I'm very tired. We can talk about it tomorrow, can't we? The fact is, I'm so upset by what's happened, I just don't know what I want. Except to sleep."

He stood up then, fighting the pain, kissed his mother, and

[443]

got himself to the stairs. His mother's last words followed Brooks and chilled him more deeply than he thought words from those kind lips could ever do.

"Don't think too much about her, dear: she isn't worth it. She never was."

The rebel bullet that destroyed his kneecap was nothing at all compared to the casual, vulgar, greedy means Caroline had chosen to shatter his heart. The feeling was beyond pain, for physical pain carried with it the promise that it might one day cease, and Brooks knew that the hurt he had suffered this day would haunt him and torture his affections until he died. For if what Caroline had been, and so lately, could turn so easily into what she now was, how could there ever be hope for any woman? And somehow his pain was more intense for finding out, at last, that his family had known about Caroline from the beginning. Caroline was the reason for the distance that had grown between them, between him and Neddy!

Slowly, dragging now, and no longer bothering to hide his handicap, he climbed the stairs. Down the hall he knew by heart. Past Neddy's door. All the way to his boyhood room with its neat narrow bed, the banner from Yale, the schoolbooks and novels, the rack of clay pipes he'd felt so grown-up smoking. There might be some old clothes still, or maybe some of Neddy's. *Wear Neddy's clothes?* A shudder went through him. That would be either a sacrilege or an honor. *Can't think about that just now, thank you all the same. No, think. It would be an honor. What would Neddy want? Surely if things were different, I would want him to use my things. Some possessions rightly ought to be shared, passed on. Some things. But decidedly, oh, most decidedly, not wives!* His crutches clattered to the wooden floor, and Brooks hardly heard them fall. He sank onto the bed and slept at once, in his clothes, and for one merciful night he dreamt no dreams at all.

⋞ 36 ⋟

Lily looked up at the perfectly blue and cloudless sky and cursed it. *Six weeks now, and not a drop of rain, and none in sight, not, surely, in this fair sky.*

The spring drought of 1863 came riding in on the heels of a dry winter, and now it was apparent that this was a serious long-range unbalance of the normally well-watered coastal hills north of the city. Only the dew that trailed behind the inevitable morning fog left some small residue of moisture on the land. But cattle couldn't drink the dew, nor crops thrive on it.

Lily and Fred Baker watched the new shoots of spring turn brown and curl in the relentless sun. The hacienda's well was deep and generous, and gave enough water for the people on the huge ranch, and for the cows and sheep to drink. If the well held out. But they had never thought to make plans for such a drought, for there had never been such a drought, at least not within the memory of anyone Lily or Fred had talked to. Sheep eat almost anything, but the cattle were another matter.

If there were no crops, then there could be no fodder, and the poor beasts would starve. Lily thought of her bank account at Wells Fargo, but even that was no consolation, for there was no fodder to be bought: each farmer grew what he needed, and in this drought they were all in the same sad predicament. Day by day, as spring wore into summer, the dust rose higher and the cattle grew thinner. Squads of Mexicans were sent into the highest hills to cut what grass they could, for the fog-shrouded hilltops still supported some green. But it was not enough, nor close enough to do any real good. Fred calculated they could hold out for another two weeks, cutting grass in the hills. Then, unless something turned up, they'd have to begin the slaughter.

Fred and Lily rode the length and breadth of the ranch, seeking everywhere, anywhere, for an answer.

There were two fine streams that usually came tumbling

down from the hills. Both were dry now, parched and empty, expectant and sad to look at in their sudden deprivation. *When the rains do come,* thought Lily, *we will build a dam up here, and a fine reservoir, and pipes down to the fields, so this will never happen again.*

It was a fine thought but small consolation as she and Fred sat on their horses looking down over the toast-brown hills to the immensity of water that was the Pacific Ocean, mocking and unusable. *If only there were a way to take the salt out of the sea!*

"Could it be done," Lily asked almost idly, "to dig a great well up here, Fred, and pipe the water to the fields?"

"It'd cost a fortune, and with no guarantees."

"Let's try."

The well diggers came two days later and stayed three weeks, and in those three weeks not a drop of water was found in their drillings, and not a drop fell from the unforgiving sky.

The dust was suddenly everywhere. Lily choked with it; it was all through the house, in their clothes, in their beds even. You couldn't hang clean-washed laundry out to dry, for it would be coated with dust in ten minutes, fine brown dust light as air, dust that lined your nostrils and grated in your throat, dust that made plumes of dust smoke in every footfall, dust that made eyes red, that coated every needle of the pines and made the desiccated leaves on the thirsting eucalyptus look like something carved from the living earth.

Lily watched the cattle slowly starving, and it cut her to the heart. *Was it for this that I worked and slaved and debased myself? To find this magic world and see it bake away before my eyes, as though the fires of hell itself were turned on me? Is it a punishment after all, a judgment on my wickedness?*

Lily was in the kitchen, making tea, in the third month of the drought when Fred Baker walked in. She smiled, but thought: *He's changed too, he's drying up like the land itself, poor Fred, he cares for it all as much as I do, and what can either of us do?*

"Will you take tea, Fred, or something stronger?"

"What I would truly like is a fine cool beer."

Lily dropped her spoon. *Beer!* She jumped up, realizing as she did so that Fred might think she'd lost her senses.

"Beer! Fred, that's it."

"If you haven't any, tea's fine."

"No, silly, beer is the answer. The Japanese use it to fatten their cattle. We can't buy fodder, Fred Baker, but we can buy beer."

"Are you sure? I've heard of hogs eating brewery wastes, but they'll eat anything."

"No, 'tis true, I swear it. I read it in one of the British journals. Tomorrow, Fred, you'll go into town and buy all the beer they can spare, thousands of gallons. You'll see."

Two days later a procession of heavily laden wagons began to arrive at the hacienda. Fred had bought forty thousand gallons of beer. A special trough had been knocked together in the cattle yard and lined with tin.

The cows and steers took to the beer like old-time topers. In a day Lily and Fred could see the difference. In a week, two hundred head of cattle had consumed nearly all the beer, and they bought more. The place stank of it. But cows that had looked like living skeletons, all ribs and empty udders, now waddled about, fat and happy and, Lily guessed, more than a little tipsy. Still and all, her inspiration worked. They lost not one cow. *God knows what the brewers of San Francisco think we're up to out here*, she thought, as they ordered and reordered enough lager to float the navy.

But still the sun shone relentlessly on the parched, dust-haunted land. And still there was no rain.

After the third month Lily stopped going out much, for the sight of this land that she loved so well, in its present state, depressed her profoundly. Still, she would not give up. It was her little kingdom, and she would fight for it, and even die for it if that were necessary.

At the end of the third month—July—Lily walked over to the Bakers' house one evening after supper to bring Mary some preserves Gloria had put up that afternoon, a special Mexican paste made from dried apricots, which was the only kind of fruit they had these days, and that imported from town.

Lily paused for a moment in the big courtyard, looking up at the dazzling summer sky, blue and—dammit!—cloudless, but beautiful all the same. It was then that she smelled the smoke.

Lily knew all the smells of the ranch, and she loved them all, even the most basic barnyard odors, even the stench of warm beer in the cattle trough, for these pungent smells reminded her of where she was and what she was building here. She stood still, wondering, her head already lifted back to see the stars. No, this was not chimney smoke, not from her chimney nor the Bakers', and there were no other houses for miles.

Yet smoke it surely was, faint but a definite presence none-theless. *Of course, the woods and the hills would be like tin-der after three months of no rain at all!* First drought and then fire. Lily had heard of this pattern, but only remotely. *Drought and then fire. Like the Bible it sounded, another punishment, then? Must she now roast in the very fires of hell?*

She walked quickly to the Baker house and got Fred.

"You're right, I'm afraid. Can't hear her, nor less see her, but she's out there all the same. Depends on the wind, Lily, it might not come our way at all, but if she does . . ."

"Why," Lily asked from a brief trance of fear, "do you call fire 'she'?"

"Always has been, like ships, and even the wind, for isn't the wind a woman?"

She laughed, not a happy laugh. "You mean fickle? Really, Fred Baker!"

"We can't take chances, Lily. The trees can go like torches in a thing like this. We'd best get the men up now, and dig a fire-break trench, and make ready to douse everything on the compound with water, and thank God the roofs are of tile."

Lily stood silent, and looked at him, and nodded. *Yes, of course, they must begin right away.*

"The cattle are here, enclosed," Lily began. "Can we send men after the sheep without risking our lives?"

"We can try. Stupid as those creatures are, there's no tell-ing what they'd do in a fire, probably walk right into it and volunteer themselves as roast lamb!"

"I'll set up the kitchen. Let's organize shifts, Fred, so that we'll always have some men well-rested if there is a special need."

Lily did not want to let herself think what that special need might be. Again she lifted her head and sniffed. She was sure the smell was stronger now. And wasn't that a kind of a glow, there, off behind the tallest hills?

They felt the fire before they could truly see it. All night long Lily worked with Gloria and two helpers in the kitchen, baking bread, brewing vats of coffee, sending the younger ser-vants out with baskets of food for the men who were even now frantically digging the firebreak.

The glow in the sky was very evident now, and growing. And the smoke was a presence like the morning fog, dense and pungent and threatening.

Soon a strange and frightening noise began to make itself heard on the ranch. It was a rushing, crackling sound all mixed in with a sort of unearthly wailing and short reports like gunfire.

"Trees," said Fred Baker gravely, "exploding."

There was a big stand of eucalyptus near the main ranch house, and Fred ordered it cut down. Lily thought to protest, for she loved the graceful trees and their strange heady smell, but he told her a new tree could grow far quicker than a new ranch house, and she saw the sense in it.

They baked their bread to the groaning and crunching of hand-saws and the dramatic crash of hundred-year-old trees falling. *Still,* thought Lily, *it could be the saving of us.*

Two great water towers served the ranch, and they were both near-filled. Fred's plan was to wet down the buildings with wooden roofs if the fire came too close, and to dampen the firebreak with hoses and bucket brigades, the better to stop flying sparks. Within the compound itself, half the buildings were tile-roofed adobe and reasonably safe from fire. The newer outbuildings—the chicken coops and storage barns and the ranch hands' bunkhouse—were all of wood and all vulnerable.

The firebreak was completed before dawn.

Before the first light of day came filtering through the hills, they could see the flames. There was almost no wind at all, yet the course of the fire was obviously toward them. Lily looked out from her bedroom window, where she'd gone to take a brief rest, and thought: *Wind or no wind, she's burning everything that will burn.* Lily felt the fatigue in her heart and in her bones, but an anger was rising in her that swept the tiredness away. *By what right was she being punished?* She bathed her face, grimy as it was with smoke, and sighed, and went back downstairs.

The flames were eating the foothills now, red and greedy, their thousand eager tongues lapping at the unresisting scrub, a slow but steady carpet of fire punctuated by great tall torches that had once been fine trees. It was the devil's own army marching at them, and Lily feared for all their lives, for surely it looked invincible. Yet she trusted in Fred and his firebreak, and the water in their two storage tanks. *And if we have to, we'll feed it on beer, too, for there's plenty of that!*

The fatigue of an hour ago had been melted by her outrage. Lily found herself everywhere—in the kitchen gesturing with a wooden spoon like a general, with Fred at the firebreak seeing that there were enough buckets for his men, borrowing pots and pans from her own kitchen, shouting encouragement, cursing a recalcitrant horse, patting a waddling steer to ease it into the corral. There were thirty-seven ranch hands in all, and twenty of them were manning the firebreak.

They could feel the heat of the flames now, even as the day's heat grew stronger. There was a hissing, crackling hellfire sound to it, a noise like grease on a hot griddle, popping and snapping, a live and menacing presence coming straight at them, ravenous, deadly, untamed. For one bad moment Lily thought of running, of taking Katie and a horse and galloping for Tiburon and the safety of the bay. Then she looked at the activity all around her, at Fred urging on his men, at the men themselves, and their spirit, and even the poor dumb animals who seemed to be cooperating, if only out of fear. *No, I'll never leave, not while there's a breath in me!* And suddenly Lily felt herself smile. *God hasn't made the fire that will get the best of me!* She passed a bucket and then went back to the kitchen to see about lunch.

By three o'clock in the afternoon the ranch compound was completely encircled by fire. Fred's firebreak held. One chicken coop went up, victim of a flying ember, but all of the other buildings were miraculously intact. Ranch hands were posted on every roof now, armed with buckets and wet blankets to beat out flames. The noise was less now, as the fire advanced beyond them.

Lily and Fred and Mary Baker stood together in the central courtyard, silent, exhausted, breathing deeply yet flushed with a kind of triumph.

For they had survived, and that in itself was a victory. They had stayed and fought the monster, and sent the monster on its way.

Lily looked around her, at the buildings black with smoke but still intact. She looked up at her beloved hills and saw them bare and blackened. And in that moment, beyond logic, Lily knew that she loved the ranch more, right now in its ruin, than she had ever done. The hills would be green again, trees could be planted again. She had fought for this sweet land and thus made it her own—more than by just paying for the place, indeed; and hadn't she killed for it, killed Tiberio Velasquez himself? And wouldn't she do the same again? Lily touched a finger to her cheek. It came away black with soot. She looked at it and burst out laughing. She put her arms around Mary Baker and gave that calm, quiet woman a great squeeze.

"We've done it! We've done it!"

Then she went upstairs and had a long hot bath and went to sleep immediately. When Lily woke, late that night, it was to a strange and unfamiliar sound.

Raindrops were spattering on the tile roof! She leaped out of bed and ran downstairs and out into the courtyard and stood there, barefoot, in her nightgown, until she was drenched. Lily threw back her head and raised her arms and laughed.

It might be too late for the fire, but wasn't it rain all the same, and delicious sweet rain, too, rain to soak into the parched earth, rain to make the seeds sprout, rain to build a new life on, for all of them, and starting tomorrow.

Then she realized where she was and how foolish she must look, and ran quickly back into the ranch house, laughing all the way.

❧ 37 ❧

Brooks Chaffee sat in his father's great tufted-leather wing chair in the front parlor of the Washington Square house and looked out at the vividly blue August day. And he hated himself for a coward.

Just as the battle at Antietam creek had forced Brooks to face up to horrors whose existence he hadn't even suspected, the discovery of Caroline's unfaithfulness had come as a shock that unsettled the very foundations of his soul.

It was a revelation deeper than shame, a hurt that blasted all of his feelings into a kind of moral numbness beyond pain, for if Caroline could be false to him, who, ever, could be true?

For months he had cowered in the big house, going out only rarely, using his game leg as an excuse and hating himself for needing excuses, hoping that this bitterness would fade, mellow, praying that time would help him to forgive Caroline, to understand her, or to forget.

Of Caroline herself, he saw nothing, and heard no word, nor wanted to. With his parents Brooks carried on a pale, polite imitation of their old life, smiling at mealtime over food he could barely force down, delicious as it was, laughing at his father's dry jokes, and all the time wondering what kind of life was left for him, wounded as he was in body, shattered as he was in spirit. For Brooks Chaffee could not forgive Caroline, and no more could he forget the careless ease with which she had tossed away his love and broken that love into a thousand sharp, irreparable fragments.

Friends came to visit, once the word seeped out that he was back. Their careful silence on the subject of Caroline told him more than he cared to know of their pity, of their disgust at the situation. And with the older generation, with his parents' friends, it was worse.

For now all the casual arrogance with which Caroline had treated these people came home to roost, dripping venom. In all justice, he had to admit they were a stuffy lot; maybe it had been a healthy thing for Caroline not to kowtow to these waddling old dowagers, these penguin-suited old gentlemen.

But these same people were an inescapable part of the Chaffees' world: Brooks had known them since infancy, and rather liked them for all their formality, for all their impossible social standards.

They had always suspected the worst of Caroline Ledoux, and now she had confirmed their fears to a degree that not even the most spiteful among them would have dared dream.

At twenty-nine Brooks Chaffee was the most famous cuckold in New York.

There were streets he could not walk, houses he could not visit, tunes he could not hear because they were haunted for him by the terrible undead ghosts of a love turned to poison. The very sunshine mocked him because it also shone on her.

One advantage of being a Chaffee was that there were regiments of lawyers at hand, and good financial advice. He'd need it all for the divorce.

When his parents realized Brooks was serious about divorcing Caroline, they took it in surprisingly good part. For divorce was simply not done. In all his acquaintance, Brooks knew no one who had ever been divorced, or seriously considered it. Yet such a thing was possible, it existed upon the lawbooks, and he was bound and determined he'd do it.

What a blessing there were no children!

Brooks sat in the sunlit room, sipping tea that had grown cold, as the morning dragged on. He hated himself for a weakling, but neither could he stop feeling what he felt. To have gone through the horrors of Antietam, of Neddy's death, and be faced with this! The world he had always taken so much for granted was entirely spoiled for him now, broken beyond repairing. He reached for his cane—the crutches were gone now, he was getting much stronger—stood up, and walked to the window.

Five small boys were flying kites in the park just across the street. The Old Gent was at the office. His mother had gone calling. He watched the boys laughing, shouting, running, tumbling in the warm sunshine, and wondered if he'd ever laugh like that again. Twice she had written to him, and twice he had forwarded the letters to his lawyers, unopened. He watched a big red kite soaring up and up into the unclouded blue sky over Washington Square. What a grand, free thing it was! How he and Neddy had loved to fly kites in that very park a thousand years ago! And how the memory of it stabbed him now. The red kite flew impossibly high; the little boy ran with it, and his small clear voice rose too, a crescendo of glee. Up and up went the kite, glorious, the tension on the string increasing as the wind took it ever higher.

Then the string broke.

Higher it went, and higher still, until the kite seemed to be nearly scraping the roof of the sky. Brooks watched it out of sight, then lowered his eyes to the earth again, to the lush green grass of the park. The kite-flying boy was being led away by his friends, sobbing bitterly. *And that's the way of it, lad, you must beware of the thing too fine and too free, too alluring, for the higher you soar, the harder you'll come crashing down.*

Brooks thought of that kite, soaring and dancing in the breeze, but out of control now, a little crazy. Soon the vagrant wind would tire of its sport and dash the fragile bright plaything down, and all its fine brave red paper would lie in tatters, the sticks of its frame shattered, string ends tangled, forlorn.

In that moment Brooks Chaffee made a decision that would change his life.

The morning after the rain, Lily woke with a child's bubbling energy, ran to her window, and looked out at a world turned black by the fire. *Well, sure and 'tis not a beautiful sight, but there is a kind of beauty in our victory, for the drought did not defeat us, nor the damned fire either, and if we can come through all that, we can come through anything.*

Then Lily smiled, thinking about the replanting.

The next few weeks passed in a frenzy of planning, plowing, seeding, sweat, and dreams. The long drought was over for sure: a week after the first rain, it rained hard again. Slowly the water-storage tanks filled up again, and now the creeks ran clear and bright. Lily sat long into the night with Fred Baker, planning, sketching where the reservoir would sit, for they were determined to have a reservoir, scooped out of the earth and lined with stones, cemented to keep the water in, fed by the two creeks, with pipes to the major fields and cattle troughs. Never again would they be so completely at the weather's mercy.

"Barring," said Fred, "an earthquake."

"Oh, I've lived through two of them since 1857, Fred, and the first time they had to tell me what it was, just a bit of a bumping. The next one, in sixty-one, was a little rougher, but nothing to speak of."

"They can get rough, though, and when they do, there's little enough can be done about it."

"Then I guess we can't worry too much, can we?"

The land seemed as eager as Lily and Fred were to heal its wounds. New grass sprouted out of the blackened hills almost as they watched, and where the stumps of great old trees stuck charred and tragic out of the earth, new shoots poked up. These were small signs, but heartening, for dead as it looked, the land was not dead. The loss was enormous in both time and in money: half of their sheep were gone, and there would be no real harvest this year. Yet there were some advantages in it too: hundreds of acres marked for clearing had been cleared all too completely by the roaring flames. The rattlesnake population, never large, seemed to have vanished along with the trees and the grass.

And for the first time, Lily found herself thinking about landscape plantings.

In those first hectic years, Lily had been far too busy to do more than get the house and outbuildings into good working order. What flowers had survived the generations of neglect, she cultivated tenderly. But no new gardens had been laid out, nor ornamental shrubs set in. Only when Fred ordered the stand of eucalyptus cut down did Lily realize how much she loved those tall fragrant trees with their dancing silvergreen leaves. The great house looked naked without them, and Lily determined that this would not go unamended for long. Just as she had learned about turnips and carrots and oats, Lily now turned to studying nature's more frivolous inventions. She looked at her long curving driveway with eyes newly educated to the tempting possibilities of rhododendrons clumped en masse, and underplantings of perennial lilies, of rare peonies and great shade trees. For here in this golden climate, almost everything could grow, given love and enough water, and Lily was determined there would be an abundance of both. For what was she to love, now, if not this good land?

Brooks steeled himself as though he were going into battle rather than merely down the hall to the Old Gentleman's library. He had been summoned, and from earliest boyhood that had meant only one thing: he was going to be put on the carpet, for sure! How he and Neddy had dreaded those gentle, implacable interviews! How he dreaded this one tonight. Leaning on the cane as lightly as comfort would allow, he made his way down the hall. The library was a small room, completely his father's, lined with bookshelves floor to ceiling, dark, with dark woods and dark leather bookbindings touched with gilt. The chairs were green leather and the brass kerosene lamp had a green shade; the bright brasswork of the lamp's stem was the only vivid note in the room. The Old Gentleman was sitting where he always sat, in the swiveling desk chair, his back to the bookshelves.

Brooks sat. There was a moment of quiet. *He's as nervous as I am*, thought Brooks as his father cleared his throat and groped for the words that soon followed.

"You're determined to go on with it, then?"

"The divorce? Absolutely. And if I can prevent her from using my name, I will do that too. The disgrace she's brought all of us is sufficient as it is, and I've no intention of letting her go on with it, dragging the name Chaffee through whatever gutters her fate may lead her to."

"I'd scarcely dare say it in public, son, but I feel you are right. That wasn't what I meant. I meant the . . . other."

"My going West? It's that or Europe, and I've never been out West. It may not be permanent, in fact it almost surely won't be. But these last few months, when I've stayed inside like a hunted man, licking my wounds, it is very hard for me to say just what I feel, sir, but I know this: I must get away, at least for a while. She has ruined New York for me, as well as my marriage. There's no place I can go, and few things I can do, but that I'm reminded of her, and how happy we were—fool's paradise that I might have been inventing for myself—and it all seems lost and useless to me. I'd be no good here now. People would either pity me, which is death, or feel that they must avoid me, that I am somehow responsible for it. Neither situation is acceptable to me. What's more, after the war—I mean, after what happened to Neddy and me—I feel the need of a change. To sail around the Horn, now, that's a fine adventure. And there is such opportunity out there, in California. Maybe it is time Chaffee, Hudner opened a branch there. And there are other opportunities too, things we Easterners haven't even thought of yet. Soon after the war, they'll build a railroad. That's a certainty. Then it'll be only a matter of days—a couple of weeks at the most—from here to there. Why, you and Mother could—"

"You have always been very dear to us, son, as was Neddy. Now the war has taken him, and this . . . new mood of yours threatens to take you. That's what I wanted to talk to you about."

"You want me not to go?"

"I'd never ask that, if you are truly determined. I ask only that you think of all the consequences."

"I could come back regularly, and you surely could come out there, assuming I decided to stay. And what about the idea of opening up a branch of Chaffee, Hudner?"

The Old Gentleman stood up then, and walked to an old globe that stood yellowing on its own handsomely turned pedestal. It was far from up-to-date, this globe; Brooks could remember it from his childhood, and it had been an ancient curiosity then. Mr. Chaffee spun the globe to California, which was inscribed as being part of Mexico.

"Half a world away."

"No one knows me there. There I can make my own future, with no extra burden of the world's pity or scorn."

"You're a well-set-up young man, Brooks. With your grandfather's trust, and what you inherited from your brother, and what you will inherit—"

"Please, don't speak of it. I need very little for myself. It may be that a settlement of some sort will be necessary for Caroline."

Brooks found himself shuddering, and it dawned on him that this was the first time since he'd come home that he had actually said her name out loud. It hung there between him and his father like a cloud of noxious smoke.

"We will do whatever must be done on that score, never fear it."

The Old Gentleman, as always, spoke quietly, but gathered into his words was enough venom to wipe out regiments of Carolines.

"Even now," said Brooks in a whisper, "just saying her name makes me quake like some weed in the wind."

His father turned from the globe and walked to Brooks's chair. He put his hand on his son's shoulder and looked him in the eye, clear blue to clear blue. "I had never thought," he said softly, "that I could hate a human being so very deeply. For what she has done to you, and to all of us, I can never forgive her."

Brooks dropped his eyes first. He had known for weeks that he was beyond questions as superficial as forgiving: he would settle, gladly, for even a small dose of forgetting.

His father squeezed Brooks's shoulder a little and went on: "Go to your California, son, if you think it will help. And our blessings will go with you."

Then, overcome by what he had said, the Old Gentleman turned quickly and walked from the library.

Brooks sat where he was for several minutes. Well he knew what his father's words had cost. Well he knew that if he did go West he might never see his parents again, or at any rate, not for years. It was not a journey anyone undertook lightly. But he wasn't undertaking it lightly. He was doing it to save his sanity, to see if there was any chance at all for happiness, for a productive life in this world for a young man who had been brutally wounded both in his body and in his spirit.

Then he smiled, a quick and bitter smile, but a smile none-theless. *Tomorrow I'll book passage on the best and quickest clipper in New York!* And, who knew? Maybe by this time next week he'd be off, bound for California, where the streets were paved with gold and everyone was happy, and no one cared about where—or what—you'd come from.

✌ 38 ➳

Lily stood in her driveway surveying the new-planted stand of sapling eucalyptus, and tried unsuccessfully to think about the war raging in the East.

By the time a newspaper reached the ranch, the news in it was weeks old. The new telegraph wires, wonder of the age, now spanned the country all the way from New York to St. Louis to Salt Lake City to San Francisco. The telegraph wires quivered and hummed with tantalizing flashes of news, but detailed reports still must come overland, and there was no way of telling what had been amplified or diminished in the passage.

The war was a distant rumble, like some remembered earthquake, unsettling but too easy to ignore or gloss over. Even the bustle and flash of San Francisco, not twenty-five miles away, seemed remote as some distant twinkling planet. Lily was so entirely absorbed in building her own small world here in San Rafael that had San Francisco vanished in a puff of smoke, she would hardly have noticed it but for Fergy. She worried about Fergy but saw him almost never: this was his choice, Lily painfully forced herself to admit, for Fergy had nothing but leisure, whereas Lily lived for Katie and for the farm, and what time the one didn't fill, the other was sure to.

Not that Lily regretted an instant of it. The hours with Kate were a joy, the more so for all the endless years of deprivation, that now, magically, had ended. Lily would ride with her daughter—and a fine little rider she was, too, on her gentle Shetland pony—all afternoon and into the evening, chattering gaily or in easy silence. Lily looked at the child, going onto seven years old now, and already felt the pangs of parting, and wondered if it would be possible, when the inevitable moment came, to let her go, to school, or to a husband. Well, it would be years, and in the meanwhile Lily intended to savor every second of every minute with the girl.

Kate was a joy and a revelation, and the more time Lily

spent with the child, the more new and delightful things Lily learned about her daughter and herself. Not, thank heaven, that Kate was perfect. Far from it. Lily doubted that she could have dealt with perfection, so far from perfect was her image of herself. Like every child in the world, there was mischief in Kate Malone, and sometimes a fit of sulking, and sometimes tears. But for all that, Kate was sunshine and rainbows and all bright magical things, a good child at heart and generous, kind to the Baker children, whom she still considered her brother and sister, even accepting Lily as her true blood mother. This had come easily to Kate after the first adjustment, and Lily thanked the angels that she hadn't waited longer to break the news.

The ranch was pulling itself up from the wreckage of the drought and the fire faster than Lily had dared to hope. Their biggest problem now was a shortage of help, for the lure of gold had never dimmed, and many a good farmer had emigrated, not to farm the land but to sift the fickle rivers of the north and scratch in the unforgiving high Sierra. Lily had a plan, and soon would put it to the test: she wanted to import entire families of farmers, to pay for their moving on their signed assurance that they would settle on her land and farm it for a stated length of time. It seemed fair, and Fred Baker was enthusiastic. The next autumn might allow him the leisure to go recruiting in the Midwestern states.

In the meantime, the ranch buzzed and crackled with activity. The new reservoir was surveyed and dug and lined. Lily and Fred looked at its filling as at a miracle. It was set in a sort of nest between three hills, and from a fourth, higher hill they could look down on it as an object of beauty under whose rippling, festive surface lived the potential to save them from another drought.

Between Kate and the ranch's endless demands on her time, Lily scarcely had a moment to herself, and this, she soon realized, was a blessing. The days were long and busy and physically tiring. She hardly ever looked in the mirror, but for a few seconds in the morning while sweeping the long red-gold hair into a functional chignon. And she hardly ever thought of Sophie's words, intended though they undoubtedly had been, to be prophetic: "*You could be anything, Lily, you could be a queen.*" Poor Sophie! Kind Sophie. Sophie had meant well, but Sophie's dreams were of silk and glory, and Lily had worn silk and suffered, and for glory she cared not a pin.

Yet still Lily wondered, sometimes in the quiet of her

white-painted bedroom just before sleep came, if ever she would meet a man and truly love him. It had been—how long?—months now since Stanford's last visit, and Lily, knowing him as she did, was certain he'd found consolation elsewhere. *And more power to him*, she thought, *for hasn't he been a good and honest friend, better, in some ways, than Fergy?* If Lily could have loved Stanford, she would have been glad to. But what was not, was not. Pigs can't fly, and they had better get used to that, and live their lives as best they can, wingless. Sometimes, creeping out of some deep corner of her brain with the practiced stealth of a bandit, would come her old daydream, taking her unaware, quick and painful. In a wink she'd be a girl again, arranging flowers for the Wallingfords' dining table in the mansion on Fifth Avenue in New York. And then the big mahogany door would open and a young blond god would look in on her and smile, asking his courteous way to the library, and move on, barely seeing the girl, and surely never realizing that by this simple act of misdirection he had changed her young life unalterably.

When the dream came, which was mercifully seldom these days, Lily knew from practice just how to deal with it.

She would get up from whatever she was doing, even if she was half-asleep in her bed. She would get up and go to Kate, wherever the child was, and give the girl a kiss. For Kate was a dream, too, and so much better than the other for being real and warm and right at hand. Yet the blond young man in her dream would not stay buried. *Someday*, Lily told herself rather grimly, *some fine day, maybe when I am old and gray and a grandmother, he'll simply go away and never come back, and I'll forget all about him!*

Lily told herself these things, but she never quite believed them.

The clipper *Anne Wallach* was brand new and tuned to set records. Just looking at her for the first time made Brooks feel better about his voyage, about his prospects for the future. There she sat at Pier Nine, her paint green and shiny as emeralds, white trim and varnished decks glittering in the sunlight, a proud golden lady on her bowsprit.

And now, six weeks out of New York, the *Anne Wallach* more than justified his fondest expectations. She cut through the sea like a knife through warm butter. The crew and their officers had pride and great skill, and the six passengers were a congenial lot, although Brooks still found that congeniality did not come easily to him. The one true luxury he had allowed himself in his otherwise Spartan luggage was books. He had brought literally hundreds of them and found the voyage ideal for continuing his studies.

How fine it was to sit on the fresh-stoned deck in the vibrating blue of a tropical afternoon reading histories of the West, or the latest English novels, or refreshing his rusty French out of Molière! The easy rhythms of the clipper as she sliced through the sea were restful to him, soothing. Sometimes it almost seemed as though they'd sailed into a bright new world where there were no wars, no death, no ravaged love to linger like a cancer in his heart. Each day, though in many ways the same as the day past and the days to come, came to Brooks Chaffee fresh-wrapped in expectations like some childhood surprise in bright crisp paper waiting under the Christmas tree. Even his game knee felt better. Time and again he walked the decks, circling and circling until he feared the passengers and crew might think him daft, walking slowly at first, and with his cane, but growing stronger and putting more and more will into it, now making the full circuit with no help from the stick, touching the handrail sometimes, but more for reassurance than from any physical need, now able to walk the ship from stem to stern and back six times, now eight, now an even dozen!

What a small victory, and yet how large it loomed! The knee joint was fused, almost rigid, it would never flex properly, and it hurt. But he had conquered it. Now he was walking regularly, up and down the steep-cut gangways and ladders, pacing the deck, all without the cane. Willpower. Brooks could smile at his folly now, to think what a very deep swamp of self-pity he had gotten himself into in those dreadful first days after coming back to New York, after finding out about Caroline.

Caroline!

There, he could think it, say it, even say it aloud, run her name through his memory without leaving bloody tracks. Oh, for sure, his knee would always be stiff. And the memory of her would ever be burnt into his soul with a searing flame. Caroline would never lose her dread power to wound Brooks Chaffee in the place where every young man is most vulnerable, in the very core and center of his heart.

The knee would always be stiff, and yet he could circle the deck with it, smiling cordially above his pain, and more than a little drunk with pride at carrying it off.

How stiff, then, would his heart be, and for how long?

What merry female eyes, what red smile, what laugh or whisper, what soft lips and silken body would come to him and be believed?

What woman could he trust, much less love? Could he ever love again, who had loved so very deeply, only to be wounded deeper still? These were the questions, unanswerable questions, that Brooks Chaffee asked himself as he walked and walked around and around the decks of the clipper *Anne Wallach*, smiling a thin little smile. What a bloody miracle it was that there were no women on board!

So Brooks read, and walked the deck, and smiled his little smile.

You wouldn't call it good luck. As he inched away from his despair, Brooks developed an inclination he had never known before: he was no longer content merely to glide through his life as he always had done. Now he thought, hard, and analyzed every action before taking it. *You wouldn't call it luck,* he thought. *Luck would be having Caroline still, or somehow having the memory of her untarnished. Luck would be having Neddy back, and being able to bend your knee like a normal man.* But still and all, how many men with shattered lives got a chance to recreate their lives in a new place, with plenty of money, with the backing of a powerful family? Maybe taking this ship to California was taking a coward's path away from his troubles, away, for that matter, from the Union's troubles, too.

There was luck in simply being able to do it.

The clipper *Anne Wallach* raced down the coast of South America, rounded the Horn in record time, and looked to be fair along the way to setting a quicker time than *Flying Cloud*'s famous eighty-nine days. Even the sea itself seemed to conspire to help them: they hadn't hit a major storm. For the first time in many months Brooks Chaffee felt the small, quivering, unmistakable twitching of hope. And for the first time since Antietam he thought it might—might just barely!—be possible for him to have a future.

He stood at the slender bow of the clipper and followed the gaze of the proud golden girl. The bow wave curled below him. Somewhere in the mist a hundred miles to his right was Valparaiso, a town he'd never see. And ahead! Ahead was the future, obscured by mists more dense than ever hid the coast of Chile, but unmistakably out there, north, in the golden land called California, waiting. *And how many other foolish young men have carried this same shopworn little dream to this same, far place, and seen it turn to—what? To mud? To gold? To death itself?*

Well, there was no denying this: whatever his future was, it would have to go some to be sadder than his past.

On the highest hilltop on the ranch, six miles back from the main house, there was a spot more dear to Lily than anyplace else on earth.

The hill was high, indeed, so high that even the most surefooted of her horses had his work cut out for him climbing the thing. But at the very top itself, for reasons best known to God or nature, the hill flattened and made a kind of small tabletop not half an acre from end to end, and roughly square, with wild grass and rounded rocks to sit on, and one twisted old pine that was a perfect natural tethering place for the horses.

From Lily's Hill, as Fred Baker and Kate had begun to call it, the other, lesser hills tumbled down to the ranch house, the barns, the small perfect circle of the new reservoir, to the sea beyond.

It was always quiet here, but for the wind's music and bird calls, and on a clear day you could see the tiny ivory-colored sails of great oceangoing clippers moving inch by inch across the view like little toys in a child's dream of nautical adventures. They came for picnics now, nearly every fair Sunday, Lily and Kate alone sometimes, and often with the Bakers.

More and more, Lily found herself riding there alone at odd moments, for the hilltop was a peaceful place, and being there seemed to help her put the ever-more-busy, ever-more-complicated world into focus.

The hilltop soothed Lily, and brought her peace, and she had come here alone on this fine blue Thursday in the late August of 1864.

Somewhere back East, Lily knew, in some other bright field, on some other fine hill, young men in blue were shooting at young men in gray, gray rags if the newspapers were to be believed, and blood was spilling, fateful things were happening. In smoky rooms back East, fat men with nervous eyes were plotting to run Frémont against Lincoln in the coming election, and across the bay, said the *Chronicle*, all of fashionable San Francisco was enthralled at the prospect of a concert at the new opera house, at which the ladies would be allowed to wear only red, white, or blue. And that, Lily thought, was just how the aristocracy of California viewed

[464]

the great war: as another chance to primp and parade their wealth, and to swagger safe patriotism at a distance.

Yet high on Lily's Hill all was at peace. The lightest possible breeze whispered through the grass and rippled the surface of the new reservoir. Her pet horse, Pedro, grazed happily, untethered, on the ripening straw, and the blue sky soared all the way to China with never a cloud to weight it down. Lily sat on a smooth, rounded rock, comfortable in the riding costume she had designed and sewn for herself: an old gingham dress with its wide skirt slit into trousers. She rode long and hard these days, rode astride like a gaucho, and hardly cared for appearances out here, in her own domain—and hadn't that crazy Amelia Bloomer done it all years ago, and in public, crusading for rights in her oddly shaped knickers? Lily played with a twig and looked out to sea.

There was one slender clipper far out at sea, not hugging the coast the way clippers usually did. How far away it seemed, in time as well as distance! And where was it going, and who was on it? The easy, idle, unanswerable questions slipped off her consciousness the way raindrops roll down a windowpane.

The stillness was palpable. Only the wind moved, its murmur blending with the occasional muffled chomping of the horse. A hawk circled overhead, its wings seeming motionless, riding the wind. From far down the valley there came a faint, persistent sound of hammering. Fred's coolies building the new milkhouse, more likely than not. The dairy operation was coming into its own this season. By next season the cheeses that were aging now would be ready for market, and the year after that their production ought to double.

Lily wished that Kate were with her, and that they could preserve this lovely day forever, that night would never come, nor the seasons change, nor either of them grow so much as a day older. There was magic on her hilltop, Lily had felt that from the first, and somehow this day gathered all the magic right out of the bright clear air and gave it to Lily Malone, free gift, just for coming here. *How very lovely it would be*, she thought, *to have a little house up here, just a couple of rooms, but with great big windows and a huge porch, to be able to wake up in the morning and see this view!* It might just be possible! Not this year, maybe, but next year, or the year after, it wouldn't cost all that much, and Kate would love it.

On Lily's hilltop in the August of the year 1864, everything seemed possible.

Brooks Chaffee stood in his favorite place at the bow of the clipper, a little apart from the others, enthralled by the sight of the soaring hills, this vast untouched land that might well be his future home.

The *Anne Wallach* had passed many a ship out of San Francisco these last few days, but now, now that they were nearly into the port itself, the immense Pacific was empty but for them. They were far out at sea, farther than Brooks expected, but cutting in now toward the mouth of the bay, the Golden Gate, hidden between its guardian hills.

He was all packed, all ready to disembark, and sad that the fine journey was ending.

For the first time, Brooks understood the call of the sea, how seductively it presented its own little world, its own choreography of adventures and challenges and amusements, all remote from the greater problems of the world left behind or the world yet to come.

The sea might be treacherous, but it could never break your heart like a woman. The sea might be beautiful, but all the secrets it held, and all its sparkling allure, were nothing compared to the charm and the mystery that could live in a girl's eyes, alive with rippling changes, overflowing with promise, brimming with invitation to try what snug harbor, what jagged reef?

They don't know me here, they can't see the empty space where my heart once lived. Here I am what I am, or what I choose to make myself. Here I can walk down a street or into a restaurant without the rippling whispers coming after me; here I can hold my head up because even if the streets of San Francisco run with mud, my name hasn't been dragged through it.

Brooks stood at the rail unsmiling. He felt better now than he had since Antietam, both physically and in his mind, yet the road back to ease and happiness was a long and treacherous one, and Brooks knew that he might never be able to go the distance. Yet even the small progress he had made on the voyage was precious to him, a faint flash of hope in the blackness of his despair, something to be cherished and nurtured like the flame from your last match on a freezing night.

The great clipper sailed smartly through the Golden Gate, sailors chanting, horns blaring, passengers cheering, all unaware of the doubts and fears and half-formed hopes that raced uninvited through the heart and mind of the lone, embittered young man at the rail.

❧ 39 ☙

The new maid was named Carmelita, and while she was a sweet little thing and willing, Lily feared that she had been giggling in the vestibule when brains were being handed out. Patiently smiling, practicing her growing knowledge of Spanish, Lily was trying to show the girl how to clean lamp chimneys. Carmelita had never seen a proper lamp, much less its chimney. The chimney-cleaning lesson was going on in the kitchen of the big house, Lily in faded calico with her workday cotton kerchief binding her hair, an apron around her waist all smudged with lamp soot.

Lily didn't hear the knocker. The housekeeper, Gloria Sanchez, appeared on silent feet to announce rather grandly: *"Un señor para la señora."*

"Quién?"

Lily was annoyed: whoever it was, was unannounced. Maybe it was someone Fred could handle.

"Un hombre muy hermoso."

Handsome, was he? Lily smiled.

Such value judgments were rare for the middle-aged and militantly virtuous Gloria Sanchez. If Gloria thought the visitor handsome, the visitor was probably Stanford. Lily got up, washed her hands, and went into the great hall. It would be good to see Stanford after all these months.

But her visitor was not Stanford Dickinson.

The door stood open behind him, and Lily's visitor was framed in the bright early-afternoon sunlight, a tall, slim shadow in fine Mexican riding clothes, a loose white shirt, black leather vest, whipcord trousers, black tooled-leather boots, hatless. The sun touched his fair, windblown hair with platinum.

Brooks Chaffee, impossibly handsome, stood in her doorway.

Lily had forgotten his voice, or maybe his voice had deepened and grown weary these ten years past.

"Mrs. Malone? My name is Brooks Chaffee, and I apolo-

[467]

gize for intruding. Stanford Dickinson suggested that you might be able to give me some advice."

How did he come here? What cruel fate is mocking me? How does he know Stanford? What might Stanford have told him about me? For a moment Lily trembled, literally felt a quiver of emotion flowing from head to toe.

Then she stepped forward, smiling, and gave him her hand, sure as she had ever been sure of anything that the touch of him would probably kill her on the spot.

"Welcome, Mr. Chaffee. If we can help you, we'll be glad to. Won't you come in and have tea or a glass of wine? I fear you've caught me in the middle of some chores, I must look a fright."

The first obstacle is passed, Lily thought, chattering gaily over her fears; *his hand has five fingers, just like anyone else's hand. And God did not strike me dead for touching it. But it is not just any hand, it's his hand, the hand of fate come to destroy my little world, just as I was getting so comfortable in it, just as the first bit of happiness I've ever known was taking root.* And for an instant Lily wished the unwishable, that he had never come to shine the merciless light of reality onto the unfledged wings of her girlhood dream.

She led him into the library, trying to see the room through his eyes, thanking the old Velasquez who had first built the place for making it so grand, hoping he wouldn't think her a ninny for chattering nervously, hoping, please God, to survive the next hour without fainting or spilling something or making an irreparable ass of herself.

Lily asked him to sit down, then fled to the kitchen to order tea. Then she raced upstairs and changed into a more presentable dress, tore off the peasant's kerchief, and gave her flaming hair five fast strokes of the silver brush, splashed her face with water, and took a quick look at the result in the mirror. *Well,* she thought, grining wryly at the freckled urchin in the glass, *if he takes me for one of the servants, he won't be far from wrong.*

Then she walked briskly out the door and down the stairs to her guest. *As though I'm just like other women, as though I'm a decent farmwoman with nothing to hide, the sort of woman a young man could talk to without harming his reputation, the sort of woman a man could touch without wondering what armies of others have been there before him. . . .* Lily stopped herself by raw willpower from continuing down this bleak line of reasoning, for she knew that if she didn't stop quickly she might never have the courage to face the poor man again.

I am what I am, and he must know that, if he knows Stanny D. And still he came here! Well, it could be that what Fergy says is true, that I'm still a bit of a tourist attraction, even in absentia. Maybe I should light up a cigar and tell him a bawdy tale or two and put an end to it here and now.

Her hand trembled on the big iron door handle.

When Lily returned to the library Brooks was on his feet, examining the books.

"I'm afraid they're mostly farming journals and horticultural books, Mr. Chaffee, we are very rustic out here." *He'll think I'm a moron, a bumpkin, and he'll be right.*

He turned at the sound of her voice, smiling. *He's changed,* Lily thought, *or it's me, my foolish dreams, painting him prettier than he is.* Oh, very handsome, *muy hermoso,* to be sure. But without quite the glow she remembered so vividly. Even his smile had a cutting edge to it. *He's been damaged somehow, that's it, wounded in some way. And haven't we all?* He walked toward her and she noticed the slight limp. *Of course, the war. I'll bet anything he was injured in some battle. Lucky it is he's alive.*

"But that's why I'm here. Stanford Dickinson was telling me only yesterday that Malone Produce is the only really modern farming operation in the West, and I've been thinking I might want to get into farming myself, if you wouldn't mind competition."

"Oh, far from it, Mr. Chaffee. There's no keeping up with the demand. California has room for a hundred Malone Produce companies. We were only the first, we never thought of being a monopoly. My manager and I will be glad to help you, in any way we can."

Gloria herself arrived with the tea, and in the best silver pot, on a silver tray, with tiny sweet cakes on a flowered dish. *Brooks Chaffee,* thought his hostess, *will never know what a tribute he is getting from Mrs. Sanchez.*

They talked for an hour; then Lily took him on a brief tour of the ranch buildings and introduced him to the Bakers. Brooks talked easily with the Bakers, asked shrewd questions, showed himself to be a keen observer, noticing things that only a bright and genuinely interested student of agriculture could be expected to see. Lily thought of her own first months on the ranch, when the great farming enterprise was really only a gleam in her eye, asking and learning and relying on Fred Baker.

Oh, and of course he's a smart one, bright as he is beautiful, she thought, *and married, too, for didn't I read that in the papers? And maybe he will settle out here and truly do farming, and try for a bit of a fling with the notorious Lily Cigar, and then bring out his fine wife with her dark eyes and fancy airs, who'd die rather than ever speak to the likes of me.* And she thought of that day, so long ago, when she had seen Brooks and Caroline in Wallingford's store.

Lily suppressed a sigh and told her eager guest about the various sizes of harrows that were being made in St. Louis, and why two small ones were better suited to these hilly fields than one of the larger sizes.

Suddenly, in what seemed like minutes, the afternoon was nearly gone, and the inevitable late-day coolness was settling on the ranch.

"We'd be pleased, Mr. Chaffee, if you could join us for supper."

"Oh," he said, smiling, "thank you, but I must get back to town. Perhaps another time. You have been terribly kind as it is, Mrs. Malone."

Of course, she thought, and the thought stung her heart, *dine with a whore? Not likely, not for a man like Brooks Chaffee*.

"It has been a pleasure," she said softly. "Mr. Dickinson is an old friend, and anything I can do to oblige him will soon be done."

"I have some business that must be done in town tomorrow," he said slowly, considering, "but on Thursday I am free, and perhaps I can persuade you to give me a more extensive tour of the farm."

Lily looked at him and as quickly looked away, not daring to believe her luck. *He must not know about me, then, Stanford must not have told him, for surely had he known, he would never have come this far*. But whatever strange magic had created her luck, Lily knew enough not to fight it. She smiled with both surprise and pleasure, and once again extended her hand.

"Consider it an appointment. We can take a picnic, and a day will be sufficient to show you nearly all of it.

"Good-bye, Mr. Chaffee."

"Good-bye, and thank you. Until Thursday."

His horse was big and black and he rode superbly. As he cantered away from the big house, Lily wondered about the limp, about Mrs. Brooks Chaffee, about what Stanford might have told him, or what he might learn on his own. Did they still sell those ridiculous photographs of her in the souvenir stores? Could he have run into Fergy and—God forbid—gotten his first impressions of the Malones from him? In the pit of Lily's stomach a thousand butterflies were playing at war games. In her throat, coils that felt like steel were tying themselves into knots that might never be undone. *So here he is, this man you've dreamed of half your life, the sea has tossed him up on your doorstep, and what good does it do, but twist the knife a little deeper, a bit more painfully, in your heart? For what could you ever be to him, or he to you?* Still, he had come once, he was coming back. The future would bring what it would bring. Lily watched the dust settling, sifting down slowly through the yellow light of late afternoon, long after his horse had vanished from her sight, and she thought of all the men who had left her, and added Brooks Chaffee to that long, sad list.

Brooks could barely hold the horse to a canter as he rode down her long carriage drive. It would be rude to start the gallop so soon, it would make him seem too eager to flee.

Yet that was his first and only impulse, on seeing her, to flee!

He had been in San Francisco more than a month now, and found it both familiar and strange, a loud striving urchin of a town, barefoot and bejeweled, a place of extremes, a place that lived for the instant, where tomorrow had far more reality than yesterday. The San Franciscans were always assuring him what a coming place it was, and how cosmopolitan. They said these things a bit too insistently, protesting too much, as though they found a kind of reassurance in the telling.

That there was a real excitement here could not be denied. The city throbbed with it. The air crackled with anticipation of . . . it hardly mattered what. The next invention, the newest scandal, the latest gold or silver or copper strike in the farthest hills—all of these things were enough to set the city rippling and quivering with pleasure. All of San Francisco's nostalgia was for tomorrow, and the days ahead of that.

This suited Brooks Chaffee down to his elegantly shod toes.

His letters of introduction led him instantly to the highest circles of San Francisco banking, which led to Stanford Dickinson, and Stanford had told him about Lily and her ranch. In his hearty, convivial style, but without mentioning his own connection to Lily, Dickinson had outlined her spectacular career and her even more spectacular gesture of leaving it all behind, trading the silks and champagne for calico and a farmer's endless contest with nature.

Brooks looked at the beautiful landscape of San Rafael as he rode down to Tiburon bay. *She had come from trouble, then, and found peace in these gentle hills, in this tonic air. Here under the immensity of the California sky, one determined woman had carved out a new life for herself, built a private kingdom where she made the rules and lived her life as she pleased.*

The rhythm of his horse was soothing. Brooks felt the peace of the countryside soaking into him like some magical healing balm. Sure, the glitter and bustle of San Francisco had appeal. The raw heedless energy of the place spoke to him, the headlong rush into the future, moving so fast that there seemed to be no time to ponder the niceties of manners, or breeding, or the honor of one's wife. A man could lose himself in San Francisco's boom just as easily as in the darkest jungle of Africa. But here, across the bay, Brooks sensed another, greater freedom. Lily had found it first, but that didn't mean he couldn't come seeking, too. *God knows there's land enough!*

Brooks urged his horse on faster, and he smiled a slow and thoughtful smile. He could feel the impact of her even now, galloping away from her ranch as if pursued by wolves.

He had stood in the great doorway of the big house, the sun warming his back, mumbling something to a maid who might or might not understand. The maid disappeared, and soon a slim girl in a faded blue dress appeared, her incredibly red-gold hair carelessly tucked behind a kerchief, green eyes blazing, not a trace of powder or pretension to her.

Dammit, dammit, dammit! And why did she have to be so damnably beautiful?

There was a strange expression on her face for a moment, as though she were trying to place him, asking herself some secret question. Then she found herself, and smiled, and held out her hand.

And the shock went through him quick and clean, like a sword.

He hadn't wanted to feel that much electricity in a woman's touch, not for a long time to come. Brooks bore down hard on his game leg, using the pain of it as a drug, overstating the limp, for who would love a cripple? She left him then, only to come back, all too soon and all too beautiful, changed now, the hair hanging free, in a most becoming dress, more in control of herself. *It's an act, a performance;*

*after all, isn't she a professional, the most famous whore
there ever was in California?* This insistence had almost no
impact at all, for Brooks knew too well, and had it burned ir-
removably into his heart, that no one could behave more like
a whore than Mrs. Brooks Chaffee of West Eleventh Street in
New York.

Her face was grave for all its beauty, and her manner
businesslike. He saw how she talked to the fellow Baker, her
partner, and the workmen on the ranch.

And she asked him for supper. He made up some excuse,
feeling a fool, feeling like a schoolboy caught truant, praying
he hadn't offended her.

He said he'd come back. *Tread gently, Chaffee, treat her
like an enemy, be very wary, for she'll knife you in the heart
quick as lightning, and twice in the same year in the same
place might be fatal.*

It was ridiculous. He was a grown man, after all, a veteran
of the great war, a New York banker, a Chaffee too, if it
came to that, and here he was quivering like some rabbit confronted by a snake.

She looked like anything but a snake. The snakes were all
inside him, and well he knew it, coiled around his memory,
strangling his heart. He made the horse go faster.

What glorious hills, what richness seemed to lie everywhere. And how very peaceful it all was, and how green.
Even the vastness of the sea was far enough removed to seem
merely decorative instead of the cataclysmic force it could
be.

And so Brooks Chaffee galloped down to Tiburon, fighting
with emotions that raced ahead of him no matter how he
struggled, raced back to West Eleventh Street, and ahead, to
Thursday, to the time he'd see her again.

As much as she tried to plan the day, rehearse what she'd
say, what they'd eat and where they'd eat it, Lily found herself in a rare state of girlish indecision. *What a little fool you
are, Lily, getting so worked up, and for what?* But however
she might chide herself, and whatever logic told her about the
situation, Lily felt as young and as vulnerable as that small
orphaned girl of long ago, trembling at the edge of her
mother's grave, fighting against a terrible urge to run away.

*What would she wear? What would she say? What did it
matter?*

Thursday came creeping at her like a bandit in the underbrush, menacing, silent, slow-moving now, but poised to lunge.

The day dawned clear after a sleepless night.

How very foolish. How entirely silly. How deadly frightening.

Lily sighed the sigh of a condemned prisoner and dragged herself out of bed, washed and dressed, and went down to have her morning tea. She would show herself and her ranch simply, without any special fuss. Let him see the worst, then, and make what he would of it. There had been temptations, many and strong they were, too, that led her mind in other directions: put on a show, wear your finest, give him champagne. The good Lord knew she could afford that. But Lily didn't want to remind the man of her wealth or how she'd earned it. That part of her life was over, and for good, buried in her own mind, if not in others'.

So when Lily dressed that August morning she put on her familiar black riding dress with its skirt split and sewn into flowing pantaloons, a simple white cotton blouse, high-necked, that tied at the throat in a kind of scarf. Over this went her black riding jacket, the black vaquero's flat-brimmed hat, and her flame of hair tied back like a pony's tail to keep it from flying in the wind.

If Brooks Chaffee wanted fashion, he would have to look elsewhere.

Their picnic would be simple too, but of the ranch's best produce. Cider, they'd have, from Fred's orchard, and cold roast chicken from their own hatchery. Bread from Malone wheat with sweet fresh butter from Malone cows. And berries and Mrs. Sanchez' spicy pickled vegetables as a refreshing salad. Already, from yesterday afternoon, the cider was chilling in a brook near her favorite hilltop place. But this would be no lonesome, romantic idyll, no indeed! Fred and Mary Baker would be joining them for lunch, even if it did mean taking Fred away from the harvest, where he usually had a sandwich on horseback while supervising the hundred-some workers.

Lily paced the big kitchen, checking the picnic basket and checking it again. *Suppose he didn't come?* She looked at the clock. A quarter to ten. Ten, he'd said. *His ferryboat sank. That's it. He's dead. He died cursing the name of Lily Cigar.* Lily felt Mrs. Sanchez' eyes on her, and she grinned. Gloria Sanchez no doubt sensed how her mistress felt, now, facing the prospect of a whole day with the *hombre muy hermoso.*

Lily smiled at her own foolishness, poured herself some more tea, and sat down.

Precisely at ten o'clock his knock came echoing through the empty halls. Lily's heart froze. *It is just another day, Lily, you goose, just one more out of thousands, the sun came up like it always has done, and it will go down just as surely, and your poor little life doesn't depend on Brooks Chaffee's smile, nor on the love of any man, and don't you forget it. What in the devil have you been slaving for all these years, if not to get away from having to depend on any man, on anything at all but your own sweat and willpower and brains?*

Trembling still, Lily went to the door.

Brooks found he could hardly eat the delicious Lick House breakfast he'd ordered before dawn. He drank two cups of sugared coffee, nibbled at a brioche, slipped on the supple Mexican riding boots he'd bought just last week, and decided to walk the six blocks to the Commercial Wharf at the foot of Sacramento Street.

He loved San Francisco in the still soft mornings, dense with fog. It was a change, and a welcome one, to see the city resting, to hear it quiet. Just before he left the drawing room of his suite at the hotel, he glanced once again at the thick envelope that had arrived from New York the day before. It held a threat and a promise. His divorce was now final, so the papers had brought him the promise of freedom at the same time they had also brought him the threat of despair, the natural unwillingness of the child who has played with fire and been burned to venture near the warm, enticing flames again. *Why, why hadn't he sent Lily Malone a note, called the thing off, waited until he had more control over his runaway heart?*

It's just because she's lovely, and you haven't had a woman since Caroline. He walked faster, boot heels pounding angrily on the pavement of Sacramento Street. *And what a fool you were, in the army, being true to Caroline!* Not, come to think on it, that there had been many chances to be untrue. Then, Antietam, and the hospital, and his nerves scrambled like eggs, and the coming back to West Eleventh Street. Where he'd been so miserable, he could barely leave the house, let alone chase a woman.

And now, this void, this huge endless empty space inside him where only ghosts and devils played, where nothing grew or flourished, this dry parched husk that once had been the dwelling place of love. Brooks grinned, but the grin left him quickly. Good, at least, that he could still laugh at his own self-pity.

Not that it made the hurt disappear.

He got to the wharf in good time and boarded the little yawl he'd hired to take him to Tiburon. The sun came peeking over Russian Hill as they set sail. It promised to be fair, a good clear California day like so many other California days. Brooks sat on the hard wooden bench and wondered what else this day might promise. He thought of Lily, and of the packet of divorce papers that sat upon his dresser with the implacable weight and finality of a stone. Brooks tried to force his mind backward in time, tried and tried to recall just how he'd felt the moment he first set eyes on Caroline. In a ballroom, it had been: he remembered the music, crowds, a big formal room, probably the Vanderbilts', music, chatter, people laughing. And a hush, the crowd parting like the sea for the Israelites, and one dark slender girl all in white, the image of chastity. *Better to have been bitten by a rattlesnake and get it over with all at once!*

He could remember the impact of her but not the feeling. He could remember doors opening in his life, the sun shining bright out of a previously clouded sky, flowers blooming, all the glittering facets of happiness dazzling as a thousand diamonds, and all turned to glass in an instant—cheap glass, and broken at that.

Only a fool could take such a risk again, knowing what love could turn into.

The shore of Tiburon came steadily closer and the far hills of San Rafael loomed behind, glowing pink in the light of dawn. *It isn't too late to turn around. You don't really want to be a farmer anyway, that was just a pretext to meet the famous—notorious—Lily Cigar, fabulous courtesan, slayer of bandits, temptress of men's souls.*

Never in the country summers of his boyhood had Brooks felt any special fondness for the earth or what grew there. He had liked to swim with Neddy, and play with the animals that roamed the wide flat meadows near his grandparents' house at East Hampton, but he was a city boy in essence, with a city boy's tastes and a city boy's soul.

On the other hand, Brooks had never seen land like this, great epic sweeps of land, land that seemed more fit for gods and legends than mere men, land that went on forever, that held all eternity in the cradle of its soaring, circling hills. The land of California had literally taken his breath away. The raw force of it spoke to him, the vast promise of it overrode his doubts with a gentle violence like the surge of the great waves in the Pacific ocean, relentless, engulfing, and in some mysterious way, fulfilling.

Brooks could look at this land and feel its strength strengthening him in a way that no city, no office-based business ever could. For the land was real, alive, breathing hope. The land must be coaxed and tended like a lover. The land could give great gifts, inflict great loss. It was a challenge that Brooks felt he could handle, once he learned how.

And she would help him learn how.

He could still turn back, he didn't have to go there, or see her, or run that terrible risk again. No one was holding a gun on him, he was a free agent after all.

Brooks thought of her eyes. He'd never seen eyes like that, clear and deeply green, of a greenness very like jade, a green that seemed to soak up the light rather than to reflect it, the green of bottomless pools in orchid jungles, the green of some fern so rare that no one had discovered it yet. He thought of her hair, and her shy smile, and he did not turn the boat back.

~§ 40 §~

Brooks stretched out in the sunlight, legs straight in front of him, his back propped against a rounded rock, and sipped chilled cider from a thick glass mug.

If there had ever been a more perfect morning, it would come as news to Brooks Chaffee.

They had ridden for miles, through Lily's fields and orchards, past her cattle sheds and chicken coops and the rabbits' hutches, through an ocean of ripe wheat and corn enough to feed all the Indians that ever were.

Just the scope of the ranch was awesome to Brooks's Eastern eyes, but there was more than sheer size to impress him here, and what impressed him the most was Lily Malone.

Oh, and not the beauty of her, either, although beyond doubt she was very lovely.

It was the intensity with which Lily obviously cared for the place, her well-tuned intelligence describing, in clear and unstinting detail, what they had done and were planning to do, and how, precisely, they had achieved so very much in such a relatively short time. For Malone Produce was a phenomenon, despite Lily's modest deprecations. In only a few years they had turned this raw land into a disciplined and highly productive farm. And what might they not do a few years hence! When Lily spoke of the ranch, her voice took on a special color. Brooks felt that she was shy with him on more general ground, on any level that might seem to be personal. This was so apparent that he wondered if for some reason she feared him, or if perchance he had offended her in some way. So reserved was her manner that he found it increasingly hard to credit the stories of her career at the Fleur de Lis, although beyond doubt that had happened.

But when she walked with him out of the great ranch house in that simple, graceful black riding outfit, then—astonishment!—swung herself right up into the saddle nimbly as any boy, and soon showed herself to be the best horsewoman he'd ever seen, the skirt cunningly split to allow her to ride astride, and when she began warming to the subject of her ranch, Brooks saw a new Lily, a woman at ease with herself and her work, in love with the land and loved by those who worked it for her.

She had led him on a grand tour, and finally higher and higher into the hills, to this lovely spot where a picnic had appeared, magically all laid out for them by invisible hands, the delicate cider all chilled, and the Bakers—fine people they—soon to join them. He turned from the incredible view to where Lily was sitting on a blanket, her legs tucked gracefully behind her, hands busy with napkins and silver.

"This is," said Brooks, "the most beautiful place in California."

She laughed, at ease now, finally. "Well, 'tis the finest spot on the ranch, sir. I come here so often they call it Lily's Hill."

"And who could blame you? If it were mine, I believe I'd build a house here, to have this view by me always."

She looked at him quickly, and something changed in her face, a small ripple of doubt, possibly. Then she smiled again. "You must be . . . what is the word? Able to read my mind."

"Psychic?"

"Exactly. For that is just what I hope to do one day, when we're more settled. Nothing grand, of course, but just a sort of cottage, for picnics like this, and maybe to sleep over in the hot weather: it's far cooler up here, you know, on a truly warm day."

"It is heaven. You know, Mrs. Malone, if anyone had told me a year ago that I'd be thinking of becoming a California rancher, I would have thought them mad. I never cared for the land until I saw land like this."

"Nor I, although I'm afraid my motives were more practical than just loving the country—not, mind you, that I don't love it, for truly I do."

"I can see that. It sings in your voice."

Again she laughed, a small rippling laugh, a young girl's laugh. "And in my turnips, you may be sure! Well, I guess there are many kinds of love for the land, and loving the view is surely part of it. My father was a city man—a Dublin man—and we have nothing of farmers in our blood, so far as I know. I am the first."

"Well, you're setting a fine example for those to come."

"It is partly luck and mostly the good help of . . . But here they are now."

The Bakers came huffing and puffing up the hill just then, having left their horses tethered below because of Mary's fear of riding sidesaddle up the rock-strewn hill. They began eating the delicious food, and the conversation became more general.

Lily was very glad she had invited the Bakers. The morning had gone well, better, by far, than she had ever dared to hope. Yet the Bakers made a welcome diversion, kept the thing on a fine impersonal level, the talk about farming, weather, seeds and equipment, labor and wages, transportation and a hundred other things Fred Baker knew very well and Brooks Chaffee was afire to learn.

Slowly, with the subtle finality of a lifting fog, Brooks Chaffee the man was emerging as a separate being from the golden lad of Lily's adolescent dream. The boy in the dream, she knew by some deep and almost primitive instinct, would never entirely leave her mind or her heart. And Brooks as he truly was, here before her, would never entirely measure up to that dream, for surely nothing could, not man or angel. The reality had some few imperfections, and Lily treasured every one of them, for they made Brooks Chaffee in some small degree attainable. The limp might cause him pain that needed soothing. The thin bitter edge that sometimes slid across his smile might be the echo of some deeper hurt that she could try to make him forget. If she ever got the chance. If she wasn't just spinning out a girl's wild dream she had no right to, a simpleminded backstairs kind of dream, a dream whose weight was far too much for the frail wings of chance that flapped and fluttered, desperately trying to raise it into a golden light of possibility. *A plan: she must have a plan!*

Brooks looked at her note for a long moment before he opened it, savoring the possibilities of it, warming to the hope that it might be an invitation, that he might be seeing her again soon. For there was no doubt that he wanted to see her again. On the other hand, it might be nothing more than a thank-you note for the double volume on botany he'd sent her, the latest thing, all leather and gilt and hand-colored plates. He sat by the fire in his drawing room at the Lick House and opened the creamy envelope.

Dear Mr. Chaffee [she had written in a young girl's rounded hand]:

You were exceedingly kind to send me the handsome books on botany, which I am enjoying already and shall no doubt continue to enjoy through the years. As you know, it is a subject dear to my heart and I thank you for being so thoughtful as to remember me in this generous fashion. Fred Baker came to me today with news that we feel may be of interest to you. A large property quite near my ranch is coming on the market: it is an old royal grant—as was mine—and comprises about three and a half thousand acres of fine rolling hills about an hour's ride north and west of Tiburon. It is the old Varga y Salamanca grant, and the heirs had offered it to me, a highly tempting offer, I must say, but the truth of the matter is that we are fully committed to developing what we have, and shall be for the foreseeable future. Naturally, it occurred to us that the grant might appeal to you as a means of starting your proposed agricultural enterprise on a handsome scale. The Varga y Salamanca heirs are represented in San Francisco by Mr. Jenkins of Wells Fargo. It is good land, Mr. Chaffee, similar in character to what you saw on our ranch in that it has never been farmed and therefore never been abused. This information is, by the way, rather confidential, although I have Mr. Jenkins' permission to mention it to you. Surely it is worth considering, since such large properties come onto the market only rarely. With thanks, again, for the delightful books, I remain,

Yours truly,
   Lillian Malone

Brooks put down the letter and stared into the fire for a moment, contemplating the rebirth of his good luck. It was a wary contemplation, for the moment he realized how completely Caroline had betrayed him, Brooks had fallen into the habit of doubting and testing any random hint of happiness or good fortune that might come his way. But this! To have such a chance dropped in his lap! A grant of more than three thousand fine acres. The Malone ranch, he knew, was more than twice that size, but still and all, thirty-five hundred would be huge, an empire almost.

But how would it go with Lily? Surely she must hold some good feelings for him, or why would she relay this offer? Was there some small tender emotion stirring in Lily, the tentative beginning of . . . what? For what could a rich and beautiful and successful woman see in him? Wounded both inside and out, hardly fit company for a happy person, burdened by a vast invisible weight of sadness; why, it was only her generosity that led her to see him at all, that and her friendship for Stanford Dickinson. That was it! He'd ask Dickinson's advice. And tomorrow.

Fred Baker sighed the sigh of a man who will never understand the nature of women.

"If you say so, Lily. But we're missing a great chance. The Salamanca grant practically adjoins the north range; if we picked up a few little farms in between, we could have the whole spread—more than ten thousand acres."

"I know that, Fred. But it just seems we've come so far, and so quickly, that this is a time to be cautious. And you admit yourself, we've got a handful just farming half of the acres we own right now."

"Sure, but . . . Oh, well, I'm a farmer, not a businessman."

Lily smiled and urged her horse on faster. It was one way to end the unwelcome conversation. Because Fred was perfectly right: by every law of prudent business, she should have bought the old Salamanca place. But there were other laws, and other considerations. Even though there might be no chance at all of anything more than a neighborly relationship with Brooks Chaffee, Lily liked him enough to be willing to settle for that. And always, always, there was the possibility, the barest gleam of hope. If he were on the next ranch . . . There had been no reply to her letter. *For all you know, my fine proud Lily, he is right this minute on some clipper ship heading back to New York and his haughty dark-eyed beauty of a wife.* The horse was galloping now, free as the wind itself. And for no reason of logic, Lily could feel the winds of luck in her own life changing, blowing stronger.

Fred Baker looked at Lily's diminishing figure as she rode furiously down the valley. Women!

Brooks looked at his dinner guest and wondered if he was making any progress. He'd invited Stanford Dickinson to talk about the possibility of buying the Varga y Salamanca grant. What he really wanted to know more about was the life and times of Lily Cigar.

They were in the huge paneled, palm-decked dining saloon of the Lick House Hotel; the air was filled with delicious smells, and laughter, and music. Dickinson was all in favor of Brooks' buying the Salamanca grant.

"Only Lily understands about land," he said, sipping his wine, "but then, Lily understands everything."

And Brooks wondered just what kind of a friend this man had been to the famous Lily Cigar.

"I've never met anyone like her."

"No one else has, either," said Stanford softly. "Lily's an original, and I've seen them all."

"Meeting her out there on her ranch, it's hard to imagine . . ."

"That she was Lily Cigar? That men fought for the honor of paying the highest price any whore ever got in this town?" Dickinson laughed, but it was a kindly laugh. "The answer is," he went on, chuckling still, "that Lily never imagined herself in that role, Chaffee. It never came naturally to her, you see. Lily was broke, had the little girl to take care of, what was she to do? Scrub floors, you say? Not in this town, not when you can get five Chinese to do it practically free. The fact is, there was very little a girl could do in those days except maybe be a servant, and who wants a maid with a baby?"

"You knew her then?"

"I was her first customer, lad, and if it weren't for the child, I would have sworn I was her first man, that's how pure she seemed to me. There was—still is, for all that—a kind of glow about her, a radiance. There is a kind of purity to her, even now, an integrity you hardly see anywhere."

Brooks felt the shuddering start in his game leg then. He hadn't been prepared for the depth of his reaction when he began fishing for Lily's history. To know, theoretically, that she had been a whore was a very different thing from sharing a table with one of her best customers. He slid a hand under the table and gripped the quivering leg. It would do that, begin trembling, whenever he was very tired or deeply upset. He smiled and gathered his strength for a reply. *Well, I asked for it, then, and don't I deserve what I get? Dickinson's a decent man, he doesn't know what I'm suffering, or what I feel for her. And exactly what do I feel?* It was only willpower that kept Brooks's voice level when he answered his guest.

"Especially not in a whorehouse."

"To call Lily a whore is like calling Michelangelo a bricklayer. She transcends the category, my boy. There was a moment when I was in love with her—oh, yes. Love, not lust. All set to leave my wife for Lily Cigar, was I. And she wasn't having any."

"Why not?"

"That's what makes Lily Lily. She's dead honest, is Lily. There are those," he said, and dropped his eyes, and spoke gently, thoughtfully, as if debating the question with unseen opponents, "who might consider Stanford Dickinson something of a catch. Not our Lily. 'Let us be friends, Stanford,' says she, and kisses me on the cheek like a sister."

"She speaks most highly of you."

"Oh, I am sure she does, and I of her. But take care, Chaffee, when you look into those green eyes, for a man could drown there, and never be seen again."

Brooks smiled at his guest. Stanford Dickinson was not the kind of man he was used to, any more than Lily was like the girls he had known all his life. But he was a stranger in a far country, and all that had been so easy and familiar to him had also betrayed him. Dickinson might be rough-hewn and flashy, there might be clubs in New York where such a man would never be admitted, and yet there was a fine blunt honesty about him, a sense that he was at ease with himself and his ambitions.

"I'm glad you like her," Brooks said, "for I do too, and it may be that I was afraid of her, of her past."

"You needn't be. Good as gold, Lily is, and better. You'll look a long, long time before you find her match for plain natural refinement of character. Oh, well I know she's not an educated girl, poor and Irish her folks were, but decent I am sure. And the Lord knows Fergy's a scamp pure and simple. But Lily, ah, Lily!"

"I haven't met her brother."

"It could happen in any family. He isn't a bad fellow, to be sure, but weak as water. When they were handing out the determination in that family, I'm afraid Lily got it all. And good for her, for what she has is more than enough for two."

"She has been very generous advising me."

"Yes," said Dickinson, snipping the end off a cigar with a small golden cigar cutter, "yes, she would be."

The waiter came with their brandy then, and they began talking about Frémont's withdrawal as the presidential candidate for the splinter-group radicals in the Republican party for the coming election.

Lily looked at him and smiled for his happiness. She thought of the strain on his face that first day, three months ago now, when Brooks had come calling, and how he had practically fled at the sight of her, and all that had happened since.

They had cantered briskly over the dusty lanes for nearly an hour now, her first official visit to his ranch.

For Brooks Chaffee was now the owner of the Varga y Salamanca grant. The house and its outbuildings were smaller than those on Lily's place, but they had been kept in far better condition, so all that remained was for Brooks to move in and find reliable help and turn the old ranch into a working farm.

In this Lily and Fred Baker had been generous with both advice and real physical assistance. Scarcely able to believe that any small part of her wild dream was coming true, Lily had persuaded a reluctant Fred Baker that another thriving farm in the vicinity would be good for all of them, and that it was their duty as pioneers in residence to do all they reasonably could to assist the newcomer.

Lily had made arrangements, lent Brooks horses and workmen and even some furniture until he could settle himself properly.

But then she withdrew, left it all up to Fred, kept herself scarce, and waited for the invitation that surely must come.

And it came!

Brooks delivered it in person one fine November afternoon: would she come the next Sunday and spend the afternoon, and see what wonders were being worked? *Would she, indeed!*

Although the trip was not long and nor was it dangerous, he insisted on calling for her in person.

And what a fine sight he made, in his riding clothes, on the great black stallion. He had been so much out-of-doors, getting the ranch in shape, that the sun had painted his fair skin with a blush of copper, and made the pale hair even paler. Brooks Chaffee looked younger than the day Lily had first seen him. But more than that, he was looking happier, more relaxed. The hard edges seemed softened a little, but maybe this was her imagination, wishful thinking. God knew she did enough of that, and especially on the subject of the young man riding so gracefully beside her.

Lily had thought of the propriety of visiting him alone, had considered bringing the Bakers as chaperons, the way she had done on the day of their picnic. *Lily Cigar, well-known whore, requires chaperoning. Lily Cigar, slayer of bandits, is frightened to venture out alone.* She could laugh at the irony of it, but the fact was, Lily did feel fear, and the fear she felt was of the simplest and most fundamental kind. She was afraid he would scorn her, mock her, call her what she surely had been. Nothing in Brooks's gentle manner had ever so much as hinted that he would be capable of behaving that way, but the place where Lily's fears lived was deep and secret, and the fears fed upon themselves and grew to monstrous size, greedy and all-consuming and never quite at rest.

They rode for half an hour on her land, through air crisp as cider on a bright day that would warm toward noon and be deliciously chilly at night. They passed the marker at the end of the Malone ranch, cantered briskly over two small farms, and sooner than Lily remembered reached another old stone marker carved with an elaborate crest. Fred Baker had been right: the two properties were very close indeed. And the little farms they'd crossed were in poor repair; almost certainly they could be bought for the right price.

Lily's mind took a leap into a beautiful if very improbable future. Then she came quickly back to reality, turned to Brooks and said, "Congratulations."

He beamed. "I would have none of it, were it not for you, Mrs. Malone."

"I'm eager to hear all your plans for it."

"You may find yourself bored, for I have a head teeming with such plans."

"Nothing to do with land improvement bores me, Mr. Chaffee, you can bet on it."

He smiled, and they rode on.

In fifteen minutes they crested a ridge and the heart and core of the ranch lay before them. The buildings were neatly laid out and sparkling with fresh whitewash. The corrals had new fence rails, and there was a new and generous watering trough for the animals. From their vantage point on the ridge, it looked like a toy farm, a rich child's plaything. Instinctively they reined their horses to a halt.

"Oh," said Lily, "truly it's a fair sight, and how neat you've made it."

"Well, it is a beginning, nothing very grand as yet, and it may be years before it earns a penny. Yet, the important thing, for me, at least, is that I am liking it. This business of being a farmer keeps on having all the appeal I hoped it would."

"I am happy for you, then. How seldom does it come to anyone, to find a thing that makes him happy."

"You are philosophical today, Mrs. Malone."

"I'm philosophical every day—just ask my horse, or my chickens, or my strawberry patch."

"The philosophy of strawberries. That could become a major religion with me, for I'm mad about them."

"And I, not to mention the fact that they'll fetch five dollars a basket in San Francisco."

"That," he said gently, "is another thing I must learn, what things cost, what things fetch."

She looked at him quickly and as quickly looked away, and thought that there are some things in life so costly that nothing they might fetch in a market would be enough.

"We can help you do that, and gladly, Mr. Chaffee."

"Now that we are neighbors, can I ask you to call me Brooks?"

"Indeed you can, but only if you call me Lily."

"Lily it is, then, and a lovely name too."

"Thank you . . . Brooks." She said his name quickly, as though it might escape her, or do her harm.

He looked in her eyes for just a moment, said nothing, and flicked the reins.

They galloped down to the Chaffee ranch house, each afraid to speak for fear of saying a thing that would smash this small fragile bit of magic that seemed to be growing between them, and in them.

❧ 41 ❧

The seasons changed, fall into winter into another spring.

Lily saw him often, for there was much coming and going between the two ranches. Lily saw him drenched with sweat, helping the hands she had lent him to build and rebuild, and plant and clear land. She saw him in all his New York finery, at the Christmas party she gave for the Bakers and Brooks and two other neighboring farm families.

It was a quiet party, with candles and a big tree and presents for the children, who were all invited too. And then, a great candlelit dinner in the dining hall of the old ranch house. And they had carol-singing to the accompaniment of Fred's son, Bill, on a Spanish guitar. Brooks had given Kate a wonderful music box that played "Silent Night," and the child played it so often that Lily was sure she'd wear the delicate workings right out.

Lily loved her little Christmas party, for in truth it was the first party she had ever given, and the people she had invited seemed to like it too. It was at the party that Lily first sensed the enormous sadness in Brooks Chaffee. He smiled, and laughed with the children, and sang the carols in a fine clear baritone. But Lily sensed his heart was elsewhere, that only good manners carried him through the evening. *Well, and for sure! And hasn't he all his fine family and that beautiful dark-haired wife? Not to mention the possibility of children. Maybe he saw Katie and thought of some other little child, his own child, thousands of miles away, on a night like this!*

But Brooks had never mentioned his family in any particular, and when he took his leave of Lily after the Christmas party, he took her hand and smiled, and paused a moment before he spoke. "How can I thank you for the nicest evening I've had in California?"

Lily stood in the doorway of her ranch house, a white woolen shawl around her shoulders against the chill December night. She wanted to prolong this moment, as she had wanted to make many another moment in his company last longer—forever! But no, he must be the most casual of friends until . . . what? If nothing more came of it, the friendship alone would be more than she had ever dared dream. So all Lily did was to give his hand the smallest of squeezes and say, "But you made us happy by being here, and Kate especially, with the music box. Really, Brooks, you will spoil her!"

"And who better?" He laughed and said a quick good-bye and galloped off into a night edged with silver from a crescent moon that looked like some enormous celestial Christmas ornament. The moon turned the dusty drive to silver too, and Lily's last sight of him was the golden-haired man in his fine black city clothes galloping on his black stallion down her driveway, head bared to the chill, horse spurred to his utmost. *Why is he always running away?* For truly it seemed so; however glad he might seem to see her, and however kind his words and actions, the hard fact remained that Brooks Chaffee seemed always in a hurry to leave her after a certain time, riding away as if fleeing for his very life. *Well, maybe he is, painted temptress that I am!*

But Lily's heart barely dared to speculate on any part of her dream coming true. Brooks was what he was, and that would have to be enough.

As the weeks of their friendship turned into months, Lily got to know the many moods of the man, the sudden unexplained silences, the warmth of his laughter, more dear to Lily because it came so seldom. There was bitterness in him too, and a temper.

Brooks never raised his voice when he was angry, and his anger carried more force for the quiet way he expressed it. Once Lily came on him in earnest conversation with Fred Baker. From a distance they might have been talking about the weather. She waved, unseen, and crossed the courtyard to them. But as she drew closer, Lily could see that Fred's face was red with indignation, and that Brooks was quietly berating him about something. She only heard the end of their talk.

". . . I should have known better than to count on you, Fred," said Brooks in a voice that was iced with contempt, "and I shall know better in future."

"As you say, Mr. Chaffee." Fred turned in his tracks then and stalked off toward the barns.

"What," asked Lily, smiling, "was that all about?"

Brooks turned suddenly, the anger still burning in his eyes, saw her, paused, and managed a smile. "I'm afraid," he said quietly, "that I lost my silly temper, and about a thing that wasn't really Fred's fault. He's ordered me that new plow and harrow rig, and there's been a six-week delay, and he never told me, so I'd been counting on it. Now the planting will be delayed, or we'll have to use the old gear, which means a delay just from slowness."

"He should have told you, then, Brooks. Can we lend you one of our plows?"

"Let me think on it, and calm myself down. It's childish to get so upset, especially with poor Fred, who's been so kind to me. I'll find him before I leave, and apologize."

"Can I cool your temper with some hot tea first?"

"I'd be delighted."

He smiled for real then, but it made Lily sad to see his beauty flawed by the tight-strung cords of tension that could so quickly alter his small boy's grin, turning it into a cynic's sneer.

Sometimes Lily felt it would have been better if she had never met Brooks Chaffee, if he had lived his life back East, if her old dream had continued to haunt her all glittering and impossible and untouched by even the barest hint that it might come true. For painful as the dream had been, it was at least a dream, and Lily was beset by fear that her fragile heart might not be able to cope with that dream if ever it should take on flesh and blood and come knocking upon her bedroom door. *And would you give yourself to him, or any man, ever again, knowing the pain that comes when they leave you, as they always have and always shall?*

Lily thought more about her neighbor than she would admit even to herself. She weighed and measured each little fragment of time they had together like a miser counting his hoard. He had said this, she had said that, he'd smiled—or frowned, or looked away—and then, suddenly it was over and there he was galloping away as though all the bandits in Mexico were hot upon his trail. For all she knew, it would go on like this forever.

And then, one spring day, it all changed.

She had sent Brooks some divisions of her beloved strawberry plants, two dozen fat little clumps, enough to sire hundreds, maybe thousands, if they thrived. He rode over the next day to thank her in person. She asked him to lunch. He suggested a picnic, for it was the prettiest day of the year thus far. Lily readily agreed, and sped to the kitchen to ask Gloria to pack whatever was at hand, knowing full well that the resourceful Gloria would do her proud on any occasion, but especially for the *hombre muy hermoso*. They rode to Lily's hilltop, and this time they were alone.

They dismounted and he tethered their horses to the old gnarled tree while she set out the lunch. There was cold ham, and bread still fragrant from Gloria's oven, and three cheeses, two salads, apple and raisin turnovers, and some new red wine.

"She must think," said Lily, laughing, "that you brought a dozen friends."

He sat down next to her, looked into her eyes, and for a moment said nothing. Then, very softly: "I have."

"Have what?"

"I have brought many friends, Lily. For you have been more of a friend to me, and in more different ways, than any stranger has a right to expect."

Seriously flustered, Lily dropped her eyes to the array of food and began filling plates. Never, never, had he said anything so personal to her. She could feel the flush rising to her face like a floodtide, sudden, unstoppable. Finally she found words, inadequate as she felt them to be.

"Ah, but in such a strange wild place, we must all help each other, don't you think? More, perhaps, than in a fine civilized town like . . . New York, for instance."

She looked at him then and saw something change in his eyes. *New York. Why did I mention New York? Maybe his memories of it are no better than my own.*

And while she pondered this, and tried to make the blushing go away, his next words startled her even more profoundly.

"Have you ever been in love, Lily?"

"Once, long, long ago, I thought . . . I had a silly girl's idea of what it might be like to be in love. But it was only a dream, for I never met the boy—he was a boy, truly—and since then, and in spite of all I've been through, no. No, I've not ever been in love."

"Do you think it shocking that I ask?"

She met his eyes, and saw a fleeting twinkle in them.

"You know who I am—what I have been. There are many who would say that Lily Cigar is far beyond the reach of anyone who tries to shock her."

"Lily, I know more than what you were. I know what you are, what you have made of yourself. And if there is a woman alive with more fine qualities than yours, why . . ."

"You'd like to meet her?"

[491]

"You mock me."

"No, Brooks, never that. I guess that my wicked life had one effect on me: I sometimes find it hard to take myself very seriously."

"There are others, Lily, who might take you very seriously indeed."

"Will you have some more ham?"

He gave a short, harsh laugh. "Now you mock me. If you've never been in love, Lily, it may have been for the good. I fell in love, and the word 'fall' hardly describes it. And in one mad instant I gave all that I valued in the world to secure that love: my heart, my name, my future. She smashed it, Lily. She treated my love like some gaudy plaything, to be worn one time to a ball and then trampled thoughtlessly underfoot, like yesterday's flowers. She disgraced herself, and me, and so tarnished my name that I could no longer live in New York."

Lily caught her breath and blinked back tears. Then she reached out and touched his arm. It was stiff with tension.

"Oh, my dear Brooks, I am terribly sorry. Of all the men in the world who deserve a woman's trust, you must be first."

He said nothing, but only sipped the dark red wine. When he spoke again, it was in a tone so low she had to bend near to catch it: he might have been talking to himself alone.

"I came to California a runaway, Lily, an exile, wounded in body and spirit, with no hope, no dream, no expectation of ever finding happiness again. I had lost—the war and my wife had conspired to take away from me everything I held most dear. When I sailed, it didn't seem to matter whether the ship floated or sank. There were times, indeed, when I felt it might be better simply to end it."

Brooks paused, and turned to her, and took her hand in his. "And then," he said, "I met you."

If the sky had fallen or the earth opened up to swallow her, Lily could hardly have been more thoroughly startled.

"Oh," she said, "you poor man."

"No man is poor, Lily, who can lay even the smallest claim to your affection."

"I had no idea, truly."

This is not happening. This is a dream. Soon I shall wake up, weeping, in my solitary bed at the ranch.

"When first I saw you, Lily, I was frightened as I have seldom been frightened in all my life."

"But why?"

"Because you are so very lovely, and I thought that to meet a lovely woman might be fatal to me."

"You think, then, that we are all alike?"

"I know you are not like . . . her."

"I am what I am—and what I have been can never be altered."

"You do yourself an injustice, Lily. Without knowing—or wanting to know—the details of it, I am sure you did what you did from necessity. The woman who did me such mischief is a true wanton, a harlot to her bones, incapable of an honest thought or action, degenerate. No one is more of a whore than the former Mrs. Brooks Chaffee!"

His voice had risen as he spoke, until it was something like a shout. He turned from her and covered his face with his hands.

Lily could not bear to see him thus. She moved closer and touched his hair, as if comforting a small child.

"She must be wicked, who can make you feel so unhappy."

He turned to her then and put both of his arms around her and kissed her fiercely on the lips. The electricity of it raced through Lily to her toes. For a moment she struggled in his arms, more from surprise than from reticence. Then, with a sigh, he released her.

"Lily, Lily, Lily! Now you have heard my confession. Now you know what no one outside my parents knows. And now I must ask you a terrible question."

"If I can do anything at all to help, you may be sure that I will."

"Do you think you could ever love me, Lily? Knowing me as you do, could you consider becoming my wife?"

Lily stood bolt upright as if someone had warned her of rattlesnakes in the vicinity. She turned from him and looked out over the spectacular view, down the rolling hills to the blue ocean. But the view was blurred by her tears.

There was silence, and only the restless wind could be heard on the hilltop. She heard him stir, felt him close behind her, felt his strong arms encircling her forcefully, tenderly. For a moment she just stood there, feeling the warmth of him, glorying in his closeness, in his touch, in the heartbreaking suddenness of his proposal. That it was a true and honorable offer, Lily had no doubt whatsoever. But to have her ancient dream come so close, so quickly, threw her into several kinds of confusion. *How in heaven could it ever work? She was the only reasonably attractive woman around—that was it, Brooks was a man and he'd probably*

*been without a woman for some time, that was all. But, of
course, that wasn't all.*

Finally she turned in his arms and looked up at him.

"I admire you, I like you, I trust you absolutely Brooks.
And it is even possible that I love you, for all I know of love.
But we must be cautious. This is not a thing to be rushed. It
is kind of you—but then, you are ever kind—to forgive my
past. But you must know all about me. My background is so
very different from yours, I'm a simple Irish girl, and if I
hadn't taught myself to read and write, you can be sure no
one else would have. I'm an orphan . . ."

"Was that ever a crime, my darling, to be an orphan? Or
to be ambitious for an education? I daresay half the girls I
knew in New York could scarcely read or write either, when
it comes to that."

"My brother is a born troublemaker."

"I'm not proposing to your brother."

"Not only was I a whore, Brooks, but a very famous one
too: they wrote songs about Lily Cigar, and sold my picture
in the public souvenir shops."

"You aren't telling me anything I don't know, my darling.
Why do you fight it so?"

His arms were still tight around her; Lily didn't dare to
move away for fear she'd faint. Instead, she lowered her head
until it was nestled against his chest.

"Because I'm afraid," she said in a small, small voice. "I
am afraid because I never dared to hope for real happiness,
or a decent marriage, and it seems like some magical wish
granted in an old fairy story. It seems so magical to me,
Brooks, that I tremble to my toes in fear that it will vanish
and go away, and perhaps some sad voice inside me says:
*'Don't take the chance, for if you take the chance, you only
risk the failing, and what you have, small happiness as it is, is
better than that.'* "

He roared with laughter then, and she looked up, startled,
sure in her heart he'd gone mad.

"Don't you see, Lily, we're the same person: afraid to walk
for fear we might stumble. Well, I, for one, want to walk
again. No! To run! To fly!"

He kissed her again, softly this time. "Fly with me, Lily.
Say you will."

Lily looked up at him and felt as though she were falling,
and falling through some enormous dark space, a little fragment spilling off the moon. But it wasn't a dangerous feeling
now, but rather a lovely warm floating, for his arms were

[494]

around her, and nothing in the world or the hereafter could bring her harm.

"Oh, Brooks. Of course I will."

He led her back to the picnic and they sat down and quietly finished the meal, shy, suddenly, after such a tidal wave of love and revelation.

Finally he said, musing, "We earn it, you know, my darling. It doesn't seem to work very well when it is simply handed to us upon a silver salver, as so many things have been given to me over the years."

"Earn what?"

"Happiness, you goose! I am happier right now, on this hilltop, Lily, than I ever dared to hope."

"Do you believe in dreams coming true?"

"Of course. One just did."

"Ah, but you say that lightly. I mean a real, long-term, heavily mortgaged dream, of the kind we keep locked away in the deepest vault, even from ourselves."

"Have I made you daft, Lily? Whatever do you mean?"

"You asked me had I ever been in love. And I answered truly. That once, long ago, when I was a silly girl, I saw— quite by chance, mind you!—the most beautiful young man in all the world. Just for a moment did I see him, he said not ten words to me, and saw me not at all, for what was I but an underparlormaid in a fine New York mansion?"

"And . . ."

"And that boy was you."

Brooks looked at her as though he had seen a ghost. It seemed almost impossible, a miracle, yet this was a day made of miracles. For surely it was a miracle that she could love him, that the winds of fate had driven them together, and here, high upon this hill, with all the world before them, bathed in the golden sun of California. When he spoke, his voice was breathless with astonishment.

"Lily! Why did you never tell me?"

"Because . . . I didn't know what you'd think—maybe you'd think that I had set my cap for you, that I was more wicked than I am."

"And how long ago was that, and in whose house?"

"It was the world ago, Brooks, and the house was the Wallingfords'."

She paused, wondering if she'd gone too far, if she should tell him the full story. A quick dark force inside her urged Lily to leave the history of her relations with Jack Wallingford for another day. Enough was enough.

"No! But Jack was one of my closest friends, damn him to hell."

"Why do you say that?"

"Because . . . I have reason to think he was one of my wife's lovers. One, dear Lily, out of very many. But it seems that for Jack to do that to a friend . . . Ah, well, let it be. He was always a wild one, and I am perfectly sure he received plenty of encouragement."

"I think," she said quietly, "that my heart will burst if I have one penny's worth more of happiness this day. Let's go home and talk to Kate: she loves you already, Brooks, and to have you as a father . . . well, that will be the wonder of wonders."

But even as she spoke Kate's name, Lily shuddered, and a chill crept through her soul. How could she ever tell Brooks the truth about Kate, without breaking his damaged heart yet again? Surely he had the right to ask. And just as surely she had the right to spare him the knowledge that Jack Wallingford had despoiled the only two women Brooks had ever loved? To tell it plain would be more than Brooks could bear, more than she could bear telling. Her mind raced. She would tell him as much of the truth as would do no harm—to either of them. And if the angels despised her for that, she would face them in her time. Anything would be preferable to endangering this bright fragile thing that had come to her so unexpectedly: his love.

Lily took a deep breath. She looked into his eyes and spoke softly. "Kate's father was a wild lad. He did not marry me. That is why I came out here, to make a new life for the child. She has never known a father."

There. It is done, and he'll never know more while I live. It's almost the truth, for if Jack Wallingford isn't a wild lad, then who is? Such a small bending of the truth, to spare a good man so much pain. How could the angels punish her for that?

He took her hand. "Kate will have a father now, my darling. You'll see."

They rode back slowly, close together, talking softly of many things. The wedding, perforce, would be soon and simple. The two great ranches would be conjoined, the small intervening farms bought up. There were many plans and many dreams, and every one of them would come true. That was exactly what happened in the fairy stories Kate loved so well, and Lily was ready to bet her life that the same glorious magic that had suffused them on her hilltop would shine and glimmer down all the days of their lives.

Brooks courted her now like a shy young man, and paid formal visits and brought her gifts. The wedding date was set for May 30, a month hence. And when they parted now, kissing warmly, easily, and with building passion, never did he ask of her what she would readily have given him; the joys of her body, the comforts of her bed, would wait until after the great day of their wedding.

It was as though they had made a secret pact, each with the other, to start the future fresh, newborn upon Lily's hilltop on the beautiful day he had first opened his heart to her, and she to him.

The two ranches teemed with activity, for small as the wedding would be, every effort was made to create a fine and festive occasion. Lily entrusted Fergy with the wine-buying, and spent long afternoons closeted with Gloria Sanchez over the menu. A banquet it would be, for a dozen guests, and a Spanish gypsy violinist playing.

And Lily puzzled about what to wear: it must be new, for the sake of the fresh start she and Brooks were making. It must definitely not be a maiden's white. Finally, and for the first time in months, Lily went into San Francisco to shop. There, in the Maison de Ville, she found the perfect gown: rich it was, but simple, an afternoon dress of dull cocoa-colored satin, with a high collar like a daffodil's trumpet, edged at collar and sleeve with the finest ivory Brussels lace. It cost a fortune and she paid it gladly, and for new shoes to match and new underclothing too, made by French nuns of the finest lawn and edged in lace. She would wear no hat, but rather her mother's dowry scarf cherished in tissue paper all these years, draped as Gloria had shown her in the manner of a Spanish *mantilla*. And Kate, as a bridesmaid, would wear in her own red-gold hair the lovely little ribbon that Frances O'Farrelley had embroidered with a hundred flowers all those years ago in St. Patrick's orphanage. Lily wondered where Fran was now, and wished she were here to share in her old friend's happiness.

After shopping, Lily met her brother for luncheon. Fergy had suggested the Lick House, it being the newest and finest of the city's hotels. Lily would have preferred someplace less conspicuous, for fear of being recognized, dreading any kind of publicity. But Fergy was Fergy, and she let him have his way. As usual.

Fergy was already at a choice table when Lily was escorted

in by a fawning headwaiter. She wondered, seeing the head-waiter's sleek and mercenary smile, how much her brother was spending to ensure such obsequiousness. Fergus Malone Junior was, as ever, overdressed. He shimmered with silk facings on the finest English woolen suit coat. He gleamed with gold watch chains and studs and cufflinks. And among the gold flashed the hot white light of diamonds. *I wouldn't trust him any further than I could throw Russian Hill*, she thought, smiling wryly at the sight of him.

He flashed his little boy's grin and rose to kiss her. "Ah, Lil, but sure and you're a sight for these tired old eyes!"

"You're looking prosperous, Fergy."

Lily wished she could say he was looking well, but in fact Fergy at the age of thirty looked more like a hard-living fifty. The green eyes that once had such sparkle were dulled now, as though some opaque veil had closed over them, and rimmed with the red of late hours and many whiskeys they were, and puffed up underneath so that he seemed to be squinting when no squinting was necessary. His skin was too pale, and Lily thought she could detect just the slightest trembling in his perfectly manicured hands.

"What'll you be drinking, Lil?"

"Tea, please, China tea with lemon."

"Tea, is it? Well, tea it'll be. You'll excuse me if I refrain from joining you."

He ordered tea for Lily and champagne for himself. The champagne arrived with such suspicious speed that Lily felt it must be a standing order for Fergy, which would be perfectly in character.

"Won't you be joining me in a toast, Lil? To your connubial happiness, and all that?"

She laughed and said, "Sure, if I can toast back in tea, Fergy. For I'll have to be getting back to the ranch soon, maybe we'd better order now."

Menus were brought, orders were given. Fergy lifted his glass and smiled. "I wish you joy, Lil, for no one deserves it more."

"Thanks, Fergy. I was hoping you'd find time to come over and meet him. It would be fitting, with you being the best man and all. Why not come someday next week, for supper, and stay over with us? We've plenty of room, and Kate would love to see her wicked uncle."

"Does she call me that?"

"Of course not. Little does the child know of wickedness,

and little may she ever know. But she loves you, Fergy, and you hardly ever see her."

"She'll have a real father now. Tell me about him. Chaffee of the New York Chaffees, isn't he? That's quite a catch, Lil, not that you need the money."

"He is a very fine man, Fergy, who had an unhappy marriage, and a bad time in the war. Brooks was wounded, and his leg is still a bit stiff from it, and he saw his only brother die at Antietam. So it hasn't been easy for him, Chaffee or not. He is kind, and good, and I love him dearly, and I want you to love him too."

"For you, old girl, I would love a one-eyed Turk with a full harem. I'll come next Wednesday, in the full flower of brotherhood."

He sipped his champagne and swallowed an oyster.

"I am happy for you, Lil, do you know it?"

"I think I do, and I thank you."

They finished the sumptuous luncheon talking quietly of many things. Fergy, as ever, was filled to overflowing with new schemes and projects; entire celestial continents could be populated with his castles in the air. Lily listened with a fraction of her brain, nodding and making the appropriate murmurs of wonder and encouragement, even though she had long since stopped paying any serious attention to Fergy's pipe dreams. But when they parted, it was on a happy note, and he renewed his promise of coming to the ranch on Wednesday.

Lily glanced about the huge, glittering dining room as they left. She recognized no one, and so far as she could tell, no one recognized her. The room itself, and the hotel that housed it, were already famous landmarks, and yet how strange she felt here, on her first visit, a year after the hotel had been erected. She, who had so lately been part of the glitter herself! San Francisco was in a state of permanent change. The first sounds Lily remembered hearing when she came to town were the clang of hammers and the rasp of saws, and these same noises filled the air still as the city flexed its muscles and continued pell-mell on the habitual orgy of building, building, building. *Well, and let them build to their heart's content,* she thought as Fergy drove her to the waiting sloop. *Brooks and I are building too, and not so much with nails and mortar as with love and dreams.*

And to Lily Malone on this beautiful day in early May of 1865, there was nothing more solid than that.

Kate looked at her mother with all the gravity of nine years. "Mama," she said quietly, "when you marry Mr. Chaffee, shall I call him 'Father'?"

Lily looked up from her sewing and smiled. She had told the girl that her father was dead, and prayed that the angels would forgive the white lie.

"I hope so, my pumpkin, for I know he'd like that. In fact, Katie-Kate, when I become Mrs. Chaffee, we might decide to call you Miss Chaffee. It would be simpler, and it sounds well, don't you think? Kate Chaffee."

"Katie Chaffee."

"Do you like it?"

"I think so."

Lily put down her sewing and ran to Kate and gave her a big hug. "I like it too, darling, I like it very much."

Fergy arrived as promised, rather to Lily's surprise, on time and sober and, for Fergy, relatively sober in his dress. He was loaded with presents, so many that his carriage was followed up the driveway by a mule cart bulging with mysterious boxes on top of his own luggage.

There were three splendid French dolls and a real China tea set in miniature for Kate. For Lily, as a wedding gift, he brought a dazzling brooch in the form of one large gracefully curving lily whose stem and leaves were carved from the rarest deep green jade, whose flower was all canary diamonds set pavé, with one perfect dewdrop of a blue-white diamond cunningly mounted upon an invisible spring so that it was forever dancing and sparkling with the slightest movement of its wearer. And for Brooks, Fergy had a magnificent Mexican saddle of the finest black leather subtly mounted in pure silver, with a chased-silver placque on the pommel that contained Brooks's monogram and the date of the marriage.

Lily was truly touched by all this, not so much by its splendor as by the mere fact that the usually careless Fergy had obviously gone to a great deal of trouble to find suitable presents. And she could see in his eyes that Brooks was impressed.

All through the long formal supper, Fergy drank little and was at his most charming. Lily had forgotten precisely how charming her brother could be at the top of his form, and now, seeing that through the eyes of her fiancé, she had a sudden happy vision of Fergy as he could be, given the right motivation, under the right circumstances. To Lily, in the flush of her own romantic happiness, this meant nothing more than the love of the proper woman. But she'd attend to that later, after the wedding.

For the wedding was now only two weeks away!

Lily never knew what Brooks wrote to his parents by way of announcing the marriage. It would be impossible, naturally, for the senior Chaffees to attend in person, or even to reply to their son's announcement.

"By the time they hear the news, my love," Brooks said one morning, "we will be old married people by at the very least a week."

"They'll never approve. They'll hate me."

"That is very unlikely, Lily, and even if they were to disapprove, what would it matter? I love them, and they love me, and what makes me happy will make them happy."

"I would hate to be the cause of their sorrow—or of anyone's."

He took both of her hands in his, and pulled her close. "Lily, my Lily, when will you learn? One of the many things I love in you is this concern for others. But, for my parents, consider this: they have lived their lives, and by a certain standard, and that standard has worked for them. Probably—no, surely!—I share many of their standards. And here I stand, loving you, wanting you to be my wife. You must trust me, Lily, that old as they are and set as they may be in their ways, my parents are far from stupid. Don't worry, dear: promise me you'll worry only about important things, like the colors of the flowers in your wedding bouquet."

And he kissed her quick and hard and Lily forgot about everything in the world but Brooks and the day she would be his forever.

In later years Lily could recall every precious detail of her wedding day clearly as if it had been engraved in crystal. But the day itself passed in such a rush of love and happiness that it seemed to last only a few blazing minutes.

The day dawned blue and perfect, the air warm but dry, a light breeze blowing in from China and only a few fat white puffs of cloud grazing the sky to point up the intensity of sapphire that seemed to vibrate with anticipation above the ranch.

The ceremony was scheduled for four o'clock, but Lily was dressed fully an hour before that, bustling about the ranch house, checking on details that had been checked many times before: the coolness of the champagne, the freshness of the flowers, the arrangement of seats in the great hall to make an informal chapel for the ceremony itself.

The Paris dress looked wonderful; even the unshakable Gloria was delighted with it. Lily wore Fergy's pin to do him honor, even though she felt it a bit flashy for daytime. And she also wore Brooks's wedding gift to her, a magnificent rope of Oriental pearls, each precisely the same size as the next, their color an elusive blush that just hinted at pink, clasped with diamonds, with single-pearl ear studs to match. The pearls, she guessed, must be worth a fortune, but more valuable to Lily were the words that Brooks had said when he gave them to her: *"They are warm, and true, and pure, my Lily, and that is how I think of you, and how I always shall think of you."* And even while one part of her mind knew full well that his reassurance was a deliberate thing to overcome her fears, Lily sensed a kind of magic in the pearls themselves: they glowed, and they must glow with the warm reflection of her love for him, and his for her. There was luck in the pearls. They radiated good magic. Lily promised herself most solemnly that she would do anything in her power to live up to the radiant expectations that gleamed from these perfect, unearthly little globes.

It was a happy promise, for Lily never imagined it would be put to the test.

The minister had been brought from San Francisco by Fergy, for Brooks was Episcopalian and Lily had long since given up the pretense of adhering to the stringent dictates of Rome.

Reverend Weith read the service in a voice so muted it gave no indication whether or not he was aware that the bride was the notorious Lily Cigar. The ceremony was quickly over with an exchange of rings and kisses, and the guests went into the garden for champagne and little cakes before supper. It was a small party and a mixed one: the minister, Weith, who was a stranger to all the rest; Stanford Dickinson, who'd invited himself, whom Lily could not bring herself to refuse; Fergy, glowing with love but, luckily, not whiskey; the Bakers; Kate; and the two neighboring farmers and their wives, who had also been guests at Lily's Christmas party.

The slow twilight enveloped them as they strolled in the small, perfect rose garden that was Lily's special pride of all her restorations after the fire. White climbing roses were espaliered against the whitewashed walls of the ranch house, and beds of specimen flowers in a dozen shades of pink and yellow and red made a rectangular outdoor room, dancing with color, fragrant with new blooms. The violin made haunting love music from behind a hedge.

Supper was predictably splendid, six courses in all, and each with its appropriate wine. Lily barely touched the wine and only nibbled at the food. The only reason she ate at all was fear of offending Gloria. For Lily was so filled with love this day that she fed on it. At last the meal was over and the final toasts were drunk and the good-byes said at the door. *Their door!* For they had long since agreed that Brooks would simply move in with Lily. Her house was much the bigger and better equipped to become the nerve center of their combined properties, and more.

She looked up at him, standing tall and proud beside her, and once again Lily could not credit her luck. This time Brooks Chaffee would not go galloping down her moonlit drive, away from her into some darker kingdom inhabited by his own haunted past. This night he was by her side, his black stallion groomed and stabled, and by her side he'd stay. And forever! *If there is such a thing as forever.* How natural it seemed, and how very frightening. How fine he looked, framed in the strong old beams of dark oak.

For one long moment they stood silent in the doorway watching Fergy's rented landau grow smaller and smaller in the purple night until it disappeared altogether, and the drumming of the horses' hooves, leaving them silent in the quiet night, and suddenly Lily found herself wondering if she was strong enough to bear this much happiness. He turned to her then, and took her in his arms and whispered, "Lily, my Lily, my Lily!"

He took her hand in his and led her down the spacious hall and up the wide staircase. It seemed to Lily that this was the first time she had climbed these stairs, or walked down this corridor, or watched the guttering celebration candles throwing mysterious shadows on the whitewashed walls. Slowly, dreaming or waking, it mattered not, they moved toward Lily's bedroom.

Brooks opened the door.

It was the same dear bedroom Lily had chosen for herself before she ever knew she would share it with a man. The room was tall and white, with old dark beams in the ceiling and three tall windows that looked up to the hills.

The bed was plain and white and covered in a fine white wool coverlet. And on the coverlet, turned down for the night, someone had written in fresh pink rose petals: "SIEMPRE FELICIDADES." Happiness forever.

Lily looked at her husband and smiled. "That must be Gloria, bless her. Do you know what it means?"

"I don't."

"It means she wishes us to be happy always."

Brooks held her close and said, "If ever a man can promise anything, my darling, I promise you that her wish will come true."

Then he turned from her and went to the bed and scooped up a handful of rose petals. He came back close to Lily and lifted his hand high in the air over her head and caused the pale fragrant things to fall down in a gentle rain on her head. Slowly he unloosed the fine lace-edged scarf that had been her mother's and set it upon the dresser.

And soon they were sharing the big white bed with the pale silver moonlight that filtered in through the half-open windows, and the fragrance of the rose petals and an exaltation of love that surpassed anything that Lily had dared to imagine.

Her one secret fear all these weeks, from the moment she had told Brooks she would be his, was that when this moment came, nothing in the reality of it could possibly live up to Lily's years of dreams and yearnings.

It was better. Brooks was gentle and strong and the fires that burned in him were bright pure fires that did not burn but only made a new alchemy of love in whose dear crucible dark dreams and secrets were magically transformed into a new and golden thing, a strong and happy cage of love that promised to hold them both, together, always.

In the gentle fury of his lovemaking, Brooks seemed to become younger, although he surely was far from old. In quiet interludes Lily would look at him, and touch his face, and see the boy of long ago.

He said very little but her name.

That was more than enough.

And when she woke to find this young god sharing her bed, Lily blinked with shock. Then a slow, soft smile crept across her face. She reached out as though to touch him, but feared waking him, and contented herself with lightly tracing the outline of his face in the air, as if she held a magic sorcerer's wand.

Lily had never thought there could be this much happiness in the world, and especially not in her world. She stretched lazily, and yawned, and nestled back against the pillows to watch her husband till he woke.

∽§ 42 §∽

Mrs. Brooks Chaffee sat at her desk in the small ranch office off the kitchen. Lily was frowning over her ledgers, even though the ledgers told a tale of ever-building prosperity for Chaffee Produce, which had started life so long ago as Malone Produce.

The more than ten thousand acres of ranchland that made up the core of Chaffee Produce was fully developed now, and what wasn't farmed was grazed, or used for poultry, cider-making, and the other small but vital enterprises that fleshed out a great produce supplier. And they'd invested, wisely, in other farmland, down near Los Angeles, for growing citrus. Now there were Chaffee lemons and oranges and tangerines. Hawaii beckoned, but they were considering that at some length: Hawaii was paradise, and tremendously fertile, and available. But it was also the very devil to control, what with irregular shipping and the basic communications problems attendant on anything several weeks away by ship. Hawaii, as far as Lily was concerned, could wait.

But the other thing that troubled her couldn't wait.

Lily could look back on the ten years of her marriage as a great success. Happiness had followed happiness, success had piled upon success. Brooks, who loved children, and dearly loved Kate, had been overwhelmed in 1868 when Lily presented him with a squirming, screaming, but nevertheless handsome son, Edward Hudner Chaffee, named for poor dead Neddy. Jonathan Fergus Chaffee had followed two years later. And here it was 1875, with the war long over and new scientific and economic wonders appearing almost daily.

Back East the wounds of the great war still bled and festered, and scandals rocked the land. But the West had a destiny of its own, and during these ten years the raw land seemed to open up like a flower, revealing unsuspected treasures whose profit would find its way down from the craggy granite and sandstone mountains to San Francisco, there to finance undreamed-of pleasures. And if gold would forever be the battle cry in the avant-garde of greed, now there was a wider, deeper, and apparently endless flow of silver out of the Sierra Nevada, and a millionaire's palace was none the less ornate for being founded even on such homely items as copper, sulfur, gypsum, or even iron. A British team prospecting for gold in Montana found gem sapphires beside a roaring trout stream called the Yogo River. There was a sense of magic to all this abundance, a feeling of being inside Aladdin's cave.

Little Neddy Chaffee was barely a year old when the continent was linked in fact and in symbol by a solid gold railroad spike. Now the journey that was three months at least by clipper around the Horn could be achieved in relative comfort in plush-trimmed parlor cars in just two weeks, New York to Sacramento.

San Francisco now boomed more than ever. Excess was the norm, and new extravagances appeared with the impulsive thrust of gilded mushrooms after a silver rain, so thick and so fast that today's wonder carried with it the seeds of destruction, doomed by the very seething spirit that called it into being to become tomorrow's half-remembered novelty. The biggest theatrical stage in all America was in the California Theater. The Occidental Hotel somehow contrived to outclass even the grandiose Lick House, which had set new standards of opulence not a decade past.

Lily was aware of these things, but they touched the core of her life hardly at all.

If she went into the city once in six months, that was a lot, and then it would be to see Fergy or to go with Brooks to some business conference, for he asked her advice in all his transactions, and especially those that affected the Chaffee Produce Company.

All the fire and gaiety in her were reserved for those she loved, and whom Lily Malone Chaffee loved she worked like a demon to keep close by her so the sharing could be stretched and made to last the longer and enjoyed to its fullest. This was unconscious, done partly from pure love, partly for convenience, and partly from fear that this magic and sacred circle might somehow be broken. For it was ever close to the surface of Lily's feelings that she was living a charmed life, as though she had stolen her happiness rather than earned it, as though her happiness might somehow be recalled like a bad debt and forever locked away out of her grasp. Lily remembered with an almost physical revulsion all the people she had loved in her life who had left her or been taken from her, and every time she stood in the big doorway and waved to Brooks as he rode off to town, a small and quite terrifying voice inside her would whisper: "Maybe this time he won't be coming back!" But he always did come back, and every day of her life she loved him more than the day before, if that were possible, if such things could be measured. Lily could laugh at herself and her fears, and they would go away meekly then. But always, always, they would come back, sneaking, probing, hissing, building a cage of self-doubt that was no less terrifying for being imaginary.

When Brooks's aged parents had risked the long train journey across the continent to see their new grandchildren, they had been kindness itself to Lily. Whatever they knew about her past affected their joy in seeing Brooks again not one whit. Old Mrs. Chaffee had brought Lily a touching gift: an antique English necklace set with Roman cameos framed in gold. The necklace had belonged to Mrs. Chaffee Senior's mother, and the gift of it had hardly been a sign of disapproval.

Once, during the month-long visit of Brooks's parents, old Mrs. Chaffee had taken Lily aside and said, "It is plain as sunrise, my dear, that you have made my son happy, and there are no words in the language to tell you how happy that makes me and his father. Thank you, Lily."

Lily had said nothing, but gasped, and suddenly found herself in tears. The old lady had comforted her, and when at last the visit was over, Lily felt they parted good friends, for she had liked both of his parents, and felt they liked her in return. And there was a special sadness in their leaving, for despite the speed of the train compared to the old clipper routes, they all knew this was probably a final visit.

Kate was blossoming into a lovely girl, and the boys were shooting up with a velocity that both amazed and delighted their parents.

But there was a problem, and it was a persistent and worrisome one. Brooks was growing restless. Not—and Lily thanked the gods for it—in any romantic sense: their love flourished and seemed to increase with the years. But having nurtured the produce business to spectacular success, Brooks was looking for new worlds to conquer.

The peaceful and isolated life that Lily had striven to create here in the remote hills of San Rafael had served an important purpose for Brooks. It had healed his emotional wounds and given him a new sense of himself, of who he was and what he could do. And Brooks was truly devoted to the ranch. Yet, as Fred Baker and Lily herself got the place ever better organized, the day-to-day business of sowing and harvesting and shipping and selling seemed to take care of itself.

And every time Brooks went into San Francisco, he seemed to come back fairly teeming with new ideas. After all, Lily told herself, he was a city man, he had a banking background, his mind was a fine far-reaching thing that could see an infinite distance beyond the next cornfield.

And Lily supported him in his enterprises. For, unlike Fergy's ever-wilder schemes, the plans of Brooks Chaffee made sense, and they made money.

Every year since he'd arrived—long before he fell in love with Lily—Brooks had invested in San Francisco real estate, and his investments had prospered and grown year by year. Now he had considerable holdings in the city and its growing suburbs. And now Lily could see a pattern forming, a pattern that she feared and dreaded to the bottom of her heart.

Lily could see a time coming when Brooks would want to move into the city and take a more active part in its life.

As he had every right to. As she had every reason to support him in so doing.

And Lily feared it like death itself.

For she knew that Brooks would want a full social life, should he set himself up in town. And Lily knew that the past could and would reach out and damage her, and Brooks, and the children. How Mamie Dickinson would jump at a chance to snub Stanford's former lover! How all the smug dowagers who hung on Mamie's gilded apron strings would cackle with glee at such a performance. And how Lily would be mortified at the prospect.

Lily looked from the ledgers out the window to her well-tended green hills. But still she was frowning.

Lily sat in the little office thinking about Brooks's restlessness until she could stand it no longer, then stood up so quickly she made herself laugh. Always, in the past, whenever a mood of doubt or of sadness would come on her, Lily had one certain cure: to busy herself with something else, some new task or an old one that had temporarily been put aside.

It was in search of such a project that she strode purposefully out of the ranch house into the pure clear spring afternoon.

Lily walked smiling into a scene of well-ordered activity. Two of Fred Baker's new mule trains waited patiently by the warehouse for their drivers, six mules in each, with each team of six pulling four large wagons—gentle, patient, stupid, and immensely strong they were, special mules whose proper name Lily could never remember, imported by Fred from Mexico, and well worth it. The wagons behind them were heaped with baskets and crates filled with the earliest cabbages and lettuce, with a consignment of honey, poultry both dressed and alive, eggs in baskets lined with fresh straw, fresh milk and cream in glass bottles, and small fat tubs of sweet butter made daily by the farmers' wives and older children. When the mule trains got to Tiburon they would meet with coastal freighters carrying lemons and oranges and limes from the Chaffee citrus ranches north of Los Angeles, with pineapples bought on subcontracts from Hawaii, but culled to Chaffee standards and bearing the Chaffee label. Lily could look at these mule trains and see a perfect little cross section of her world, of the new world she loved so well and felt so happy in, the world she had given herself to building these last thirteen years.

As if on purpose to make this smiling picture of Lily's world complete, Kate came running, whooping, laughing into the yard, pursued by seven-year-old Neddy, who was running even faster, yelling even louder. Lily smiled as Kate let herself be caught, then caught her captor, picking Neddy up by the arms and swinging him round and round until he squealed for mercy. They were both brown as walnuts and most undignified. As she wished them to be, innocent of the world and its whalebone-and-pulpit standards.

Katie! It was really for Katie, more than for herself, and long before Brooks had come to California, that Lily had bought the ranch and made it into a separate world where the real world couldn't harm them. Lily knew that with every passing month, with every inch the child grew, the time was drawing closer when Kate must go out into that world, for better or for worse. She was already, at eighteen, taller than her mother, and ripe with the promise of beauty. Kate's hair had the same shimmering copper glints as did Lily's, but her eyes were Jack's eyes, dark and sometimes distant, now merry, now impenetrable. Lily had never told the girl about her past, much less her true parentage. Kate knew that Lily was her blood mother, that her father was dead—and for all Lily knew, he might be.

Now, in just two weeks' time, Kate would be off. They'd escort her to Sacramento and put her on the train, there to go all the way across this wild country to enroll at the Mount Holyoke Seminary for Young Ladies in Massachusetts. This had been Kate's own idea, and Brooks was in agreement. Lily buried her own doubts, for she could see the thirst for learning glow bright in the girl's eyes, and the little school at Tiburon, to which all the children rode their horses every day, was surely less than adequate at Katie's age. But to see Kate go and be gone for at least half a year, unless Lily went chasing after her, which Lily well knew would be impossible, for that would surely be the worst of all the partings, if she were to leave Brooks and Neddy and little Jon . . .

Still, Lily smiled and watched her children for a moment before she called to them.

"Kate! Neddy! Where's your brother?"

They came running across the courtyard. Neddy spoke first, grinning his father's grin. "He's making an Indian raid on Gloria's pantry."

"And you, Edward Hudner Chaffee," said Lily, scooping the boy up in her arms and holding him high, which she could do for only a moment, so fine and fast was he growing, "are a blackguard, to be informing on him."

She kissed Neddy and set him down. "Now," said Lily, "why don't we all go and join Jon in his raid? I happen to know where some of Gloria's lace cookies are hidden, and I'll bet I could eat three of 'em right now."

This scheme met with the expected reaction, and they all joined hands and headed back across the courtyard toward the kitchen.

It was Neddy, born with the ears of a prowling fox, who first heard his father's approach. "There," he piped, "comes Black Prince."

"Pish," said Kate, "you hear the mules stamping. Father never comes home this early."

"Bet a cookie?"

"You're on."

But the bet was no sooner made than Kate lost it, for Brooks Chaffee came cantering smartly into the courtyard on the echo of her words. He slid gracefully out of the saddle, hitched the black stallion to the new wrought-iron hitching bar, and walked across to his family, kissing them each in turn, beginning with Lily.

How very handsome he looks in his city clothes, she thought, as though she were seeing him for the first time. *Forty-one years old, and stronger than he ever was, the limp's almost gone now, it only hurts on the coldest, wettest days, and some of the hurt inside him is less now, too, for surely it's been a year and more since he woke me up in the night screaming for his dead brother. And the other one, his first wife, there is no knowing how often he thinks of her, and surely he'll never forget her, any more than I'll forget the Fleur de Lis, yet it is a gentler kind of pain by now, there have been so many happy things in the meantime to fill the empty fearful space inside him.*

Lily looked up at her husband with a discoverer's eyes and thought that there must be many a female heart broken every time Brooks Chaffee turned his back on San Francisco and headed home for the ranch.

"You look," she said, "like the sourdough miner who just won a no-good claim in a poker game and struck gold on it."

Brooks laughed. There was a special look about him this afternoon, hinting at some happy secret, some new triumph.

"I would love," he said, "some tea. Then I'll tell you all some good news."

They trooped into the great kitchen and sat around the big round oak table. Lily made tea for Brooks and herself, and got milk and cookies for the children.

Kate spoke first. "I know. You've been nominated for governor."

Lily smiled at this and shivered in her heart, for it was not impossible: Brooks now had many friends in San Francisco, and of such prominence that politics was ever in the background of their lives, and often it played a role more prominent than that.

But he only laughed and denied it.

Neddy spoke next. "You're a general in the army and they want you to lead the war on Mexico and I'm your lieutenant."

Lily could see a flickering of pain come onto her husband's face and go again in a flash, for the child was only being like all boys, in love with the dash and the trumpet calls of anything to do with the military, knowing not at all how hideous it could be and how his father still carried the scars of Antietam both on his body and in his heart. She knew it would be her turn to guess now, and the fear of it almost choked her, for whatever his news was, it probably meant change, and Lily's world was perfect right now, as it was, so small and tight and happy that it was hard to imagine a change that might improve it.

She fought her fear by making light of it. "You have found gold under my turnip patch."

They all laughed, and turned expectantly to Brooks.

He paused a moment for dramatic effect, then began, as if

telling a children's story. "Once upon a time," he said portentously, "there was a beautiful hilltop."

He's building me my dream house, Lily thought joyously, *a little cottage high on my hill, just for the two of us!* They had often talked of doing just that, but somehow they had never gotten around to it.

"This hilltop was very special," Brooks continued, "for it was higher than the other hills, and it commanded a wonderful view down to the ocean—"

"And all the way to China?" Neddy forgot his manners in the excitement.

"That," said Brooks gravely, "is quite possible, but only on a very clear day. In any event, the hilltop is so special, and the Chaffee family has been so happy in this house, that when I saw this other hilltop, I thought we could only be twice as happy in two houses. So I bought it, and just closed the deal today, and before very long we will have a fine new house in town as well as our fine old house here at the ranch. And your old father won't have to spend so much time running back and forth, for I'll be able to stroll down California Street to my new office."

His eyes were on Lily as he spoke, for Brooks knew her fears, her deep love for the ranch and the little world she had built there. He knew, too, that he could count on Lily to control herself in front of the children, that it had been just a bit sly of him to announce this new development so publicly. There was a message in his glance, and the message was: *Don't fail me now, whatever your problem is, we'll work it out somehow, it is important to me, this move, growing, seeing more of the great world.*

Lily's smile froze on her face as the shock sank in. So he had done the thing she dreaded most. There went her dream of a cottage on her hillside at the ranch! Instead there would be a gaudy palace on Nob Hill, probably not a few blocks from the Fleur de Lis, or where the Fleur de Lis had been, for it was gone now, torn down these last five years; a bank filled that site now, all very respectable. But you couldn't tear down Lily's secret shame, nor halt the wagging tongues of scandal-loving San Francisco.

Lily looked at Brooks, and as quickly looked away.

Her eyes passed to Kate, lovely Kate, innocent Kate: *And how do you tell your only daughter her mother was a whore?* She looked at Neddy, bubbling with charm and good spirits, and thought of the parties he might not be invited to on her account, and how he'd roamed these gentle hills for years, blissfully unaware that there were such things in the world as spite, and shame, and discrimination.

Lily sighed and thought: *If I had died ten minutes ago, I would have died happy.* Then she stood up and left the kitchen without a word.

✥ 43 ✥

Brooks found her in their bedroom, standing at one of the three tall windows, standing so straight and still she might have been part of the furniture, staring out over their hills with unfocused eyes, too shocked for tears or for rage.

Lily heard his step, but said nothing, nor moved a muscle.

Brooks came up behind her and gently enfolded her in his arms.

Lily shuddered and sighed a sigh that might have come from any condemned prisoner. Finally she found her tongue. "It is done, then? It's final?"

He kissed her cheek. Lily moved her head away as if to elude a bothersome housefly.

"I thought you'd be pleased, Lily."

She spun around in his arms, and there was no way to hide the pain in her eyes or mute the anger so suddenly unleashed in her voice. "Pleased? When you never even discussed the thing with me? Pleased! When you know what that town did to me, what it can do to me still, and our children? When you know what I've built here on the ranch and how much it means to me, and you throw it all away in one idle gesture, and to achieve . . . what? No, Brooks. Love you as I do, I am not pleased."

His thoughts raced, for her reaction shocked him. Brooks knew Lily disliked the town, but he had never known, for the occasion had never come up, how very deep and intense her hatred and fear of the place could be.

"I was thinking of the children, too."

"The children? That's what disturbs me the most. Have you ever seen happier children than ours, or healthier? What do they need with the crowded, smelly city and the spoiled little rich boys and girls who'd be their playmates there—assuming my children would be allowed to play with them. The town loves scandal, Brooks, and it would be a true shame to visit that on the little ones."

[514]

"That's the heart of it, isn't it? You, the bravest woman I have ever known, are afraid of some silly gossip."

Lily turned from him then and walked slowly across the room and sat on their big white bed. For a moment she said nothing. Then she covered her face with her hands and spoke in a voice so empty of hope it might have been the wind scrubbing gravestones. Nor could she look at him.

"I knew . . . I always knew, deep in my heart, that my luck was too good to last, that sooner or later I would have to pay for my sins, and sins they surely were, Brooks. I knew that no matter how much you loved me, this moment would come, the time when for all your fine protestations that my past didn't matter, it would come sneaking back to haunt us. Can't you see that's why I love the ranch so much? Can't you see that here we are safe—I'm safe, and the children—that here there is no one who would dare to rake over the past that should be allowed to rest forever? Yes. I'm afraid. I'm more afraid than ever I have been. I am afraid of losing your respect—your love—and for the children, who are innocent. The city is a dangerous place for me, Brooks. Yet, if you ask it of me, I will go there."

He came and sat beside her and put his arm around her. His voice was gentle as his touch, but for the first time that touch did not warm her, and the comfort in his words rang hollow.

"Lily, Lily, my Lily. When did I ever say a thing to you that wasn't true? Well, on the basis of that, my darling, I must ask you to trust me now. You have kept yourself so close out here at the ranch, you really haven't seen San Francisco in years. 'Tis a glorious place now, Lily, magnificent! Great things are happening. And, like it or not, we are part of it, a bigger part than you probably suspect. And the time has come to take our place there, not just for our own sakes, but also for the children. Kate and Neddy and Jon are going to be leaders in this part of the world, Lily, if they choose to take what will be available to them. And we must prepare them for that. It is all very well to have them running about the ranch like so many farmers' children, but they must learn to deal as equals in the world they will inherit."

"They'll inherit the ranch too, I hope?"

"And much more, and if they're to know what to do with it, we must prepare them. That's why Mount Holyoke is such a good idea for Kate. It'll turn her into a fine young lady."

"That's exactly what I fear the most."

"You're joking."

"In my experience, small as it is, the fine young ladies—and gentlemen—of this world are a very mixed lot, at best."

"You married one."

"Shall I remind you, my darling, that once you did, too? Let us not fight, Brooks. I have seen this coming for some time, and as with too many other unpleasant things in my life, I simply refused to admit it. Aside from everything else, the life of a rich woman in the city appeals to me not at all. They are such idle creatures, Brooks, far more idle than you guess. They spend their time in trembling delight over the cut of a sleeve or the tilt of a bonnet, they gather in buzzing swarms to try with a kind of sad desperate energy to outdo each other in the splendor of their dress, their houses, the distinction of their guest lists. I was not a maid in the Wallingford house for nothing. It is shallow, hypocritical, and extravagant. It creates nothing useful. It is boring and demeaning. And I would think these things even if I didn't feel that there is a grave risk of the gossips of the town hurting you and our children through my reputation."

"You are Mrs. Brooks Chaffee of Chaffee Produce, and you could buy and sell the lot of them."

"I am Lily Cigar."

She stood quickly, as if stung. Lily walked to the middle of the room and turned in her tracks with a panther's grace. Her voice when she spoke was low, but there was an unmistakable ripple of menace in it.

"You can't know what that means, Brooks. No man could know. Your name and our money may impress the climbers. It is never a trick to fill a room with people if you're serving fine food and good liquor and plenty of it. But for those who have already climbed, those who play the game of who is highest upon the greased pole at any given moment, they are another matter altogether. I was born too close to the gutter to ever lose sight of it entirely, Brooks. When I took up whoring, it was for one reason only, to free myself from ever again being dependent upon anyone, or on any system of society. I hated it, but it was a game I played to win, and win I did, handsomely. And as soon as I could, I came out here and made myself a world of my own, and it works, my little world. Is it so bad, what we have here, that you must flee?"

Brooks looked at the woman he loved more than anyone or anything in the world and tried, as though his life hung in the balance, to feel what she felt. That Lily was in deep pain was obvious. But he had seen her overcome too many problems with an easy-seeming, offhand grace and courage to credit her fear. *Women are silly sometimes, all of them, and this must be one of those times for Lily. And she's wrong, and I'll prove it to her! For haven't I seen the best San Francisco has to offer, its finest women and richest houses, and is there one of those women who could come within miles of Lily for beauty, outside or in, for wit and brains and decency? Not one. Lily will shine there, she'll have the town eating out of her hand, and she'll be happier for it.*

"There's more in the world than our ranch, Lily."

"If you hadn't come, I'd have stayed here always."

"Then I'm glad I came, for you are too fine and lovely to stay bottled up on a farm, however big and thriving."

For the first time, then, she smiled, a thin and fleeting smile. "If you were going into the darkest jungle, or off to some bloody war, Brooks darling, I would follow you unquestioningly, no matter what the cost. And I'll follow you even to San Francisco, for even on the ranch I love I'd be miserable without you."

Brooks came to her then and took her in his arms. She felt all the warmth of him flowing into her with the strong steady glow of a well-made fire. And when she shuddered now, it was with pleasure. Her anger quieted, and for the moment her fears crept away. This was his magic, the blessing of his love, and she knew it was magic and that magic spells could be taken as quickly as they came, out of nowhere, and to nowhere return.

In her mind's eye San Francisco loomed tall and dark and glowering like some cruel enemy's fortress, a citadel strongly defended, that she must attack alone and unarmed.

"I'm afraid," she said softly, as much to herself as to him.

"What was that?"

Lily sighed. "Nothing, my darling. Nothing at all."

She held him tight then, for the room was reeling. It seemed that all her world was flying to pieces, and only Brooks could keep her from falling into some dark and unmeasurable void forever.

Lily was more frightened in that moment than she could ever remember: frightened for herself, for Brooks, and for what the coming failure that she could feel in her bones might do to both of them.

One week later found Lily and Kate in a frenzy of last-minute shopping and packing and making plans. Kate would spend a week with the senior Caffees in New York before proceeding by train to the seminary.

As far as they knew, Kate would be the only California girl to make this epic journey, and the thought of her eighteen-year-old innocent traveling all those thousands of miles of wild country alone, unchaperoned, sent Lily fluttering back and forth from the brink of deciding to go with the girl, at least to Chicago, or to send one of the more reliable servants.

But Kate would have none of this; she looked on the trip as a great adventure, a wonderful lark, the watershed of her childhood, the gateway to womanhood.

Lily looked at her daughter and thought of herself at the same age, or nearly, alone and terrified on the clipper *Eurydice*, under the chaperonage of Sophie Delage.

And Lily knew that Kate would be fine on this journey, for Kate was a strong and sensible girl, high-spirited and full of fun, sure of herself and unsusceptible to the snares of strangers or cities. Lily looked at Kate and thought: *This is the moment. Now is the time for me to tell the child who her mother is and what I've done—here, on the ranch, and before someone else does it, as they most certainly will do.* But Lily could find no words to say these things. Instead, she tried to be lighthearted, tried not to show how very much she would miss the girl when the time of parting came, just next week.

Kate's room was in that condition of siege halfway between chaos and organization that always attends big-scale packing. The closets and drawers were flung open, half-empty, with the clothes chosen for the journey neatly arrayed on the bed and in trunks, and the rejects more casually piled for repairs or to be distributed among the servants.

Lily went to Kate's small white-painted bookcase, presided over by a worn but ever-game Hortense, the rag doll of Lily's childhood and Kate's. "You'll want this," said Lily, picking out a Bible and handing it to Kate, "and surely the dictionary."

Lily picked up the dictionary and was about to hand it on when something fell out, a rectangle of cardboard, and fluttered to the floor. Kate was on it with the speed of a hawk on a mouse, but Lily was closer and therefore quicker. And even as she crouched to pick the thing up, Lily knew with dreadful certainty what it was.

Holding the card in two fingers as if it might contaminate her, Lily handed it to her daughter.

"Where did you get this?"

"In the city, a year ago, in a souvenir shop."

"Then you know."

Kate came to her and took her hand. "Mama, I have known for years and years. And it's all right. I love you, Mama. I bought the picture because it's so pretty."

The picture was one of the old souvenir postcards that showed Lily as she had been in Sophie's house, chastely gowned in pure white and holding a white lily. The photograph was simply captioned. It just said: "LILY CIGAR."

To Lily it was about as pretty as a death's-head. She turned from Kate to gather her thoughts. *So here it was, the truth seeping out at last, poisonous, inescapable, even here at the ranch.*

If her past could infiltrate this private domain so very easily, what might it not do in the city itself? Lily turned back to Kate and said quietly, "All these years, Kate, ever since you were born, I have been dreading this moment, praying you might never have to know. Who told you?"

"It doesn't really matter, does it? Small children have big ears, Mama, and they are not always very kind. I don't even know how old I was, but I surely didn't know what that word meant."

"The word was 'whore'?"

"Yes."

"A sad thing it is to lose you to the East and to lose your respect at the same time."

Kate looked at her mother and thought of the day—how many years ago—when another child at the Tiburon schoolyard had taunted her with the ugly revelation. Kate hadn't known the meaning of "whore," but the tone Sadie had used said it all. And that night when Brooks got back from town, Kate had sought him out.

"When I first heard about it," said Kate softly, "I went to Father. And I will never forget what he said then, for there was no hiding the truth in it, or the way he looked when he spoke of you. He said that Lily Cigar was the best and most honorable woman he had ever known, and that's why he loved you, and loves you still. And all at once I knew that nothing a mean little girl might say could truly harm me—or us. So you see, you're wrong on all counts, Mama: you will never lose me. Wherever I am, I will love you and Father, for aren't I part of you, and you of me, and all of us together? And how could a girl have better parents, I ask you."

"Oh, Kate, Katie-Kate! You're better than your old mother deserves, girl."

Then they were in each other's arms, half-sobbing and half-laughing, and it seemed to Lily that the world that had made her the gift of a child so loving could never do her harm.

Brooks looked at his wife as he helped her off the Chaffee Produce tender that had sailed them across the bay. *Thirty-eight, and she never looked better,* he thought. *Even if she refuses to dress in the height of fashion or wear much jewelry, other women look pale beside her.*

Brooks was happy this fine summer's afternoon.

The visit to town was an act of conciliation on Lily's part, a gesture more symbolic than functional, viewing the site of their new house and meeting the architects. Brooks knew Lily still hated the town and dreaded living any part of the year there, but he was proud that she would come here, thus, for his sake, and he vowed to make it worth her while.

The town glittered: it seemed to reflect his happiness. A bright July sun burnished the new brick and limestone facades that seemed to be springing up everywhere. Brass sparkled, glass shone, and the very hides of the horses that pulled their carriage up California Street to the building site seemed more silk than stallion.

The horses strained with the effort of climbing to the very summit of Nob Hill, but that was the destination. And when they alighted, there, just as Brooks had described it, was the finest building lot in all of San Francisco, five acres right on the crest of the hill, with views in every direction. From here they would see the first rays of dawn and the sunset's last glowing. From here they could count the clippers pouring through the Golden Gate, see their own busy barges plying back and forth from Tiburon.

Lily stood silent for a moment. Then she said, taking Brooks by the hand, "If one has to live/here, my darling, there could hardly be a more beautiful place to do it."

He squeezed her hand, delighted. "You can look down on all the city."

And the city can look down on me. Lily's mind was still infested with doubts, but she kept them to herself.

The architect came just then, and for a pleasant hour they looked at sketches and talked of elevations. Lily began to see the site in terms of terraced gardens, and her farmer's eye imagined flowering plum and cherry trees, banked evergreens, beds of flowers, a reflecting pool, terraces upon terraces, and a tall, simple house with a great deal of glass to let in the light and let out the view.

"Not," she said emphatically, "one of these vulgar fun-fair creations with so many fancy towers and carpenter's lacework everywhere."

"Something a bit Palladian, perhaps?" The architect spoke in a too-refined voice that was neither English nor Eastern but somewhere in between.

"What," asked Lily, "does that mean?"

The architect's eyebrows rose just a fraction of an inch. "A very famous architect, madame, of Italy in its great days. He reinterpreted the classical feeling quite beautifully."

The man's pen flew over a sheet of paper and a light but sober design took form, with a pillared Grecian portico flanked by tall, wide, pedimented windows, and the windows starting at ground level so that they could also serve as French doors opening out onto terraces.

"And the whole thing, you see, opening onto courtyards and terraces on all sides, and the stables and carriage houses built underneath the gardens, down the hillside a bit, so that nothing at all interferes with the main house—the great house—itself."

Lily could see the essential elegance of the scheme, for all its great size and stately proportions. It had a simplicity that looked as though it might last, as opposed to the suddenly fashionable and quickly outdated styles that proliferated elsewhere on these hills.

"I think," she said, "that it could be lovely."

These words fell like music on Brooks's ears. He would have agreed to building a million-dollar doghouse if it made her happy.

They ended their excursion on a happy note, with a quiet tea in a small hotel nearby, where—Lily was delighted to note—no one recognized her. Soon they were back on the Chaffee tender and headed into the westering sun toward Tiburon.

The great house was eight months building, and yet it seemed to rise overnight, looming tall and dark in Lily's imagination, haunted by her old doubts and fears long before she ever set foot in the place.

Oh, sure and it would be beautiful. All of the grace and taste and richness that money could buy were being bought, regardless of cost, for the Chaffee place.

That's what the people on the streets of San Francisco

called it already, "the Chaffee place on Nob Hill." And the rumors of its great cost and elegance spread like fire.

"They'll be fighting to get in," Brooks said.

Fighting to get in they well might be, and fighting to see who'd be the first to snub the pretensions of Lily Cigar.

But Lily had made a bargain with herself to hide her fears, to give no voice to the doubts that plagued her now more vividly than they had ever done, or her terror of letting her husband down, of disgracing him by the simple juxtaposition of her lurid fame with his blameless honor.

Well and good, Lily told herself when the fear crept up on her in the night, *you've fought and won many a battle before this one, and you will fight now, and you may win or die trying, but fight you shall, and with every weapon at your command.*

Who, precisely, the enemy was in this dreaded contest, Lily could never be entirely sure. Her frightened brain distilled all the respectable and disapproving matrons of the town into the stiff, chinless, sneering form of Mamie Dickinson, so well remembered from that harsh interview of long ago when Lily had been seeking work as a seamstress.

Lily's nightmares included an avenging Mamie on a tall white horse, leading an army, racing up Nob Hill with lances leveled and drawn swords glittering in the sun, charging the Chaffee place, all set to skewer Lily Cigar to make San Francisco safe for respectable women like themselves. They had lowered lances and swords drawn, and for some inexplicable reason, in the other hand of every galloping matron was a neatly filled cup of China tea.

The dream had comical aspects that were obvious even to Lily, yet there was a dreadful reality to it that never failed to move her.

She would awake in the night stifling a scream, and feel Brooks next to her, warm and easy and confident, and then Lily would smile in the darkness and ridicule her own fears and gather her courage again.

For the next assault could not be long in coming.

Furnishing the new house and staffing it were occupations that required constant generalship, and these tasks fell to Lily.

She was a commuter into the city now, and the Chaffee tenders plied their way back and forth across the bay carrying Mrs. Brooks Chaffee along with their golden burden of fruits and vegetables, poultry and beef, and dairy produce.

[522]

Lily never learned to like the architect, but she gave good taste its due, and he had taste to spare.

Living in the handsomely proportioned and simply furnished old Spanish-colonial ranch house had altered Lily's taste.

Whereas the Fleur de Lis had been calculatedly furnished to dazzle the eye and delight all the other senses, and although Brooks assured her that the standard of decor in the great new mansions of the town was indistinguishable from a good class of whorehouse, Lily wanted a different feeling entirely for their new house on Nob Hill.

She wanted elegance, but it must be a simple, understated sort of elegance.

Lily found herself in the bookstores more often than in the decorators' showrooms, for the decorators were forever spilling over with the latest and the newest and the costliest fancies from Paris or London or New York, a vulgar cornucopia where silk jostled velvet, where gilt-bronze writhed as if in agony and androgynous marble maidens cast chaste unseeing eyes toward heaven in vain supplication, as if asking for release from the clutter.

Lily was too well used to the clear open air and soaring skies of San Rafael, and to the spare clean-lined sweep of her own ranch house, to tolerate the fussiness she found everywhere in this strange new San Francisco. The overcrowded rooms seemed to close in on her, even if they were not filled with people. And the people she saw were as cluttered and overfussy in their dress as the houses they lived in. There was a sense of suffocation in the corseted, hooped, bustled women draped with overskirts and fringes and peplums, furred and jeweled and bonneted, hair sculptured like bronze, trimmed and tinseled, booted and parasoled within an inch of their lives. The most fashionable women seemed to be wearing enough clothes for a whole village: they were unable to walk, really, and so they had cultivated a peculiar gait somewhere between a glide and a waddle, made up of innumerable tiny restricted steps whose effect was rather like a not very well-rehearsed ballet dancer in a hurry to go nowhere.

It was comical, and sad, and Lily vowed to have none of it.

She read her architecture books with the same growing interest with which she had once scoured the farming journals.

Slowly, as the walls and terraces began to take shape, a plan for decorating the great house took shape in Lily's mind.

It would be simple, and vastly underfurnished by the standards of the day. And it would be spectacular.

Where the fashion was for fat gilded chairs and sofas and draperies over draperies, and marble inlaid and carved and tortured, the Chaffee house would glow with the warmth of old wood, and come alive with pale light colors, the colors of faded frescoes instead of the overripe plums and murky umbers and malachite greens that fashion decreed. There would be space, and only the simplest of rare old lace draperies at the many windows, so that the vistas over the courtyards and terraces and sunken gardens would forever be a part of the furnishings in every room. The fashion of the day so draped windows that little light came in, and it was a matter of some physical exertion to look out. This seemed nonsensical to Lily: Why, indeed, have windows then? It would be more economical to live in a cave.

Lily began to tour the antique shops, but she bought little. She wrote to New York for dealers' catalogs, and began corresponding with three of the leading dealers. Lily learned to value one fine object above six mediocre examples. And with her inborn sense of the dramatic, she evolved simple but unexpected ways of displaying her treasures.

The things that attracted her most were simple and fine. An unadorned old Chinese vase, for example, shaped like an elongated teardrop, whose glaze faded from near-raspberry to a pale bluish white. It entranced her, and she splurged on it. Country French furniture from the period of Louis XVI pleased Lily with its warm fruitwoods and gentle curves, its sense of containment and ease. This was radical taste in an era that valued everything lush and plush and golden, where there was no such thing as an excess of Baroque curlicues, where no velvet was too deep or too red, where Society with a capital S glided through its days and its nights in a perpetual murky twilight, where the difference between midnight and noon was more a matter of changing costumes than of a change in the atmosphere in the rooms.

And it happened that Lily began to take a kind of unexpected pride in the house that Brooks had forced on her.

She found, and had the wit to grin at her folly in resisting the thing, that much of what Brooks had said was true: the new house was opening up new vistas in her imagination. She was learning new things, acquiring new tastes, deepening her education, and thus making herself more valuable to Brooks. This was a pleasure and a consolation, and for a time it kept her fears at bay.

There were days when Lily wished the house would never quite be finished, when she secretly hoped they'd never have to move into the place, that she could just go on forever planning gardens and vistas and the colors of rooms.

But the eight months passed like a week, and suddenly Lily found herself in a frenzy of hiring servants. This was vastly different and more complicated than getting help for the ranch. Here, she must have a serious chef, legions of maids, coachmen and footmen, gardeners and grooms. Brooks must have a proper valet and she a maid for her own wardrobe and for Kate's. The boys must have a nursemaid, although they would surely rebel at the thought.

It was only when she was well along in her seemingly endless interviews that Lily realized she was now to play the role of Mrs. Wallingford, mistress of a huge and ambitious establishment more like a grand hotel than a home.

This made her shudder with foreboding.

Lily wondered where Mr. and Mrs. Groome were, not to mention the estimable Louise Dulac. And wouldn't that be a fine ironic twist of fortune's wheel, to have all those good people at her beck and call, who once had been the lowliest and most thoroughly terrified serving maid at the Wallingfords'? But the Wallingford mansion was no more, or at least the Wallingfords were no longer holding forth there. Lily wondered if that huge white limestone pile still stood, or was New York as fickle in its fashions now as San Francisco had become? Surely the house had been big enough to be a small hotel, or a school even, or who knew what?

She thought of Jack Wallingford then, and his bitterness, how he'd laughed at his parents and their world, how he'd laughed at them and taken from them and taken from Lily, and taken from her own dear Brooks the thing Brooks had loved most in all the world.

Jack Wallingford!

Well, the past was the past. She'd never see Jack again, and she'd be the better for that. Lily thought of Kate and how fine a girl Kate had become, and how little Jack cared or knew. *How little he deserves a daughter like my Katie.* Jack Wallingford, indeed. Lily had wondered more than once: had she never laid eyes on Brooks Chaffee in those days, would she have tolerated the advances of young Master Jack?

Like all the most disturbing questions, this one had no proper answer.

When it came time to move into the new house, which

Brooks faithfully promised would be only a seasonal thing, October until May, so that the boys could have the advantage of proper schooling instead of the makeshift one-room establishment that was Lily's pride at the ranch, Lily found that there was little to move, since everything in the San Francisco establishment had been acquired anew. Even their clothing and linens were fresh from the tailors and department stores and dressmakers. So there was no element of rush or flurry about the moving, no question of deadlines.

Lily and Brooks walked through the empty rooms on the week before they moved in. All of the essentials were in place: waxed floors gleamed, old mirrors reflected a sense of mystery along with the beholder's image, and hundreds of windows danced with light and framed gardens that bloomed more with promise than with flowers.

She felt the pressure of his hand increase with his pleasure. "You have done just what I expected, my darling," he said softly. "You've made a miracle. It's delightful, Lily. It looks just like you."

"Then," she said laughing, "it must look tired, for if I see one dealer's catalog ever again, 'twill be one too many."

"The colors are enchanting—light yet subtle."

"I stole them out of picture books of old, old places in Italy."

"And the furniture! It's fine, but not . . . not competitive, if you know what I mean."

"You mean it doesn't scream to all the world how rich you are. Well, don't be fooled, my dear, for it cost a very pretty penny all the same."

"What I like most about it—aside from its mistress—is the views, and the way you've let us all see them."

Lily turned and walked to a small fruitwood console and moved a vase four inches to the right.

"I'm very pleased with the house, Brooks. More than pleased: if we must be grand, then this is a most pleasant way to do it. But the house itself was never a problem for me. The life that goes with such a house, as you know, is another matter altogether."

"You are afraid I'll become a social butterfly, my Lily, my love? Fill the place with drunks and bores at all hours? Come, darling, surely you know me better than that."

"Why did you want it, then?"

"Because," he said softly, kissing her cheek, "a rare jewel deserves a rare setting. And because I want certain things for our children, things that may seem superficial but that will serve them well—I believe—in their future life. I want to see our Katie married in this garden, I want to be an old man dozing in his easy chair at that window, and wake to hear the grandchildren playing around that fountain. I want to look out our bedroom window at the city we have helped to build, and the ocean that brought us here, that brought us together."

They stood in the window and looked out over the terraced gardens and down onto the rooftops of the city. San Francisco Bay was a splash of melted silver far below. And somewhere, somewhere near, although she could not actually make it out, was the building—now a bank—that had once held all the glitter and shame of the Fleur de Lis.

Lily sighed. "I hope," she whispered as though all the world was listening, "that it makes you happy."

And as she stood there in the big and beautifully proportioned room, looking out upon one of the most glorious views in all of the world and standing warm in the arms of the man she had loved nearly all her life, Lily could feel the happiness draining out of her like blood from a wound.

⋙ 44 ⋘

The party would be the talk of San Francisco.

Fergy assured his sister of that fact, confirming her very worst fears.

For it was not possible, it seemed, to simply move in. One must open the place officially, as if it were some gambling casino or whorehouse. One must have a big glittering party. One must certify one's arrival on the scene, and it must be writ large like a stage direction in a play: ENTER THE CHAFFEES, ARMED FOR BEAR.

So now it would begin—or end.

How she had wished to take up life in San Francisco slowly, by small degrees, a few little dinners for close friends, possibly—just possibly—a few ladies in for tea. *If they'd come. If they'd sully their fine reputations by mingling with a "soiled dove."*

But no. It would be a party, a reception, a soiree, and a big one. Music, lights, champagne: a major event in the social arena.

It had been Brooks, of course, who suggested the thing. "A small party, my darling, just a few of my business friends, and anyone you'd like."

"Small" meant some hundred and fifty names, three hundred people if all the men brought lady guests. *I'll get sick. I'll leave town. I'll burn the damned place down!* But Lily knew she would do none of these things, that she would make the party as fine and as beautiful as she could, simply because Brooks wanted it done. *And is it such a great thing for a man to ask, for his wife to serve as a hostess for his friends?* Lily caught her reflection in one of the old mirrors, a bluish, rippling image, more like a reflection in a pond than in glass. And she thought: *But I am not like other men's wives, and this is not like other towns, and it is a great thing he's asking of me, greater far than he knows, or will let himself know.*

Lily had long ceased to read the San Francisco papers, but

she knew their tone all too well, their love of scandal and sensation, their old maid's devotion to local gossip, their irresistible thirst for stirring up the social caldrons of the town, making mischief out of thin air when none fell ready-made to their hand.

Lily remembered her farewell from the Fleur de Lis and regretted it now, for it had only built the legend of Lily Cigar. She felt her old notoriety waiting in ambush now, like a bandit army.

Brooks smiled and told her not to worry, that she was thinking too much on it. *And maybe,* she told herself grimly, *he's right.* Lily smiled and wrote the cards of invitation herself and sent them round by the coachman, sure in her heart that they were tickets to her own funeral. But she had promised herself that if she must preside over the extinction of her husband's dream of a fuller social life in town, she would do it in style, and smiling, whatever the smiles might cost her. *Riding for a fall, that's what we are,* she thought, writing in her boudoir at the little pearwood escritoire. She looked up at him and spoke gently. "You know, my darling, that there are only two possibilities in this: they won't come, or they'll come only to sneer, and never invite us back."

He came to the desk and put his arms around her neck. "I've never known my Lily to think the worst of anyone, or to expect the worst. It will be a huge success, dearest, for all the town is perishing to see what glories you've wrought here."

"All the town is perishing to see me fall on my face, more likely."

"Nonsense. Why, Stanford Dickinson was saying just yesterday—"

"Brooks, dear, you don't understand. You are too good to be able to even contemplate the way some of their minds work. If Mamie Dickinson ever sets foot in my house, it would be a miracle on the level of the loaves and the fishes. To women like that, I am worse than a leper. They must see me punished, humbled, put in my place. And for them, my proper place is in the gutter."

"I can't believe that."

"That's because you are a kind and generous man, and you have no fears about your position in the world. But to women like Mamie, position is everything, it is like the Chinese gaining or losing 'face,' as they call it. The ultimate disgrace. If a scarlet woman like me can lead a life of wickedness and then triumph and be happy, why, that undermines the very fabric of their existence. It means that all their stiff and hypocritical rules of decorum might not matter a damn. So they must strike out at me if God won't do it for them. I understand that thoroughly, Brooks, and I even forgive them for it, for they cannot help being what they are."

"Well, my love, I hear you clearly, and I can only pray you are wrong about that, and the party will confirm me."

"Three weeks will tell, my darling," said Lily in a voice so low it was barely audible. "Then we shall see."

She busied herself with the preparations and determined to stop worrying about what was beyond her control in any case. Lily began feeling more like a general than a housewife: extra butlers and maids would be hired for the occasion, and an orchestra, plus strolling violinists, and special tables must be built for the buffet on the terrace, and extra tables too, in case of bad weather, and a wooden dancing floor too, cunningly made in sections so it could be the more easily stored and expanded and used on the other terraces for other parties. If there were other parties.

Lily sometimes found herself smiling at the irony of how very well her time served at the Wallingford mansion and at the Fleur de Lis worked for her now, for the similarities were greater in many respects than the differences: all huge establishments must have them. Lily insisted on interviewing all of the servants herself, and she learned why rich women seem so obsessed by "the servant problem," for indeed, it was a problem.

"Tell me," Lily said to the trembling sixteen-year-old girl who stood awkwardly before her in a dress so worn it aroused Lily's sympathy at once, "tell me, Mary, what do you want most in the world?"

It was a question Lily asked every girl she interviewed, and most of the men, too, for the answers were revealing. Mary's large blue eyes raced about the luxurious drawing room and finally alighted, meeting Lily's kindly gaze.

"Oh, madame," she said very softly, "it would be to eat regular."

Lily stood up then, and went to the girl and embraced her gently, feeling the child's shudder, her fear, the tremor of a trapped animal.

"There's no better reason, Mary, for wanting work than that one. And we will find work for you, my dear, never doubt it."

To Lily's astonishment, the responses to their invitations came back promptly, and for the most part, positively.

"My mother always figures that two-thirds is about normal, unless there's an epidemic, or it's the wrong season. And she—"

"Is Mrs. Chaffee of Washington Square. I am Mrs. Chaffee formerly of the Fleur de Lis."

Lily put down a small pile of acceptances that had come with the morning's mail.

"Still," she went on, " 'tis better than their refusing outright."

His laugh surprised her. "And I," he said, laughing still, "thought I'd married an optimist."

Lily stood and went to him and kissed him. "You did," she said, smiling, "or by now I'd be in China and still running."

Saturday, June 28, 1876, dawned with the perfect blue clarity common to summer in northern California. *At least,* Lily thought, looking out from her bedroom window, *the weather did not fail me.*

The last few days had been mayhem, but now all was in order. The new parlormaid, Mary, proved a wonder; she seemed to have magical powers that enabled her to be in three places at once.

All that remained to be done was to drape the lace cloths on the terrace buffets and to arrange the flowers that would arrive this morning from San Francisco's three best florists and from the ranch, supplemented by a few roses already in bloom here on the hill. The food would be laid out at the last minute, and the chafing dishes filled and ignited after the guests had arrived.

Lily could not but look on these rooms, these terraces, with pleasure, nor miss the anticipation that hung in the air, for the household fairly quivered with it.

Yet mixed with the beauty that no one's eyes could deny was something else, a nameless fear, and no matter how gently Brooks might soothe her doubts, no matter how she might chide herself for being a ninny, Lily walked through the grand rooms and thought that they might have been fixed up for a funeral instead of a gala supper dance.

One thousand tall white candles stood expectantly at attention in one thousand polished candleholders throughout the house, and the five main terraces were strung, in addition, with pastel-colored Chinese paper lanterns. The five-piece string orchestra would be heard, but not seen, being concealed behind a hedge of white roses.

Twenty-five cases of Clicquot champagne were on ice in the cellar, and ten silver tubs big enough to bathe in had been rented to display the wine on the terraces and in the main reception rooms of the house. It was rose season, and there were roses everywhere, white and pale pink and a rare shade that was nearly apricot. The Occidental Hotel had lent two chefs and five waiters to supplement the Chaffees' own staff, and the buffet would be startling in its variety and richness. There would be immense lobster salads, and hams and turkeys sliced thin as paper, hot curried dishes, French pâtés thick with truffles and aspics; an entire sturgeon poached and stuffed and glazed with sauce duglère seemed to swim on a vast silver tray in the center. There were sorbets and petits fours and nine varieties of chilled mousse, and cookies and coffee laced with rare cognac.

The guests had been invited for eight-thirty.

Lily was dressed by seven, and making the rounds of the great house, checking on the last-minute details. It was impressive, if she did say so herself. But Brooks was still dressing, and there was no one but the servants to hear, so Lily kept her counsel and moved smiling through the huge rooms, approving, making small suggestions, rearranging a flower here, straightening a fork there.

Squeaks and groans issued from the far end of the terrace, where the orchestra was tuning up.

At eight Lily ordered half of the thousand candles lit. The other half would be lighted at ten-thirty. The afterglow had faded now, and the candles flickered defiantly in the falling night.

Lily stood in the main drawing room looking out through the open French doors across her terrace and down onto the pinpoint lights of San Francisco. It was so clear and still that she could even detect a faint sparkle of diamond dust across the bay—the lights of Tiburon.

And behind Tiburon, unseen but deeply felt, the welcoming hills of San Rafael, the ranch!

What would she not have given to be there now, in gingham by the kitchen fire, reading to Neddy and little Jon?

Lily sighed softly, and turned, and touched her upswept hair to make sure it was in place.

Brooks walked into the room, dramatic in his finely cut black evening clothes, smiling. He was carrying something, she couldn't quite see what.

"You are," he said, kissing her, "the loveliest sight in a city of lovely sights."

"I am a tired old woman and you are a shameless flatterer."

[532]

But she was pleased because she pleased him.

"Let me show you where everything is," she said with a little laugh, "seeing as how you'll be getting the bills."

He took her hand in his. "First, a small token of admiration."

Lily looked first at her husband and then at the thing he was carrying. Of course. A black leather jeweler's box. She had more jewels now than she ever cared to wear. Tonight, for example, she wore only the lovely strand of pearls he had given her for a wedding present, just the pearls, no ornament in her hair, no rings or bracelets or fancy buttons on her simply cut dull-satin gown of dark amethyst, its neckline an unadorned oval scoop, its sleeves slightly puffed at the shoulder and tapering sleekly past her elbows, where they met the ivory kidskin gloves. It was a startling gown, having nothing to do with the current vogue, with a full skirt to the floor but no hoops or bustles, a slender but uncorseted waist, and a slightly medieval look about it all, which was only natural, since the style had been adapted from something Lily had found in a picture book of tapestries.

"Really, Brooks . . ."

"Open it." His voice was just like Neddy's when Neddy had captured some especially spectacular and frightening frog or turtle—eight years old and eager.

She took the little box: from the foursquare shape of it, a ring box. Lily slowly opened the lid. Green fires leaped up at her from a huge square of perfectly faceted emerald flanked by a small regiment of baguette diamonds. The stone was clear as air, deep and alive. She turned it in the candlelight and it seemed to flash blue among the sparkling green and pure white refractions.

Lily slipped it on her finger, on the third finger of her left hand next to the simple wedding band.

"My darling," she whispered, "this is . . ."

"If I could scoop up the moon, Lily, and put it on your finger, I would do it."

Lily kissed him slowly, softly. "I would love you no less if you were a beggarman, Brooks Chaffee, but since you seem to be quite the opposite, I thank you for a lovely ring."

"There is no way I can ever thank you, my darling, for the gifts you have given me every day since first I saw you: the gift of love, of hope, of our children, but most of all the gift of yourself."

They stood close, entwined thus, the youngest lovers in all the world, until the sound of a carriage in the driveway called them back to the real world, to this great haughty house perched so high above the booming town, to their aspirations and their duties. The first carriage was quickly followed by others, and the sound of wheels on gravel and clopping hooves became a low counterpoint to the distant waltzing strings and the scent of roses everywhere, corks popping, and laughter.

Lily, being primed for what happened next, was less surprised than her husband.

It amounted to a complete social boycott by all the ladies of San Francisco.

More than a hundred men came to the party, but only half a dozen of them brought women, and the women, more often than not, were not wives or daughters.

She and Brooks stood in the great foyer, underneath the sweeping curve of the main staircase. They stood flanked by rose trees in white tubs, stood close together in the candlelight, stood smiling, greeting, shaking hands.

And before the first twenty guests had arrived, Lily could see the pattern forming. "There seems," she whispered to Brooks through her most dazzling smile, "to be an epidemic in the town that attacks only women."

A man in San Francisco, Lily knew all too well, could go anywhere, and with anyone, and never make a scandal. He could go gaming or whoring or to the races. He could break laws and keep mistresses and be roaring, rampaging drunk and disorderly from dawn until dusk and no one would lift an eyebrow.

It was left to the womenfolk to preserve the sanctity of the hearth, the morality of the family circle, the standards of Queen Victoria. *And,* Lily thought with a bitter grin, *that is just where they are tonight, the good ladies of San Francisco. They are at home, upholding their damned standards.* She looked anxiously at Brooks, wondering how it would affect him. For herself, Lily cared not a jot for the approval or scorn of the righteous matrons of the town. For her family, for the man she loved more than life itself, that was another matter. They stood by the staircase for an hour, until most of the guests had arrived. Then Brooks turned to her, smiling his most dazzling smile, and said, "I, for one, intend to have a very good time at our party. How about you, Mrs. Chaffee?"

"I could have a good time," she said with a laugh that came more from her head than her heart, "in the bottom of a mineshaft at midnight, if you were there, Mr. Chaffee. How about a glass of champagne?"

Hand in hand, they strolled out into the glittering throng.

The night seemed to last years. Lily tried to remember who had accepted and who had not. The mayor, she knew, had promised to come but was nowhere to be seen. *In the most scandal-ridden town in America,* she thought bitterly, *we are too scandalous for his Honor.*

Lily moved among the guests, her head held high, a smile never far from her lightly rouged lips, afraid of nothing, laughing, charming, the perfect hostess.

It was a tribute to her performance that even Brooks thought she was having a good time.

The wine and the food and the flowers were perfection. Lily danced, Lily talked gently to the shy and listened attentively to the loquacious, introduced strangers to each other, who were also strangers to her. And she looked at her guests very carefully, wondering exactly why they had come, and what they had said to the wives who were so militantly and so successfully boycotting the occasion. They all seemed to know Brooks, and to like him, as why should they not? Many of these men were no doubt business partners to some degree of the many and widely flung parts of Chaffee Produce, or the Chaffee real-estate interests, or maybe they simply hoped that some of the wealth and glory that were so vividly in evidence tonight in the Chaffee mansion might come their way, seekers of crumbs from the banquets of the great.

And Lily found herself feeling sorry for the few ladies who had come, for they were either too ignorant or too insignificant to have been caught up in the general snubbing. To these females, Lily extended herself, and was her most witty, her kindest, showed them the upper floors of the great house, discussed the furnishings with an expert's appreciation, for indeed Lily had become something of an expert during the months of building and furnishing.

Fergy came with an actress friend, a dark little thing with a pretty face and snake's eyes. But she was a woman, and decently dressed, and Lily was glad to have her. Fergy himself was flushed with wine but on his best behavior. Lily had forbidden reporters, and she extracted from her brother a promise to keep his silence about the party when next he saw his journalist pals. But she knew very well that there could be no counting on such discretion from the hundred-and-some other men in the rooms.

San Francisco would have a great laugh at her expense tomorrow, her expense and Brooks's. Lily could hardly have felt more pain had she been publicly flogged in Golden Gate

Park, and her pain was deeper, more intense because she felt it on his account more than her own. *To have brought this on him, to have my sins come home to roost at last.* She moved through the gardens, smiling, chatting, sipping champagne. And every sip tasted bitter as hemlock, and every smile cost the earth.

It was past three o'clock when the last candle flickered out and the last carriage crunched down the drive.

Hand in hand, Brooks and Lily walked up the curving staircase to their bedroom suite on the second floor. Slowly silently, they moved down the wide hallway. In their bedroom, Lily moved mechanically to the window. Servants were extinguishing the last of the fairy lanterns on the terrace. The gas jets of San Francisco's street-lights were still alight, and lights still shone in some of the houses of the town.

Lily stood there for a moment, saying nothing, for there seemed to be nothing to say. Brooks came up behind her and put his hands on the silky skin of her shoulders, and bent his head to nuzzle gently at the lovely curve where her slender neck resolved itself into the delicacy of her shoulder. His voice was a hoarse whisper, loud in the silence of a gathering dawn.

"You're far, far better than all of them put together, my Lily, my Lily, my love. Never forget that."

"Ah, poor Brooks, you had such fine hopes, and now where are they? I truly don't care, my darling, but that you wanted it thus, not a damn do I care for the lot of them, 'tis you and only you I care for, and always have, and always will."

"Damn her."

Lily didn't have to ask whom he meant: the sheepish, lopsided grin on Stanford Dickinson's face had confirmed every suspicion and magnified every fear.

"Now do you understand why I so love the ranch?"

"I never doubted your reasons, Lily, but I never dreamed of anything like this, such small-mindedness, either."

" 'Tis because there isn't a small-minded bone in your body. Don't worry, my darling, they aren't going to get the best of Lily Cigar. I won't run, far from it. If it's San Francisco you want, I will stay here and work and fight and do whatever I have to do until they come crawling up Nob Hill on their knees to us."

He laughed then, and Lily smiled in the darkness. It couldn't be that bad a wound if he could laugh thus already. And in that secret smile was a promise: she'd do what she said, and do it well, and quickly. Tomorrow wasn't a moment too soon to begin, either.

Lily turned in his arms and kissed him, and the night and their love closed around her, warm and reassuring and throbbing with passion.

❧ 45 ❧

Lily found the key to all the drawing rooms of San Francisco in the pages of the daily newspapers she had always scorned.

On the morning after their party, Lily slept very late.

It was past eleven when she woke, and Brooks was gone. Lily rang for her maid, ordered breakfast in her bedroom, and asked for the morning editions of the town's four best-read newspapers.

The party was mentioned in every paper, but only one had the nerve to hint at the snubbing that was the most vivid memory of that night for Lily and Brooks.

Lily's self-imposed program of educating herself included much reading, but few newspapers. Politics interested her very little and gossip not at all, and these seemed to be the two singularly unattractive rocks upon which the popular press was founded.

But now, like an attacking general gathering intelligence, Lily read every page of every paper with burning attention.

What she saw in those flimsy pages was an enormous thirst for culture.

The bawdy, brawling, strike-it-rich little mining town was desperately anxious for the approval of its older, more polished counterparts back East and abroad. Anything to do with serious painting, sculpture, and especially music was coveted and revered out of all proportion to its possible artistic worth.

Lily smiled as she formed a plan, for the city's thirst for culture and respectability was very like her own.

The difference was one of degree and of publicity: while San Francisco needed, in fact demanded, public approval in the eyes of the world, Lily would hardly blink an eye if all the world outside her family moved to China tomorrow morning.

But Brooks wanted San Francisco, and San Francisco she would get him.

Lily sat luxuriously on a chaise longue, uncharacteristically lazy this fine June morning, and schemed. And as she schemed, Lily's good spirits came back to her, and she found herself, all alone in the big bedroom, laughing out loud. San Francisco, indeed! She'd give her husband Mamie Dickinson on a silver platter.

Brooks saw the humor in it too.

"It's quite simple," Lily said over a quiet supper, just the two of them alone that night. "Who leads the cultural life of the town can also lead its social life. If I—we—have access to some conductor or opera star that Mamie Dickinson has not, then she must come to us or be ostracized."

"So you will go lion-hunting?"

"Not for love of the lions, my darling, but for love of you. With your permission."

"Granted and granted. And the day I see Mamie Dickinson and her gang cross this threshold, I will . . ."

"Build me my cottage on Lily's Hill?"

"Of solid silver, if you like."

"And possibly spend some time with me there?"

"My darling, I am with you wherever I go. But yes, and as much as you like."

She looked at him and wondered at her luck. "I won't hold you to your word, my darling, because the time I would want is forever."

Lily knew that the cultivation of San Francisco's uppermost social circle would take time and willpower. In fact, it took more than a year, and the cost to her spirit was incalculable, for the prize was nothing she cared for in the least. The values of these women were so shallow as to be transparent, and what Lily saw very clearly through the transparency was fear and jealousy and bitterness. In their own cruel way the dowagers of the city were easily as insecure as Lily had ever been, and once she realized that, they became fair game for her plans. In the meantime she forced herself to endure small afternoon concerts in the second drawing room, now equipped with a fine rosewood grand piano and an antique harp and renamed the music room.

Now Lily used her brother's connections with the press, and suddenly her musical afternoons were mentioned, and favorably, in the newspapers and the details of the mansion were described with wonderment. Lily chose her guests with care and shrewdness, and steeled herself for the refusals that often came. But slowly, painfully, the little afternoons acquired a certain small fame. The Chaffees gave no more large parties, but only small and meticulously organized dinner parties, often including visiting business acquaintances of Brooks's, and sometimes people connected with the opera house. The Chaffees' table became famous for the quality of its food and wines, and for the selectivity of the guest list. Slowly, slowly. Conquest by conquest Lily built up a circle of lady friends who saw no scandal in accepting her magnificant hospitality.

Still, she bided her time.

Then, one day in the spring of 1877, Lily saw a small item in one of Brooks's New York papers, and she knew the time was ripe.

Mamie Dickinson looked at her reflection in the huge gilded mirror that was the most striking feature of her bedroom in the gray mansion on Rincon Hill. What she saw did not please her.

The gown had arrived from Paris only last week, and was the very pinnacle of fashion, but the gown did not please her. Her jewels were famous for their size and rarity, vast rubies and diamonds vaster still, but the jewels, tonight, seemed to glitter for their own amusement, and they did not please her.

No more did the sardonic expression on the cheerful damned face of the cad she'd married please Mamie, cad he was, and bounder! The fact that Stanford Dickinson was one of the richest, and handsomest—and most fickle!—men in all of California did not please Mamie at all this night, for he fairly gloated.

That she, Mamie Dickinson, unquestioned leader, arbitress and setter of trends for all of San Francisco, should be obliged to dance attendance on a whore! And not only was Lily Cigar notorious for having been a whore, but for having been the particular favorite whore of Stanford Dickinson himself!

Lily might be forgiven her past, but not—at least not by Mamie—could she ever be forgiven her cleverness.

It was nothing less than diabolical.

There was no question of not going to the concert: all of San Francisco would be there, and not to go might imply not having been invited. And not having been invited meant your star had fallen, or, worse, had never risen at all.

Mamie frowned at the Paris satin and Venetian lace, at the rubies and diamonds, at the past and the future.

The tables had been fairly turned, and this night might mark the certification of Lily Cigar Malone Chaffee as the new leader! And with Mamie right there, helpless, watching.

Well, Mamie thought, maybe not helpless, not altogether. She wasn't dead yet, nor the battle over.

And the worst thing was, Mamie had no idea how this vulgar little upstart had pulled it off.

How did one get the world-famous Swedish soprano Christine Nilsson to travel all the way to California and give one very private recital, "just for a few friends" as the handwritten note had suggested? Nilsson was the toast of New York, of London, of Paris, of anywhere and everywhere. Everywhere but San Francisco. A tour was rumored, but not until next season, if it happened at all. And yet, here she was, staying with the Chaffees, singing for the Chaffees "and just a few friends"!

It was intolerable. Not that Mamie hadn't tried to organize another boycott. The good Lord knew she'd tried. But even He seemed to have turned against her.

When Mrs. Hitchkok Coit had flatly told Mamie she had every intention of going, and even been so presumptuous as to laugh out loud at Mamie's gently offered suggestion of their getting up a theater party that night, Mamie knew it was all over. If Mrs. Hitchkok Coit was going, then they'd all be going, traitors all: the senior Coits would surely be there, Jim Lick beyond a doubt, the Reeses, and W. C. Ralston, the lot. Damn! The simple fact of it was that Mamie dared not to conduct her boycott alone, for it might fail, and to fail might be to risk losing her authority once and for all. No, better far to infiltrate the enemy camp. Who knew what mischief might not be worked from within?

But it was a small and insufficient satisfaction. Mamie frowned as she descended the staircase. Stanford held her wrap.

"You're getting fat, Stanford."

His reply was couched in laughter.

Lily stood so close to Brooks that she could feel the warmth of him. They stood at the foot of the great staircase, receiving their guests, and the guests came in matched pairs now, with a woman for nearly every man, and the women glittering in all their finest, jewels sparkling under the light of the uncountable candles, and with another kind of sparkle in their eyes, caught up as they were in the glow of expectation, to hear the famous Christine Nilsson, who had never sung in California, who might never sing here again!

Lily smiled and shook hands, waiting for the moment she knew must come.

And it came.

There was no roll of drums. No angels sang or trumpets blared, but there, walking slowly through the door, walking up the three marble stairs, across the foyer, coming right to her, there were Stanford and Mamie Dickinson.

Lily looked at the woman who had caused her so much misery, and there was no triumph in her glance. *How sad it must be for her,* Lily thought, forcing herself to smile, to say the words of welcome, *for this is all she cares for in the world, playing this silly game, and she has lost, and in public.*

"It is kind of you to come, Mrs. Dickinson," said Lily softly, "very kind indeed."

The woman's lips quivered into a simulation of a smile; then she quickly walked on. Stanford kissed Lily heartily.

"Congratulations, my dear!" was all he said, and all he had to say.

Soon all the hundred guests had arrived and had been served with champagne. The music room was banked with white flowers, almost as if for a wedding. The rosewood piano had been elevated for the occasion onto a specially built platform at the far end of the room, hastily constructed but made attractive by being covered with an old Persian carpet in soft shades of ivory and rose. After forty-five minutes of party talk, Lily sensed a restlessness in the crowd. She went to the small library where Christine Nilsson was waiting, and led her into the room.

There was a ripple of anticipation, then a hush. Lily didn't have to signal for silence, the silence was waiting for her as she mounted to the platform, leading Madame Nilsson by the hand.

Lily looked at her guests and smiled. All of San Francisco was here: the hundred richest and most distinguished people that it would be possible to gather under any roof in town for any reason. She bowed her head slightly, as if searching for words, then spoke in a low, clear voice.

"We thank you for coming. Madame Nilsson has been kind enough to offer to sing for us, and unless we can persuade her to alter her tour program, this may be the only time she ever sings in California. I give you Christine Nilsson, in her famous aria from Gounod's *Faust* . . . Marguerite's jewel song!"

There was applause, murmurs, more applause. Nilsson smiled, turned to her accompanist, and nodded. Then, standing very straight, with her striking single-braid hairstyle inspired by Marguerite, all twined with daisies, Christine sang, in a voice as sweet and pure as meadow flowers: "*Ah, je ris de me voir si belle en ce miroir . . .*"

Lily had stepped down from the platform. She stood next to Brooks and held his hand. The silence in the big room was a physical thing, and Nilsson's voice rippled over it with unforgettable clarity and grace. Lily squeezed his hand. It was going to be a success!

Christine Nilsson tossed her dark, strikingly pretty head so that the single long braid cunningly entwined with daisies fairly flew back over her elegant shoulder. She laughed a rippling, mountain-brook kind of laugh. "It was, then, not a failure?" They were alone now, sitting in the small library having cordials, at nearly three o'clock in the morning after Madame Nilsson's little concert.

Lily smiled at her guest: she had come to feel close to the Swedish woman in these few days. Christine knew how to enjoy life, how to laugh, how not to take herself seriously despite the fame and the money and the endless hours of practicing. And she sang the way Lily had always imagined the angels singing, with a clear true voice whose power was perhaps less in sheer volume than in the vast artistry with which Madame Nilsson projected it, burning each phrase unforgettably into your memory. Lily had never especially liked opera, although Brooks kept a box for business friends. Now, hearing the legendary Nilsson, Lily awoke for the first time to the potential of great singing.

"It will be remembered forever, Madame Nilsson," said Brooks.

"And tomorrow," Lily added with a laugh, "half the women in San Francisco will be braiding their hair as you do, or buying false braids."

"Forever?" Christine Nilsson smiled the smile of one who has, perhaps, seen forever come and go more than once. "I am happy, in any event, if I please you kind people."

A hundred thousand dollars' worth of kindness, Lily thought, *and well worth it*. For that was the fee that Chaffee, Hudner had negotiated with Madame Nilsson's agent in New York: one hundred thousand dollars for one evening's performance, and all expenses paid, and the fee never to be discussed. Lily would have gladly paid—how much?—to see the expression on Mamie Dickinson's face, and on Stanford's.

"I must," Lily said, "tell you a secret. Tonight I won a bet."

"Which I," said Brooks, laughing, "must pay, or I will never hear the end of it."

"What was this famous bet?"

"A certain woman . . ."

"Who shall be nameless." Brooks laughed louder.

". . . thought I was not elegant enough to visit, and Brooks bet me a cottage if ever she came here."

"Which proves, madame," said Brooks, "that you are irresistible."

"Let me guess," said Christine, entering in the spirit of their laughter. "She is not a nice woman. With many rubies and no chin, and a face like one who has swallowed a rotten egg?"

"Exactly. That's Mamie to the bone."

"Not," repeated the soprano, with some emphasis, "nice."

"Why do you say that? I give you great credit for your instincts, madame, for you are quite right. She is not a nice woman—on the contrary, quite cruel if she can be."

"Indeed." Christine Nilsson smiled, sipped her apricot cordial, and spoke. "After supper—which was delicious!—this one, this Mamie, finds me, to my sorrow, in a corner. She smiles the smile of a cat who has stolen little fishes from the fishbowl. And she whispers something into my ear that I do not like whispered."

There was a pause, for both Lily and Brooks could well imagine what Mamie had said, and they were disgusted by such behavior under their own roof.

It was the soprano who broke the silence, and in a way that startled Lily and her husband.

Nilsson laughed, a loud, sudden, fishwife's laugh. "You are," said Christine, "afraid. Do not be. Is not necessary. Shall I tell you what that one said, and what I have replied?"

"Do." It took more strength than Lily imagined to say that one small word.

"She whispers, that you are . . . something not nice."

"A whore, is probably what she said."

"A whore." Christine's nose wrinkled at the word, and Lily thought: *She'll leave right now, and scandalize us before all the world—that is the price of my boldness.* "Well," continued the singer, "I must say this did not produce the response I am thinking she wanted, that one."

"What did you say?" Brooks spoke softly, and there was no laughter in his voice now.

"First, a little pause . . . for the drama, you see, my stage training. Then I laugh—ha-ha-ha, trilling, a merry little laugh, and then I take her arm, thus . . ." Christine rose and took Lily's arm in a most seductive manner. "And then I say loudly, *'But, madame, I too am whoring, all the time, this singing is but a hobby for me.'* She ran, this nasty woman."

Brooks roared. Lily, laughing too, rose and kissed her guest on the cheek.

"That was a brave and very kind thing to do, madame, and I will never forget you for it."

Nilsson laughed, and suddenly the empty halls of three o'clock resounded with it. They said good night then, and, laughing still, climbed the great stairway to bed.

Undressing in the pale light of emerging dawn, Lily found herself laughing again.

"I would give," she said softly, "almost anything to have seen that."

"Madame Nilsson is a great lady." Brooks came to her, and enfolded her in his strong arms, and whispered into her ear: "But no one is as great as my Lily."

"Not even Lily Cigar?"

"My Lily," he said, between kisses, stroking her, finally sweeping her up in his arms and carrying her to the bed, "is a thousand Lilys, and they are all wonderful, and there is no way I can ever love even one of them enough."

"Try . . ." she whispered, praying that, in the smoky blue light of early dawn, he wouldn't see her tears. "Oh, please try, my darling."

And he tried.

⊷ 46 ⊷

Lily sat on the veranda of her little cottage high on Lily's Hill, writing a long, long list.

Social lists had no power to harm her now, especially not this one. How much had altered in the two years since the house was built in San Francisco, and how delightfully! Here she sat, on the porch of the beautiful little cottage Brooks had built for her, true to his bet, starting the very week after her triumph over Mamie Dickinson and the prudes who had hung on Mamie's social apron strings.

Lily had always been happy with Brooks, but that happiness had ever been mixed with her fears and her doubts, with her sense of inadequacy that seemed to grow deeper as their position in the world grew more prosperous and commanding.

The evening with Christine Nilsson had changed her outlook. Many of Lily's old fears had faded then, to be replaced by the astonishing discovery that she really cared much less for acceptance in the eyes of the world than she had imagined: it was like watching a children's game from a distance, for the prizes to be won seemed insignificant in proportion to the effort involved. Lily knew there were still people in the town who would never really accept her, or forgive her, and it seemed to matter hardly at all: a priceless lesson had been learned that night.

And here she sat, happy task, writing the guest list for Katie's wedding, sure that whoever she might ask would come.

It seemed impossible, but here it was 1878 and Kate was twenty-one, an advanced age, some people thought, for a young lady to still go unmarried.

Yet Katie had her mother's determination, and determined she was to finish the course of education at the Mount Holyoke Seminary. That being done, her engagement to young Dane Atkinson, of the New York Atkinsons, would be culminated in the finest wedding Brooks and Lily could provide. Which, Lily reflected with irrepressible pride, would be very fine indeed.

Chaffee Produce was producing revenues at an ever-increasing rate, but for all that, Brooks's other activities were doing as well, some of them better.

Lily's heart and the true home of her mind's voyaging would forever be the ranch. Yet they seemed to be spending more and more time in town these days, and Lily found herself minding that much less than she had ever dared to hope.

After the triumph of the Christine Nilsson concert, invitations had poured into the big house on Nob Hill. Lily and Brooks were selective about accepting them, but the inevitable result was that their social life was busier now than it ever had been.

And there was the orphanage.

Lily had long wanted to involve herself in some useful work, and now that the ranch was organized to a fare-thee-well by Fred Baker, and now that their social position in the town seemed assured, a kind of restlessness came over her.

This was a new and unpleasant sensation: to have time and leisure and no specific way to fill the long golden afternoons. Brooks was more and more involved in his office, and traveling to find new lands to buy, new possibilities for investment. The boys were at school now almost all day long. Lily began a systematic investigation of the schools, hospitals, and orphanages of the town, and before very long reached the conclusion that none of the existing orphanages were satisfactory.

And she decided then and there to found her own.

The memory of her own days at St. Patrick's orphanage on Prince Street in New York was vivid for Lily to this day. And while the nuns and priests had surely been kind to her, and the place had been clean and well-run in many respects, it was far from ideal.

The teaching, to name one example, had been slapdash: a child could count himself lucky if St. Paddy's taught him the bare essentials of reading and writing, much less science or history or any of the other subjects that might help an orphan make his way in the world. Lily had, indeed, learned to sew a fine seam there, and to embroider nicely, but these things came from her own interest rather than the guidance of St. Paddy's.

Lily began to dream of an ideal orphanage, and being Lily, she soon found means to start this dreaming along the road to reality.

It would, to begin with, be in the countryside. There would be trees and green lawns and maybe even a small working farm. There would be, instead of one large jail-like building, clusters of individual houses, each holding no more than ten or twelve children, each the permanent home of a married, teaching couple. Thus the militaristic atmosphere that contaminated so many otherwise worthy institutions could be largely avoided. The children would have close supervision, a familylike atmosphere, and, God willing, love. There would be sports and games and music and a regular program of serious study. There would be useful training for the older children, each according to his or her abilities. Some might even go on to college!

In this, as in all her plans, Lily had the full and enthusiastic support of Brooks.

"I can't think," he had said when she proudly showed him her prospectus, all neatly written out in great detail, "of a better thing to do, my dear, and anything I can do that might help will surely be done."

"It will come down to a question of money, and quite a lot of it, I'm afraid."

"You and I can give a handsome sum to get the place started, then we'll see. There are many ways to raise money for a good cause."

"The hundred-dollar dinners, you mean? I've always hated those."

"We'll see. The important thing is to find the site, and find the right people to teach there."

The very next day Brooks set up a special bank account at Wells Fargo for the Fergus and Mary Malone Academy. Lily insisted that nowhere would the sad word "orphan" appear in the academy's literature, although every child enrolled would indeed be at the least half-orphaned. They found a good site high on a hill in San Mateo, close enough to town to get there in under an hour on the new coastal road, more than one hundred acres, and not expensive, since it wasn't really prime farmland. Then came the discussions with architects, the approval of plans, the interviewing of teaching couples, administrators, and other workers to run the establishment smoothly.

The children would come by referral from any number of churches—the Malone Academy would be nondenominational—schools, and even the police.

In less than a year the academy was opened, while still a

building, with just three of its houses finished and thirty-one children enrolled.

Before it was finished, Lily and Brooks had spent more than a quarter-million dollars on the academy, and the endless details of organizing it seemed to fill more hours than there were in the day.

But Lily had only to visit the academy and see the blooming faces of the children to be rewarded out of all proportion to the time and energy and money she had invested there.

Sometimes, impulsively, she'd take one of the new arrivals by the hand and show the child his new home. The new ones were almost always speechless with fear, and this was a feeling that Lily remembered very well, even after all these years.

"You must remember, dear, that no one here will harm you. We love children, and that is why the Malone Academy exists."

"They won't harm us, then, or put us to work in the mills?"

The child was a boy, thin as a sparrow, maybe seven years old.

"Nothing like that, Joe. If you were to be very, very naughty, I'm not saying you might not get spanked properly. But you'll have classes, too, and learn useful things: see, there's the schoolhouse, we're just finishing it, and over there, the playground, and there, just over the hill, is the farm, where you can learn how animals live, and even milk the cows one day, maybe."

She saw the wonder blooming in the boy's eyes like a flower, and felt his fear melting, and at times like that Lily thought that if she had done nothing but this in her life, she would have done a good thing.

In imagining the academy, Lily had gone by her own sure instincts about what sort of environment would be the happiest for an orphaned child. She had remembered bitterly the shock of her separation from Fergy in St. Paddy's, and it was considered a radical innovation that brothers and sisters be kept together under the same roof, and separated as little as possible. Before many months had passed, Lily found that she had created a model orphanage, that educators had begun writing about it, visiting the place, and holding it up as an example for orphanages everywhere.

"Model be damned," she said, laughing, reading one such complimentary article in a learned journal. "It's no more than good common sense, that's all."

"Common for you, my love, is anyone else's rare." Brooks looked up from his breakfast of coddled eggs and sausages and smiled. "I'm very proud of you, Lily—I hope you know that."

She said nothing, but just reached across the small table and touched his hand, as if for luck.

The academy had consumed the year 1877 in one quick gulp, it seemed to Lily. And now that the academy was on a relatively even keel in its second year of life, Lily's energies were focused on fund-raising to secure the academy's endowment, and on the forthcoming wedding of Katie.

Kate, modest as ever, had wanted a simple family wedding at the ranch, and her mother agreed. Brooks, bursting with pride in both of his womenfolk, wanted to make a bigger splash in town.

The inevitable compromise consisted in giving Katie her way about the ceremony itself, which would be so intimate as to virtually duplicate Lily's own wedding to Brooks. But it would be preceded two days earlier by a grand supper party and dance in the mansion on Nob Hill. And it was over this guest list that Lily was toiling now, high on her hill at the ranch.

Kate had missed out on the social life that lay waiting for Neddy and little Jon like a gilded trap.

Growing up on the ranch, she lacked the coveys of girlfriends that a girl in her position might be expected to have. She was bringing three girlfriends from the seminary to be bridesmaids, however, and young Dane's party would include his brother and another college friend, not to mention the senior Atkinsons and Mr. Atkinson's brother. It would be a jolly party on the two private railroad cars Brooks had ordered for the cross-country journey.

And they were arriving in just three weeks! Lily looked at her list and wrote faster. It seemed that the wedding day was gaining on her, that there were a million details yet to be considered, from the wine and the flowers to the food and the music. She knew, from experience, that these things would seem, to their guests, to fall into place apparently by magic, and that the only magic involved would be plenty of hard work on the part of Mrs. Brooks Chaffee herself. Well, it could hardly be in a happier cause.

Yet the wedding meant losing Katie, for they would be living in the East, in New York, where Dane would become a partner in his family's law firm. Well, the trains were getting much more reliable these days, and there was even talk of a canal to be cut in Colombia or Panama that would drastically reduce the sailing time. When the boys were a little older, long visits would be possible in both directions. Kate and her children could come to California in the summer, perhaps.

Kate and her children! Lily laughed out loud at her surprise. To be a grandmother. Well, and why not—she had celebrated her fortieth birthday last year. A grandmother. Lily Cigar a granny, and quite a respectable one too, thank you very much. How old Sophie Delage would roar with laughter at the thought.

And suddenly a rush of the old fears came back at Lily, chilling her happiness. She wondered, but had never dared to ask, what Kate might have told her fiancé about her mother's past. And would he care, and would his family be scandalized?

Well, Katie was a grown girl now, loyal and smart, and Lily trusted her instincts. If anyone could find a way to be true to both parents and lover, it would be Kate. Frowning just slightly, Lily went back to her lists.

The next day found Lily and her lists in town again.

Now the generalship would begin in earnest, and all of the final arrangements for the ball and the wedding itself must be made and confirmed. Luckily, Kate being away so much of the year, Maison de Ville had a dressmaker's dummy of the girl, and so the wedding dress was nearly completed, awaiting only the final fitting. Lily smiled at the thought of her Katie wearing the fine linen scarf that was all they owned from her maternal grandmother's trousseau. *Something old, something new* . . . Well, the old pain, the ancient shame, all seemed buried now and nearly forgotten, and everything that was new had a special, happy glow.

Lily was in the silver closet counting forks when the maid brought her the letter.

It was a cheap envelope, sealed, bearing the name of a hotel Lily did not recognize. No more did she recognize the bold, uneven handwriting. "Mrs. Brooks Chaffee" was all that was written on the envelope.

"Who brought this?"

"A man, madame."

"A gentleman?"

"I . . . wouldn't say that, ma'am."

Lily frowned and opened the letter. Then she frowned some more, and walked quickly out of the silver closet and up the stairs to her room. Lucky it was that Brooks was out of town today.

In her bedroom, Lily closed the door and, uncharacteristically, locked it behind her. Then she sat down at her little French desk and read the terrible thing over and over again.

Dear Lily [it began]:

Just like the proverbial bad penny, here I am, turning up in San Francisco after these more than twenty years. I hear you've done right well by yourself, Lily, which is more than I can say for myself. I don't know if you heard that my poor father went bust, but he did, and with a crash that is echoing still in certain circles. Well, that's ancient history now, Lily, but I just wanted to say hello and I also want very much to see you and my old true friend Brooks Chaffee, and of course the kid, who must be anything but a kid by now. The truth of it is, I need your help, Lily dear, for old times' sake. How well I remember your beauty, my dear, and the good times we had. Meet me tonight at the Belle Hélène restaurant on Market Street, at eight o'clock. I know you will not fail your old friend

Jack Wallingford

Lily's hand trembled as she read the letter, and she read it over again through eyes blurring with tears.

Jack! Jack, whom she hadn't thought of in years. Jack, whose name alone could send Brooks into a fury because it recalled Caroline, and Jack had been Caroline's lover, and Lily's too, and Katie's father. Suddenly all of their happiness revolved around Jack Wallingford: their future as a family lay in his hands—and they were careless, careless hands even in the old days. God only knew what they might be like now. Jack would have no way of knowing that Lily had never told Brooks of Kate's true parentage, nor Katie either. But even if Brooks and Katie knew—and Lily determined they never should—Jack could still cause incredible, wanton damage, especially now, on the eve of the wedding. She must see Jack and deal with him. The threatening tone in his letter was unmistakable. It must be a try at blackmail. She paced the big sunny room, frantic, wondering how much cash might be in the house, and how much Jack might ask, and what might be his conditions. *Suppose he wanted her?*

For a moment Lily's mind froze with horror. She stood, stiff with fright, at the window, looking out over the town she

[552]

had conquered, seeing nothing. Then she rang for her maid and dispatched the coachman to fetch Fergy.

Fergy would know what to do. Fergy was the only one in the world, besides Jack Wallingford, who knew Lily's whole story. And Fergy had the kind of friends who could arrange things in ways that skirted the law. If Jack Wallingford woke up tomorrow on a freighter bound for China, Lily would not be at all displeased. Fergy would help. Fergy would know what to do. For half an hour Lily paced her bedroom like a trapped cat.

Then he came, and relief flooded through her with the sudden welcoming rush of sun breaking through clouds. She ran to her brother and kissed him, and thought: *Thank God, he's sober.* For Fergy wasn't always sober at three in the afternoon. It was a continual amazement to Lily that Fergy hadn't killed himself with drink, or in a fight with some of his low-life pals, and that he'd held onto some of the Fleur de Lis money.

He took her in his arms and gave her a big squeeze. It had been more than a month since she'd seen him.

"Why the summons, Lily of my heart?"

She said nothing, but handed him the letter.

"Damn, damn, damn! Lil, this stinks of blackmail."

"Yes," she said evenly, "that's what it looks like, and he's the only one in the world who could."

"Why?"

"Because Brooks, who knows everything else about me, doesn't know about Jack. Katie doesn't either. And Jack was Brooks's friend."

"Brooks is better than that, Lil. He's seen you through everything. He'll see you through this."

"I'm not so sure. There was a time, perhaps, when I could have told it all—and should have. But that time's past, and . . . and I don't want to take the chance, Fergy. It would hurt so many people, not just me."

"Good old Jack. You'll have to pay him, then. You're lucky you can afford to."

"That's just it: I can't. That is, I can't draw out big sums without telling Brooks. All our funds are jointly held, and always have been."

"What do you want me to do?"

"First, I want you to come with me tonight. I can't go to a place like that alone. Whatever kind of place it is. Who knows what a man like Jack has in mind?"

"It would be convenient if Mr. Jack Wallingford had a very serious accident, wouldn't it, Lil?"

She looked at him for a moment that stretched out to an eternity. Lily knew perfectly well that her brother could arrange such an accident. Jack could disappear into the cold swirling waters of the bay and never be seen again except by fishes.

"No. Definitely not that. But there might be some way to induce him to leave."

"Such as a pistol behind the ears?"

Lily looked at him quickly then, with a new awareness, for there was something in his voice that convinced her he was serious, and capable of doing Jack real violence. She felt herself trembling. Lily had always thought of Fergy as being a danger to himself. Suddenly, and for the first time, she sensed what violence was in him, and how dangerously close to the surface it might be. She reached for his hand.

"You must promise me, Fergy, that you won't do anything before we plan it out together, and carefully. After all, we don't know what Jack wants of us, do we?"

"I can smell it from here, Lily. He wants cash, and fast, and plenty of it."

"Let's hope," she said as the precarious balance of her situation sank deeper and deeper into her brain, "that it will be that simple."

They hired a cab, for Lily would not be seen in one of the Chaffee carriages on such an errand. And as the cab rattled down the great hill, Lily was glad of Fergy's strong presence beside her, for she felt like a prisoner going to the gallows.

She had dressed carefully for this fateful meeting, dressed simply and in black, and with her only hooded cloak, black velvet and designed more for operagoing than assignations with one's twenty-two-years-lost lover. Still, it covered her hair, for which she was justly famous, and it thrust most of her face into shadow.

She felt like a criminal, and hated Jack for making her feel thus.

But more than hate and more than any fear for herself was the greater fear of what Jack might do, even unintentionally, to wreck Kate's happiness.

The Belle Hélène was elegant and sly, precisely the sort of French restaurant where Lily had gone, so long ago, for supper with Luke Ransome, to be seduced by his words of love, and wake to his leather sack of gold nuggets. And that, too, had been for Kate. She took one quick look at the place and knew it cost money, knew there would be discreet little rooms upstairs with locks on the inside only, and that in one of those rooms Jack would be waiting.

And after all I've been through, she thought, shivering, *it will end here, in this sleazy restaurant, because Jack Wallingford needs money.* She stopped in her tracks and whispered to Fergy, "I can't do it."

"You have to, Lil. The only thing worse than going would be not going. It'd make the man desperate, and by the sound of him, he's desperate enough as it is."

It was unarguable. She took a deep breath and followed the leering headwaiter up the stairs.

It was only by his mocking laughter and by the danger in his eyes that Lily recognized Jack Wallingford.

Her Jack, the Jack of 1856, had been a sleek dark boy, very grown up for twenty-one, handsome in his way, although never a patch on Brooks Chaffee, but with a defiant grace to him and a reckless air, a sense of riding upon the wind and laughing at risky heights and caring never a damn about the fall that must surely one day come.

And how he had fallen, that sleek dark boy.

Bloated now to twice his boyhood size, none too clean, and balding, his well-cut dark suit shiny with wear, boots cracked and uncared for, Jack sprawled rather than sat on a French settee that looked far too small for him. A champagne glass tilted in his pudgy hand, and a big silver bucket held one bottle empty and inverted, one open, and two untouched. Jack heard the door and looked in their direction, his eyes moving with a quick furtive motion followed more slowly by the bulk of his head. He struggled to rise, slopping champagne on the red-flowered carpet. The headwaiter paused, surveyed Jack with undisguised disdain, turned, and left them.

Lily suddenly found herself thinking of the limestone palace on Fifth Avenue, of its gilded bronze and marble, of Jack's mother holding up a bracelet of enormous sapphires, of Marianne and her English baron.

Jack's laugh cut into her dreams, mocking the dream and her place in it, mocking himself and all the world and its follies.

"A vision, that's what you are, my Lily, a vision, but then, you always were a vision, even—heh-heh—when my vision wasn't quite clear. But who may this be. Surely not—no, it is not!—my dearest, oldest chum. Brooks?"

She wondered if the liquor had completely rotted his brain,

or what was left of it. "Fergus Malone, meet Jack Wallingford. Jack, this is my brother."

"Aha! The long-lost brother. Well I remember Lily's tales of you. Lost at sea, were you not?"

"That," said Fergy with unaccustomed gravity, "is what Lily thought."

Jack reconsidered his attempt to rise, and waved them rather grandly into the two available chairs.

"Do, do sit down, and perhaps you'll take a glass of wine with old Jack, in fond memory of times past."

And your no-good bank draft, and buying me off for a thousand dollars, and for all the other servant girls you've ruined, Lily though with a rush of unexpected bitterness, *and we'll toast the good gone days with champagne that I'll end up paying for, and at inflated prices, too, in this gilt-edged whorehouse.*

But then she thought of what he might do, and the dangers of angering him, and Lily accepted the glass Jack offered with his none-too-steady hand.

She swept the black velvet hood from her head and looked at the man whose lust had changed her life forever, and found that she could not hate him.

What Lily felt was more like pity, for she thought of all the happiness the years had brought her, even when mixed with shame and with suffering, and it was all too obvious what sad changes the same amount of time had wrought on Jack Wallingford.

"And how," she asked, for want of any better thing to say, "are your parents?"

"Dead, both dead, and better for it, the way things turned out. The last of the famous Wallingford sapphires went to bury them in fine style, finer far than they'd known these last years." He lifted the champagne glass high, as if making some silent toast, then in one quick gesture emptied it. "No one came, of course. They don't, in New York, come to the funerals of dead nouveaux riches with the bad grace to lose their riches. Twelve funeral carriages, I ordered, and nine of them went empty."

"And how have you been, Jack?"

"I? How have I been? I've been exemplary, my dear Lily, quite exemplary. How often in this fickle world does one get the chance to so spectacularly fulfill all the prophecies the bon-ton of New York made about me in my feckless youth? They all said I'd come to a bad end, and . . . here I am!"

He said it with a little note of triumph, pathetic in its childlike enthusiasm. Then he refilled his wineglass.

"Here I am," he said, as if to an empty room, "on my uppers and blackmailing servant girls. A bounder, that's what I am, Lily, and that's what they all expected me to be. Bounding Jack Wallingford. Well, dearie, I've come bounding right straight across the wide prairies and into your life."

"What do you want from me?"

"Money, of course. An income. A bit of security for my old age."

Lily stood up. Green fire flashed from her eyes. "There is no way, my dear Jack, to blackmail Lily Cigar. What would you accuse me of that the gossips of the town haven't accused me of already, time and again?"

"I wasn't thinking so much of you, Lily. I was thinking of Lily Cigar's daughter, of the fair Katharine, of her upcoming marriage to young Mr. Dane Atkinson of New York City, an event that seems to delight the local newspapers nearly as much as might the revelation of the girl's parentage."

Lily looked at him, shocked beyond disgust, angered beyond fear. Suddenly she understood why murders happen, and she knew that if the little revolving pistol Stanford had given her long ago were in her reticule now, she might well use it. And she thought of Katie, and thanked all the angels for sparing the child this dark, dark side of her heritage. When Lily replied, it was in a low, even tone, a voice drained of all emotion.

"You wouldn't dare do such a thing to your own daughter."

"Aha! Then she is my daughter. I wasn't quite sure. One of the luxuries we bounders can't afford, Lily, is tender feelings for the family tie, even when bound to it by law. Nor am I sure how the good Brooks Chaffee might react to learning I've made horns for him twice now, in a manner of speaking, first with you, dear Lily, first of all men, and then with the sainted Caroline."

Lily's temper came back to her then, back from the cold, dead place where Jack's words had sent her feelings into hiding. The worst part was that Jack seemed to be enjoying himself so. It wasn't just a question of money, that was clear now: it was the pleasure he got from inflicting pain. The rage built in Lily until she couldn't trust herself to speak. Helpless, fuming, she looked to Fergy. Anything Fergy wanted to do or have done to this monster, Lily would agree to, and give her blessing. Death was too kind for Jack Wallingford.

Then Fergy spoke, and his voice was quiet, measured, and very unlike the usual hotheaded response Lily had come to expect of him.

"I think," he began evenly, "that there's a solution that may make us all happy. How," he asked Jack gently, "would you like an easy position at a very good salary—guaranteed—in one of the most beautiful places on this earth, inhabited by some of the most beautiful women on earth, and with a good cash settlement to help you get started?"

"Where is this paradise?"

"Hawaii, and paradise is the right word for it. We are expanding into the pineapple trade there, and a general overseer is just what we need. You'll have a big house and servants, high on a hill overlooking the sea. The native women are lovely and very fond of making love. The salary will be generous and the work minimal, and you'll have plenty of help. And, let us say, a hundred thousand dollars in the bank."

Lily looked at her brother in barely concealed wonderment. He was making it all up. There were no such plans, although they had discussed the prospect vaguely from time to time over the years, and always put it aside as unmanageable. Then she looked at Jack, and saw his interest growing.

Jack looked at them both. "It's all too easy-sounding," he said, as if to himself. "There's got to be a hook in it somewhere."

"There certainly is," Lily said quickly, "for while we will go some distance to avoid . . . complications, we are not fools altogether. First, you must stay in Hawaii for five years no less. Secondly, you must never attempt to contact Kate or my husband. And third, you must put that in writing, on a contract that will be in your hands by this time tomorrow along with the money and your passage to Honolulu."

He looked at her blankly for a moment and then smiled. "You learn fast, my little Lily, you learn very fast."

Jack turned to Fergy, then back to Lily. "I'll do it, and thank you both very kindly. More wine?"

For an instant Lily thought she had heard him wrongly. *He'll do it, then! He will actually do it. Fergy has saved me from being a murderess.* With a quick, involuntary gesture Lily cast her eyes to the ceiling, fully expecting to find a band of angels up there, watching over her. For surely this was a miracle! She came out of her daze, blinking, flustered and she was still fighting for control of her voice when she replied.

"Really, we must be going. Fergy will visit you tomorrow with a bank draft and the rest of it."

He sipped his wine and peered at her over the rim of the glass. " 'Really, we must be going,' My, my. I found an upstairs maid, but what did I lose? I salute you, Lily Cigar, for it's a fast track and you are indeed some kind of a thoroughbred."

"Thank you, and good-bye."

She turned and left, with Fergy quick behind her. They were halfway out the door when his voice came back at them, sharp and startling.

"Wait!"

Fergy turned back to face the room. Jack laughed. "I forgot this." He held up the restaurant's check. Fergy took out his wallet and left several large bills on a table.

"Thanks, pal."

"I'll see you here at five tomorrow." Then Fergy took his sister's arm and walked her down the stairs.

Only in the hansom cab did she dare speak. "Fergy, if I live forever, I can never thank you enough. I was trembling back there. I didn't know whether to kill him . . . or myself."

He looked at her, and smiled, and bent across the short distance to kiss her cheek. "And what have I ever done for you, Lil, but caused you pain and sorrow? You think it's a good plan?"

"Anything that gets that beast out of town is a good plan, Fergy. Yes, it's a fine plan. Better far than anything that came into my poor head. I was thinking only of Kate."

"I'll be sad to miss the wedding, but she'll forgive her feckless old uncle, I hope."

"But why miss it?"

"To go with him, silly girl. You don't think I'd ever turn a man like that loose with a hundred thousand dollars and his good word? I know the type very well, Lily, my love, far too well for my own good, and but for the grace of God and my sister, I might *be* like Jack Wallingford. His promises are written in smoke, Lil, no matter what he signs. He'd be back like a shot to bother you more. No, think not another thought on it: I'll sail with him, and very soon, and see that he stays put, at least for a good while. And in any event, I've always wanted to go out there, truly I have. If what they say about those native girls is true, well, there's no answering for just when I'll be back."

Lily looked at him, reflected for a moment, and saw the sense in it. *Maybe I've underestimated Fergy*, she thought, *maybe we all have.* "You come back right quick, or I'll come after you. I don't know what I'd do without you, Fergy. You've saved my life."

"As you have saved mine, and time and again. Now, how about buying your old brother a glass of celebration?"

"Champagne, 'twill be, to wash the foul taste of Jack Wallingford out of our mouths forever!"

"Don't be too hard on him, Lil, it's only weak he is, and spoiled, and he didn't cause that to happen. If there's a blame to blame, it must be on his parents."

"Who spoiled him rotten."

"If he relaxed more—and were a bit cleaner—why, he might not be such a bad sort after all."

"Better for you than me," she said, laughing for the first time since Jack's letter had come.

And laughing they walked up the white stone steps of the Chaffee mansion on Nob Hill.

⊰ 47 ⊱

Brooks was delayed down the peninsula, negotiating for land.

So Lily had her farewell supper for Fergy quite alone in the library of her house on the hill, just the two of them at a round table near the fire, for the dining salon was of a size to make any number less than two dozen seem like mice in a cathedral. Lily preferred the library in any event, with its warm oak panels and jewel-colored leather bindings, its brass fireplace fitments and tall French windows giving onto a terrace.

It had worked better than Lily dared hope.

Wallingford had signed the paper—for whatever that was worth—had accepted a draft on the Bank of Honolulu for one hundred thousand dollars of Fergy's money, and passage for the pair of them had been hastily booked on the clipper *East Wind* that sailed at dawn.

Lily had invited her brother to choose the menu and the wines: a bisque of lobster, sautéed trout from the Sierras, a small roasted turkey, Chaffee Produce's finest asparagus, and strawberry ice for dessert, with champagne served throughout. Lily sipped and nibbled, Fergy ate and drank prodigiously, laughed, sang snatches of popular tunes, and generally kept his sister in stitches.

Fergy sang with a pure lilting tenor, and some songs were bawdy and some were sad. And always he sang the song about Lily. She sat now, slowly turning her glass, as he sang it again:

> Her golden hair in ringlets hung,
> Her dress was spangled o'er,
> She had rings upon her fingers,
> Brought from a foreign shore:
> She'd entice both kings and princes,
> So costly was she dressed,
> She far exceeds Diana bright,
> She's the Lily of the West!

[561]

Lily smiled. She was wearing the emerald ring Brooks had given her, and now she waved it flagrantly in the air, breathed on it with an exaggerated gesture, and polished it on her bosom. They dissolved in laughter.

But there was a strangeness in the air. *Maybe,* Lily thought, *it's just that we've seen so little of each other, alone like this, these last several years. Maybe he couldn't afford the hundred thousand.* Not, God knew, that he had to worry about her making good on it. Or maybe it was coming from inside herself, this strangeness, this feeling that Fergy's gaiety was only the first and most opaque of many veils, that it might or might not lift to reveal other veils, layers of meaning, things he meant to say, serious things, hopes, untold joys or losses. And how could she know for sure? It might well be the wine, or the simple fact of his long-buried wanderlust calling him to the sea again.

She looked at him over the sorbet and said gently, "Do you remember, back at St. Paddy's, when it looked like the end of the world, you vowed you'd come back and rescue me, Fergy? You were going to come for me in a coach with seven footmen. And that's just what you have done."

His laugh had an edge to it. "God help you, Lil, if you'd been holding your breath, waiting for that to happen all these years."

"I feel closer to you right now than I have in a long, long time."

"I love you, Lily, and I ever have, even though I've taken some strange ways of showing it."

"You've just saved me from becoming a murderess, more likely than not, and saved Kate from God knows what. Not to mention the loan of a hundred thousand."

"It's a gift, Lil."

"I won't hear of it."

"A wedding gift to Katie. I've wasted my life, Lil, don't think I don't know it. I've been drunk and gone whoring and dreamed mad dreams. I've taken from you a thousand, thousand times more than ever I've given. Sometimes I think that all the good in Big Fergus, in Mama, all came out in you, and all the bad—however much there was—came to me."

Lily looked at him in quiet astonishment, for what he said was true, and sad, and sadder for his being aware of it. Until these last few days, Lily would not have given him credit for such keen awareness. She reached across the table and took his hand, and smiled.

"Get on with you! You've been a fine brother, the best a girl could want."

"I've been nothing of the kind, and well you know it. I've run away from every problem life ever threw my way. Ran away from you, even, with hardly a thought. Could have tried a lot harder than I did to find you, too. I've been weak, Lil, very weak, and that's a fact."

"You've just not . . . found yourself."

"Ha! I've found myself all too well, and not liked the look of what I found. But it's glad I am if I can help you this little bit, at least, even after all these years."

"Well"—she laughed, willing to try anything to change the subject—"they do sail by, don't they? Katie to be married. It doesn't seem like more than twenty years, not with all that's happened."

"You did it all yourself, and God bless you for it."

"Bless is highly unlikely to be what that gentleman has in mind for your wicked sister, Fergy, quite the contrary, I expect."

So finally she got him laughing, and his mood lifted. He poured a second brandy and Lily had more coffee and they talked for hours about the old days, and the days to come. At last she saw him to the door.

"Have a good voyage, Fergy dear." Lily stood on tiptoe to kiss him.

"My love to Katie, and Brooks, and her young man." Fergy spoke softly now, almost in a whisper, although there was no one to hear. "I'll be thinking of you, wherever I am, with great love."

"Come back to us soon, Fergy."

"Good-bye, my Lily."

She looked at him as he climbed into the waiting landau and drove off down Nob Hill. *"Vaya con Dios, Fergy,"* she whispered to the purple night. And God go with you. And angels watch over you. Then she turned and walked slowly back into the great stone house.

The wedding came and went all too quickly, vanished in a cloud of happy memories, without incident or scandal. Soon, too soon, Katie and her charming new husband had climbed aboard the private cars once more, after two blissful weeks of honeymooning in Lily's small cottage on the hill. Kate's happiness was an almost physical thing; she glowed and radiated joy to everyone around her, and most of all to Lily. Thus Lily's sadness at her departure was leavened by the general

[563]

and unmistakable pleasure that the newlyweds took in each other and in all the world around them.

It seemed to Lily that she stood with Brooks for an eternity upon the station platform, waving until the last of Katie was the tiny white flutter of her handkerchief against the dark side of the diminishing train.

It was almost one month later to the day that Lily got the news.

She looked up from her little desk in their bedroom on Nob Hill, and was startled to see the expression on Brooks's face.

He hadn't looked this grave in years and years, not since that terrible, wonderful day when he'd told her about his first marriage and asked if she could love him.

Instinctively she stood up and quickly went to him. "My darling, what's wrong?" Instantly she thought of Kate, of their two boys, of . . . what?

He held her tightly, with both of his arms around her, comforting her and cradling her as if that alone could defuse the words he hardly dared to speak.

"It is," he said gently, "very bad, my dearest. We must be brave."

"Quickly, tell me. What? What?" Whatever the news might be, not knowing, not to share his grief, was the worst possible torture for Lily.

"Fergy is dead."

"Fergy? He can't be."

"A reporter came calling, just now, to ask if you had any comment."

He handed her a fresh, folded copy of the day's *Chronicle*. And even as she reached for the paper, Lily felt herself drowning in a dream. For was this not the second time in her life that she'd been handed a newspaper account of her brother's death? She looked at the headlines.

SWEPT OVERBOARD! FERGUS MALONE PERISHES IN MYSTERIOUS TRAGEDY AT SEA.
Mr. Wallingford of New York Also Missing

Honolulu, July 27, 1878. The clipper *East Wind* docked here yesterday with a strange tale of violent death at sea. The captain's report to the local police indicates that on the night of July 12, Mr. Fergus Malone, well-known businessman and gambler of San Francisco, and one Jack Wallingford, late of New York, fell or were swept overboard after a violent struggle on deck. Some witnesses suggest that one of the men might have thrown the other overboard and then jumped after him, but in the darkness it was impossible to discern the details of the fight. The clipper turned back in an attempt to find the two passengers, but all efforts failed in the moonless night. It is certain, in those shark-infested waters, and more than a thousand miles from the nearest landfall, that both men must have perished. The Hawaiian police labeled the tragedy "death by misadventure," and since both participants in the struggle were lost, no charges have been brought. Mr. Malone is survived by his sister, Mrs. Brooks Chaffee, of Nob Hill and San Rafael, whose daughter, Katharine, was lately married to Mr. Dane Atkinson of New York. Mr. Wallingford is survived by his sister, Marianne, Baroness West, of Westover, England.

All she could see was Fergy at fourteen, just before he'd run away from St. Paddy's, and another vision, of Fergy just lately, just before he'd left her to sail on the *East Wind*. And over the years a faint lifeless voice, her mother's voice, dying, rang loud in Lily's brain, *"Save your tears, child, for one day you may truly need them."* She did need them, and they came, those tears. For a long moment Lily just stood there, her head buried in Brooks's chest, and then she gave out a sigh that might have come all the way round Cape Horn, all the way from New York, a sigh that echoed through all the years of Fergy's mad adventures, his wild dreams, flashes of charm and of real kindness, and now this final gallantry, the ultimate justification of his love for her.

For Lily knew as surely as she had ever known anything that what the newspaper article really spoke of was a simple case of murder and suicide, and that the cause of it all was Lily Cigar, and that she could never tell a soul in all the world, not even Brooks, to whom she always told everything.

The sigh built into a sob, and the first sob was followed by many more.

Brooks tried to comfort her with words, with kisses, and failed.

For Lily, who had cried so seldom in her life, was crying now for herself as much as for Fergy, and for the sins of the past that had a way of sneaking back to attack you where and when you least expected them. Finally she stopped, gasping, runner of a long and losing race, breathless, defeated.

"I know," Brooks said gently, "what it is to lose your only brother. I am terribly sorry, my darling."

Lily looked up at him. "He was as good a brother as he knew how to be, poor, poor Fergy."

"I'm sure he tried."

"And Jack Wallingford." Lily feared that when she said his name some bolt of lightning might come down from on high and strike her dead for a murderess.

"Jack's no loss to anyone, but still it's a terrible coincidence."

"It is that."

"Well, my darling, you have me, and Kate, and the boys."

"And I thank God for you all, every day."

"About the funeral services . . ."

"I think not, darling. Fergy wouldn't have wanted that. We can leave a memorial at the academy, build something in his name. That's a fine way to remember someone, orphan that he was."

"We'll do that. Lily, is there anything I can do, anything you'd like me to get for you?"

She stretched up to kiss him. "No, thank you, my dear. But I think I will go to the ranch for a few days, if you'll excuse me, and think about him, and try to get over it all."

"Of course."

She left the next day and went directly to her little cottage on the top of Lily's Hill. There she stayed for five days, bright blue summer days, days of blazing noon and chilled nights, nights when the stars seemed to reach out for her, days when the distant blue sea looked more like an ornament than Fergy's grave.

And peace came to her there, as it always had, a troubled peace, maybe, but when Lily came back into town, she was calmer. The thought of Fergy no longer sent her quivering with unnamed dreads. And she could say the name "Jack Wallingford" without feeling nauseous.

And for the first time in her life Lily felt old.

This was not a physical feeling but an emotional one. Fergy's death, Katie's wedding, somehow the two events conspired against her usual soaring hopeful spirit. Kate a radiant bride and Fergy a murdering suicide, or very likely. That was quite a weight for Lily to carry in secret. Now her debt to Fergy could never be rightly paid, not if she lived to be a hundred.

She thought of all the forces that had shaped her life and how very little control she—or anyone—had over them. But as the Chaffee Produce tender brought her to the San Francisco side of the great bay, Lily thought, too, of other and happier things.

She thought of Brooks, whose love and strength were and always had been like a friendly beacon for her darkest hours. She thought of Kate, and the boys, glowing with health and promise. She thought of the ranch and all she had dreamed of there, and how the dreams had come sprouting, thrustingly true. Lily looked up at the seven haughty hills of the town and realized that they held no threat for her now, that no secret fears lurked behind any doorway in the city.

For that she could thank Fergy, and Brooks, and her own force of will.

A sailor helped her down the gangway. Lily thanked him. And, for the first time in days, she found herself smiling. For there, unexpectedly, stood Brooks Chaffee with a bouquet of fresh white roses, and her two sons. She ran to them, laughing, and was young again.

৵ঙ 48 ৡৰ

Lily stood in the open door of the ranch and watched him come galloping up the long drive, a tall hatless figure all in black and riding on a huge black stallion, his hair flying in the breeze, hair in which pure white now competed with the gold. *I never saw a finer figure of a man, on horseback or off.*

Lily smiled to herself and wondered how many thousands of times she had stood thus, waiting for Brooks Chaffee to come riding home to her.

Well, at least he always came.

Yes, he'd always come home, and through all the years of their life together Lily had learned to live with the insistent whispering terror inside her that said: *One day he won't be coming back to you. One day there will be another woman, younger, prettier, fancier. One day will come the bandit on the lonely road, the sinking ship, the maddened horse.*

Lily could not stop the doubts and the questions, silly as she knew them to be. But she had a way of dealing with them. Now, and for some years, every time the doubts crept in, Lily would simply thank God and all his angels for the good years that could never be taken from her, the years, she felt, that Brooks had given her for no reason but luck so extraordinary it would not be false to call it miraculous. For she never felt she deserved this man, this love, and for that reason Lily cherished it all the more, and the man who brought love to her in hundreds of ways, knowing and unknowing, every day and night of their lives, apart or together.

These days, they were more and more together, for the boys were grown, Neddy fast learning to take over the many businesses that had sprouted from this very ranch, and Jon back East practicing law in Boston.

Lily didn't feel anywhere near sixty-three, but sixty-three she would be, shortly after the century turned, which it would, at the end of the year, irrevocable as any ocean's tide.

1900!

Lily remembered the excitements of 1876, Centennial year,

but in '76 her life had been a flurry of taking care of the children, of moving into town, followed the next year by her great triumph over Mamie Dickinson.

How small that seemed now, and what an overblown word "triumph" was, a word fit for the deeds of emperors, hardly to be applied to the case of scheming hostesses on Nob Hill!

A new century was rushing at them with the velocity of an express train, glittering and unstoppable, the past gathering all of its awesome energies in one mad dash for the future that held . . . who knew what?

America was in love with its future and ever had been. Lily felt that this was not a bad thing, for the future had always held fine promises for her, for Lily personally, and more often than not those promises had been fulfilled beyond her modest expectations.

Brooks dismounted with a boy's elastic grace, tethered the great horse with a flick of his hand, and ran to her.

He still ran to her! And the grin he grinned was a boy's grin. Lily stretched out her slender arms to receive him. No. She very decidedly did not feel sixty-three.

Brooks laughed out loud to himself as he galloped up the drive. It was a day to make a man laugh, a day on which the sky itself seemed to smile and the wind teased the trees. And there was a letter from young Jon!

Young Jon indeed: the boy was twenty-nine and quite on his own in Boston, cutting a merry swath among the debutantes of Beacon Hill. How glad Brooks and Lily had been when Jon decided not to join some of his chums in the Cuban invasion that had attracted so many fine young men to the trumped-up cause of freeing the Spanish-dominated island. Jon had a good head on him, and Neddy too, as why should they not, with the blood that flowed in their veins?

Brooks pressed on his horse and thought in passing how very much this dear, familiar drive had changed in the thirty-five years he'd known it, changed, and for the better, and yet always remaining the same. Oh, sure, the flowering shrubs were a fine sight, a happy replacement for the random sage and scrub oaks that had once served as God's own decoration, back before the great brushfire. The whole place was neat and trig as twelve gardeners and many years could make it. And it still was the same: its proud Mexican heritage had not been hidden. Here was the same well-loved curve of the hill, the same dearly remembered foothills climbing into the blue distance, the opening of the drive into the courtyard, the simple, noble proportions of the ranch house, that huge dark-oak doorway and . . . Lily!

Lily waiting.

Lily, who had done nothing less than give him back a life in that dark time when he had written himself off as lost to happiness forever. Lily, straight and slender and smiling. Lily, whose flame of hair was only slightly brushed with an occasional white hair. Lily, who had loved him more than he ever deserved, fine and steadfast all these years, loved him even while fighting the devils that haunted her, playing a role if he asked it, the best mother a man could want for his children, sweet and strong and . . . Lily!

There was no calculating the breadth and depth of his good luck. Brooks thought of Neddy, Neddy the first, his brother. He thought of Fergy and poor Jack Wallingford and all the other luckless devils and wondered what in God's green world he had ever done to deserve even a fraction of what had been given him. But then he stopped thinking and spurred the horse and raced for his woman. There was Lily, and there was a letter to read, and in his heart it was springtime, whatever the calendar might say about his age!

They had tea in the kitchen, as of old, and ate Gloria's cookies, and read Jon's letter.

Jon was getting married. His letter vibrated with love. It was the first time in the history of the world that a young man had been so blessed. To fall in love! To be loved in return! If only his parents could understand. There was no girl like her, not anywhere, nor had there ever been. To what heights his mad heart soared, no astronomer would ever be able to measure. Her name was Felicity. Felicity! The best name a girl could have. The letter went on, three pages' worth, and before it was half-read, both Brooks and Lily were dissolved in laughter.

"Stop, do stop, I'll spill my tea!"

He stopped reading. "She sounds nice, for a goddess."

"Well, it was bound to happen. I suppose we shall have to make the journey."

"Maybe they'll elope, and come out here."

"Never, my dear, not if I read between those lines. He'll have the most proper of proper weddings in a brick Pilgrim church, and all the maiden aunts will frown on us as parvenus."

"We'll frown right back."

"On the contrary, we will have a lovely time, my dear. You forget we are old and dignified these days."

"You are young as young, Lily, and my love is young, whatever ravages the years have wrought on me."

"If we must go East, why not make a proper trip of it and go on to France? I loved it the last time."

"We had the children the last time." There was a note of regret in his voice, and Lily knew just what her husband was thinking. The goddess had taken the last one away from them: they would never really have their children again.

"But this time we will know people. The Harringtons are in London, the DuBoises in Nice, and—"

"I will not call on Marianne Wallingford."

"It might be a lark, for the wicked baroness to be visited by her mother's former maid."

"She is, one hears, very wicked indeed."

"Poor girl. Think what they forced her to marry."

"Quite set the style, though. Now there are more titles for sale in France and England and Italy than Chaffee oranges on Market Street."

"And rich American mothers fighting for them."

He took her hand and squeezed it. "There isn't a title in the world I'd trade for the one I've got: 'Husband of Lily.' "

And the warmth of him and the urgency of his love flowed through her as it always did, undiminished by time, and Lily decided that she most definitely did not feel her age, whatever her age was supposed to feel like.

"Husband of Lily Cigar?"

"Especially."

"Need I tell you I feel the same, my dearest Brooks, even after all this time? I thought that as you came up the drive just now, and it must be that age is making me silly, for it all seemed just as it was—how I feel for you—only, perhaps, even better now."

His reply was a kiss. Then he bent and whispered into her ear, even though there was no one to hear them, "Why do you think I gallop?"

And Lily laughed, but it was a laugh wrapped in all the shimmering garments of love.

They told her to use one of the coachmen, but Lily merely smiled. Her horses were tame, the little landau was light and easy to handle, and she would be damned if the mere fact of being in her late sixties was going to certify her as an invalid forever. She climbed up into the driver's seat with a light enough step if she did say so herself. And the sleek bottle-green carriage was soon tripping merrily along the smooth road to San Mateo. Her only dread was running into one or another of San Francisco's eight motorcars, smelly clanging inventions that they were, well-calculated to frighten a horse and its driver clear into Marin County. At least they gave plenty of warning, with their wheezing and rattling.

She was on her way to the academy.

The day was fine, as only early April can be in San Francisco: the morning fog had gone questing back beyond the hills—from whence it would come pouring back again in late afternoon, seeking its mother, the sea. The sun that broke through was still tempered by mist. Later, it would be warm.

When Lily thought about her long life, which happened much more often now than she could ever remember, it seemed to her that aside from Brooks and her children, the best thing she had done was to found the academy.

And what a fine place it had grown to!

For all of her revulsion at San Francisco society, Lily had to admit that it was her own diligent work among the rich of the city that had built the academy into the model institution it had become.

Every winter, right at the height of the season, she gave the Academy Assembly Ball, and that was beyond any question the major event of the year. And year by glittering year the profits rose, until last January they had raised more than a hundred thousand dollars.

Fergy had no heir but his sister, and Lily had diverted her share of his estate to the academy. The Fergus Malone Junior Gymnasium was better equipped than the sports facilities of most universities, or so her own sons told her, and they surely had reason to know. From the simple cluster of cottages that had been the inception of the academy, the physical plant had grown impressive. The hundred and sixteen acres of the original purchase were none too many for the present size of the place. They had nearly a thousand students there now, and a real school, a proper infirmary, and many more cottages. The place still had the countrified atmosphere that Lily had wanted, but San Mateo itself was growing ever less rustic, and the effects of this were inevitably felt at the academy. It was a happy place, Lily knew, and a productive one: now the students of the Fergus and Mary Malone Memorial Academy entered college on a regular basis, often winning scholarships on their own, sometimes with financial help from the academy on a special loan arrangement that Brooks had invented, whereby the students' college expenses were paid for by the academy, and then the academy was paid back in small no-interest installments by the student himself after he found work. In the twelve years that this had been in effect, there had been not one default on those loans.

Lily went to the academy regularly, not because she felt that she was particularly necessary there—although the administration naturally consulted her on every important decision—but rather because it pleased her to see her plan so beautifully carried into action.

She would walk the well-trimmed paths of the place, and sometimes peek into classrooms, take apples to the children in the infirmary and read them stories, joke with one or another of the teaching staff. But she took great care never to become intrusive; the academy was run by the finest professionals to be found, a group on the young side, teeming with enthusiasm and ideas.

This was reflected in the children, who came in virtually every size and shade and color from Chinese to red Indian. Yet for all their physical diversity, these children had one strong bond in common: almost without exception they were alert, and interested, and happy. This happiness reflected directly into Lily's heart, and warmed her in the most secret corners of her being.

The little green landau climbed the last hill. There was the academy, all spread out before her, gleaming with care and promise.

Lily smiled, as she almost always did just at this turning in the road. *How very fine it is to have a dream, and have it come true!*

⪻ 49 ⪼

Lily sat in their biggest formal carriage and wondered, as the
driver rattled down Market Street, when in the world they'd
replace the outmoded cable cars with their clumsy-looking
overhead wires. She was far from sure that every new development in the booming town represented any real
progress: Mr. Claus Spreckels had his huge eighteen-story
building, pride of the city, bristling with all the newest electrical devices and those swaying, clanging elevators. This was a
noisy, vulgar kind of progress, if progress it was. Nor was she
overjoyed at the huge white Greek Revival bulk of the new
Fairmont Hotel that had lately sprung up at the top of California Street, intruding on the Chaffee view of sunsets and
the western bay.

Still, the city was a magnet for money, the city must grow,
and there were some attractive plans in the air. Cutting great
new boulevards around the seven hills rather than the silly
pioneer-day grids of streets that ran straight up and down the
steepest slopes—there was an idea that made sense.

And the culture of the town was booming too, hand in
hand with trade. It was culture, in the form of the Metropoli-
tan Opera tour, that brought Lily downtown on this warm
Tuesday morning of April 17, 1906. Ever since her adventure
with the soprano Christine Nilsson, Brooks had left all oper-
atic arrangements to Lily, and she was on her way to make
sure their seats for Caruso's performance of *Carmen* tonight
were as specified, with the extra four chairs in their regular
box for the guests. On an evening that had generated such
anticipation, it would pay to inspect the setup in person, and
to secure the tickets in her own hands. Thinking of Caruso
reminded Lily of Italy, and of the recent disastrous eruption
of Vesuvius, in which uncounted hundreds of villagers in the
Neapolitan area had been killed. Just Saturday, they had attended an Italian Relief dinner, and Brooks, with his typical
generosity, had given a substantial check to the cause. But the
tempestuous behavior of Vesuvius seemed very far away to

[574]

Lily as she gazed out of the carriage at the imposing commercial buildings of Market Street.

The city had learned its lesson about fires long ago. Well she remembered the earthquake and fire of 1868, and the panic that followed. But these new buildings were stone and bronze and glass, warranted fireproof.

There was still Chinatown, of course, a shambles of narrow wood hovels and narrower alleys. There were bad fires regularly in that section, but they were quickly put out, and the place was as quickly rebuilt, only to wait for the next fire, and the next. The men in City Hall were always just about to do something about this, but like so many other somethings, it never seemed to get done.

The carriage made its way into the workingmen's district everyone called simply South of the Slot, by which they meant the slot that ran the length of Market Street for the use of the cable cars. The old Grand Opera House was an anachronism in the Slot, built thirty years ago in a neighborhood no one suspected would change so dramatically. The dusty old structure stood gathering the remnants of its faded grandeur about it, a forlorn dowager among the rabble, hoping for rescue.

The manager led Lily deferentially up to their box. How sad the old place looked in the dim light of day; a harsh gray light leaked through sooty windows and spilled over the dusty gilt and fading plush of the big theater. The box had been arranged as Lily asked, and the tickets were ready. From backstage came the sound of a big tenor voice doing scales. She looked inquiringly at the manager. He nodded wisely, guardian of a great treasure. Caruso himself was about to begin a dress rehearsal!

Lily was half-tempted to stay and hide herself in the box like some naughty schoolgirl, but she had many things to do before the night's performance.

There was shopping that must be done, gifts to be sent for the third birthday of Jon's little boy, her fourth grandchild, and with the mails as they were, a month in advance was none too soon. Then, she must see to the final arrangements of the dinner party they were giving after the performance. This would be a small, informal group, only a dozen close friends, but there were details that Lily would leave to no one else. She was superstitious, for example, about arranging the flowers herself. Sometimes she thought that this was because of that afternoon several eternities ago, back on Fifth Avenue in the Wallingford mansion, when she had been arranging flowers and first caught sight of Brooks. But the fact was that she had a great flair with flowers, and other people's arrangements of them rarely pleased her. It would be a busy day, but what a night! Lily thanked the manager, tucked the tickets into her purse, and climbed into her carriage.

Lily sat tall in the Chaffee box and reached out for Brooks's hand. It was a tribute to the raw power of Enrico Caruso's voice that he could send such shivers through her in his performance as Don Jose, for it must be admitted that the pudgy Italian tenor was not the physical image of the romantic and impetuous Jose. Yet still she thrilled to his singing.

Madame Fremstad, however, was another matter entirely. She sang Carmen like Brunhilde, and not an especially fine Brunhilde at that. Well, still and all, this was the place to be in San Francisco tonight: the California debut of the legendary Caruso!

Lily held her husband's hand and listened intently. It was a fine time of the year, after an especially cold and rainy winter. Or, maybe, it was simple old age that made the winters seem harder every year. Suddenly Lily had to repress a giggle. Madame Fremstad was flirting. Madame Fremstad was being saucy.

It was like watching Russian Hill try to waltz.

Lily took great care not to meet Brooks's eyes, for she knew he must be thinking along similar lines, and it would never do for the dignified patrons of the arts, Mr. and Mrs. Brooks Chaffee, of Nob Hill, to be found giggling at such a solemn moment in the history of art. She buried her face in her lace handkerchief and pretended to hide a sneeze.

The final curtain rang down to a roar of applause, and both of the principals took many a bow. Out of politeness to Caruso, the usually more discriminating audience, including the Chaffees and their party, clapped generously for Madame Fremstad as well.

Caruso came out alone, sweat gleaming from his two chins. He bowed and smiled, and gestured elegantly to the farthest balcony.

Three thousand pairs of hands responded as if on strings. It was deafening, and the tenor's bright dark eyes flashed hungrily, flicking from corner to corner of the great theater absorbing their praise through his very pores.

Soon they were in the carriage, and soon after that the small and very happy group was gathered around Lily's rosewood dining table doing justice to one of her well-known late uppers. It was relaxed, low-key, and the last guests left a bit ast one in the morning.

Brooks blew out the last of the candles, and they climbed he great staircase together, hand in hand.

"Was it fun for you?" she asked, thinking that he looked a it tired, that maybe the opera bored him.

"The best part was watching you try not to laugh at that valrus playing Carmen. And I must say Hettie Mills is getting more boring by the minute, either that or my tolerance rows less. All she talked about at dinner was how fat Stanord Dickinson has gotten since Mamie died, and who really ares about that?"

"Not Mamie, for sure. He is getting fat. Well, my love, it vas nice to hear Caruso."

"Speaking of fat."

"You are a wicked man. He's a great artist."

"And great in girth."

Brooks was proud of his physical condition. At seventy-two e could still ride all day or hike over farmland with his sons nd their friends and never tire.

"Any evening I spend in your company, Lily, is fun no natter what else intrudes."

She said nothing, but squeezed his hand tighter. Soon they vere in the warmth and quiet of their big bed and the only ound in the room was the barely audible rise and fall of neir breathing.

Lily woke quickly. Someone was shaking her, shaking the vhole bed, the whole house. There was a jolt and a great uiver, then another jolt, then an ominous stillness. Lily lay till, her mind racing. *The gasworks had exploded! It was pring thunder. The Russian Navy was shelling them.*

The shock had lasted only seconds. Or had she dreamed it? he sat bolt upright in the great bed and reached for Brooks. hen Lily smiled. There he was, asleep like a great baby!

Then came the second jolt, more violent than the first. *This no thunder. This is no distant explosion. This is an earthuake!* There was a pause, then an enormous crash inside the ouse that sounded like all the china on a banquet table reaking at once. Lily thought of the great chandelier in the airwell, with its thousands of crystal pendants. *Could it ave broken loose and crashed to the marble below?* For a noment she lay as if paralyzed, afraid to leave the bed. She eached for Brooks and called his name.

"What happened?" Brooks was out of the bed like a shot, nd pulling on a robe. Slowly, moving with the heavy motion of a sleepwalker, Lily got out of bed and put on her robe. "I think," she said softly, "that we've had an earthquake."

There was a pause while they both seemed to weigh the ominous silence that filled the San Francisco night. Brooks walked to the big French windows and threw them open.

"Don't! The balcony might be loose."

Brooks turned quickly and gave her an appraising look, as if to see whether Lily had gone crazy. She wondered whether it would be safe to investigate that terrible crash, and decided to wait: whatever was down, was down.

"I can't see a thing," said Brooks, "nor hear anything, either."

"Then something is very wrong out there."

"Listen, there's only the wind."

"What time is it?" Lily asked, as if that could make some difference.

He went to his dressing chest and lit a match. "Fifteen after five, if this thing's right."

"Just a little quake."

"I'll never take them for granted, though, there's something eerie about them. Until I came here, I'd always thought the earth was . . . well, pretty solid."

"They come and go so quickly—remember sixty-eight?"

"Sixty-eight was pretty bad, Lily, not the quake, but the fires."

"Yes, but we have so many more brick and stone buildings now."

"The instant someone tells me a thing is fireproof, or unbreakable, or warranted forever, I get very suspicious."

"Stop being so suspicious and come kiss your wife."

"You," he said, stooping to kiss her cheek, "are truly warranted forever."

The next jolt caught him that way, leaning across the bed.

It rocked the room, the house, the hill, and the whole town. There was a violent rumbling, a sound of big rocks rolling downhill. Then silence. Then a series of crashes, tearing, ripping sounds, and a great rushing, heavy-breathing sound as though some incalculably huge giant was drawing in his breath for a final assault upon the wicked city. Brooks lay where he fell on the bed, clutching Lily. *If this,* he thought instantly, *is how we die, then thank God it is together, for what in the world would I do without her?*

Brooks thought these things but did not say them, for fear of frightening Lily.

It was impossible for either of them to tell how long he lay there, just holding her, or how long the terrifying stillness lasted.

But a moment came when the stillness slowly altered in texture.

There was no sudden loud sound, but rather a gathering of sounds, a building concerto of doom.

A horse screamed. There were distant rumblings, stone on stone. A man's hoarse voice pierced the dawn. "Harry?" he cried pitifully, "Harry?"

There was no answer for him.

Brooks stood up and once again went to the window. This time Lily stood too, and joined him there.

They could see some lights flickering in the Fairmont Hotel three blocks to the right.

"Candles," Brooks said softly. "Their electricity must be cut off."

"And I don't see streetlights."

"If the gas mains burst, that could be real trouble." *And,* he thought, but gave the thought no tongue, *if the water mains break, too, the whole shooting match could go up in smoke, just like that.*

There were people in the streets now, but the darkness conspired with silence to hide the damage. Brooks and Lily could only guess, and wonder, and they had no way of telling how bad it might be. Yet for all the mystery, the worst seemed to be over now. There, out beyond their garden wall, they could begin to see people moving in the slow-gathering dawn. They heard the clatter of a horse-drawn wagon going full tilt, and somehow this reassured them. A soft insistent knocking came at their door.

"Come in."

It was Mary, Lily's maid. "Oh, madame, you're all right."

"We're fine, thank you, Mary. And how are you, and the others?"

"None injured, ma'am, but scared, that's for sure."

"Well, then," said Lily smiling with confidence she did not feel, "let us see what damage there is, and how to fix it."

"The bathrooms, ma'am, the reservoirs, you know, are all overflowed."

Lily thought of the big brass tanks encased in mahogany that held the flushing water high over the toilets. Of course, they'd be most vulnerable. Lily followed her maid, who chattered to keep her fears at bay.

But Brooks stayed at the window, looking down on the city. There, down by the docks—his docks—he could see the first thin plume of smoke, pale gray as the dawn that bore it, slender it was, and curling upward slowly, gently. The plume of smoke had the false innocence of a cabin's chimney smoke. But it was just that much wider, and it came just that much faster. This was no one's chimney.

Instinctively Brooks began dressing, wondering if his country boots were in the closet where he'd left them. Wondering if he could get to the Chaffee Produce offices above the warehouse at the foot of Market Street in time to do any good.

Lily stood at the stair rail looking down fifty feet to the ruins of the immense gilt-bronze-and-crystal chandelier that had once graced the palace of Vaux le Vicomte. The chandelier had survived the wrath of Louis XIV, who had jailed the château's owner, Fouquet, for fiscal indiscretions. The chandelier had also survived the mobs of the Terror. But it had not survived the wrath of nature in the early morning of April 18, 1906, in San Francisco. It was a sad twisted thing now, its graceful arms awry, its carved and faceted crystals smashed, candles broken. Lily looked at it in awe for a moment that seemed to last an hour.

Then she heard his footsteps on the stairs behind her. Lily turned and saw that he was dressed, but in country clothes, rough clothes, the sort of thing they wore in bad weather at the ranch.

"You're not going to the ranch?"

"No, my darling, I just want to check the warehouse, and the offices, you just can't tell from here what the damage might be—and I fear it's more than we think."

"Brooks. Don't go."

"I'll be back in a few hours. There may be looting, if there's enough destruction. I must go, Lily."

She looked at him and thought: *I am acting like the kind of silly, weak-hearted woman I despise most. Of course he must go. Then why does it shake me worse than the damned earthquake?* She took a deep breath and tried to regain control of her voice.

"I do understand how you feel, my darling," she said gently. "But promise me you won't take foolish chances, and that you'll come back to me soon."

"You can," he replied casually, with an assurance that must have been snatched out of the eerie silence, for it surely did not grow inside him, "count on me for luncheon. The only thing to fear, Lily, is fire. We're luckier than most, having our own well and our own pump. You must rally the servants and fill every bathtub, every horse trough, and all the biggest pots and pans in the kitchen. 'Tis better, far, to be prepared."

"I'll do that." Lily tried to smile, but the memory of the brushfire on the ranch burned vividly in her mind and heart.

"I won't be long, my love." He kissed her and walked down the great staircase, casually as though twenty thousand dollars' worth of antique chandelier were not lying in fragments on the marble floor below.

Lily stood for a moment watching his fine straight back until he vanished from her range of vision. The young maid watched her, awestruck. The madame's lips were moving, but she said nothing. Lily formed a prayer. Her heart prayed, but she had no strength to give it voice. Then she turned to the maid and briskly commenced her tour of inspection.

Brooks turned toward the stables, and then turned away. With a ground shock as violent as this had been, and maybe more coming, it would be folly to take a carriage out, much less his gleaming new electric motorcar. The roads might well be impassable even on foot. In any event, it wasn't that much of a walk to his offices; on fine mornings he often did it for pleasure: across Mason to California, then down California, through Chinatown all the way down to its confluence with Market Street near the docks. It was a vibrant half-hour's stroll downhill, and he had even done the uphill leg a few times, although that, admittedly, was work.

But now, as Brooks turned right at his own front gate and walked along Mason Street, he might have been a visitor from a distant planet, so awed was he by the changes all around him and the anticipation of other, more severe changes soon to be encountered.

The first few houses looked secure enough, but then, this was the richest part of town, and the houses were mostly big and solid and well set back in their gardens. The third house he passed had all its chimneys cut off like mown grass. One chimney, and a big one, had obviously crashed through the roof. Brooks hoped no one was sleeping in the room where it struck. He passed a railroad magnate's stone château and found himself laughing out loud, for there, having dived headfirst from her pedestal, was a chaste but definitely nude Grecian slave girl in marble, buried to her improbable bosom in a patch of tea roses, her boiled-asparagus legs, whiter than snow, pointing straight up toward the unkind heaven that had wrought such havoc on her calculated sexless dignity.

He paused at the corner of California Street. The wideness

of the street and the extreme steepness of its slope allowed the best view in the vicinity: Brooks could see over all the town.

There were six fires now.

Half an hour ago, if that, he had seen two. Part of the town's lurid history was the history of fire after devastating fire. In the old jerry-built gold-rush days, San Francisco had been leveled five times in ten years by fire, and just as quickly—and shoddily—rebuilt. But they'd learned: the buildings were brick and stucco and stone now, and the biggest of them, like Spreckels' Call building, were framed in steel on top of that. And the fire department was famous throughout America for its speed and effectiveness.

Six fires. Six columns of smoke. It could only mean that the water mains had been destroyed by the shock. The best fire department in the world was impotent without water.

Brooks Chaffee quickened his pace.

The silence that had marked his first glimpse of the shaken city was still heavy in the air.

There was a startling urgency in the fact that in this boisterous, bustling, booming caldron of a town, and at just the time of day when most people were usually operating at full steam to get their chores started, there was such a cryptic hush. It was not the reassuring calm of a starlit mountain midnight, the kind of lovely stillness that both he and Lily so loved in their little cottage high on Lily's Hill in San Rafael. This was a stunned silence, the reflexive quiet of someone who has just received a violent, undeserved, and entirely unexpected blow.

The entire city was in shock.

There were people in the streets now, fully dressed, some of them dressed bizarrely, as if for an evening party. One woman wore a gingham housedress and five ropes of pearls. A very fat man stood in silent grandeur wearing an evening tailcoat and miner's red-flannel long underwear and gleaming English riding boots.

They stood like sentinels, silent, in little clusters or alone, watching. Saying nothing. A few men, like Brooks, seemed to be going about their normal routines.

But no cable cars ran, no electric lights burned, no horse carriages or motorcars could be seen on the streets. There were just the watchers, and the silence.

Now the six plumes of smoke were eight.

Lily's tour of inspection was quickly over. Big as it was,

she knew the mansion well, and all the details of its running were familiar to her. Only the stables and the coachmen's quarters were a mystery to her, and especially the details of the keeping and running of Brooks's new Brewster electric automobile, which frightened her still, even though it was far quieter-running than the horrendous gas motors.

The chandelier had been the first casualty of the earthquake, and it remained the most serious one. There was broken glass, naturally, and some broken dishes. But, for the most part, the big stone house seemed intact. Lily obeyed Brooks's orders to fill every possible receptacle with water. The well and its mechanical pump still worked, although the electrical pump system had failed. None of the electric lights were working, nor the gas lights, either. Lily was pleased that she had such an ample supply of candles: in time, they might need every one of them. Thinking about what they might need in time, if the quake was as bad as Brooks seemed to fear, Lily had a conference with her cook, and sent servants out to buy whatever could be bought in the way of food and canned goods.

It was impossible to tell what kind of siege they might be in for. The larder, needless to say, was tremendously well-stocked. Still and all, who knew how long they might be cut off from gas and electricity and the stores closed? And there might be others to feed, if the quake had done any extensive harm.

For the first time ever, Lily was glad that two of her children were back East, out of the path of this particular danger. And where was Neddy at this moment, and his brood, and how would things be at the ranch?

Lily's head was filled with questions as she bustled about the big house, checking supplies, calming the servants' fears, keeping herself very busy for fear of what she might do if she had a moment to think.

Brooks stopped to watch a crew of firemen, sharing their frustration. He was nearing Market Street now, at the corner of California and Front. And there was a wide six-story office building with shops on the street floor, just starting to blaze. The flames were flashing and flickering out the top-story windows. *It must have been flying sparks, getting to the roof, to light it from the top like that,* Brooks thought almost idly, as though he were observing some scientific phenomenon of passing interest instead of a deadly threat to the whole town. Someone had alerted the firemen, or perhaps they were just patrolling continuously now, for there were so many fires that Brooks had long stopped counting.

The horse-drawn fire wagon came smartly trotting up to the corner, all brass and bright red paint, but Brooks could see the instant it stopped that something was wrong. The something was the men. Their neat uniforms were disheveled, there was soot on their faces, but what startled Brooks to his marrow was something else. The expression on the faces of these brave men was a sad revelation of what was happening to San Francisco. It was an expression of defeat, despair, a hopeless kind of resignation.

Still, they went gamely through the motions.

Here was a fire plug, part of what City Hall claimed was the most extensive, most advanced prevention system of any city in the world.

Up went two men with the threaded hose. They had a special kind of wrench to open the hydrant. Open it they did, and stood there expectantly. Brooks found himself sharing their hopelessness. The open plug gaped black, dry as a lizard's backside, with not one drop of water to quench the blaze. For one long moment the two firemen simply stood there staring into the dry hydrant in barely repressed despair mixed with rage, for there was nothing in all the world that they could do to stop the ravenous flames.

Finally Brooks walked on, holding his handkerchief to his nose now, for the smoke was ever thicker, and the heat more intense.

After she had seen to the inventory and restocking of her larder, Lily moved on to the linen closets. She could plainly see the ever-building cloud of smoke coming from the city below, and it was in vain that she tried to shut her ears to the one rapid system of communication that seemed to be working in the city: the servants' underground gossip grapevine.

Mary was a good-natured girl, and willing, but she could not, for the life of her, stop chattering. And every time Lily sent the girl on some errand to the kitchen or the stables, back she came bubbling over with fragments of news dire enough to make Cassandra seem optimistic. Cliff House, for sure, had fallen right into the sea, and everyone in it. Martial law was being declared momentarily, to stop the terrible rioting, looting, drinking, and raping that seethed in the streets. Soldiers were marching from the Presidio, with orders to shoot to kill. A woman cooking breakfast had set the chimney on fire over Van Ness Avenue way, and now all that part of the town was in flames, too, the ham-and-eggs fire they were calling it, closing in on Nob Hill from behind. Doomed they all were, and only God could save them.

"Mary, my dear," said Lily in her gentlest voice, "if you don't stop chattering, I may strangle you with my own two hands, and surely you would not wish to make a murderess of me, now, would you, dear?"

Mary looked at her mistress, dazed, not knowing if Lily was joking or not. With Lily Cigar, you could never tell.

Lily looked at the blankets, the sheets, the towels. There looked to be enough to serve an army, but an army was exactly what they might end up serving. Even if she discounted half of what Mary said, the situation was bad and building to worse.

Here, in their own walled garden, with their own well and their vast resources for guests and entertaining, they were a kind of island insulated from the rest of Nob Hill even on the finest day of the year. Now that insulation might save them from the fire. Now she must be prepared for refugees: there would surely be hundreds of burned-out families needing care, and especially the women and children.

Suddenly Lily thought of the academy, and wondered how it had fared, and to what use its fine buildings might be put, should the city be overflowing.

Lily thought of everything, in fact, but the one thought that underlay all of the others, so big and so frightful that it must be more tightly caged than the wildest jungle beast.

It was only when Mary timidly asked her about luncheon that Lily realized nearly seven hours had passed since the first shock of the earthquake had jolted them out of bed.

There was no way to climb over the tumbled limestone facade of the Denver and St. Louis Trust Company building, so Brooks had to detour a whole block out of his way. The business district near Market Street was a dream to him now, a nightmare no more real and no less terrifying than the eighth circle of hell. Dense, sooty smoke enveloped everything, and the stench was terrible, a harsh, scorched, burned-toast smell mixed with unlikely minor-key odors: a chemical kind of stench here, the smell of roasted meat there, rotten eggs somewhere else, all building into an olfactory dirge for fallen greatness.

There were fewer civilians on the streets now, and more police, firemen, and some soldiers. Brooks was stopped once

by an armed corporal, asked his business, identified himsel
and was allowed to proceed.

"Begging your pardon Mr. Chaffee, it's the looters, see?"

"I see." But he didn't. In all of his walk down Nob Hi
Brooks had seen every kind of disorder but nary a loote
Still and all, the dockside and South of the Slot populatio
being what it surely was, looting must be a possibility. *The*
why do you resent that soldier?

Brooks walked on, to face he knew not what.

He walked over scattered bricks, past an abandoned churc
from inside of whose Gothic-arched and paneless window
curls of smoke were still escaping, past a motorcar speedin
swerving, darting in and out of the cluttered street on som
mad errand, five silent men clinging to the vehicle with th
grim resolve of sea captains sworn to go down with their shi
It was at the same time comical and sad.

Thinking of the soldier suddenly rocked Brooks's mind t
the core. *Antietam. That was what this all reminded him o*
Antietam. The noise, the stench, the chaos, the being caugh
unaware, unprepared, the underlying sense that this was a
the prank of some mad god.

Brooks stopped in his tracks and thought about tha
Thinking about Antietam made him think about Neddy, an
then about everyone else in this insane world whom he love
The other Neddy, his son. Jon and Katie. And Lily, Lil
Lily, without whose love his entire life might have become
landscape as bleak and burnt-out as the one he walked i
now.

He would keep his promise, and get back to her soon.

Just as soon as he found out the status of Chaffee Pr
duce, and its records, and its office building on the docks.

Lily sat in her bedroom with a bit of lunch on a tray. Sh
sipped the tea and ate nothing. *Damn the phones for bein*
out! Damn the earthquake, for that matter, or anything els
that took him away. She looked out the window.

No longer could she tell one fire from another.

At one o'clock, which had just chimed on the little Frenc
clock he had given her at Christmas, the city seemed engulfe
in a dark and sinister fog. A wall of smoke shrouded th
lower part of the town. The part where the Chaffee Buildin
was. The part where Brooks must have been for hours no
If he got there at all. If, and if, and if. The floodgates opene
now, and all of the doubts and fears that Lily had s
resolutely kept locked in the strictest repression all the mor

ing now came tumbling out, armed and well-practiced in tormenting her.

Brooks stood at the end of Market Street looking up at the smoldering shell that had once been the Chaffee Produce office building.

It had been gutted by fire, the windows blown out, the roof caved in. His walk downtown had been for nothing, then.

He stood with his hands in his pockets, forgetting to hold the handkerchief over his face, forgetting everything but his dumb, blind rage at the waste and futility of it all.

God's mad jest held no mirth for Brooks Chaffee. He thought of the records lost, the contracts gone, the enormously detailed lists of prices and promises that must, still, somehow be kept.

Immediately his quick mind began rebuilding the structure itself brick by brick, the records, the business.

Of course, the business wasn't really destroyed at all. The office building might be the nerve center of Chaffee Produce and his real-estate ventures and investment trusts, but the actual brawn and muscle of his fortune lay elsewhere, in the safety of Marin County, across the bay, in the ten thousand fertile acres that had been the nucleus of the empire when his ranch had joined with Lily's ranch so long ago. There were other ranches now, stretching as far to the north and east as Sacramento, as far to the south as Los Angeles, with a branch flourishing in Hawaii, as if in Fergy's memory. No, the quake would barely touch the surface of Chaffee Produce. It was the small manufacturer in his loft, deep in debt for new machinery, underinsured, who would be destroyed.

Brooks stared into the ruined building, then walked closer, picked his way through the rubble and up the stoop to the front door, whose cinders lay under his boots where they'd burned.

The first explosion took him by surprise. The ground trembled under him, and then he heard the noise, a roar like distant cannonfire, then another roar, closer, and another, closer still. He stopped in his tracks. *I'm losing my sanity, for certain, I'm imagining Antietam again, haven't done that for years, not this vividly, not with such an ear-bursting rumble of sound.*

Another explosion followed quick on the heels of the first three, then another. Brooks imagined Antietam, pushed that image out of his mind, and tried to guess what it might be for real.

Of course. They were dynamiting. With the water mains gone, they were trying to create firebreaks to stop the invading flames. Brooks looked up, choked at the smoke, thought of the freshening wind from the sea, and wished them luck with it.

They'd need luck, and maybe miracles on this black day.

He stood in the doorway of his building feeling like an uninvited guest at a funeral. Inside, everything was black and broken. Almost everything. For there, just a few feet from where he stood, was a dull gleam of Chinese red. The tin box! Somehow the tin records box from his own office three floors up had survived. It was a square box, eighteen inches by eighteen, and about six inches deep, and in it—if they'd survived—were all of the most important contracts of the last six months.

Brooks edged his way across the blackened floorboards toward the box. *Easy, now, the floor might be burned nearly through; there, slowly, that's the way, now!*

He bent his knees slowly, fearing that any sudden move might set off an avalanche of rubble or cave in the floor. Brooks grabbed the box, tugged it gently, firmly out from its robe of charred wood—his desk! Finally, quivering, he held the thing in his hands. Dented, charred, but solid, its brass handle gleaming as it had gleamed the last time he'd seen it, just a few days ago. Damn! He didn't have the key. Well, he'd pry it open at home. Brooks turned where he stood, just a few feet from the door.

Then he froze, trembling. He could feel the floorboards slowly, slowly sagging underneath him. *Quick now!* The floor creaked, groaned, and shuddered as Brooks lurched forward.

It fell in with a roar as he jumped with the last ounce of energy in him, and attained the marble door stoop at the last second. He stood there in shock, clutching the red tin box, his mind a merciful blank.

Behind him the floor fell into the gutted cellar. In that moment Brooks heard her voice just as clear as if they were in bed together: "Promise me you'll come back soon. . . ."

He shook his head as if to clear it, paused for an instant longer, and then, clutching the tin box like a football, he began running up Market Street in the direction of Nob Hill.

It was a run through the obstacle course of all his worst dreams.

The blackened buildings loomed over him and the air itself was nearly black, laden with soot and ashes, and the stench was everywhere. The proud towers of commerce, sickened by their helplessness in the face of the blaze, had vomited bricks and glass and timbers into the wide street, pride of San Francisco. The steel bones of buildings under construction vied in their naked horror with the fresh ruins beside them. He could hear distant shouting, a church bell clanging in alarm, the clatter of frantic hooves. Brooks kept his head down and ran, and ran. Past Drum Street and Davis and Front he ran, feeling the breathwork of it now, gasping at the smoke, holding the tin box as though his very soul depended on it, his mind empty but for one engulfing thought: *Lily! Lily! Lily!*

The two soldiers stood in the shadow of a gutted, smoldering bank. The flask of bourbon was half empty now. They'd found it in the wreckage of a law office on a side street. How long ago? The tall soldier drank deep. Then he wiped his unshaven chin with the back of his hand and passed the flask to his companion.

"Thanky," said the other. "Just what the doctor ordered."

He drank, and licked his lips. There was a pleasant low-tuned humming in his head. He didn't mind the smoke so much now, or the distant rumble of dynamiting. They stood for a moment in companionable silence, leaning on their rifles like shepherds with no flocks in sight.

Market Street was deserted.

"Look there." The short one pointed.

A man was running up the broken street, running hard, a good runner he was, too. Hatless, in countryman's clothes, carrying something with as much care as if it were a tender baby. A red tin box.

" 'S got himself someone's cashbox, looks like to me."

"Can't let 'im just run away with it."

"Nope."

The tall soldier shifted his weight. He picked up his rifle and slowly, almost casually raised it into position. He squeezed the trigger, saw the result of his first round, grunted, squeezed again. And again.

Brooks winced.

The pain in his chest was sudden and sharp, but still he kept on running, dodging the heaps of rubble, the burnt-out wagons, a woman's incongruously beplumed hat, a child's toy. Four blocks he'd run, nearly five. His chest hurt. Another searing pain.

Then he felt the wetness and looked down, hearing nothing, still clutching the tin box. There was another shade of red mingling with the red of the tin box.

It was blood.

Brooks Chaffee stopped, astonished, and looked about him and saw nothing.

The third bullet took half his head off.

Brooks sank to the sooty pavement slowly, slowly, turning as he fell. He forgot where he was or what he was doing and what had been done to him.

He was riding the black stallion, galloping up the driveway of the ranch, the sun clear and hot on his face, a smile coming just as it always came when he rounded that last curve and could see the big house, white and gleaming in the pure light of noon, and the big door open and Lily there, waiting.

He slid off the great rampaging horse.

She opened her arms and lifted her head for the kiss.

Brooks went to her, smiling a welcome.

One of the soldiers was fat, the other so tall and thin that together they looked like a comic drawing. They were both drunk now, but the thin one was the drunker. He squinted as he reloaded the carbine.

The fat one looked at his friend with new respect. "For a man with half a snootful, you aim right good, Charlie."

Charlie fumbled with the bullet, slid it in, cocked the rifle. "Nothin' to it, soldier, jest followin' old Funston's orders, you heered him plain as day, *'Shoot them looters,'* says he, *'and shoot to kill, gotta teach them a lesson, that's what we got.'*"

They stood side by side and looked down at the body.

"Why's he smilin'?"

"Beats me."

"Looks like he knows a right good joke, that 'un."

"Yep. Joke. I'll drink to that."

The fat soldier clapped the thin one on the back and they ambled up Market Street, laughing.

❧ 50 ❧

By three in the afternoon Lily could stand it no longer. She knew in her heart that something must be wrong, that Brooks would never delay this long without so much as a message, and the thought of him down there somewhere, injured maybe, needing her, and with no way of getting in touch, was sure to drive her mad.

Well she knew how slight her chances were of finding him in the confusion that must be rampant in the city. However unreliable the servants' rumors might be, there was some grain of fact buried in them, and even discounting for hysteria and ignorance, the picture of San Francisco besieged by fire was a terrifying one.

Still, she would never rest easy again if she did not try.

Lily paced her bedroom, turned to a closet, and found an old gingham dress, something she had worn in from the ranch one morning in the rain.

It would not do to look too much like Mrs. Brooks Chaffee, nor Lily Cigar, either, if half of what Mary said was true.

Lily found an old shawl, an inconspicuous purse, and bound her head with a dark blue silk scarf. For even mixed as it was with silver now, the gold of her hair was too well-known to leave uncovered. *What, precisely, was she afraid of?* Lily would not take the time to answer her own question, for some mocking voice inside her suggested that the answer might be a long time coming.

She found some money, debated on how much to take, and finally took quite a lot: more than one hundred dollars was tucked in the bottom of her purse. There might be cabs to hire, or people to bribe.

Lily had no necessity to go out into the city alone, but she knew that alone was how she'd be going. Mary protested, but Mary would drive her mistress even crazier, by her side. Gloria, bent with rheumatism but still bright and clever and willing, also offered, as did the butler and both coachmen.

She thanked them all and gave detailed instructions on how to run the house in her absence.

Then Lily walked down the stairs and out into the storm of fire.

She knew the route Brooks must have taken in the morning, and she followed it now as best she could: across Mason and down California to Market.

Her eyes squinting against the smoke, her desperate heart pounding, Lily walked through a landscape of devastation. All the north side of Market Street was burning now, the south side having long since been consumed. The lower quarter of the city was one vast blackened ruin, what could be seen of it when the smoke temporarily shifted a little. Smoke was everywhere. Hell itself could have no more smoke than this, nor flames either. It was a retribution. Sodom and Gomorrah punished, San Francisco, bawd of the Pafific, brought low for its sins.

And my own sins, too, let us not forget them.

Lily walked through the smoke and ruins, a condemned woman going to the gallows and not counting the steps or the minutes or the reasons why, but concentrating the entire force of her mind on one single purpose: *Find him for me please, God in heaven, just find him, find him!*

She saw a little girl timidly making her way up Mulberry Street in New York fifty-some years ago, on her futile way to St. Paddy's, to light a candle to Saint Jude.

There isn't even a church left standing, if I wanted to do that now.

The walking was slow, partly because the streets were filled with refugees where they weren't filled with rubble. No one seemed to notice Lily, and she saw no one she knew.

Lily saw sights that were bizarre, and almost comical, and unbearably sad. People who had obviously lost everything but the clothes on their backs milled about, silent, disoriented, not knowing where to go or what to do. And there was no one to tell them what to do.

An occasional soldier was visible, but the soldiers seemed to be wandering as aimlessly as the people they had been called in to protect.

The sky rained soot, the air was hot, and the first time Lily looked at her hands, she didn't recognize them: they were that blackened. *Two blocks farther, and I can sign up for the minstrel show,* she thought grimly, imagining coming on Brooks and him passing her by thinking she was a free black slave woman.

She walked down the hill, past men and women and children of all ages and conditions, most of them pulling and hauling household goods to some unspecified destination. An old lady and someone who might have been her grandson struggled valiantly with a big upright piano. A girl of perhaps six staggered under the weight of a bird cage bigger than she was. A very dignified man in full evening dress carried a potted palm tree stiffly before him like a bride's bouquet. A pair of young lovers strolled hand in hand through the throng, oblivious of everything but each other.

The crowd thinned out as Lily approached the Chinatown district.

Suddenly there came a snorting, a stamping of hooves, and the high-pitched but unmistakably angry screams of a Chinese mob.

For the first time that day Lily felt a real, personal, physical fear. She backed into a burnt-out doorway as the noises came closer and closer.

What she saw sickened her profoundly. A huge dark brown bull came staggering around the corner, his eyes bulging with terror, kicking up his heels, rearing and arching his back against his tormentors.

They were many. A mob of coolies pursued the beast with knives and garden tools, with anything that could wound the bull, no matter how slightly, no matter at what risk. Lily looked away, then found her gaze drawn back to the macabre scene against her will. As she looked, a small wiry boy of perhaps ten darted up to the bull's flank and plunged in a long kitchen knife. It stuck there, despite the spurting blood, despite the animal's frantic motions. Now Lily saw that there were other weapons sticking out of the bull: knives of several sizes, and two long steel objects that might have been gigantic hat pins or skewers. Still the poor beast charged away, and still the mob pursued him. Then a soldier appeared and mercifully shot the creature through the head. It fell, twitching, and the Chinese just stood there silently watching it die.

A voice at her elbow startled Lily nearly as much as the gruesome spectacle she had just witnessed. It was a man's voice, and gentle. "The bull, don't you know, caused the earthquake."

Lily looked at him, so thoroughly astonished she forgot her fear. He was her boys' age, and scholarly-looking, with gold-rimmed eyeglasses.

"I beg your pardon?"

"No, madame, I beg yours, for I see I have frightened you.

But Chinese customs fascinate me, even the cruel ones. You see, they believe that the earth rests on the backs of three giant bulls. So, naturally, when the quake came, it only meant that one of those bulls had gone astray. They were trying to drive it back to its rightful position in the scheme of things."

"I would wish," Lily said quietly, thinking of other things, "that it were that simple."

"And I. Good day to you, madame."

And he was gone in the smoke.

Lily stepped past the Chinese and their victim and walked on down California Street.

The lower parts of the Chinese sector were nearly abandoned. Everything that could burn had burned, and everything else was a blackened shell of stone or brickwork. In some cases the intense heat had melted the mortar, reduced it to sand, and the bricks came tumbling down of their own weight and the velocity of the fire storm.

The city was drowning in fire, and there seemed to Lily no way at all to save it.

And she knew as she walked through this black, ruined landscape, this three-dimensional, searing, burning, crumbling nightmare, what she would almost surely find at the bottom of Market Street—and what she would not find.

Still, Lily must go there and see for herself.

She walked on, glad of her country walking boots and inconspicuous dress.

The bottom of Market Street was deserted as a stage setting long after the final curtain had been rung down. The skull-eyed, blackened fronts of the once-elegant office buildings seemed to stare at Lily as she picked her lonely way through the ruins.

She hardly recognized the Chaffee Building when she finally got there. She stood for a moment in the street, staring up at the gutted structure, and then, slowly, as if hypnotized by the quiet of the place and the blackness inside it, Lily climbed up the seven marble steps to the empty space that once held the fine mahogany-and-etched-glass door. She paused in the opening, looking down into a blackness where the floor had been, a blackness that might easily have been a grave.

"Brooks? Brooks?"

Her voice rose, and a faint echo came mocking back at her, a ghost's voice, barely audible above the almost constant rumble of far-off dynamiting.

"Brooks . . ." whispered the echo. "Brooks . . ." The echo came from a place that Lily feared more than death itself. The echo seemed to come from the darkest corner of her own heart, that buried, secret place where all along, over all these golden years, she had known the profound and inadmissible truth that the cards had turned up lucky for her one time too many, that she was living upon borrowed luck, that she didn't deserve Brooks, or his love, or the thousand kinds of happiness that his love had brought her.

That it would all be taken away from her in some evil, unimaginable manner.

Lily turned slowly, and slowly she walked down the rubble-strewn marble stairs. She would try the hospitals. She would try the morgue. Up Market Street she walked, not sure where the hospital was anymore, if indeed it was still standing. Lily walked two blocks alone, then felt the tugging at her sleeve. She looked down and saw a girl, small and thin, no more than eighteen, surely, greatly disheveled, eyes big with the urgency of her mission. The girl wore a bathrobe over a torn nightgown, and she had no shoes at all. In her hand was a small oval photograph of a pretty child, a boy, perhaps two years old. The girl tried to speak, but her voice had been reduced to croaking.

"Have . . . you seen my boy? Have you seen my little Albert?"

Lily looked at the pathetic creature and thought how very many lives must endure the bottom dropping out from underneath them on this awful day.

"I'm terribly sorry, my dear, but I have not." The girl just nodded. Lily wondered how many times since dawn she must have asked this question and been disappointed. Lily reached in her purse and found a ten-dollar bill and pressed it into the girl's hand.

"Buy yourself something to eat, child. Keep your strength up. For Albert's sake."

The girl looked at Lily, made a neat little curtsy, smiled a faint thin wire-drawn line of a smile, and said gently, "Have . . . you seen my boy? Have you seen my little Albert?"

Lily turned away to hide the tears that suddenly filled her eyes. When she had recovered her composure and turned back, the girl was halfway down the block, moving determinedly in the direction of a big fireman. Lily's ten dollars lay forgotten in the street. She picked up the bill and tucked it in her purse. *I should have a picture of him, famous as he is, not everyone in town knows Brooks by sight.*

And Lily herself headed for the fireman, who, a study in weariness, muttered that the temporary central hospital in this quarter had been set up in the huge halls of the Mechanics Institute.

Lily stood as tall as fatigue would let her, and carried her head high, and all the way to the Mechanics Institute she forced herself to think of a hundred minor accidents—very minor, please, God!—that could have put Brooks in the hospital and out of communication.

A stray brick, a speeding fire engine, a tumble on a bit of rubble, breaking up a fight, stopping a looter, helping the firemen—there were endless possibilities.

And there were endless possibilities for other, maybe fatal mishaps.

The Mechanics Institute, scene of a thousand balls and banquets, now looked like something imagined by Dante on an especially gloomy midnight. The late-afternoon sunlight was so diminished by the smoke and soot that it could have been nighttime. Inside the vast hall was jammed from wall to wall with hastily improvised cots, with mattresses flung any which way on the floor, with the screams and moanings and prayers of the wounded, with anxious friends and relatives searching, with bloodstained doctors and nurses and volunteers rushing this way and that with never enough time or supplies.

Lily soon realized that only the gravely injured, and women in childbirth, were likely to receive any attention at all.

She stood at one end of the vast chamber and knew what she must do. An hour and a half later Lily had seen every patient in the institute with her own eyes. She had seen men with their legs crushed, children burned black and screaming for want of anesthetics, an entire section of insane people cruelly but necessarily tied to their cots. Lily had seen more kinds of suffering than she had ever imagined or wanted to imagine.

But she had not seen Brooks.

In a daze, she walked out of the door.

More patients were being rushed into nonexistent spaces every minute, but Lily knew that whatever had happened to her husband must have happened long ago—this morning.

This morning! It was longer than long ago, decades it was, a lifetime ago, an eternity.

Now she must go to the morgue.

A policeman told her there was a temporary morgue under

tents in a vacant lot three blocks away. She nodded, and thanked him, and started walking, moving mechanically now in her tiredness and despair.

What had been very bad at the hospital was much worse at the morgue, for the quake and the fire and the violence that followed between man and man had worked strange and terrible ends for over a hundred people. The attendant, a police captain, assured Lily that, had Brooks died anywhere downtown, he would have been brought here. At first the basic decencies were observed, but the death toll had mounted through the day, and now there were no sheets to cover them, and no more cots to lay them on; the dead were stacked on the ground like firewood, close, side by side. As she had seen all of the wounded, now Lily saw all of the dead. And Brooks was not among them.

She felt like a ghost herself now, doomed forever to wander among the dead and the dying, seeking what she could never find.

Lily turned and walked the length of the army tents, oblivious of the torn and burned and battered bodies all around her, sick beyond repugnance at the sight of death or the smell of it.

In the street she paused, holding on to a lamppost, making one last valiant effort to organize her thoughts, to focus what little was left of her energy on the great problem that haunted her, and on the smaller problem of mere survival.

Home. She must go home!

It could be, by a miracle, that he'd gone home and was waiting for her. He'd have the sense not to go looking for her—or would he? Lily looked up the street, up the hill, whose top was obscured in the persistent smoke, steeling herself for the long climb home. *If the damned house was still standing!* But standing or flaming, that's where he'd be—if he was capable, anymore, of being anyplace.

Lily walked slowly for half a block. She sensed the shape emerging from the sooty smoke ahead before she actually saw him. She stopped dead, unbelieving. Then he saw her, and ran, shouting, his arms outstretched to catch her.

"Mamma! Thank God! We've been frantic."

Lily looked at her eldest son and smiled, incapable of speaking. He had always looked like his father, and never more than in this moment: tall, was Neddy, and fair—only Katie had inherited her mother's flame of hair—tall was her Neddy, and beautiful to look on, like his father. So Lily

[597]

smiled wearily above the knife wound in her heart, for love her son as she surely did, he was not Brooks Chaffee.

Neddy had his motorcar nearby, and he helped her into it. Soon they were up the hill and home. And home was still standing: Brooks's instructions had worked their wonders, for every house around them had been scorched and gutted. All the servants had pitched in to save the Chaffee mansion, servants upon the rooftops squirting vagrant sparks with seltzer bottles, maids in upstairs bathrooms bailing out the filled-up bathtubs to wet down the walls, an orgy of water-splashing as the flames danced all around the garden walls for hours.

It was only when they were safely inside and Lily had washed and changed and they were sitting in something like comfort, drinking tea, that Neddy broke the news.

An army officer had come looking for Lily and, not finding her, had found Ned.

Lily listened to her son, feeling sorry for him as he spoke the terrible words, knowing what they cost him, anticipating his fears of the effect those words might have on her.

Neddy finished his story and took his mother's hand, as much to reassure himself as her. "He couldn't have known what hit him," he said softly. "At least we can thank God for that."

"Take me to him."

"Mamma, he was badly shot."

"Take me to him."

They had lain Brooks Chaffee in the dining room. He lay on the big rosewood table, which had been covered by a sheet, and Neddy had somehow found an undertaker to cleanse his father's body and prepare it for burial.

Lily walked slowly into the room and up to the table.

So he had come home after all.

She looked down at the face she had loved more than any other, loved nearly all her life, loved to distraction, beyond hoping, loved with all that her heart and her mind and body could give. She bent and kissed that dear face, damaged as it was.

Then she turned and left the room. There was so much to be done, so many people to help.

The next three days passed in a blur for Lily and Ned and their servants. The fire raged in every part of the city. Golden Gate Park became one huge refugee camp. There were more deaths, and much illness developed, and Lily would hear of nothing but turning her house into a refuge for the homeless. They all worked virtually around the clock. When the household supplies were exhausted, Lily prevailed upon the army, and more rations were sent. Lily would have helped in any case, but now the work had a new and special meaning for her. The busier she kept, the less chance she had to think about her loss.

She worked herself until the point of mere exhaustion had passed, worked until she could work no more, and then worked longer. She comforted the homeless, sympathized with those who had lost loved ones, played with the children, helped her own staff in the kitchen, got medical aid where it was needed, and organized a remarkably effective intelligence-gathering system about long-range opportunities for the victims under her roof.

And finally, late at night, she would drag herself upstairs to bed, tired beyond thinking: only then Lily would sink into a numbed and dreamless sleep.

On Friday the rain came. The last of the fires sputtered out, and the three days of horror ground painfully to a halt. The human loss and the loss of property could never accurately be calculated, yet already the irrepressible city was bounding back, as it had bounded back many times before, looking only into the future, building with the burnt stones of ruin, leapfrogging the black canyons of despair. Permanent refugee camps were quickly organized, and Lily assisted in evacuating her temporary guests to one of them. For nearly a week she had fed, clothed, sheltered, and comforted more than two hundred refugees. The newspapers that had quickly sprung out of their own ashes made her one of the heroines of the disaster, and when they made reference to her colorful past, it was in the most reverent and symbolic manner, for in Lily Cigar they suddenly saw an image of the city itself, determined, a little brazen, a touch of bawdiness but supremely gallant for all that, and a beauty too, don't forget it, and with drive and spunk and a loving heart.

That was how the papers described her, and how one more chapter was added to the legend.

But Lily never read those stories.

She had another, more important job to do.

On Wednesday, April 25, just one week after the earthquake, Brooks Chaffee was buried high on a hilltop on the ranch at San Rafael, just down the slope from the getaway cottage on Lily's Hill. Only Lily and Ned and the servants were there; it was a brief ceremony and a simple one.

Lily stood at the graveside, saying nothing, until the last spadeful of earth had been shoveled on his coffin. And she thought that all she had ever cherished, ever since she could remember, had passed this way, gone to the grave. Then her son's hand found hers and led her up the slope to the little cottage.

They stood together on the porch, looking out over the hills to the blue sea in the distance. Then she spoke, softly, remembering.

"He was always so happy here."

Neddy looked at her. "He had good reason to be. Will you be staying here, Mamma?"

Lily looked out at the view, and felt the sun warm on her face. She thought of the days she had spent here with Brooks, and of the time she had come here to lick her wounds when Fergy died.

Then she turned to her son and smiled. "No, darling, there's far too much for me to do."

Together they walked down the hill hand in hand, to where the horses were waiting. And Lily, still spry as a girl, climbed up onto her mount and cantered off down the hill to the ranch. She knew as she rode away from his grave that there would be no separation from Brooks, not now or ever, that he would be with her in every word she uttered, in every thought that formed in her mind, in every beat of her heart. For theirs was a love of such depth and sympathy that death was powerless against it.

Ned Chaffee looked at his mother as she rode, rode easily, expertly, enjoying the ride and the day, and suddenly he was smiling too, for he thought what a very lucky man his father had been, to win the love of Lily Cigar.

Epilogue

CHAFFEE-DICKINSON NUPTIALS UNITE
PROMINENT PIONEER DYNASTIES

From the San Francisco *Chronicle*, May 30, 1918:

Perfect weather was the order of the day for what many Bay Area socialites consider the Wedding of the Year 1918, uniting Miss Elizabeth Hudner Chaffee of Nob Hill and San Rafael, and Major Stanford Dickinson III at Miss Chaffee's grandmother's ranch in San Rafael. Miss Chaffee wore an heirloom gown of ivory satin reembroidered with antique Point de Venise lace, and a short veil of the same lace, and carried a country bouquet of white roses and stephanotis from her grandmother's famous garden.

She was attended by five recent debutantes, the Misses Hillary Coit, Malvina Crocker, Judith Winchester, Livia Dickinson (sister of the groom), and Edythe Hitchkok, all of San Francisco.

Major Dickinson had as his best man his younger brother, Jeb Dickinson, and as ushers, five classmates from Yale: Mr. Derek DuBois, Mr. Anton Hartmann, Mr. James Connor, Mr. Jay Cavior, and Mr. Nicholas Crocker.

Both the bride and the groom are descended from third-generation San Francisco families, Mrs. Dickinson being the granddaughter of Mr. Brooks Chaffee, well-known produce tycoon and landowner, whose tragic accidental shooting during the 1906 fire saddened all San Francisco, and his widow, Mrs. Lillian Malone Chaffee, remarkable at age 81, who is active in many local arts and charities to this day. Major Dickinson is the grandson of Stanford Dickinson I and Mrs. Mamie Dickinson, both of San Francisco, both deceased.

When asked to comment upon her granddaughter's

[601]

wedding, Mrs. Brooks Chaffee said: "Well, it was absolutely lovely, I'm sure. And young Stanford is a fine lad, very heroic in France, as you know. My one regret," said Mrs. Chaffee with perhaps the only look of sadness that intruded upon the otherwise joyous occasion, "is that my dear husband didn't live to see it. And, of course, Stanford and Mamie Dickinson. What would I not give to see the expression on dear Mamie's face were she here today!"

The bride and bridegroom will spend the first part of their honeymoon in what has come to be known as "The Honeymoon Cottage" high on a hill on the Chaffee ranch, after which they will sail for an extended cruise of the Far East. On returning, Major Dickinson expects to enter the family real-estate business, and to make his home in Hillsborough.

ABOUT THE AUTHOR

Tom Murphy is a vice-president of the New York advertising company, Bozell & Jacobs. His previous novels are BALLET! and ASPEN INCIDENT.